Robert Harris

ENIGMA

ARCHANGEL

This edition published by Hutchinson in 2004

Enigma first published in the United Kingdom in 1995 by Hutchinson
Archangel first published in the United Kingdom in 1998 by Hutchinson

Hutchinson Books
The Random House Group Limited
20 Vauxhall Bridge Road, London, SW1V 2SA

Random House Australia (Pty) Limited
20 Alfred Street, Milsons Point, Sydney
New South Wales 2061, Australia

Random House New Zealand Limited
18 Poland Road, Glenfield, Auckland 10, New Zealand

Random House (Pty) Limited
Endulini, 5a Jubilee Road, Parktown 2193, South Africa

The Random House Group Limited Reg. No. 954009

www.randomhouse.co.uk

A CIP catalogue record for this book
is available from the British Library

Papers used by Random House
are natural, recyclable products made from wood grown in
sustainable forests. The manufacturing processes conform to
the environmental regulations of the country of origin

Typeset by MATS, Southend-on-Sea, Essex
Printed and bound in Germany by
Elsnerdruck, Berlin

ISBN 0 09 1904080

ENIGMA

For Gill,
and for Holly and Charlie
QXQF VFLR TXLG VLWD PRUA

Author's Note

This novel is set against the background of an actual historical event. The German naval signals quoted in the text are all authentic. The characters, however, are entirely fictional.

'It looks as if Bletchley Park is the single greatest achievement of Britain during 1939-45, perhaps during this century as a whole.'

George Steiner

'A mathematical proof should resemble a simple and clear-cut constellation, not a scattered cluster in the Milky Way. A chess problem also has unexpectedness, and a certain economy; it is essential that the moves should be surprising, and that every piece on the board should play its part.'

G.H. Hardy, *A Mathematician's Apology*

ONE

WHISPERS

WHISPERS: the sounds made by an enemy wireless transmitter immediately before it begins to broadcast a coded message.

A Lexicon of Cryptography
('Most Secret', Bletchley Park, 1943)

CAMBRIDGE IN THE fourth winter of the war: a ghost town.

A ceaseless Siberian wind with nothing to blunt its edge for a thousand miles whipped off the North Sea and swept low across the Fens. It rattled the signs to the air-raid shelters in Trinity New Court and battered on the boarded-up windows of King's College Chapel. It prowled through the quadrangles and staircases, confining the few dons and students still in residence to their rooms. By mid-afternoon the narrow cobbled streets were deserted. By nightfall, with not a light to be seen, the university was returned to a darkness it hadn't known since the Middle Ages. A procession of monks shuffling over Magdalene Bridge on their way to Vespers would scarcely have seemed out of place.

In the wartime blackout the centuries had dissolved.

It was to this bleak spot in the flatlands of eastern England that there came, in the middle of February 1943, a young mathematician named Thomas Jericho. The authorities of his college, King's, were given less than a day's notice of his arrival – scarcely enough time to reopen his rooms, put sheets on his bed, and have more than three years' worth of dust swept from his shelves and carpets. And they would not have gone to even that much trouble, it being wartime and servants so scarce – had not the Provost himself been telephoned at the Master's Lodge by an obscure but very senior official of His Majesty's Foreign Office, with a request that 'Mr Jericho be looked after until he is well enough to return to his duties'.

'Of course,' replied the Provost, who couldn't for the life of him put a face to the name of Jericho. 'Of course. A pleasure to welcome him back.'

As he spoke, he opened the college register and flicked through it until he came to: Jericho, T. R. G.; matriculated, 1935; Senior Wrangler, Mathematics Tripos, 1938; Junior Research Fellow at two hundred pounds a year; not seen in the university since the outbreak of war.

Jericho? Jericho? To the Provost he was at best a dim memory, a fuzzy adolescent blob on a college photograph. Once, perhaps, he would have remembered the name, but the war had shattered the sonorous rhythm of intake and graduation and all was chaos – the Pitt Club was a British Restaurant, potatoes and onions were growing in the gardens of St John's . . .

'He has recently been engaged upon work of the gravest national importance,' continued the caller. 'We would appreciate it if he were not disturbed.'

'Understood,' said the Provost. 'Understood. I shall see to it he is left alone.'

'We are obliged to you.'

The official rang off. *Work of the gravest national importance*, by God . . . The old man knew what that meant. He hung up and looked thoughtfully at the receiver for a few moments, then went in search of the domestic bursar.

A Cambridge college is a village, with a village's appetite for gossip – all the keener when that village is nine-tenths empty – and the return of Jericho provoked hours of analysis among the college staff.

There was, for a start, the manner of his arrival – a few hours after the call to the Provost, late on a snowy night, swaddled in a travelling rug, in the back of a cavernous official Rover driven by a young chauffeuse in the dark blue uniform of the Women's Royal Navy. Kite, the porter, who offered to carry the visitor's bags to his rooms, reported that Jericho clung to his pair of battered leather suitcases and refused to let go of either, even though he looked so pale and worn out that Kite doubted he would make it up the spiral staircase unaided.

Dorothy Saxmundham, the bedder, saw him next, when she went in the following day to tidy up. He was propped on his pillows staring out at the sleet pattering across the river, and he never turned his head, never even looked at her, didn't seem to know she was there, poor lamb. Then she went to move one of his cases and he was up in a flash – 'Please don't touch that, thank you so much, Mrs Sax, thank you' – and she was out on the landing in a quarter of a minute.

He had only one visitor: the college doctor, who saw him twice, stayed for about fifteen minutes on each occasion, and left without saying a word.

He took all his meals in his room for the first week

– not that he ate very much, according to Oliver Bickerdyke, who worked in the kitchens: he took up a tray three times a day, only to take it away again an hour later, barely touched. Bickerdyke's great coup, which led to at least an hour of speculation around the coke stove in the Porter's Lodge, was to come upon the young man working at his desk, wearing a coat over his pyjamas, a scarf and a pair of mittens. Normally, Jericho 'sported his oak' – that is to say, he kept the heavy outer door to his study firmly shut – and called politely for his tray to be left outside. But on this particular morning, six days after his dramatic arrival, he had left it slightly ajar. Bickerdyke deliberately brushed the wood lightly with his knuckles, so quietly as to be inaudible to any living creature, save possibly a grazing gazelle, and then he was across the threshold and within a yard of his quarry before Jericho turned round. Bickerdyke just had time to register piles of papers ('covered in figures and circuits and Greek and suchlike') before the work was hastily covered up and he was sent on his way. Thereafter the door remained locked.

Listening to Bickerdyke's tale the next afternoon, and not wishing to be outdone, Dorothy Saxmundham added a detail of her own. Mr Jericho had a small gas fire in his sitting room and a grate in his bedroom. In the grate, which she had cleaned that morning, he had obviously burned a quantity of paper.

There was silence while this intelligence was digested.

'Could be *The Times*,' said Kite eventually. 'I puts a

copy of *The Times* under his door every morning.'

No, declared Mrs Sax. It was not *The Times*. They were still in a pile by the bed. 'He doesn't seem to read them, not as I've noticed. He just does the crosswords.'

Bickerdyke suggested he was burning letters. 'Maybe love letters,' he added, with a leer.

'Love letters? Him? Get away.' Kite took off his antique bowler hat, inspected its frayed brim, then replaced it carefully on his bald head. 'Besides, he ain't had any letters, not a single one, not since he's been here.'

And so they were forced to the conclusion that what Jericho was burning in his grate was his work – work so secret, nobody could be allowed to see even a fragment of the waste. In the absence of hard fact, fantasy was piled upon fantasy. He was a government scientist, they decided. No, he worked in Intelligence. No, no – he was a genius. He had had a nervous breakdown. His presence in Cambridge was an official secret. He had friends in high places. He had met Mr Churchill. He had met the King . . .

In all of which speculation, they would have been gratified to learn, they were absolutely and precisely correct.

Three days later, early on the morning of Friday 26 February, the mystery was given a fresh twist.

Kite was sorting the first delivery of mail, stuffing a small sackful of letters into the few pigeon holes whose owners were still in college, when he came across not one but three envelopes addressed to T. R. G. Jericho

Esq, originally sent care of the White Hart Inn, Shenley Church End, Buckinghamshire, and subsequently forwarded to King's. For a moment, Kite was taken aback. Did the strange young man, for whom they had constructed such an exotic identity, in reality manage a *pub?* He pushed his spectacles up on to his forehead, held the envelope at arm's length, and squinted at the postmarks.

Bletchley.

There was an old Ordnance Survey map hanging at the back of the lodge, showing the dense triangle of southern England enclosed by Cambridge, Oxford and London. Bletchley sat astride a big railway junction exactly midway between the two university towns. Shenley Church End was a tiny hamlet about four miles north-west of it.

Kite studied the more interesting of the three envelopes. He raised it to his bulbous, blue-veined nose. He sniffed it. He had been sorting mail for more than forty years and he knew a woman's handwriting when he saw it: clearer and neater, more looped and less angular than a man's. A kettle was boiling on the gas ring at the back of the stove. He glanced around. It was not yet eight, and barely light outside. Within seconds he had stepped into the alcove and was holding the flap of the envelope to the steam. It was made of thin, shoddy wartime paper, sealed with cheap glue. The flap quickly moistened, curled, opened, and Kite extracted a card.

He had just about read through to the end when he heard the lodge door open. A blast of wind shook the windows. He stuffed the card back into the envelope, dipped his little finger into the glue pot kept ready by the stove, stuck down the flap, then casually poked his head round the corner to see who had come in. He almost had a stroke.

'Good heavens – morning – Mr Jericho – sir . . .'

'Are there any letters for me, Mr Kite?' Jericho's voice was firm enough, but he seemed to sway slightly and held on to the counter like a sailor who had just stepped ashore after a long voyage. He was a pale young man, quite short, with dark hair and dark eyes – twin darknesses that served to emphasise the pallor of his skin.

'Not as I've noticed, sir. I'll look again.'

Kite retreated with dignity to the alcove and tried to iron out the damp envelope with his sleeve. It was only slightly crumpled. He slipped it into the middle of a handful of letters, came out to the front, and performed – even if he said so himself – a virtuoso pantomime of searching through them.

'No, no, nothing, no. Ah, yes, here's something. Gracious. And two more.' Kite proffered them across the counter. 'Your birthday, sir?'

'Yesterday.' Jericho stuffed the envelopes into the inside pocket of his overcoat without glancing at them.

'Many happy returns, sir.' Kite watched the letters disappear and gave a silent sigh of relief. He folded his arms and leaned forward on the counter. 'Might I hazard a guess at your age, sir? Came up in 'thirty-five, as I recall. Would that make you, perhaps, twenty-six?'

9

'I say, is that my newspaper, Mr Kite? Perhaps I might take it. Save you the trouble.'

Kite grunted, pushed himself back up on his feet and fetched it. He made one last attempt at conversation as he handed it over, remarking on the satisfactory progress of the war in Russia since Stalingrad and Hitler being finished if you asked him – but, of course, that he, Jericho, would surely be more up to date about such matters than he, Kite . . . ? The younger man merely smiled.

'I doubt if my knowledge about anything is as up to date as yours, Mr Kite, not even about myself. Knowing your methods.'

For a moment, Kite was not sure he had heard correctly. He stared sharply at Jericho, who met his gaze and held it with his dark brown eyes, which seemed suddenly to have acquired a glint of life. Then, still smiling, Jericho nodded 'Good morning', tucked his paper under his arm and was gone. Kite watched him through the lodge's mullioned window – a slender figure in a college scarf of purple and white, unsteady on his feet, head bowed into the wind. 'My methods,' he repeated to himself. *'My methods?'*

That afternoon, when the trio gathered for tea as usual around the coke stove, he was able to advance a whole new explanation for Jericho's presence in their midst. Naturally, he could not disclose how he came by his information, only that it was especially reliable (he hinted at a man-to-man chat). Forgetting his earlier scorn about love letters, Kite now asserted with confidence that the young fellow was obviously suffering from a broken heart.

2

Jericho did not open his letters immediately. Instead he squared his shoulders and tilted forwards into the wind. After a week in his room, the richness of the oxygen pummelling his face made him feel light-headed. He turned right at the Junior Combination Room and followed the flagstone path that led through the college and over the little hump-back bridge to the water meadow beyond. To his left was the college hall, to his right, across a great expanse of lawn, the massive cliff-face of the chapel. A tiny column of choirboys was bobbing through its grey lee, gowns flapping in the gale.

He stopped, and a gust of wind rocked him on his heels, forcing him half a step backwards. A stone passageway led off from one side of the path, its arch grown over with untended ivy. He glanced, by force of habit, at the set of windows on the second floor. They were dark and shuttered. Here, too, the ivy had been allowed to grow unchecked, so that several of the small, diamond-shaped panes were lost behind thick foliage.

He hesitated, then stepped off the path, under the keystone, into the shadows.

The staircase was just as he remembered it, except that now this wing of the college was closed and the

11

wind had blown dead leaves into the well of the steps. An old newspaper curled itself around his legs like a hungry cat. He tried the light switch. It clicked uselessly. There was no bulb. But he could still make out the name, one of three painted on a wooden board in elegant white capitals, now cracked and faded.

TURING, A.M.

How nervously he had climbed these stairs for the first time – when? in the summer of 1938? a world ago – to find a man barely five years older than himself, as shy as a freshman, with a hank of dark hair falling across his eyes: the great Alan Turing, the author of *On Computable Numbers,* the progenitor of the Universal Computing Machine . . .

Turing had asked him what he proposed to take as his subject for his first year's research.

'Riemann's theory of prime numbers.'

'But I am researching Riemann myself.'

'I know,' Jericho had blurted out, 'that's why I chose it.'

And Turing had laughed at this outrageous display of hero worship, and had agreed to supervise Jericho's research, even though he hated teaching.

Now Jericho stood on the landing and tried Turing's door. Locked, of course. The dust smeared his hand. He tried to remember how the room had looked. Squalor had been the overwhelming impression. Books, notes, letters, dirty clothes, empty bottles and tins of food had been strewn across the floor. There had been a teddy bear called Porgy on the mantelpiece above the gas fire, and a battered violin

12

leaning in the corner, which Turing had picked up in a junk shop.

Turing had been too shy a man to get to know well. In any case, from the Christmas of 1938 he was hardly ever to be seen. He would cancel supervisions at the last minute saying he had to be in London. Or Jericho would climb these stairs and knock and there would be no reply, even though Jericho could sense he was behind the door. When, at last, around Easter 1939, not long after the Nazis had marched into Prague, the two men had finally met, Jericho had nerved himself to say: 'Look, sir, if you don't want to supervise me . . .'

'It's not that.'

'Or if you're making progress on the Riemann Hypothesis and you don't want to share it . . .'

Turing had smiled. 'Tom, I can assure you I am making no progress on Riemann whatsoever.'

'Then what . . . ?'

'It's not Riemann.' And then he had added, very quietly: 'There are other things now happening in the world, you know, apart from mathematics . . .'

Two days later Jericho had found a note in his pigeonhole.

'Please join me for a glass of sherry in my rooms this evening. F.J. Atwood.'

Jericho turned from Turing's room. He felt faint. He gripped the worn handrail, taking each step carefully, like an old man.

Atwood. Nobody refused an invitation from Atwood, professor of ancient history, dean of the college before Jericho was even born, a man with a spider's web of connections in Whitehall. It was tantamount to a summons from God.

'Speak any languages?' had been Atwood's opening question as he poured the drinks. He was in his fifties, a bachelor, married to the college. His books were arranged prominently on the shelf behind him. *The Greek and Macedonian Art of War. Caesar as Man of Letters. Thucydides and His History.*

'Only German.' Jericho had learned it in adolescence to read the great nineteenth-century mathematicians – Gauss, Kummer, Hilbert.

Atwood had nodded and handed over a tiny measure of very dry sherry in a crystal glass. He followed Jericho's gaze to the books. 'Do you know Herodotus, by any chance? Do you know the story of Histiaeus?'

It was a rhetorical question; Atwood's questions mostly were.

'Histiaeus wished to send a message from the Persian court to his son-in-law, the tyrant Aristagoras, at Miletus, urging him to rise in revolt. However, he feared any such communication would he intercepted. His solution was to shave the head of his most trusted slave, tattoo the message onto his naked scalp, wait for his hair to grow, then send him to Aristagoras with a request that he be given a haircut. Unreliable but, in his case, effective. Your health.'

Jericho learned later that Atwood told the same stories to all his recruits. Histiaeus and his bald slave gave way to Polybius and his cipher square, then came Caesar's letter to Cicero using an alphabet in which *a* was enciphered as *d, b* as *e, c* as *f,* and so forth. Finally, still circling the subject, but closer now, had come the lesson in etymology.

'The Latin *crypta,* from the Greek root κρυπτη meaning "hidden, concealed". Hence *crypt,* burial place of the dead, and *crypto,* secret. Crypto-communist, crypto-fascist . . . By the way, you're not either, are you?'

'I'm not a burial place of the dead, no.'

'*Cryptogram* . . .' Atwood had raised his sherry to the light and squinted at the pale liquid. '*Cryptanalysis* . . . Turing tells me he thinks you might be rather good . . .'

Jericho was running a fever by the time he reached his rooms. He locked the door and flopped face down on his unmade bed, still wearing his coat and scarf. Presently he heard footsteps and someone knocked.

'Breakfast, sir.'

'Just leave it outside. Thank you.'

'Are you all right, sir?'

'I'm fine.'

He heard the clatter of the tray being set down, and steps retreating. The room seemed to be lurching and swelling out of all proportion, a corner of the ceiling was suddenly huge and close enough to touch. He closed his eyes and the visions came up at him through the darkness –

– Turing, smiling his shy half smile: 'Tom, I can assure you, I am making no progress on Riemann whatsoever . . .'

– Logie, pumping his hand in the Bombe Hut, shouting above the noise of the machinery, 'The Prime

Minister has just been on the telephone with his congratulations . . .'

– Claire, touching his cheek, whispering, 'Poor you, I've really got under your skin, haven't I, poor you . . .'

– 'Stand back' – a man's voice, Logie's voice – 'Stand back, give him air . . .'

And then there was nothing.

When he woke, the first thing he did was look at his watch. He'd been unconscious for about an hour. He sat up and patted his overcoat pockets. Somewhere he had a notebook in which he recorded the duration of each attack, and the symptoms. It was a distressingly long list. He found instead the three envelopes.

He laid them out on the bed and considered them for a while. Then he opened two of them. One was a card from his mother, the other from his aunt, both wishing a happy birthday. Neither woman had any idea what he was doing and both, he knew, were guiltily disappointed he wasn't in uniform and being shot at, like the sons of most of their friends.

'But what do I tell people?' his mother had asked him in despair during one of his brief visits home, after he had refused yet again to tell her what he did.

'Tell them I'm in government communications,' he had replied, using the formula they had been instructed to deploy in the face of persistent enquiries.

'But perhaps they'd like to know a little more than that.'

'Then they're acting suspiciously and you should call the police.'

His mother had contemplated the social catastrophe of her bridge four being interviewed by the local inspector, and had fallen silent.

And the third letter? Like Kite before him, he turned it over and sniffed it. Was it his imagination or was there a trace of scent? Ashes of Roses by Bourjois, a minuscule bottle of which had practically bankrupted him just a month earlier. He used his slide rule as a paperknife and slit the envelope open. Inside was a cheap card, carelessly chosen – it showed a bowl of fruit, of all things – and a standard message for the circumstances, or so he guessed, never having been in this situation before. 'Dearest T . . . always see you as a friend . . . perhaps in the future . . . sorry to hear about . . . in haste . . . much love . . .' He closed his eyes.

Later, after he had filled in the crossword, after Mrs Sax had finished the cleaning, after Bickerdyke had deposited another tray of food and taken it away again untouched, Jericho got down on his hands and knees and tugged a suitcase from beneath his bed and unlocked it. Folded into the middle of his 1930 Doubleday first edition of *The Complete Sherlock Holmes* were six sheets of foolscap covered in his tiny writing. He took them over to the rickety desk beside the window and smoothed them out.

'The cipher machine converts the input(plain language, P) into the cipher (Z) by means of a function f. Thus Z=f(P,K) where K denotes the key . . .'

He sharpened his pencil, blew away the shavings and bent over the sheets.

'Suppose K has N possible values. For each of the N assumptions we must see if $f^{-1}(Z,K)$ produces plain language, where f^{-1} is the deciphering function which produces P if K is correct...'

The wind ruffled the surface of the Cam. A flotilla of ducks rode the waves, without moving, like ships at anchor. He put down his pencil and read her card again, trying to measure the emotion, the meaning behind the flat phrases. Could one, he wondered, construct a similar formula for letters – for love letters or for letters signalling the end of love?

'The input (sentiment, S) is converted into a message (M) by the woman, by means of the function w. Thus $M=w(S,V)$ where V denotes the vocabulary. Suppose V has N possible values...'

The mathematical symbols blurred before his eyes. He took the card into the bedroom, to the grate, knelt and struck a match. The paper flared briefly and twisted in his hand, then swiftly turned to ash.

Gradually his days acquired a shape.

He would rise early and work for two or three hours. Not at cryptanalysis – he burned all that on the day he burned her card – but at pure mathematics. Then he would take a nap. He would fill in *The Times* crossword before lunch, timing himself on his father's old pocket watch – it never took him more than five minutes to complete it, and once he finished it in three minutes forty. He managed to solve a series of complex chess problems – 'the hymn tunes of mathematics', as G.H. Hardy called them – without using pieces or a board. All this reassured him his brain had not been permanently impaired.

After the crossword and the chess he would skim through the war news while trying to eat something at his desk. He tried to avoid the Battle of the Atlantic (DEAD MEN AT THE OARS: U-BOAT VICTIMS FROZEN IN LIFEBOATS) and concentrated instead on the Russian Front: Pavlograd, Demiansk, Rzhev . . . the Soviets seemed to recapture a new town every few hours and he was amused to find *The Times* reporting Red Army Day as respectfully as if it were the King's Birthday.

In the afternoon he would walk, a little further on each occasion – at first confining himself to the college grounds, then strolling through the empty town, and finally venturing into the frozen countryside – before returning as the light faded to sit by the gas fire and read his Sherlock Holmes. He began to go into Hall for dinner, although he declined politely the Provost's offer of a place at High Table. The food was as bad as at Bletchley, but the surroundings were better, the candlelight flickering on the heavy-framed portraits and gleaming on the long tables of polished oak. He learned to ignore the frankly curious stares of the college staff. Attempts at conversation he cut off with a nod. He didn't mind being solitary. Solitude had been his life. An only child, a stepchild, a 'gifted' child – always there had been something to set him apart. At one time he couldn't speak about his work because hardly anyone would understand him. Now he couldn't speak of it because it was classified. It was all the same.

By the end of his second week he had actually started to sleep through the night, a feat he hadn't managed for more than two years.

Shark, Enigma, kiss, bombe, break, pinch, drop, crib – all the weird vocabulary of his secret life he slowly succeeded in erasing from his conscious mind. To his astonishment, even Claire's image became diffuse. There were still vivid flashes of memory, especially at night – the lemony smell of newly washed hair, the wide grey eyes as pale as water, the soft voice half amused, half bored – but increasingly the parts failed to cohere. The whole was vanishing.

He wrote to his mother and persuaded her not to visit him.

'Nurse Time,' the doctor had said, snapping shut his bag of tricks, 'that's who'll cure you. Mr Jericho. Nurse Time.'

Rather to Jericho's surprise it seemed that the old boy was right. He was going to be well again. 'Nervous exhaustion' or whatever they called it was not the same as madness after all.

And then, without warning, on Friday 12 March, they came for him.

The night before it happened he had overheard an elderly don complaining about a new air base the Americans were building to the east of the city.

'I said to them, you do realise you're standing on a fossil site of the Pleistocene era? That I myself have removed from here the horncores of *Bos primigenius?* D'you know, the fellow merely *laughed . . .*'

Good for the Yanks, thought Jericho, and he decided there and then it would make a suitable destination for his afternoon walk. Because it would take him at least three miles further than he had attempted so far, he left earlier than usual, straight after lunch.

He strode briskly along the Backs, past the Wren Library and the icing sugar towers of St John's, past the sports field in which two dozen little boys in purple shirts were playing football, and then turned left, trudging beside the Madingley Road. After ten minutes he was in open country.

Kite had gloomily predicted snow, but although it was still cold it was sunny and the sky was a glory – a pure blue dome above the flat landscape of East Anglia, filled for miles with the silver specks of aircraft and the white scratches of contrails. Before the war he had cycled through this quiet countryside almost every week and had barely seen a car. Now an endless succession of big American trucks lumbered past him, forcing him on to the verge – brasher, faster, more modern than British Army lorries, covered over at the back with camouflaged tarpaulins. The white faces of the US airmen peered out of the shadows. Sometimes the men shouted and waved and he waved back, feeling absurdly English and self-conscious.

Eventually he came within sight of the new base and stood beside the road watching three Flying Fortresses take off in the distance, one after the other – vast aircraft, almost too heavy, or so it seemed to Jericho, to escape the ground. They lumbered along the fresh concrete runway, roaring with frustration, clawing at the air for liberation until suddenly a crack of daylight appeared beneath them, and the crack widened, and they were aloft.

He stood there for almost half an hour, feeling the air pulse with the vibrations of their engines, smelling the faint scent of aviation spirit carried on the cold air. He had never seen such a demonstration of power. The fossils of the Pleistocene era, he reflected with grim delight, must now be so much dust. What was that line of Cicero that Atwood was so fond of quoting? *'Nervos belli, pecuniam infinitam.'* The sinews of war, unlimited money.

He looked at his watch and realised he had better turn back if he was going to reach the college before dark.

He had gone about a mile when he heard an engine behind him. A jeep overtook him, swerved and stopped. The driver, wrapped in a heavy overcoat, stood up and beckoned to him.

'Hey, fella! Wanna lift?'

'That would be kind. Thank you.'

'Jump in.'

The American didn't want to talk, which suited Jericho. He gripped the edges of his seat and stared ahead as they bounced and rattled at speed down the darkening lanes and into the town. The driver dropped him at the back of the college, waved, gunned the engine, and was gone. Jericho watched him disappear, then turned and walked through the gate.

Before the war, this three-hundred-yard walk, at this

time of day, at this time of year, had been Jericho's favourite: the footpath running across a carpet of mauve and yellow crocuses, the worn stones lit by ornate Victorian lamps, the spires of the chapel to the left, the lights of the college to the right. But the crocuses were late, the lanterns had not been switched on since 1939, and a static water tank disfigured the famous aspect of the chapel. Only one light gleamed faintly in the college and as he walked towards it he gradually realised it was *his* window.

He stopped, frowning. Had he left his desk light on? He was sure he hadn't. As he watched, he saw a shadow, a movement, a figure in the pale yellow square. Two seconds later the light went on in his bedroom.

It wasn't possible, was it?

He started to run. He covered the distance to his staircase in thirty seconds and took the steps like an athlete. His boots clattered on the worn stone. 'Claire?' he shouted. 'Claire?' On the landing his door stood open.

'Steady on, old thing,' said a male voice from within, 'you'll do yourself a mischief.'

3

Guy Logie was a tall, cadaverous man, ten years older than Jericho. He lay on his back on the sofa facing the door, his neck on one armrest, his bony ankles dangling over the other, long hands folded neatly on his stomach. A pipe was clamped between his teeth and he was blowing smoke rings at the ceiling. Distended haloes drifted upwards, twisted, broke and melted into haze. He took his pipe from his mouth and gave an elaborate yawn which seemed to take him by surprise.

'Oh, God. Sorry.' He opened his eyes and swung himself into a sitting position. 'Hello, Tom.'

'Oh please. Please, don't get up,' said Jericho. 'Please, I insist, make yourself at home. Perhaps I could get you some tea?'

'Tea. What a grand idea.' Before the war Logie had been head of mathematics at a vast and ancient public school. He had a Blue in rugger and another in hockey and irony bounced off him like pebbles off an advancing rhinoceros. He crossed the room and grasped Jericho by the shoulders. 'Come here. Let me look at you, old thing,' he said, turning him this way and that towards the light. 'Oh dear oh dear, you do look bloody terrible.'

Jericho shrugged himself free. 'I *was* fine.'

'Sorry. We did knock. Your porter chap let us in.'

'Us?'

There was a noise from the bedroom.

'We came in the car with the flag on it. Greatly impressed your Mr Kite.' Logie followed Jericho's gaze to the bedroom door. 'Oh, that? That's Leveret! Don't mind him.' He took out his pipe and called: 'Mr Leveret! Come and meet Mr Jericho. The *famous* Mr Jericho.'

A small man with a thin face appeared at the entrance to the bedroom.

'Good afternoon, sir.' Leveret wore a raincoat and trilby. His voice had a slight northern accent.

'What the hell are you doing in there?'

'He's just checking you're alone,' said Logie sweetly.

'Of course I'm bloody well alone!'

'And is the whole staircase empty, sir?' enquired Leveret. 'Nobody in the rooms above or below?'

Jericho threw up his hands in exasperation. 'Guy, for God's sake!'

'I think it's all clear,' said Leveret to Logie. 'I've already closed the blackout curtain in there.' He turned to Jericho. 'Mind if I do the same here, sir?' He didn't wait for permission. He crossed to the small leaded window, opened it, took off his hat and thrust his head out, peering up and down, left and right. A freezing mist was off the river and a blast of chill air filled the room. Satisfied, Leveret ducked back inside, closed the window and drew the curtains.

There was a quarter of a minute's silence. Logie broke it by rubbing his hands and saying: 'Any chance of a fire, Tom? I'd forgotten what this place was like in winter. Worse than school. And tea? You mentioned tea? Would you like some tea, Mr Leveret?'

'I would indeed, sir.'

'And what about some toast? I noticed you had some bread, Tom, in the kitchen over there. Toast in front of a college fire? Wouldn't that take us back?'

Jericho looked at him for a moment. He opened his mouth to protest then changed his mind. He took a box of matches from the mantelpiece, struck a light and held it to the gas fire. As usual the pressure was low

25

and the match went out. He lit another and this time it caught. A worm of flame glowed blue and began to spread. He went across the landing to the little kitchen, filled the kettle and lit the gas ring. In the bread bin there was indeed a loaf – Mrs Saxmundham must have put it there earlier in the week – and he sawed off three grey slices. In the cupboard he found a pre-war pot of jam, surprisingly presentable after he had scraped the white fur of mould from its surface, and a smear of margarine on a chipped plate. He arranged his delicacies on a tray and stared at the kettle.

Perhaps he *was* having a dream? But when he looked back into his sitting room, there was Logie stretched out again on the sofa, and Leveret perched uneasily on the edge of one of the chairs, his hat in his hands, like an unreliable witness waiting to go into court with an under-rehearsed story.

Of course they had brought bad news. What else could it be but bad news? The acting head of Hut 8 wouldn't travel fifty miles across country in the deputy director's precious bloody car just to pay a social call. They were going to sack him. *'Sorry, old thing, but we can't carry passengers . . .'* Jericho felt suddenly very tired. He massaged his forehead with the heel of his hand. The familiar headache was beginning to return, spreading up from his sinuses to the back of his eyes.

He had thought it was her. That was the joke. For about half a minute, running towards the lighted window, he had been happy. It was pitiful.

The kettle was beginning to boil. He prised open the tea caddy to find age had reduced the tea leaves to dust.

Nevertheless he spooned them into the pot and tipped in the hot water.

Logie pronounced it nectar.

Afterwards they sat in silence in the semi-darkness. The only illumination was provided by the faint gleam of the desk lamp behind them and the blue glow of the fire at their feet. The gas jet hissed. From beyond the blackout curtains came a faint flurry of splashes and the mournful quacking of a duck. Logie sat on the floor, his long legs outstretched, fiddling with his pipe. Jericho slouched in one of the two easy chairs, prodding the carpet absent-mindedly with the toasting fork. Leveret had been told to stand guard outside: 'Would you mind closing both doors, old thing? The inner door and the outer door, if you'd be so kind?'

The warm aroma of toast hung over the room. Their plates had been pushed to one side.

'This really is most companionable,' murmured Logie. He struck a match and the objects on the mantelpiece threw brief shadows on the damp wall. 'Although one appreciates that one is, in a sense, *fortunate* to be in a place like Bletchley, given where else one might be, one does start to get rather *down* with the sheer *drabness* of it all. Don't you find?'

'I suppose so.' Oh, do get on with it, thought Jericho, stabbing at a couple of crumbs. Just sack me and leave.

Logie made a contented sucking noise through his pipe, then said quietly: 'You know, we've all been terribly worried about you, Tom. I do hope you haven't felt abandoned.'

27

At this unexpected display of concern, Jericho was surprised and humiliated to find tears pricking at his eyes. He kept looking down at the carpet. 'I'm afraid I made the most frightful ass of myself, Guy. The worst of it is, I can't remember much of what happened. There's almost a week that's pretty well a blank.'

Logie gave a dismissive wave of his pipe. 'You're not the first to bust his health in that place, old thing. Did you see in *The Times* poor Dilly Knox died last week? They gave him a gong at the end. Nothing too fancy – CMG, I think. Insisted on receiving it at home, personally, propped up in his chair. Dead two days later. Cancer. Ghastly. And then there was Jeffreys. Remember him?'

'He was sent back to Cambridge to recover as well.'

'That's the man. Whatever happened to Jeffreys?'

'He died.'

'Ah. Shame.' Logie performed a bit more pipe smoker's business, tamping down the tobacco and striking another match.

Just don't let them put me in admin, prayed Jericho. Or Welfare. There was a man in Welfare, Claire had told him, in charge of billeting, who made the girls sit on his knee if they wanted digs with a bathroom.

'It was Shark, wasn't it,' said Logie, giving him a shrewd look through a cloud of smoke, 'that did for you?'

'Yes. Perhaps. You could say that.'

Shark nearly did for all of us, thought Jericho.

'But you broke it,' pursued Logie. 'You broke Shark.'

28

'I wouldn't put it quite like that. *We* broke it.'

'No. *You* broke it.' Logie twirled the spent match in his long finger. 'You broke it. And then it broke you.'

Jericho had a sudden memory-flash of himself on a bicycle, under a starlit sky. A cold night and the cracking of ice.

'Look,' he said, suddenly irritated 'd'you think we could get to the point here, Guy? I mean, tea in front of the college fire talking about old times? It's all very pleasant, but come on –'

'This *is* the point, old thing.' Logie drew his knees up under his chin and wrapped his hands around his shins. 'Shark, Limpet, Dolphin, Oyster, Porpoise, Winkle. The six little fishes in our aquarium, the six German naval Enigmas. And the greatest of these is Shark.' He stared into the fire and for the first time Jericho was able to have a good look at his face, ghostly in the blue light, like a skull. The eye sockets were hollows of darkness. He looked like a man who hadn't slept for a week. He yawned again. 'You know, I was trying to remember, in the car coming over, who decided to call it Shark in the first place.'

'I can't recall,' said Jericho. 'I've an idea it was Alan. Or maybe it was me. Anyway, what the devil does it matter? It just emerged. Nobody argued. Shark was the perfect name for it. We could tell at once it was going to be a monster.'

'And it was.' Logie puffed on his pipe. He was starting to disappear in a bank of fumes. The cheap wartime tobacco smelled like burning hay. 'And it is.'

Something in the way he delivered that last word –

some slight hesitation – made Jericho look up sharply.

The Germans called it Triton, after the son of Poseidon, the demigod of the ocean who blew through a twisted seashell to raise the furies of the deep. 'German humour,' Puck had groaned when they discovered the code name, 'German fucking humour . . .' But at Bletchley they stuck to Shark. It was a tradition, and they were British and they liked their traditions. They named all the enemy's ciphers after sea creatures. The main German naval cipher they called Dolphin. Porpoise was the Enigma key for Mediterranean surface vessels and shipping in the Black Sea. Oyster was an 'officer only' variation on Dolphin. Winkle was the 'officer only' variant of Porpoise.

And Shark? Shark was the operational cipher of the U-boats.

Shark was unique. Every other cipher was produced on a standard three-rotor Enigma machine. But Shark came out of an Enigma with a specially adapted fourth rotor which made it twenty-six times more difficult to break. Only U-boats were allowed to carry it.

It came into service on 1 February 1942 and it blacked out Bletchley almost completely.

Jericho remembered the months that followed as a prolonged nightmare. Before the advent of Shark, the cryptanalysts in Hut 8 had been able to break most U-boat transmissions within a day of interception, allowing ample time to re-route convoys around the wolf packs of German submarines. But in the ten months after the introduction of Shark they read the traffic on just three occasions, and even then it took them seventeen days each time, so that the intelligence, when it did arrive, was virtually useless, was ancient history.

To encourage them in their labours a graph was posted in the code-breakers' hut, showing the monthly tonnages of shipping sunk by the U-boats in the North Atlantic. In January, before the blackout, the Germans destroyed forty-eight Allied ships. In February they sank seventy-three. In March, ninety-five. In May, one hundred and twenty . . .

'The weight of our failure,' said Skynner, the head of the Naval Section, in one of his portentous weekly addresses, 'is measured in the bodies of drowned men.'

In September, ninety-five ships were sunk. In November, ninety-three . . .

And then came Fasson and Grazier.

Somewhere in the distance the college clock began to toll. Jericho found himself counting the chimes.

'Are you all right, old thing? You've gone terribly silent.'

'Sorry. I was just thinking. Do you remember Fasson and Grazier?'

'Fasson and who? Sorry, I don't think I ever met them.'

'No. Nor did I. None of us did.'

Fasson and Grazier. He never knew their Christian names. A first lieutenant and an able-bodied seaman. Their destroyer had helped trap a U-boat, the *U-459,* in the eastern Mediterranean. They had depth-charged

31

her and forced her to the surface. It was about ten o'clock at night. A rough sea, a wind blowing up. After the surviving Germans had abandoned the submarine, the two British sailors had stripped off and swum out to her, lit by searchlights. The U-boat was already low in the waves, holed in the conning tower by cannon fire, shipping water fast. They'd brought off a bundle of secret papers from the radio room, handing them to a boarding party in a boat alongside, and had just gone back for the Enigma machine itself when the U-boat suddenly went bows up and sank. They went down with her – half a mile down, the Navy man had said when he told them the story in Hut 8. *'Let's just hope they were dead before they hit the bottom.'*

And then he'd produced the code books. This was on 24 November 1942. More than nine and a half months into the blackout.

At first glance they scarcely looked worth the cost of two men's lives: two little pamphlets, the Short Signal Book and the Short Weather Cipher, printed in soluble ink on pink blotting paper, designed to be dropped into water by the wireless operator at the first sign of trouble. But to Bletchley they were beyond price, worth more than all the sunken treasure ever raised in history. Jericho knew them by heart even now. He closed his eyes and the symbols were still there, burned into the back of his retina.

T = Lufttemperatur in ganzen Celsius-Graden. –28C = a. –27C = b. –26C = c . . .

U-boats made daily weather reports: air temperature, barometric pressure, wind-speed, cloud-cover . . .

The Short Weather Cipher book reduced that data to a half-dozen letters. Those half-dozen letters were enciphered on the Enigma. The message was then broadcast from the submarine in Morse code and picked up by the German Navy's coastal weather stations. The weather stations used the U-boats' data to compile meteorological reports of their own. These reports were then re-broadcast, an hour or two later, in a standard three-rotor Enigma weather cipher – *a cipher Bletchley could break* – for the use of every German vessel.

It was the back door into Shark.

First, you read the weather report. Then you put the weather report back into the short weather cipher. And what you were left with, by a process of logical deduction, was the text that had been fed into the four-rotor Enigma a few hours earlier. It was a perfect crib. A cryptanalyst's dream.

But still they couldn't break it.

Every day the code-breakers, Jericho among them, fed their possible solutions into the bombes – immense electro-mechanical computers, each the size of a walk-in wardrobe, which made a noise like a knitting machine – and waited to be told which guess was correct. And every day they received no answer. The task was simply too great. Even a message enciphered on a three-rotor enigma might take twenty-four hours to decode, as the bombes clattered their way through the billions of permutations. A four-rotor Enigma, multiplying the numbers by a factor of twenty-six, would theoretically take the best part of a month.

For three weeks Jericho worked round the clock, and when he did grab an hour or two's sleep it was only to dream fitfully of drowning men. *'Let's just hope they were dead before they hit the bottom . . .'* His brain was beyond tiredness. It ached physically, like an over-worked muscle. He began to suffer blackouts. These only lasted a matter of seconds but they were frightening enough. One moment he might be working in the Hut, bent over his slide-rule, and the next everything around him had blurred and jumped on, as if a film had slipped its sprockets in a projector. He managed to beg some Benzedrine off the camp doctor but that only made his mood swings worse, his frenzied highs followed by increasingly protracted lows.

Curiously enough, the solution, when it came, had nothing to do with mathematics, and afterwards he was to reproach himself furiously for becoming too immersed in detail. If he had not been so tired, he might have stepped back and seen it earlier.

It was a Saturday night, the second Saturday in December. At about nine o'clock Logie had sent him home. Jericho had tried to argue, but Logie had said: 'No, you're going to kill yourself if you go on at this rate, and that won't be any use to anyone, old love, especially you.' So Jericho had cycled wearily back to his digs above the pub in Shenley Church End and had crawled beneath the bedclothes. He heard last orders called downstairs, listened as the final few regulars departed and the bar was closed up. In the dead hours after midnight he lay looking at the ceiling wondering if he would ever sleep again, his mind churning like a piece of machinery he couldn't switch off.

It had been obvious from the moment Shark had first surfaced that the only acceptable, long-term solution was to redesign the bombes to take account of the fourth rotor. But that was proving a nightmarishly slow process. If only they could somehow complete the mission Fasson and Grazier had begun so heroically and steal a Shark Enigma. That would make the redesign easier. But Shark Enigmas were the crown jewels of the German Navy. Only the U-boats had them. Only the U-boats and, of course, U-boat communication headquarters in Sainte-Assise, southeast of Paris.

A commando raid on Sainte-Assise, perhaps? A parachute drop? He played with the image for a moment and then dismissed it. Impossible. And, in any case, useless. Even if, by some miracle, they got away with a machine, the Germans would know about it, and switch to a different system of communications. Bletchley's future rested on the Germans continuing to believe that Enigma was impregnable. Nothing could ever be done which might jeopardise that confidence.

Wait a minute.

Jericho sat upright.

Wait a bloody minute.

If only the U-boats and their controllers in Saint-Assise were allowed to have four-rotor Enigmas – and Bletchley knew for a fact that that was the case – how the hell were the coastal weather stations deciphering the U-boat's transmissions?

It was a question no one had bothered to stop and ask, yet it was fundamental.

To read a message enciphered on a four-rotor machine you had to have a four-rotor machine.

Or did you?

If it is true, as someone once said, that genius is 'a zigzag of lightning across the brain', then, in that instant, Jericho knew what genius was. He saw the solution lit up like a landscape before him.

He seized his dressing gown and pulled it over his pyjamas. He grabbed his overcoat, his scarf, his socks and his boots and in less than a minute he was on his bike, wobbling down the moonlit country lane towards the Park. The stars were bright, the ground was iron-hard with frost. He felt absurdly euphoric, laughing like a madman, steering directly into the frozen puddles along the edge of the road, the ice crusts rupturing under his tyres like drum skins. Down the hill he free-wheeled into Bletchley. The countryside fell away and the town spread out beneath him in the moonlight, familiarly drab and ugly but on this night beautiful, as beautiful as Prague or Paris, perched on either bank of a gleaming river of railway tracks. In the still air he could hear a train half a mile away being shunted in the sidings – the sudden, frantic chugging of a locomotive followed by a series of clanks, then a long exhalation of steam. A dog barked and set off another. He passed the church and the war memorial, braked to avoid skidding on the ice, and turned left into Wilton Avenue.

He was panting with exertion by the time he reached the Hut, fifteen minutes later, so much so he could

36

barely blurt out his discovery and catch his breath and stop himself from laughing at the same time: '– They're – using – it – as – a – three-rotor – machine – they're – leaving – the – fourth – rotor – in – neutral – when – they – do – the – weather – stuff – the – silly – bloody – buggers –'

His arrival caused a commotion. The night shift all stopped working and gathered in a concerned half-circle round him – he remembered Logie, Kingcome, Puck and Proudfoot – and it was clear from their expressions they thought he really had gone mad. They sat him down and gave him a mug of tea and told him to take it again, slowly, from the beginning.

He went through it once more, step by step, suddenly anxious there might be a flaw in his logic. Four-rotor Enigmas were restricted to U-boats and Sainte-Assise: correct? Correct. Therefore, coastal stations could only decipher three-rotor Enigma messages: correct? Pause. Correct. Therefore, when the U-boats sent their weather reports, the wireless operators must logically disengage the fourth rotor, probably by setting it at zero.

After that, everything happened quickly. Puck ran along the corridor to the Big Room and laid out the best of the weather cribs on one of the trestle tables. By 4 A.M. they had a menu for the bombes. By breakfast one of the bombe bays was reporting a drop and Puck ran through the canteen like a schoolboy shouting: 'It's out! It's out!'

It was the stuff of legend.

At midday Logie telephoned the Admiralty and told

the Submarine Tracking Room to stand by. Two hours later, they broke the Shark traffic for the previous Monday and the Teleprincesses, the gorgeous girls in the Teleprinter Room, began sending the translated decrypts down the line to London. They were indeed the crown jewels. Messages to raise the hairs on the back of your neck.

FROM: U–BOAT TO CAPTAIN SCHRÖDER
FORCED TO SUBMERGE BY DESTROYERS. NO CONTACT.
LAST POSITION OF ENEMY AT 0815 NAVAL GRID SQUARE
1849.
COURSE 45 DEGREES, SPEED 9 KNOTS.

FROM: GILADORNE
HAVE ATTACKED. CORRECT POSITION OF CONVOY IS
AK1984. 050 DEGREES. AM RELOADING AND KEEPING
CONTACT.

FROM: HAUSE
AT 0115 IN SQUARE 3969 ATTACKED, FLARES AND
GUNFIRE, DIVED, DEPTH CHARGES. NO DAMAGE. AM IN
NAVAL GRID SQUARE AJ3996. ALL TIN FISH, 70 CBM.

FROM: FLAG OFFICER, U–BOATS
TO: 'DRAUFGÄNGER' WOLF PACK
TOMORROW AT 1700 BE IN NEW PATROL LINE FROM
NAVAL GRID SQUARE AK2564 TO 2994. OPERATIONS
AGAINST EASTBOUND CONVOY WHICH AT 1200/7/12 WAS
IN NAVAL GRID SQUARE AK4189. COURSE 050 TO 070
DEGREES. SPEED APPROX 8 KNOTS.

By midnight they had broken, translated and teleprinted to London ninety-two Shark signals giving the Admiralty the approximate whereabouts and tactics of half the Germans' U-boat fleet.

Jericho was in the Bombe Hut when Logie found him. He had been chasing about for the best part of nine hours and now he was supervising a changeover on one of the machines, still wearing his pyjamas under his overcoat, to the great amusement of the Wrens who tended the bombe. Logie clasped Jericho's hand in both of his and shook it vigorously.

'The Prime Minister!' he shouted in Jericho's ear, above the clattering of the bombes.

'What?'

'The Prime Minister has just been on the telephone with his congratulations!'

Logie's voice seemed a long way away. Jericho bent forward to hear better what Churchill had said and then the concrete floor melted beneath his feet and he was pitching forward into darkness.

'Is,' said Jericho.

'What, old thing?'

'Just now, you said Shark *was* a monster and then you said it *is* a monster.' He pointed the fork at Logie. 'I know why you've come. You've lost it, haven't you?'

Logie grunted and stared into the fire and Jericho felt as though someone had laid a stone on his heart. He sat back in his chair, shaking his head, then gave a snort of laughter.

'Thank you, Tom,' said Logie, quietly. 'I'm glad you find it funny.'

'And all the time I thought you'd come here to give me the push. That's funny. That's pretty funny, isn't it, *old thing?*'

'What day is it today?' asked Logie.

'Friday.'

'Right, right.' Logie extinguished his pipe with his thumb and stuffed it into his pocket. He sighed. 'Let me see. That means it must have happened on Monday. No, Tuesday. Sorry. We haven't had a lot of sleep lately.'

He passed a hand through his thinning hair and Jericho noticed for the first time that he'd turned quite grey. So it's not just me, he thought, it's all of us, we're all falling to pieces. No fresh air. No sleep. Not enough fresh food. Six-day weeks and twelve-hour days . . .

'We were still just about ahead of the game when you left,' said Logie. 'You know the drill. Of course you do. You wrote the bloody book. We'd wait for Hut 10 to break the main naval weather cipher, then, by lunchtime, with a bit of luck we'd have enough cribs to tackle the day's short weather codes. That would give us three of the four rotor settings and then we'd get stuck into Shark. The time-lag varied. Sometimes we'd break it in one day, sometimes three or four. Anyway, the stuff was gold-dust and we were Whitehall's blue-eyed boys.'

'Until Tuesday.'

'Until Tuesday.' Logie glanced at the door and

40

dropped his voice. 'It's an absolute tragedy, Tom. We'd cut losses in the North Atlantic by 75 per cent. That's about three hundred thousand tons of shipping a month. The intelligence was amazing. We knew where the U-boats were almost as precisely as the Germans did. Of course, looking back, it was too good to last. The Nazis aren't fools. I always said: "Success in this game breeds failure, and the bigger the success, the bigger the failure's likely to be." You'll remember me saying it. The other side gets suspicious, you see. I said –'

'What happened on Tuesday, Guy?'

'Right-ho. Sorry. Tuesday. It was about eight in the evening. We got a call from one of the intercept stations. Flowerdown, I think, but Scarborough heard it too. I was in the canteen. Puck came and fetched me out. They'd started picking up something in the early afternoon. A single word, broadcast on the hour, every hour. It was coming out of Sainte-Assise on both main U-boat radio nets.'

'This word was enciphered in Shark, I take it?'

'No, that's just it. That's what they were so excited about. It wasn't in cipher. It wasn't even in Morse. It was a human voice. A man. Repeating this one word: *Akelei.*'

'*Akelei,*' murmured Jericho. '*Akelei* . . . That's a flower, isn't it?'

'Ha!' Logie clapped his hands. 'You are a bloody marvel, Tom. See how much we miss you? We had to go and ask one of the German swots on Z-watch what it meant. *Akelei:* a five-petalled flower of the buttercup

41

family, from the Latin *Aquilegia*. We vulgarians call it columbine.'

'*Akelei*,' repeated Jericho. 'This is a prearranged signal of some sort, presumably?'

'It is.'

'And it means?'

'It means trouble, is what it means, old love. We found out just how much trouble at midnight yesterday.' Logie leaned forwards. The humour had left his voice. His face was lined and grave. '*Akelei* means: "Change the Short Weather Code Book." They've gone over to a new one and we haven't a bloody clue what to do about it. They've closed off our way into Shark, Tom. They've blacked us out again.'

It didn't take Jericho long to pack. He'd bought nothing since he arrived in Cambridge except a daily newspaper, so he took out exactly what he'd carried in three weeks earlier: a pair of suitcases filled with clothes, a few books, a fountain pen, a slide rule and pencils, a portable chess set and a pair of walking boots. He laid his cases on the bed and moved slowly about the room collecting his possessions while Logie watched him from the doorway.

Running round and round in his head, unbidden from some hidden depth in his subconscious, was a nursery rhyme: 'For want of a nail, the horse was lost; for want of a horse, the rider was lost; for want of a rider, the battle was lost; for want of a battle, the kingdom was lost; and all for the want of a horseshoe nail . . .'

42

He folded a shirt and laid it on top of his books.

For want of a Short Weather Code Book they might lose the Battle of the Atlantic. So many men, so much material, threatened by so small a thing as a change in weather codes. It was absurd.

'You can always tell a boarding-school boy,' said Logie, 'they travel light. All those endless train journeys, I suppose.'

'I prefer it.'

He stuffed a pair of socks down the side of the case. He was going back. They wanted him back. He couldn't decide whether he was elated or terrified.

'You don't have much stuff in Bletchley, either, do you?'

Jericho swung round to look at him. 'How do you know that?'

'Ah.' Logie winced with embarrassment. 'I'm afraid we had to pack up your room, and, ah, give it to someone else. Pressure of space and all that.'

'You didn't think I'd be coming back?'

'Well, let's say we didn't know we'd need you back so soon. Anyway, there's fresh digs for you in town, so at least it'll be more convenient. No more long cycle rides late at night.'

'I rather like long cycle rides late at night. They clear the mind.' Jericho closed the lids on the suitcases and snapped the locks.

'I say, you are up to this, old love? Nobody wants to force you into anything.'

'I'm a damn sight fitter than you are, by the look of you.'

'Only I'd hate you to feel pressured . . .'

'Oh do shut up, Guy.'

'Right-ho. I suppose we haven't left you with much choice, have we? Can I help you with those?'

'If I'm well enough to go back to Bletchley, I'm well enough to manage a couple of suitcases.'

He carried them to the door and turned off the light. In the sitting room he extinguished the gas fire and took a last look around. The overstuffed sofa. The scratched chairs. The bare mantelpiece. This was his life, he thought, a succession of cheaply furnished rooms provided by English institutions: school, college, government. He wondered what the next room would be like. Logie opened the doors and Jericho turned off the desk light.

The staircase was in darkness. The bulb had long since died. Logie got them down the stone steps by striking a series of matches. At the bottom, they could just make out the shape of Leveret, standing guard, his silhouette framed against the black mass of the chapel. He turned round. His hand went to his pocket.

'All right, Mr Leveret,' said Logie. 'It's only me. Mr Jericho's coming with us.'

Leveret had a blackout torch, a cheap thing swathed in tissue paper. By its pale beam, and by the faint residue of light still left in the sky, they made their way through the college. As they walked alongside the Hall they could hear the clatter of cutlery and the sound of the diners' voices, and Jericho felt a pang of regret. They passed the Porter's Lodge and stepped through the man-sized gate cut in the big oak door. A crack of light appeared in one of the lodge's windows as someone inside pulled back the curtain a fraction. With Leveret in front of him and Logie behind, Jericho had a curious sensation of being under arrest.

The deputy director's Rover was pulled up on the cobbled pavement. Leveret carefully unlocked it and ushered them into the back seat. The interior was cold and smelled of old leather and cigarette ash. As Leveret was stowing the suitcases in the boot Logie said suddenly: 'Who's Claire, by the way?'

'Claire?' Jericho heard his voice in the darkness, guilty and defensive.

'When you came up the staircase I thought I heard you shouting "Claire". Claire?' Logie gave a low whistle. 'I say, she's not the arctic blonde in Hut 3, is she? I bet she is. You lucky bugger . . .'

Leveret started the engine. It stuttered and backfired. He let out the brake and the big car rocked over the cobbles on to King's Parade. The long street was deserted in both directions. A wisp of mist shone in the shaded headlamps. Logie was still chuckling to himself as they swung left.

'I bet she jolly well is. You lucky, lucky bugger . . .'

Kite stayed at his post by the window, watching the red tail-lights until they vanished past the corner of Gonville and Caius. He let the curtain drop.

Well, well . . .

This would give them something to talk about the next morning. Listen to this, Dottie. Mr Jericho was taken away at dead of night – oh, all right then, eight o'clock – by two men, one a tall fellow and the other very obviously a plain clothes copper. Escorted from the premises and not a word to anyone. The tall chap and the copper had arrived about five o'clock while the young master was still out walking and the big one – the detective, presumably – had asked Kite all sorts of questions: 'Has he seen anyone since he's been here? Has he written to anyone? Has anyone written to him? What's he been doing?' Then they'd taken his keys and searched Jericho's room before Jericho got back.

It was murky. Very murky.

A spy, a genius, a broken heart – and now what? A criminal of some sort? Quite possibly. A malingerer? A runaway? A deserter! Yes, that was it: a deserter!

Kite went back to his seat by the stove and opened his evening paper.

NAZI SUB TORPEDOES PASSENGER LINER, he read. WOMEN AND CHILDREN LOST.

Kite shook his head at the wickedness of the world. It was disgusting, a young man of that age, not wearing uniform, hiding away in the middle of England while mothers and kiddies were being killed.

TWO

CRYPTOGRAM

CRYPTOGRAM: message written in cipher or in some other secret form which requires a key qy for its meaning to be discovered.

A Lexicon of Cryptography
('Most Secret', Bletchley Park, 1943)

1

THE NIGHT WAS impenetrable, the cold irresistible. Huddled in his overcoat inside the icy Rover, Tom Jericho could barely see the flickering of his breath or the mist it formed on the window beside him. He reached across and rubbed a porthole in the condensation, smearing his fingers with cold, wet grime. Occasionally their headlamps flashed on white-washed cottages and darkened inns, and once they passed a convoy of lorries heading in the opposite direction. But mostly they seemed to travel in a void. There were no street lights or signposts to guide them, no lit windows; not even a match glimmered in the blackness. They might have been the last three people alive.

Logie had started to snore within fifteen minutes of leaving King's, his head dropping further forwards onto his chest each time the Rover hit a bump, a motion which caused him to mumble and nod, as if in profound agreement with himself. Once, when they turned a corner sharply, his long body toppled sideways and Jericho had to fend him off gently with his forearm.

In the front seat Leveret hadn't uttered a word, except to say, when Jericho asked him to turn it on, that the heater was broken. He was driving with exaggerated care, his face hunched inches from the windscreen, his right foot alternating cautiously between the brake pedal and the accelerator. At times they seemed to be travelling scarcely faster than walking-pace, so that although in daylight the journey to Bletchley might take little more than an hour and a half, Jericho calculated that tonight they would be lucky to reach their destination before midnight.

'I should get some sleep if I were you, old thing,' Logie had said, making a pillow of his overcoat. 'Long night ahead.'

But Jericho couldn't sleep. He stuffed his hands deep into his pockets and stared uselessly into the night.

Bletchley, he thought with disgust. Even the sensation of the name in the mouth was unpleasant, stranded somewhere between blanching and retching. Of all the towns in England, why did they have to choose *Bletchley?* Four years ago he'd never even heard of the place. And he might have lived the rest of his life in happy ignorance had it not been for that glass of sherry in Atwood's rooms in the spring of 1939.

How odd it was, how absurd to trace one's destiny and to find that it revolved around a couple of fluid ounces of pale manzanilla.

It was immediately after that first approach that Atwood had arranged for him to meet some 'friends' in London. Thereafter, every Friday morning for four months, Jericho would catch an early train and make his way to a dusty office block near St James's tube station. Here, in a shabby room furnished by a blackboard and a clerk's desk, he was initiated into the

50

secrets of cryptography. And it was just as Turing had predicted: he loved it.

He loved the history, all of it, from the ancient runic systems and the Irish codes of the Book of Ballymote with their exotic names ('Serpent through the heather', 'Vexation of a poet's heart'), through the codes of Pope Sylvester II and Hildegard von Bingen, through the invention of Alberti's cipher disk – the first poly-alphabetic cipher – and Cardinal Richelieu's grilles, all the way down to the machine-generated mysteries of the German Enigma, which were gloomily held to be unbreakable.

And he loved the secret vocabulary of cryptanalysis, with its homophones and polyphones, its digraphs and bigraphs and nulls. He studied frequency analysis. He was taught the intricacies of superencipherment, of placode and enicode. At the beginning of August 1939 he was formally offered a post at the Government Code and Cipher School at a salary of three hundred pounds a year and was told to go back to Cambridge and await developments. On 1 September he woke to hear on the wireless that the Germans had invaded Poland. On 3 September, the day Britain declared war, a telegram arrived at the Porter's Lodge ordering him to report the following morning to a place called Bletchley Park.

He left King's as instructed, as soon as it was light, wedged into the passenger seat of Atwood's antiquated sports car. Bletchley turned out to be a small Victorian railway town about fifty miles west of Cambridge. Atwood, who liked to cut a dash, insisted on driving with the roof off, and as they rattled down the narrow streets Jericho had an impression of smoke and soot, of little, ugly terraced houses and the tall, black chimneys of brick kilns. They passed under a railway bridge, along a lane, and were waved through a pair of high gates by armed sentries. To their right, a lawn sloped down to a lake fringed by large trees. To their left was a mansion – a long, low, late-Victorian monstrosity of red brick and sand-coloured stone that reminded Jericho of the veterans' hospital his father had died in. He looked around, half expecting to see wimpled nurses wheeling broken men in Bath chairs.

'Isn't it perfectly hideous?' squeaked Atwood with delight. 'Built by a Jew. A stockbroker. *A friend of Lloyd George.*' His voice rose with each statement, suggesting an ascending scale of social horror. He parked abruptly at a crazy angle, with a spurt of gravel, narrowly missing a sapper unrolling a large drum of electrical cable.

Inside, in a panelled drawing room overlooking the lake, sixteen men stood around drinking coffee. Jericho was surprised at how many he recognised. They glanced at one another, embarrassed and amused. *So,* their faces said, *they got you too.* Atwood moved serenely among them, shaking hands and making sharp remarks they all felt obliged to smile at.

'It's not fighting the Germans I object to. It's going to war on behalf of these beastly Poles.' He turned to a handsome, intense-looking young man with a broad, high forehead and thick hair. 'And what's your name?'

'Pukowski,' said the young man, in perfect English. 'I'm a beastly Pole.'

Turing caught Jericho's eye and winked.

In the afternoon the cryptanalysts were split into teams. Turing was assigned to work with Pukowski, redesigning the 'bombe', the giant decryptor which the great Marian Rejewski of the Polish Cipher Bureau had built in 1938 to attack Enigma. Jericho was sent to the stable block behind the mansion to analyse encrypted German radio traffic.

How odd they were, those first nine months of the war, how unreal, how – it seemed absurd to say it now – *peaceful.* They cycled in each day from their digs in various country pubs and guesthouses around the town. They lunched and dined together in the mansion. In the evenings they played chess and strolled through the grounds before cycling home to bed. There was even a Victorian maze of yew hedges to get lost in. Every ten days or so, someone new would join the party – a classicist, a mathematician, a museum curator, a dealer in rare books – each recruited because he was a friend of someone already resident in Bletchley.

A dry and smoky autumn of golds and browns, the rooks whirling in the sky like cinders, gave way to a winter off a Christmas card. The lake froze. The elms drooped under the weight of snow. A robin pecked at breadcrumbs outside the stable window.

Jericho's work was pleasantly academic. Three or four times a day, a motorcycle dispatch-rider would clatter into the courtyard at the back of the big house bearing a pouch of intercepted German cryptograms. Jericho sorted them by frequency and call sign and

marked them up on charts in coloured crayons – red
for the Luftwaffe, green for the German Army – until
gradually, from the unintelligible babble, shapes
emerged. Stations in a radio net allowed to talk freely
to one another made, when plotted on the stable wall,
a crisscross pattern within a circle. Nets in which the
only line of communication was two-way, between a
headquarters and its out-stations, resembled stars.
Circle-nets and star-nets. *Kreis und Stern.*

This idyll lasted eight months, until the German
offensive in May 1940. Up to then, there had been
scarcely enough material for the cryptanalysts to make
a serious attack on Enigma. But as the Wehrmacht
swept through Holland, Belgium, France, the babble
of wireless traffic became a roar. From three or four
motorcycle pouches of material, the volume increased
to thirty or forty; to a hundred; to two hundred.

It was late one morning about a week after this had
started that Jericho felt a touch on his elbow and
turned to find Turing, smiling.

'There's someone I want you to meet, Tom.'

'I'm rather busy at present, Alan, to be honest.'

'Her name's Agnes. I really think you ought to see
her.'

Jericho almost argued. A year later he would have
argued, but at that time he was still too much in awe of
Turing not to do as he was told. He tugged his jacket
off the back of his chair and walked out, shrugging it
on, into the May sunshine.

By this time the Park had already started to be
transformed. Most of the trees at the side of the lake

had been chopped down to make way for a series of large wooden huts. The maze had been uprooted and replaced by a low brick building, outside which a small crowd of cryptanalysts had gathered. There was a sound coming from within it, of a sort Jericho had never heard before, a humming and a clattering, something between a loom and a printing press. He followed Turing through the door. Inside, the noise was deafening, reverberating off the whitewashed walls and the corrugated iron ceiling. A brigadier, an air commodore, two men in overalls and a frightened-looking Wren with her fingers in her ears were standing round the edge of the room staring at a large machine full of revolving drums. A blue flash of electricity arced across the top. There was a fizz and a crackle, a smell of hot oil and overheated metal.

'It's the redesigned Polish bombe,' said Turing. 'I thought I'd call her Agnes.' He rested his long, pale fingers tenderly on the metal frame. There was a bang and he snatched them away again. 'I do hope she works all right . . .'

Oh yes, thought Jericho, rubbing another window into the condensation, oh yes, she worked all right.

The moon slid from beneath a cloud, briefly lighting the Great North Road. He closed his eyes.

She worked all right, and after that the world was different.

Despite his earlier wakefulness Jericho must have fallen asleep, for when he next opened his eyes Logie was sitting up and the Rover was passing through a small

town. It was still dark and at first he couldn't get his
bearings. But then they passed a row of shops, and
when the headlights flickered briefly on the billboard
of the County Cinema (NOW SHOWING: 'THE NAVY
COMES THROUGH', 'SOMEWHERE I'LL FIND YOU'), he
muttered to himself, and heard the weariness already
creeping back into his voice: 'Bletchley.'

'Too bloody right,' said Logie.

Down Victoria Road, past the council offices, past a
school . . . The road curved and suddenly, in the
distance, above the pavements, a myriad of fireflies
were swarming towards them. Jericho passed his hands
across his face and found that his fingers were numb.
He felt mildly sick.

'What time is it?'

'Midnight,' said Logie. 'Shift change.'

The specks of light were blackout torches.

Jericho guessed the Park's workforce must now be
about five or six thousand, toiling round the clock in
eight-hour shifts – midnight till eight, eight till four,
four till midnight. That meant maybe four thousand
people were now on the move, half coming off shift,
half going on, and by the time the Rover had turned
into the road leading to the main gate it was barely
possible to advance a yard without hitting someone.
Leveret was alternately leaning out of the window,
shouting and hammering on the horn. Crowds of
people had spilled out into the road, most on foot,
some on bicycles. A convoy of buses was struggling to
get past. Jericho thought: the odds are two to one that
Claire's among them. He had a sudden desire to shrink

down in his seat, to cover his head, to get away.

Logie was looking at him curiously. 'Are you *sure* you're up to this, old thing?'

'I'm fine. It's just – it's hard to think it started with sixteen of us.'

'Wonderful, isn't it? And it'll be twice the size next year.' The pride in Logie's voice abruptly gave way to alarm. 'For God's sake, Leveret, look out man, you nearly ran that lady over!'

In the headlights a blonde head spun angrily and Jericho felt a rush of nausea. But it wasn't her. It was a woman he didn't recognise, a woman in an army uniform, a slash of scarlet lipstick like a wound across her face. She looked as if she was tarted up and on her way to meet a man. She shook her fist and mouthed 'Bugger off' at them.

'Well,' said Logie, primly, 'I *thought* she was a lady.'

When they reached the guard post they had to dig out their identity cards. Leveret collected them and passed them on through the window to an RAF corporal. The sentry hitched his rifle and studied the cards by torchlight, then ducked down and directed the beam in turn on to each of their faces. The brilliance struck Jericho like a blow. Behind them he could hear a second sentry rummaging through the boot.

He flinched from the light and turned to Logie. 'When did all this start?' He could remember a time when they weren't even asked for passes.

'Not sure now you mention it.' Logie shrugged. 'They seem to have tightened up in the last week or two.'

Their cards were returned. The barrier rose. The sentry waved them through. Beside the road was a freshly painted sign. They had been given a new name some time around Christmas and Jericho could just about read the white lettering in the darkness: 'Government Communication Headquarters'.

The metal barrier came down after them with a crash.

2

Even in the blackout you could sense the size of the place. The mansion was still the same, and so were the huts, but these were now just a fraction of the overall site. Stretching away beyond them was a great factory of intelligence: low, brick-built offices and bombproof bunkers of concrete and steel, A-Blocks and B-Blocks and C-Blocks, tunnels and shelters and guard posts and garages . . . There was a big military camp just beyond the wire. The barrels of anti-aircraft batteries poked through camouflaged netting in the nearby woods. And more buildings were under construction. There had never been a day when Jericho hadn't heard the racket of mechanical diggers and cement mixers, the ringing of pickaxes and the splintering of falling trees. Once, just before he left, he had paced out the distance from the new assembly hall to the far perimeter fence and had reckoned it at half a mile. What was it all for? He had no idea. Sometimes he thought they must be monitoring every radio transmission on the planet.

Leveret drove the Rover slowly past the darkened mansion, past the tennis court and the generators, and drew up a short distance from the huts.

Jericho clambered stiffly from the back seat. His legs had gone to sleep and the sensation of the blood returning made his knees buckle. He leaned against the side of the car. His right shoulder was rigid with cold. A duck splashed somewhere on the lake and its cry made him think of Cambridge – of his warm bed and his crosswords – and he had to shake his head to clear the memory.

Logie was explaining to him that he had a choice: Leveret could take him over to his new digs and he could have a decent night's kip, or he could come in straight away and take a look at things immediately.

'Why don't we start now?' said Jericho. His re-entry into the hut would be an ordeal. He'd prefer to get it over with.

'That's the spirit, old love. Leveret will look after your cases, won't you, Leveret? And take them to Mr Jericho's room?'

'Yes, sir.' Leveret looked at Jericho for a moment, then stuck out his hand. 'Good luck, sir.'

Jericho took it. The solemnity surprised him. Anyone would think he was about to make a parachute jump into hostile territory. He tried to think of something to say. 'Thank you very much for driving us.'

Logie was fiddling with Leveret's blackout torch. 'What the hell's wrong with this thing?' He knocked it against his palm. 'Bloody thing. Oh, sod it. Come on.'

He strode away on his long legs and after a moment's hesitation Jericho wrapped his scarf tight around his neck and followed. In the darkness they had to feel their way along the blastproof wall surrounding Hut 8. Logie banged into what sounded like a bicycle and Jericho heard him swear. He dropped the torch. The impact made it come on. A trickle of light revealed the entrance to the hut. There was a smell of lime and damp here – lime and damp and creosote: the odours of Jericho's war. Logie rattled the handle, the door opened and they stepped into the dim glow.

Because he had changed so much in the month he had been away, somehow – illogically – he had expected that the hut would have changed as well. Instead, the instant he crossed the threshold, the familiarity of it almost overwhelmed him. It was like a recurrent dream in which the horror lay in knowing precisely what would happen next – the certainty that it always had been, and always would be, exactly like this.

A narrow, ill-lit corridor, perhaps twenty yards long, stretched in front of him, with a dozen doors leading off it. The wooden partitions were flimsy and the noise of a hundred people working at full stretch leaked from room to room – the clump and thud of boots and shoes on the bare boards, the hum of conversation, the occasional shout, the scrape of chair legs, the ringing of telephones, the *clack clack clack* of the Type-X machines in the Decoding Room.

The only tiny difference was that the walk-in

cupboard on the right, immediately next to the entrance, now had a nameplate on it: 'Lt. Kramer US Navy Liaison Officer'.

Familiar faces loomed towards him. Kingcome and Proudfoot were whispering together outside the Catalogue Room and drew back to let him pass. He nodded to them. They nodded in return but didn't speak. Atwood hurried out of the Crib Room, saw Jericho, gawped, then put his head down. He muttered, 'Hello, Tom,' then almost ran towards Research.

Clearly, nobody had ever expected to see him again. He was an embarrassment. A dead man. A ghost.

Logie was oblivious, both to the general astonishment and to Jericho's discomfort. 'Hello, everybody.' He waved to Atwood. 'Hello, Frank. Look who's back! The prodigal returns! Give them a smile, Tom, old thing, it's not a ruddy funeral. Not yet, anyway.' He stopped outside his office and fiddled with his key for half a minute, then discovered the door was unlocked. 'Come in, come in.'

The room was scarcely bigger than a broom store. It had been Turing's cubbyhole until just before the break into Shark, when Turing had been sent to America. Now Logie had it – his tiny perquisite of rank – and he looked absurdly huge as he bent over his desk, like an adult poking around in a child's den. There was a fireproof safe in one corner, leaking intercepts, and a rubbish bin labelled CONFIDENTIAL WASTE. There was a telephone with a red handset. Paper was everywhere – on the floor, on the table, on the top of the radiator

61

where it had baked crisp and yellow, in wire baskets and in box files, in tall stacks and in piles that had subsided into fans.

'Bugger, bugger, bugger.' Logie had a message slip in his hands and was frowning at it. He took his pipe out of his pocket and chewed on the stem. He seemed to have forgotten Jericho's presence until Jericho coughed to remind him.

'What? Oh. Sorry, old love.' He traced the words of the message with his pipe. 'The Admiralty's a bit exercised, apparently. Conference in A-Block at eight o'clock with Navy brass up from Whitehall. Want to know the score. Skynner's in a spin and demands to see me forthwith. Bugger, bugger.'

'Does Skynner know I'm back?' Skynner was the head of Bletchley's Naval Section. He'd never cared for Jericho, probably because Jericho had never concealed his opinion of him: that he was a bombast and a bully whose chief war aim was to greet the peace as Sir Leonard Skynner, OBE, with a seat on the Security Executive and a lease on an Oxford mastership. Jericho had a vague memory of actually telling Skynner some of this, or all of it, or possibly more, shortly before he was sent back to Cambridge to recover his senses.

'Of course he knows you're back, old thing. I had to clear it with him first.'

'And he doesn't mind?'

'Mind? No. 'The man's desperate. He'd do anything to get back into Shark.' Logie added quickly: 'Sorry, I don't mean . . . that's not to say that bringing you back is an act of desperation. Only, well, you know . . .' He sat down heavily and looked again at the message. He rattled his pipe against his worn yellow teeth. 'Bugger, bugger, bugger . . .'

Looking at him then it occurred to Jericho that he knew almost nothing about Logie. They had worked together for two years, would regard themselves as friends, yet they'd never had a proper conversation. He didn't know if Logie was married, or if he had a girl.

'I'd better go and see him, I suppose. Excuse me, old love.'

Logie squeezed past his desk and shouted down the corridor: 'Puck!' Jericho could hear the cry being taken up somewhere in the recesses of the hut by another voice. 'Puck!' And then another: 'Puck! Puck!'

Logie ducked his head back into the office. 'One analyst per shift co-ordinates the Shark attack. Puck this shift, Baxter next, then Pettifer.' His head disappeared again. 'Ah-ha, here he comes. Come on, old thing. Look alive. I've a surprise for you. See who's in here.'

'So there you are, my dear Guy,' came a familiar voice from the corridor. 'Nobody knew where to find you.'

Adam Pukowski slid his lithe frame past Logie, saw Jericho and stopped dead. He was genuinely shocked. Jericho could almost see his mind struggling to regain control of his features, forcing his famous smile back on to his face. At last he managed it. He even threw his arms round Jericho and hugged him. 'Tom, it's . . . I had begun to think you were never returning. It's marvellous.'

63

'It's good to see you again, Puck.' Jericho patted him politely on the back.

Puck was their mascot, their touch of glamour, their link with the adventure of war. He had arrived in the first week to brief them on the Polish bombe, then flown back to Poland. When Poland fell he had fled to France, and when France collapsed he had escaped across the Pyrenees. Romantic stories clustered around him: that he had hidden from the Germans in a goatherd's cottage, that he had smuggled himself aboard a Portuguese steamer and ordered the captain to sail to England at pistol-point. When he had popped up again in Bletchley in the winter of 1940 it was Pinker, the Shakespearian, who had shortened his name to Puck ('that merry wanderer of the night'). His mother was British, which explained his almost perfect English, distinctive only because he pronounced it so carefully.

'You have come to give us assistance?'

'So it seems.' He shyly disengaged himself from Puck's embrace. 'For what it's worth.'

'Splendid, splendid.' Logie regarded them fondly for a moment, then began rummaging among the litter on his desk. 'Now where is that thing? It was here this morning . . .'

Puck nodded at Logie's back and whispered: 'Do you see, Tom? As organised as ever.'

'Now, now, Puck, I heard that. Let me see. Is this it? No. Yes. Yes!'

He turned and handed Jericho a typewritten document, officially stamped and headed 'By Order of

64

the War Office'. It was a billeting notice, served on a Mrs Ethel Armstrong, entitling Jericho to lodgings in the Commercial Guesthouse, Albion Street, Bletchley.

'I'm afraid I don't know what it's like, old thing. Best I could do.'

'I'm sure it's fine.' Jericho folded the chit and stuffed it into his pocket. Actually, he was quite sure it *wasn't* fine – the last decent rooms in Bletchley had disappeared three years ago, and people now had to travel in from as far away as Bedford, twenty miles distant – but what was the point in complaining? On past experience he wouldn't be using the room much anyway, except to sleep in.

'Now don't you go exhausting yourself, my boy,' said Logie. 'We don't expect you to work a full shift. Nothing like that. You just come and go as you please. What we want from you is what you gave us last time. Insight. Inspiration. Spotting that something we've all missed. Isn't that so, Puck?'

'Absolutely.' His handsome face was more haggard than Jericho had ever seen it, more tired even than Logie's. 'God knows, Tom, we are certainly up against it.'

'I take it then we're no further forward?' said Logie. 'No good news I can give our lord and master?'

Puck shook his head.

'Not even a glimmer?'

'Not even that.'

'No. Well, why should there be? Damn bloody *admirals.*' Logie screwed up the message slip, aimed it at his rubbish bin and missed. 'I'd show you round

65

myself, Tom, but the Skynner waits for no man, as
you'll recall. All right with you, Puck? Give him the
grand tour?'

'Of course, Guy. As you wish.'

Logie ushered them out into the passage and tried to
lock the door, then gave up on it. As he turned he
opened his mouth and Jericho nerved himself for one
of Logie's excruciating housemaster's pep talks –
something about innocent lives depending on them,
and the need for them to do their best, and the race
being not to the swift nor the battle to the strong (he
had actually said this once) – but instead his mouth just
widened into a yawn.

'Oh, dear. Sorry, old thing. Sorry.'

He shuffled off down the corridor, patting his
pockets to make sure he had his pipe and tobacco
pouch. They heard him mutter again, something about
'bloody admirals', and he was gone.

Hut 8 was thirty-five yards long by ten wide and
Jericho could have toured it in his sleep, probably *had*
toured it in his sleep, for all he knew. The outside walls
were thin and the damp from the lake seemed to rise
through the floorboards so that at night the rooms were
chilly, cast in a sepia glow by bare, low-wattage bulbs.
The furniture was mostly trestle tables and folding
wooden chairs. It reminded Jericho of a church hall on
a winter's night. All that was missing was a badly tuned
piano and somebody thumping out 'Land of Hope and
Glory'.

It was laid out like an assembly line, the main stage

in a process that originated somewhere far out in the darkness, maybe two thousand miles away, when the grey hull of a U-boat rose close to the surface and squirted off a radio message to its controllers. The signals were intercepted at various listening-posts and teleprinted to Bletchley and within ten minutes of transmission, even as the U-boats were preparing to dive, they were emerging via a tunnel into Hut 8's Registration Room. Jericho helped himself to the contents of a wire basket labelled 'Shark' and carried them to the nearest light. The hours immediately after midnight were usually the busiest time. Sure enough, six messages had been intercepted in the last eighteen minutes. Three consisted of just eight letters: he guessed they were weather reports. Even the longest of the other cryptograms was no more than a couple of dozen four-letter groups:

JRLO GOPL DNRZ LOBT —

Puck made a weary face at him, as if to say: What can you do?

Jericho said: 'What's the volume?'

'It varies. One hundred and fifty, perhaps two hundred messages a day. And rising.'

The Registration Room didn't just handle Shark. There was Porpoise and Dolphin and all the other different Enigma keys to log and then pass across the corridor to the Crib Room. Here, the cribsters sifted them for clues – radio station call signs they recognised (Kiel was JDU, for example, Wilhelmshaven KYU), messages whose contents they could guess at, or cryptograms that had already been enciphered in one key and then retransmitted in another (they marked these 'XX' and called them 'kisses'). Atwood was the champion cribster and the Wrens said cattily behind his back that these were the only kisses he had ever had.

It was in the big room next door – which they called, with their solemn humour, the Big Room – that the cryptanalysts used the cribs to construct possible solutions that could be tested on the bombes. Jericho took in the rickety tables, the hard chairs, the weak lighting, the fug of tobacco, the college-library atmosphere, the night chill (most of the cryptanalysts were wearing coats and mittens) and he wondered why – *why?* – he had been so ready to come back. Kingcome and Proudfoot were there, and Upjohn and Pinker and de Brooke, and maybe half a dozen newcomers whose faces he didn't recognise, including one young man sitting bold as you please in the seat which had once been reserved for Jericho. The tables were stacked with cryptograms, like ballot papers at an election count.

Puck was muttering something about back-breaks but Jericho, fascinated by the sight of someone else in his place, lost track and had to interrupt him. 'I'm sorry, Puck. What was that?'

'I was saying that from twenty minutes ago we are up to date. Shark is now fully read to the point of the code change. So that there is nothing left to us. Except history.' He gave a weak smile and patted Jericho's shoulder. 'Come. I'll show you.'

Enigma

When a cryptanalyst believed he'd glimpsed a possible break into a message, his guess was sent out of the hut to be tested on a bombe. And if he'd been skilful enough, or lucky enough, then in an hour, or a day, the bombe would churn through a million permutations and reveal how the Enigma machine had been set up. That information was relayed back from the bombe bays to the Decoding Room.

Because of its noise, the Decoding Room was tucked away at the far end of the hut. Personally, Jericho liked the clatter. It was the sound of success. His worst memories were of the nights when the building was silent. A dozen British Type-X enciphering machines had been modified to mimic the actions of the German Enigma. They were big, cumbersome devices – typewriters with rotors, a plugboard and a cylinder – at which sat young and well-groomed debutantes.

Baxter, who was the hut's resident Marxist, had a theory that Bletchley's workforce (which was mainly female) was arranged in what he called 'a paradigm of the English class system'. The wireless interceptors, shivering in their coastal radio stations, were generally working-class and laboured in ignorance of the Enigma secret. The bombe operators, who worked in the grounds of some nearby country houses and in a big new installation just outside London, were petit-bourgeois and had a vague idea. And the Decoding Room girls, in the heart of the Park, were mostly upper-middle-class, even aristocratic, and they saw it all – the secrets literally passed through their fingers. They typed out the letters of the original cryptogram,

69

and from the cylinder on the right of the Type-X a strip
of sticky-backed paper, the sort you saw gummed
down on telegram forms, slowly emerged, bearing the
decrypted plaintext.

'Those three are doing Dolphin,' said Puck,
pointing across the room, 'and the two by the door are
just starting on Porpoise. And this charming young
lady here, I believe' – he bowed to her – 'has Shark.
May we?'

She was young, about eighteen, with curly red hair
and wide hazel eyes. She looked up and smiled at him,
a dazzling *Tatler* smile, and he leaned across her and
began uncoiling the strip of tape from the cylinder.
Jericho noticed as he did so that he left one hand
resting casually on her shoulder, just as simply as that,
and he thought how much he envied Puck the ease of
that gesture. It would have taken him a week to pluck
up the nerve. Puck beckoned him down to read the
decrypt.

VONSCHULZEQU88521DAMPFER1TANKERWAHRSCHEINLICHAM6
3TANKERFACKEL ...

Jericho ran his finger along it, separating the words
and translating it in his mind: U-boat commander von
Schulze was in grid square 8852 and had sunk one
steamship (for certain) and one tanker (probably) and
had set one other tanker on fire . . .

'What date is this?'

'You can see it there,' said Puck. '*Sechs drei*. The
sixth of March. We've broken everything from this

70

week up to the code change on Wednesday night, so now we go back and pick up the intercepts we missed earlier in the month. This is – what? – six days old. Herr Kapitän von Schulze may be five hundred miles away by now. It is of academic interest only, I fear.'

'Poor devils,' said Jericho, passing his finger along the tape for a second time. *IDAMPFERITANKER . . .* What freezing and drowning and burning were concentrated in that one line! What were the ships called, he wondered, and had the families of the crews been told?

'We have approximately a further eighty messages from the sixth still to run through the Type-Xs. I shall put two more operators on to it. A couple of hours and we should be finished.'

'And then what?'

'Then, my dear Tom? Then I suppose we shall make a start on back-breaks from February. But that barely qualifies even as history. February? February in the Atlantic? Archaeology!'

'Any progress on the four-wheel bombe?'

Puck shook his head. 'First, it is impossible. It is out of the question. Then there is a design, but the design is theoretical nonsense. Then there is a design that should work, but doesn't. Then there is a shortage of materials. Then there is a shortage of engineers. . .' He made a weary gesture with his hand, as if he were pushing it all out of the way.

'Has anything else changed?'

'Nothing that affects us. According to the direction finders, U-boat HQ has moved from Paris to Berlin. They have some wonderful new transmitter at

Magdeburg they say will reach a U-boat forty-five feet under water at a range of two thousand miles.'

Jericho murmured: 'How very ingenious of them.'

The red-headed girl had finished deciphering the message. She tore off the tape, stuck it on the back of the cryptogram and handed it to another girl, who rushed out of the room. Now it would be turned into recognisable English and teleprinted to the Admiralty.

Puck touched Jericho's arm. 'You must be tired. Why don't you go now and rest?'

But Jericho didn't feel like sleeping. 'I'd like to see all the Shark traffic we haven't been able to break. Everything since midnight on Wednesday.'

Puck gave a puzzled smile. 'Why? There's nothing you can do with it.'

'Maybe so. But I'd like to see it.'

'Why?'

'I don't know.' Jericho shrugged. 'Just to handle it. To get a feel of it. I've been out of the game for a month.'

'You think we may have missed something, perhaps?'

'Not at all. But Logie has asked me.'

'Ah yes. The celebrated Jericho "inspiration" and "intuition".' Puck couldn't conceal his irritation. 'And so from science and logic we descend to superstition and "feelings".'

'For heaven's sake, Puck!' Jericho was starting to become annoyed himself. 'Just humour me, if that's how you prefer to look at it.'

Puck glared at him for a moment, and then, as quickly as they had arisen, the clouds seemed to pass. 'Of course.' He held up his hands in a gesture of surrender. 'You must see it all. Forgive me. I'm tired. We're all tired.'

Five minutes later, when Jericho walked into the Big Room carrying the folder of Shark cryptograms, he found his old seat had been vacated. Someone had also laid out in his place a new pile of jotting paper and three freshly sharpened pencils. He looked around, but nobody seemed to be paying him any attention.

He laid the intercepts out on the table. He loosened his scarf. He felt the radiator – as ever, it was lukewarm. He blew some warmth on to his hands and sat down.

He was back.

3

Whenever anyone asked Jericho why he was a mathematician – some friend of his mother, perhaps, or an inquisitive colleague with no interest in science – he would shake his head and smile and claim he had no idea. If they persisted, he might, with some diffidence, direct them to the definition offered by G. H. Hardy in his famous *Apology*: 'a mathematician, like a painter or a poet, is a *maker* of patterns'. If that didn't satisfy them, he would try to explain by quoting the most basic illustration he could think of: pi – 3.14 – the ratio of a circle's circumference to its diameter. Calculate pi to a thousand decimal places, he would say, or a million or more, and you will discover no pattern to its unending sequence of digits. It appears random, chaotic, ugly. Yet Leibnitz and Gregory can take the same number and tease from it a pattern of crystalline elegance:

$$\frac{pi}{4} = 1 - \frac{1}{3} + \frac{1}{5} - \frac{1}{7} + \frac{1}{9} - -$$

and so on to infinity. Such a pattern had no practical usefulness, it was merely beautiful – as sublime, to Jericho, as a line in a fugue by Bach – and if his questioner still couldn't see what he was driving at, then, sadly, he would give up on them as a waste of time.

On the same principle, Jericho thought the Enigma machine was beautiful – a masterpiece of human ingenuity that created both chaos and a tiny ribbon of meaning. In the early days at Bletchley he used to fantasise that some day, when the war was over, he would track down its German inventor, Herr Arthur Scherbius, and buy him a glass of beer. But then he'd heard that Scherbius had died in 1929, killed – of all ludicrously illogical things – by a runaway horse, and hadn't lived to see the success of his patent.

If he had, he would have been a rich man. By the end of 1942 Bletchley estimated that the German had manufactured at least a hundred thousand Enigmas. Every Army headquarters had one, every Luftwaffe base, every warship, every submarine, every port, every big railway station, every SS brigade and Gestapo HQ.

Never before had a nation entrusted so much of its secret communications to a single device.

In the mansion at Bletchley the cryptanalysts had a roomful of captured Enigmas and Jericho had played with them for hours. They were small (little more than a foot square by six inches deep), portable (they weighed just twenty-six pounds) and simple to operate. You set up your machine, typed in your message, and the ciphertext was spelled out, letter by letter, on a panel of small electric bulbs. Whoever received the enciphered message merely had to set up his machine in exactly the same way, type in the cryptogram, and there, spelled out on the bulbs, would be the original plaintext.

The genius lay in the vast number of different permutations the Enigma could generate. Electric current on a standard Enigma flowed from keyboard to lamps via a set of three wired rotors (at least one of which turned a notch every time a key was struck) and a plugboard with twenty-six jacks. The circuits changed constantly; their potential number was astronomical, but calculable. There were five different rotors to choose from (two were kept spare) which meant they could be arranged in any one of sixty possible orders. Each rotor was slotted on to a spindle and had twenty-six possible starting positions. Twenty-six to the power of three was 17,576. Multiply that by the sixty potential rotor-orders and you got 1,054,560. Multiply *that* by the possible number of plugboard connections – about 150 million million – and you were looking at a machine that had around 150 million million *million* different starting positions. It didn't matter how many Enigma machines you captured or how long you played with them. They were useless unless you knew the rotor order, the rotor starting positions and the plugboard connections. And the Germans changed these daily, sometimes twice a day.

The machine had only one tiny – but, as it turned out, crucial – flaw. It could never encipher a letter as itself: an *A* would never emerge from it as an *A*, or *a B* as a *B*, or a *C* as *a C* . . . *Nothing is ever itself:* that was the great guiding principle in the breaking of Enigma, the infinitesimal weakness that the bombes exploited.

Suppose one had a cryptogram that began:

```
IGWH BSTU XNTX EYLK PEAZ ZNSK UFJR CADV _
```

And suppose one knew that this message originated from the Kriegsmarine's weather station in the Bay of Biscay, a particular friend of the Hut 8 cribsters, which always began its reports in the same way:

```
WEUBYYNULLSEQSNULLNULL
```

('Weather survey 0600', WEUB being an abbreviation for WETTERÜBERSICHT and SEQS for SECHS; YY and NULL being inserted to baffle eavesdroppers).

The cryptanalyst would lay out the ciphertext and slide the crib beneath it and on the principle that *nothing is ever itself* he would keep sliding it until he found a position in which there were no matching letters between the top and bottom lines. The result in this case would be:

Enigma

BSTUXNTXEYLKPEAZZNSKUF
WEUBYYNULLSEQSNULLNULL

And at this point it became theoretically possible to calculate the original Enigma settings that alone could have produced this precise sequence of letter pairings. It was still an immense calculation, one which would have taken a team of human beings several weeks. The Germans assumed, rightly, that whatever intelligence might be gained would be too old to be of use. But Bletchley – and this was what the Germans had never reckoned on – *Bletchley didn't use human beings.* It used bombes. For the first time in history, a cipher mass-manufactured by machine was being broken by machine.

Who needed spies now? What need now of secret inks and dead-letter drops and midnight assignations in curtained *wagons-lits?* Now you needed mathematicians and engineers with oilcans and fifteen hundred filing clerks to process five thousand secret messages a day. They had taken espionage into the machine age.

But none of this was of much help to Jericho in breaking Shark.

Shark defied every tool he could bring to bear on it. For a start, there were almost no cribs. In the case of a surface Enigma key, if Hut 8 ran out of cribs, they had tricks to get round it – 'gardening', for example. 'Gardening' was arranging for the RAF to lay mines in a particular naval grid square outside a German harbour. An hour later, you could guarantee, the harbour master, with Teutonic efficiency, would send a message using that day's Enigma settings, warning ships to beware of mines in naval grid square such-and-such. The signal would be intercepted, flashed to Hut 8, and give them their missing crib.

But you couldn't do that with Shark and Jericho could make only the vaguest guesses at the contents of the cryptograms. There were eight long messages originating from Berlin. They would be orders, he supposed, probably directing the U-boats into 'wolf packs' and stationing them in front of the oncoming convoys. The shorter signals – there were a hundred and twenty-two, which Jericho sorted into a separate pile – had been sent by the submarines themselves. These could contain anything: reports of ships sunk and of engine trouble; details of survivors floating in the water and of crewmen washed overboard; requests for spare parts and fresh orders. Shortest of all were the U-boats' weather messages or, very occasionally, contact reports: 'Convoy in naval grid square BE9533 course 70 degrees speed 9 knots . . .' But these were encoded, like the weather bulletins, with one letter of the alphabet substituting for each piece of information. And then they were enciphered in Shark.

He tapped his pencil against the desk. Puck was quite right. There was not enough material to work with.

And even if there had been, there was still the wretched fourth rotor on the Shark Enigma, the innovation that made U-boat messages twenty-six times more difficult to break than those of surface ships. One hundred and fifty million million million multiplied by twenty-six. A phenomenal number. The engineers had been struggling for a year to develop a four-rotor bombe – but still, apparently, without success. It seemed to be just that one step beyond their technical ability.

No cribs, no bombes. Hopeless.

Hours passed during which Jericho tried every trick he could think of to prompt some fresh inspiration. He arranged the cryptograms chronologically. Then he arranged them by length. Then he sorted them by frequency. He doodled on the pile of paper. He prowled around the hut, oblivious now to who was looking at him and who wasn't. This was what it had been like for ten interminable months last year. No wonder he had gone mad. The chorus-lines of meaningless letters danced before his eyes. But they were not meaningless. They were loaded with the most vital meaning imaginable, if only he could find it. But where was the pattern? Where was the pattern? Where was the *pattern*?

It was the practice on the night shift at about four o'clock in the morning for everyone to take a meal-break. The cryptanalysts went off when they liked, depending on the stage they'd reached in their work. The Decoding Room girls and the clerks in the Registration and Catalogue rooms had to leave according to a rota so that the hut was never caught short-staffed.

Jericho didn't notice the drift of people towards the door. He had both elbows on the table and was leaning over the cryptograms, his knuckles pressed to his temples. His mind was eidetic – that is to say, it could hold and retrieve images with photographic accuracy, be they mid-game positions in chess, crossword puzzles or enciphered German naval signals – and he was working with his eyes closed.

'"Below the thunders of the upper deep,"' intoned a muffled voice behind him, '"Far, far beneath in the abysmal sea,/His ancient, dreamless, uninvaded sleep . . ."'

'". . . The Kraken sleepeth."' Jericho finished the quotation and turned to find Atwood pulling on a purple balaclava. 'Coleridge?'

'Coleridge?' Atwood's face abruptly emerged wearing an expression of outrage. *Coleridge?* It's Tennyson, you barbarian. We wondered whether you'd care to join us for refreshment.'

Jericho was about to refuse, but decided that would be rude. In any case, he was hungry. He'd eaten nothing except toast and jam for twelve hours.

'That's kind. Thank you.'

He followed Atwood, Pinker and a couple of the others along the length of the hut and out into the night. At some stage while he'd been lost in the cryptograms it must have rained and the air was still moist. Along the road to the right he could hear people moving in the shadows. The beams of torches glistened on the wet tarmac. Atwood conducted them past the mansion and the arboretum and through the main gate. Discussing work outside the hut was forbidden and Atwood, purely to annoy Pinker, was declaiming on the suicide of Virginia Woolf, which he held to be the greatest day for English letters since the invention of the printing press.

'I c-c-can't believe you mmm-mmm-mmm...' When Pinker snagged himself on a word, his whole body seemed to shake with the effort of trying to get himself free. Above his bow-tie, his face bloomed scarlet in the torchlight. They stopped and waited patiently for him. 'Mmm-mmm...'

'Mean that?' suggested Atwood.

'Mean that, Frank,' gasped Pinker with relief. 'Thank you.'

Someone came to Atwood's support, and then Pinker's shrill voice started to argue again. They moved off. Jericho lagged behind.

The canteen, which lay just behind the perimeter fence, was as big as an aircraft hangar, brightly lit and thunderously noisy, with perhaps five or six hundred people sitting down to eat or queuing for food.

One of the new cryptanalysts shouted to Jericho: 'I bet you've missed this!' Jericho smiled and was about to say something in return but the young man went off to collect a tray. The din was dreadful, and so was the smell – a blended steam of institutional food, of cabbage and boiled fish and custard, laced with cigarette smoke and damp clothes. Jericho felt simultaneously intimidated by it and detached from it, like a prisoner returning from solitary confinement, or a patient from an isolation ward released on to the street after a long illness.

He queued and didn't pay much attention to the food being slopped on his plate. It was only after he had handed over his two shillings and sat down that he took a good look at it – boiled potatoes in a curdled yellow grease and a slab of something ribbed and grey. He stabbed at the lump with his fork, then lifted a fragment cautiously to his mouth. It tasted like fishy liver, like congealed cod liver oil. He winced.

'This is perfectly vile.'

Atwood said, through a full mouth: 'It's whale meat.'

'Good heavens.' Jericho put his fork down hurriedly.

'Don't waste it, dear boy. Don't you know there's a war on? Pass it over.'

Jericho pushed the plate across the table and tried to swill the taste away with the milk-water coffee.

The pudding was some kind of fruit tart, and that was better, or, rather, it tasted of nothing more noxious than cardboard, but halfway through it, Jericho's wavering appetite finally died. Atwood was now giving them his opinion of Gielgud's interpretation of Hamlet, spraying the table in the process with particles of whale, and at that point Jericho decided he'd had enough. He took the leftovers that Atwood didn't want and scraped them into a milk churn labelled 'PIG SWILL'.

When he was halfway to the door he was suddenly overcome with remorse at his rudeness. Was this the behaviour of a good colleague, what Skynner would call 'a team player'? But then, when he turned and looked back, he saw that nobody had missed him. Atwood was still talking, waving his fork in mid-air, Pinker was shaking his head, the others were listening.

Enigma

Jericho turned once more for the door and the salvation of the fresh air.

Thirty seconds later he was out on the pavement, picking his way carefully in the darkness towards the guard post, thinking about Shark.

He could hear the *click click* of a woman's heels hurrying about twenty paces in front of him. There was no one else around. It was between sittings: everyone was either working or eating. The rapid footsteps stopped at the barrier and a moment later the sentry shone his torch directly in the woman's face. She glanced away with a murmur of annoyance, and Jericho saw her then, for an instant, spot-lit in the blackout, looking straight in his direction.

It was Claire.

For a fraction of a second, he thought she must have seen him. But he was in the shadows and reeling backwards in panic, four or five steps backwards, and she was dazzled by the light. With what seemed like infinite slowness she brought her hand up to shield her eyes. Her blonde hair gleamed white.

He couldn't hear what was said but very quickly the torch was quenched and everything was dark again. And then he heard her moving off down the path on the other side of the barrier, *click click click*, obviously in a rush about something, fading into the night.

He had to catch her up. He stumbled quickly to the guard post, searching for his wallet, searching for his pass, nearly tripping off the kerbstone, but he couldn't find the damned thing. The torch came on, blinding him – *'evening sir'*, *'evening corporal'* – and his fingers were useless, he couldn't make them work, and the pass wasn't in his wallet, wasn't in his overcoat pockets, wasn't in his jacket pockets, breast pocket – he couldn't hear her footsteps now, just the sentry's boot tapping impatiently – and, yes, it *was* in his breast pocket, *'here you are'*, *'thank you sir'*, *'thank you corporal'*, *'night sir'*, *'night corporal'*, night, night, night . . .

She was gone.

The sentry's light had robbed him of what little vision he had. When he closed his eyes there was only the imprint of the torch and when he opened them the darkness was absolute. He found the edge of the road with his foot and followed its curve. It took him once again past the mansion and brought him out close to the huts. Far away, on the opposite bank of the lake, someone – perhaps another sentry — started to whistle 'We'll Gather Lilacs in the Spring Again', then stopped.

It was so quiet, he could hear the wind moving in the trees.

While he was hesitating, wondering what to do, a dot of light appeared along the footpath to his right, and then another. For some reason Jericho drew back into the shadows of Hut 8 as the torches bobbed towards him. He heard voices he didn't recognise – a man's and a woman's – whispered but emphatic. When they were almost level with him, the man threw his cigarette into the water. A cascade of red points ended in a hiss. The woman said: 'It's just a week, darling,' and went to embrace him. The fireflies danced and separated and moved on.

He stepped out onto the path again. His night vision was coming back. He looked at his watch. It was 4.30. Another ninety minutes and it would start to get light.

On impulse he walked down the side of Hut 8, keeping close to the blastproof wall. This brought him to the edge of Hut 6, where the ciphers of the German Army and Luftwaffe were broken. Straight ahead was a narrow alleyway of rough grass separating Hut 6 from the end wall of the Naval Section. And at the end of that, crouched low in the darkness, just about visible, was the side of another hut – Hut 3 – to which the decrypted ciphers from Hut 6 were sent for translation and dispatch.

Hut 3 was where Claire worked.

He glanced around. There was no one in sight.

He left the path and started to stumble down the passage. The ground was slippery and uneven and several times something grabbed at his ankle – ivy, maybe, or a tendril of discarded cable – and almost sent him sprawling. It took him about a minute to reach Hut 3.

Here, too, was a concrete wall, designed, optimistically, to shield the flimsy wooden structure from an exploding bomb. It was neck-high, but although he was short he was just about able to peer over the top.

A row of windows was set into the side of the building. Over these, from the outside, blackout shutters were fastened every day at dusk. All that was visible was the ghosts of squares, where the light seeped around the edges of the frames. The floor of Hut 3, like Hut 8's, was made of wood, suspended above a concrete base, and he could hear the muffled clumps and thuds of people moving about.

She must be on duty. She must be working the midnight shift. She might be three feet from where he stood.

He was on tiptoe.

He had never been inside Hut 3. For reasons of security, workers in one section of the Park were not encouraged to stray into another, not unless they had good reason. From time to time his work had taken him over the threshold of Hut 6, but Hut 3 was a mystery to him. He had no idea of what she did. She'd tried to tell him once, but he'd said gently that it was best he didn't know. From odd remarks he gathered it was something to do with filing and was 'deadly dull, darling'.

He stretched out as far as he could, until his fingertips were brushing the asbestos cladding of the hut.

What are you doing, darling Claire? Are you busy with your boring filing, or are you flirting with one of the night-duty officers, or gossiping with the other girls, or puzzling over that crossword you can never do?

Suddenly, about fifteen yards to his left, a door opened. From the oblong of dim light a uniformed man emerged, yawning. Jericho slid silently to the ground until he was kneeling in the wet earth and pressed his chest against the wall. The door closed and the man began to walk towards him. He stopped about ten feet away, breathing hard. He seemed to be listening. Jericho closed his eyes and shortly afterwards he heard a pattering and then a drilling noise and when he opened them he saw the faint silhouette of the man pissing against the wall, very hard. It went on for a wondrously long time and Jericho was close enough to get a whiff of pungent, beery urine. A fine spray was being borne downwind on the breeze. He had to put his hand to his nose and mouth to stop himself gagging. Eventually, the man gave a deep sigh – a groan, almost – of satisfaction, and fumbled with the buttons of his fly. He moved away. The door opened and closed again and Jericho was alone.

There was a certain humour in the situation, and later even he was to see it. But at the time he was on the edge of panic. What, in the name of reason, did he think he was doing? If he were to be caught, kneeling in the darkness, with his ear pressed to a hut in which he had no business, he would have – to put it mildly – a hard time explaining himself. For a moment he considered simply marching inside and demanding to see her. But his imagination recoiled at the prospect. He might be thrown out. Or she might appear in fury and create a scene. Or she might appear and be the soul of sweetness, in which case what did he say? *'Oh, hello, darling. I just happened to be passing. You look in good form. By the way, I've been meaning to ask you, why did you wreck my life?'*

He used the wall to help him scramble to his feet. The quickest way back to the road was straight head, but that would take him past the door of the hut. He decided that the safest course would be to go back the way he had come.

He was more cautious after his scare. Each time he took a step he planted his foot carefully and on every fifth pace he paused to make sure that no one else was moving around in the blackout. Two minutes later he was back outside the entrance to Hut 8.

He felt as if he had been on a cross-country run. He was out of breath. There was a small hole in his left shoe and his sock was wet. Bits of damp grass were sticking to the bottoms of his trouser legs. His knees were sodden. And where he had rubbed against the concrete wall the front of his overcoat was streaked luminously white. He took out his handkerchief and tried to clean himself up.

He had just about finished when he heard the others coming back from the canteen. Atwood's voice carried in the night: 'A dark horse, that one. Very dark. I recruited him, you know,' to which someone else chimed in: 'Yes, but he was once very good, wasn't he?'

Jericho didn't stop to hear the rest. He pushed open the door and almost ran down the passage, so that by the time the cryptanalysts appeared in the Big Room he was already seated at his desk, bent over the intercepts, knuckles to his temples, eyes closed.

He stayed like that for three hours.

At about six o'clock, Puck stopped by to drop on the table another forty encrypted signals, the latest batch of Shark traffic, and to enquire – not without a degree of sarcasm – if Jericho had 'solved it yet?' At seven, there was a rattle of step ladders against the outside wall and the blackout shutters were unfastened. A pale grey light filtered into the hut.

What was she doing, hurrying into the Park at that time of night? That was what he did not understand. Of course, the mere fact of seeing her again after a month spent trying to forget her was disturbing. But it was the circumstances, in retrospect, that troubled him more. She had not been in the canteen, he was sure of that. He had scrutinised every table, every face – had been so distracted he had barely even looked at what he was being given to eat. But if she had not been in the canteen, where had she been? Had she been with someone? Who? Who? And the way she was walking so hurriedly. Was there not something furtive, even panicky, about it?

His memory replayed the scene frame by frame: the footsteps, the flash of light, the turn of her head, her cry, the halo of her hair, the way she had vanished . . . That was something else. Could she really have walked the entire distance to the hut in the time it took him to fumble for his pass?

Just before eight o'clock he gathered the crypto-grams together and slipped them into the folder. All around him, the cryptanalysts were preparing to go off shift – stretching and yawning and rubbing at tired eyes, pulling together their work, briefing their replacements. Nobody noticed Jericho walk quickly down the corridor to Logie's office. He knocked once. There was no reply. He tried the door. As he remembered: unlocked.

He closed it behind him and picked up the

telephone. If he delayed for a second his nerve would fail him. He dialled '0' and on the seventh ring, just as he was about to give up, a sleepy operator answered.

His mouth was almost too dry to get the words out. 'Duty Officer, Hut 3, please.'

Almost immediately a man's voice said, irritably: 'Colonel Coker.'

Jericho nearly dropped the receiver.

'Do you have a Miss Romilly there?' He didn't need to disguise his voice: it was so strained and quavering it was unrecognisable. 'A Miss Claire Romilly?'

'You've come through to *completely* the wrong office. Who is this?'

'Welfare.'

'Oh bloody *hell!*' There was a deafening bang, as if the colonel had thrown the telephone across the room, but the connection held. Jericho could hear the clatter of a teleprinter and a man's voice, very cultured, somewhere in the background: 'Yes, yes, I've got that. Right-oh. Cheerio.' The man ended one conversation and started another. 'Army Index here . . .' Jericho glanced at the clock above the window. Now it was past eight. Come on, come on . . . Suddenly there was more loud banging, much closer, and a woman said softly in Jericho's ear: 'Yes?'

He tried to sound casual but it came out as a croak. 'Claire?'

'No, I'm afraid it's Claire's day off. She won't be back on duty until eight tomorrow morning. Can I help?'

Jericho gently replaced the receiver in its cradle, just

90

as the door was thrown open behind him.

'Oh, *there* you are, old thing . . .'

4

Daylight diminished the huts.

The blackout had touched them with a certain mystery but the morning showed them up for what they were: squat and ugly, with brown walls and tarred roofs and a premature air of dereliction. Above the mansion, the sky was glossy white with streaks of grey, a dome of polished marble. A duck in drab winter plumage waddled across the path from the lake looking for food, and Logie almost kicked it as he strode past, sending it protesting back to the water.

He had not been in the least perturbed to find Jericho in his office and Jericho's carefully prepared excuse – that he was returning the Shark intercepts – had been waved away.

'Just dump 'em in the Crib Room and come with me.'

Drawn across the northern edge of the lake, next to the huts, was A-Block, a long, two-storey affair with brick walls and a flat top. Logie led the way up a flight of concrete steps and turned right. At the far end of the corridor a door opened and Jericho heard a familiar voice booming: '. . . all our resources, human and material, into this problem . . .' and then the door closed again and Baxter peered down the passage towards them.

91

'So there you are. I was just coming to find you. Hello, Guy. Hello, Tom. How are you? Hardly recognised you. Upright.' Baxter had a cigarette in his mouth and didn't bother to remove it, so it bobbed as he spoke and sprayed ash down the front of his pullover. Before the war he had been a lecturer at the London School of Economics.

'What have we got?' said Logie, nodding towards the closed door.

'Our American "lee-ay-son officer", plus another American – some big shot from the Navy. A man in a suit – a lounge lizard from Intelligence by the look of him. Three from our Navy, of course, one of them an admiral. All up from London specially.'

'An admiral?' Logie's hand went automatically to his tie and Jericho noticed he had changed into a pre-war double-breasted suit. He licked his fingers and tried to plaster down his hair. 'I don't like the sound of an admiral. And how's Skynner?'

'At the moment? I'd say heavily out-gunned.' Baxter was staring at Jericho. The corners of his mouth twitched down briefly, the nearest Jericho had seen him come to a smile. 'Well, well, I suppose you don't look too bad, Tom.'

'Now, Alec, don't you go upsetting him.'

'I'm fine, Alec, thank you. How's the revolution?'

'Coming along, comrade. Coming along.'

Logie patted Jericho on the arm. 'Don't say anything when we get inside, Tom. You're only here for show, old love.'

Only here for show, thought Jericho, what the hell

does that mean? But before he could ask, Logie had opened the door and all he could hear was Skynner – 'we must expect these setbacks from time to time' – and they were on.

There were eight men in the room. Leonard Skynner, the head of the Naval Section, sat at one end of the table, with Atwood to his right and an empty chair to his left, which Baxter promptly reclaimed. Gathered around the other end were five officers in dark blue naval uniform, two of them American and three British. One of the British officers, a lieutenant, had an eye-patch. They looked grim.

The eighth man had his back to Jericho. He turned as they came in and Jericho briefly registered a lean face with fair hair.

Skynner stopped speaking. He stood and held out a meaty hand. 'Come in Guy, come in Tom.' He was a big square-faced man with thick black hair and wide bushy eyebrows that almost met above the bridge of his nose and reminded Jericho of the Morse code symbol for M. He beckoned to the newcomers eagerly, obviously thankful to see Allied reinforcements. 'This is Guy Logie,' he said to the admiral, 'our chief cryptanalyst, and Tom Jericho, of whom you may have heard. Tom was instrumental in getting us into Shark just before Christmas.'

The admiral's leathery old face was immobile. He was smoking a cigarette – they were all smoking cigarettes except for Skynner – and he regarded Jericho, as did the Americans, blankly, through a fog of

tobacco, without the slightest interest. Skynner rattled
off the introductions, his arm sweeping round the table
like the hand of a clock. 'This is Admiral Trowbridge.
Lieutenant Cave. Lieutenant Villiers. Commander
Hammerbeck —' the older of the two Americans
nodded '— Lieutenant Kramer, US Navy Liaison. Mr
Wigram is observing for the cabinet Office.' Skynner
gave a little bow to everybody and sat down again. He
was sweating.

Jericho and Logie each collected a folding chair from
a stack beside the table and took up positions next to
Baxter.

Almost the whole of the wall behind the admiral was
taken up by a map of the North Atlantic. Clusters of
coloured discs showed the positions of Allied convoys
and their escorts: yellow for the merchantmen, green
for the warships. Black triangles marked the suspected
whereabouts of German U-boats. Beneath the chart
was a red telephone, a direct link to the Submarine
Tracking Room in the basement of the Admiralty. The
only other decoration on the whitewashed walls was a
pair of framed photographs. One was of the King,
signed, looking nervous, presented after a recent visit.
The other was of Grand Admiral Karl Dönitz,
commander in chief of the German Navy: Skynner
liked to think of himself as locked in a personal battle
with the wily Hun.

Now, though, he seemed to have lost the thread of
what he was saying. He sorted through his notes and in
the time it took Logie and Jericho to take their places,
one of the Royal Navy men — Cave, the one with the

eye-patch – received a nod from the admiral and started speaking.

'Perhaps, if you've finished outlining your problems, it might be helpful for us now to set out the operational situation.' His chair scraped on the bare floor as he rose to his feet. His tone was insultingly polite. 'The position at twenty-one hundred . . .'

Jericho passed his hand over his unshaven chin. He couldn't make up his mind whether to keep his overcoat on or take it off. On, he decided – the room was cold, despite the number of people in it. He undid the buttons and loosened his scarf. As he did so, he noticed the admiral watching him. They couldn't believe it, these senior officers, whenever they came up to visit – the lack of discipline, the scarves and cardigans, the first-name terms. There was a story about Churchill, who'd visited the Park in 1941 and given a speech to the cryptanalysts on the lawn. Afterwards, as he was being driven away, he'd said to the director: 'When I told you to leave no stone unturned recruiting for this place, I didn't expect you to take me literally.' Jericho smiled at the memory. The admiral glowered and flicked cigarette ash on the floor.

The one-eyed naval officer had picked up a pointer and was standing in front of the Atlantic chart, holding a sheaf of notes.

'It must be said, unfortunately, that the news you've given us couldn't have come at a worse moment. No fewer than three convoys have left the United States in the past week and are presently at sea. Convoy SC-122.' He rapped it once with the pointer, hard, as if he had a grudge against it, and read out his notes. 'Departed New York last Friday. Carrying fuel oil, iron ore, steel, wheat, bauxite, sugar, refrigerated meat, zinc, tobacco and tanks. Fifty merchant ships.'

Cave spoke in a clipped, metallic voice, without looking at his audience. His one good eye was fixed on the map.

'Convoy HX-229.' He tapped it. 'Departed New York Monday. Forty merchant vessels. Carrying meat, explosives, lubricating oil, refrigerated dairy produce, manganese, lead, timber, phosphate, diesel oil, aviation spirit, sugar and powdered milk.' He turned to them for the first time. The whole of the left side of his face was a mass of purple scar tissue. 'That, I might say, is two weeks' supply of powdered milk for the entire British Isles.'

There was some nervous laughter. 'Better not lose that,' joked Skynner. The laughter stopped at once. He looked so forlorn in the silence Jericho almost felt sorry for him.

Again, the pointer crashed down.

'And Convoy HX-229A. Left New York Tuesday. Twenty-seven ships. Similar cargoes to the others. Fuel oil, aviation spirit, timber, steel, naval diesel, meat, sugar, wheat, explosives. Three convoys. A total of one hundred and seventeen merchant ships, with a gross registered tonnage of just under one million tons, plus cargo of another million.'

One of the Americans – it was the senior one, Hammerbeck – raised his hand. 'How many men involved?'

'Nine thousand merchant seamen. One thousand passengers.'

'Who are the passengers?'

'Mainly servicemen. Some ladies from the American Red Cross. Quite a lot of children. A party of Catholic missionaries, curiously enough.'

'Jesus Christ.'

Cave permitted himself a crimped smile. 'Quite.'

'And whereabouts are the U-boats?'

'Perhaps I might let my colleague answer that.'

Cave sat down and the other British officer, Villiers, took the floor. He flourished the pointer.

'Submarine Tracking Room had three U-boat packs operational as of zero-zero-hundred Thursday – heah, heah, and heah.' His accent barely qualified as recognisable English, it was the sort that pronounced 'cloth' as 'clawth' and 'really' as 'rarely', and when he spoke his lips hardly moved, as if it were somehow ungentlemanly – a betrayal of the amateur ethos – to put too much effort into talking. 'Gruppe Raubgraf heah, two hundred miles off the coast of Greenland. Gruppe Neuland, heah, almost precisely mid-ocean. And Gruppe Westmark heah, due south of Iceland.'

'Zero-zero *Thursday*? You mean more than thirty hours ago?' Hammerbeck's hair was the colour and thickness of steel wool, close-cropped to his scalp. It glinted in the fluorescent light as he leaned forwards. 'Where the hell are they now?'

'I'm afraid I've no ideah. I thought that was why we were heah. They've blipped awf the screen.'

Admiral Trowbridge lit another cigarette from the

tip of his old one. He had transferred his attention from Jericho and now he was staring at Hammerbeck through small, rheumy eyes.

Again, the American raised his hand. 'How many subs are we talking about in these three wolf packs?'

'I'm sorry to say, ah, they're quite large, ah, we estimate forty-six.'

Skynner squirmed in his chair. Atwood made a great show of rummaging through his papers.

'Let me get this straight,' said Hammerbeck. (He was certainly persistent – Jericho was beginning to admire him.) 'You're telling us one million tons of shipping – '

'Merchant shipping,' interrupted Cave.

'– merchant shipping, pardon me, one million tons of *merchant* shipping, with ten thousand people on board, including various ladies of the American Red Cross and assorted Catholic Bible-bashers, is steaming towards forty-six U-boats, and you have no idea where those U-boats are?'

'I'm rather afraid I am, yes.'

'Well, I'll be fucked,' said Hammerbeck, sitting back in his chair. 'And how long before they get there?'

'That's hard to say.' It was Cave again. He had an odd habit of turning his face away when he talked, and Jericho realised he was trying not to show his shattered cheekbone. 'The SC is the slower convoy. She's making about seven knots. The HXs are both faster, one ten knots, one eleven. I'd say we've got three days, at the maximum. After that, they'll be within operational range of the enemy.'

Hammerbeck had begun whispering to the other American. He was shaking his head and making short chopping motions with his hand. The admiral leaned over and muttered something to Cave, who said quietly: 'I'm afraid so, sir.'

Jericho looked up at the Atlantic, at the yellow discs of the convoys and the black triangles of the U-boats, sewn like shark's teeth across the sea lanes. The distance between the ships and the wolf packs was roughly eight hundred miles. The merchantmen were making maybe two hundred and forty miles every twenty-four hours. Three days was about right. My God, he thought, no wonder Logie was so desperate to get me back.

'Gentlemen, please, if I may?' said Skynner loudly, bringing the meeting back to order. Jericho saw he'd plastered on his 'come let us smile in the face of disaster' expression – invariably a sign of incipient panic. 'I think we should guard against too much pessimism. The Atlantic does cover thirty-two million square miles, you know.' He risked another laugh. 'That's an awful lot of ocean.'

'Yes,' said Hammerbeck, 'and forty-six is one hell of a lot of U-boats.'

'I agree. It's probably the largest concentration of hearses we've faced,' said Cave. 'I'm afraid we must assume the enemy will make contact. Unless, of course, we can find out where they are.'

He gave Skynner a significant look, but Skynner ignored it and pressed on. 'And let's not forget – these convoys are not unprotected?' He glanced around the table for support. 'They do have an escort?'

'Indeed.' Cave again. 'They have an escort of – ' he consulted his notes '– seven destroyers, nine corvettes and three frigates. Plus various other vessels.'

'Under an experienced commander . . .'

The British officers glanced at one another, and then at the admiral.

'Actually, it's his first command.'

'Jesus Christ!' Hammerbeck rocked forwards in his chair and brought his fists down on the table.

'If I might step in heah. Obviously, we didn't know last Friday when the escorts were forming up that our intelligence was going to be shut awf.'

'How long will this blackout last?' This was the first time the admiral had spoken and everyone turned to look at him. He gave a sharp, explosive cough, which sounded as if small pieces of machinery were flying around loose in his chest, then sucked in another lungful of smoke and gestured with his cigarette. 'Will it be over in four days, d'you think?'

The question was addressed directly to Skynner and they all turned to look at him. He was an administrator, not a cryptanalyst – he'd been vice-chancellor of some northern university before the war – and Jericho knew he hadn't a clue. He didn't know whether the blackout would last four days, four months or four years.

Skynner said carefully: 'It's possible.'

'Yes, well, all things are possible.' Trowbridge gave an unpleasant rasping laugh that turned into another cough. 'Is it likely? Is it likely you can break this, whatever you call it – this Shark – before our convoys come within range of the U-boats?'

'We'll give it every priority.'

'I know damn well you'll give it every priority, Leonard. You keep saying you'll give it every priority. That's not the question.'

'Well, sir, as you press me, sir, yes.' Skynner stuck his big jaw out heroically. In his mind's eye he was steering his ship manfully into the face of the typhoon. 'Yes, I think we may be able to do it.'

You're mad, thought Jericho.

'And you all believe that?' The admiral stared hard in their direction. He had eyes like a bloodhound's, red-lidded and watery.

Logie was the first to break the silence. He looked at Skynner and winced and scratched the back of his head with the stem of his pipe. 'I suppose we do have the advantage of knowing more about Shark than we did before.'

Atwood jumped in: 'If Guy thinks we can do it, I certainly respect his opinion. I'd go along with whatever he estimates.' Baxter nodded judiciously. Jericho inspected his watch.

'And you?' said the admiral. 'What do you think?'

In Cambridge, they would just about be finishing breakfast. Kite would be steaming open the mail. Mrs Sax would be rattling round with her brushes and pails. In Hall on Saturday they served vegetable pie with potatoes for lunch . . .

He was aware that the room had gone quiet and he looked up to find all eyes were on him. The fair-haired man in the suit was staring at him with particular curiosity. He felt his face begin to colour.

And then he felt a spasm of irritation.

Afterwards Jericho was to think about this moment many times. What made him act as he did? Was it tiredness? Was he simply disoriented, plucked out of Cambridge and set down in the middle of this nightmare? Was he still ill? Illness would certainly help explain what happened later. Or was he so distracted by the thought of Claire that he wasn't thinking straight? All he remembered for certain was an overwhelming feeling of annoyance. *'You're only here for show, old love.'* You're only here to make up the numbers, so Skynner can put on a good act for the Yanks. You're only here to do as you're told, so keep your views to yourself, and don't ask questions. He was suddenly sick of it all, sick of everything – sick of the blackout, sick of the cold, sick of the chummy first-name terms and the lime smell and the damp and the whale meat – *whale meat* – at four o'clock in the morning . . .

'Actually, I'm not sure I am as optimistic as my colleagues.'

Skynner interrupted him at once. You could almost hear the klaxons going off in his mind, see the airmen sprinting across the deck and the big guns swivelling skywards as HMS *Skynner* came under threat. 'Tom's been ill, sir, I'm afraid. He's been away from us for the best part of a month . . .'

'Why not?' The admiral's tone was dangerously friendly. 'Why aren't you optimistic?'

'. . . so I'm not sure he's altogether fully *au fait* with the situation. Wouldn't you admit that, Tom?'

'Well, I'm certainly *au fait* with Enigma, ah,

Leonard.' Jericho could hardly believe his own words. He plunged on. 'Enigma is a very sophisticated cipher system. And Shark is its ultimate refinement. I've spent the past eight hours reviewing the Shark material and, ah, forgive me if I'm speaking out of turn, but it seems to me we are in a very serious situation.'

'But you *were* breaking it successfully?'

'Yes, but we'd been given a key. The weather code was the key that unlocked the door. The Germans have now changed the weather code. That means we've lost our key. Unless there's been some development I'm not aware of, I don't understand how we're going to . . .' Jericho searched for a metaphor. '. . . pick the lock.'

The other American naval officer, the one who hadn't spoken so far – Jericho had momentarily forgotten his name – said: 'And you still haven't gotten those four-wheel bombes you promised us, Frank.'

'That's a separate issue,' muttered Skynner. He gave Jericho a murderous look.

'Is it?' Kramer – that was it. He was called Kramer. 'Surely if we had a few four-wheel bombes right now we wouldn't need the weather cribs?'

'Just stop there for a moment,' said the admiral, who had been following this conversation with increasing impatience. 'I'm a sailor, and an old sailor at that. I don't understand all this – *talk* – about keys and cribs and bombs with wheels. We're trying to keep the sea-lanes open from America and if we can't do that we're going to lose this war.'

'Hear, hear,' said Hammerbeck. 'Well said, Jack.'

'Now will somebody please give me a straight answer

to a straight question? Will this blackout definitely be over in four days' time or won't it? Yes or no?'

Skynner's shoulders sagged. 'No,' he said wearily. 'If you put it like that, sir, I can't say *definitely* it will be over, no.'

'Thank you. So, if it isn't over in four days, when will it be over? You. You're the pessimist. What do you think?'

Once again Jericho was conscious of everyone watching him.

He spoke carefully. Poor Logie was peering inside his tobacco pouch as if he wished he could climb in and never come out 'It's very hard to say. All we have to measure it by is the last blackout.'

'And how long did that go on?'

'Ten months.'

It was as if he had detonated a bomb. Everybody made a noise. The Navy men shouted. The admiral started coughing. Baxter and Atwood said 'No!' simultaneously. Logie groaned. Skynner, shaking his head, said: 'That really is defeatist of you, Tom.' Even Wigram, the fair-headed man, gave a snort and stared at the rafters, smiling at some private joke.

'I'm not saying it will definitely take us ten months,' Jericho resumed when he could make himself heard. 'But that's the measure of what we're up against and I think that four days is unrealistic. I'm sorry. I do.'

There was a pause, and then Wigram said, softly: '*Why*, I wonder . . .'

'Mr Wigram?'

'Sorry, Leonard.' Wigram bestowed his smile

around the table, and Jericho's immediate thought was how *expensive* he looked – blue suit, silk tie, Jermyn Street shirt, pomaded hair swept back and scented with some masculine cologne – he might have stepped out of the lobby of the Ritz. *A lounge lizard,* Baxter had called him, which was Bletchley code for *spy.*

'Sorry,' Wigram said again. 'Thinking aloud. I was just wondering *why* Dönitz should have decided to change this *particular* bit of code and *why* he should have chosen to do so *now.*' He stared at Jericho. 'From what you were saying, it sounds as though he couldn't have chosen any one thing more damaging to us.'

Jericho didn't have to reply; Logie did it for him. 'Routine. Almost certainly. They change their code books from time to time. Just our bad luck they did it now.'

'Routine,' repeated Wigram. 'Right.' He smiled once more. 'Tell me, Leonard, how many people know about this weather code and how important it is to us?'

'Really, Douglas,' laughed Skynner, 'whatever are you suggesting?'

'How many?'

'Guy?'

'A dozen, perhaps.'

'Couldn't make me a little list, could you?'

Logie looked to Skynner for approval. 'I, ah, well, I, ah . . .'

'Thanks.'

Wigram resumed his examination of the ceiling.

The silence that followed was broken by a long sigh from the admiral. 'I think I gather the sense of the meeting.' He stubbed out his cigarette and reached down beside his chair for his briefcase. He began stuffing his papers into it and his lieutenants followed suit. 'I can't pretend it's the happiest of messages to take back to the First Sea Lord.'

Hammerbeck said: 'I guess I'd better signal Washington.'

The admiral stood and immediately they all pushed back their chairs and got to their feet.

'Lieutenant Cave will act as Admiralty liaison.' He turned to Cave: 'I'd like a daily report. On second thoughts, perhaps better make that twice a day.'

'Yes, sir.'

'Lieutenant Kramer: you'll carry on here and keep Commander Hammerbeck informed?'

'I sure will, sir. Yes, sir.'

'So.' He pulled on his gloves. 'I suggest we reconvene this meeting as and when there are developments to report. Which hopefully will be within four days.'

At the door, the old man turned. 'It's not just one million tons of shipping and ten thousand men, you know. It's one million tons of shipping and ten thousand men *every two weeks*. And it's not just the convoys. It's our obligation to send supplies to Russia. It's our chances of invading Europe and driving the Nazis out. It's everything. It's the whole war.' He gave another of his wheezing laughs. 'Not that I want to put any pressure on you, Leonard.' He nodded. 'Good morning, gentlemen.'

As they mumbled their 'good morning sirs', Jericho

106

heard Wigram say quietly to Skynner: 'I'll talk to you later, Leonard.'

They listened to the visitors clatter down the concrete stairs, and then to the crunch of their feet on the path outside, and suddenly the room was quiet. A mist of blue tobacco hung over the table like smoke rising after a battle.

Skynner's lips were compressed. He was humming to himself. He gathered his papers into a pile and squared off the edges with exaggerated care. For what seemed a long time, nobody spoke.

'Well,' said Skynner eventually, 'that was a triumph. Thank you, Tom. Thank you very much indeed. I'd forgotten what a tower of strength you could be. We've missed you.'

'It's my fault, Leonard,' said Logie. 'Bad briefing. Should have put him in the picture better. Sorry. Bit of a rush first thing.'

'Why don't you just get back to the Hut, Guy? In fact, why don't you all go back, and then Tom and I can have a little chat.'

'Bloody fool,' said Baxter to Jericho.

Atwood took his arm. 'Come on, Alec.'

'Well, he is. Bloody fool.'

They left.

The moment the door closed Skynner said: 'I never wanted you back.'

'Logie didn't mention that.' Jericho folded his arms to stop his hands shaking. 'He said I was needed here.'

'I never wanted you back, not because I think you're a fool – Alec's wrong about that. You're not a fool. But you're a wreck. You're ruined. You've cracked once before under pressure and you'll do it again, as your little performance just now showed. You've outlived your usefulness to us.'

Skynner was leaning his large bottom casually against the edge of the table. He was speaking in a friendly tone and if you had seen him from a distance you would have thought he was exchanging pleasantries with an old acquaintance.

'Then why am I here? I never asked to come back.'

'Logie thinks highly of you. He's the acting head of the Hut and I listen to him. And, I'll be honest, after Turing, you probably have – or, rather, *had* – the best reputation of any cryptanalyst on the Park. You're a little bit of history, Tom. A little bit of a legend. Bringing you back, letting you attend this morning, was a way of showing our masters how seriously we take this, ah, temporary crisis. It was a risk. But obviously I was wrong. You've lost it.'

Jericho was not a violent man. He had never hit another person, not even as a boy, and he knew it was a mercy he had avoided military service: given a rifle he would have been a menace to no one except his own side. But there was a heavy brass ashtray on the table – the sawn-off end of a six-inch shell-case, brimful of cigarette stubs – and Jericho was seriously tempted to ram it into Skynner's smug face. Skynner seemed to sense this. At any rate, he pulled his bottom off the table and began to pace the floor. This must be one of the benefits of being a madman, thought Jericho, people can never take you entirely for granted.

Enigma

'It was so much simpler in the old days, wasn't it?' said Skynner. 'A country house. A handful of eccentrics. Nobody expecting very much. You potter along. And then suddenly you're sitting on the greatest secret of the war.'

'And then people like you arrive.'

'That's right, people like myself are needed, to make sure this remarkable weapon is used properly.'

'Oh is that what you do, Leonard? You make sure the weapon is used properly. I've often wondered.'

Skynner stopped smiling. He was a big man, nearly a foot taller than Jericho. He came up very close, and Jericho could smell the stale cigarette smoke and the sweat on his clothes.

'You've no conception of this place any more. No idea of the problems. The Americans, for instance. In front of whom you've just humiliated me. Us. We're negotiating a deal with the Americans that – ' He stopped himself. 'Never mind. Let's just say that when you – when you *indulge* yourself as you just did, you can't even conceive of the seriousness of what's at stake.'

Skynner had a briefcase with a royal crest stamped on it and 'G VI R' in faded gold lettering. He slipped his papers into it and locked it with a key attached to his belt by a long chain.

'I'm going to arrange for you to be taken off cryptanalytical work and put somewhere you can't do any damage. In fact, I'm going to have you transferred out of Bletchley altogether.' He pocketed the key and patted it. 'You can't return to civilian life, of course, not until the war's over, not knowing what you know.

109

Still, I hear the Admiralty's on the lookout for an extra brain to work in statistics. Dull stuff, but cushy enough for a man of your . . . delicacy. Who knows? Perhaps you'll meet a nice girl. Someone more – how shall we say? – more *suitable* for you than the person I gather you *were* seeing.'

Jericho did try to hit him then, but not with the ashtray, only with his fist, which in retrospect was a mistake. Skynner stepped to one side with surprising grace and the blow missed and then his right hand shot out and grabbed Jericho's forearm. Skynner dug his fingers very hard into the soft muscle.

'You are an ill man, Tom. And I am stronger than you, in every way.' He increased the pressure for a second or two, then abruptly let go of the arm. 'Now get out of my sight.'

5

God, but he was tired. Exhaustion stalked him like a living thing, clutching at his legs, squatting on his sagging shoulders. Jericho leaned against the outside wall of A-Block, rested his cheek against the smooth, damp concrete, and waited for his pulse to return to normal.

What had he done?

He needed to lie down. He needed to find some hole to crawl into and get some rest. Like a drunk searching for his keys, he felt first in one pocket and then another and finally pulled out the billeting chit and squinted at it. Albion Street? Where was that? He had a vague memory. He would know it when he saw it.

He pushed himself away from the wall and began to make his way, carefully, away from the lake towards the road that led to the main gate. A small, black car was parked about ten yards ahead and as he came closer the driver's door opened and a figure in a blue uniform appeared.

'Mr Jericho!'

Jericho stared with surprise. It was one of the Americans. 'Lieutenant Kramer?'

'Hi. Going home? Can I give you a ride?'

'Thank you. No. Really, it's only a short walk.'

'Aw, come on.' Kramer patted the roof of the car. 'I just got her. It'd be my pleasure. Come on.'

Jericho was about to decline again, but then he felt his legs begin to crumple.

'Whoa there, feller.' Kramer sprang forward and took his arm. 'You're all in. Long night, I guess?'

Jericho allowed himself to be guided to the passenger door and pushed into the front seat. The interior of the little car was cold and smelled as if it hadn't been used in a long while. Jericho guessed it must have been someone's pride and joy until petrol rationing forced it off the road. The chassis rocked as Kramer clambered in the other side and slammed the door.

'Not many people around here run their own cars.' Jericho's voice sounded oddly in his ears, as if from a distance. 'You have trouble getting fuel?'

'No, sir.' Kramer pressed the starter button and the engine rattled into life. 'You know us. We can get as much as we want.'

The car was carefully inspected at the main gate. The barrier rose and they headed out, past the canteen and the assembly hall, towards the end of Wilton Avenue.

'Which way?'

'Left, I think.'

Kramer flicked out one of the little amber indicators and they turned into the lane that led down to the town. His face was handsome – boyish and square-cut, with a faded tan that suggested service overseas. He was about twenty-five and looked formidably fit.

'I guess I'd like to thank you for that.'

'Thank me?'

'At the conference. You told the truth when the others all talked bull-shit. "Four days" – Jesus!'

'They were just being loyal.'

'Loyal? Come on, Tom. D'you mind if I call you Tom? I'm Jimmy, by the way. They'd been fixed.'

'I don't think this is a conversation we should be having . . .' The dizziness had passed and in the clarity that always followed it occurred to Jericho that the American must have been waiting for him to emerge from the meeting. 'This will do fine, thank you.'

'Really? But we've hardly gone any distance.'

'Please, just pull over.'

Kramer swerved into the kerb beside a row of small cottages, braked and turned off the engine.

'Listen, will you, Tom, just a minute? The Germans brought in Shark three months after Pearl Harbor –'

112

'Look –'

'Relax. Nobody's listening.' This was true. The lane was deserted. 'Three months after Pearl Harbor, and suddenly we're losing ships like we're going out of business. But nobody tells us why. After all, we're the new boys around here – we just route the convoys the way London tells us. Finally, it's getting so bad, we ask you guys what's happened to all this great intelligence you used to have.' He jabbed his finger at Jericho. 'Only *then* are we told about Shark.'

'I can't listen to this,' said Jericho. He tried to open the door but Kramer leaned across and seized the handle.

'I'm not trying to poison your mind against your own people. I'm just trying to tell you what's going on here. After we were told about Shark last year, we started to do some checking. Fast. And eventually, after one hell of a fight, we began to get some figures. D'you know how many bombes you guys had by the end of last summer? This is after two years of manufacture?'

Jericho was staring straight ahead. 'I wouldn't be privy to information like that.'

'Fifty! And d'you know how many our people in Washington said they could build within *four months*? Three hundred and sixty!'

'Well, build them, then,' said Jericho, irritably, 'if you're so bloody marvellous.'

'Oh no,' said Kramer. 'You don't understand. That's not allowed. Enigma is a British baby. Official. Any change in status has to be negotiated.'

'Is it being negotiated?'

'In Washington. Right now. That's where your Mr

Turing is. In the meantime, we just have to take whatever you give us.'

'But that's absurd. Why not just build the bombes anyway?'

'Come on, Tom. Think about it for a minute. You have all the intercept stations over here. You have all the raw material. We're three thousand miles away. Damn hard to pick up Magdeburg from Florida. And what's the point in having three hundred and sixty bombes if there's nothing to put in them?'

Jericho shut his eye sand saw Skynner's flushed face, heard his rumbling voice: '*You've no conception of this place any more . . . We're negotiating a deal with the Americans . . . You can't even conceive of the seriousness . . .*' Now, at least, he understood the reason for Skynner's anger. His little empire, so painfully put together, brick by bureaucratic brick, was mortally threatened by Shark. But the threat came not from Berlin. It came from Washington.

'Don't get me wrong,' Kramer was saying, 'I've been here a month and I think what you've all achieved is astounding. Brilliant. And nobody on our side is talking about a takeover. But it can't go on like this. Not enough bombes. Not enough typewriters. Those huts. Christ! "Was it dangerous in the war, Daddy?" "Sure was, I damned near froze to death." Did you know the whole operation almost stopped one time because you ran out of coloured pencils? I mean, what are we saying here? That men have to die because you don't have enough *pencils?*'

Jericho felt too tired to argue. Besides, he knew

enough to know it was true: all true. He remembered a night, eighteen months ago, when he'd been asked to keep an eye open for strangers at the Shoulder of Mutton, standing near the door in the blackout, sipping halves of shandy, while Turing, Welchman and a couple of the other big chiefs met in a room upstairs and wrote a joint letter to Churchill. Exactly the same story: not enough clerks, not enough typists, the factory at Letchworth that made the bombes – it used to make cash registers, of all things – short of parts, short of manpower . . . There'd been one hell of a row when Churchill got the letter – a tantrum in Downing Street, careers broken, machinery shaken up – and things had improved, for a while. But Bletchley was a greedy child. Its appetite grew with the feeding. *'Nervos belli, pecuniam infinitam.'* Or, as Baxter had put it, more prosaically, it all comes down to money in the end. The Poles had had to give Enigma to the British. Now the Brits would have to share it with the Yanks.

'I can't have anything to do with this. I've got to get some sleep. Thanks for the lift.'

He reached for the handle and this time Kramer made no attempt to stop him. He was halfway out of the door when Kramer said: 'I heard you lost your old man in the last war.'

Jericho froze. 'Who told you that?'

'I forget. Does it matter?'

'No. It's not a secret.' Jericho massaged his forehead. He had a filthy headache coming on. 'It happened before I was born. He was wounded by a shell at Ypres. He lived on for a bit but he wasn't much use after that.

He never came out of hospital. He died when I was six.'

'What did he do? Before he got hit?'

'He was a mathematician.'

There was a moment's silence.

'I'll see you around,' said Jericho. He got out of the car.

'My brother died,' said Kramer suddenly. 'One of the first. He was in the Merchant Marine. Liberty ships.'

Of course, thought Jericho.

'This was during the Shark blackout, I suppose?'

'You got it.' Kramer looked bleak, then forced a smile. 'Let's keep in touch, Tom. Anything I can do for you – just ask.'

He reached over and pulled the door shut with a bang. Jericho stood alone on the roadside and watched as Kramer executed a rapid U-turn. The car backfired, then headed at speed up the hill towards the Park, leaving a little puff of dirty smoke hanging in the morning air.

THREE

PINCH

PINCH: (1) <u>vb</u>., to steal enemy
cryptographic material; (2) <u>n</u>.,
any object stolen from the enemy
that enhances the chances of
breaking his codes or ciphers.

<u>A Lexicon of Cryptography</u>
('Most Secret', Bletchley Park, 1943)

1

BLETCHLEY WAS A railway town. The great main line from London to Scotland split it down the middle, and then the smaller branch line from Oxford to Cambridge sliced it into quarters, so that wherever you stood there was no escaping the trains: the noise of them, the smell of their soot, the sight of their brown smoke rising above the clustered roofs. Even the terraced houses were mostly railway-built, cut from the same red brick as the station and the engine sheds, constructed in the same dour, industrial style.

The Commercial Guesthouse, Albion Street, was about five minutes' walk from Bletchley Park and backed on to the main line. Its owner, Mrs Ethel Armstrong, was, like her establishment, a little over fifty years old, solidly built, with a forbidding, late-Victorian aspect. Her husband had died of a heart attack a month after the outbreak of war, whereupon she had converted their four-storey property into a small hotel. Like the other townspeople – and there were about seven thousand of them – she had no idea of what went on in the grounds of the mansion up the road, and even less interest. It was profitable, that was all that mattered to her. She charged thirty-eight shillings a week and expected her five residents, in return for meals, to hand over all their food-rationing coupons. As a result, by the spring of 1943, she had a thousand pounds in War Savings Bonds and enough edible goods hoarded in her cellar to open a medium-sized grocery store.

It was on the Wednesday that one of her rooms had become vacant, and on the Friday that she had been served a billeting notice requiring her to provide accommodation to a Mr Thomas Jericho. His possessions from his previous address had been delivered to her door that same morning: two boxes of personal effects and an ancient iron bicycle. The bicycle she wheeled into the back yard. The boxes she carried upstairs.

One carton was full of books. A couple of Agatha Christies. *A Synopsis of Elementary Results in Pure and Applied Mathematics,* two volumes, by a fellow named George Shoobridge Garr. *Principia Mathematica,* whatever that was. A pamphlet with a suspiciously Germanic ring to it – *On Computable Numbers, with an Application to the Entscheidungsproblem* – inscribed 'To Tom, with fond respect, Alan'. More books full of mathematics, one so repeatedly read it was almost falling to pieces and stuffed full of markers – bus and tram tickets, a beer mat, even a blade of grass. It fell open at a heavily underlined passage:

> there is one purpose at any rate which the real
> mathematics may serve in war. When the world is
> mad, a mathematician may find in mathematics
> an incomparable anodyne. For mathematics is, of
> all the arts and sciences, the most remote.

Well, the last line's true enough, she thought. She closed the book, turned it around and squinted at the spine: *A Mathematician's Apology* by G. H. Hardy, Cambridge University Press.

The other box also yielded little of interest. A Victorian etching of King's College Chapel. A cheap Waralarm clock, set to go off at eleven, in a black fibre case. A wireless. An academic mortarboard and a dusty gown. A bottle of ink. A telescope. A copy of *The Times* dated 23 December 1942, folded to the crossword, which had been filled in by two different hands, one very small and precise, the other rounder, probably feminine. Written above it was 2712815. And, finally, at the bottom of the carton, a map, which, when she unfolded it, proved not to be of England, or even (as she had suspected and secretly hoped) of Germany, but of the night sky.

She was so put off by this dreary collection that when, at half past midnight that night, there was a knock on the door and another two suitcases were delivered by a small man with a northern accent, she didn't even bother to open them but dumped them straight in the empty room.

Their owner arrived at nine o'clock on Saturday morning. She was sure of the time, she explained later to her next-door neighbour, Mrs Scratchwood, because the religious service was just ending on the wireless and the news was about to start. And he was exactly as she'd suspected he would be. He wasn't very tall. He was thin. Bookish. Ill-looking, and nursing his arm, as if he'd just injured it. He hadn't shaved, was as white as

– well, she was going to say 'as a sheet', but she hadn't seen sheets that white since before the war, certainly not in her house. His clothes were of good quality, but in a mess: she noticed there was a button missing on his overcoat. He was pleasant enough, though. Nicely spoken. Very good manners. A quiet voice. She'd never had any children herself, never had a son, but if she had, he would have been about the same age. Well, let's just say he needed feeding up, anyone could see that.

She was strict about the rent. She always demanded a month in advance – the request was made down in the hall, before she took them up to see the room – and there was usually an argument, at the end of which she grumpily agreed to settle for two weeks. But he paid up without a murmur. She asked for seven pounds six shillings and he gave her eight pounds, and when she pretended she hadn't any change, he said: 'Fine, give it me later.' When she mentioned his ration book he looked at her for a moment, very puzzled, and then he said (and she would remember it for the rest of her life): 'Do you mean this?'

'*Do you mean this?*' She repeated it in wonderment. As if he'd never seen one before! He gave her the little brown booklet – the precious weekly passport to four ounces of butter, eight ounces of bacon, twelve ounces of sugar – and told her she could do what she liked with it. 'I've never had any use for it.'

By this time she was so flustered she hardly knew what she was doing. She tucked the money and the ration book into her apron before he could change his mind and led him upstairs.

Now Ethel Armstrong was the first to admit that the fifth bedroom of the Commercial Guest House was not up to much. It was at the end of the passage, up a little twist of stairs, and the only furniture in it was a single bed and a wardrobe. It was so small the door wouldn't open properly because the bed got in the way. It had a tiny window flecked with soot which looked out over the wide expanse of railway tracks. In two and a half years it must have had thirty different occupants. None had stayed more than a couple of months and some had refused to sleep in it at all. But this one just sat on the edge of the bed, squeezed in between his boxes and his cases, and said wearily, 'Very pleasant, Mrs Armstrong.'

She quickly explained the rules of the house. Breakfast was at seven in the morning, dinner at six thirty in the evening, 'cold collations' would be left in the kitchen for those working irregular shifts. There was one bathroom at the far end of the passage, shared between the five guests. They were permitted one bath a week each, the depth of water not to exceed five inches (a line was marked on the enamel) and he would have to arrange his turn with the others. He would be given four lumps of coal per evening to heat his room. The fire in the parlour downstairs was extinguished at 9 p.m., sharp. Anyone caught cooking, drinking alcohol or entertaining visitors in their room, especially of the opposite sex – he'd smiled faintly at that – would be evicted, balance of rent to be paid as a forfeit.

She'd asked if he had any questions, to which he

made no reply, which was a mercy, because at that moment a nonstop express shrieked past at sixty miles an hour no more than a hundred feet from the bedroom window, shaking the little room so violently that Mrs Armstrong had a brief and horrifying vision of the floor giving way and them both plummeting downwards, down through her own bedroom, down through the scullery, crashing down to land amid the waxy legs of ham and tinned peaches so carefully stacked and hidden in her Aladdin's cave of a cellar.

'Well, then,' she said, when the noise (if not yet the house) had finally subsided, 'I'll leave you to get some peace and quiet.'

Tom Jericho sat on the edge of the bed for a couple of minutes after listening to her footsteps descending the stairs. Then he took off his jacket and shirt and examined his throbbing forearm. He had a pair of bruises just below the elbow as neat and black as damsons, and he remembered now whom Skynner had always reminded him of: a prefect at school called Fane, the son of a bishop, who liked to cane the new boys in his study at teatime, and make them all say 'thank you, Fane' afterwards.

It was cold in the room and he started to shiver, his skin puckering into rashes of gooseflesh. He felt desperately tired. He opened one of his suitcases and took out a pair of pyjamas and changed into them quickly. He hung up his jacket and thought about unpacking the rest of his clothes, but decided against it. He might be out of Bletchley by the next morning.

That was a point – he passed his hand across his face –
he'd just given away eight pounds, more than a week's
salary, for a room he might not need. The wardrobe
vibrated as he opened it and the wire coat hangers
sounded a melancholy chime. Inside it stank of
mothballs. He quickly shoved the cardboard boxes into
it and pushed the cases under the bed. Then he drew
the curtains, lay down on the lumpy mattress, and
pulled the blankets up under his chin.

For three years Jericho had led a nocturnal life,
rising with the darkness, going to bed with the light,
but he'd never got used to it. Lying there listening to
the distant sounds of a Saturday morning made him
feel like an invalid. Downstairs someone was running a
bath. The water tank was in the attic directly above his
head, and the noise of it emptying and refilling was
deafening. He closed his eyes and all he could see was
the chart of the North Atlantic. He opened them and
the bed shook slightly as a train went by and that
reminded him of Claire. The 15.06 out of London
Euston – '*calling at Willesden, Watford, Apsley,
Berkhamsted, Tring, Cheddington and Leighton
Buzzard, arriving Bletchley four-nineteen*' – he could
recite the station announcement even now, and see her
now as well. It had been his first glimpse of her.

This must have been – what? – a week after the break
into Shark? A couple of days before Christmas, anyway.
He and Logie, Puck and Atwood had been ordered to
present themselves at the office block in Broadway, near
St James's tube station, from which Bletchley Park was
run. 'C' himself had made a little speech about the value

of their work. In recognition of their 'vital breakthrough', and on the orders of the Prime Minister, they had each received an iron handshake and an envelope containing a cheque for a hundred pounds, drawn on an ancient and obscure City bank. Afterwards, slightly embarrassed, they'd said goodbye to one another on the pavement and gone their various ways – Logie to lunch at the Admiralty, Puck to meet a girl, Atwood to a concert at the National Portrait Gallery – and Jericho back to Euston to catch the train to Bletchley, '*calling at Willesden, Watford, Apsley . . .*'

There would be no more cheques now, he thought. Perhaps Churchill would ask for his money back.

A million tons of shipping. Ten thousand people. Forty-six U-boats. And that was just the beginning of it.

'*It's everything. It's the whole war.*'

He turned his face to the wall.

Another train went by, and then another. Someone else began to run a bath. In the back yard, directly beneath his window, Mrs Armstrong hung the parlour carpet over the washing line and began to beat it, hard and rhythmically, as if it were a tenant behind with his rent or some prying inspector from the Ministry of Food.

Darkness closed around him.

The dream is a memory, the memory a dream.

A teeming station platform – iron girders and pigeons fluttering against a filthy glass cupola. Tinny carols playing over the public address system. Steel light and splashes of khaki.

126

Enigma

A line of soldiers bent sideways by the weight of kitbags runs towards the guard's van. A sailor kisses a pregnant woman in a red hat and pats her bottom. School children going home for Christmas, salesmen in threadbare overcoats, a pair of thin and anxious mothers in tatty furs, a tall, blonde woman in a well-cut, ankle-length grey coat, trimmed with black velvet at the collar and cuffs. A pre-war coat, *he thinks,* nothing so fine is made now-adays . . .

She walks past the window and he realises with a jolt that she's noticed he is staring at her. He glances at his watch, snaps the lid shut with his thumb and when he looks up again she's actually stepping into his compartment. Every seat is taken. She hesitates. He stands to offer her his place. She smiles her thanks and gestures to show there's just sufficient room for her to squeeze between him and the window. He nods and sits again with difficulty.

Doors slam along the length of the train, a whistle blows, they shudder forwards. The platform is a blur of waving people.

He's wedged so tightly he can barely move. Such intimacy would never have been tolerated before the war, but nowadays, on these endless uncomfortable journeys, men and women are always being thrown together, often literally so. Her thigh is pressed to his, so hard he can feel the firmness of muscle and bone beneath the padding of her flesh. Her shoulder is to his. Their legs touch. Her stocking rustles against his calf. He can feel the warmth of her, and smell her scent.

He looks past her and pretends to stare out of the

127

window at the ugly houses sliding by. She's much younger than he thought at first. Her face in profile is not conventionally pretty, but striking – angular, strong – he supposes 'handsome' is the word for it. She has very blonde hair, tied back. When he tries to move, his elbow brushes the side of her breast and he thinks he might die of embarrassment. He apologies profusely but she doesn't seem to notice. She has a copy of The Times, folded up very small so that she can hold it in one hand.

The compartment is packed. Servicemen lie on the floor and jam the corridor outside. An RAF corporal has fallen asleep in the luggage rack and cradles his kit bag like a lover. Someone begins to snore. The air smells strongly of cheap cigarettes and unwashed bodies. But gradually, for Jericho, all this begins to disappear. There are just the two of them, rocking with the train. Where they touch his skin is burning. His calf muscles ache with the strain of neither moving too close nor drawing apart.

He wonders how far she's going. Each time they stop at one of the little stations he fears she might get off. But no: she continues to stare down at her square of newsprint. The dreary hinterland of northern London gives way to a dreary countryside, monochrome in the darkening December afternoon – frosted fields barren of livestock, bare trees and the straggling dark lines of hedgerows, empty lanes, little villages with smoking chimneys that stand out like smudges of soot in the white landscape.

An hour passes. They're clear of Leighton Buzzard and within five minutes of Bletchley when she suddenly says: 'German town partly in French disagreement with Hamelin.'

He isn't sure he's heard her properly, or even if the remark is addressed to him.

'I'm sorry?'

'German town partly in French disagreement with Hamelin.' She repeats it, as if he's stupid. 'Seven down. Eight letters.'

'Ah yes,' he says. 'Ratisbon.'

'How do you get that? I don't think I've even heard of it.' She turns her face to him. He has an impression of large features – a sharp nose, a wide mouth – but it is the eyes that hold him. Grey eyes – a cold grey, with no hint of blue. They're not dove-grey, he decides later, or pearl-grey. They're the grey of snow clouds waiting to break.

'It's a cathedral city. On the Danube, I believe. Partly in French – well, bon, *obviously. Disagreement with Hamelin. That's easy. Hamelin – Pied Piper – rats. Rat is* bon. *Rat is good. Not the view in Hamelin.'*

He starts to laugh then stops himself. Just hark at yourself, he thinks, you're babbling like an idiot.

'Fill up ten. Nine letters.'

'That's an anagram,' he says immediately. 'Plentiful.'

'Morning snack as far as it goes. Five letters.'

'Ambit.'

She shakes her heard, filling in the answers. 'How do you get it so quickly?'

'It's not hard. You learn to know the way they think. Morning – that's a.m., obviously. Snack as far as it goes – bit with the e missing. As far as it goes – well, within one's ambit. One's limit. May I?'

He reaches over and takes the paper and pencil. Half his brain studies the puzzle, the other half studies her –

how she takes a cigarette from her handbag and lights it, how she watches him, her head resting slightly to one side. Aster, tasso, loveage, landau . . . It's the first and only time in their relationship he's ever fully in control, and by the time he's completed the thirty clues and given her back the paper they're pulling through the outskirts of a small town, crawling past narrow gardens and tall chimneys. Behind her head he sees the familiar lines of washing, the air raid shelters, the vegetable plots, the little red-brick houses coated black by the passing trains. The compartment darkens as they pass beneath the iron canopy of the station. 'Bletchley,' calls the guard. 'Bletchley station!'

He says, 'I'm afraid this is my stop.'

'Yes.' She looks thoughtfully at the finished crossword, then turns and smiles at him. 'Yes. D'you know, I rather guessed it might be.'

'Mr Jericho!' someone calls. 'Mr Jericho!'

'Mr Jericho!'

He opened his eyes. For a moment he was disoriented. The wardrobe loomed over him like a thief in the dim light.

'Yes.' He sat up in the strange bed. 'I'm sorry. Mrs Armstrong?'

'It's a quarter past six, Mr Jericho.' She was shouting to him from halfway up the stairs. 'Will you be wanting supper?'

A quarter past six? The room was almost dark. He pulled his watch out from beneath his pillow and flicked it open. To his astonishment he found he had slept through the entire day.

'That would be very kind, Mrs Armstrong. Thank you.'

The dream had been disturbingly vivid – more substantial, certainly, than this shadowy room – and as he threw off the blankets and swung his bare feet on to the cold floor, he felt himself to be in a no-man's-land between two worlds. He had a peculiar conviction that Claire had been thinking of him, that his subconscious had somehow acted like a radio receiver and had picked up a message from her. It was an absurd thought for a mathematician, a rationalist, to entertain, but he couldn't rid himself of it. He found his sponge-bag and slipped his overcoat over his pyjamas.

On the first floor a figure in a blue flannel dressing gown and white paper curlers hurried out of the bathroom. He nodded politely but the woman gave a squeak of embarrassment and scuttled down the passage. Standing at the basin, he laid out his toiletries: a sliver of carbolic soap, a safety razor with a six-month-old blade, a wooden toothbrush worn down to a fuzz of bristles, an almost empty tin of pink tooth powder. The taps clanked. There was no hot water. He scraped at his chin for ten minutes until it was red and pricked with blood. This was where the devil of the war resided, he thought, as he dabbed at his skin with the hard towel: in the details, in the thousand petty humiliations of never having enough toilet paper or soap or matches or baths or clean clothes. Civilians had been pauperised. They smelled, that was the truth of it. Body odour lay over the British Isles like a great sour fog.

There were two other guests downstairs in the

dining room, a Miss Jobey and a Mr Bonnyman, and the three of them made discreet conversation while they waited for their food. Miss Jobey was dressed in black with a cameo brooch at her throat. Bonnyman wore mildew-coloured tweeds with a set of pens in his breast pocket and Jericho guessed he might be an engineer on the bombes. The door to the kitchen swung open as Mrs Armstrong brought in their plates.

'Here we go,' whispered Bonnyman. 'Brace yourself old boy.'

'Now, don't you go getting her worked up again, Arthur,' said Miss Jobey. She gave his arm a playful pinch, at which Bonnyman's hand slid beneath the table and squeezed her knee. Jericho poured them all a glass of water and pretended not to notice.

'It's potato pie,' announced Mrs Armstrong, defiantly. 'With gravy. And potatoes.'

They contemplated their steaming plates.

'How very, ah, substantial,' said Jericho, eventually.

The meal passed in silence. Pudding was some kind of stewed apple with powdered custard. Once that had been cleared away Bonnyman lit his pipe and announced that, as it was a Saturday night, he and Miss Jobey would be going to the Eight Bells Inn on the Buckingham Road.

'Naturally, you're very welcome to join us,' he said, in a tone which implied that Jericho, naturally, wouldn't be welcome at all. 'Do you have any plans?'

'It's kind of you, but as a matter of fact I do have plans. Or, rather, *a* plan.'

After the others had gone, he helped Mrs Armstrong

clear away the dishes, then went out into the back yard to check his bicycle. It was almost dark and there was a sharpness in the air that promised frost. The lights still worked. He cleaned the dirt off the regulation white patch on the mudguard and pumped some air into the tyres.

By eight o'clock he was back up in his room. At half past ten, Mrs Armstrong was on the point of laying aside her knitting to go up to bed when she heard him coming downstairs. She opened the door a crack, just in time to see Jericho hurrying along the passage and out into the night.

2

The moon defied the blackout, shining a blue torch over the frozen fields, quite bright enough for a man to cycle by. Jericho lifted himself out of the saddle and trod hard on the pedals, rocking from side to side as he toiled up the hill out of Bletchley, pursuing his own shadow, cast sharp on the road before him. From far in the distance came the drone of a returning bomber.

The road began to level out and he sat back on the saddle. For all his efforts with the pump, the tyres remained half-flat, the wheels and chain were stiff for want of oil. It was hard going, but Jericho didn't mind. He was taking action, that was the point. It was the same as code-breaking. However hopeless the situation, the rule was always to do *something*. No cryptogram, Alan Turing used to say, was ever solved by simply staring at it.

He cycled on for about two miles, following the lane as it continued to rise gently towards Shenley Brook End. This was hardly a village, more a tiny hamlet of perhaps a dozen houses, mostly farmworkers' cottages. He couldn't see the buildings, which sheltered in a slight hollow, but when he rounded a bend and caught the scent of woodsmoke he knew he must be close.

Just before the hamlet, on the left, there was a gap in the hawthorn hedge where a rutted track led to a little cottage that stood alone. He turned into it and skittered to a halt, his feet slipping on the frozen mud. A white owl, improbably huge, rose from a nearby branch and flapped soundlessly across the field. Jericho squinted at the cottage. Was it his imagination or was there a hint of light in the downstairs window? He dismounted and began to wheel his bike towards it.

He felt wonderfully calm. Above the thatched roof the constellations spread out like the lights of a city – Ursa Minor and Polaris, Pegasus and Cepheus, the flattened M of Cassiopeia with the Milky Way flowing through it. No glow from earth obscured their brilliance. *You can at least say this for the blackout,* he thought, *it has given us back the stars.*

The door was stout and iron-studded. It was like knocking on stone. After half a minute he tried again.

'Claire?' he called. 'Claire?'

There was a pause, and then: 'Who is it?'

'It's Tom.'

He took a breath and braced himself, as if for a blow.

134

The handle turned and the door opened slightly, just enough to reveal a dark-haired woman, thirtyish, about Jericho's height. She was wearing round spectacles and a thick overcoat and was holding a prayer book.

'Yes?'

For a moment he was speechless. 'I'm sorry,' he said, 'I was looking for Claire.'

'She's not in.'

'Not in?' he repeated, hopelessly. He remembered now that Claire shared the cottage with a woman called Hester Wallace (*'she works in Hut 6, she's a sweetie'*) but for some reason he had forgotten all about her. She did not look very sweet to Jericho. She had a thin face, split like a knife by a long, sharp nose. Her hair was wrenched back off a frowning forehead. 'I'm Tom Jericho.' She made no response. 'Perhaps Claire's mentioned me?'

'I'll tell her you called.'

'Will she be back soon?'

'I've no idea, I'm sorry.'

She began to close the door. Jericho pressed his foot against it. 'I say, I know this is awfully rude of me, but I couldn't possibly come in and wait, could I?'

The woman glanced at his foot, and then at his face. 'I'm afraid that's impossible. Good evening, Mr Jericho.' She pushed the door closed with surprising force.

Jericho took a step backwards on to the track. This was not a contingency envisaged in his plan. He looked at his watch. It was just after eleven. He picked up his bicycle and wheeled it back towards the lane, but at the

135

last moment, instead of going out on to the road, he
turned left and followed the line of the hedge. He laid
the bicycle flat and drew into the shadows to wait.

After about ten minutes, the cottage door opened
and closed and he heard the rattle of a bicycle being
wheeled over stone. It was as he thought: Miss Wallace
had been dressed to go out because she was working the
midnight shift. A pinprick of yellow light appeared,
wobbled briefly from side to side, and then began to
bob towards him. Hester Wallace passed within twenty
feet in the moonlight, knees pumping, elbows stuck
out, as angular as an old umbrella. She stopped at the
entrance to the lane and slipped on a luminous armlet.
Jericho edged further into the hawthorn. Half a minute
later she was gone. He waited a full quarter of an hour
in case she'd forgotten something, then headed back to
the cottage.

There was only one key – ornate and iron and big
enough to fit a cathedral. It was kept, he recalled, under
a piece of slate beneath a flowerpot. Damp had warped
the door and he had to push hard to open it, scraping
an arc on the flagstone floor. He replaced the key and
closed the door behind him before turning on the light.

He had only been inside once before, but there
wasn't much to remember. Two rooms on the ground
floor: a sitting room with low beams and a kitchen
straight ahead. To his left, a narrow staircase led up to
a little landing. Claire's bedroom was at the front,
looking towards the lane. Hester's was at the rear. The
lavatory was a chemical toilet just outside the back
door, reached via the kitchen. There was no bathroom.

A galvanised metal tub was kept in the shed next to the kitchen. Baths were taken in front of the stove. The whole place was cold and cramped and smelled of mildew. He wondered how Claire stuck it.

'Oh, but darling, it's so much better than having some ghastly landlady telling one what to do . . .'

Jericho took a couple of steps across the worn rug and stopped. For the first time he began to feel uneasy. Everywhere he looked he saw evidence of a life being lived quite contentedly without him – the ill-assorted blue-and-white china in the dresser, the vase full of daffodils, the stack of pre-war *Vogues*, even the arrangement of the furniture (the two armchairs and the sofa drawn up cosily around the hearth). Every tiny domestic detail seemed significant and premeditated.

He had no business here.

He very nearly left at that moment. All that stopped him was the faintly pathetic realisation that he had nowhere else particularly to go. The Park? Albion Street? King's? His life seemed to have become a maze of dead ends.

Better to make a stand here, he decided, than run away again. She was bound to be back quite soon.

God, but it was cold! His bones were ice. He walked up and down the cramped room, ducking to avoid the heavy beams. In the hearth was white ash and a few blackened fragments of wood. He sat first in one armchair, then tried the other. Now he was facing the door. To his right was the sofa. Its covers were of frayed pink silk, its cushions hollowed and leaking feathers. The springs had gone and when you sat in it you sank almost to the floor and had to struggle to get out. He remembered that sofa and he stared at it for a long time, as a soldier might stare at a battlefield where a war had been irretrievably lost.

They leave the train together and walk up the footpath to the Park. To their left is a playing field, ploughed into allotments for the Dig for Victory campaign. To their right, through the perimeter fence, is the familiar huddle of low buildings. People walk briskly to ward off the cold. The December afternoon is raw and misty, the day is leaking into dusk.

She tells him she's been up to London to celebrate her birthday. How old does he think she is?

He hasn't a clue. Eighteen perhaps?

Twenty, she says triumphantly, ancient. And what was he doing in town?

He can't tell her, of course. Just business, he says. Just business.

Sorry, she says, she shouldn't have asked. She still can't get the hang of all this 'need to know'. She has been at the Park three months and hates it. Her father works at the Foreign Office and wangled her the job to keep her out of mischief. How long has he been here?

Three years, says Jericho, she shouldn't worry, it'll get better.

Ah, she says, that's easy for him to say, but surely he does something interesting?

Not really, he says, but then he thinks that makes him sound boring, so he adds: 'Well, quite interesting, I suppose.'

In truth he's finding it hard to keep up his end of the conversation. It's distracting enough merely to walk alongside her. They lapse into silence.

There's a noticeboard close to the main gate advertising a performance of Bach's Musikalisches Opfer *by the Bletchley Park Music Society. 'Oh, now look at that,' she says. 'I adore Bach', to which Jericho replies with genuine enthusiasm, that Bach is his favourite composer. Grateful at last to have found something to talk about, he launches into a long dissertation about the* Musikalisches Opfer*'s six-part fugue, which Bach is supposed to have improvised on the spot for King Frederick the Great, a feat equivalent to playing and winning sixty games of blindfold chess simultaneously. Perhaps she knows that Bach's dedication to the King –* Regis Iussu Cantio et Reliqua Canonica Arte Resoluta *– rather interestingly yields the acrostic* RICERCAR, *meaning 'to seek'?*

No, oddly enough, she doesn't know that.

This increasingly desperate monologue carries them as far as the huts where they both stop and, after another awkward pause, introduce themselves. She offers him her hand – her grip is warm and firm, but her nails are a shock: painfully bitten back, almost to the quick. Her surname is Romilly. Claire Romilly. It has a pleasant ring. Claire Romilly. He wishes her a merry Christmas and turns away but she calls him back. She hopes he won't think it too fresh of her, but would he like to go with her to the concert?

He isn't sure, he doesn't know . . .

She writes down the date and time just above The Times *crossword – 27 December at 8.15 – and thrusts it*

139

into his hands. She'll buy the tickets. She'll see him there.
Please don't say no.
And before he can think of an excuse, she's gone.

He's due to be on shift on the evening of the 27ᵗʰ but he doesn't know where to find her to tell her he can't go. And anyway, he realises, he rather does *want to go. So he calls in a favour he's owed by Arthur de Brooke and waits outside the assembly hall, and waits, and waits. Eventually, after everyone else has gone in, and just when he's about to give up, she comes running out of the darkness, smiling her apologies.*

The concert is better than he'd hoped. The quintet all work at the Park and once played professionally. The harpsichordist is particularly fine. The women in the audience are wearing evening frocks, the men are wearing suits. Suddenly, and for the first time he can recall, the war seems a long way away. As the last notes of the third canon ('per Motum contrarium'*) are dying in the air he risks a glance at Claire only to discover that she is looking at him. She touches his arm and when the fourth canon (*'per Augmentationem, contrario Motu'*) begins, he is lost.*

Afterwards he has to go straight back to the hut: he's promised he'd be back before midnight. 'Poor Mr Jericho,' she says, 'just like Cinderella . . .' But at her suggestion they meet again for the following week's concert — Chopin — and when that's over they walk down the hill to the station to have cocoa in the platform buffet.

'So,' she says, as he returns from the counter bearing two cups of brown froth, 'how much am I allowed to know about you?'

'Me? Oh, I'm very boring.'

140

'*I don't think you're boring at all. In fact, I've heard a rumour you're rather brilliant.*' *She lights a cigarette and he notices again her distinctive way of inhaling, seeming almost to swallow the smoke, then tilting her head back and breathing it out through her nostrils. Is this some new fashion, he wonders?* '*I suppose you're married?*' *she says.*

He almost chokes on his cocoa. '*Good God, no. I mean, I would hardly be –* '

'*Fiancée? Girlfriend?*'

'*Now you're teasing me.*' *He pulls out a handkerchief and dabs at his chin.*

'*Brothers? Sisters?*'

'*No, no.*'

'*Parents? Even* you *must have parents.*'

'*Only one still alive.*'

'*I'm the same,*' *she says.* '*My mother's dead.*'

'*How awful for you. I'm sorry. My mother, I must say, is very much alive.*'

And so it goes on, this hitherto untasted pleasure of talking about oneself. Her grey eyes never leaving his face. The trains steam past in the darkness, trailing a wash of soot and hot air. Customers come and go. 'Who cares if we're without a light?' *sings a crooner on the wireless in the corner,* 'they can't blackout the moon . . .' *He finds himself telling her things he's never really spoken of before – about his father's death and his mother's remarriage, about his stepfather (a businessman, whom he dislikes), about his discovery of astronomy and then of mathematics . . .*

'*And your work now?*' *she says.* '*Does that make you happy?*'

'Happy?' He warms his hands on his cup and considers the question. 'No. I couldn't say happy. It's too demanding – frightening, even, in a way.'

'Frightening?' The wide eyes widen further with interest. 'Frightening how?'

'What might happen . . .' (You're showing off, he warns himself, stop it.) 'What might happen if you get it wrong, I suppose.'

She lights another cigarette. 'You're in Hut 8, aren't you? Hut 8's the naval section?'

This brings him up with a jolt. He looks around quickly. Another couple are holding hands at the next table, whispering. Four airmen are playing cards. A waitress in a greasy apron is polishing the counter. Nobody seems to have heard.

'Talking of which,' he says, brightly, 'I think I ought to get back.'

On the corner of Church Green Road and Wilton Avenue she kisses him, briefly, on the cheek.

The following week it is Schumann, followed by steak-and-kidney pudding and jam roly-poly at the British Restaurant in Bletchley Road ('two courses for eleven-pence') and this time it's her turn to talk. Her mother died when she was six, she says, and her father trailed her from embassy to embassy. Family has been a procession of nannies and governesses. At least she's learned some languages. She'd wanted to join the Wrens, but the old man wouldn't let her.

Jericho asks what London was like in the Blitz.

'Oh, a lot of fun, actually. Loads of places to go. The Milroy, the Four Hundred. A kind of desperate gaiety.

We've all had to learn to live for the moment, don't you think?'

When they say goodbye she kisses him again, her lips to one cheek, her cool hand to the other.

In retrospect, it is around this time, in the middle of January, that he should have started keeping a record of his symptoms, for it is now that he begins to lose his equilibrium. He wakes with a feeling of mild euphoria. He bounces into the hut, whistling. He goes for long walks around the lake between shifts, taking bread to feed the ducks – just for the exercise, he tells himself, but really he is scanning the crowds for her, and twice he sees her, and once she sees him and waves.

For their fourth date (the fifth, if you count their meeting on the train) she insists they do something different, so they go to the County Cinema on the High Street to see the new Noël Coward picture, In Which We Serve.

'And you really mean to tell me you've never once been here?'

They're queuing for tickets. The film's only been showing for a day and the line extends round the corner into Aylesbury Street.

'I haven't, actually, to be honest, no.'

'God, Tom, you are *a funny old darling. I think I'd die stuck in Bletchley without the flicks to go to.'*

They sit near the back and she laces her arm through his. The light from the projector high up behind them makes a kaleidoscope of blues and greys in the dust and cigarette smoke. The couple next to them are kissing. A woman giggles. A fanfare of trumpets announces a newsreel and there, on the screen, long columns of German prisoners, an impossible number, are shown trekking through snow, while the announcer talks excitedly about Red Army breakthroughs on the eastern front. Stalin appears, presenting medals, to loud applause. Someone shouts: 'Three cheers for Uncle Joe!' The lights come up, then dim again, and Claire squeezes his arm. The main film begins – 'This is the story of a ship' *– with Coward as an improbably suave Royal Navy captain. There's a lot of clipped excitement.* 'Vessel on fire bearing green three-oh . . . Torpedo track, starboard, sir . . . Carry on firing . . .' *At the climax of the sea battle, Jericho looks around at the flickering of the celluloid explosions on the rapt faces, and it strikes him that he is a part of all this – a distant, vital part – and that nobody knows, nobody will ever know . . . After the final credits the loudspeakers play* 'God Save the King' *and they all stand, many of the audience so moved by the film they begin to sing.*

They've left their bicycles near the end of an alley running beside the cinema. A few paces further on a shape rubs itself against the wall. As they come closer they can see it is a soldier with his greatcoat wrapped around a girl. Her back is to the bricks. Her white face stares at them from the shadows like an animal in its hide. The movement stops for the time it takes Claire and Jericho to collect their bicycles, then it starts again.

'What very peculiar behaviour.'

He says it without thinking. To his surprise, Claire bursts out laughing.

'What's the matter?'

144

'Nothing,' she says.

They stand on the pavement holding their bicycles, waiting for an Army lorry with dimmed headlights to pass, its gearbox grinding as it heads north along Watling Street. Her laughter stops.

'Do come and see my cottage, Tom.' She says it almost plaintively. 'It's not that late. I'd love to show it you.'

He can't think of an excuse, doesn't want to think of one.

She leads the way through the town and out past the Park. They don't speak for fifteen minutes and he begins to wonder how far she's taking him. At last, when they're rattling down the path that leads to the cottage, she calls over her shoulder, 'Isn't it a perfect sweetheart?'

'It's, ah, off the beaten track.'

'Now don't be horrible,' she says, pretending to be hurt.

She tells him how she found it standing derelict, how she charmed the farmer who owns it into letting her rent it. Inside, the furniture is shabby-grand, rescued from an aunt's house in Kensington that was shut up for the Blitz and never reopened.

The staircase creaks so alarmingly, Jericho wonders if their combined weight might pull it away from the wall. The place is a ruin, freezing cold. 'And this is where I sleep,' she says, and he follows her into a room of pinks and creams, crammed full of pre-war silks and furs and feathers, like a large dressing-up box. A loose floorboard goes off like a gunshot beneath his feet. There's too much detail for the eye to register, so many hat boxes, shoe boxes, bits of jewellery, cosmetic bottles . . . She slips off her coat and lets it fall to the floor and flings herself flat out on the bed, then props herself up on her elbows and kicks off her shoes. She seems amused by something.

'And what's this?' Jericho, in a turmoil, has retreated to the landing and is staring at the only other door.

'Oh, that's Hester's room,' she calls.

'Hester?'

'Some bureaucratic beast found out where I was and said if I had a second bedroom I had to share. So in came Hester. She works in Hut 6. She's a sweetie, really. Got a bit of a crush on me. Take a look. She won't mind.'

He knocks, there's no reply, he opens the door. Another tiny room, but this one spartan, like a cell: a brass bedstead, a jug and bowl on a washstand, some books piled on a chair. Ableman's German Primer. *He opens it.* 'Der Rhein ist etwas langer als die Elbe,' *he reads. The Rhine is somewhat longer than the Elbe. He hears the gunshot of the floorboard behind him and Claire lifts the book from his hands.*

'Don't snoop, darling. It's rude. Come on, let's make a fire and have a drink.'

Downstairs, he kneels by the hearth and rolls a copy of The Times *into a ball. He piles on kindling and a couple of small logs, and lights the paper. The chimney draws voraciously, sucking up the smoke with a roar.*

'Look at you, you haven't even taken off your coat.'

He stands, brushing the dust away, and turns to face her. Grey skirt, navy cashmere sweater, a single loop of milk-white pearls at her creamy throat — the ubiquitous, unchanging uniform of the upper-class Englishwoman. She somehow contrives to look both very young and very mature at the same time.

146

'Come here. Let me do it.'

She sets down the drinks and begins to unbutton his overcoat.

'Don't tell me, Tom,' she whispers, 'don't tell me you didn't know what they were doing behind that cinema?'

Even barefoot she is as tall as he is.

'Of course I knew . . .'

'In London nowadays the girls all call it a "wall job". What do you think? They say you can't get pregnant this way . . .'

Instinctively, he draws his coat around her. She wraps her arms about his back.

3

Damn it, damn it, damn it.

He pitched himself forwards and out of the chair, sending the images scattering and smashing on the cold stone floor. He prowled around the tiny sitting room a couple of times, then went into the kitchen. Everything was clean and swept and put away. That would be Hester's handiwork, he guessed, not Claire's. The stove had burned down very low and was lukewarm to the touch, but he resisted the temptation to shovel in some coal. It was quarter to one. Where was she? He wandered back into the sitting room, hesitated at the foot of the stairs, and began to climb. The plaster on the walls was damp and flaking beneath his fingers. He decided to try Hester's room first. It was exactly as it had been six weeks earlier. A pair of sensible shoes beside the bed. A cupboard full of dark clothes. The same German primer. *'An seinen Ufern sind Berge, Felsen und malerische Schlosser aus den ältesten Zeiten.'* On its shores are mountains, rocks and picturesque castles from the oldest times. He closed it and went back out on the landing.

And so, at last, to Claire's room.

He was quite clear now about what he was going to do, even though conscience told him it was wrong and logic told him it was stupid. And, in principle, he agreed. Like any good boy he had learned his Aesop, knew that 'listeners never hear good of themselves' – but since when, he thought, as he began opening drawers, since when has that pious wisdom stopped anybody? A letter, a diary, a message – anything that might tell him *why* – he had to see it, he had to, even though the chances of its yielding any comfort were nil. Where was she? Was she with another man? Was she doing what all the girls in London, darling, call a wall job?

He was suddenly in a rage and he went through her room like a housebreaker, pulling out drawers and upending them, sweeping jewellery and trinkets off the shelves, pulling her clothes down on to the floor, throwing off her sheets and blankets and wrenching up her mattress, raising clouds of dust and scent and ostrich feathers.

After ten minutes he crawled into the corner and laid his head on a pile of silks and furs.

'You're a wreck,' Skynner had said. *'You're ruined.*

You've lost it. Find someone more suitable than the person you were seeing.'

Skynner knew about her, and Logie had seemed to know as well. What was it he'd called her? The 'arctic blonde'? Perhaps they all knew? Puck, Atwood, Baxter, everybody?

He had to get out, get away from the smell of her perfume and the sight of her clothes.

And it was that action that changed everything, for it was only when he stood on the landing, leaning with his back to the wall and his eyes closed, that he realised there *was* something he'd missed.

He walked back slowly and deliberately into her room. Silence. He stepped across the threshold and repeated the action. Silence again. He got down on his knees. One of auntie's Kensington rugs covered the floorboards, something oriental, stained, and tastefully threadbare. It was only about two yards square. He rolled it up and laid it on the bed. The wooden planks which had lain beneath it were bowed with age, worn smooth, fixed down by rust-coloured nails, untouched for two centuries – except in one place, where a shorter length of the old planking, perhaps, eighteen inches long, was secured by four very modern, very shiny screws. He slapped the floor in triumph.

'Is there any other point to which you would wish to draw my attention, Mr Jericho?'
'To the curious incident of the creaking floorboard.'
'But the floorboard didn't creak.'
'That was the curious incident.'
In the mess of her bedroom he could see no suitable

tool. He went down into the kitchen and found a knife. It had a mother-of-pearl handle with an 'R' engraved on it. Perfect. He almost skipped across the sitting room. The tip of the knife slotted into the head of the screw and the thread turned easily, it came away like a dream. So did the other three. The floorboard lifted up to reveal the horsehair and plaster of the downstairs ceiling. The cavity was about six inches deep. He took off his overcoat and his jacket and rolled up his sleeve. He lay on his side and thrust his hand into the space. To begin with he brought out nothing except handfuls of debris, mostly lumps of old plaster and small pieces of brick, but he kept on working his way around until at last he gave a cry of delight as his hand touched paper.

He put everything back in its place, more or less. He hung the clothes back up from the beams, piled her underclothes and her scarves back into the drawers and replaced the drawers in the mahogany chest. He heaped the trinkets of jewellery into their leather case and draped others artfully along the shelves, together with her bottles and pots and packets, most of which were empty.

He did all this mechanically, an automaton.

He remade the bed, lifting off the rug and smoothing down the eiderdown, throwing the lace cover over it where it settled like a net. Then he sat on the edge of the mattress and surveyed the room. Not bad. Of course, once she began looking for things, then she would know someone had been through it, but at a casual glance it looked the same as before – apart, that is, from the hole in the floor. He didn't know yet what to do about that. It depended on whether or not he replaced the intercepts. He pulled them out from under the bed and examined them again.

There were four, on standard-size sheets, eight inches by ten. He held one up to the light. It was cheap wartime paper, the sort Bletchley used by the ton. He could practically see a petrified forest in its coarse yellow weave – the shadows of foliage and leaf-stalks, the faint outlines of bark and fern.

In the top left-hand corner of each signal was the frequency on which it had been transmitted – 12260 kilocycles per second – and in the top right its TOI, Time of Interception. The four had been sent in rapid succession on 4 March, just nine days earlier, at roughly twenty-five-minute intervals, beginning at 9.30 p.m. and ending just before midnight. Each consisted of a call sign – ADU – and then about two hundred five-letter groups. That in itself was an important clue. It meant, whatever else they were, they weren't naval: the Kriesgmarine's signals were transmitted in groups of four letters. So they were presumably German Army or Luftwaffe.

She must have stolen them from Hut 3.

The enormity of the implications hit Jericho for a second time, winding him like a punch in the stomach. He arranged the intercepts in sequence on her pillow and tried very hard, like a defending King's Counsel, to come up with some innocent explanation. A piece of silly mischief? It was possible. She had certainly never

151

paid much attention to security – shouting about Hut 8 in the station buffet, demanding to know what he did, trying to tell him what *she* did. A dare? Again, possible. She was capable of anything. But that hole in the floorboards, the cool deliberation of it, drew his gaze and mocked his advocacy.

A sound, a footstep downstairs, dragged him out of his reverie and made him jump to his feet.

He said, 'Hello?' in a loud voice that suggested more courage than he felt. He cleared his throat. 'Hello?' he repeated. And then he heard another nose, definitely a footstep, and definitely *outside* now, and a charge of adrenaline snapped in. He moved quickly to the bedroom door and turned the light off, so that the only illumination in the cottage came from the sitting room. Now, if anyone came up the stairs, he would be able to see their silhouette, while remaining hidden. But nothing happened. Perhaps they were trying to come round the back? He felt horribly vulnerable. He moved cautiously down the stairs, flinching at every creak. A blast of cold air struck him.

The front door was wide open.

He threw himself down the last half-dozen steps and ran outside, just in time to see the red rear light of a bicycle shoot out of the track and vanish down the lane.

He set off in pursuit but gave up after twenty paces. He didn't stand a chance of catching the cyclist.

There was a heavy frost. In every direction the ground shone a dull and luminous blue. The branches of the bare trees were raised against the sky like blood vessels. In the glittering ice, two sets of tyre-tracks were imprinted: incoming and outgoing. He followed them back to the door, where they ended in a series of sharp footprints.

Sharp, large, *male* footprints.

Jericho looked at them for half a minute, shivering in his shirtsleeves. An owl shrieked in the nearby copse and it seemed to him that its call had the rhythm of Morse: dee-dee-dee-*dah,* dee-dee-dee-*dah.*

He hurried back into the cottage.

Upstairs, he rolled the intercepts very tightly into a cylinder. He used his teeth to tear a small hole in the lining of his overcoat and pushed the signals into it. Then he quickly screwed down the floorboards and replaced the rug. He put on his jacket and coat, turned off the lights, locked the door, replaced the key.

His bicycle added a third set of impressions in the frost.

At the entrance to the lane he stopped and looked back at the darkened cottage. He had a strong sensation – foolish, he told himself – that he was being watched. He glanced around. A gust of wind stirred in the trees; in the blackthorn hedge beside him, icicles clinked and chimed.

Jericho shivered again, remounted the bike and pointed it down the hill, towards the south, towards Orion and Procyon, and to Hydra, which hung suspended in the night sky above Bletchley Park like a knife.

FOUR

KISS

KISS: the coincidence of two
different cryptograms, each
transmitted in a different cipher,
yet each containing the same
original plaintext, the solution
of one thereby leading to the
solution of the other.

A Lexicon of Cryptography
('Most Secret', Bletchley Park, 1943)

1

He doesn't know what wakes him — some faint sound, some movement in the air that hooks him in the depths of his dreams and hauls him to the surface.

At first his darkened room seems entirely normal — the familiar jet-black spar of the low oak beam, the smooth grey plains of wall and ceiling — but then he realises that a faint light is rising from the foot of his bed.

'Claire?' he says, propping himself up. 'Darling?'

'It's all right, darling. Go on back to sleep.'

'What on earth are you doing?'

'I'm just going through your things.'

'You're . . . what?'

His hand fumbles across the bedside table and switches on the lamp. His Waralarm shows him it is half past three.

'That's better,' she says, and she turns off the blackout torch. 'Useless thing, anyway.'

And she is doing exactly what she says. She is naked except for his shirt, she is kneeling, and she is going through his wallet. She removes a couple of one-pound notes, turns the wallet inside out and shakes it.

'No photographs?' she says.

'You haven't given me one yet.'

'Tom Jericho,' she smiles, replacing the money, 'I do declare, you're becoming almost smooth.'

She checks the pockets of his jacket, his trousers, then

157

shuffles on her knees across to his chest of drawers. He laces his hands behind his head and leans back against the iron bedstead and watches her. It is only the second time they have slept together – a week after the first – and at her insistence they have done it not in her cottage but in his room, creeping through the darkened bar of the White Hart Inn and up the creaking stair. Jericho's bedroom is well away from the rest of the household so there is no danger of them being overheard. His books are lined up on the top of the chest of drawers and she picks up each in turn, holds it upside down and flicks through the pages.

Does he see anything odd in all this? No, he does not. It merely seems amusing, flattering, even – one further intimacy, a continuation of all the rest, a part of the waking dream his life has become, governed by dream rules. Besides, he has no secrets from her – or, at least, he thinks he hasn't. She finds Turing's paper and studies it closely.

'And what are computable numbers with an application to the Entscheidungsproblem, *when they're at home?'*

Her pronunciation of the German, he registers with surprise, is immaculate.

'It's a theoretical machine, capable of an infinite number of numerical operations. It supports the assumptions of Hilbert and challenges those of Godel. Come back to bed, darling.'

'But it's only a theory?'

He sighs and pats the mattress next to him. They're sleeping in a single bed. 'Turing believes there's no inherent reason why a machine shouldn't be capable of doing everything a human brain can do. Calculate. Communicate. Write a sonnet.'

'Fall in love?'

'If love is logical.'

'Is it?'

'Come to bed.'

'This Turing, does he work at the Park?'

He makes no reply. She leafs through the paper, squinting with disgust at the mathematics, then replaces it with the books and opens one of the drawers. As she leans forwards the shirt rides higher. The lower part of her back gleams white in the shadows. He stares, mesmerised, at the soft triangle of flesh at the base of her vertebrae as she rummages among his clothes.

'Ah,' she says, 'now here is something.' She withdraws a slip of paper. 'A cheque for a hundred pounds, drawn on the Foreign Office Contingency Fund, made out to you –'

'Give me that.'

'Why?'

'Put it back.'

He is across the room and standing beside her within a couple of seconds, but she is quicker than he is. She is on her feet, on tiptoe, holding the cheque aloft, and she – absurdly – is just that half-inch taller than him. The money flutters like a pennant beyond his reach.

'I knew there would be something. Come on, darling, what's it for?'

He should have banked the damn thing weeks ago. He'd quite forgotten it. 'Claire, please . . .'

'You must have done something frightfully clever in that naval hut of yours. A new code? Is that it? You broke some new important code, my clever, clever darling?'

She may be taller than he is, she may even be stronger,

but he has the advantage of desperation. He seizes the firm muscle of her bicep and pulls her arm down and twists her round. They struggle for a moment and then he throws her back on the narrow bed. He prises the cheque out of her bitten-down fingers and retreats with it across the room.

'Not funny, Claire. Some things just aren't that funny.'

He stands there on the rough matting – naked, slender, panting with exertion. He folds the cheque and slips it into his wallet, puts the wallet into his jacket, and turns to hang the jacket in the wardrobe. As he does so, he is aware of a peculiar noise coming from behind him – a frightening, animal noise, something between a rasping breath and a sob. She has curled herself up tight on the bed, her knees drawn up to her stomach, her forearms pressed to her face.

My God, what has he done?

He starts to gabble his apologies. He hadn't meant to frighten her, let alone to hurt her. He goes across to the bed and sits beside her. Tentatively, he touches her shoulder. She doesn't seem to notice. He tries to pull her towards him, to roll her over on her back, but she has become as rigid as a corpse. The sobs are shaking the bed. It is like a fit, a seizure. She is somewhere beyond grief, somewhere far away, beyond him.

'It's all right,' he says. 'It's all right.'

He can't tug the bedclothes out from under her, so he fetches his overcoat and lays that across her, and then he lies beside her, shivering in the January night, stroking her hair.

They stay like that for half an hour until, at last, when she is calm again, she gets up off the bed and begins to dress. He cannot bring himself to look at her and he knows better than to speak. He can just hear her moving around the room, collecting her scattered clothes. Then the door closes quietly. The stairs creak. A minute later he hears the click of her bicycle being wheeled away from beneath his window.

And now his own nightmare begins.

First, there is guilt, that most corrosive of emotions, more torturing even than jealousy (although jealousy is added to the brew a few days later, when he happens to see her walking through Bletchley with a man he doesn't recognise: the man could be anyone, of course — cousin, friend, colleague — but naturally his imagination can't accept that). Why did he respond so dramatically to so small a provocation? The cheque could, after all, have been a reward for anything. He didn't have to tell her the truth. Now that she's gone, a hundred plausible explanations for the money come to mind. What had he done to provoke such terror in her? What awful memory had he reawakened?

He groans and draws the blankets over his head.

The next morning he takes the cheque to the bank and exchanges it for twenty large, crisp, white five-pound notes. Then he searches out the dreary little jewellery shop on Bletchley Road and asks for a ring, any ring as long as it is worth a hundred pounds, at which the jeweller — a ferret of a man with pebble-thick glasses, who clearly can't believe his luck — produces a diamond worth less than half that amount, and Jericho buys it.

He will make it up to her. He will apologise. It will all be right.

But luck is not with Jericho. He has become the victim

161

of his own success. A Shark decrypt discloses that a U-boat tanker – the U-459, under Korvettenkapitän von Williamowitz-Mollendorf, with 700 tons of fuel on board – is to rendezvous with, and refuel, the Italian submarine Kalvi, 300 miles east of St Paul's Rock, in the middle of the Atlantic. And some fool at the Admiralty, forgetting that no action, however tempting, must ever be taken that will endanger the Enigma secret, orders a squadron of destroyers to intercept. The attack is made. It fails. The U-459 escapes. And Dönitz, that crafty fox in his Paris lair, is immediately suspicious. In the third week of January, Hut 8 decrypts a series of signals ordering the U-boat fleet to tighten its cipher security. Shark traffic dwindles. There is barely enough material to make a menu for the bombes. At Bletchley, all leave is cancelled. Eight-hour shifts drag on to twelve hours, to sixteen hours . . . The daily battle to break the codes is almost as great a nightmare as it was in the depths of the Shark blackout, and Skynner's lash is felt on everybody's back.

Jericho's world has gone from perpetual sunshine to bleak midwinter in the space of a week. His messages to Claire, of entreaty and remorse, vanish, unanswered, into a void. He can't get out of the Hut to see her. He can't work. He can't sleep. And there's no one he can talk to. To Logie, lost and vague behind his smokescreen of tobacco? To Baxter, who would regard a dalliance with a woman like Claire Romilly as a betrayal of the world proletariat? To Atwood – Atwood! – whose sexual adventures have hitherto been confined to taking the prettier male undergraduates on golfing weekends to Brancaster, where they quickly discover that all the locks have been removed

162

from the bathroom doors? Puck would have been a possibility, but Jericho could guess at his advice – 'Take out someone else, my dear Thomas, and fuck her' – and how could he admit the truth: that he didn't want to 'fuck' anyone else, that he had never 'fucked' anyone else?

On the final day of January, collecting a copy of The Times *from Brinklow's the newsagent in Victoria Road, he spots her, at a distance, with the other man, and he shrinks into a doorway to avoid being seen. Apart from that, he never meets her: the Park has become too big, there are too many changes of shift. Eventually, he's reduced to lying in wait in the lane opposite her cottage, like a Peeping Tom. But she seems to have stopped coming home.*

And then he almost walks right into her.

It is 8 February, a Monday, at four o'clock. He's walking wearily back to the hut from the canteen; she is part of a flood of workers streaming towards the gate at the end of the afternoon shift. He has rehearsed for his moment so many times, but in the end all he manages is a whine of complaint: 'Why don't you answer my letters?'

'Hello, Tom.'

She tries to walk on, but he won't let her get away this time. He has a pile of Shark intercepts waiting for him on his desk but he doesn't care. He catches at her arm.

'I need to talk to you.'

Their bodies block the pavement. The flow of people has to pass around them, like a river round a rock.

'Mind out,' says someone.

'Tom,' she hisses, 'for God's sake, you're making a scene.'

'Good. Let's get out of here.'

He is pulling at her arm. His pressure is insistent and reluctantly she surrenders to it. The momentum of the crowd sweeps them through the gate and along the road. His only thought is to put some distance between them and the Park. He doesn't know how long they walk for – fifteen minutes, perhaps, or twenty – until, at last, the pavements are deserted and they are passing through the hinterland of the town. It is a raw, clear afternoon. On either side of them, semidetached suburban villas hide behind dirty privet hedges, their wartime gardens filled with chicken runs and the half-buried, corrugated-iron hoops of bomb shelters. She shakes her arm free.

'There's no point in this.'

'You're seeing someone else?' He hardly dares to ask the question.

'I'm always seeing someone else.'

He stops but she walks on. He lets her go for fifty yards then hurries to catch her up. By now the houses have petered out and they're in a kind of no-man's land between town and country, on Bletchley's western edge, where people dump their rubbish. A flock of seagulls cries and rises, like a swirl of waste paper caught by the wind. The road has dwindled to a track which leads under the railway to a row of abandoned Victorian brick kilns. Three red-brick chimneys, as in a crematorium, rise fifty feet against the sky. A sign says: DANGER, FLOODED CLAY PIT – VERY DEEP WATER.

Claire draws her coat around her shoulders and shivers – 'What a filthy place!' – but she still walks on ahead.

For ten minutes, the derelict brick works provide a welcome distraction. Indeed, they wander through the ruined kilns and workshops in a silence that is almost companionable. Amorous couples have scratched their formulae on the crumbling walls: AE + GS, Tony = Kath, Sal 4 Me. Lumps of masonry and brick litter the ground. Some of the buildings are open to the sky, the walls are scorched – there's clearly been a fire – and Jericho wonders if the Germans could have mistaken it for a factory, and bombed it. He turns to say as much to Claire, but she has disappeared.

He finds her outside, her back to him, staring across the flooded clay pit. It is huge, a quarter of a mile across. The surface of the water is coal-black and perfectly still, the stillness hinting at unimaginable depths.

She says: 'I ought to get back.'

'What do you want to know?' he says. 'I'll tell you everything you want to know.'

And he will, if she wants it. He doesn't care about security or the war. He'll tell her about Shark and Dolphin and Porpoise. He'll tell her about the Bay of Biscay weather crib. He'll tell her all their little tricks and secrets, and draw her a diagram of how the bombe works, if that's what she wants. But all she says is: 'I do hope you're not going to be a bore about this, Tom.'

A bore. Is that what he is? He is being a bore?

'Wait,' he calls after her, 'you might as well have this.'

He gives her the little box with the ring in it. She opens it and tilts the stone to catch the light, then snaps the lid shut and hands it back.

'Not my style.'

'Poor you,' he remembers her saying a minute or two later,

'I've really got under your skin, haven't I? Poor you . . .'

And by the end of the week he's in the deputy director's Rover, being borne back through the snow to King's.

2

The smells and sounds of an English Sunday breakfast curled up the staircase of the Commercial Guesthouse and floated across the landing like a call to arms: the hiss of hot fat frying in the kitchen, the dirge-like strains of a church service being relayed by the BBC, the muffled crack of Mrs Armstrong's worn slippers flapping like castanets on the linoleum floor.

They were a ritual in Albion Street, these Sunday breakfasts, served up with appropriate solemnity on plain white utility crockery: one piece of bread, as thick as a hymn book, dunked in fat and fried, with two spoonfuls of powdered egg, scrambled and slopped on top, the whole mass sliding freely on a rainbow film of grease.

It was not, Jericho had to acknowledge, a great meal, nor even a particularly edible one. The bread was rust-coloured, flecked with black, and obscurely flavoured by the kippers that had been cooked in the same fat the previous Friday. The egg was pale yellow and tasted of stale biscuits. Yet such was his appetite after the excitements of the night that, despite his anxiety, he ate every scrap of it, washed it down with two cups of greyish tea, mopped up the last of the grease with a fragment of bread, and even, on his way out, complimented Mrs Armstrong on the quality of her cooking – an unprecedented gesture which caused her to poke her head around the kitchen door and search his features for a trace of irony. She found none. He also attempted a cheerful 'Good morning' to Mr Bonnyman, who was just groping his way down the banisters ('Feeling a bit rough, to be honest, old boy – something wrong with the beer in that place') and by seven forty-five he was back in his room.

If Mrs Armstrong could have seen the changes he had wrought up there, she would have been astonished. Far from preparing to evacuate it after his first night, like so many of the bedroom's previous tenants, Jericho had unpacked. His suitcases were empty. His one good suit hung in the wardrobe. His books were lined along the mantelpiece. Balanced on the top of them was his print of King's College Chapel.

He sat on the edge of the bed and stared at the picture. It was not a skilful piece of work. In fact, it was rather ugly. The twin Gothic spires were hastily drawn, the sky was an improbable blue, the blob-like figures clustered around its base could have been the work of a child. But even bad art can sometimes have its uses. Behind its scratched glass, and behind the cheap Victorian mezzotint itself, laid flat and carefully secured, were the four undecrypted intercepts he had removed from Claire's bedroom.

He should have returned them to the Park, of course. He should have cycled straight from the cottage to the huts, should have sought out Logie or some other figure of authority, and handed them in.

167

Even now, he couldn't disentangle all his motives for not doing so, couldn't sort out the selfless (his wish to protect her) from the selfish (his desire to have her in his power, just once). He only knew he could not bring himself to betray her, and that he was able to rationalise this by telling himself that there was no harm in waiting till the morning, no harm in giving her a chance to explain.

And so he had cycled on, past the main gate, had tiptoed up to his room and had hidden the cryptograms behind the print, increasingly aware that he had strayed across whatever border it is that separates folly from treason, and that with every passing hour it would be harder for him to find his way back.

For the hundredth time, sitting on his bed, he ran though all the possibilities. That she was crazy. That she was being blackmailed. That her room was being used as a hiding place without her knowledge. That she was a spy.

A spy? The notion seemed fantastic to him – melodramatic, bizarre, *illogical.* For one thing, why would a spy with any sense steal cryptograms? A spy would be after decodes, surely: the answers not the riddles; the hard proof that Enigma was being broken?

He checked the door, then gently took down the picture and dismantled the frame, working the thumbtacks loose with his fingers and lifting away the hardboard backing. Now he thought about it, there *was* something distinctly odd about these cryptograms, looking at them again he realised what it was. They should have had the thin paper strips of decode produced by the Type-X machines gummed to their backs. But not only were there no strips, there weren't even any marks to show where the strips had been torn off. So, by the look of them, these signals had never even been broken. Their secrets were intact. They were virgin.

None of it made any sense.

He stroked one of the signals between finger and thumb. The yellowish paper had a slight but perceptible odour. What was it? He held it close to his nose and inhaled. The scent of a library or an archive, perhaps? Quite a rich smell – warm, almost smoky – as evocative as perfume.

He realised suddenly that despite his fear he was actually beginning to treasure the cryptograms, as another man might treasure a favourite snapshot of a girl. Only these were better than any photographs, weren't they, for photographs were merely *likenesses*, whereas these were clues to *who she was*, and therefore wasn't he, by possessing them, in a sense, possessing her . . .?

He would give her just one chance. No more.

He looked at his watch. Twenty minutes had passed since breakfast. It was time to go. He slipped the cryptograms behind the picture, reassembled the frame and replaced it on the mantelpiece, then opened the door a fraction. Mrs Armstrong's regular guests had all come in from the night-shift. He could hear their murmured voices in the dining room. He put on his overcoat and stepped out on to the landing. Such were his efforts to seem natural, Mrs Armstrong would later swear she heard him humming to himself as he descended the stairs.

'I see you smiling in the cigarette glow
Though the picture fades too soon
But I see all I want to know
They can't black out the moon . . .'

From Albion Street to Bletchley Park was a walk of less than half a mile – left out of the door and along the street of terraced houses, left under the blackened railway bridge and sharp right across the allotments.

He strode quickly over the frozen ground, his breath steaming before him in the cold sunshine. Officially it was almost spring but someone had forgotten to pass the news on to winter. Patches of ice, not yet melted from the night before, cracked beneath the soles of his shoes. Rooks called from the tops of skeletal elms.

It was well past eight o'clock by the time he turned off the footpath into Wilton Avenue and approached the main gate. The shift change was over; the suburban road was almost deserted. The sentry – a giant young corporal, raw-faced from the cold – came stamping out of the guard post and barely glanced at his pass before waving him into the grounds.

Past the mansion he went, keeping his head down to avoid having to speak to anyone, past the lake (which was fringed with ice) and into Hut 8, where the silence emanating from the Decoding Room told him all he needed to know. The Type-X machines had worked their way through the backlog of Shark intercepts and now there was nothing for them to do until Dolphin and Porpoise came on stream, probably around mid-morning. He caught a glimpse of Logie's tall figure at

170

the end of the corridor and darted into the Registration Room. There, to his surprise, was Puck, sitting in a corner, being watched by a pair of love-struck Wrens. His face was grey and lined, his head resting against the wall. Jericho thought he might be asleep but then he opened a piercing blue eye.

'Logie's looking for you.'

'Really?' Jericho took off his coat and scarf and hung them on the back of the door. 'He knows where to find me.'

'There's a rumour going around that you hit Skynner. For God's sake tell me it's true.'

One of the Wrens giggled.

Jericho had forgotten all about Skynner. He passed his hand through his hair. 'Do me a favour, Puck, will you?' he said. 'Pretend you haven't seen me?'

Puck regarded him closely for a moment, then shut his eyes. 'What a man of mystery you are,' he murmured, sleepily.

Back in the corridor Jericho walked straight into Logie.

'Ah, there you are, old love. I'm afraid we need to have a talk.'

'Fine, Guy. Fine.' Jericho patted Logie on the shoulder and squeezed past him. 'Just give me ten minutes.'

'No, not in ten minutes,' Logie shouted after him, 'now!'

Jericho pretended he hadn't heard. He trotted out into the fresh air, walked briskly round the corner, past Hut 6, towards the entrance to Hut 3. Only when he was within twenty paces of it did his footsteps slow, then stop.

The truth was, he knew very little about Hut 3, except that it was the place where the decoded messages of the German Army and Luftwaffe were processed. It was about twice the size of the other huts and was arranged in the shape of an L. It had gone up at the same time as the rest of the temporary buildings, in the winter of 1939 – a timber skeleton rising out of the freezing Buckinghamshire clay, clothed in a sheath of asbestos and flimsy wooden boarding – and to heat it, he remembered, they had cannibalised a big cast-iron stove from one of the Victorian greenhouses. Claire used to complain she was always cold. Cold, and that her job was 'boring'. But where exactly she worked within its warren of rooms, let alone what this 'boring' job entailed, was a mystery to him.

A door slammed somewhere behind him and he glanced over his shoulder to see Logie emerging from around the corner of the naval hut. Damn, damn. He dropped to one knee and pretended to fumble with his shoelace but Logie hadn't seen him. He was marching purposefully towards the mansion. That seemed to settle Jericho's resolve. Once Logie was out of sight, he counted himself down then launched himself across the path and through the entrance into the hut.

He did his best to look as if he had a right to be there. He pulled out a pen and set off down the central corridor, thrusting past airmen and Army officers, glancing officiously from side to side into the busy rooms. It was much more overcrowded even than Hut

8. The racket of typewriters and telephones was amplified by the membrane of wooden walls to create a bedlam of activity.

He had barely gone halfway down the passage when a colonel with a large moustache stepped smartly out of a doorway and blocked his path. Jericho nodded and tried to edge past him, but the colonel moved deftly to one side.

'Hold on, stranger. Who are you?'

On impulse Jericho stuck out his hand. 'Tom Jericho,' he said. 'Who are you?'

'Never mind who the hell I am.' The colonel had jug ears and thick black hair with a wide, straight parting that stood out like a firebreak. He ignored the proffered hand. 'What's your section?'

'Naval. Hut 8.'

'Hut 8? State your business here.'

'I'm looking for Dr Weitzman.'

An inspired lie. He knew Weitzman from the Chess Society: a German Jew, naturalised British, who always played Queen's Gambit Declined.

'Are you, by God?' said the colonel. 'Haven't you Navy people ever heard of the telephone?' He stroked his moustache and looked Jericho up and down. 'Well, you'd better come with me.'

Jericho followed the colonel's broad back along the passage and into a large room. Two groups of about a dozen men sat at tables arranged in a pair of semicircles, working their way through wire baskets stacked high with decrypts. Walter Weitzman was perched on a stool in a glass booth behind them.

'I say, Weitzman, d'you know this chap?'

Weitzman's large head was bent over a pile of German weapons manuals. He looked up, vague and distracted, but when he recognised Jericho his melancholy face brightened into a smile. 'Hello, Tom. Yes, of course I know him.'

'"*Kriegsnachrichten Für Seefahrer*,"' said Jericho, a fraction too quickly. 'You said you might have something by now.'

For a moment, Weitzman didn't react and Jericho thought he was done for, but then the old man said slowly, 'Yes. I believe I have that information for you.' He lowered himself carefully from his stool. 'You have a problem, colonel?'

The colonel thrust his chin forward. 'Yes, actually, Weitzman, I do, now you mention it. "Inter-hut communication, unless otherwise authorised, must be conducted by telephone or written memorandum." Standard procedure.' He glared at Weitzman and Weitzman stared back, with exquisite politeness. The belligerence seemed to leak out of the colonel. 'Right,' he muttered. 'Yes. Remember that in future.'

'Arsehole,' hissed Weitzman, as the colonel moved away. 'Well, well. You'd better come over here.'

He led Jericho to a rack of card-index files, selected a drawer, pulled it out and began riffling through it. Every time the translators came across a term they couldn't understand, they consulted Weitzman and his famous index-system. He'd been a philologist at Heidelberg until the Nazis forced him to emigrate. The Foreign Office, in a rare moment of inspiration, had dispatched him to Bletchley in 1940. Very few phrases defeated him.

'*"Kriegsnachrichten Für Seefahrer,"* *"War notices for Marines."* First intercepted and catalogued, November ninth last year. As you knew perfectly well already.' He held the card within an inch of his nose and studied it through his thick spectacles. 'Tell me, is the good colonel still looking at us?'

'I don't know. I think so.' The colonel had bent down to read something one of the translators had written, but his gaze kept returning to Jericho and Weitzman. 'Is he always like that?'

'Our Colonel Coker? Yes, but worse today, for some reason.' Weitzman spoke softly, without looking at Jericho. He tugged open another drawer and pulled out a card, apparently absorbed. 'I suggest we stay here until he leaves the room. Now here's a U-boat term we picked up in January: *"Fluchttiefe."*'

'"Evasion depth,"' replied Jericho. He could play this game for hours. *Vorhalt-Rechner* was a deflection-angle computer. A cold-soldered joint was a *kalte Lötstelle*. Cracks in a U-boat's bulkheads were *Stirnwandrisse* . . .

'"Evasion depth,"' Weitzman nodded. 'Quite right.'

Jericho risked another look at the colonel. 'He's going out of the door . . . now. It's all right. He's gone.'

Weitzman gazed at the card for a moment, then slipped it back among the rest and closed the drawer. 'So. Why are you asking me questions to which you already know the answers?' His hair was white, his small brown eyes overshadowed by a jutting forehead.

Wrinkles at their edges suggested a face that had once creased readily into laughter. But Weitzman didn't laugh much any more. He was rumoured to have left most of his family behind in Germany.

'I'm looking for a woman called Claire Romilly. Do you know her?'

'Of course. The beautiful Claire. Everyone knows her.'

'Where does she work?'

'She works here.'

'I know here. Here where?'

'"Inter-hut communication, unless otherwise authorised, must be conducted by telephone or written memorandum. Standard procedure."' Weitzman clicked his heels. 'Heil Hitler!'

'Bugger standard procedure.'

One of the translators turned round, irritably. 'I say, you two, put a sock in it, will you?'

'Sorry.' Weitzman took Jericho by the arm and led him away. 'Do you know, Tom,' he whispered, 'in three years, this is the first time I have heard you swear?'

'Walter. Please. It's important.'

'And it can't wait until the end of the shift?' He gave Jericho a careful look. 'Obviously not. Well, well again. Which way did Coker go?'

'Back towards the entrance.'

'Good. Follow me.'

Weitzman led Jericho almost to the other end of the hut, past the translators, through two long narrow rooms where scores of women were labouring over a pair of giant card indexes, around a corner and through a room lined with teleprinters. The din here was

176

terrific. Weitzman put his hands to his ears, looked over his shoulder and grinned. The noise pursued them down a short length of passage, at the end of which was a closed door. Next to it was a sign, in a schoolgirl's best handwriting: GERMAN BOOK ROOM.

Weitzman knocked on the door, opened it and went inside. Jericho followed. His eye registered a large room. Shelves stacked with ledgers and files. Half a dozen trestle tables pushed together to form one big working area. Women, mostly with their backs to him. Six, perhaps, or seven? Two typing, very fast, the others moving back and forth arranging sheaves of papers into piles.

Before he could take in any more, a plump, harassed-looking woman in a tweed jacket and skirt advanced to meet them. Weitzman was beaming now, exuding charm, for all the world as if he were still in the tearoom of Heidelberg's Europäischer Hof. He took her hand and bowed to kiss it.

'Guten Morgen, mein liebes Fräulein Monk. Wie geht's?'

'Gut, danke, Herr Doktor. Und dir?'

'Danke, sehr gut.'

It was clearly a familiar routine between them. Her shiny complexion flushed pink with pleasure. 'And what can I do for you?'

'My colleague and I, my dear Miss Monk – ' Weitzman patted her hand, then released it and gestured towards Jericho '– are looking for the delightful Miss Romilly.'

At the mention of Claire's name, Miss Monk's flirtatious smile evaporated. 'In that case you must join the queue, Dr Weitzman. Join the queue.'

'I am sorry. The queue?'

'We are all trying to find Claire Romilly. Perhaps you, or your colleague, have an idea where we might start?'

To say that the world stands still is a solipsism, and Jericho knew it even as it seemed to happen – knew that it isn't ever the world that slows down, but rather the individual, confronted by an unexpected danger, who receives a charge of adrenaline and speeds up. Nevertheless, for him, for an instant, everything did freeze. Weitzman's expression became a mask of bafflement, the woman's of indignation. As his brain tried to compute the implications, he could hear his own voice, far away, begin to babble: 'But I thought . . . I was told – assured – yesterday – she was supposed to be on duty at eight this morning . . .'

'Quite right,' Miss Monk was saying. 'It really is most thoughtless of her. And terribly inconvenient.'

Weitzman gave Jericho a peculiar look, as if to say, What have you got me into? 'Perhaps she's ill?' he suggested.

'Then surely a note would have been considerate? A message? Before I let the entire night-shift go? We can barely cope when there are eight of us. When we're down to seven . . .'

She started to prattle on to Weitzman about '3A' and '3M' and all the staffing memos she'd written and how no one appreciated her difficulties. As if to prove her point, at that moment the door opened and a woman came in with a stack of files so high she had to

wedge her chin on top of them to keep control. She let
them fall on the table and there was a collective groan
from Miss Monk's girls. A couple of signals fluttered
over the edge of the table and on to the floor and
Jericho, primed for action, swooped to retrieve them.
He got a brief glimpse of one –

```
                    ZZZ
BATTLE HEADQUARTERS GERMAN AFRIKA KORPS LOCATED
MORNING THIRTEENTH £ THIRTEENTH ONE FIVE
KILOMETRES WEST OF BEN GARDANE £ BEN GARDANE
```

– before it was snatched out of his hands by Miss
Monk. She seemed for the first time to become aware
of his presence. She cradled the secrets to her plump
breast and glared at him.

'I'm sorry, you are – who are you exactly?' she asked.
She edged to one side to block his view of the table.
'You are – what? – a friend of Claire, I take it?'

'It's all right, Daphne,' said Weitzman, 'he's a friend
of mine.'

Miss Monk flushed again. 'I beg your pardon,
Walter,' she said. 'Of course, I didn't mean to imply –'

Jericho cut in: 'I wonder, could I ask you, has she
done this before? Failed to turn up, I mean, without
telling you?'

'Oh no. Never. I will not tolerate slacking in my
section. Dr Weitzman will vouch for that.'

'Indeed,' said Weitzman, gravely. 'No slacking here.'

Miss Monk was of a type that Jericho had come to
know well over the past three years: mildly hysterical at

moments of crisis; jealous of her precious rank and her extra fifty pounds a year; convinced that the war would be lost if her tiny fiefdom were denied a gross of lead pencils or an extra typist. She would hate Claire, he thought: hate her for her prettiness and her confidence and her refusal to take anything seriously.

'She hasn't been behaving at all oddly?'

'We have important work to do. We've no time here for oddness.'

'When did you last see her?'

'That would be Friday.' Miss Monk obviously prided herself on her memory for detail. 'She came on duty at four, went off at midnight. Yesterday was her rest day.'

'So I don't suppose it's likely she came back into the hut, say, early on Saturday morning?'

'No. I was here. Anyway, why should she do that? Normally, she couldn't wait to get away.'

I bet she couldn't. He glanced again at the girls behind Miss Monk. What on earth were they all doing? Each had a mound of paperclips in front of her, a pot of glue, a pile of brown folders and a tangle of rubber bands. They seemed – could this be right? – to be compiling new files out of old ones. He tried to imagine Claire here, in this drab room, among these sensible drones. It was like picturing some gorgeous parakeet in a cage full of sparrows. He wasn't sure what to do. He took out his watch and flicked open the lid. Eight thirty-five. She had already been missing more than half an hour.

'What will you do now?'

'Obviously – because of the level of classification –

180

there's a certain procedure we have to follow. I've already notified Welfare. They'll send someone round to her room to turf her out of bed.'

'And if she isn't there?'

'Then they'll contact her family to see if they know where she is.'

'And if they don't?'

'Well, then it's serious. But it never gets that far.' Miss Monk drew her jacket tight across her pigeon chest and folded her arms. 'I'm sure there's a *man* at the bottom of this somewhere.' She shuddered. 'There usually is.'

Weitzman was continuing to give Jericho imploring glances. He touched him on the arm. 'We ought to go now, Tom.'

'Do you have an address for her family? Or a telephone number?'

'Yes, I think so, but I'm not sure I should . . .' She turned towards Weitzman, who hesitated fractionally, shot another look at Jericho, then forced a smile and a nod.

'I can vouch for him.'

'Well,' said Miss Monk, doubtfully, 'if you think it's permissible . . .' She went over to a filing cabinet beside her desk and unlocked it.

'Coker will kill me for this,' whispered Weitzman, while her back was turned.

'He'll never find out. I promise you.'

'The curious thing is,' said Miss Monk, almost to herself, 'that she'd really become much more *attentive* of late. Anyway, this is her card.'

Next-of-kin: Edward Romilly.
Relation: Father.
Address: 27 Stanhope Gardens, London SW.
Telephone: Kensington 2257.

Jericho glanced at it for a second and handed it back.

'I don't think there's any need to trouble him, do you?' asked Miss Monk. 'Certainly not yet. No doubt Claire will arrive at any moment with some silly story about oversleeping – '

'I'm sure,' said Jericho.

'– in which case,' she added shrewdly, 'who shall I say was looking for her?'

'Auf Wiedersehen, Fraulein Monk.' Weitzman had had enough. He was already half out of the room, pulling Jericho after him with surprising force. Jericho had a last vision of Miss Monk, standing bewildered and suspicious, before the door closed on her schoolroom German.

'Auf Wiedersehen, Herr Doktor, und Herr . . .'

Weitzman didn't lead Jericho back the way they had come. Instead he bundled him out of the rear exit. Now, in the cold daylight, Jericho could see why he had found it so difficult stumbling around out here the other night. They were on the edge of a building site. Trenches had been carved four feet deep into the grass. Pyramids of sand and gravel were covered in a white mould of frost. It was a miracle he hadn't broken his neck.

Weitzman shook a cigarette out of a crumpled pack

of Passing Clouds and lit it. He leaned against the wall of the hut and exhaled a sigh of steam and smoke. 'Useless for me to ask, I suppose, what in God's name is going on?'

'You don't want to know, Walter. Believe me.'

'Troubles of the heart?'

'Something like that.'

Weitzman mumbled a couple of words in Yiddish that might have been a curse and continued to smoke.

About thirty yards away, a group of workmen were huddled around a brazier, finishing a tea break. They dispersed reluctantly, trailing pickaxes and spades across the hard ground, and Jericho had a sudden memory of himself as a boy, holding hands with his mother, walking along a seaside promenade, his spade clattering on the concrete road behind him. Somewhere beyond the trees, a generator kicked into life sending a scattering of rooks cawing into the sky.

'Walter, what's the German Book Room?'

'I'd better get back,' said Weitzman. He licked the ends of his thumb and forefinger and nipped off the glowing tip of his cigarette, slipping the unsmoked portion into his breast pocket. Tobacco was far too precious to waste even a few shreds.

'Please, Walter . . .'

'Ach!' Weitzman made a sudden gesture of disgust with his arm, as if sweeping Jericho aside, and began making his way, unsteadily but wonderfully quickly for a man of his age, down the side of the hut towards the path. Jericho had to scramble to keep pace with him.

'You ask too much, you know – '

'I know I do.'

'I mean, my God, Coker already suspects I am a Nazi spy. Can you believe that? I may be a Jew, but for him one German is no different from another. Which, of course, is precisely *our* argument. I suppose I should be flattered.'

'I wouldn't – it's just – there's nobody else . . .'

A pair of sentries with rifles rounded the corner and strolled towards them. Weitzman clamped his jaw shut and abruptly turned right off the path towards the tennis court. Jericho followed him. Weitzman opened the gate and they stepped on to the asphalt. The court had been put in – at Churchill's personal instigation, so it was said – two years earlier. It hadn't been used since the autumn. The white lines were barely visible beneath the frost. Drifts of leaves had collected against the chain-link fence. Weitzman closed the gate after them and walked towards the net post.

'It's all changed since we started, Tom. Nine-tenths of the people in the hut I don't even know any more.' He kicked moodily at the leaves and Jericho noticed for the first time how small his feet were; dancer's feet. 'I've grown old in this place. I can remember a time when we thought we were geniuses if we read fifty messages a week. Do you know what the rate is now?'

Jericho shook his head.

'Three thousand a *day*.'

'Good God.' *That's a hundred and twenty-five an hour,* thought Jericho, *that's one every thirty seconds . . .*

'Is she in trouble, then, your girl?'

'I think so. I mean, yes – yes, she is.'

184

'I'm sorry to hear it. I like her. She laughs at my jokes. Women who laugh at my jokes must be cherished. Especially if they are young. And pretty.'

'Walter . . .'

Weitzman turned towards Hut 3. He had chosen his ground well, with the instinct of a man who has been forced at some time, as a matter of personal survival, to learn how to find privacy. Nobody could come up behind them without entering the tennis court. Nobody could approach from the front without being seen. And if anyone was watching from a distance – well, what was there to see but two old colleagues, having a private chat?

'It's organised like a factory line.' He curled his fingers into the wire netting. His hands were white with cold. They clenched the steel like claws. 'The decrypts arrive by conveyor belt from Hut 6. They go first to the Watch for translation – you know that, that's my post. Two Watches per shift, one for urgent material, the other for back-breaks. Translated Luftwaffe signals are passed to 3A, Army to 3M. A for air, M for military. God in heaven, it's cold. Are you cold? I'm shaking.' He pulled out a filthy handkerchief and blew his nose. 'The duty officers decide what's important and give it a Z-priority. A single Z is low-grade – Hauptmann Fischer is to be transferred to the German Air Fleet in Italy. A weather report would be three Zs. Five Zs is pure gold – where Rommel will be tomorrow afternoon, an imminent air attack. The intelligence is summarised, then three copies are dispatched – one to SIS in Broadway, one to the

185

appropriate service ministry in Whitehall, one to the relevant commander in the field.'

'And the German Book Room?'

'Every proper name is indexed: every officer, every piece of equipment, every base. For example, Hauptmann Fischer's transfer may at first seem quite worthless as intelligence. But then you consult the Air Index and you see his last posting was to a radar station in France. Now he is going to Bari. So: the Germans are installing radar in Bari. Let them build it. And then, when it is almost finished, bomb it.'

'And that's the German Book?'

'No, no.' Weitzman shook his head crossly, as if Jericho were some dim student at the bottom of his class at Heidelberg. 'The German Book is the very end of the process. All this paper – the intercept, the decode, the translation, the Z-signal, the list of cross-references, all these thousands of pages – it all comes together at the end to be filed. The German Book is a verbatim transcription of all decoded messages in their original language.'

'Is that an important job?'

'In intellectual terms? No. Purely clerical.'

'But in terms of access? To classified material?'

'Ah. Different.' Weitzman shrugged. 'It would depend on the person involved, of course, whether they could be bothered to read what they were handling. Most don't.'

'But in theory?'

'In theory? On an average day? A girl like Claire would probably see more operational detail about the German armed forces than Adolf Hitler.' He glanced at

Jericho's incredulous face and smiled. 'Absurd, isn't it? What is she? Nineteen? Twenty?'

'Twenty,' muttered Jericho. 'She always told me her job was boring.'

'Twenty! I swear it's the greatest joke in the history of warfare. Look at us: the hare-brained debutante, the weakling intellectual and the half-blind Jew. If only the master race could see what we're doing to them – sometimes the thought of it is all that keeps me going.' He held his watch up very close to his face. 'I must get back. Coker will have issued a warrant for my arrest. I fear I have talked too much.'

'Not at all.'

'Oh, I have, I have.'

He turned towards the gate. Jericho made a move to follow but Weitzman held up a hand to stop him. 'Why don't you wait here, Tom? Just for a moment. Let me get clear.'

He slipped out of the court. As he passed by on the other side of the fence, something seemed to occur to him. He slowed and beckoned Jericho closer to the wire netting.

'Listen,' he said softly, 'if you think I can help you again, if you need any more information – please, don't ask me. I don't want to know.'

Before Jericho could answer he had crossed the path and disappeared around the back of Hut 3.

Within the grounds of Bletchley Park, just beyond the mansion, in the shadow of a fir tree, stood an ordinary red telephone box. Inside it, a young man in

ROBERT HARRIS

motorcycle leathers was finishing a call. Jericho,
leaning against the tree, could hear his singsong accent,
muffled but audible.

'Right you are . . . OK, doll . . . See you.'

The dispatch rider put the receiver down with a
clatter and pushed open the door.

'All yours, pal.'

The motorcyclist didn't move away at first. Jericho
stood in the kiosk, pretending to fish in his pockets for
change, and watched him through the glass. The man
adjusted his leggings, put on his helmet, fiddled with
the chin strap . . .

Jericho waited until he had moved away before
dialling zero.

A woman's voice said: 'Operator speaking.'

'Good morning. I'd like to make a call, please, to
Kensington double-two five seven.'

She repeated the number. 'That'll be fourpence,
caller.'

A sixty-mile land line connected all Bletchley Park
numbers to the Whitehall exchange. As far as the operator could tell, Jericho was merely calling one London
borough from another. He pressed four pennies into the
slot and after a series of clicks he heard a ringing tone.

It took fifteen seconds for a man to answer.

'Ye-es?'

It was exactly the voice Jericho had always imagined
for Claire's father. Languid and assured, it stretched
that single short syllable into two long ones. Immediately there was a series of pips and Jericho pushed the
A-button. His money tinkled into the coin-box.

188

Already, he felt at a disadvantage – an indigent without access to a telephone of his own.

'Mr Romilly?'

'Ye-es?'

'I'm so sorry to trouble you, sir, especially on a Sunday morning, but I work with Claire . . .'

There was a faint noise, and then a pause, during which he could hear Romilly breathing. A crackle of static cut across the line. 'Are you still there, sir?'

The voice, when it came again, was quiet, and it sounded hollow, as if emanating from a vast and empty room. 'How did you get this number?'

'Claire gave it me.' It was the first lie that came into Jericho's head. 'I wondered if she was with you.'

Another long pause. 'No. No, she isn't. Why should she be?'

'She's not turned up for her shift this morning. Yesterday was her day off. I wondered if she might have gone down to London.'

'Who is this speaking?'

'My name is Tom Jericho.' Silence. 'She may have spoken of me.'

'I don't believe so.' Romilly's voice was barely audible. He cleared his throat. 'I'm awfully sorry, Mr Jericho. I'm afraid I can't help you. My daughter's movements are as much a mystery to me as they seem to be to you. Goodbye.'

There was a fumbling noise and the connection was broken off.

'Hello?' said Jericho. He thought he could still hear somebody breathing on the line. 'Hello?' He held on to the heavy bakelite receiver for a couple of seconds, straining to hear, then carefully replaced it.

He leaned against the side of the telephone box and massaged his temples. Beyond the glass, the world went silently about its business. A couple of civilians with bowler hats and rolled umbrellas, fresh from the London train, were being escorted up the drive to the mansion. A trio of ducks in winter camouflage came in to land on the lake, feet splayed, ploughing furrows in the grey water.

'My daughter's movements are as much a mystery to me as they seem to be to you.'

That was not right, was it? That was not the reaction one would expect of a father on being told his only child was missing?

Jericho groped in his pocket for a handful of change. He spread the coins out on his palm and stared at them, stupidly, like a foreigner just arrived in an unfamiliar country.

He dialled zero again.

'Operator speaking.'

'Kensington double-two five seven.'

Once again, Jericho inserted four pennies into the metal slot. Once again there was a series of short clicks, then a pause. He tightened his finger on the button. But this time there was no ringing tone, only the *blip-blip-blip* of an engaged signal, pulsing in his ear like a heartbeat.

Over the next ten minutes Jericho made three more attempts to get through. Each met the same response.

Either Romilly had taken his telephone off the hook, or he was involved in a long conversation with someone.

Jericho would have tried the number a fourth time, but a woman from the canteen with a coat over her apron had turned up and started rapping a coin on the glass, demanding her turn. Finally, Jericho let her in. He stood on the roadside and tried to decide what to do.

He glanced back at the huts. Their squat, grey shapes, once so boring and familiar, now seemed vaguely threatening.

Damn it. What did he have to lose?

He buttoned his jacket against the cold and turned towards the gate.

3

St Mary's Parish Church, eight solid centuries of hard white stone and Christian piety, lay at the end of an avenue of elderly yew trees, less than a hundred yards beyond Bletchley Park. As Jericho walked through the gate he saw bicycles, fifteen or twenty of them, stacked neatly around the porch, and a moment later heard the piping of the organ and the mournful lilt of a Church of England congregation in mid-hymn. The graveyard was perfectly still. He felt like a late guest approaching a house where a party was already in full swing.

*'We blossom and flourish as leaves on a tree,
And wither, and perish, but naught changeth thee . . .'*

Jericho stamped his feet and beat his arms. He considered slipping inside and standing at the back of the nave until the service ended, but experience had taught him there was no such thing as a quiet entry into a church. The door would bang, heads would turn, some officious sidesman would come hurrying down the aisle with a prayer sheet and a hymn book. Such attention was the last thing he wanted.

He left the path and pretended to study the tombstones. Frosted cobwebs of improbable size and delicacy shone like ectoplasm between the memorials: marble monuments for the well-to-do, slate for the farmworkers, weathered wooden crosses for the poor and infants. Ebenezer Slade, aged four years and six months, asleep in the arms of Jesus. Mary Watson, wife of Albert, taken after a long illness, rest in peace . . . On a few of the graves, bunches of dead flowers, petrified by ice, testified to some continuing flicker of interest among the living. On others, yellow lichen had obscured the inscriptions. He bent and scratched away at it, hearkening to the voices of the righteous beyond the stained glass window.

'O ye Dews and Frosts, bless ye the Lord: praise him and magnify him for ever.

O ye Frost and Cold, bless ye the Lord: praise him and magnify him for ever . . .'

Odd images chased through his mind.

He thought of his father's funeral, on just such a

day as this: a freezing, ugly Victorian church in the industrial Midlands, medals on the coffin, his mother weeping, his aunts in black, everyone studying him with sad curiosity, and he all the time a million miles away, factoring the hymn numbers in his head ('Forward out of error,/Leave behind the night' – number 392 in *Ancient and Modern* – came out very prettily, he remembered, as $2 \times 7 \times 2 \times 7 \times 2 \ldots$)

And for some reason he thought of Alan Turing, restless with excitement in the hut one winter night, describing how the death of his closest friend had made him seek a link between mathematics and the spirit, insisting that at Bletchley they were creating a new world: that the bombes might soon be modified, the clumsy electro-mechancial switches replaced by relays of pentode valves and GT1C-thyatrons to create computers, machines that might one day mimic the actions of the human brain and unlock the secrets of the soul . . .

Jericho wandered among the dead. Here was a small stone cross garlanded with stone flowers, there a stern-looking angel with a face like Miss Monk. All the time he kept listening to the service. He wondered whether anyone from Hut 8 was among the congregation and, if so, who. With all else failing, might Skynner be offering up a prayer to God? He tried to imagine what fresh reserves of sycophancy Skynner would draw on to communicate with a being even higher than the First Lord of the Admiralty, and found he couldn't do it.

'The blessing of God Almighty, the Father, the Son, and

the Holy Ghost, be amongst you and remain with you always. Amen.'

The service was over. Jericho wove quickly through the headstones, away from the church, and stationed himself behind a pair of large bushes. From here he had a clear view of the porch.

Before the war the faithful would have emerged to an uplifting peal of grandsire triples. But church bells now were to be rung only in the event of invasion, so that when the door opened and the elderly priest stationed himself to say farewell to his parishioners, the silence gave the ceremony a subdued, even melancholy air. One by one the worshippers stepped into the daylight. Jericho didn't recognise any of them. He began to think he might have come to the wrong conclusion. But then, sure enough, a small, lean young woman in a black coat appeared, still holding the prayer book from the night before.

She shook hands briefly, even curtly, with the vicar, said nothing, looped her carpetbag over the handles of her bicycle and wheeled it towards the gate. She walked quickly, with short, rapid steps, her sharp chin held high. Jericho waited until she had gone some way past him, then stepped out from his hiding place and shouted after her: 'Miss Wallace!'

She stopped and glanced back in his direction. Her weak eyesight made her frown. Her head moved vaguely from side to side. It wasn't until he was within two yards of her that her face cleared.

'Why, Mr . . .'

'Jericho.'

Enigma

'Of course. Mr Jericho. The stranger in the night.'
The cold had reddened the sharp point of her nose and
painted two neat discs of colour, the size of half-
crowns, on her white cheeks. She had long, thick, black
hair which she wore piled up, shot through and secured
by an armoury of pins. 'What did you make of the
sermon?'

'Uplifting?' he said, tentatively. It seemed easier
than telling the truth.

'Did you really? I thought it the most frightful rot
I've heard all year. "Suffer not a woman to teach, nor
to usurp authority over the man, but to be in
silence . . ."' She shook her head furiously. 'Is it a
heresy, do you suppose, to call St Paul an *ass*?'

She resumed her brisk progress towards the lane.
Jericho fell in beside her. He had picked up a few
details about Hester Wallace from Claire – that before
the war she'd been a teacher at a girls' private school in
Dorset, that she played the organ and was a
clergyman's daughter, that she received the quarterly
newsletter of the Jane Austen Society – just enough
clues to suggest the sort of woman who might indeed
go straight from an eight-hour night-shift to Sunday
matins.

'Do you attend most Sundays?'

'Always,' she said. 'Although increasingly one
wonders why. And you?'

He hesitated. 'Occasionally.'

It was a mistake and she was on to it at once.

'Whereabouts d'you sit? I don't recall ever seeing
you.'

'I try to keep at the back.'

'So do I. Exactly at the back.' She gave him a second look, her wire-framed round spectacles flashing in the winter sun. 'Really, Mr Jericho, a sermon you obviously didn't hear, a pew you never occupy: one might almost suspect you of laying claim to a piety you don't rightly possess.'

'Ah . . .'

'I'll bid you good day.'

They had reached the gate. She swung herself on to the saddle of her bicycle with surprising grace. This was not how Jericho had planned it. He had to reach out and hold on to the handlebars to stop her pedalling away.

'I wasn't in church. I'm sorry. I wanted to talk to you.'

'Kindly remove your hand from my machine, Mr Jericho.' A couple of elderly parishioners turned to stare at them. 'At once, if you please.' She twisted the handlebars back and forth but Jericho held on.

'I am so sorry. It really won't take a moment.'

She glared at him. For an instant he thought she might be about to reach down for one of her stout and sensible shoes and hammer his fingers loose. But there was curiosity as well as anger in her eyes, and curiosity won. She sighed and dismounted.

'Thank you. There's a bus shelter over there.' He nodded to the opposite side of Church Green Road. 'Just spare me five minutes. Please.'

'Absurd. Quite absurd.'

The wheels of her bicycle clicked like knitting

needles as they crossed the road to the shelter. She refused to sit. She stood with her arms folded, looking down the hill towards the town.

He tried to think of some way of broaching the subject. 'Claire tells me you work in Hut 6. That must be interesting.'

'Claire has no business telling you where I work. Or anyone else for that matter. And, no, it is not interesting. Everything interesting seems to be done by men. Women do the rest.'

She could be pretty, he thought, if she put her mind to it. Her skin was as smooth and white as Parian. Her nose and chin, though sharp, were delicate. But she wore no make-up, and her expression was permanently cross, her lips drawn into a thin, sarcastic line. Behind her spectacles, her small, bright eyes glinted with intelligence.

'Claire and I, we were . . .' He fluttered his hands and searched for the word. He was so hopeless at all this. '"Seeing one another" I suppose is the phrase. Until about a month ago. Then she refused to have anything more to do with me.' His resolution was wilted by her hostility. He felt a fool, addressing her narrow back. But he pressed on. 'To be frank, Miss Wallace, I'm worried about her.'

'How odd.'

He shrugged. 'We were an unlikely couple, I agree.'

'No.' She turned to him. 'I meant how *odd* that people always feel obliged to disguise their concern for themselves as concern for other people.'

The corners of her mouth twitched down in her

version of a smile and Jericho realised he was beginning to dislike Miss Hester Wallace, not least because she had a point.

'I don't deny an element of self-interest,' he conceded, 'but the fact is, I am worried about her. I think she's disappeared.'

She sniffed. 'Nonsense.'

'She hasn't turned up for her shift this morning.'

'An hour late for work hardly constitutes a disappearance. She probably overslept.'

'I don't think she went home last night. She certainly wasn't back by two.'

'Then perhaps she overslept *somewhere else*,' said Miss Wallace, maliciously. The spectacles flashed gain. 'Incidentally, might I ask *how* you know she didn't come home?'

He had learned it was better not to lie. 'Because I let myself in and waited for her.'

'So. A housebreaker as well. I can see why Claire wants nothing more to do with you.'

To hell with this, thought Jericho.

'There are other things you should know. A man came to the cottage last night while I was there. He ran away when he heard my voice. And I just called Claire's father. He claims he doesn't know where she is, but I think he's lying.'

That seemed to impress her. She chewed on the inside of her lip and looked away, down the hill. A train, an express by the sound of it, was passing through Bletchley. A curtain of brown smoke, half a mile long, rose in percussive bursts above the town.

'None of this is my concern,' she said at last.

'She didn't mention she was going away?'

'She never does. Why should she?'

'And she hasn't seemed odd to you lately? Under any sort of strain?'

'Mr Jericho, we could probably fill this bus shelter – no, we could probably fill an entire double-decker bus – with young men who are worried about their relationships with Claire Romilly. Now I'm really very tired. Much too tired and inexpert in these matters to be of any help to you. Excuse me.'

For the second time she mounted her bicycle, and this time Jericho didn't try to stop her. 'Do the letters ADU mean anything to you?'

She shook her head irritably and pushed herself away from the kerb.

'It's a call sign,' he shouted after her. 'Probably German Army or Luftwaffe.'

She applied the brakes with such force she slid off the saddle, her flat heels skittering in the gutter. She looked up and down the empty road. 'Have you gone utterly mad?'

'You'll find me in Hut 8.'

'Wait a moment. What has this to do with Claire?'

'Or, failing that, the Commercial Guesthouse in Albion Street.' He nodded politely. 'ADU, Miss Wallace. Angels Dance Upwards. I'll leave you in peace.'

'Mr Jericho . . .'

But he didn't want to answer any of her questions. He crossed the road and hurried down the hill. As he

199

turned left into Wilton Avenue towards the main gate he glanced back. She was still where he had left her, her thin legs planted either side of the pedals, staring after him in astonishment.

4

Logie was waiting for him when he got back to Hut 8. He was prowling around the confined space of the Registration Room, his bony hands clasped behind his back, the bowl of his pipe jerking around as he chomped furiously on its stem.

'This your coat?' was his only greeting. 'Better bring it with you.'

'Hello, Guy. Where are we going?' Jericho unhooked his coat from the back of the door and one of the Wrens gave him a rueful smile.

'*We're* going to have a chat, old cock. Then *you're* going home.'

Once inside his office, Logie threw himself into his chair and swung his immense feet up on to his desk. 'Close the door then, man. Let's at least *try* and keep this between ourselves.'

Jericho did as he was told. There was nowhere for him to sit so he leaned his back against it. He felt surprisingly calm. 'I don't know what Skynner's been telling you,' he began, 'but I didn't actually land a punch.'

'Oh, well, that's fine, then.' Logie raised his hands in

mock relief. 'I mean to say, as long as there's no *blood*, none of your actual *broken bones* – '

'Come on, Guy. I never touched him. He can't sack me for that.'

'He can do whatever he sodding well likes.' The chair creaked as Logie reached across the desk and picked up a brown folder. He flicked it open. 'Let us see what we have here. "Gross insubordination," it says. "Attempted physical assault," it says. "Latest in a long series of incidents which suggest the individual concerned is no longer fit for active duties."' He tossed the file back on his desk. 'Not sure I disagree, as a matter of fact. Been waiting for you to show your face around here ever since yesterday afternoon. Where've you been? Admiralty? Taking a swing at the First Sea Lord?'

'You said not to work a full shift. "Just come and go as you please." Your very words.'

'Don't get smart with me, old love.'

Jericho was silent for a moment. He thought of the print of King's College Chapel with the intercepts hidden behind it. Of the German Book Room and Weitzman's frightened face. Of Edward Romilly's shaken voice. *My daughter's movements are as much a mystery to me as they seem to be to you.* He was aware that Logie was studying him carefully.

'When does he want me to go?'

'Well, now, you bloody idiot. "Send him back to King's and this time letter the bugger walk" – I seem to recall those were my specific instructions.' He sighed and shook his head. 'You shouldn't have made him look a fool, Tom. Not in front of his clients.'

'But he *is* a fool.' Outrage and self-pity were welling in him. He tried to keep his voice steady. 'He hasn't the foggiest idea of what he's talking about. Come on, Guy. Do you honestly believe, for one minute, that we can break back into Shark within the next three days?'

'No. But there are ways of saying it and there are ways of saying it, if you follow me, especially when our dearly beloved American brethren are in the same room.'

Someone knocked and Logie shouted: 'Not now, old thing, thanks all the same!'

He waited until whoever it was had gone and then said, quietly: 'I don't think you quite appreciate how much things have changed round here.'

'That's what Skynner said.'

'Well, he's right. For once. You saw it for yourself at the conference yesterday. It's not 1940 any more, Tom. It's not plucky little Britain stands alone. We've moved on. We have to take account of what other people think. Just look at the map, man. Read the newspapers. These convoys embark from *New York*. A quarter of the ships are American. The cargo's *all* American. American troops. American crews.' Logie suddenly covered his face with his hands. 'My God, I can't believe you tried to hit Skynner. You really are pretty potty, aren't you? I'm not at all sure you're safe to walk the streets.' He lifted his feet off the desk and picked up the telephone. 'Look, I don't care what he says, I'll see if I can get the car to take you back.'

'No!' Jericho was surprised at the vehemence in his

voice. In his mind he could see, perfectly replicated, the Atlantic plot – the brown landmass of North America, the Rorschach inkblots of the British Isles, the blue of the ocean, the innocent yellow discs, the shark's teeth, set and loaded like a mantrap. And Claire? Impossible to find her even now, when he had access to the Park. Shipped back to Cambridge, stripped of his security clearance, he might as well be on another planet. 'No,' he said, more calmly. 'You can't do that.'

'It's not my decision.'

'Give me a couple of days.'

'What?'

'Tell Skynner you want to give me a couple of days. Give me a couple of days to see if I can find a way back into Shark.'

Logie stared at Jericho for five seconds, then started to laugh. 'You get madder and madder as the week wears on, old son. Yesterday you're telling us Shark can't be broken in three days. Now you're saying you might be able to do it in two.'

'Please, Guy. I'm begging you.' And he was. He had his hands on Logie's desk and was leaning over it. He was pleading for his life. 'Skynner doesn't just want me out of the hut, you know. He wants me out of the Park altogether. He wants me locked up in some garret in the Admiralty doing long division.'

'There are worse places to spend the war.'

'Not for me there aren't. I'd hang myself. I belong here.'

'I have already stuck my neck out so far for you, my lad.' Logie jabbed his pipe into Jericho's chest.

'"Jericho?" they said. "You can't be serious. We're in a crisis and you want *Jericho*?"' He jabbed his pipe again. 'So I said: "Yes, I know he's half bloody cracked and keeps on fainting like a maiden bloody aunt, but he's got something, got that extra two per cent. Just trust me."' Jab, jab. 'So I beg a bloody car – no joke round here, as you've gathered – and instead of getting my kip I come and drink stale tea in King's and plead with you, bloody *plead*, and the first thing you do is make us all look idiots and then you slug the head of section – all right, all right, *try* to slug him. Now, I ask you: who's going to listen to me now?'

'Skynner.'

'Come off it.'

'Skynner will have to listen, he will if you insist you need me. I know – ' Jericho was inspired. 'You could threaten to tell that admiral, Trowbridge, that I've been removed – at a vital moment in the Battle of the Atlantic – just because I spoke the truth.'

'Oh, I could, could I? Thank you. Thanks very much. Then we'll both be doing long division in the Admiralty.'

'"There are worse places to spend the war."'

'Don't be cheap.'

There was another knock, much louder this time. 'For God's sake,' yelled Logie, 'piss off!' But the handle started to turn anyway. Jericho moved out of the way, the door opened and Puck appeared.

'Sorry, Guy. Good morning, Thomas.' He gave them each a grim nod. 'There's been a development, Guy.'

'Good news?'

'Frankly, no, to be entirely honest. It is probably not good news. You had better come.'

'Hell, *hell.*' muttered Logie. He gave Jericho a murderous look, grabbed his pipe and followed Puck out into the corridor.

Jericho hesitated for a second, then set off after them, down the passage and into the Registration Room. He had never seen it so full. Lieutenant Cave was there, along, it seemed, with almost every cryptanalyst in the hut – Baxter, Atwood, Pinker, Kingcome, Proudfoot, de Brooke – as well as Kramer, like a matinee idol in his American naval uniform. He gave Jericho a friendly nod.

Logie glanced around the room with surprise. 'Hail, hail, the gang's all here.' Nobody laughed. 'What's up, Puck? Holding a rally? Going on strike?'

Puck inclined his head towards the three young Wrens who made up the Registration Room's day shift.

'Ah yes,' said Logie, 'of course,' and he flashed his smoker's teeth at them in an ochre smile. 'Bit of business to attend to, girls. Hush hush. I wonder if you wouldn't mind leaving the gentlemen alone for a few minutes.'

'I happened to show this to Lieutenant Cave,' said Puck, when the Wrens had gone. 'Traffic analysis.' He held aloft the familiar yellow log sheet, as if he were about to perform a conjuring trick. 'Two long signals intercepted in the last twelve hours coming out of the

Nazis' new transmitter near Magdeburg. One just
before midnight: one hundred and eight four-letter
groups. One just after: two hundred and eleven groups.
Rebroadcast twice, over both the Diana and Hubertus
radio nets. Four-six-oh-one kilocycles. Twelve-nine-
fifty.'

'Oh, do get on with it,' said Atwood, under his
breath.

Puck affected not to hear. 'In the same period, the
total number of Shark signals intercepted from the
North Atlantic U-boats up to oh-nine-hundred this
morning: five.'

'Five?' repeated Logie. 'Are you sure, old love?' He
took the log sheet and ran his finger down the neatly
inked columns of entries.

'What's the phrase?' said Puck. '"As quiet as the
grave"?'

'Our listening posts,' said Baxter, reading the log
sheet over Logie's shoulder. 'There must be something
wrong with them. They must have fallen asleep.'

'I rang the intercept control room ten minutes ago.
After I'd spoken to the lieutenant. They say there's no
mistake.'

An excited murmur of conversation broke out.

'And what say you, O wise one?'

It took Jericho a couple of seconds to realise that
Atwood was talking to him. He shrugged. 'It's very
few. Ominously few.'

Puck said: 'Lieutenant Cave believes there's a
pattern.'

'We've been interrogating captured U-boat crew

about tactics.' Lieutenant Cave leaned forwards and Jericho saw Pinker flinch at the sight of his scarred face. 'When Dönitz sniffs a convoy, he draws his hearses up line abreast across the route he expects it to take. Twelve boats, say, maybe twenty miles apart. Possibly two lines, possibly three – nowadays he's got the hearses to put on a pretty big show. Our estimate, before the blackout, was forty-six operational in that sector of the North Atlantic alone.' He broke off, apologetically. 'Sorry,' he said, 'do stop me if I'm telling my grandmothers how to suck eggs.'

'Our work's rather more – ah – theoretical,' said Logie. He looked around and several of the crypt-analysts nodded in agreement.

'All right. There are basically two types of line. There's your picket line, which basically means the U-boats stay stationary on the surface waiting for the convoy to steam into them. And there's your patrol line, which involves the hearses sweeping forwards in formation to intercept it. Once the lines are established, there's one golden rule. Absolute radio silence until the convoy's sighted. My hunch is that that's what's happening now. The two long signals coming out of Magdeburg – those are most likely Berlin ordering the U-boats into line. And if the boats are now observing radio silence . . .' Cave shrugged: he was sorry to have to state the obvious. 'That means they must be on battle stations.'

Nobody said anything. The intellectual abstractions of cryptanalysis had taken solid form: two thousand German U-boat men, ten thousand Allied seamen and passengers, converging to do battle in the North Atlantic winter, a thousand miles from land. Pinker looked as if he might be sick. Suddenly the oddity of their situation struck Jericho. Pinker was probably personally responsible for sending – what? – a thousand German sailors to the bottom of the ocean, yet Cave's face was the closest he had come to the brutality of the Atlantic war.

Someone asked what would happen next.

'If one of the U-boats finds the convoy? It'll shadow it. Send a contact signal every two hours – position, speed, direction. That'll be picked up by the other hearses and they'll start to converge on the same location. Same procedure, to try to draw in as many hunters as possible. Usually, they try to get right inside the convoy, in among our ships. They'll wait until nightfall. They prefer to attack in the dark. Fires from the ships that have been hit illuminate other targets. There's more panic. Also, night-time makes it harder for our destroyers to catch them.'

'Of course, the weather's appalling,' added Cave, his sharp voice cutting in to the silence, 'even for the time of year. Snow. Freezing fog. Green water breaking over the bows. That's actually in our favour.'

Kramer said: 'How long do we have?'

'Less time than we originally thought, that's for certain. The U-boat is faster than any convoy, but it's still a slow beast. On the surface it moves at the speed of a man on a bicycle, underwater it's only as fast as a man on foot. But if Dönitz knows about the convoys? Perhaps a day and a half. The bad weather will give them visibility problems. Even so – yes – I'd guess a day and a half at the outside.'

Cave excused himself to go and telephone the bad news to the Admiralty. The cryptanalysts were left alone. At the far end of the hut a faint clacking noise began as the Type-X machines started their day's work.

'That'll be D-D-Dolphin,' said Pinker. 'Will you excuse me, G-G-Guy?'

Logie raised a hand in benediction and Pinker hurried out of the room.

'If only we had a four-wheel bombe,' moaned Proudfoot.

'Well, we ain't got one, old love, so don't let's waste time on that.'

Kramer had been leaning against one of the trestle tables. Now he pushed himself on to his feet. There wasn't room for him to pace, so he performed a kind of restless shuffle, smacking his fist into the palm of his left hand.

'Goddamn it, I feel so *helpless*. A day and a half. A measly, goddamn *day and a half.* Jesus! There must be *something*. I mean, you guys did break this thing once, didn't you, during the last blackout?'

Several people spoke at once.

'Oh, yes.'

'D'you remember that?'

'That was Tom.'

Jericho wasn't listening. Something was stirring in his mind, some tiny shift in the depths of his subconscious, beyond the reach of any power of analysis. What was it? A memory? A connection? The more he tried to concentrate on it, the more elusive it became.

'Tom?'

He jerked his head up in surprise.

'Lieutenant Kramer was asking you, Tom' said Logie, with weary patience, 'about how we broke Shark during the blackout.'

'What?' He was irritated at having his thoughts interrupted. His hands fluttered. 'Oh, Dönitz was promoted to admiral. We took a guess that U-boat headquarters would be pleased as Punch. So pleased, they'd transmit Hitler's proclamation verbatim to all boats.'

'And did they?'

'Yes. It was a good crib. We put six bombes onto it. Even then it still took us nearly three weeks to read one day's traffic.'

'With a good crib?' said Kramer. 'Six bombes. *Three weeks?*'

'That's the effect of a four-wheel Enigma.'

Kingcome said: 'It's a pity Dönitz doesn't get a promotion every day.'

This immediately brought Atwood to life. 'The way things are going, he probably will.'

Laughter momentarily lightened the gloom. Atwood looked pleased with himself.

'Very good, Frank,' said Kingcome. 'A daily promotion. Very good.'

Only Kramer refused to laugh. He folded his arms and stared down at his gleaming shoes.

They began to talk about some theory of de Brooke's which had been running on a pair of bombes for the past nine hours, but the methodology was hopelessly skewed, as Puck pointed out.

'Well, at least I've had an idea,' said de Brooke, 'which is more than you have.'

'That is because, my dear Arthur, if I have a terrible idea, I keep it to myself.'

Logie clapped his hands. 'Boys, boys. Let's keep the criticism constructive, shall we?'

The conversation dragged on but Jericho had stopped listening a long time ago. He was chasing the phantom in his mind again, searching back through his mental record of the past ten minutes to find the word, the phrase, that could have stirred it into life. Diana, Hubertus, Magdeburg, picket line, radio silence, contact signal . . .

Contact signal.

'Guy, where d'you keep the keys to the Black Museum?'

'What, old thing? Oh, in my desk. Top right-hand drawer. Hey, where're you going? Just a minute, I haven't finished talking to you yet . . .'

It was a relief to get out of the claustrophobic atmosphere of the hut and into the cold, fresh air. He trotted up the slope towards the mansion.

He seldom went into the big house these days but whenever he did it reminded him of a stately home in a twenties murder mystery. (*'You will recall, inspector, that the colonel was in the library when the fatal shots*

211

were fired . . .') The exterior was a nightmare, as if a giant handcart full of the discarded bits of other buildings had been tipped out in a heap. Swiss gables, Gothic battlements, Greek pillars, suburban bay windows, municipal red brick, stone lions, the entrance porch of a cathedral – the styles sulked and raged against one another, capped by a bell-shaped roof of beaten green copper. The interior was pure Gothic horror, all stone arches and stained glass windows. The polished floors rang hollow beneath Jericho's feet and the walls were decorated with dark wooden panelling of the sort that springs open in the final chapter to reveal a secret labyrinth. He was hazy about what went on here now. Commander Travis had the big office at the front looking out over the lake while upstairs in the bedrooms all sorts of mysterious things were done: he'd heard rumours they were breaking the ciphers of the German Secret Service.

He walked quickly across the hall. An Army captain loitering outside Travis's office was pretending to read that morning's *Observer*, listening to a middle-aged man in tweeds trying to chat up a young RAF woman. Nobody paid any attention to Jericho. At the foot of the elaborately carved oak staircase, a corridor led off to the right and wound around the back of the house. Midway along it was a door which opened to reveal steps down to a secondary passage. It was here, in a locked room in the cellar, that the cryptanalysts from huts 6 and 8 stored their stolen treasures.

Jericho felt along the wall for the light switch.

The larger of the two keys unlocked the door to the

museum. Stacked on metal shelves along one wall were a dozen or more captured Enigma machines. The smaller key fitted one of a pair of big iron safes. Jericho knelt and opened it and began to rummage through the contents. Here they all were, their precious pinches: each one a victory in the long war against the Enigma. There was a cigar box with a label dated February 1941, containing the haul from the armed German trawler *Krebs:* two spare rotors, the Kriegsmarine grid map of the North Atlantic and the naval Enigma settings for February 1941. Behind these was a bulging envelope marked *München* – a weather ship whose capture three months after the *Krebs* had enabled them to break the meterological code – and another labelled 'U-110'. He pulled out armfuls of papers and charts.

Finally, from the bottom shelf at the back, he withdrew a small package wrapped in brown oilcloth. This was the haul for which Fasson and Grazier had died, still in its original covering, as it had been passed out of the sinking U-boat. He never saw it without thanking God that they'd found something waterproof to wrap it in. The smallest exposure to water would have dissolved the ink. To have plucked it from a drowning submarine, at night, in a high sea . . . It was enough to make even a mathematician believe in miracles. Jericho removed the oilcloth tenderly, as a scholar might unwrap the papyri of an ancient civilisation, or a priest uncover holy relics. Two little pamphlets, printed in Gothic lettering on pink blotting paper. The second edition of the U-boats' Short Weather Cipher, now useless, thanks to the code book change. And – exactly as he had remembered – the Short Signal Book. He flicked through it. Columns of letters and numbers.

A typed notice was stuck on the back of the safe door: 'It is strictly forbidden to remove any item without my express permission. (Signed) L.F.N. Skynner, Head of Naval Section.'

Jericho took particular pleasure in slipping the Short Signal Book into his inside pocket and running with it back to the hut.

Jericho tossed the keys to Logie who fumbled and then just caught them.

'Contact signal.'

'What?'

'Contact signal,' repeated Jericho.

'Praise the Lord!' said Atwood, throwing up his hands like a revivalist preacher. 'The Oracle has spoken.'

'All right, Frank. Just a minute. What about it, old love?'

Jericho could see it all much faster than he could convey it. Indeed, it was quite hard to formulate it in words at all. He spoke slowly, as if translating from a foreign language, reordering it in his mind, turning it into a narrative.

'Do you remember, in November, when we got the Short Weather Cipher Book off the U-459? When we also got the Short Signal Book? Only we decided not to concentrate on the Short Signal Book at the time, because it never yielded anything long enough to make a worthwhile crib? I mean, a convoy contact signal on its own, it isn't worth a damn, is it? It's just five letters once in a blue moon.' Jericho withdrew the little pink pamphlet carefully from his pocket. 'One letter for the speed of the convoy, a couple for its course, a couple more for the grid reference . . .'

Baxter stared at the code book as if hypnotised. 'You've removed that from the safe *without permission?*'

'But if Lieutenant Cave is correct, and whichever U-boat finds the convoy is going to send a contact signal every *two hours*, and if it's going to shadow it till nightfall, then it's possible – theoretically possible – it might send as many as four, or even five signals, depending on what time of day it makes its first sighting.' Jericho sought out the only uniform in the room. 'How long does daylight last in the North Atlantic in March?'

'About twelve hours,' said Kramer.

'Twelve hours, you see? And if a number of other U-boats attach themselves to the same convoy, on the same day, in response to the original signal, and *they* all start sending contact signals every two hours . . .'

Logie, at least, could see what he was driving at. He withdrew his pipe slowly from his mouth. 'Bloody hell!'

'Then again, *theoretically*, we could have, say, twenty letters of crib off the first boat, fifteen off the second – I don't know, if it's an attack by eight boats, let's say, we could easily get to a hundred letters. It's just as good as the weather crib.' Jericho felt as a proud as a father, offering the world a glimpse of his newborn child. 'It's beautiful, don't you see?' He gazed at each of the cryptanalysts in turn: Kingcome and Logie were beginning to look excited, de Brooke and Proudfoot seemed thoughtful, Baxter, Atwood and Puck appeared downright hostile. 'It was never possible till this moment, because until now the Germans have never been able to throw so many U-boats against such a mass of shipping. It's the whole story of Enigma in a nutshell. The very scale of the Germans' achievement breeds such a mass of material for us, it'll sow the seeds of their eventual defeat.'

He paused.

'Aren't there rather a lot of *ifs* there?' said Baxter drily. '*If* the U-boat finds the convoy early enough in the day, *if* it reports every two hours, *if* the others all do the same, *if* we manage to intercept every transmission . . .'

'And *if,*' said Atwood, 'the Short Signal Book we pinched in November wasn't changed last week at the same time as the Weather Cipher Book . . .'

That was a possibility Jericho hadn't considered. He felt his enthusiasm crumble slightly.

Now Puck joined in the attack. 'I agree. The concept is quite brilliant, Thomas. I applaud your – inspiration, I suppose. But your strategy depends on failure, does it not? We will only break Shark, on your admission, if the U-boats find the convoy, which is exactly what we want to avoid. And suppose we do come up with that day's Shark settings – so what? Marvellous. We can read all the U-boats' signals to Berlin, boasting to Dönitz about how many Allied ships they've sunk. And twenty-four hours later, we're blacked out again.'

Several of the cryptanalysts groaned in agreement.

'No, no,' Jericho shook his head emphatically. 'Your logic is flawed, Puck. What we hope, obviously, is that the U-boats don't find the convoys. Yes – that's the whole point of the exercise. But if they do, we can at least turn it to our advantage. And it won't just be one day, not if we're lucky. If we break the Shark settings for twenty-four hours, then we'll pick up the encoded weather messages for that entire period. And, remember, we'll have our own ships in the area, able to give us the precise weather data the U-boats are encoding. We'll have the plaintext, we'll have the Shark cipher settings, so we'll be able to make a start on reconstructing the new Weather Code Book. We could get our foot back in the door again. Don't you see?'

He ran his hands through his hair and tugged at it in exasperation. Why were they all being so dim?

Kramer had been scribbling furiously in a notebook. 'He's on to something, you know.' He tossed his pencil into the air and caught it. 'Come on. It's worth a try. At least it puts us back in the fight.'

Baxter grunted. 'I still don't see it.'

'Nor do I,' said Puck.

'I suppose you don't see it, Baxter,' said Atwood, 'because it doesn't represent a triumph for the world proletariat?'

Baxter's hands curled into fists. 'One of these days, Atwood, someone's going to knock your bloody smug block off.'

'Ah. The first impulse of the totalitarian mind: violence.'

'Enough!' Logie banged his pipe like a gavel on one

of the trestle tables. None of them had ever heard him shout before and the room went quiet. 'We've had quite enough of that already.' He stared hard at Jericho. 'Now, it's quite right we should be cautious. Puck, your point's taken. But we've also got to face facts. We've been blacked out four days and Tom's is the only decent idea we've got. So bloody good work, Tom.'

Jericho stared at an ink stain on the floor. *Oh God,* he thought, *here comes the housemaster's pep talk.*

'Now, there's a lot resting on us here, and I want every man to remember he's part of a team.'

'No man is an island, Guy,' said Atwood, deadpan, his chubby hands clasped piously on his wide stomach.

'Thank you, Frank. Quite right. No they're not. And if ever any of us – any of us – is tempted to forget it, just think of those convoys, and all the other convoys this war depends on. Got it? Good. Right. Enough said. Back to work.'

Baxter opened his mouth to protest, but then seemed to think better of it. He and Puck exchanged grim glances on their way out. Jericho watched them go and wondered why they were so determinedly pessimistic. Puck couldn't abide Baxter's politics and normally the two men kept their distance. But now they seemed to have made common cause. What was it? A kind of academic jealousy? Resentment that he had come in after all their hard work and made them look like fools?

Logie was shaking his head. 'I don't know, old love, what are we to do with you?' He tried to look stern, but he couldn't hide his pleasure. He put his hand on

Jericho's shoulder.

'Give me my job back.'

'I'll have to talk to Skynner.' He held the door open and ushered Jericho out into the passage. The three Wrens watched them. 'My God,' said Logie, with a shudder. 'Can you imagine what he's going to say? He's going to love it, isn't he, having to tell his friends the admirals that the best chance of getting back into Shark is if the convoys are attacked? Oh, bugger, I suppose I'd better go and call him.' He went halfway into his office, then came out again. 'And you're quite sure you never actually hit him?'

'Quite sure, Guy.'

'Not a scratch?'

'Not a scratch.'

'Pity, said Logie, half to himself. 'In a way. Pity.'

5

Hester Wallace couldn't sleep. The blackout curtains were drawn against the day. Her tiny room was a study in monochrome. A nosegay of lavender sent a soothing fragrance filtering through her pillow. But even though she lay dutifully on her back in her cotton nightgown, her legs pressed together, her hands folded on her breast, like a maiden on a marble tomb, oblivion still eluded her.

'ADU, Miss Wallace. Angels Dance Upwards . . .'

The mnemonic was infuriatingly effective. She

couldn't get it out of her brain, even though the arrangement of letters meant nothing to her.

'It's a call sign. Probably German Army or Luftwaffe . . .'

No surprise in that. It was almost bound to be. After all, there were so many of them: thousands upon thousands. The only reliable rule was that Army and Luftwaffe call-signs never began with a D, because D always indicated a German commercial station.

ADU . . . ADU . . .

She couldn't place it.

She turned on her side, brought her knees up to her stomach and tried to fill her mind with soothing thoughts. But no sooner had she rid herself of the intense, pale face of Tom Jericho than her memory showed her the wizened priest of St Mary's, Bletchley, that croaking mouthpiece of St Paul's misogynies. 'It is a shame for women to speak in the church . . .' (1 Corinthians 14.xxxv). 'Silly women laden with sins, led away with divers lusts . . .' (2 Timothy 3.vi). From such texts he had woven a polemical sermon against the wartime employment of the female sex – women driving lorries, women in trousers, women drinking and smoking in public houses unaccompanied by their husbands, women neglecting their children and their homes. 'As a jewel of gold in a swine's mouth, so is a fair woman which is without discretion.' (Proverbs 11.xxii).

If only it were true! she thought. If only women *had* usurped authority over men! The Brylcreemed figure of Miles Mermagen, her head of section, rose greasily before her inner eye. 'My dear Hester, a transfer at the present moment is really quite out of the question.' He had been a manager at Barclays Bank before the war and liked to come up behind the girls as they worked and massage their shoulders. At the Hut 6 Christmas Party he had manoeuvred her under the mistletoe and clumsily taken off her glasses. ('Thank you, Miles,' she'd said, trying miserably to make a joke of it, 'without my spectacles you too look almost tolerably attractive . . .') His lips on hers were unpleasantly moist, like the underside of a mollusc, and tasted of sweet sherry.

Claire, of course, had known immediately what to do.

'Oh, darling, poor you, and I suppose he's got a wife?'

'He says they were married too young.'

'Well, she's your answer. Tell him you think it's only fair you go and have a talk with her first. Tell him you want to be her friend.'

'But what if he says yes?'

'Oh, God! Then I suppose you'll just have to kick him in the balls.'

Hester smiled at the memory. She shifted her position in the bed again and the cotton sheet rode up and corrugated beneath her. It was quite hopeless. She reached out and switched on the little bedside lamp, fumbling around its base for her glasses.

Ich lerne deutsch, ich lernte deutsch, ich habe deutsch gelernt . . .

German, she thought: German would be her

221

salvation. A working knowledge of written German would lift her out of the grind of the Intercept Control Room, away from the clammy embrace of Miles Mermagen, and propel her into the rarefied air of the Machine Room, where the *real* work was done – where she should have been put in the first place.

She propped herself up in bed and tried to focus on *Abelman's German Primer.* Ten minutes of this was usually quite enough to send her off to sleep.

'Intransitive verbs showing a change of place or condition take the auxiliary *sein* instead of *haben* in the compound tenses . . .'

She looked up. Was that a noise downstairs?

'In subordinate word order the auxiliary must stand last, directly after the past participle or the infinitive . . .'

And there it was again.

She slipped her warm feet into her cold outdoor shoes, wrapped a woollen shawl about her shoulders, and went out onto the landing.

A knocking sound was coming from the kitchen.

She began to descend the stairs.

There had been two men waiting for her when she arrived back from church. One had been standing on the doorstep, the other had emerged casually from the back of the cottage. The first man was young and blond with a languid, aristocratic manner and a kind of decadent Anglo-Saxon handsomeness. His companion was older, smaller, slim and dark, with a northern accent. They both had Bletchley Park passes and said they'd come from Welfare and were looking for Miss Romilly. She hadn't turned up for work: any idea

222

where she might be?

Hester had said she hadn't. The older man had gone upstairs and had spent a long time searching around. The blond, meanwhile – she never caught his name – had sprawled on the sofa and asked a lot of questions. There was something offensively patronising about him, for all his good manners. This is what Miles Mermagen would be like, she found herself thinking, if he'd had five thousand pounds' worth of private education. What was Claire like? Who were her friends? Who were the men in her life? Had anyone been asking after her? She mentioned Jericho's visit of the previous night and he made a note of it with a gold propelling pencil. She almost blurted out the story of Jericho's peculiar approach in the churchyard (*'ADU, Miss Wallace . . .'*) but by this time she had taken so strongly against the blond man's manner she bit back the words.

Knock, knock, knock from the kitchen . . .

Hester took the poker that stood beside the sitting-room fireplace and slowly opened the kitchen door.

It was like stepping into a refrigerator. The window was banging in the wind. It must have been open for hours.

At first she felt relieved, but that lasted only until she tried to close it. Then she discovered that the metal catch, weakened by rust, had been snapped clean off. Part of the wooden window frame around it was splintered.

She stood in the cold and considered the implications and quickly concluded there was only one plausible explanation. The dark-haired man who had appeared from behind the cottage on her return from church had obviously been in the process of breaking in.

They had told her there was nothing to worry about. But if there was nothing to worry about, why had they been prepared to force entry into the house?

She shivered and drew the shawl around her.

'Oh Claire,' she said aloud, 'oh, Claire, you silly, stupid, *stupid* girl, what *have* you done?'

She used a piece of blackout tape to try and secure the window. Then, still holding the poker, she went back upstairs and into Claire's room. A silver fox was hanging over the end of the bed, its glass-bead eyes staring, its needle teeth bared. Out of habit, she folded it neatly and placed it on the shelf where it normally lived. The room was such an expression of Claire, such an extravagance of colour and fabric and scent, that it seemed to resonate with her presence, even now, when she was away, to hum with it, like the last vibrations of a tuning fork . . . Claire, holding some ridiculous dress to herself and laughing and asking her what she thought, and Hester pretending to frown with an older sister's disapproval. Claire, as moody as an adolescent, on her stomach on the bed, leafing through a pre-war *Tatler*. Claire combing Hester's hair (which, when she let it down, fell almost to her waist), running her brush through it with slow and languorous strokes that made Hester's limbs turn weak. Claire insisting on painting Hester in her make-up, dressing her up like a doll and standing back in mock surprise: *'Why, darling, you're*

224

beautiful! Claire, in nothing but a pair of white silk knickers and a string of pearls, prancing about the room in search of something, long-legged as an athlete, turning and seeing that Hester was secretly watching her in the mirror, catching the look in her eyes, and standing there for a moment, hip thrust forward, arms outstretched, with a smile that was something between an invitation and a taunt, before sweeping back into motion . . .

And on that cold, bright Sabbath afternoon, Hester Wallace, the clergyman's daughter, leaned against the wall and closed her eyes and pressed her hand between her legs with shame.

An instant later the noise from the kitchen started again and she thought her heart might burst with panic. She fled across the landing and into her room, pursued by the dry whine of the vicar of St Mary's – or was it really the voice of her father? – reciting from the Book of Proverbs:

'For the lips of a strange woman drop as an honeycomb, and her mouth is smoother than oil: But her end is bitter as wormwood, sharp as a two-edged sword. Her feet go down to death; her steps take hold on hell . . .'

6

For the first time in more than a month, Tom Jericho found that he was busy.

He had to supervise the copying of the Short Signal Code Book, six typewritten transcripts of which were duly produced and stamped MOST SECRET. Every line had to be checked, for a single error could spell the difference between a successful break and days of failure. The intercept controllers had to be briefed. Teleprinted orders had to be sent to all the duty officers of every Hut 8 listening post – from Thurso, clinging to the cliffs on the northernmost tip of Scotland, right down to St Erth, near Land's End. Their brief was simple: concentrate everything you have on the known Atlantic U-boat frequencies, cancel all leave, bring in the lame and the sick and the blind if you have to, and pay even greater attention than usual to very short bursts of Morse preceded by E-bar – *dot dot dash dot dot* – the Germans' priority code which cleared the wavelength for convoy contact reports. Not one such signal was to be missed, understand? *Not one.*

From the Registry, Jericho withdrew three months' worth of Shark decrypts to bring himself back up to speed, and, that afternoon, sitting in his old place by the window in the Big Room, proved by slide-rule calculation what he already knew by instinct: that seventeen convoy contact reports, if harvested in the same twenty-four-hour stretch, would yield eighty-five letters of cipher encode which might – *might*, if the cryptanalysts had the requisite percentage of luck – give them a break into Shark, provided they could get at least ten bombes working in relay for a minimum of thirty-six hours . . .

And all the time he thought of Claire.

There was very little, practically, he could do about her. Twice during the day he managed to get out to the telephone box to try to call her father: once as they all went off to lunch, when he was able to drop back, unnoticed by the rest, just before they reached the main gate; and the second time in the late afternoon when he pretended he needed to stretch his legs. On each occasion, the connection was made, but the phone merely rang, unanswered. He had a vague but growing feeling of dread, made worse by his powerlessness. He couldn't return to Hut 3. He didn't have the time to check out her cottage. He would have liked to go back to his room to rescue the intercepts – hidden behind a *picture* on top of the *mantelpiece*? was he *insane*? – but the round trip would have taken him the best part of twenty minutes and he couldn't get away.

In the event, it was to be well past seven before he got away. Logie was passing through the Big Room when he stopped off at Jericho's table and told him, for God's sake, to get back to his digs and get some rest. 'There's nothing more for you to do here, old love. Except wait. I expect it'll be around this time tomorrow that we'll start to sweat.'

Jericho reached thankfully for his coat. 'Did you talk to Skynner?'

'About the plan, yes. Not about you. He didn't ask and I certainly wasn't going to bring it up.'

'Don't tell me he's forgotten?'

Logie shrugged. 'There's some other flap on that seems to have taken his mind off things.'

'What other flap?'

But Logie had moved away. 'I'll see you in the morning. You just make sure you get some kip.'

Jericho returned the stack of Shark intercepts to the Registry and went outside. The March sun, which had barely risen above the trees all day, had sunk behind the mansion, leaving a fading streak of primrose and pale orange at the rim of an indigo sky. The moon was already out and Jericho could hear the sound of bombers, far away, a lot of them, forming up for the night's attack on Germany. As he walked, he gazed around him in wonder. The lunar disc on the still lake, the fire on the horizon – it was an extraordinary conjunction of lights and symbols, almost like a portent. He was so engrossed he had almost passed the telephone box before he realised that it was empty.

One last try? He glanced at the moon. Why not?

The Kensington number still wasn't answering so he decided, on a whim, to try the Foreign Office. The operator put him through to a duty clerk and he asked for Edward Romilly.

'Which department?'

'I don't know, I'm afraid.'

The line went silent. The chances of Edward Romilly being at his desk on a Sunday night were slim. He rested his shoulder against the glass panel of the booth. A car went past slowly, then pulled up about ten yards down the road. Its brake lights glowed red in the dusk. There was a click and Jericho returned his attention to the call.

'Putting you through.'

A ringing tone, and then a cultured female voice said: 'German Desk.'

German Desk? He was momentarily disconcerted. 'Ah, Edward Romilly, please.'

'And who shall I say is calling?'

My God, he *was* there. He hesitated again.

'A friend of his daughter.'

'Wait, please.'

His fingers were clamped so tight around the receiver that they were aching. He made an effort to relax. There was no good reason why Romilly *shouldn't* work on the German Desk. Hadn't Claire told him once that her father had been a junior official at the Berlin Embassy, just as the Nazis were coming to power? She would have been about ten or eleven. That must have been where she learned her German.

'I'm afraid, sir, Mr Romilly's already left for the evening. Who shall I say called?'

'Thank you. It doesn't matter. Good night.'

He hung up quickly. He didn't like the sound of that. And he didn't like the look of this car, either. He came out of the telephone box and began to walk towards it – a low, black machine with wide running boards, edged white for the blackout. Its engine was still running. As he came closer it suddenly catapulted forwards and shot round the curving road towards the main gate. He trotted after it but by the time he reached the entrance it had gone.

As Jericho went down the hill, the vague outline of the town evaporated into the darkness. No generation for at least a century could have witnessed such a spectacle. Even in his great-grandfather's day there would have been some illumination – the gleam of a gaslight or a carriage lantern, the bluish glow of a night watchman's paraffin lamp – but not any more. As the light faded, so did Bletchley. It seemed to sink into a black lake. He could have been anywhere.

He was aware, now, of a certain paranoia, and the night magnified his fears. He passed an urban pub close to the railway bridge, an elaborate Victorian mausoleum with FINE WHISKYS, PORTS AND STOUTS inlaid in gold on the black masonry like an epitaph. He could hear a badly tuned piano playing 'The Londonderry Air' and for a moment he was tempted to go in, buy a drink, find someone to talk to. But then he imagined the conversation –

'So, what's your line then, pal?'

'Just government work.'

'Civil service?'

'Communications. Nothing much. Look, I say, can I get you another drink?'

'Local are you?'

'Not exactly . . .'

– and he thought: no, better to keep clear of strangers; best, really, not to drink at all. As he was turning into Albion Street he heard the scrape of a footstep behind him and spun round. The pub door had opened, there was a moment of colour and music, then it closed and the road was dark again.

The guesthouse was about half way down Albion Street, on the right and he had almost reached it when he noticed, on the left, a car. He slowed his pace. He couldn't be sure it was the same one that had behaved so oddly at the Park, although it looked quite similar. But then, when he was almost level with it, one of the occupants struck a match. As the driver leaned over to cup his hand to the light, Jericho saw on his sleeve the three white stripes of a police sergeant.

He let himself into the guesthouse and prayed he could make the stairs before Mrs Armstrong rose like a night fighter to intercept him in the hall. But he was too late. She must have been waiting for the sound of his key in the latch. She appeared from the kitchen through a cloud of steam that smelled of cabbage and offal. In the dining room, somebody made a retching noise and there was a shout of laughter.

Jericho said weakly, 'I don't think I'm very hungry, Mrs Armstrong, thanks all the same.'

She dried her hands on her apron and nodded towards a closed door. 'You've got a visitor.'

He had just planted his foot defiantly on the first stair. 'Is it the police?'

'Why, Mr Jericho, whatever would the police be doing here? It's a very nice-looking young gentleman. I've put him,' she added, with heavy significance, 'in the parlour.'

The parlour! Open nightly to any resident from eight till ten on weekdays, and from teatime onwards, Saturday and Sunday: as formal as a ducal drawing room, with its matching three-piece suite and antimacassars (made by the proprietress herself), its mahogany standard lamp with tasselled shade, its row

231

of grinning Toby jugs, precisely lined above its freezing hearth. Who had come to see him, wondered Jericho, who warranted admission to the *parlour*?

At first he didn't recognise him. Golden hair, a pale and freckled face, pale blue eyes, a practised smile. Advancing across the room to meet him, right hand outstretched, left hand holding an Anthony Eden hat, fifty guineas' worth of Savile Row coat draped over manly shoulders. A blur of breeding, charm and menace.

'Wigram. Douglas Wigram. Foreign Office. We met yesterday but weren't introduced properly.'

He took Jericho's hand lightly and oddly, a finger crooked back into his palm, and it took Jericho a moment to realise he had just been the recipient of a masonic handshake.

'Digs all right? Super room, this. Super. Mind if we go somewhere else? Whereabouts are you based? Upstairs?'

Mrs Armstrong was still in the hall, fluffing up her hair in front of the oval mirror.

'Mr Jericho suggests we might have our little chat upstairs in his room, if that's OK with you, Mrs A?' He didn't wait for a reply. 'Let's go then, shall we?'

He held out his arm, still smiling, and Jericho found himself being ushered up the stairs. He felt as though he had been tricked or robbed but he couldn't work out how. On the landing he rallied sufficiently to turn and say, 'It's very small, you know, there's barely room to sit.'

'That's perfectly all right, my dear chap. As long as it's private. Onwards and upwards.'

Jericho switched on the dim light and stood back to

let Wigram go in first. There was a faint whiff of eau de cologne and cigars as he brushed past. Jericho's eyes went straight to the picture of the chapel, which, he was relieved to note, looked undisturbed. He closed the door.

'See what you mean about the room,' said Wigram, cupping his hands to the glass to peer out of the window. 'The hell we have to go through, what? And a railway view thrown in. Bliss.' He closed the curtains and turned back to Jericho. He was cleaning his fingers on a handkerchief with almost feminine delicacy. 'We're rather worried.' His smile widened. 'We're rather worried about a girl called Claire Romilly.' He folded the blue silk square and thrust it back into his breast pocket. 'Mind if I sit down?'

He shrugged off his overcoat and laid it on the bed, then hitched up his pinstriped trousers a fraction at the knees to avoid damaging the crease. He sat on the edge of the mattress and bounced up and down experimentally. His hair was blond; so were his eyebrows, his eyelashes, the hairs on the back of his neat white hands . . . Jericho felt his skin prickle with fear and disgust.

Wigram patted the eiderdown beside him. 'Let's talk.' He didn't seem the least put out when Jericho stayed where he was. He merely folded his hands contentedly in his lap.

'All right,' he said, 'we'll make a start, then, shall we? Claire Romilly. Twenty. Clerical grade staff. Officially missing for –' he looked at his watch '– twelve hours. Failed to show for her morning shift. Actually, when you start to check, not seen since midnight, Friday – dear oh

233

dear, that's nearly two days ago now – when she left the Park after work. Alone. The girl she lives with swears she hasn't seen her since Thursday. Her father says he hasn't seen her since before Christmas. Nobody else – girls she works with, family, so forth – nobody seems to have the foggiest. Vanished.' Wigram snapped his fingers. 'Just like that.' For the first time he'd stopped smiling. 'Rather a good friend of yours, I gather?'

'I haven't seen her since the beginning of February. Is this why there are police outside?'

'But good enough? Good enough that you've *tried* to see her? Out to her cottage last night, according to our little Miss Wallace. Scurry, scurry. Questions, questions. Then, this morning, into Hut 3 – questions, questions, again. Phone call to her father – oh, yes,' he said, noticing Jericho's surprise, 'he rang us straight away to say you'd called. You've never met Ed Romilly? Lovely bloke. Never achieved his full potential, so they say. Rather lost the plot after his wife died. Tell me, Mr Jericho, why the interest?'

'I'd been away for a month. I hadn't seen her.'

'But surely you've got plenty more important things to worry about, especially just now, than renewing one acquaintance?'

His last words were almost lost in the roar of a passing express train. The room vibrated for fifteen seconds, which was the exact duration of his smile. When the noise was over, he said: 'Were you surprised to be brought back from Cambridge?'

'Yes. I suppose I was. Look, Mr Wigram, who are you, exactly?'

'Surprised when you were told *why* you were needed back?'

'Not surprised. No.' He searched for the word. 'Shocked.'

'Shocked. Ever talk to the girl about your work?'

'Of course not.'

'Of course not. Strike you as odd, though – possibly more than a coincidence, possibly even sinister – that one day the Germans black us out in the North Atlantic and two days later the girlfriend of a leading Hut 8 cryptanalyst goes missing? Actually on the same day he comes back?'

Jericho's gaze flickered involuntarily to the print of the chapel. 'I told you. I never talked to Claire about my work. I hadn't seen her for a month. And she wasn't my girlfriend.'

'No? What was she then?'

What was she then? A good question. 'I just wanted to see her,' he said lamely. 'I couldn't find her. I was concerned.'

'Got a photo of her? Something recent?'

'No. Actually, I don't have any pictures of her.'

'Really? Now here's another funny thing. Pretty girl like that. But can we find a picture? We'll just have to use the ID copy from her Welfare file.'

'Use it for what?'

'Can you fire a gun, Mr Jericho?'

'I couldn't hit a duck at a funfair.'

'Now that's what I would have thought, though one shouldn't always judge a chap by his looks. Only the Bletchley Park Home Guard had a little burglary at their armoury on Friday night. Two items missing. A Smith and Wesson .38 revolver, manufactured in Springfield, Massachusetts, issued by the War Office last year. And a box containing thirty-six rounds of ammunition.'

Jericho said nothing. Wigram looked at him for a while, as if he were making up his mind about something. 'No reason why *you* shouldn't know, I suppose. Trustworthy fellow like you. Come and sit down.' He patted the eiderdown again. 'I can't keep shouting the biggest frigging secret in the British Empire across your frigging bedroom. Come on. I won't bite, I promise.'

Reluctantly, Jericho sat down. Wigram leaned forwards. As he did so, his jacket parted slightly, and Jericho glimpsed a flash of leather and gunmetal against the white shirt.

'You want to know who I am?' he said softly. 'I'll tell you who I am. I'm the man our masters have decreed should find out just what's what down here in your little *anus mundi*.' He was speaking so quietly, Jericho was obliged to move his head in close to hear. 'Bells are going off, you see. Horrible, horrible bells. Five days ago, Hut 6 decoded a German Army signal from the Middle East. General Rommel's becoming a bit of a bad sport. Seems to think the only reason he's losing is that somehow, by some miracle, we always appear to know where exactly he's going to attack. Suddenly, the Afrika Korps want an enquiry into cipher security. Oh dear. *Ding dong.* Twelve hours later, Admiral Dönitz, for reasons as yet unknown, suddenly decides to tighten Enigma procedure by changing the U-boat weather code. *Ding dong* again. Today, it's the Luftwaffe. Four German merchant ships loaded with goodies for the aforementioned Rommel were recently "surprised" by the RAF and sunk halfway to Tunisia. This morning, we read that the German C-in-C, Mediterranean, Field Marshal Kesselring himself, no less, is demanding to know whether the enemy could have read his codes.' Wigram patted Jericho's knee. 'Peals of alarms, Mr Jericho. A Westminster-Abbey-on-Coronation-Day peal of alarms. And in the middle of them all, your lady friend disappears, at the same time as a shiny new shooter and a box of bullets.'

'Exactly who or what are we dealing with here?' said Wigram. He had taken out a small black leather notebook and a gold propelling pencil. 'Claire Alexandra Romilly. Born: London, twenty-first of the twelfth, 'twenty-two. Father: Edward Arthur Macauley Romilly, diplomat. Mother: the Honourable Alexandra Romilly, *née* Harvey, deceased in motor accident, Scotland, August 'twenty-nine. The child is educated privately abroad. Father's postings: Bucharest, 'twenty-eight to 'thirty-one; Berlin, 'thirty-one to 'thirty-four; Washington, 'thirty-four to 'thirty-eight. A year in Athens, then back to London. The girl by now is at some fancy finishing school in Geneva. She returns to London on the outbreak of war, aged seventeen. Principal occupation for the next three years, as far as one can gather: having a good time.' Wigram licked his finger and turned the page. 'Some voluntary civil defence work. Nothing too arduous. July 'forty-one:

translator at the Ministry of Economic Warfare. August 'forty-two: applies for clerical position, Foreign Office. Good languages. Recommended for position at Bletchley Park. See attached letter from father, blah, blah. Interviewed 10th of September. Accepted, cleared, starts work the following week.' Wigram flicked the pages back and forth. 'That's the lot. Not exactly a rigorous process of selection, is it? But then she does come from a *frightfully* good family. And Papa *does* work down at head office. And there *is* a war on. Care to add anything to the record?'

'I don't think I can.'

'How'd you meet her?'

For the next ten minutes Jericho answered Wigram's questions. He did this carefully and – mostly – truthfully. Where he lied it was only by omission. They had gone to a concert for their first date. After that they had gone out in the evenings a few times. They had seen a picture. Which one? *In Which We Serve.*

'Like it?'

'Yes.'

'I'll tell Noël.'

She had never talked about politics. She had never discussed her work. She had never mentioned other friends.

'Did you sleep with her?'

'Mind your own bloody business.'

'I'll put that down as yes.'

More questions. No, he had noticed nothing odd about her behaviour. No, she had not seemed tense or nervous, secretive, silent, aggressive, inquisitive, moody, depressed or elated – no, none of these – and at the end, they hadn't quarrelled. Really? No. So they had . . . what, then?

'I don't know. Drifted apart.'

'She was seeing someone else?'

'Perhaps. I don't know.'

'Perhaps. You don't know.' Wigram shook his head in wonder. 'Tell me about last night.'

'I cycled over to her cottage.'

'What time?'

'About ten, ten-thirty. She wasn't there. I talked with Miss Wallace for a bit. Then I came home.'

'Mrs Armstrong says she didn't hear you come in until around two o'clock this morning.'

So much for tiptoeing past her door, thought Jericho.

'I must have cycled around for a while.'

'I'll say you did. In the frost. In the blackout. You must have cycled around for about three hours.'

Wigram gazed down at his notes, tapping the side of his nose. 'Not right, Mr Jericho. Can't quite put my finger on it, but definitely *not right*. Still.' He snapped the notebook shut and gave a reassuring smile. 'Time to go into all that later, what?' He put his hand on Jericho's knee and pushed himself to his feet. 'First, we must catch our rabbit. You've no idea where she might be, I suppose? No favourite haunts? No little den to run to?' He gazed down at Jericho, who was staring at the floor. 'No? No. Thought not.'

By the time Jericho felt he could trust himself to look up again, Wigram had draped his beautiful over-coat back around his shoulders and was preoccupied picking tiny pieces of lint from its collar.

'It could all be a coincidence,' said Jericho. 'You do realise that? I mean, Dönitz always seems to have been suspicious about Enigma. That's why he gave the U-boats Shark in the first place.'

'Oh absolutely,' said Wigram cheerfully. 'But let's look at it another way. Let's imagine the Germans *have* got a whisper of what we're up to here. What would they do? They couldn't exactly chuck out a hundred thousand Enigma machines overnight, could they? And then what about all those experts of theirs, who've always said Enigma is unbreakable? They're not going to change their minds without a fight. No. They'd do what they look as though they might be doing. They'd start checking every suspicious incident. And in the meantime, they'd try and find hard proof. A person, perhaps. Better still, a person with documentary evidence. God, there are enough of them about. Thousands right here, who either know all the story, or a bit of it, or enough to put two and two together. And what kind of people are they?' He withdrew a sheet of paper from his inside pocket and unfolded it. 'This is the list I asked for yesterday. Eleven people in the Naval Section knew about the importance of the Weather Code Book. Some rum names here, if you stop to think about them. Skynner we can exclude, I suppose. And Logie – he seems sound enough. But Baxter? Now Baxter's a communist, isn't he?'

'I think you'll find that communists don't have much time for Nazis. As a rule.'

'What about Pukowski?'

'Puck lost his father and his brother when Poland was invaded. He loathes the Germans.'

'The American, then. Kramer. *Kramer*? He's a second-generation German immigrant, did you know that?'

'Kramer also lost a brother to the Germans. Really, Mr Wigram, this is ridiculous . . .'

'Atwood. Pinker. Kingcome. Proudfoot. de Brooke. *You* . . . Who *are* you all, exactly?' Wigram looked around the tiny room with distaste: the frayed blackout curtains, the tatty wardrobe, the lumpy bed. For the first time he seemed to notice the print of the chapel above the mantelpiece. 'I mean, just because a bloke's been to King's College, Cambridge . . .'

He picked up the picture and held it at an angle under the light. Jericho watched him, transfixed.

'E. M. Forster,' said Wigram thoughtfully. 'Now he's still at King's, isn't he?'

'I believe so.'

'Know him?'

'Only to nod to.'

'What was that essay of his? How did it go? The one about choosing between your friend and your country?'

'"I hate the idea of causes, and if I had to choose between betraying my country and betraying my friend, I hope I should have the guts to betray my country." But he did write that before the war.'

Wigram blew some dust off the frame and set the print carefully back on the top of Jericho's books.

'So I should hope,' he said, standing back to admire it. He turned and smiled at Jericho. 'So I should frigging well hope.'

After Wigram had gone, it was some minutes before Jericho felt able to move.

He lay full length on the bed, still wearing his scarf and overcoat, and listened to the sounds of the house. Some mournful string quartet which the BBC judged suitable entertainment for a Sunday night was scraping away downstairs. There were footsteps on the landing. A whispered conversation ensued which ended with a woman – Miss Jobey, was it? – having a fit of the giggles. A door slammed. The cistern above his head emptied and refilled. Then silence again.

When he did move, after about a quarter of an hour, his actions had a frantic, fumbling haste. He carried the chair over from the bedside to the door and tilted it against the flimsy panelling. He took the print and laid it face down on the threadbare carpet, pulled out the tacks, lifted off the back, rolled the intercepts into a tube, and took them over to the grate. On top of the little bucket of coal beside the hearth was a matchbox containing two matches. The first was damp and wouldn't strike but the second did, just, and Jericho twisted it round to make sure the yellow flame caught and grew, then he applied it to the bottom of the intercepts. He held on to them as they writhed and blackened until the very last moment, until the pain obliged him to drop them in the grate, where they disintegrated into tiny flakes of ash.

FIVE

CRIB

CRIB: a piece of evidence (usually
a captured code book or a length
of plaintext) which provides clues
for the breaking of a cryptogram;
'without question, the crib . . .
is the single most essential tool
of any cryptanalyst' (Knox
et al., op. cit., page 27).

A Lexicon of Cryptography
('Most Secret', Bletchley Park, 1943)

1

THE WARTIME LIPSTICK was hard and waxy – it was like trying to colour your lips with a Christmas candle. When, after several minutes of hard rubbing, Hester Wallace replaced her glasses, she peered into the mirror with distaste. Make-up had never featured much in her life, not even before the war, when there had been plenty in the shops. But now, when there was nothing to be had, the lengths one was expected to go to were quite absurd. She knew of girls in the hut who made lipstick out of beetroot and sealed it in place with Vaseline, who used shoe polish and burnt cork for mascara and margarine wrappers as a skin softener, who dusted bicarbonate of soda into their armpits to disguise their sweat . . . She formed her lips into a cupid's bow, which she immediately drew back into a grimace. Really, it was quite, quite absurd.

The shortage of cosmetics seemed to have caught up at last even with Claire. Although there was a profusion of pots and bottles all over her little dressing table – Max Factor, Coty, Elizabeth Arden: each name redolent of pre-war glamour – most of them turned out on closer inspection to be empty. Nothing was left except a trace of scent. Hester sniffed at each in turn and her mind was filled with images of luxury – of satin cocktail dresses by Worth of London and gowns with

245

daring *décolletage*, of fireworks at Versailles and the Duchess of Westminster's summer ball, and a dozen other wonderful nonsenses that Claire had prattled on about. Eventually she found a half-full pot of mascara and a glass-stoppered jar with an inch of rather lumpy face powder and set to work with those.

She had no qualms about helping herself. Hadn't Claire always told her she should? Making-up was fun, that was Claire's philosophy, it made one feel good about oneself, it turned one into someone else, and, besides, '*if this is what it takes, then, darling heart, this is simply what one does*'. Very well. Hester dabbed grimly at her pallid cheeks. If *this* was what it bloody well *took* to help persuade Miles Mermagen to approve a transfer, this was what he'd bloody well *get*.

She regarded her reflection without enthusiasm, then carefully replaced everything in its proper place and went downstairs. The sitting room was freshly swept. Daffodils above the hearth. A fire laid. The kitchen, too, was spotless. She had made a carrot flan earlier in the evening, enough for two, with ingredients she had grown herself in the little vegetable patch outside the kitchen door, and now she laid a place for Claire, and left a note telling her where to find the flan and instructions on how to heat it. She hesitated, then added at the end: 'Welcome back – from wherever you've been! – much love, H.' She hoped it didn't sound too fussy and inquisitive; she hoped she wasn't turning into her mother.

'ADU, *Miss Wallace . . .*'

Of course Claire would come back. It was all a stupid panic, too absurd for words.

She sat in one of the armchairs and waited for her until a quarter to midnight, when she dared leave it no longer.

As her bicycle bounced along the track towards the lane she startled a white owl which rose silently like a ghost in the moonlight.

In a way it was all Miss Smallbone's fault. If Angela Smallbone hadn't pointed out in the common room after prep that the *Daily Telegraph* was holding a crossword competition, then Hester Wallace's life would have gone on undisturbed. It was not a particularly thrilling life – a placid, provincial life in a remote and eccentric girls' preparatory school near the Dorset town of Beaminster, less than ten miles from where Hester had grown up. And it was not a life much touched by war, either, save for the pale faces of the evacuee children on some of the nearby farms, the barbed wire along the beach near Lyme Regis, and the chronic shortage of teaching staff – a shortage which meant that when the Michaelmas term began in the autumn of 1942, Hester was having to take divinity (her usual subject) *and* English *and* some Latin and Greek.

Hester had a gift for crosswords and when Angela read out that night that the prize-money was twenty pounds . . . well, she thought, why not? The first hurdle, an abnormally difficult puzzle printed in the next day's paper, she passed with ease. She sent off her solution and a letter arrived almost by return of post inviting her to the final, to be held in the *Telegraph's* staff canteen, a fortnight hence, a Saturday. Angela agreed to take over hockey practice, Hester caught the train from Crewkerne up to London, joined fifty other finalists – and won. She completed the crossword in three minutes and twenty-two seconds and Lord Camrose himself presented her with the cheque. She gave five pounds to her father for his church restoration fund, she spent seven pounds on a new winter coat (second-hand, actually, but good as new), and the rest she put in her Post Office savings account.

It was on the Thursday that the second letter had arrived, this one very different. Registered post, long buff envelope. On His Majesty's Service.

Afterwards, she could never quite decide. Had the *Telegraph* held the competition at the instigation of the War Office, as a way of trawling the country for men and women with an aptitude for word puzzles? Or had some bright spark at the War Office merely seen the results of the competition and asked the *Telegraph* for a list of the finalists? Whatever the truth, five of the most suitable were summoned to be interviewed in a grim Victorian office block on the wrong side of the Thames, and three of them were ordered to report to Bletchley.

The school hadn't wanted her to go. Her mother had cried. Her father had detested the idea, just as he detested all change, and for days beforehand he was filled with foreboding ('He shall return no more to his house, neither shall his place know him any more' Job 7.x). But the law was the law. She had to go. Besides, she thought, she was twenty-eight. Was she doomed to live out the rest of her life in the same place, tucked away in this drowsy quilt of tiny fields and honey-stoned villages? Here was her chance of escape. She had picked up enough clues at the interview to guess that the work would be codes, and her fantasies were all of quiet, book-lined libraries and the pure, clear air of the intellect.

Arriving at Bletchley station in her second-hand coat on a soaking Monday morning, she was taken straight by shooting brake to the mansion and given a copy of the Official Secrets Act to sign. The Army Captain who inducted them laid his pistol on the desk and said that if any of them, ever, breathed a word of what they were about to be told, he'd use it on them. Personally. Then they were assigned. The two male finalists became cryptanalysts, while she, the woman who had beaten them, was dispatched to a bedlam called Control.

'You take this form here, see, and in this first column you enter the code name of the intercept station. Chicksands, right, that's CKS, Beaumanor is BMR, Harpendon is HPN – don't worry, dear, you'll soon get used to it. Now here, see, you put the time of interception, here frequency, here call sign, here number of letter groups . . .'

Her fantasies were dust. She was a glorified clerk, Control a glorified funnel between the intercept stations and the cryptanalysts, a funnel down which poured the ceaseless output of some forty thousand different radio call signs, using more than sixty separately identified Enigma keys.

'German Air Force, right, they're usually either

insects or flowers. So you've got Cockroach, say, that's the Enigma key for western fighters, based in France. Dragonfly is Luftwaffe in Tunis. Locust is Luftwaffe, Sicily. You've got a dozen of those. Your flowers are the Luftgau – Foxglove: eastern front, Daffodil: western front, Narcissus: Norway. Birds are for the German Army. Chaffinch and Phoenix, they're Panzerarmee Afrika. Kestrel and Vulture – Russian front. Sixteen little birdies. Then there's Garlic, Onion, Celery – all the vegetables are weather Enigmas. They go straight to Hut 10. Got it?'

'What are Skunk and Porcupine?'

'Skunk is Fliegerkorps VIII, eastern front. Porcupine is ground-air cooperation, southern Russia.'

'Why aren't they insects as well?'

'God knows.'

The charts they had to fill in were called either 'blists' or 'hankies', the filing cabinet for miscellaneous trivia was known as Titicaca ('an Andes lake fed by many rivers,' said Mermagen portentously, 'but with no outflow'). The men gave one another silly names – 'the Unicorn-Zebra', 'the Mock Turtle' – while the girls mooned after the handsomer cryptanalysts in the Machine Room. Sitting in the freezing hut that winter, compiling her endless lists, Hester had a sense of Nazi Germany only as an endless, darkened plain, with thousands of tiny, isolated lights, flickering at one another in the blackness. Oddly enough, she thought, it was all, in its way, as remote from the war as the meadows and thatched barns of Dorset.

*

Enigma

She parked her bicycle in the shed beside the canteen and was borne along by the stream of workers to be deposited near the entrance to Hut 6. Control was already in a fine state of uproar, Mermagen bustling self-importantly between the desks, knocking his head against the low-hanging lampshades, sending pools of yellow light spilling crazily in all directions. Fourth Panzer Army was reporting the successful recapture of Kharkov from the Russians and the ninnies in Hut 3 were demanding that *every* frequency in the southern sector, eastern front, be double-backed *immediately*.

'Hester, Hester, just in time. Will you talk to Chicksands, there's a good girl, and see what they can do? And while you're on, the Machine Room reckon they've got a corrupt text on the last batch of Kestrel – the operator needs to check her notes and re-send. Then the eleven o'clock from Beaumanor all need blisting. Grab someone to help you. Oh, and the Index could do with a sorting out.'

All this before she had even taken off her coat.

It was two o'clock before there was enough of a lull for her to get away and talk to Mermagen in private. He was in his broom-cupboard office, his feet up on the desk, studying a handful of papers through half-closed eyes, in a terrific man-of-destiny pose she guessed he'd copied from some actor in the pictures.

'I wondered if I might have a word, Miles.'

Miles. She found this insistence on first-name terms a tiresome affectation, but informality was a rigid rule, an essential part of the Bletchley ethos: *we*, the civilian amateurs shall defeat *them*, the disciplined Hun.

Mermagen continued to study his papers.

She tapped her foot. 'Miles?'

He flicked over a page. 'You have my completely divided attention.'

'My request for a transfer –'

He groaned and turned over another page. 'Not that again.'

'I've been learning German –'

'How brave.'

'You did say that *not* having German made a transfer impossible.'

'Yes, but I didn't say that *having* it made a transfer *likely*. Oh, bloody hell! Well, come in, then.'

With a sigh he put aside his papers and beckoned her over the threshold. Someone must have told him once that Brylcreem made him look racy. His oily black hair, swept back off his forehead and behind his ears, glistened like a swimmer's cap. He was trying to grow a Clark Gable moustache but it was slightly too long on the left-hand side.

'Transfers of personnel from section to section are, as I've told you before, extremely rare. We do have security to consider.'

Security to consider: this must have been how he turned down loans before the war. Suddenly he was staring at her intently and she realised he had noticed the make-up. He couldn't have looked more startled if she'd painted herself with woad. His voice seemed to drop an octave.

'Look here, Hester, the last thing I want is to be difficult. What you need is a change of scene for a day

252

or two.' He touched his moustache lightly and gave a faint smile of recognition, as if he were surprised to find it still in place. 'Why don't you go up and take a look round one of the intercept stations, get a feel for where you fit into the chain? I know,' he added, 'I could do with a refresher myself. We could go up together.'

'Together? Yes . . . Why not? And find a little pub somewhere we could stop off for lunch?'

'Excellent. Make a real break of it.'

'Possibly a pub with rooms, so we could stay overnight if it got late?'

He laughed nervously. 'I still couldn't guarantee a transfer, you know.'

'But it would help?'

'Your words.'

'Miles?'

'Mmmm?'

'I'd rather die.'

'Frigid little bitch.'

She filled the basin with cold water and splashed her face furiously. The icy water numbed her hands and stung her face. It trickled down inside the neck of her shirt and up the sleeves. She welcomed the shock and the discomfort. She deserved it as a punishment for her folly and delusion.

She pressed her flat stomach against the edge of the basin and stared myopically at the chalk-white face in the mirror.

Useless to complain, of course. It was her word against his. She would never be believed. And even if she was – so what? My dear, it was *simply* the way of the world. Miles could ram her up against Lake bloody Titicaca if he liked, and put his hand up her skirt, and they'd still never let her go: nobody, once they'd seen as much as she had, was ever allowed to leave.

She felt a pricking of self-pity in the corners of her eyes and immediately lowered her head back over the basin and drenched her face, scrubbing at her cheeks and mouth with a sliver of carbolic soap until the powder stained the water pink.

She wished she could talk to Claire.

'*ADU, Miss Wallace . . .*'

Behind her in the cubicle the toilet flushed. Hurriedly, she pulled the plug out of the basin and dried her face and hands.

Name of intercept station, time of interception, frequency, call sign, letter groups . . . Name of intercept station, time of interception, frequency, call sign, letter groups . . .

Hester's hand moved mechanically across the paper.

At four o'clock the first half of the night-shift began drifting off to the canteen.

'Coming, Hetty?'

'Too much to do, unfortunately. I'll catch you up.'

'Poor you!'

'Poor you and *bloody* Miles,' said Beryl McCann, who had been to bed with Mermagen, once, and wished to God she hadn't.

Hester bent her head lower over her desk and continued to write in her careful schoolmistress

254

copperplate. She watched the other women putting on their coats and filing out, their shoes clumping on the wooden floor. Ah, but Claire had been so *funny* about them. It was one of the things Hester loved in her the most, the way she mimicked everyone: Anthea Leigh-Delamere, the huntswoman, who liked to come on shift in jodhpurs; Binnie with the waxy skin who wanted to be a Catholic nun; the girl from Solihull who held the telephone a foot away from her mouth because her mother had told her the receiver was full of germs . . . As far as Hester knew, Claire had never even *met* Miles Mermagen, yet she could impersonate him to perfection. The ghastliness of Bletchley had been their shared and private joke, their conspiracy against the bores.

The opening of the outside door let in a sudden blast of freezing air. Blists and hankies rustled and fluttered in the chill.

Bores. Boring. Claire's favourite words. The Park was boring. The war was boring. The town was *terrifically* boring. And the men were the biggest bores of all. The men – my God, what scent was it she gave off? – there were always two or three of them at least, hanging round her like tomcats on heat. And how she mocked them, on those precious evenings when she and Hester were alone together, sitting companionably by the fireside like an old married couple. She mocked their clumsy fumblings, their corny dialogue, their absurd self-importance. The only man she didn't mock, now Hester came to think of it, was the curious Mr Jericho, whom she had never even mentioned.

'*ADU, Miss Wallace . . .*'.

Now that she had made up her mind to do it – and hadn't she always *known*, secretly, that she was going to do it? – she was astonished at how calm she felt. It would only be the briefest of glances, she told herself, and where was the harm in that? She even had the perfect excuse to slip across to the Index, for hadn't the beastly Miles, in everybody's hearing, commanded her to ensure the volumes were all arranged in proper order?

She finished the blist and slotted it into the rack. She forced herself to wait a decent interval, pretending to check the others' work, and then moved as casually as she could towards the Index Room.

2

Jericho drew back the curtains to unveil another cold, clear morning. It was only his third day in the Commercial Guesthouse but already the view had acquired a weary familiarity. First came the long and narrow garden (concrete yard with washing line, vegetable patch, bomb shelter) which petered out after seventy yards into a wilderness of weeds and a tumbledown, rotted fence. Then there was a drop he couldn't see, like a ha-ha, and then a broad expanse of railway lines, a dozen or more, which led the eye, at last, to the centrepiece: a huge Victorian engine shed with LONDON MIDLAND & SCOTTISH RAILWAY in white letters just visible beneath the grime.

What a day in prospect: the sort of day one waded through with no aim higher than to reach the other end intact. He looked at his Waralarm. It was a quarter past seven. It would be dark in the North Atlantic for at least another four hours. By his reckoning there would be nothing for him to do until – at the earliest – midnight, British time, when the first elements of the convoy would begin to enter the U-boat danger zone. Nothing to do except sit around the hut and wait and brood.

There had been three occasions during the night when Jericho had made up his mind to seek out Wigram and make a full confession, on the last of which he had actually got as far as putting on his coat. But in the end the judgement was too fine a one to call. On the one hand, yes, it was his duty to tell Wigram all he knew. On the other, no, what he knew would make little practical difference to the task of finding her, so why betray her? The equations cancelled one another out. By dawn he had surrendered, gratefully, to the old inertia, the product of always seeing both sides of every question.

And it could all still be some ghastly mistake – couldn't it, just? Some prank gone badly wrong? Eleven hours had passed since his conversation with Wigram. They might have found her by now. More likely, she would have turned up, either at the cottage or the hut – wide-eyed and wondering, darlings, what on earth the fuss was all about.

He was on the point of turning away from the

window when his eye was caught by a movement at the
far end of the engine shed. Was it a large animal of
some sort, or a big man crawling on all fours? He
squinted through the sooty glass but the thing was too
far away for him to make it out exactly, so he fetched
his telescope from the bottom of the wardrobe. The
window sash was stuck but a few heavy blows from the
heel of his hand were enough to raise it six inches. He
knelt and rested the telescope on the sill. At first he
couldn't find anything to focus on amid the dizzying
crisscross of tracks but then, suddenly, it was filling his
eye – an Alsatian dog as big as a calf, sniffing under the
wheels of a goods wagon. He shifted the telescope a
fraction to his left and there was a policeman dressed in
a greatcoat that came down below his knees. Two
policemen, in fact, and a second dog, on a leash.

He watched the little group for several minutes as
they searched the empty train. Then the two teams
split up, one passing further up the tracks and the other
moving out of sight towards the little railway cottages
opposite. He snapped the telescope shut.

Four men and two dogs for the railway yard. Say, a
couple more teams to cover the station platforms. How
many in the town? Twenty? And in the surrounding
countryside?

'*Got a photo of her? Something recent?*'

He tapped the telescope against his cheek.

They must be watching every port and railway
station in the country.

What would they do if they caught her?

Hang her?

Come on, Jericho. He could practically hear his housemaster's voice at his elbow. *Brace up, boy.*

Get through it somehow.

Wash. Shave. Dress. Make a little bundle of dirty laundry and leave it on the bed for Mrs Armstrong, more in hope than expectation. Go downstairs. Endure attempts to make polite conversation. Listen to one of Bonnyman's interminable, off-colour stories. Be introduced to two of the other guests: Miss Quince, rather pretty, a teleprincess in the naval hut, and Noakes, once an expert on Middle High German court epics, now a cryptanalyst in the weather section, vaguely known since 1940: a surly creature, then and now. Avoid all further conversation. Chew toast as stale as cardboard. Drink tea as grey and watery as a February sky. Half-listen to the wireless news: 'Moscow Radio reports the Russian Third Army under General Vatutin is making a strong defence of Kharkov in the face of the renewed German offensive . . .'

At ten to eight Mrs Armstrong came in with the morning post. Nothing for Mr Bonnyman ('thank God for that,' said Bonnyman), two letters for Miss Jobey, a postcard for Miss Quince, a bill from Heffers bookshop for Mr Noakes and nothing at all for Mr Jericho – oh, except this, which she'd found when she came down and which must have been put through the door some time in the night.

He held it carefully. The envelope was poor-quality, official-issue stuff, his name printed on it in blue ink, with 'By hand, Strictly Personal' added underneath and double-underlined. The 'e' in Jericho and in

'Personal' was in the Greek form. His nocturnal correspondent was a classicist, perhaps?

He took it into the hall to open, Mrs Armstrong at his heels.

Hut 6
4.45 A.M.

Dear Mr Jericho,

As you expressed such a strong interest in medieval alabaster figurework when we met yesterday, I wondered if you might care to join me at the same place at 8 this morning to view the altar tomb of Lord Grey de Wilton (15th cent. and really *very fine*)?

Sincerely,

H.A.W.

'Bad news, Mr Jericho?' She couldn't quite suppress the note of hope in her voice.

But Jericho was already dragging on his overcoat and was halfway out of the door.

Even after taking the hill at a fast trot he was still five minutes late by the time he passed the granite war memorial. There was no sign of her or anyone else in the graveyard so he tried the door to the church. At first he thought it was locked. It took both hands to turn the rusty iron ring. He put his shoulder to the weathered oak and it shuddered inwards.

The church inside was cave-like, cold and dark, the shadows pierced by shafts of dusty, slate-blue light, so solid they seemed to have been propped like slabs against the windows. He hadn't been in a church for years and the chilly stink of candle wax and damp and incense brought memories of childhood crawling back. He thought he could make out the shape of a head in one of the pews nearest the altar and began to walk towards it.

'Miss Wallace?' His voice was hollow and seemed to travel a great distance. But when he came closer he saw it wasn't a head, just a priest's vestment, draped neatly over the back of the pew. He passed on up the nave to the wood-panelled altar. To the left was a stone coffin with an inscription; next to it, the smooth, white effigy of Richard, Lord Grey de Wilton, dead these past five hundred years, reclining in full armour, his head resting on his helmet, his feet on the back of a lion.

'The armour is especially interesting. But then warfare in the fifteenth century was the highest occupation for a gentleman.'

He wasn't sure where she'd come from. She was simply there when he turned round, about ten feet behind him.

'And the face, I think, is also good, if unexceptional. You weren't followed, I trust?'

'No. I don't think so, no.'

She took a few steps towards him. With her dead complexion and tapering white fingers she might have been an alabaster effigy herself, climbed down from Lord Grey's tomb.

'Perhaps you noticed the royal arms above the north door?'

'How long have you been here?'

'The arms of Queen Anne, but, intriguingly, still of the Stuart pattern. The arms of Scotland were only added as late as 1707. Now that *is* rare. About ten minutes. The police were just leaving as I arrived.' She held out her hand. 'May I have my note back, please?'

When he hesitated she presented her palm to him again, more emphatically this time.

'The *note*, please, if you'd be so good. I'd prefer to leave no trace. Thank you.' She took it and stowed it away at the bottom of her voluminous carpet bag. Her hands were shaking so much she had trouble fastening the clasp. 'There's no need to whisper, by the way. We're quite alone. Apart from God. And He's supposed to be on our side.'

He knew it would be wise for him to wait, to let her come to it in her own time, but he couldn't help himself.

'You've checked it?' he said. 'The call sign?'

She finally snapped the bag shut. 'Yes. I've checked it.'

'And is it Army or Luftwaffe?'

She held up a finger. 'Patience, Mr Jericho. Patience. First there's some information I'd like from you, if you don't mind. We might begin with what made you choose those three letters.'

'You don't want to know, Miss Wallace. Believe me.'

She raised her eyes to heaven. 'God preserve me: another one.'

'I'm sorry?'

'I seem to move in an endless round, Mr Jericho, from one patronising male to another, for ever being

262

told what I am and am not allowed to know. Well, that
ends here.' She pointed to the flagstone floor.

'Miss Wallace,' said Jericho, catching the same tone
of cool formality, 'I came in answer to your note. I have
no interest in alabaster figurework – medieval,
Victorian or ancient Chinese, come to that. If you've
nothing else to tell me, good morning to you.'

'Then good morning.'

'Good morning.'

If he'd had a hat he would have raised it.

He turned and began his progress down the aisle
towards the door. You fool, said a voice at his inner ear,
you bloody conceited fool. By the time he'd gone half
way his pace had slowed and by the time he reached the
font he stopped. His shoulders sagged.

'Checkmate, I believe, Mr Jericho,' she called
cheerfully from beside the altar.

'ADU was the call sign on a series of four intercepts our
. . . mutual friend . . . stole from Hut 3.' His voice was
weary.

'How do you know she stole them?'

'They were hidden in her bedroom. Under the floorboards. As far as I know, we're not encouraged to take
our work home.'

'Where are they now?'

'I burned them.'

They were sitting in the second row of pews, side by
side, facing straight ahead. Anyone coming into the
church would have thought it was a confession – she
playing the priest and he the sinner.

'Do you think she's a spy?'

'I don't know. Her behaviour is suspicious, to put it charitably. Others seem to think she is.'

'Who?'

'A man from the Foreign Office called Wigram, for one.'

'Why?'

'Obviously because she's disappeared.'

'Oh, come. There must be more to it than that. All this fuss for one missed shift?'

He ran his hand nervously through his hair.

'There are . . . indications – and don't, for God's sake, ask me to tell you what they are – just indications, all right, that the Germans may suspect Enigma is being broken.'

A long pause.

'But why would our mutual friend wish to help the *Germans?*'

'If I knew that, Miss Wallace, I wouldn't be sitting here with you, passing the time of day breaking the Official Secrets Act. Now, really, please, have you heard enough?'

Another pause. A reluctant nod of the head.

'Enough.'

She told it like story, in a low voice, without looking at him. She used her hands a lot, he noticed. She couldn't keep them still. They fluttered like tiny white birds – now pecking at the hem of her coat, pulling it demurely across her knees, now perching on the back of the pew in front, now describing, in rapid, circling motions, how she had gone about her crime.

She waits until the other girls have gone off on their meal break.

She leaves the door to the Index Room open a fraction, so as not to look suspicious and to ensure a good warning of anyone's approach.

She reaches up to the dusty metal shelf and drags down the first volume.

AAA, AAB, AAC . . .

She flicks through to the tenth page.

And there it is. The thirteenth entry.

ADU.

She runs her finger along the line to the row and column entries and notes their numbers on a scrap of paper.

She puts the index volume back. The row ledger is on a higher shelf and she has to fetch a stool to get it.

She stops off on her way to bob her head around the door and check the corridor.

Deserted.

Now she is nervous. Why? she asks herself. What is she doing that's so terribly wrong? She smooths her hands down over her grey skirt to dry her palms, then opens the book. She turns the pages. She finds the number. Again, she follows the line across.

She checks it once, and then a second time. There's no mistake.

ADU is the call sign of *Nachrichten-Regimenter* 537 – a motorised German Army signals unit. Its transmissions are on wavelengths monitored by the

Beaumanor intercept station in Leicestershire. Direction-finding has established that, since October, Unit number 537 has been based in the Smolensk military district of the Ukraine, presently occupied by Wehrmacht Army Group Centre under the command of Field Marshal Gunther von Kluge.

Jericho had been leaning forwards in anticipation. Now he drew back in surprise. 'A signals unit?'

He felt obscurely disappointed. What exactly had he been expecting? He wasn't sure. Just something a little more . . . *exotic*, he supposed.

'537,' he said, 'is that a front-line unit?'

'The line in that sector is shifting every day. But according to the situation map in Hut 6, Smolensk is still about a hundred kilometres inside German territory.'

'Ah.'

'Yes. That was my reaction – at first, anyway. I mean, this is a standard, rear-echelon, low-priority target. This is workaday in the extreme. But there are several . . . complications.' She fished in her bag for a handkerchief and blew her nose. Again, Jericho observed the slight trembling of her fingers.

After replacing the row volume it is the work of less than a minute to pull down the appropriate column book and make a note of the intercept serial numbers.

When she comes out of the Index Room, Miles ('that's Miles Mermagen,' she adds in parenthesis, 'Control Room duty officer: a bear of *very* little brain')

Miles is on the telephone, his back to the door, oiling up to someone in authority – 'No, no, that's absolutely fine, Donald, a pleasure to be of service . . .' – which suits Hester beautifully for it means he never even notices her collect her coat and leave. She clicks on her blackout torch and steps out into the night.

A gust of wind swirls down the alley between the huts and buffets her face. At the far end of Hut 8 the path forks: right will take her to the main gate and the warm bustle of the canteen, left leads into the blackness along the edge of the lake.

She turns left.

The moon is wrapped in a tissue of cloud but the pale light is just luminous enough to show her the way. Beyond the eastern perimeter fence lies a small wood which she can't see, but the sound of the wind moving through the invisible trees seems to pull her on. Past A- and B-Blocks, two hundred and fifty yards, and there it is, straight ahead, faintly outlined: the big, squat, bunkerlike building, only just completed, that now houses Bletchley's central Registry. As she comes closer her torch flashes on steel-shuttered windows, then finds the heavy door.

Thou shalt not steal, she tells herself, reaching for the handle.

No, no. Of course not.

Thou shalt not steal, thou wilt merely take a quick look, and then depart.

And, in any case, don't 'the secret things belong unto the Lord our God' (Deuteronomy 29.xxix)?

The rawness of the white neon is a shock after the

gloom of the hut, and so is the calm, ruffled only by the
distant clatter of the Hollerith punch-card machines.
The workmen still haven't finished. Brushes and tools
are stacked to one side of a reception area that is thick
with the smell of building work – fresh concrete, wet
paint, wood-shavings. The duty clerk, a corporal in the
Women's Auxiliary Air Force, leans across the counter
in a friendly way as if she is serving in a shop.

'Cold night?'

'Rather.' Hester manages to smile and nod. 'I've got
some serials to check.'

'Reference or loan?'

'Reference.'

'Section?'

'Hut 6 Control.'

'Pass?'

The woman takes the list of numbers and disappears
into a back room. Through the open door Hester can
see stacks of metal shelving, infinite rows of cardboard
files. A man strolls past the doorway and takes down
one of the boxes. He stares at her. She looks away. On
the whitewashed wall is a poster, a Bateman cartoon
showing a woman sneezing, accompanied by some
typical, fatuous Whitehall busybodying:

THE MINISTRY OF HEALTH says:-
Coughs and sneezes spread diseases
Trap the germs by using your handkerchief
Help to keep the Nation Fighting Fit

There is nowhere to sit. Behind the counter is a large

clock with 'RAF' stamped on its face – so large, in fact, that Hester can actually see the big hand moving. Four minutes pass. Five minutes. The Registry is unpleasantly hot. She can feel herself starting to sweat. The stench of paint is nauseating. Seven minutes. Eight minutes. She would like to flee, but the corporal has taken her identity card. Dear God, how could she have been so utterly stupid? What if the clerk is now on the phone to Hut 6, checking up on her? At any instant, Miles will come crashing into the Registry: 'What the hell d'you think you're doing, woman?' Nine minutes. Ten minutes. Try to focus on something else. Coughs and sneezes spread diseases . . .

She's in such a state, she actually fails to hear the clerk come up behind her.

'I'm sorry to have been so long, but I've never come across anything like this . . .'

The girl, poor thing, is rather shaken.

'Why?' asked Jericho.

'The file,' said Hester. 'The file I'd asked her for? It was empty.'

There was a loud metallic crack behind them and then a series of short scrapes as the church door was pushed open. Hester closed her eyes and dropped to her knees on one of the cassocks, tugging Jericho down beside her. She clasped her hands and lowered her head and he did the same. Footsteps came halfway up the aisle behind them, stopped, and then resumed slowly on tiptoe. Jericho glanced surreptitiously to his left in time to see the elderly priest bending to retrieve his vestment.

269

'Sorry to interrupt your prayers,' whispered the vicar. He gave Hester a little wave and a nod. 'Hello there. So sorry. I'll leave you to God.'

They listened to his fussy tread fading towards the back of the church. The door was tugged shut. The latch fell with a crash. Jericho sat back on the pew and laid his hand over his heart and swore he could feel it beating through four layers of clothing. He looked at Hester – 'I'll leave you to *God?*' he repeated – and she smiled. The change it wrought in her was remarkable. Her eyes shone, the hardness in her face softened – and for the first time he briefly glimpsed the reason why she and Claire might have been friends.

Jericho contemplated the stained-glass window above the altar and made a steeple of his fingers. 'So what exactly are we to make of this? That Claire must have stolen the entire contents of the file? No –' he contradicted himself immediately ' – no, that can't be right, can it, because what she had in her room were the original cryptograms, not the decodes . . .?'

'Precisely,' said Hester. 'There was a typewritten slip in the Registry file which the clerk showed me – words to the effect that the enclosed serial numbers had been reclassified and withdrawn, and that all enquires should be addressed to the office of the Director-General.'

'The *Director-General?* Are you sure?'

'I *can* read, Mr Jericho.'

'What was the date on the slip?'

'March the 4th.'

270

Jericho massaged his forehead. It was the oddest thing he'd ever heard. 'What happened after the Registry?'

'I went back to the hut and wrote my note to you. Delivering that took the rest of my meal break. Then it was a matter of getting back into the Index Room whenever I could. We deep a daily log of all intercepts, made up from the blists. One file for each day.' Once again she rummaged in her bag and withdrew a small index-card with a list of dates and numbers. 'I wasn't sure where to start so I simply went right back to the beginning of the year and worked my way through. Nothing recorded till February the 6th. Only eleven interceptions altogether, four of which came on the final day.'

'Which was what?'

'March the 4th. The same day the file was removed from the Registry. What do you make of that?'

'Nothing. Everything. I'm still trying to imagine what a rear-echelon German signals unit could possibly say that would warrant the removal of its entire file.'

'The Director-General is who, as a matter of interest?'

'The chief of the Secret Intelligence Service. "C". I don't know his real name.' He remembered the man who had presented him with the cheque just before Christmas. A florid face and hairy country tweeds. He had looked more like a farmer than a spy master. 'Your notes,' he said, holding out his hand. 'May I?'

Reluctantly she handed him the list of interceptions. He held it towards the pale light. It certainly made a

271

bizarre pattern. Following the initial interception, just after noon on 6 February, there had been two days of silence. Then there had been another signal at 1427 hours on the 9th. Then a gap of ten days. Then a broadcast at 1807 on the 20th, and another long gap, followed by a flurry of activity: two signals on 2 March (1639 and 1901), two on the 3rd (1118 and 1727), and finally four signals, in rapid succession, on the night of the 4th. These were the cryptograms he had taken from Claire's room. The broadcasts had begun just two days before his final conversation with Claire at the flooded clay pit. And they had ended a month later, while he was still at Cambridge, less than a week before the Shark blackout.

There was no shape to it at all.

He said: 'What Enigma key were they transmitted in? They *were* enciphered in Enigma, I take it?'

'In the Index they were catalogued as Vulture.'

'Vulture?'

'The standard Wehrmacht Enigma key for the Russian front.'

'Broken regularly?'

'Every day. As far as I know.'

'And the signals – how were they sent? They were, what, just carried on the usual military net?'

'I don't know, but I'd say almost certainly not.'

'Why?'

'There's not enough traffic, for a start. It's too irregular. And the frequency's not one I recognise. It feels to me like something rather more special – a private line, as it were. Just the two stations: a mother

272

and a lone star. But we'd need to see the log sheets to be certain.'

'And where are they?'

'They should have been in the Registry. But when we checked we found they'd all been removed as well.'

'My, my,' murmured Jericho, 'they really have been thorough.'

'Short of tearing the sheets out of the Control Room Index, they couldn't have done much more. And *you* think *she's* behaving suspiciously? I'll have that back now, if I may.'

She took the record of the interceptions and bent forwards to hide it in her bag.

Jericho rested his head on the back of the pew and stared up at the vaulted ceiling. Special? he though. I'll say it was special, more than special for the Director-General himself to palm the entire bloody file, plus all the log sheets. There was no sense to it. He wished he weren't so damned tired. He needed to shut his study door for a day or two, sport his oak, find a good, fresh pile of clean notepaper and a set of sharpened pencils . . .

He slowly let his gaze descend to take in the rest of the church – the saints in their windows, the marble angels, the stone memorials to the respectable dead of Bletchley parish, the ropes from the belfry looped together like a hanging spider beneath the gloomy organ loft. He closed his eyes.

Claire, Claire, what have you done? Did you see something you weren't supposed to in that 'deadly dull' job of yours? Did you rescue a few scraps from the confidential waste when nobody was looking and spirit them home? And if you did that, why? And do they know you did it? Is that why Wigram's after you? Have you learned too much?

He saw her on her knees in the darkness at the foot of his bed, heard his own voice slurred with sleep – *'What on earth are you doing?'* – and her ingenuous reply: *'I'm just going through your things . . .'*

You were always looking for something, weren't you? And when I couldn't provide it, you just went on to someone else. (*'There's always someone else,'* you said: almost the last words you ever spoke to me, remember?) What is it, then, this thing you want so badly?

So many questions. He realised he was beginning to freeze. He huddled down into his coat, burying his chin in his scarf, thrusting his hands deep into his pockets. He tried to recall the images of the four cryptograms – LCNNR KDEMS LWAZA – but the letters were blurred. He had found this before. It was impossible mentally to photograph pages of gibberish: there had to be some meaning to them, some structure, to fix them in his mind.

'A mother and a lone star . . .'

The thick walls held a silence that seemed as old as the church itself – an oppressive silence, interrupted only occasionally by the rustling of a bird nesting in the rafters. For several minutes neither of them spoke.

Sitting on the hard bench, Jericho felt as though his bones had turned to ice, and this numbness, combined with the silence and the reliquaries everywhere and the sickly smell of incense, made him morbid. His father's funeral came to him for the second time in two days – the gaunt face in the coffin, his mother forcing him to kiss it goodbye, the cold skin beneath his lips giving off a sour reek of chemicals, like the school lab, and then the even worse stench at the crematorium.

'I need some air,' he said.

She gathered her bag and followed him down the aisle. Outside they pretended to study the tombs. To the north of the churchyard, screened by trees, was Bletchley Park. A motorcycle passed noisily down the lane towards the town. Jericho waited until the crack of its engine had dwindled to a drone in the distance and then said, almost to himself: 'The question I keep asking myself is why did she steal *cryptograms*? I mean, given what else she could have taken. If one was a spy –' Hester opened her mouth to protest and he held up his hand. 'All right, I'm not saying that she is, but if one was, surely one would want to steal proof that Enigma was being broken? What earthly use is an intercept?' He lowered himself to his haunches and ran his fingers over an inscription that had almost crumbled away. 'If only we knew more about them . . . To whom they were sent, for instance.'

'We've been over this. They've removed every trace.'

'But someone must know something,' he mused. 'For a start, someone must have broken the traffic. And someone else must have translated it.'

'Why don't you ask one of your cryptanalyst friends? You're all terrifically good chaps together, aren't you?'

'Not especially. In any case I'm afraid we're encouraged to lead quite separate lives. There *is* a man in Hut 3 who might have seen them . . .' But then he remembered Weitzman's frightened face (*'please don't ask me, I don't want to know . . .'*) and he shook his head. 'No. He wouldn't help.'

'Then what a pity it is,' she said, with some asperity, 'that you burned our only clues.'

'Keeping them was too much of a risk.' He was still rubbing slowly at the stone. 'For all I knew, you might have told Wigram I'd asked you about the call sign.' He looked up at her uneasily. 'You didn't, I take it?'

'Credit me with some sense, Mr Jericho. Would I be here talking to you now?' She stamped off down the row of graves and began furiously studying an epitaph.

She regretted her sharpness almost at once. ('He that is slow to anger is better than the mighty; and he that ruleth his spirit than he that taketh a city.' Proverbs 16.xxxii.) But then, as Jericho pointed out later, when relations between them had improved sufficiently for him to risk the observation, if she hadn't lost her temper, she might never have thought of the solution.

'Sometimes,' he said, 'we need a little tension to sharpen our wits.'

She was jealous, that was the truth of it. She had thought she knew Claire as well as anyone but it was fast becoming apparent that she knew her hardly at all, scarcely better even than he did.

She shivered. There was no warmth in this March

sun. It fell on the stone tower of St Mary's as cold as light from a looking glass.

Jericho was back on his feet now, moving between the graves. She wondered whether she might have been like him if she'd been allowed to go to university. But her father wouldn't stand for it and her brother George had gone instead, as if it were God's law: men go to university, men break codes; women stay at home, women do the filing.

'*Hester, Hester, just in time. Will you talk to Chicksands, there's a good girl, and see what they can do? And while you're on, the Machine Room reckon they've got a corrupt text on the last batch of Kestrel — the operator needs to check her notes and re-send. Then the eleven o'clocks from Beaumanor . . .*'

She had been standing slack with defeat, gazing at a tombstone, but now she felt her body slowly coming to attention.

'*The operator needs to check her notes . . .*'

'Mr Jericho!'

He turned at the sound of his name to see her stumbling through the graves towards him.

It was almost ten o'clock and Miles Mermagen was combing his hair in his office, preparatory to returning to his digs, when Hester Wallace appeared at his office door.

'No,' he said, with his back to her.

'Miles, listen, I've been thinking, you were right, I've been an utter fool.'

He squinted suspiciously at her in the mirror.

'My application for a transfer – I want you to withdraw it.'

'Fine. I never submitted it.'

He returned his attention to himself. The comb slid through the thick black hair like a rake through oil.

She forced a smile. 'I was thinking about what you said, about needing to know where one fits into the chain . . .' He finished his grooming and turned his profile to the mirror, trying to look at his reflection sideways on. 'If you remember, we talked about my possibly going to an intercept station.'

'No problem.'

'I thought, well, I'm not due on shift till tomorrow afternoon – I thought I might go today.'

'Today?' He looked at his watch. 'Actually, I'm tied up, rather.'

'I *could* go on my own, Miles. And report my finding –' behind her back she dug her nails into her palm '– one evening.'

He gave her another narrowed look and she thought, No, no, really this is too obvious, even for him, but then he shrugged. 'Why not? Better call them first.' He waved his hand grandly. 'Invoke my name.'

'Thank you, Miles.'

'Lot's wife, what?' He winked. 'Pillar of salt by day, ball of fire by night . . .?'

On the way out he patted her bottom.

Thirty yards away, in Hut 8, Jericho was knocking on the door marked US NAVY LIAISON. A loud voice told him to 'come on in'.

Kramer didn't have a desk – the room wasn't big enough – just a card table with a telephone on it and wire baskets filled with papers stacked on the floor. There wasn't even a window. On one of the wooden partitions separating him from the rest of the hut he'd taped a recent photograph, torn out of *Life* magazine, showing Roosevelt and Churchill at the Casablanca conference, sitting side by side in a sunny garden. He noticed Jericho staring at it.

'When you fellers get me really down I look at it and think – well, hell, if they can do it, so can I.' He grinned. 'Got something to show you.' He opened his attaché case and pulled out a wad of papers marked MOST SECRET: ULTRA. 'Skynner finally got the order to give them me this morning. I'm supposed to get them off to Washington tonight.'

Jericho flicked through them. A mass of calculations that were half familiar, and some complex technical drawings of what looked like electronic circuitry.

Kramer said: 'The plans for the prototype four-wheel bombes.'

Jericho looked up in surprise. 'They're using valves?'

'Sure are. Gas-filled triode valves. GTIC thyatrons.'

'Good God.'

'They're calling it Cobra. The first three wheel-settings will be solved in the usual way on the existing bombes – that is, electro-mechanically. But the fourth – the *fourth* – will be solved purely electronically, using a relay rack and valves, linked to the bombe by this fat cable form, that looks like a –' Kramer cupped his hands into a circle '– well, that looks like a cobra, I

279

guess. Using valves in sequence – that's a revolution. Never been done before. Your people say it should make the calculations a hundred times, maybe a thousand times, as fast.'

Jericho said, almost to himself: 'A Turing machine.'

'A what?'

'An electronic computer.'

'Well, whatever you want to call it. It works in theory, that's the good news. And from what they're saying, this may be just the start. It seems they're planning some kind of super-bombe, all electronic, called Colossus.'

Jericho had a sudden vision of Alan Turing, one winter afternoon, sitting cross-legged in his Cambridge study while the lamps came on outside, describing his dream of a universal calculating machine. How long ago had that been? Less than five years?

'And when will this happen?'

'That's the bad news. Even Cobra won't be operational till June.'

'But that's appalling.'

'Same old goddamn story. No components, no workshops, not enough technicians. Guess how many men are working on this thing right now, as we speak.'

'Not enough, I expect.'

Kramer held up one hand and spread his fingers close to Jericho's face. 'Five. *Five!*' He stuffed the papers back into his case and snapped the lock. 'Something's got to be done about this.' He was muttering and shaking his head. 'Got to get something moving.'

'You're going to London?'

'Right now. Embassy first. Then on across Grosvenor Square to see the admiral.'

Jericho winced with disappointment. 'I suppose you're taking your car?'

'Are you kidding. With this?' He patted the case. 'Skynner's making me go with an escort. Why?'

'I was just wondering – I know this is an awful cheek, but you said if I had a favour to ask – I was wondering if I might possibly borrow it?'

'Sure.' Kramer pulled on his overcoat. 'I'll probably be gone a couple of days. I'll show you where she's parked.' He collected his cap from the back of the door and they went out into the corridor.

By the entrance to the hut they ran into Wigram. Jericho was surprised at how unkempt he looked. He had obviously been up all night. A dusting of reddish-blond stubble glinted in the sunlight.

'Ah, the gallant lieutenant and the great cryptanalyst. I heard you two were friends.' He bowed with mock formality and said to Jericho: 'I'll need to talk to you again later, old chap.'

'Now there's a guy who gives me the creeps,' said Kramer, as they walked up the path towards the mansion. 'Had him in my room for about twenty minutes this morning, asking me questions about some girl I know.'

Jericho almost trod on his own feet.

'You know Claire Romilly?'

'There she is,' said Kramer, and for an instant Jericho thought he meant Claire but actually he was

pointing to his car. 'She's still warm. The tank's full
and there's a can in the back.' He fished in his pocket
for the key and threw it to Jericho. 'Sure I know Claire.
Doesn't everybody? Hell of a girl.' He patted Jericho
on the arm. 'Have a nice trip.'

3

It was another half-hour before Jericho was able to get
away.

He climbed the concrete steps to the Operations
Room where he found Cave sitting alone at the end of
the long table, telephones on either side of him, staring
up at the Atlantic Plot. Eleven Shark signals had been
intercepted since midnight, he said, none of them from
the anticipated battle zone, which was bad news.
Convoy HX-229 was within 150 miles of the suspected
U-boat lines, steaming directly due east, full tilt
towards them, at a speed of 10.5 knots. SC-122 was
slightly ahead of her, to the north east. HX-229A was
well back, heading north up the coast of Newfoundland. 'Nearly light,' he said, 'but the weather's getting
worse, poor sods.'

Jericho left him to it and went in search, first, of
Logie, who dismissed him with a wave of his pipe
('Fine, old love, you rest up, curtain rises twenty
hundred'), and then of Atwood, who eventually agreed
to lend him his pre-war AA touring atlas of the British
Isles. ("'Roll up that map,'" he quoted wistfully, as he

produced it from beneath his desk, "'it will not be wanted these ten years.'")

After that he was ready.

He sat in the front seat of Kramer's car and ran his hands over the unfamiliar controls and it occurred to him that he'd never quite got round to learning how to drive. He knew the basic principles, of course, but it must have been six or seven years since his last attempt, and that had been in his stepfather's huge and tanklike Humber – a vastly different proposition to this little Austin. Still, at least he wasn't doing anything illegal: in a country where one nowadays practically needed a permit to visit the lavatory, it was for some reason no longer necessary to have a driving licence.

He took several minutes trying to sort out clutch pedal from accelerator, handbrake from gear lever, then pulled out the choke and switched on the ignition. The car rocked and stalled. He put the gears into neutral and tried again and this time, miraculously, as his left foot lifted off the clutch, the car crawled forwards.

At the main gate he was waved down and managed to bring the car gliding to a halt. One of the sentries opened his door and he had to climb out while another got in to search the interior.

Half a minute later the barrier was rising and he was through.

He drove at a cyclist's pace along the narrow lanes towards Shenley Brook End, and it was this low speed that saved him. The plan he had agreed with Hester Wallace – assuming he could get Kramer's car – was that he would pick her up from the cottage, and he was just rounding the bend a quarter of a mile before the turning when something flashed dark in the field up ahead on the right. Immediately, he swerved up on to the verge and braked. He left the engine running then cautiously opened the door and clambered out on the running board to get a better view.

Policemen again. One moving stealthily around the edge of the field. Another half hidden in the hedge, apparently watching the road outside the cottage.

Jericho dropped back into the driver's seat and tapped his fingers on the steering wheel. He wasn't sure whether he had been seen but the sooner he got out of their range of vision the better. The gear change was stiff and it took both hands to jam the lever into reverse. The engine clanked and whined. First he nearly backed into the ditch, then he overcorrected and the car went weaving drunkenly across the road, mounted the opposite bank and stalled. It was not an elegant piece of parking but at least he was sufficiently far back around the curve for the policemen to be out of sight.

They had to have heard him, surely? At any moment one of them would come strolling down the lane to investigate, and he tried to think up some excuse for his lunatic behaviour, but the minutes passed and nobody appeared. He switched off the ignition and the only sound was birdsong.

No wonder Wigram looked so tired, he thought. He appeared to have taken over command of half the police force of the county – probably of the country, for all Jericho knew.

Suddenly, the scale of the odds stacked against them struck him as so overwhelming, he was seriously tempted to jack in the whole damn fool project. (*'We must go to the intercept station, Mr Jericho – go to Beaumanor and get hold of the operator's handwritten notes. They keep them for at least a month and they'll never have dreamed of removing those – I'll take a wager on it. Only we poor drones have anything to do with them.'*) Indeed, he might well have turned the car round that very minute and driven back to Bletchley if there hadn't been a loud tapping noise at the window to his left. He must have jumped a full inch in his seat.

It was Hester Wallace, although at first he didn't recognise her. She had exchanged her skirt and blouse for a heavy tweed jacket and a thick sweater. A pair of brown corduroy trousers were tucked into the tops of grey woollen socks, and her stout boots were so clogged with mud they seemed the size of a carthorse's hooves. She hefted her bulging carpetbag into the back of the Austin and sank down low in the passenger seat. She gave a long sigh of relief.

'Thank God. I thought I'd missed you.'

He leaned over and closed the door very quietly.

'How many are there?'

'Six. Two in the fields opposite. Two going from house to house in the village. Two in the cottage – one upstairs, dusting Claire's bedroom for fingerprints, and a policewoman downstairs. I told her I was going out. She tried to stop me but I said it was my one day off this week and I'd do as I pleased. I left by the back door and worked my way round to the road.'

285

'Did anybody see you?'

'I don't think so.' She blew warmth on her hands and rubbed them. 'I suggest we drive, Mr Jericho. And don't go back into Bletchley, whatever you do. I overheard them talking. They're stopping all cars on the main road out of town.'

She slid further down the seat so that she was invisible from outside the car unless someone came right up to the window. Jericho turned on the engine and the Austin rolled forwards. If they couldn't go back to Bletchley, he thought, then really he had no choice except to drive straight ahead.

They came round the curve and the road was clear. The turning to the cottage was on the left, deserted, but as they came level with it a policeman suddenly stepped out from the hedge opposite and held up his hand. Jericho hesitated and then pressed his foot down on the accelerator. The policeman stepped smartly out of the way and Jericho had a momentary impression of an outraged brick-red face. Then they were dropping down into the hollow and rising again and passing through the village. Another policeman was talking to a woman on the doorstep of her thatched cottage and he turned to stare at them. Jericho trod on the accelerator again and soon the village was behind them and the road was corkscrewing down into another leafy hollow. They rose into Shenley Church End, passed the White Hart Inn, where Jericho used to live, and then a church, and almost at once they had to stop at the junction of the A5.

Jericho glanced in his mirror to check there was no

one behind them. It seemed safe enough. He said to
Hester: 'You can get up now.' He was in a daze. He
couldn't believe what he was doing. He waited to let a
couple of lorries go by, indicated, and then swung left
on to the old Roman road. It ran straight and true
ahead of them, northwest, for as far as they could see.
Jericho changed up a gear, the Austin gathered speed,
and they were clear.

Wartime England opened up before them – still the
same but somehow subtly different: a little bit
smudged, a little bit knocked about, like a prosperous
estate going fast to ruin, or a genteel elderly lady fallen
on hard times.

They didn't encounter any bomb damage until they
reached the outskirts of Rugby, where what looked
from a distance to be a ruined abbey turned out to be
the roofless shell of a factory, but the depredations of
war were everywhere. Fences beside the road, after
three years without repairs, were sagging or collapsed.
The gates and railings had gone from the fine country
parks to be melted down for munitions. The houses
were shabby. Nothing had been painted since 1940.
Broken windows were boarded over, ironwork was
rusted or coated in tar. Even the inn signs were
blistered and faded. The country was degraded.

And we, too, thought Jericho, as they overtook yet
another stooped figure trudging beside the road, don't
we look slightly worse each year? In 1940 there had at
least been the galvanising energy unleashed by the
threat of invasion. And in 1941 there had been some

hope when Russia and then America had entered the war. But 1942 had dragged into 1943, the U-boats had wrought murder on the convoys, the shortages had worsened and, despite the victories in Africa and on the eastern front, the war had begun to look endless – an unbroken, unheroic vista of rationing and exhaustion. The villages seemed almost lifeless – the men away, the women drafted into factories – while in Stony Stratford and in Towcester the few people who were about had mostly formed into queues outside shops with empty windows.

Beside him, Hester Wallace was silent, monitoring their progress with obsessive interest on Atwood's atlas. Good, he thought. With all the signposts and place names taken down, they would have no idea where they were if they once got lost. He didn't dare drive too quickly. The Austin was unfamiliar and (he was discovering) idiosyncratic. From time to time the cheap wartime petrol caused it to emit a loud bang. It tended to drift towards the centre of the road, and the brakes weren't too hot, either. Besides, a private car was such a rarity, he feared some officious policeman would pull them over if they went too fast and demand to see their papers.

He drove on steadily for more than an hour until, just before a market town she declared was Hinckley, she told him to turn off right on to a narrower road.

They had left Bletchley under a clear sky but the further north they had gone, the darker it had become. Grey clouds heavy with snow or rain had rolled across the sun. The tarmac pushed across a bleak, flat landscape, with not a vehicle to be seen, and for a second time Jericho experienced the curious sense that history was going backwards, that not for a quarter of a century could the roads have been this empty.

Fifteen miles further on she made him turn right again and suddenly they were climbing into much more hilly country, thickly wooded, with startling outcrops of bare rock striped white by snow.

'What place is this?'

'Charnwood Forest. We're almost there. You'd better pull over in a minute. Here, look,' she said, pointing to a deserted picnic area set just off the road. 'Here will do. I shan't be long.'

She hauled her bag from the back seat and set off towards the trees. He watched her go. She looked like a farm boy in her jacket and trousers. What was it Claire had said? *'She's got a bit of a crush on me'?* More than a bit, he thought, much more than a bit, to risk so much. It struck him that she was almost the exact physical opposite of Claire, that where Claire was tall and blonde and voluptuous, Hester was short and dark and skinny. Rather like him, in fact. She was changing her clothes behind a tree which wasn't quite wide enough and he got a sudden glimpse of her thin white shoulder. He looked away. When he looked back she was emerging from the dark woodland in an olive-green dress. The first drop of rain plopped on to the windscreen just as she got back into the car.

'Drive on then, Mr Jericho.' She found their position on the atlas again and rested her finger on it.

His hand paused on the ignition key. 'Do you think,

Miss Wallace,' he said, hesitantly, 'in view of the circumstances, we might now risk first-name terms?'

She gave him a faint smile. 'Hester.'

'Tom.'

They shook hands.

They followed the road through the forest for about five miles and then the trees thinned and they were into high, open country. The rain and melted snow had turned the narrow lane into a mud track and for five minutes they were forced to crawl in second gear behind a pony and trap. At last the driver raised his whip in apology and turned off to the right, towards a tiny village with curls of smoke rising from half a dozen chimneys, and very soon afterwards Hester shouted: 'There!'

If they hadn't been travelling so slowly, they might have missed it: a pair of lodge gates, a private road with a red-and-white pole slung across it, a sentry box, a cryptic sign: WOYG, BEAUMANOR.

War Office 'Y' Group, Beaumanor, 'Y' being the code name for the wireless interception service.

'Here we go.'

Jericho had to admire her nerve. While he was still fumbling sweatily for his pass, she had leaned across him to proffer hers to the guard and had announced briskly that they were expected. The Army private checked her name off on a clipboard, went round to the back of the car to make a note of their registration number, returned to the window, gave Jericho's card a cursory glance, and nodded them in.

Beaumanor Hall was another of those huge, secluded country houses that had been commandeered by the military from their grateful, almost bankrupt owners, and that would never, Jericho guessed, return to private use. It was early Victorian, with an avenue of dripping elms to one side and a stable yard to the other, into which they were directed. They drove under a fine arch. Half a dozen giggling ATS girls, their coats held over their heads like tents to ward off the rain, ran out in front of them and disappeared into one of the buildings. The courtyard held a couple of small Morris commercial trucks and a row of BSA motorcycles. As Jericho parked, a uniformed man hurried over to them carrying a vast and battered umbrella.

'Heaviside,' he said, 'Major Heaviside, as in the eponymous layer. And you must be Miss Wallace and you must be . . .?'

'Tom Jericho.'

'Mr Jericho. Excellent. Splendid.' He shook their hands vigorously. 'This is a treat for us, I must say. A visit from head office to the country cousins. Commander sends a thousand sorrows and says d'you mind if I do the honours? He'll try and catch us later. 'Fraid you've missed lunch, but tea? Cup of tea? *Filthy* weather . . .'

Jericho had been braced for some suspicious questions, and had used the journey to rehearse some careful answers, but the major merely ushered them under his leaking umbrella and guided them into the house. He was young, tall and balding, with spectacles so smeared with debris it was a wonder he could see through them. He had sloping shoulders, like a bottle, and the collar of his tunic was blanched white with dandruff. He took them into a cold and musty drawing room and ordered tea.

By now he'd finished his potted history of the house ('designed by the same bloke who built Nelson's Column, so they tell me') and was well embarked on a detailed history of the wireless interception service ('started out in Chatham till the bombing got too bad . . .'). Hester was nodding politely. A woman Army private brought them tea as thick and brown as shoe polish and Jericho sipped it and glanced impatiently around the empty walls. There were holes in the plaster where the picture hooks had been pulled out, and grimy shadows traced the outlines of large frames, now removed. An ancestral seat without ancestors, a house without a soul. The windows looking out on to the garden were crossed with strips of sticky tape.

He pointedly took out his watch and opened it. Almost three o'clock. They would need to be moving soon.

Hester noticed he was fidgeting. 'Perhaps,' she said, leaping into a brief lull in the major's monologue, 'we might take a look around?'

Heaviside looked startled and clattered his teacup into his saucer. 'Oh, crumbs, sorry. Right. If you're fit, then, we'll make a start.'

The rain was mixed with snow now, and the wind was blowing it hard, in waves, from the north. It lashed their faces as they came around the side of the big house and as they picked their way through the mud of a flattened rose garden they had to raise their arms against it, like boxers warding off blows. There was an odd keening, howling noise, like nothing Jericho had ever heard before, coming from beyond a wall.

'What the devil's that?'

'The aerial farm,' said Heaviside.

Jericho had only visited an intercept station once before, and that had been years ago, when the science was still in its infancy: a shack full of shivering Wrens perched on top of the cliffs near Scarborough. This was of a different order. They went through a gate in the wall and there it was – dozens of radio masts laid out in odd patterns, like the stone circles of the Druids, across several acres of fields. The metal pylons were bound together by thousands of yards of cable. Some of the taut steel hummed in the wind, some screamed.

'Rhombic and Beveridge configurations,' shouted the major above the racket. 'Dipoles and quadra-hedrons . . . Look!' He tried to point and his umbrella was abruptly snapped inside out. He smiled hopelessly and waved it in the direction of the masts. 'We're about three hundred feet up here, hence this bloody wind. The farm's got two main harvests, can you see? One's pointing due south. That picks up France, the Med, Libya. The other's targeted east to Germany and the Russian front. The signals go by coaxial cables to the intercept huts.' He spread his arms wide and bellowed, 'Beautiful, isn't it? We can pick up everything for the best part of a thousand miles.' He laughed and waved his hands as if he were conducting an imaginary choir. 'Sing to me, you buggers.'

The wind slashed sleet in their faces and Jericho cupped his hands to his ears. It felt as though they were interfering with nature, tapping into some rushing elemental force they had no business dabbling in, like Frankenstein summoning down lightning into his laboratory. Another gust of wind knocked them backwards and Hester clutched at his arm for support.

'Let's get out of here,' yelled Heaviside. He gestured for them to follow him. Once they were on the other side of the wall they had some shelter from the wind. An asphalt road girdled what looked, at a distance, to be an estate village nestling in the grounds of the big house: cottages, farm sheds, a greenhouse, even a cricket pavilion with a clock tower. All dummy front-ages, explained Heaviside, cheerfully, designed to fool German air reconnaissance. This was where the work of interception was done. Was there anything they were especially interested in?

'How about the eastern front?' said Hester.

'Eastern front?' said Heaviside. 'Fine.'

He bounded ahead of them through the puddles, still trying to shake out his broken umbrella. The rain worsened and their fast walk turned into a run as they sprinted for the hut. The door banged shut behind them.

'We rely on the feminine element, as you can see,' said Heaviside, taking off his spectacles and drying them on the corner of his tunic. 'Army girls and civilian women.' He replaced his glasses and blinked around the hut. 'Good afternoon,' he said to a stout woman with sergeant's stripes. 'The supervisor,' he explained, then added in a whisper: 'Bit of a dragon.'

Enigma

Jericho counted twenty-four wireless receivers, arranged in pairs, on either side of a long aisle, each with a woman hunched over it wearing headphones. The room was quiet apart from the hum of the machines and the occasional rustle of intercept forms.

'We've three types of sets,' Heaviside went on quietly. 'HROs, Hallicrafter 28 Skyriders and American AR-88s. Each girl has her own frequencies to patrol, though we'll double back if things get busy.'

'How many people d'you have working here?' asked Hester.

'Couple of thousand.'

'And you intercept everything?'

'Absolutely. Unless you tell us not to.'

'Which we never do.'

'Right, right.' Heaviside's bald head was glistening with rainwater. He bent forwards and shook himself vigorously, like a dog. 'Except that time the other week, of course.'

Afterwards, what Jericho would remember most was how coolly she handled it. She didn't even blink. Instead she actually changed the subject and asked Heaviside how fast the girls had to be ('we insist on a speed of ninety Morse characters a minute, that's the absolute minimum') and then the three of them began to stroll down the central aisle.

'These are sets tuned to the eastern front,' said Heaviside, when they were about halfway down. He stopped and pointed to the elaborate pictures of vultures stuck on the side of several of the receivers.

295

'Vulture's not the only German Army key in Russia, of course. There's Kite and Kestrel, Smelt for the Ukraine –'

'Are the nets particularly active at the moment?' Jericho felt it was time he should say something.

'Very much so, since Stalingrad. Retreats and counterattacks all along the front. Alarms and excursions. You've got to hand it to these Reds, you know – they can't half fight.'

Hester said casually: 'It would have been a Vulture station you were told not to intercept?'

'That's right.'

'And this would have been around the 4th of March?'

'Bang on. About midnight. I remember because we'd just sent four long signals and were feeling fairly well chuffed when your chap Mermagen comes on the blower in a frightful panic and says: "No more of *that*, thanks very much, not now, not tomorrow, not for ever more."'

'Any reason?'

'No reason. Just stop. Thought he was going to have a heart attack. Oddest damned thing I ever heard.'

'Perhaps,' suggested Jericho, 'knowing you were busy, they wanted to knock out low-priority traffic?'

'Balls,' said Heaviside, 'pardon me, but really!' His professional pride was wounded. 'You can tell your Mr Mermagen from me that it was nothing we couldn't handle, was it, Kay?' He patted the shoulder of a strikingly pretty ATS operator, who took off her headphones and pushed back her chair. 'No, no, don't get up, didn't mean to interrupt. We were just discussing our mystery station.' He rolled his eyes. 'The one we're not supposed to hear.'

'Hear?' Jericho looked at Hester sharply. 'You mean it's still broadcasting?'

'Kay?'

'Yes, sir.' She had a rather melodious Welsh accent. 'Not so often now, sir, but he was awful busy last week.' She hesitated. 'I don't, like, try to listen, on purpose, sir, but he does have the most beautiful fist. Real old school. Not like some of the *kids –*' she spat out the word '– they're using nowadays. Nearly as bad as the Italians, they are.'

'A man's style of Morse,' said Heaviside pompously, 'is as distinctive as his signature.'

'And what is his style?'

'Very fast but very clear,' said Kay. 'Rippling, I'd say. Fist like a concert pianist, he has.'

'Think she rather fancies this chap, don't you, Mr Jericho?' Heaviside laughed and gave her shoulder another pat. 'All right, Kay. Good work. Back to it.'

They moved on. 'One of my best,' he confided. 'Can be pretty ghastly, you know, eight hours listening at a stretch, just taking down gibberish. Specially at night, in the winter. Bloody freezing out here. We have to issue 'em with blankets. Ah, now, here, look: here's one coming in.'

They stood at a discreet distance behind an operator who was frantically copying down a message. With her left hand she kept fractionally adjusting the dial on the wireless set, with her right she was fumbling together message forms and carbon paper. The speed with which she then started to take down the message was astonishing. 'GLPES,' read Jericho over her shoulder, 'KEMPG NXWPD . . .'

'Two forms,' said Heaviside. 'Log sheet, on which she records the whispers: that's tuning messages, Q-code and so forth. And then the red form which is the actual signal.'

'What happens next?' whispered Hester.

'There are two copies of each form. Top copy goes to the Teleprinter Hut for immediate transmission to your people. That's the hut we passed that looks like the cricket pavilion. The other copies we keep here, in case there's a garble or something goes missing.'

'How long do you keep them?'

'Couple of months.'

'Can we see?'

Heaviside scratched his head. 'If you want. Not much to it, though.'

He led them to the far end of the hut, opened a door, turned on the light and stood back to show them the interior. A walk-in cupboard. A bank of about a dozen dark green filing cabinets. No window. Light switch on the left.

'How are they arranged?' asked Jericho.

'Chronologically.' He closed the door.

Not locked, noted Jericho, continuing his inventory. And the entrance not really visible, except to the four operators nearest to it. He could feel his heart beginning to thump.

'Major Heaviside, sir!'

298

They turned to find Kay standing, beckoning to them, one of her headphones pressed to her ear.

'My mystery piano player, sir. He's just started doing his scales again, sir, if you're interested.'

Heaviside took the headset first. He listened with a judicious expression, his eyes focused on the middle distance, like an eminent doctor with a stethoscope being asked to give a second opinion. He shook his head and shrugged and passed the headphones to Hester.

'Ours not to reason why, old chap,' he said to Jericho.

When it was Jericho's turn, he removed his scarf and placed it carefully on the floor next to the cable form that connected the wireless set to the aerials and the power supply. Putting on the headphones was rather like putting his head under water. There was a strange rush of sounds. A howl that reminded him of the wind in the aerial farm. A gunfire crackle of static. Two or three different and very faint Morse transmissions braided together. And suddenly, and most bizarrely, a German diva singing an operatic aria he vaguely recognised as being from the second act of *Tannhäuser*.

'I can't hear anything.'

'Must have drifted off frequency,' said Heaviside.

Kay turned the dial minutely anticlockwise, the sound wowed up and down an octave, the diva evaporated, more gunfire, and then, like stepping into an open space, a rapid, staccato *dah-dah-dah-dah-dah* of Morse, pulsing clearly and urgently, more than a thousand miles distant, somewhere in German-occupied Ukraine.

*

They were halfway to the Teleprinter Hut when Jericho raised his hand to his throat and said, 'My scarf.'

They stopped in the rain.

'I'll get one of the girls to bring it over.'

'No, no, I'll fetch it, I'll catch you up.'

Hester took her cue. 'And how many machines did you say you have?' She began to walk on.

Heaviside hesitated between the two of them, then hurried after Hester. Jericho could have kissed her. He never heard the major's answer. It was whipped away by the wind.

You are calm, he told himself, you are confident, you are doing nothing wrong.

He went back into the hut. The woman sergeant had her fat back to him, leaning over one of the interceptors. She never saw him. He walked swiftly down the central aisle, looking straight ahead, and let himself into the storeroom. He closed the door behind him and turned on the light.

How long did he have? Not long.

He tugged at the first drawer of the first filing cabinet. Locked. Damn it. He tried it again. Wait. No, it *wasn't* locked. The cabinet was fitted with one of these irritating anti-tilt mechanisms, which prevented two drawers being opened at once. He looked down and saw that the bottom drawer was protruding slightly. He closed it gently with his foot and to his relief the top drawer slid open.

Brown cardboard folders. Bundles of smudged carbons, held together by metal paperclips. Log sheets and W/T red forms. Day, Month and Year in the top right-hand corner. Meaningless jumbles of handwritten letters. This folder for 15 January 1943.

He stepped back and counted quickly. Fifteen four-drawer cabinets. Sixty drawers. Two months. Roughly a drawer a day. Could that be right?

He strode over to the sixth cabinet and opened the third drawer down.

February the 6th.

Bingo.

He held the image of Hester Wallace's neat notation steady in his mind. 6.2./1215. 9.2/1427. 20.2/1807. 2.3./1639, 1901 . . .

It would have helped if his fingers hadn't swollen to the size of sausages, if they weren't shaking and slippery with sweat, if he could somehow catch his breath.

Someone must come in. Someone must hear him, surely, opening and closing the metal drawers like organ stops, pulling out two, three, four cryptograms and the log sheets, too (Hester had said they'd be useful), stuffing them into his inside coat pocket, five, six – dropped it, damn – seven cryptograms. He almost gave up at that – 'Quit while you're ahead, old love' – but he needed the final four, the four Claire had hidden in her room.

He opened the top drawer of the thirteenth filing cabinet, and there they were, towards the back, virtually in sequence, thank you, God.

A footstep outside the storeroom. He grabbed the logs and red forms and had just about got them into his pocket and the drawer shut when the door opened to silhouette the trim figure of Kay the intercept girl.

'I thought I saw you come in,' she said, 'only you left your scarf, see?' She held it up and closed the door behind her, then slowly advanced down the narrow room towards him. Jericho stood paralysed with an idiot grin on his face.

'I don't mean to bother you, sir, but it is important, isn't it?' Her dark eyes were wide. He dimly registered again that she was very pretty, even in her Army uniform. The tunic was belted tight at her waist. Something about her reminded him of Claire.

'I'm sorry?'

'I know I shouldn't ask, sir – we're never meant to ask, are we? – but, well, *is it*? Only no one ever tells us, see? Rubbish, that's all it is to us, just rubbish, rubbish, all day long. And all night, too. You try to go to sleep and you can still hear it – beep-beep-bloody-beep. Drives you barmy after a bit. I joined up, see, volunteered, but it's not what I expected, this place. Can't even tell my mum and dad.' She had come up very close to him. 'You *are* making sense of it? It *is* important? I won't tell,' she added, solemnly, 'honest.'

'Yes,' said Jericho. 'We are making sense of it, and it is important. I promise you.'

She nodded to herself, smiled, looped his scarf around his neck and tied it, then walked slowly out of the storeroom, leaving the door open. He gave it twenty seconds, then followed her. Nobody stopped him as he went out through the hut and into the rain.

4

Heaviside didn't want them to leave. Jericho tried
feebly to protest – the light was bad, he said, they had
a long journey ahead, they had to beat the blackout –
but Heaviside was horrified. He insisted, *insisted* they
at least take a look at the direction finders and the high-
speed Morse receivers. He was so enthusiastic, he
looked as though he might burst into tears if they said
no. And so they trailed meekly after him across the slick
wet concrete, first to a row of wooden huts dressed up
to look like a stable block and then to another fake
cottage.

The chorus of the aerial farm sang weirdly in the
background, Heaviside became increasingly excited
describing abstruse technicalities of wavelength and
frequency, Hester pretended heroically to be interested
and carefully avoided meeting Jericho's eye, and all the
time Jericho walked around unhearing, in a cocoon of
anxiety, nerved for the distant sounds of discovery and
alarm. Never had he been more desperate to get away
from anywhere. From time to time his hand stole into
his inside coat pocket, and once he left it there,
reassured to feel the roughness of the intercepts safely
between his fingers, until he realised he was doing a
passable impersonation of Napoleon, whereupon he
promptly snatched it out again.

As for Heaviside, such was his pride in Beaumanor's
work, he clearly would have kept them there for
another week if he could. But when, an interminable

half-hour later, he suggested a visit to the motor pool
and the auxiliary generators, it was Hester, so cool until
then, who finally snapped and said, rather too firmly in
retrospect, that no, thank you, but really they did have
to get going.

'Honestly? It's a heck of a long way to have come for
just a couple of hours.' Heaviside looked mystified.
'The commander will be disappointed to miss you.'

'Alas,' said Jericho. 'Some other time.'

'Up to you, old boy,' said Heaviside huffily. 'Don't
want to press ourselves on you.' And Jericho cursed
himself for hurting his feelings.

He walked them round to their car, halting on the
way to point out an antique ship's figurehead of an
admiral, perched on top of an ornamental horse
trough. Some wit had draped a pair of Army knickers
over the admiral's sword and they hung limply in the
raw damp. 'Cornwallis,' said Heaviside. 'Found him in
the grounds. Our lucky charm.'

When they said goodbye he shook hands with them
each in turn, Hester first, then Jericho, and saluted as
they got into the Austin. He turned as if to go, then
froze, and suddenly ducked down to the window.

'What was it you said you did again, Mr Jericho?'

'Actually, I didn't.' Jericho smiled and turned the
engine on. 'Cryptanalytic work.'

'Which section?'

'Can't say, I'm afraid.'

He jammed the gear stick into reverse and executed
a clumsy three-point turn. As they pulled away he
could see Heaviside in the rear-view mirror, standing in

the rain, his hand protecting his eyes, watching them. The curve of the drive took them off to the left and the image vanished.

'Pound to a penny,' muttered Jericho, 'he's on his way to the nearest telephone.'

'You got them?'

He nodded. 'Let's wait till we get clear of here.'

Out through the gates, along the lane, past the village, towards the forest. The rain was blowing across the dark slope of woodland in ghostly white columns, like the banners of a phantom army. A large and lonely bird was flying through the cloudburst, very high and far away. The windscreen wipers scudded back and forth. The trees closed in around them.

'You were very good,' said Jericho.

'Until the end. By the end it was unendurable, not knowing if you'd managed it.'

He started to tell her about the storeroom, but then he noticed a track coming up, leading off from the side of the road into the privacy of the wood.

The perfect spot.

They bounced along the rough trail for about a hundred yards, plunging into puddles that turned out to be potholes a foot deep. Water fountained out on either side of them, tearing against the underside of the chassis. It spouted through a hole at Hester's feet and drenched her shoes. When at last the headlights showed a patch of bog too wide to negotiate, Jericho turned off the engine.

There was no sound except for the pattering of the rain on the thin metal roof. Overhanging branches blotted out the sky. It was almost too dark to read. He turned on the interior light.

'VVVADU QSA?K,' said Jericho, reading off the whispers on the first log sheet. 'Which, if I remember my days in traffic analysis, roughly translates as: This is station call sign ADU requesting reading of my signal strength, over.' He ran his finger down the carbon copy. Q-code was an international language, the Esperanto of wireless operators; he knew it off by heart. 'And then we get VVVCPQ BT QSA4 QSA?K. This is station call-sign CPQ, break, your signal strength is fine, what is my signal strength? Over.'

'CPQ,' said Hester, nodding. 'I recognise that call sign. That has something to do with Army High Command in Berlin.'

'Good. One mystery solved, then.' He returned his attention to the log sheet. 'VVVADU QSA3 QTC1 K: Smolensk to Berlin, your signal strength is reasonable, I have one message for you, over. QRV, says Berlin: I am ready. QXH K: broadcast your traffic, over. Smolensk then says QXA109: my message consists of 109 cipher groups.'

Hester fluttered the first cryptogram triumphantly. 'Here it is. One hundred and nine exactly.'

'OK. Fine. So that goes through – straight away, presumably, because Berlin replies: VVVCPQ R QRU HHVA. Message received and understood, I have nothing for you, Heil Hitler and good night. All very smooth and methodical. Right out of the manual.'

'That girl in the Intercept Hut said he was precise.'

'What we don't have, unfortunately, is Berlin's replies.' He riffled through the log sheets. 'Easy contact on the 9th as well, and again on the 20th. Ah,' he said, 'now on the 2nd of March it looks to have been more tricky.' The form was indeed a mass of terse dialogue. He held it up to the light. Smolensk to Berlin: QZE, QRJ, QRO. (Your frequency is too high, your signals are too weak, increase your power.) And Berlin snapping back: QWP, QRX10 (observe regulations, wait ten minutes) and finally an exasperated QRX (shut up). 'Now this is interesting. No wonder they suddenly start to sound like strangers.' Jericho squinted at the carbon copy. 'The call sign in Berlin has changed.'

'Changed? Absurd. Changed to what?'

'TGD.'

'*What?* Let me see that.' She snatched the form out of his hand. 'That's not possible. No, no. TGD simply isn't a Wehrmacht call sign.'

'How can you be sure?'

'Because I know it. There's a whole Enigma key named after TGD. It's never been broken. It's famous.' She had started to wind a lock of hair nervously around her right index finger. 'Notorious might be a better word.'

'What is it?'

'It's the call sign of Gestapo headquarters in Berlin.'

'Gestapo?' Jericho fumbled through the remaining log sheets. 'But all the messages from March the 2nd onwards,' he said, 'that's eight out of the eleven, all the long ones, including the four in Claire's room – they're all addressed to that sign.' He gave the forms to her so she could check for herself and sat back in his seat.

A gust of wind stirred the branches above them, sending a shower of rainwater rattling like a volley across the windscreen.

'Let's try and construct a thesis,' said Jericho after a minute or two, as much to hear a human voice as anything. The random pattering of the downpour and the crepuscular gloom of the forest were beginning to affect his nerves. Hester had pulled her feet up from the sodden floor and was huddled up very small on the front seat, staring out at the forest, hugging her legs, occasionally massaging her toes through her damp stockings.

'March the 4th is the key day,' he went on. (*Where was I on 4 March? In another world: reading Sherlock Holmes in front of a Cambridge gas fire, avoiding Mr Kite and learning to walk again.*) 'Up to that day, everything is proceeding normally. A signals unit hibernating in the Ukraine, dormant all winter, has come to life in the warmer weather. First, a few signals to Army HQ in Berlin, and then a burst of longer traffic to the Gestapo –'

'That's not normal,' said Hester scathingly. 'An Army unit transmitting reports in a Russian-front Enigma key to the headquarters of the secret police? Normal? I'd call that unprecedented.'

'Quite.' He didn't mind being interrupted. He was glad of a sign she was listening. 'In fact, it's so unprecedented, someone at Bletchley wakes up to what's happening and starts to panic. All previous signals are removed from the Registry. And just before midnight on that same day your Mr Mermagen telephones Beaumanor and tells them to stop interception. Ever happen before?'

'Never.' She paused, then moved her shoulder slightly in concession. 'Well, all right, *maybe*, when traffic's very heavy, a low-priority target *might* be neglected for a day or so. But you saw the size of Beaumanor. And that's not as big as the RAF's station at Chicksands. And there must be a dozen smaller places, maybe more. We're always being told by people like you that the whole point of the exercise is to monitor *everything*.'

He nodded. This was true. It had been their philosophy from the beginning: be inclusive, miss nothing. It isn't the big boys who give you the cribs – they're too good. It's the little fellows – the long-forgotten incompetents stuck in out-of-the-way places, who always begin their messages 'situation normal, nothing to report' and then use the same nulls in the same places, or who habitually encipher their own call-signs, or who set the rotors every morning with their girlfriend's initials . . .

Jericho said: 'So he wouldn't have told them to stop on his own authority?'

'Miles? God, no.'

'Who gives him his orders?'

'That depends. Hut 6 Machine Room, usually. Sometimes the Hut 3 Watch. They decide priorities.'

'Could he have made a mistake?'

'In what sense?'

'Well, Heaviside said Miles called Beaumanor just

before midnight on the 4th in a panic. I was wondering: what if Miles had been told earlier in the day that this unit was no longer to be intercepted, but forgot to pass on the message.'

'Eminently possible. Likely, in fact, knowing Miles. Yes, yes *of course.*' Hester turned round to face him. 'I see what you're driving at. In the time between Miles being told to pull the plug and the order reaching Beaumanor, four more messages had been intercepted.'

'Exactly. Which came into Hut 6 late on the night of the 4th. But by then the order had already been issued that they weren't to be decoded.'

'So they just got caught up in the bureaucracy and were passed along the line.'

'Until they ended up in the German Book Room.'

'In front of Claire.'

'Undecrypted.'

Jericho nodded slowly. Undecrypted. That was the crucial point. That explained why the signals in Claire's bedroom had showed no signs of damage. There had never been any strips of Type-X decode gummed to their backs. They had never been broken.

He peered into the wood but he didn't see trees, he saw the German Book Room on the morning after the night of 4 March, when the cryptograms would have arrived to be filed and indexed.

Would Miss Monk herself have rung the Hut 6 duty officer, or would she have delegated the task to one of her girls? 'We've got four orphan intercepts here, without the solutions. What, pray, are we supposed to do with them?' And the reply would have been – what?

Oh, Christ! File them? Forget them? Dump them in the bin marked CONFIDENTIAL WASTE?

Only none of those things had happened.

Claire had stolen them instead.

'*In theory?*' Weitzman had said. '*On an average day? A girl like Claire would probably see more operational detail about the German armed forces than Adolf Hitler. Absurd, isn't it?*'

Ah, but they weren't supposed to *read* it, Walter, that was the point. Well-bred young ladies wouldn't dream of reading someone else's mail, unless they were told to do so for King and country. They certainly wouldn't read it for themselves. That was the reason why Bletchley employed them.

But what was it Miss Monk had said of Claire? '*She'd really become much more attentive of late . . .*' Naturally she had. *She* had begun to read what was passing through her hands. And at the end of February or the beginning of March she had seen something that had changed her life. Something to do with a German rear-echelon signals unit whose wireless operator played Morse code to the Gestapo as if it were a Mozart sonata. Something so utterly 'un-boring, darling', that when Bletchley had decided they couldn't bear to read the traffic any more, she had felt compelled to steal the last four intercepts herself.

And why had she stolen them?

He didn't even need to pose the question. Hester had reached the answer ahead of him, although her voice was faint and disbelieving and almost drowned out by the rain.

'She stole them to read them.'

She stole them to read them. The answer slid beneath the random pattern of events and fitted it like a crib.

She stole the cryptograms to read them.

'But is it really feasible?' asked Hester. She seemed bewildered by the destination to which her logic had led her. 'I mean, could she really have done it?'

'Yes. It's possible. Hard to imagine. Possible.'

Oh, the nerve of it, thought Jericho. Oh, the sheer breathtaking bloody *nerve* of it, the cool deliberation with which she must have plotted it. Claire, my darling, you really are a wonder.

'But she couldn't have managed it on her own,' he said, 'not locked away at the back of Hut 3. She'd have needed help.'

'Who?'

He raised his hands from the steering wheel in a hopeless gesture. It was hard to know where to begin. 'Someone with access to Hut 6 for a start. Someone who could look up the Enigma settings for German Army key Vulture on March the 4th.'

'Settings?'

He glanced at her in surprise, then realised that the actual workings of an Enigma was not the sort of information she would have needed to know. And in Bletchley, what you didn't need to know you were never told.

'*Walzenlage,*' he said. '*Ringstellung. Stecker-verbindungen.* Wheel order, ring setting and cross-plugging. If Vulture was being read every day, they'd

312

already have had those in Hut 6.'

'Then what would you have had to do?'

'Get access to a Type-X machine. Set it up in exactly the right way. Type in the cryptograms and tear off the plaintext.'

'Could Claire have done that?'

'Almost certainly not. She'd never have been allowed anywhere near the decoding room. And anyway she wasn't trained.'

'So her accomplice would have needed some skill?'

'Skill, yes. And nerve. And time, come to that. Four messages. A thousand cipher groups. Five thousand individual characters. Even an expert operator would need the best part of half an hour to decode that much. It *could* have been done. But she would have needed a superman.'

'Or woman.'

'No.' He was remembering the events of Saturday night: the sound downstairs in the cottage, the big male footprints in the frost, the cycle tracks and the red rear light of the bicycle shooting away from him into the darkness. 'No. It's a man.'

If only I'd been thirty seconds quicker, he thought. I'd have seen his face.

And then he thought: Yes, and maybe got a bullet in my own for my trouble: a bullet from a stolen Smith and Wesson .38, manufactured in Springfield, Massachusetts.

He felt a sudden prickle of ice-cold moisture on the back of his wrist and glanced up. He followed its trajectory to a spot in the roof, just before the windscreen. As he watched, another dark bubble of rainwater slowly swelled, ripened to a rich rust colour, and dropped.

Shark.

He realised guiltily he had nearly forgotten it.

'What's the time?'

'Almost five.'

'We should be getting back.'

He rubbed at his hand and reached for the ignition.

The car wouldn't start. Jericho twisted the key back and forth and pumped away frantically at the accelerator but all he managed to coax from the engine was a dull turning noise.

'Oh, hell!'

He turned up his collar, got out and went round to the boot. As he opened the lid a brace of pigeons took off behind him, wings snapping like firecrackers. There was a starting handle under the spare can of petrol and he inserted that into the hole in the front bumper. '*You do this the wrong way, lad,*' his stepfather had told him, '*and you can break your wrist.*' But which was the right way? Clockwise or anticlockwise? He gave the handle a hopeful tug. It was horribly stiff.

'Pull out the choke,' he shouted to Hester, 'and press your foot down on the third pedal if she starts to fire.'

The little car rocked as she slid across into the driver's seat.

He bent to his task again. The forest floor was only a couple of feet from his face, a pungent brown carpet of decaying leaves and fir cones. He heaved a couple more

314

times until his shoulder ached. He was beginning to
sweat now, perspiration mingling with the rainwater,
dripping off the end of his nose, trickling down his
neck. The insanity of their whole undertaking seemed
encapsulated in this moment. The greatest convoy
battle of the war was about to start, and where was he?
In some primeval bloody forest in the middle of bloody
nowhere poring over stolen Gestapo cryptograms with
a woman he barely knew. What in the name of reason
did they think they were doing? They must be – he
tightened his grip – *crazy* . . . He jerked viciously on the
starting handle and suddenly the engine caught, splut-
tered, nearly died, then Hester revved it loudly. The
sweetest sound he'd ever heard, it split the forest. He
slung the handle into the boot and slammed the lid.

The gearbox whined as he reversed along the track
towards the road.

The overhanging branches made a tunnel of the
soaking lane. Their headlights glinted on a film of
running water. Jericho drove slowly around and
around the same course, trying to find some landmark
in the gloom, trying not to panic. He must have taken
a wrong turning coming out of the clearing. The
steering wheel beneath his hands felt as wet and
slippery as the road. Eventually they came to a
crossroads beside a vast and decaying oak. Hester bent
her head again to the map. A lock of long black hair fell
across her eyes. She used both hands to pile it up. She
clenched a pin between her teeth and muttered
through it: 'Left or right?'

'You're the navigator.'

'And you're the one who decided to drive us off the main road.' She skewered her hair savagely back in place. 'Go left.'

He would have chosen the other way but thank God he didn't because she was right. Soon the road ahead began to brighten. They could see patches of weeping sky. He pressed his foot down and the speedometer touched forty as they passed out of the forest and into the open. When, after a mile or so, they came to a village, she told him to pull up outside the tiny post office.

'Why?'

'I need to find out where we are.'

'You'd better be quick.'

'I've really no intention of sight-seeing.'

She slammed the door behind her and ran through the rain, sidestepping the puddles with a gym mistress's agility. A bell tinkled inside the shop as she opened the door.

Jericho glanced ahead, then checked in his mirror. The village appeared to consist of nothing more than this one street. No parked vehicles that he could see. No one about. He guessed that a private car, especially one driven by a stranger, would be a rarity, a talking-point. In the little red-brick cottages and the half-timbered houses he could already imagine the curtains being twitched back. He turned off the windscreen wipers and sank lower in his seat. For the twentieth time his hand went to the bulge of cryptograms in his inside pocket.

316

Two Englands, he thought. One England – this one – familiar, safe, obvious. But now another, secret England, secluded in the grounds of stately houses – Beaumanor, Gayhurst, Woburn, Adstock, Bletchley – an England of aerial farms and direction finders, clattering bombes and, soon, the glowing green and orange valves of Turing machines (*'it should make the calculations a hundred times, maybe a thousand times as fast'*). A new age beginning to be born in the parklands of the old. What was it that Hardy had written in his *Apology*? 'Real mathematics has no effect on war. No one has yet discovered any warlike purpose to be served by the theory of numbers.' The old boy couldn't guess the half of it.

The bell tinkled again and Hester emerged from the post office holding a newspaper over her head like an umbrella. She opened the car door, shook the paper and threw it, not very gently, into his lap.

'What's this for?' It was the *Leicester Mercury*, the local rag: that afternoon's edition.

'They print appeals for help, don't they? From the police? When someone is missing?'

It was a good idea. He had to concede it. But although they checked the paper carefully – twice, in fact – they could find no photograph of Claire and no mention of the hunt for her.

Dropping southwards, heading for home. A different route for the return journey, more easterly – this was Hester's plan. To keep their spirits up, she occasionally recited the names of the villages and checked them in the gazetteer as they rattled down their empty high streets. Oadby, she said, ('note the early English to Perpendicular church'), Kibworth Harcourt, Little Bowden, and on across the border out of Leicestershire and into Northamptonshire. The sky over the distant pale hills brightened from black to grey and finally to a kind of glossy, neutral white. The rain slowed, then stopped. Oxendon, Kelmarsh, Maidwell . . . Square Norman towers with arrow-slits, thatched pubs, tiny Victorian railway stations nesting in a bosky countryside of high hedges and dense copses. It was enough to make you want to burst into a chorus of 'There'll Always Be an England' except that neither of them felt like singing.

Why had she run? That was what Hester said she couldn't understand. Everything else seemed logical enough: how she would have got hold of the cryptograms in the first place, why she might have wanted to read them, why she would have needed an accomplice. But why then commit the one act guaranteed to draw attention to yourself? Why fail to turn up for your morning shift?

'You,' she said to Jericho, after she had thought it over for a few more miles. There was a hint of accusation in her voice. 'I think it must be you.'

Like a prosecuting counsel she took him back over the events of Saturday night. He had gone to the cottage, yes? He had discovered the intercepts, yes? A man had arrived downstairs, yes?

'Yes.'

'Did he see you?'

318

'No.'

'Did you *say* anything?'

'I may have shouted "Who's there?" or something of the sort.'

'So he could have recognised your voice?'

'It's possible.'

But that would mean I knew him, he thought. Or at least that he knew me.

'What time did you leave?'

'I don't know exactly. About half past one.'

'There you are,' she said. 'It *is* you. Claire returns to the cottage after you've gone. She discovers the intercepts are missing. She realises that you must have them because this mysterious man has told her you were there. She believes you'll take them straight to the authorities. She panics. She runs . . .'

'But that's madness.' He took his eyes off the road to stare at her. 'I'd never have betrayed her.'

'So *you* say. But did *she* know that?'

Did she know that? No, he realised, returning his attention to the wheel, no, she did not know that. Indeed, on the basis of his behaviour on the night she found the cheque, she had good reason to assume he was a fanatic about security – a pretty ironic conclusion, given he now had eleven stolen cryptograms stuffed inside his overcoat pocket.

A twenty-year-old bus with an outside staircase to its upper deck, like something out of a transport museum, pulled over to the grass verge to let them overtake. The schoolchildren on board waved frantically as they passed.

'Who were her boyfriends? Who was she seeing apart from me?'

'You don't want to know. *Believe me.*' There was relish in the way she threw back at him the words he had used to her in church. He couldn't blame her for it.

'Come on, Hester.' He gripped the steering wheel grimly and glanced into the mirror. The bus was receding from view. A car was emerging from behind it. 'Don't spare my blushes. Let's keep it simple. Just confine it to men from the Park.'

Well, they were impressions, she said, rather than names. Claire had never mentioned names.

Give me the impressions, then.

And she did.

The first one she'd encountered had been young, with reddish hair, clean-shaven. She'd met him on the stairs with his shoes in his hand one morning in early November.

Reddish hair, clean-shaven, repeated Jericho. It didn't sound familiar.

A week later she'd cycled past a colonel parked in the lane in an Army staff car with the headlights dowsed. And then there was an Air Force man called Ivo Something, with a weird vocabulary of 'prangs' and 'crates' and 'shows' that Claire used to mimic fondly. Was he Hut 6 or 3? She was fairly sure Hut 3. There was an Honourable Evelyn double-barrelled someone-or-other – 'thoroughly *dis*honourable, darling' – whom Claire had met in London during the Blitz and who now worked in the mansion. There was an older man who Hester thought had something to do with the

Navy. And there was an American: he was definitely Navy.

'That would be Kramer,' said Jericho.

'You know him?'

'He's the man who lent me the car. How recent was that?'

'About a month ago. But I got the impression he was just a friend. A source of Camels and nylons, nothing special.'

'And before Kramer there was me.'

'She never talked about you.'

'I'm flattered.'

'Given the way she used to talk about the others, you should be.'

'Anyone else?'

She hesitated. 'There may have been someone new in the last month. She was certainly away a good deal. And once, about two weeks ago, I had a migraine and came home early off shift and I *thought* there was a man's voice coming from her room. But if there was they stopped talking when they heard me on the stairs.'

'That's eight then, by my count. Including me. And leaving out any others you've forgotten or don't know about.'

'I'm sorry, Tom.'

'It's quite all right.' He managed to arrange his face into a parody of a smile. 'If anything it's rather fewer than I'd thought.' He was lying, of course, and he guessed she knew it. 'Why is it, I wonder, that I don't hate her for it?'

'Because that's the way she is,' said Hester, with

unexpected ferocity. 'Well, she never made much secret of it, did she? And if one hates her for what she is – then, really, one can't have loved her very much in the first place, can one?' Her neck had blushed a deep pink. 'If all one wants is a reflection of oneself – well, honestly, there's always the mirror.'

She sat back, apparently as surprised by this speech as he was.

He checked the road behind them. Still empty apart from the same, solitary car. How long since he'd first noticed it? About ten minutes? But now he came to think of it, it had probably been there a good while longer, certainly since before they overtook the school bus. It was lying about a hundred yards back, low and wide and dark, its belly close to the ground, like a cockroach. He squeezed his foot harder on the accelerator and was relieved to see the gap between them widen until at last the road dipped and turned and the big car disappeared.

A minute later it was back again, maintaining exactly the same distance.

The narrow lane ran between high, dark hedges flecked with buds. Through them, as through a magic lantern, Jericho caught odd glimpses of tiny fields, a ruined barn, a bare, black elm, petrified by lightning. They came to a longish stretch of flat road.

There was no sun. He calculated there must be about half an hour of daylight left.

'How far is it to Bletchley?'

'Stony Stratford coming up, then about six miles. Why?'

He looked again in the mirror and had just begun to say, 'I fear –' when a bell started to clamour behind them. The big car had finally tired of following and was flashing its headlights, ordering them to pull over.

Until this moment, Jericho's encounters with the police had been rare, brief and invariably marked by those exaggerated displays of mutual respect customary between the guardians of the law and the lawful middle classes. But this one would be different, he saw that at once. An unauthorised journey between secret locations, without proof of ownership of the car, without petrol coupons, at a time when the country was being scoured for a missing woman: what would that earn them? A trip to the local police station, for sure. A lot of questions. A telephone call to Bletchley. A body search.

It didn't bear contemplating.

And so, to his astonishment, he found himself measuring the road ahead, like a long-jumper at the start of his run. The red roofs and the grey church spire of Stony Stratford had begun to poke above the distant line of trees.

Hester grabbed the edges of her seat. He jammed his foot down hard to the floor.

The Austin gathered speed slowly, as in a nightmare, and the police car, responding to the challenge, began to gain on them. The speedometer climbed past forty, to fifty, to fifty-five, to nearly sixty. The countryside seemed to be racing directly at them, only swerving at the last second to flash by narrowly on either side. A

main road appeared ahead. They had to stop. And if
Jericho had been an experienced driver that is what he
would have done, police or no police. But he hesitated
until there was nothing he could do but brake as hard
as he dared, change down into second gear and yank
the steering wheel hard left. The engine screamed.
They spun and cornered on two tyres, he and Hester
pitched sideways by the force. The clanging bell was
drowned by the roar of an engine and suddenly the
radiator grille of a tank transporter was rushing to fill
the rear-view mirror. Its bumper touched them. An
outraged blast from its hooter, as loud as a foghorn,
seemed to blow them forwards. They shot across the
bridge over the Grand Union Canal and a swan turned
lazily to watch them and then they were doglegging
through the market town – right, left, right,
shuddering over cobbled alleys, the wheel shaking in
Jericho's hands – anything to get off this wretched
Roman road. Abruptly the houses receded and they
were out in open country again, running alongside the
canal. A narrowboat was being towed by a weary
carthorse. The bargeman, lying stretched out beside
the tiller, raised his hat to them.

'Left here,' said Hester, and they swung away from
the canal into a lane that was not much better than the
forest track: just two strips of potholed, tarmaced road,
extending ahead like tyre tracks, separated by a mound
of grass that scraped the bottom of the car. Hester
turned and knelt on her seat, staring out of the back
window for any sign of the police, but the countryside
had closed behind them like a jungle. Jericho drove on

324

slowly for two miles. They passed through a tiny
hamlet. A mile the other side of it a space had been dug
out to allow cars – or, more likely, carts – to pass one
another. He drove up into it and switched off the
engine.

They did not have much time.

Jericho kept watch on the lane while she changed in
the back seat of the Austin. According to the map, they
were only about a mile due west of Shenley Brook End
and she was insistent she could make it back to the cottage on foot across open country before dark. He
marvelled at her nerve. To him, after the encounter
with the police, everything had taken on a sinister
aspect: the trees gesticulating at one another in the
wind, the patches of dense shadow now gathering at the
edges of the fields, the rooks that had erupted, cawing,
from their nests and were now circling high above them.

'Can't we read them?' Hester had asked, after they
had parked. He had taken the cryptograms from his
pocket so that they could decide what to do with them.
'Come on, Tom. We can't just burn them. If she
thought she could read them, why can't we?'

Oh, a dozen reasons, Hester. A hundred. But here
were three to be going on with. First, they would need
the Vulture settings that were in use on the days the
signals were sent.

'I can try to get those,' she had said. 'They must be
in Hut 6 somewhere.'

Very well, maybe she could. But even if she
managed it, they would still need several *hours* to

themselves on a Type-X machine – and not one of the Type-Xs in Hut 8, either, because naval Enigmas were wired differently from Army ones.

She had made no answer to that.

And, third, they would need to find a place to hide the cryptograms, because otherwise, if they were caught with them, they'd both be on trial *in camera* at the Old Bailey.

No answer to that, either.

There was a movement in the hedge about thirty yards ahead of him. A fox came nosing out of the undergrowth and stepped into the lane. Halfway across it stopped and stared directly at him. It held itself perfectly still and sniffed the air, then slouched off into the opposite hedgerow. Jericho let out his breath.

And yet, and yet . . . Even as he had ticked off all the obvious objections, he had known that she was right. They couldn't simply destroy the cryptograms now, not after all they had gone through to get them. And once that was conceded then the only logical reason for keeping them was to try to break them. Hester would have to steal the settings somehow while he looked for a way of gaining access to a Type-X machine. But it was dangerous – he prayed that she could see that. Claire was the last person to steal the cryptograms and there was no telling what had happened to her. And somewhere – maybe looking for them now, for all they knew – was a man who left large footprints in the frost; a man apparently armed with a stolen pistol; a man who knew that Jericho had been in Claire's room and had taken away the signals.

I am no hero, he thought. He was scared half to death.

The car door opened and Hester emerged, dressed again in trousers, sweater, jacket and boots. He took her bag and stowed it in the Austin's boot.

'Are you sure you don't want me to drive you?'

'We've been over this. It's safer if we split up.'

'For God's sake then be careful.'

'You should worry about yourself.' The air was milky with the approaching dusk – damp and cold. Her face was beginning to blur. She said: 'I'll see you tomorrow.'

She swung herself easily over the gate and set off directly across the field. He thought she might turn and wave but she never looked back. He watched her for about two minutes, until she had safely reached the far side. She searched briefly for a gap in the hedge, then vanished like the fox.

5

The lane led him up over the Chase, past the big wireless masts of the Bletchley Park out-station at Whaddon Hall, and down to the Buckingham Road. He peered along it, cautiously.

According to the map, only five roads, including this one, connected Bletchley with the outside world, and if the police were still watching the traffic they would stop him, he was certain. Short of flying a swastika the

327

Austin could hardly have looked more suspicious. Mud was spattered over the bodywork to the height of the windows. Grass was wrapped tightly around the axles. The back bumper was buckled where the tank transporter had struck it. And the engine, after Stony Stratford, had acquired a kind of urgent death rattle. He wondered what on earth he would say to Kramer.

The road was quiet in both directions. He passed a couple of farmhouses and within five minutes he was entering the outskirts of the town. He drove on past the suburban villas with their white pebble-dashed frontages and their fake Tudor beams, then left up the hill towards Bletchley Park. He turned into Wilton Avenue and immediately braked. Parked at the end of the street beside the guard post was a police car. An officer in a greatcoat and cap was talking earnestly to the sentry.

Once again, Jericho had to use both hands to jam the gear lever into reverse, then he backed out very slowly into Church Green Road.

He had moved beyond panic now and was in some calm place at the centre of the storm. 'Act as normally as possible', that had been his advice to Hester when they had decided to keep the cryptograms. 'You're not on duty until four tomorrow afternoon? Fine, then don't go in before that time.' The injunction must apply to him as well. Normality. Routine. He was expected in Hut 8 for the night's attack on Shark? He would be there.

He drove on up the hill and parked the car in a street of private houses about three hundred yards from St

Mary's Church. Where to hide the cryptograms? The Austin? Too risky. Albion Street? Too likely to be searched. A process of elimination brought him to the answer. Where better to hide a tree than in a forest? Where better to conceal a cryptogram than in a code-breaking centre? He would take them into the Park.

He transferred the wad of paper from the inside pocket of his overcoat to the hiding place he had made in the lining and locked the car. Then he remembered Atwood's atlas and unlocked it again. Bending to retrieve the book he casually checked the road. A woman in the house opposite was standing on her doorstep, in an oblong of yellow light, calling her children in from play. A young couple strolled past, arm in arm. A dog loped miserably along the gutter and stopped to cock its leg against the Austin's front tyre. An ordinary, English provincial street at twilight. *The world for which we fight.* He closed the door quietly. Head down, hands in pockets, he set off at a brisk walk for the Park.

It was a matter of pride with Hester Wallace that, when it came to walking, she had the stamina of any man. But what had looked on the map to be a straight and easy mile had turned into a crooked ramble three times as long, across tiny fields enclosed by tangled hedges and by ditches swollen wide as moats with brown meltwater, so that it was almost dark by the time she reached the lane.

She thought she might be lost but after a minute or two the narrow road began to seem familiar to her – a pair of elms grown too close together, as if from the same root; a mossy and broken stile – and soon she could smell the fires in the village. They were burning green wood and the smoke was white and acrid.

She kept a look out for policemen, but saw none – not in the field opposite the cottage, nor in the cottage itself, which had been left unlocked. She bolted the front door behind her, stood at the bottom of the stairs and called out a greeting.

Silence.

Slowly she climbed the stairs.

Claire's room was in chaos. *Desecrated* was the word that came to mind. The personality it had once reflected was disarranged, destroyed. Her clothes had all been strewn about, the sheets stripped off her bed, her jewellery scattered, her cosmetics opened up and spilled by clumsy male hands. At first she thought the surfaces were coated in talcum, but the fine white dust had no smell, and she realised it must be fingerprint powder.

She made a start at clearing it up, but soon abandoned it and sat on the edge of the naked mattress with her head in her hands until a great wave of self-disgust made her leap to her feet. She blew her nose angrily and went downstairs.

She lit a fire in the sitting room and set a kettle full of water on the hearth. In the kitchen she riddled the stove and managed to coax a glow from the pale ash, piled on some coal and set a saucepan to boil. She carried in the tin bath from the outhouse, bolting and locking the back door behind her.

She would stifle her terrors with routine. She would bathe. She would eat the remains of last night's carrot flan. She would retire early and hope for sleep.

Because tomorrow – *tomorrow* – would be a frightening day.

Inside Hut 8 there was a crowded, nervous atmosphere, like the green room of a theatre on opening night.

Jericho found his usual place next to the window. To his left: Atwood, leafing through Dilly Knox's edition of the mimes of Herodas. Pinker opposite, dressed as if for Covent Garden, his black velvet jacket slightly too long in the sleeve, so that his stubby fingers protruded like mole's paws. Kingcome and Proudfoot were playing with a pocket chess-set. Baxter was rolling a series of spindly cigarettes with a little tin contraption that didn't work properly. Puck had his feet up on the desk. The Type-Xs clacked sporadically in the background. Jericho nodded a general good evening, gave Atwood back his atlas – 'Thank you, dear boy. Good trip?' – and draped his overcoat over the back of his slatted chair. He was just in time.

'Gentlemen!' Logie appeared in the doorway and clapped twice to draw their attention, then stepped aside to allow Skynner to precede him into the room.

There was a general clatter and scraping of chair legs as they all clambered to their feet. Someone stuck their head round the door of the Decoding Room and the racket of the Type-Xs ceased.

'Easy, everybody,' said Skynner and waved them

back into their seats. Jericho found that by tucking his feet under his chair he could rest his ankle against the stolen cryptograms. 'Just stopped by to wish you luck.' Skynner's heavy body was swathed like a Chicago gangster's in half an acre of pre-war, double-breasted pinstripe. 'I'm sure you're all aware of what's at stake here as well as I am.'

'Shut up, then,' whispered Atwood.

But Skynner didn't hear him. This was what he loved. He stood with his feet planted firmly apart, his hands clasped behind his back. He was Nelson before Trafalgar. He was Churchill in the Blitz. 'I don't think I'm exaggerating when I say this could be one of the most decisive nights of the war.' His gaze sought out each of them in turn, coming last of all to Jericho and sliding away with a flicker of distaste. 'A mighty battle – probably the greatest convoy battle of the war – is about to start. Lieutenant Cave?'

'According to the Admiralty,' said Cave, 'at nineteen hundred hours this evening, convoys HX-229 and SC-122 were both warned they had entered the presumed operational area of the U-boats.'

'There we are, then. "Out of this nettle, danger, may we pluck this flower, safety."' Skynner nodded abruptly. 'Go to it.'

'Haven't I heard that before somewhere?' said Baxter.

'*Henry IV* Part One.' Atwood yawned. 'Chamberlain quoted it before he went off to meet Herr Hitler.'

After Skynner had gone, Logie went round the room handing out copies of the convoy contact section of the

332

Short Signal Code Book. To Jericho, as a mark of
recognition, he gave the precious original.

'We're after convoy contact reports, gentlemen: as
many of them as possible in the twenty-four hours
between midnight tonight and midnight tomorrow –
in other words, the maximum amount of crib covering
one day's Enigma settings.'

The instant an E-bar signal was heard, the duty
officer of the receiving station would telephone to alert
them. When the contact report arrived by teleprinter a
minute later, ten copies would be made and distributed. No fewer than twelve bombes – Logie had the
personal guarantee of the Hut 6 bombe controller –
would be placed at their disposal the moment they had
a worthwhile menu to run.

As he finished his speech, the blackout shutters
began to be fixed to the windows and the hut battened
down for the night.

'So, Tom,' said Puck pleasantly. 'How many contact
reports do you think we will need for this scheme of
yours to succeed?'

Jericho was leafing through the Short Signal Code
Book. He glanced up. 'I tried to work it out yesterday.
I'd say about thirty.'

'Thirty?' repeated Pinker, his voice rising in horror.
'But that would m-m-mean a mmm-mmm-mmm –'

'Massacre?'

'Massacre. Yes.'

'How many U-boats would be needed to produce
thirty signals?' asked Puck.

Jericho said: 'I don't know. That would depend on the time between the initial sighting and the start of the attack. Eight. Perhaps nine.'

'Nine,' muttered Kingcome. 'Christ! Your move, Jack.'

'Will someone tell me, then, please,' said Puck, 'for what I am supposed to be hoping? Am I hoping that the U-boats find these convoys or not?'

'Not,' said Pinker, looking round the table for support. 'Obviously. We w-w-want the convoys to escape the U-boats. That's what this is all about.'

Kingcome and Proudfoot nodded but Baxter shook his head violently. His cigarette disintegrated, sprinkling shreds of tobacco down the front of his cardigan. 'Damn it,' he said.

'You'd really s-s-sacrifice a c-c-convoy?' asked Pinker.

'Of course.' Baxter carefully brushed the loose tobacco into his palm. 'For the greater good. How many men has Stalin had to sacrifice so far? Five million? Ten million? The only reason we're still in the war is the butcher's bill on the eastern front. What's a convoy in comparison, if it gets us back into Shark?'

'What do you say, Tom?'

'I don't have an answer. I'm a mathematician, not a moral philosopher.'

'Bloody typical,' said Baxter.

'No, no, in terms of moral logic, Tom's is actually the only rational reply,' said Atwood. He had laid aside his Greek. This was the sort of discussion he liked. 'Consider. A madman seizes both your children at knife-point and says to you: "One must die, make your choice." Towards whom do you direct your reproaches? Towards yourself, for having to make a decision? No. Towards the madman, surely?'

Jericho said, staring at Puck: 'But that analogy doesn't answer Puck's point about what one should *hope* for.'

'Oh, but I would argue that that is *precisely* what it does answer, in that it rejects the premise of his question: the presumption that the onus is on us to make a moral choice. *Quod erat demonstrandum.*'

'Nobody can split a hair f-finer than F-Frank,' said Pinker, admiringly.

'"The *presumption* that the onus is on us to make a moral choice,"' repeated Puck. He smiled across the table at Jericho. 'How very Cambridge. Excuse me. I think I must visit the lavatory.'

He made his way towards the back of the hut. Kingcome and Proudfoot returned to their chess game. Atwood picked up Herodas. Baxter fiddled with his cigarette-rolling machine. Pinker closed his eyes. Jericho leafed through the Short Signal Code Book and thought of Claire.

Midnight came and went without a sound from the North Atlantic and the tension which had been building all evening began to slacken.

The 2 a.m. offering from the cooks of the Bletchley Park canteen was enough to make even Mrs Armstrong blanch – boiled potatoes in cheese sauce with barracuda, followed by a pudding made from two slices of bread stuck together with jam and then deep-fried in batter – and by four, the digestive effects of this, combined with the dim light in Hut 8 and the fumes from the paraffin heater, were casting a soporific pall over the naval cryptanalysts.

Atwood was the first to succumb. His mouth dropped open and the top plate of his dentures came loose so that he made a curious clicking sound as he breathed. Pinker wrinkled his nose in disgust and went off to make a nest for himself in the corner, and soon afterwards Puck, too, fell asleep, his body bent forwards, his left cheek resting on his forearms on the table. Even Jericho, despite his determination to stand guard over the cryptograms, found himself slipping over the edge of unconsciousness. He pulled himself back a couple of times, aware of Baxter watching him, but finally he couldn't fight it any longer and he slid into a turbulent dream of drowning men whose cries sounded in his ears like the wind in the aerial farm.

SIX

STRIP

STRIP: to remove one layer of
encipherment from a cryptogram
which has been subjected to the
process of super-encipherment (US,
qv), i.e., a message which has been
enciphered once, and then
re-enciphered to provide double
security.

A Lexicon of Cryptography
('Most Secret', Bletchley Park, 1943)

LATER, IT WOULD transpire that Bletchley Park knew almost everything there was to know about *U-653*.

They knew she was a Type VIIc – 220 feet long, 20 feet wide, with a submerged displacement of 871 tons and a surface range of 6,500 miles – and that she had been manufactured by the Howaldts Werke of Hamburg, with engines by Blohm und Voss. They knew she was eighteen months old, because they had broken the signals describing her sea-trials in the autumn of 1941. They knew she was under the command of Kapitänleutnant Gerhard Feiler. And they knew that on the night of 28 January 1943 – the final night, as it happened, that Tom Jericho had spent with Claire Romilly – *U-653* had slipped her moorings at the French naval port of Saint-Nazaire and had moved out under a dark and moonless sky into the Bay of Biscay to begin her sixth operational tour.

After she had been at sea for a week, the cryptanalysts in Hut 8 broke a signal from U-boat headquarters – then still in their grand apartment building off the Bois de Boulogne in Paris – ordering *U-653* to proceed on the surface to naval grid square KD 63 'AT MAXIMUM MAINTAINABLE SPEED WITHOUT REGARD TO THE THREAT FROM THE AIR'.

On 11 February she joined ten other U-boats in a new mid-Atlantic patrol line code-named Ritter.

Weather conditions in the North Atlantic were particularly foul in the winter of 1942-3. There were a hundred days when the U-boats reported winds topping force 7 on the Beaufort scale. Sometimes the gales reached over 100 miles per hour, whipping up waves more than 50 feet high. Snow, sleet, hail and frozen spray lashed submarines and convoys alike. One Allied ship rolled over and sank in minutes simply from the weight of ice on her superstructure.

On 13th February, Feiler broke radio silence to report that his watch officer, one Leutnant Laudon, had been washed overboard – a blatant disregard of operational procedure on Feiler's part which brought no condolences but a terse rebuke from his controllers, broadcast to the entire submarine fleet:

```
FEILER'S MESSAGE ABOUT LOSS OF WATCH OFFICER
SHOULD NOT HAVE BEEN SENT UNTIL W/T SILENCE WAS
BROKEN BY GENERAL CONTACT WITH ENEMY.
```

It was only on the 23rd, after nearly four weeks at sea, that Feiler redeemed himself by at last making contact with a convoy. At 6 p.m. he dived to avoid an escorting destroyer, and then, when night came, rose to attack. He had at his disposal twelve torpedoes, each 23 feet long with its own electric motor, capable of running through a convoy, turning in a half circle and running back, turning again and so on, and on, until either its power ran out or a ship was sunk. The sensing mechanism was crude; it was not unknown for a U-boat to find itself being pursued by its own armaments. They were called FATs: *Flachenabsuchendertorpedos*, or 'shallow searching torpedoes'. Feiler fired four of them.

```
FROM: FEILER
IN NAVAL GRID SQUARE BC 6956 AT 0116. FOUR-FAN
AT A CONVOY PROCEEDING ON A SOUTHERLY COURSE AT
7 KNOTS. ONE STEAMSHIP OF 6,000 GROSS REGISTERED
TONS: LARGE EXPLOSION AND A CLOUD OF SMOKE, THEN
NOTHING MORE SEEN. ONE STEAMSHIP OF 5,500 GRT
LEFT BURNING. 2 FURTHER HITS HEARD, NO
OBSERVATIONS.
```

On the 25th, Feiler radioed his position.
On the 26th, his luck turned bad again.

```
FROM: U-653
AM IN NAVAL GRID SQUARE BC 8747. HIGH PRESSURE
GROUP 2 AND STARBOARD NEGATIVE BUOYANCY TANK
UNSERVICEABLE. BALLAST TANK 5 NOT TIGHT. IS
MAKING ODD NOISES. DIESEL PRODUCING DENSE WHITE
SMOKE.
```

Headquarters took all night to consult its engineers and replied at ten the following morning.

```
TO: FEILER
THE CONDITION OF BALLAST TANK NO 5 IS THE ONLY
THING WHICH MAY ENFORCE RETURN PASSAGE. DECIDE
FOR YOURSELF AND REPORT.
```

By midnight, Feiler had made his decision.

FROM: U-653

AM NOT RETURNING.

On 3 March, in mountainous seas, *U-653* came alongside a U-boat tanker and took on board 65 cubic metres of fuel and provisions sufficient for another fourteen days at sea.

On the 6th, Feiler was ordered into station in a new patrol line, code-named *Raubgraf* (Robber Baron).

And that was all.

On 9 March the U-boats abruptly changed their Weather Code Book, Shark was blacked out, and *U-653*, along with one hundred and thirteen other German submarines then known to be operating in the Atlantic, vanished from Bletchley's view.

At 5 a.m. GMT on Tuesday 16 March, some nine hours after Jericho had parked the Austin and walked into Hut 8, *U-653* was heading due east on the surface, returning to France. In the North Atlantic it was 3 a.m.

After ten days on station in the *Raubgraf* line, with no sign of any convoy, Feiler had finally decided to head for home. He had lost, along with Leutnant Laudon, four other ratings washed overboard. One of his petty officers was ill. The starboard diesel was still giving trouble. His one remaining torpedo was defective. The boat, which had no heating, was cold and damp, and everything – lockers, food, uniforms – was covered in a greenish-white mould. Feiler lay on his wet bunk, curled up against the cold, wincing at the irregular beat of the engine, and tried to sleep.

Up on the bridge, four men made up the night watch: one for each point of the compass. Cowled like monks in dripping black oilskins, lashed to the rail by metal belts, each had a pair of goggles and a pair of Zeiss binoculars clamped firmly to his eyes and was staring blindly into his own sector of darkness.

The cloud cover was ten-tenths. The wind was a steel attack. The hull of the U-boat thrashed beneath their feet with a violence that sent them skidding over the wet deck plates and knocking into one another.

Facing directly ahead, towards the invisible prow, was a young Obersteurmann, Heinz Theen. He was peering into such an infinity of blackness that it was possible to imagine they might have fallen off the edge of the world, when suddenly he saw a light. It flared out of nowhere, several hundred yards in front of him, winked for two seconds, then disappeared. If he hadn't had his binoculars trained precisely upon it, he would never have seen it.

Astonishing though it seemed, he realised he had just witnessed someone lighting a cigarette.

An Allied seaman lighting a cigarette in the middle of the North Atlantic.

He called down the conning tower for the captain.

By the time Feiler had scrambled up the slippery metal ladder to the bridge thirty seconds later the cloud had shifted slightly in the high wind and shapes were moving all around them. Feiler swivelled through 360 degrees and counted the outlines of nearly twenty ships, the nearest no more than 500 yards away on the port side.

A whispered cry, as much of panic as command: 'Alarrrmm!'

The *U-653* came out of her emergency dive and hung motionless in the calmer water beneath the waves.

Thirty-nine men crouched silently in the semidarkness listening to the sounds of the convoy passing overhead: the fast revs of the modern diesels, the ponderous churning of the steamers, the curious singing noises of the turbines in the warship escorts.

Feiler let them all go by. He waited two hours, then surfaced.

The convoy was already so far ahead as to be barely visible in the faint dawn light – just the masts of the ships and a few smudges of smoke on the horizon, and then, occasionally, when a high wave lifted the U-boat, the ironwork of bridges and funnels.

Feiler's task under standing orders was not to attack – impossible in any case, given his lack of torpedoes – but to keep his quarry in sight while drawing in every other U-boat within a radius of 100 miles.

'Convoy steering 070 degrees,' said Feiler. 'Naval grid square BD 1491.'

The first officer made a scrawled note in pencil then dropped down the conning tower to collect the Short Signal Code Book. In his cubbyhole next to the captain's berth the radioman pressed his switches. The Enigma came on with a hum.

2

At 7 a.m., Logie had sent Pinker, Proudfoot and Kingcome back to their digs to get some decent rest. 'Sod's law will now proceed to operate,' he predicted, as he watched them go, and sod's law duly did. Twenty-five minutes later, he was back in the Big Room with the queasy expression of guilty excitement which would characterise the whole of that day.

'It looks like it may have started.'

St Erith, Scarborough and Flowerdown had all reported an E-bar signal followed by eight Morse letters, and within a minute one of the Wrens from the Registration Room was bringing in the first copies. Jericho placed his carefully in the centre of his trestle table.

RGHC DMIG. His heart began to accelerate.

'Hubertus net,' said Logie. '4601 kilocycles.'

Cave was listening to someone on the telephone. He put his hand over the mouthpiece. 'Direction finders have a fix.' He clicked his fingers. 'Pencil. Quick.' Baxter threw him one. '49.4 degrees north,' he repeated. '38.8 degrees west. Got it. Well done.' He hung up.

Cave had spent all night plotting the convoys' courses on two large charts of the North Atlantic – one issued by the Admiralty, the other a captured German naval grid, on which the ocean was divided into thousands of tiny squares. The cryptanalysts gathered round him. Cave's finger came down on a spot almost

345

exactly midway between Newfoundland and the British Isles. 'There she is. She's shadowing HX-229.' He made a cross on the map and wrote 0725 beside it.

Jericho said: 'What grid square is that?'

'BD 1491.'

'And the convoy course?'

'070.'

Jericho went back to his desk and in less than two minutes, using the Short Signal Code Book and the current Kriegsmarine address book for encoding naval grid squares ('Alfred Krause, Blucherplatz 15': Hut 8 had broken that just before the blackout) he had a five-letter crib to slide under the contact report.

R G H C D M I G
D D F G R X ? ?

The first four letters announced that a convoy had been located steering 070 degrees, the next two gave the grid square, the final two represented the code name of the U-boat, which he didn't have. He circled R-D and D-R. A four-letter loop on the first signal.

'I get D-R/R-D,' said Puck a few seconds later.

'So do I.'

'Me too,' said Baxter.

Jericho nodded and doodled his initials on the pad. 'A good omen.'

After that, the pace of events began to quicken.

At 8.25, two long signals were intercepted emanating from Magdeburg, which Cave at once surmised would be U-boat headquarters ordering every submarine in the North Atlantic into the attack zone. At 9.20, he put down the telephone to announce that the Admiralty had just signalled the convoy commander with a warning that he was probably being shadowed. Seven minutes later, the telephone rang again. Flowerdown intercept station. A second E-bar flash from almost the same location as the first. The Wrens hurried in with it: KLYS QNLP.

'The same hearse,' said Cave. 'Following standard operating procedure. Reporting every two hours, or near as damn it.'

'Grid square?'

'The same.'

'Convoy course?'

'Also the same. For now.'

Jericho went back to his desk and manipulated the original crib under the new cryptogram.

```
K L Y S Q N L P
D D F G R X ? ?
```

Again, there were no letter clashes. The golden rule of Enigma, its single, fatal weakness: *nothing is ever itself – A can never be A, B can never be B* . . . It was working. His feet performed a little tap dance of delight beneath the table. He glanced up to find Baxter staring at him and he realised, to his horror, that he was smiling.

'Pleased?'

'Of course not.'

But such was his shame that when, an hour later, Logie came through to say that a second U-boat had just sent a contact signal, he felt himself personally responsible.

SOUY YTRQ.

At 11.40, a third U-boat began to shadow the convoy, at 12.20, a fourth, and suddenly Jericho had seven signals on his desk. He was conscious of people coming up and looking over his shoulder – Logie with his burning hayrick of a pipe and the meaty smell and heavy breathing of Skynner. He didn't look round. He didn't talk. The outside world had melted for him. Even Claire was just a phantom now. There were only the loops of letters, forming and stretching out towards him from the grey Atlantic, multiplying on his sheets of paper, turning into thin chains of possibility in his mind.

They didn't stop for breakfast, nor for lunch. Minute by minute, throughout the afternoon, the cryptanalysts followed, at third hand, the progress of the chase two thousand miles away. The commander of the convoy was signalling to the Admiralty, the Admiralty had an open line to Cave, and Cave would shout each time a fresh development looked like affecting the hunt for cribs.

Two signals came at 13.40 – one a short contact report, the other longer, almost certainly originating from the U-boat that had started the hunt. Both were for the first time close enough to be fixed by direction finders on board the convoy's own escorts. Cave

348

listened gravely for a minute, then announced that HMS *Mansfield*, a destroyer, was being dispatched from the main body of merchantmen to attack the U-boats.

'The convoy's just made an emergency turn to the southeast. She's going to try to shake off the hearses while *Mansfield* forces them under.'

Jericho looked up. 'What course is she steering?'

'What course is she steering?' repeated Cave into the telephone. 'I *said*,' he yelled, 'what fucking *course* is she steering?' He winced at Jericho. The receiver was jammed tight to his scarred ear. 'All right. Yes. Thank you. Convoy steering 118 degrees.' Jericho reached for the Short Signal Code Book.

'Will they manage to get away?' asked Baxter.

Cave bent over his chart with a rule and protractor. 'Maybe. It's what I'd do in their place.'

A quarter of an hour passed and nothing happened.

'Perhaps they have done it,' said Puck. 'Then what do we do?'

Cave said: 'How much more material do you need?'

Jericho counted through the signals. 'We've got nine. We need another twenty. Another twenty-five would be better.'

'Jesus!' Cave regarded them with disgust. 'It's like sitting with a flock of carrion.'

Somewhere behind them a telephone managed half a ring before it was snatched out of its cradle. Logie came in a moment later, still writing.

'That was St Erith reporting an E-bar signal at 49.4 degrees north, 38.1 degrees west.'

'New location,' said Cave, studying his charts. He made a cross, then threw his pencil down and leaned back in his chair, rubbing his face. 'All she's managed to do is run straight from one hearse into another. Which is what? The fifth? Christ, the sea must be teeming with them.'

'She isn't going to get away,' said Puck, 'is she?'

'Not a chance. Not if they're coming in from all around her.'

A Wren moved among the cryptanalysts, doling out the latest cryptogram: BKEL UUXS.

Ten signals. Five U-boats in contact.

'Grid square?' said Jericho.

Hester Wallace was not a poker player, which was a mistake on her part as she had been blessed with a poker face that could have made her a fortune. Nobody watching her wheel her bicycle into the shed beside the canteen that afternoon, or seeing her flick her pass at the sentry, or squeezing up against the corridor wall in Hut 6 to let her march by, or sitting opposite her in Intercept Control – nobody would have guessed the turmoil in her mind.

Her complexion was, as ever, pale, her forehead slightly creased by a frown that discouraged conversation. She wore her long, dark hair like a headache, savagely twisted up and speared. Her costume was the usual uniform of the West Country schoolmistress: flat shoes, grey woollen stockings, plain grey skirt, white shirt and an elderly but well-cut tweed jacket which she would shortly take off and hang over the back of the

350

chair, for the afternoon was warm. Her fingers moved across the blist in a short, staccato pecking motion. She had hardly slept all night.

Name of intercept station, time of interception, frequency, call sign, letter groups . . .

Where was the record of settings kept? That was the first matter to determine. Not in Control, obviously. Not in the Index Room. Not in the Registry. And not next door in the Registration Room, either: she had already made a quick inspection there. The Decoding Room was a possibility, but the Type-X girls were always complaining they were cramped for space, and sixty separate Enigma keys, their settings changed daily – in the case of the Luftwaffe, sometimes twice a day – well, that was a minimum of five hundred pieces of information every week, 25,000 in a year, and this was the war's fourth year. That would suggest a sizeable catalogue; a small library, in fact.

The only conclusion was that they had to be kept where the cryptanalysts worked, in the Machine Room, or else close by.

She finished blisting Chicksands, noon till three, and moved towards the door.

Her first pass through the Machine Room was spoiled by nerves: straight through it to the other end of the hut without even glancing from side to side. She stood outside the Decoding Room, cursing her fears, pretending to study the noticeboard. With a shaking hand she made a note about a performance of *Die Fledermaus* by the Bletchley Park Music Society which she had no intention of ever attending.

The second run was better.

There was no machinery in the Machine Room – the origin of its name was lost in the glorious mists of 1940 – just desks, cryptanalysts, wire baskets filled with signals and, on the wall to the right, shelf after shelf of files. She stopped and looked around distractedly, as if searching for a familiar face. The problem was, she knew nobody. But then her gaze fell upon a bald head with a few long, ginger hairs combed pathetically across a freckled crown, and she realised that wasn't entirely true.

She knew Cordingley.

Dear old, dull old Donald Cordingley, the winner – in a crowded field – of the Dullest Man in Bletchley contest. Ineligible for military service due to a funnel chest. By profession: actuary. Ten years' service with the Scottish Widows Assurance Society in the City of London, until a lucky third place in the *Daily Telegraph* crossword competition won him a seat in the Hut 6 Machine Room.

Her seat.

She watched him for a few more seconds, then moved away.

When she got back to Control Miles Mermagen was standing by her desk.

'How was Beaumanor?'

'Engrossing.'

She had left her jacket over her chair and he ran his hand over the collar, feeling the material between his thumb and forefinger, as if checking it for quality.

'How'd you get there?'

'A friend gave me a lift.'

'A male friend, I gather.' Mermagen's smile was wide and unfriendly.

'How do you know that?'

'I have my spies,' he said.

The ocean was alive with signals. They were landing on Jericho's desk at the rate of one every twenty minutes.

At 16.00 a sixth U-boat fastened on to the convoy and soon afterwards Cave announced that HX-229 was making another turn, to 028 degrees, in her latest and (in his opinion) hopeless attempt to escape her pursuers.

By 18.00 Jericho had a pile of nineteen contact signals, out of which he had conjured three four-letter loops and a mass of half-sketched bombe menus that looked like the plans for some complex game of hopscotch. His neck and shoulders were so knotted with tension he could barely straighten up.

The room by now was crowded. Pinker, Kingcome and Proudfoot had come back on shift. The other British naval lieutenant, Villiers, was standing next to Cave, who was explaining something on one of his charts. A Wren with a tray offered Jericho a curling Spam sandwich and an enamel mug of tea and he took them gratefully.

Logie came up behind him and tousled his hair.

'How are you feeling, old love?'

'Wrecked, frankly.'

'Want to knock off?'

'Very funny.'

'Come into my office and I'll give you something. Bring your tea.'

The 'something' turned out to be a large, yellow Benzedrine tablet, of which Logie had half a dozen in an hexagonal pillbox.

Jericho hesitated. 'I'm not sure I should. These helped send me funny last time.'

'They'll get you through the night, though, won't they? Come on, old thing. The commandos swear by them.' He rattled the box under Jericho's nose. 'So you'll crash out at breakfast? So what? By then we'll either have this bugger beaten. Or not. In which case it won't matter, will it?' He took one of the pills and pressed it into Jericho's palm. 'Go on. I won't tell Nurse.' He closed Jericho's fingers around it and said quietly: 'Because I can't let you go, you know, old love. Not tonight. Not you. Some of the others, maybe, but not you.'

'Oh, Christ. Well, since you put it so nicely.'

Jericho swallowed the pill with a mouthful of tea. It left a foul taste and he drained his mug to try and swill it away. Logie regarded him fondly.

'That's my boy.' He put the box back in his desk drawer and locked it. 'I've been protecting your bloody back again, incidentally. I had to tell him you were much too important to be disturbed.'

'Tell who? Skynner?'

'No. Not Skynner. Wigram.'

'What does he want?'

'You, old cock. I'd say he wants you. Skinned, stuffed and mounted on a pole somewhere. Really, I don't know, for such a quiet bloke, you don't half make some enemies. I told him to come back at midnight. All right by you?'

Before Jericho could reply the telephone rang and Logie grabbed it.

'Yes? Speaking.' He grunted and stretched across his desk for a pencil. 'Time of origin 19.02, 52.1 degrees north, 37.2 degrees west. Thanks, Bill. Keep the faith.'

He replaced the receiver.

'And then there were seven . . .'

It was dark again and the lights were on in the Big Room. The sentries outside were banging the blackout shutters into place, like prison warders locking up their charges for the night.

Jericho hadn't set foot out of the hut for twenty-four hours, hadn't even looked out of the window. As he slipped back into his seat and checked his coat to make sure the cryptograms were still there, he wondered vaguely what kind of day it had been and what Hester was doing.

Don't think about that now.

Already, he could feel the Benzedrine beginning to take effect. The muscles of his heart seemed feathery, his body charged. When he glanced across his notes, what had seemed inert and impenetrable a half-hour ago was suddenly fluid and full of possibility.

The new cryptogram was already on his desk: YALB DKYF.

'Naval grid square BD 2742,' called Cave. 'Course 055 degrees. Convoy speed nine and a half knots.'

355

Logie said: 'A message from Mr Skynner. A bottle of Scotch for the first man with a menu for the bombes.'

Twenty-three signals received. Seven U-boats in contact. Two hours to go till nightfall in the North Atlantic.

20.00: nine U-boats in contact.
20.46: ten.

The Control Room girls took a table near the serving hatch for their evening meal. Celia Davenport showed them all some pictures of her fiancé, who was fighting in the desert, while Anthea Leigh-Delamere brayed endlessly about a meet of the Bicester Hunt. Hester passed on the photographs without looking at them. Her eyes were fixed on Donald Cordingley, queuing to collect his lump of coelacanth, or whatever other obscure example of God's aquatic creatures they were now required to eat.

She was cleverer than he, and he knew it.

She intimidated him.

Hello, Donald, she thought. *Hello, Donald . . . Oh, nothing much, just this new back-break section, coming along with bucket and shovel after the Lord Mayor's parade . . . Now, listen, Donald, there's this funny little wireless net, Konotop-Prihiki-Poltava, in the southern Ukraine. Nothing vital, but we've never quite broken it and Archie – you must know Archie? – Archie has a theory it may be a variant on Vulture . . . Traffic runs through February and the first few days in March . . . That's right . . .*

She watched him as he sat alone and picked at his

lonely supper. She watched him, indeed, as if she *were* a vulture. And when, after fifteen minutes, he rose and scraped the leftovers from his plate into the swill bins, she rose as well, and followed him.

She was vaguely aware of the other girls staring after her in astonishment. She ignored them.

She tracked him all the way back to Hut 6, gave him five minutes to settle down, then went in after him.

The Machine Room was shaded and somnolent, like a library at dusk. She tapped him lightly on the shoulder.

'Hello, Donald.'

He turned round and blinked up at her in surprise. 'Oh, hello.' The effort of memory was heroic. 'Hello, Hester.'

'It's almost dark out there,' said Cave, looking at his watch. 'Not long now. How many have you had?'

'Twenty-nine,' said Baxter.

'I believe you said that would be enough, Mr Jericho?'

'Weather,' said Jericho, without looking up. 'We need a weather report from the convoy. Barometric pressure, cloud cover, cloud type, wind speed, temperature. Before it gets too dark.'

'They've got ten U-boats on their backs and you want them to tell you the *weather*?'

'Yes, please. Fast as they can.'

The weather report arrived at 21.31.

There were no more contact signals after 21.40.

*

357

Thus convoy KX-229 at 22.00.

Thirty-seven merchant vessels, ranging in size from the 12,000-ton British tanker *Southern Princess* to the 3,500-ton American freighter *Margaret Lykes*, making slow progress through heavy seas, steering a course of 055 degrees, direct to England, lit up like a regatta by a full moon to a range of ten miles visibility – the first such night in the North Atlantic for weeks. Escort vessels: five, including two slow corvettes and two clapped out, elderly ex-American destroyers donated to Britain in 1940 in exchange for bases, one of which – HMS *Mansfield* – had lost touch with the convoy after charging down the U-boats because the convoy commander (on his first operational command) had forgotten to signal her with his second change of course. No rescue ship available. No air cover. No reinforcements within a thousand miles.

'All in all,' said Cave, lighting a cigarette and contemplating his charts, 'what you might fairly call a bit of a cock-up.'

The first torpedo hit at 22.01.

At 22.32, Tom Jericho was heard to say, very quietly, 'Yes.'

3

It was chucking-out time at the Eight Bells Inn on the Buckingham Road and Miss Jobey and Mr Bonnyman had virtually exhausted the main topic of their

evening's conversation: what Bonnyman dramatically
termed the 'police raid' on Mr Jericho's room.

They had heard the details at supper from Mrs
Armstrong, her face still flushed with outrage at the
memory of this violation of her territory. A uniformed
officer had stood guard all afternoon on the doorstep
('in full view of the entire street, mind you'), while two
plain-clothes men carrying a box of tools and waving a
warrant had spent the best part of three hours searching
the upstairs back bedroom, before leaving at teatime
with a pile of books. They had dismantled the bed and
the wardrobe, taken up the carpet and the floorboards,
and brought down a heap of soot from the chimney.
'That young man is out,' declared Mrs Armstrong,
folding her hamlike arms, 'and all rent forfeit.'

'"*All rent forfeit*,"' repeated Bonnyman into his beer,
for the sixth or seventh time. 'I love it.'

'And such a quiet man,' said Miss Jobey.

A handbell rang behind the bar and the lights
flickered.

'Time, gentlemen! Time, please!'

Bonnyman finished his watery bitter, Miss Jobey her
port and lemon, and he escorted her unsteadily, past
the dartboard and the hunting prints, towards the
door.

The day that Jericho had missed had given the town
its first real taste of spring. Out on the pavement the
night air was still mild. Darkness touched the dreary
street with romance. As the departing drinkers
stumbled away into the blackout, Bonnyman playfully
pulled Miss Jobey towards him. They fell back slightly

into a doorway. Her mouth opened on his, she pressed herself up against him, and Bonnyman squeezed her waist in return. Whatever she might have lacked in beauty – and in the blackout, who could tell? – she more than made up for in ardour. Her strong and agile tongue, sweet with port, squirmed against his teeth.

Bonnyman, by profession a Post Office engineer, had been drafted to Bletchley, as Jericho had guessed, to service the bombes. Miss Jobey worked in the upstairs back bedroom of the mansion, filing Abwehr hand-ciphers. Neither, in accordance with regulations, had told the other what they did, a discretion which Bonnyman had extended somewhat to cover in addition the existence of a wife and two children at home in Dorking.

His hands slipped down her narrow thighs and began to hoist her skirt.

'Not here,' she said into his mouth, and brushed his fingers away.

Well (as Bonnyman would afterwards confide with a wink to the unsmiling police inspector who took his statement), the things a grown man has to do in wartime, and all for a simple you-know-what.

First, a cycle ride, which took them along a track and under a railway bridge. Then, by the thin beam of a torch, over a padlocked gate and through mud and brambles towards the hulk of a broken building. A great expanse of water somewhere close by. You couldn't see it, but you could hear the lapping in the breeze and the occasional cry of a waterfowl, and you could sense a deeper darkness, like a great black pit.

Complaints from Miss Jobey as she snagged her precious stockings and wrenched her ankle: loud and bitter imprecations against Mr Bonnyman and all his works which did not augur well for the purpose he had in mind. She started whining: 'Come on, Bonny, I'm frightened, let's go back.'

But Bonnyman had no intention of turning back. Even on a normal evening, Mrs Armstrong monitored every peep and squeak in the ether of the Commercial Guesthouse like a one-woman intercept station; tonight, she'd be on even higher alert than usual. Besides, he always found this place exciting. The light flashed on bare brick and on evidence of earlier liaisons – *AE + GS, Tony = Kath*. The spot held an odd erotic charge. So much had clearly happened here, so many whispered fumblings . . . They were a part of a great flux of yearning that went back long before them and would go on long after them – illicit, irrepressible, eternal. This was *life*. Such, at any rate, were Bonnyman's thoughts, although naturally he didn't express them at the time, nor afterwards to the police.

'And what happened next, sir? Precisely.'

He won't admit to this either, thank you very much, precisely or imprecisely.

But what did happen next was that Bonnyman wedged the torch in a gap in the brickwork where something had been torn from the wall, and threw his arms around Miss Jobey. He encountered a little light resistance at first – some token twisting and turning and 'stop it', 'not here' – which quickly became less convincing, until suddenly her tongue was up to its tricks again and they were back where they'd left off outside the Eight Bells Inn. Once again his hands began to ride up her skirt and once again she pushed him away, but this time for a different reason. Frowning slightly, she ducked and pulled down her knickers. One step, two steps, and they had vanished into her pocket. Bonnyman watched, enraptured.

'What happened next, inspector, *precisely*, is that Miss Jobey and myself noticed some hessian sacking in the corner.'

She with her skirt up above her knees, he with his trousers down around his ankles, shuffling forwards like a man in leg-irons, dropping heavily to his knees, a cloud of dust from the sacks rising and blossoming in the torch-beam, then much squirming and complaining on her part that something was digging into her back.

They stood and pulled away the sacks to make a better bed.

'And that was when you found it?'

'That was when we found it.'

The police inspector suddenly brought his fist down hard on the rough wooden table and shouted for his sergeant.

'Any sign of Mr Wigram yet?'

'We're still looking, sir.'

'Well, bloody well find him, man. Find him.'

4

The bombe was heavy – Jericho guessed it must weigh more than half a ton – and even though it was mounted on castors it still took all his strength, combined with the engineer's, to drag it away from the wall. Jericho pulled while the engineer went behind it and put his shoulder to the frame to heave. It came away at last with a screech and the Wrens moved in to strip it.

The decryptor was a monster, like something out of an H. G. Wells fantasy of the future: a black metal cabinet, eight feet wide and six feet tall, with scores of five-inch-diameter drum wheels set into the front. The back was hinged and opened up to show a bulging mass of coloured cables and the dull gleam of metal drums. In the place where it had stood on the concrete floor there was a large puddle of oil.

Jericho wiped his hands on a rag and retreated to watch from a corner. Elsewhere in the hut a score of other bombes were churning away on other Enigma keys and the noise and the heat were how he imagined a ship's engine room might be. One Wren went round to the back of the cabinet and began disconnecting and replugging the cables. The other moved along the front, pulling out each drum in turn and checking it. Whenever she found a fault in the wiring she would hand the drum to the engineer who would stroke the tiny brush wires back into place with a pair of tweezers. The contact brushes were always fraying, just as the belt which connected the mechanism to the big electric motor had a tendency to stretch and slip whenever there was a heavy load. And the engineers had never quite got the earthing right, so that the cabinets had a tendency to give off powerful electric shocks.

Jericho thought it was the worst job of all. A pig of a job. Eight hours a day, six days a week, cooped up in this windowless, deafening cell. He turned away to look at his watch. He didn't want them to see his impatience. It was nearly half past eleven.

His menu was at that moment being rushed into bombe bays all across the Bletchley area. Eight miles north of the Park, in a hut in a clearing in the forested estate of Gayhurst Manor, a clutch of tired Wrens near the end of their shift were being ordered to halt the three bombes running on Nuthatch (Berlin-Vienna-Belgrade Army administration), strip them and prepare them for Shark. In the stable block of Adstock Manor, ten miles to the west, the girls were actually sprawled with their feet up beside their silent machines, drinking Ovaltine and listening to Tommy Dorsey on the BBC Light Programme, when the supervisor came storming through with a sheaf of menus and told them to stir themselves, fast. And at Wavendon Manor, three miles northeast, a similar story: four bombes in a dank and windowless bunker were abruptly pulled off Osprey (the low-priority Enigma key of the Organisation Todt) and their operators told to stand by for a rush job.

Those, plus the two machines in Bletchley's Hut 11, made up the promised dozen bombes.

The mechanical check completed, the Wren went back to the first row of drums and began adjusting them to the combination listed on the menus. She called out the letters to the other girl, who checked them.

'Freddy, Butter, Quagga . . .'

'Yes.'

'Apple, X-ray, Edward . . .'

'Yes.'

The drums slipped on to their spindles and were fixed into place with a loud metallic click. Each was wired to mimic the action of a single Enigma rotor: 108 in all, equivalent to thirty-six Enigma machines running in parallel. When all the drums had been set, the bombe was trundled back into place and the motor started.

The drums began to turn, all except one in the top row which had jammed. The engineer gave it a whack with his spanner and it, too, began to revolve. The bombe would now run continuously on this menu – certainly for one day; possibly, according to Jericho's calculations, for two or three – stopping occasionally when the drums were so aligned they completed a circuit. Then the readings on the drums would be checked and tested, the machine restarted, and so it would go on until the precise combination of settings had been found, at which point the cryptanalysts would be able to read that day's Shark traffic. Such, at any rate, was the theory.

The engineer began dragging out the other bombe and Jericho moved forward to help, but was stopped by a tugging on his arm.

'Come on, old love,' shouted Logie above the din.

'There's nothing more we can do here.' He pulled at his sleeve again.

Reluctantly, Jericho turned and followed him out of the hut.

He felt no sense of elation. Maybe tomorrow evening or maybe on Thursday, the bombes would give them the Enigma settings for the day now ending. Then the real work would begin – the laborious business of trying to reconstruct the new Short Weather Code Book – taking the meteorological data from the convoy, matching it to the weather signals already received from the surrounding U-boats, making some guesses, testing them, constructing a fresh set of cribs . . . It never ended, this battle against Enigma. It was a chess tournament of a thousand rounds against a player of prodigious defensive strength, and each day the pieces went back to their original positions and the game began afresh.

Logie, too, seemed rather flat as they walked along the asphalt path towards Hut 8.

'I've sent the others home to their digs for some kip,' he was saying, 'which is where I'm going. And where you ought to go, too, if you're not too high to sleep.'

'I'll just clear up here for a bit, if that's all right. Take the code book back to the safe.'

'Do that. Thanks.'

'And then I suppose I'd better face Wigram.'

'Ah, yes. Wigram.'

They went into the hut. In his office, Logie tossed Jericho the keys to the Black Museum. 'And your prize,' he said, holding up a half-bottle of scotch. 'Don't let's forget that.'

Jericho smiled. 'I thought you said Skynner was offering a full bottle.'

'Ah, well, yes, I did, but you know Skynner.'

'Give it to the others.'

'Oh, don't be so bloody pious.' From the same drawer Logie produced a couple of enamel mugs. He blew away some dust and wiped their insides with his forefinger. 'What shall we drink to? You don't mind if I join you?'

'The end of Shark? The future?'

Logie splashed a large measure of whisky into each mug. 'How about,' he said, shrewdly, offering one to Jericho, 'how about *your* future?'

They clinked mugs.

'*My* future.'

They sat in their overcoats, in silence, drinking.

'I'm defeated,' said Logie at last, using the desk to pull himself to his feet. 'I couldn't tell you the year, old love, never mind the day.' He had three pipes in a rack and he blew noisily through each of them, making a harsh, cracking sound, then slipped them into his pocket. 'Now don't forget your scotch.'

'I don't want the bloody scotch.'

'Take it. Please. For my sake.'

In the corridor, he shook Jericho's hand, and Jericho feared Logie was going to say something embarrassing. But whatever it was he had in mind, he thought better of it. Instead, he merely gave a rueful salute and lurched along the passage, banging the door behind him.

*

The Big Room, in anticipation of the midnight shift, was almost empty. A little desultory work was being done on Dolphin and Porpoise at the far end. Two young women in overalls were on their knees around Jericho's desk, gathering every scrap of waste paper into a couple of sacks, ready for incineration. Only Cave was still there, bent over his charts. He looked up as Jericho came in.

'Well? How's it going for you?'

'Too early to tell,' said Jericho. He found the code book and slipped it into his pocket. 'And you?'

'Three hit so far. A Norwegian freighter and a Dutch cargo ship. They just went straight to the bottom. The third's on fire and going round and round in circles. Half the crew lost, the other half trying to save her.'

'What is she?'

'American Liberty ship. The *James Oglethorpe*. Seven thousand tons, carrying steel and cotton.'

'American,' repeated Jericho. He thought of Kramer. *'My brother died, one of the first . . .'*

'It's a slaughter,' said Cave, 'an absolute bloody slaughter. And shall I tell you the worst of it? It's not going to finish tonight. It's going to go on and on like this for days. They're going to be chased and harried and torpedoed right the way across the bloody North Atlantic. Can you imagine what that feels like? Watching the ship next to you blow up? Not being allowed to stop and search for survivors? Waiting for your turn?' He touched his scar, then seemed to realise what he was doing and let his hand fall. There was a terrible resignation in the gesture. 'And now, apparently, they're picking up U-boat signals swarming all around SC-122.'

His telephone began to ring and he swung away to answer it. While his back was turned, Jericho quietly placed the half-empty half-bottle of scotch on his desk, then made his way out into the night.

His mind, on a fuel of Benzedrine and scotch, seemed to be wheeling away on a course of its own, churning like the bombes in Hut 11, making bizarre and random connections – Claire and Hester and Skynner, and Wigram with his shoulder holster, and the tyre tracks in the frost outside the cottage, and the blazing Liberty ship going round and round over the bodies of half her crew.

He stopped by the lake to breathe some fresh air and thought of all the other occasions when he had stood here in the darkness, gazing at the faint silhouette of the mansion against the stars. He half-closed his eyes and saw it as it might have been before the war. A midsummer evening. The sounds of an orchestra and a bubble of voices drifting across the lawn. A line of Chinese lanterns, pink and mauve and lemon, stirring in the arboretum. Chandeliers in the ballroom. White crystal fracturing on the smooth surface of the lake.

The vision was so strong that he found he was sweating in his overcoat against the imagined heat, and as he climbed the slope towards the big house he fancied he saw a line of silver Rolls-Royces, their chauffeurs leaning against the long bonnets. But as he drew closer he saw that the cars were merely buses, come to drop off the next shift, pick up the last, and that the music in the mansion was only the percussion of telephone bells and the tapping of hurrying footsteps on the stone floor.

In the labyrinth of the house he nodded cautiously to the few people he passed – an elderly man in a dark grey suit, an Army captain, a WAAF. They appeared seedy in the dingy light and he guessed, by their expressions, he must look pretty odd himself. Benzedrine could do funny things to the pupils of your eyes, he seemed to remember, and he hadn't shaved or changed his clothes for more than forty hours. But nobody in Bletchley was ever thrown out for simply looking strange, or the place would have been empty from the start. There was old Dilly Knox, who used to come to work in his dressing gown, and Turing who cycled in wearing a gas mask to try to cure his hay fever, and the cryptanalyst from the Japanese section who had bathed naked in the lake one lunchtime. By comparison, Jericho was as conventional as an accountant.

He opened the door to the cellar passage. The bulb must have blown since his last visit and he found himself peering into a darkness as chill and black as a catacomb. Something gleamed very faintly at the foot of the stairs and he groped his way down the steps towards it. It was the keyhole to the Black Museum, traced in luminous paint: a trick they had learned in the Blitz.

Inside the room the light switch worked. He unlocked the safe and replaced the code book and for a moment he was seized by the crazy notion of hiding the stolen cryptograms inside it as well. Folded into an envelope they might pass unnoticed for months. But when, after tonight, was he likely to pass this way again? And one day they would be discovered. And then all it would take would be a telephone call to Beaumanor and everything would be unravelled – his involvement, Hester's . . .

No, no.

He closed the steel door.

But still he couldn't quite bring himself to leave. So much of his life was here. He touched the safe and then the rough, dry walls. He drew his finger through the dust on the table. He contemplated the row of Enigmas on the metal shelf. They were all encased in light wood, mostly in their original German boxes, and even in repose they seemed to exude a compelling, almost menacing power. These were far more than mere machines, he thought. These were the synapses of the enemy's brain – mysterious, complex, *animate*.

He stared at them for a couple of minutes, then began to turn away.

He stopped himself.

'Tom Jericho,' he whispered. 'You bloody fool.'

The first two Enigmas he lifted down and inspected turned out to be badly damaged and unusable. The third had a luggage label attached to its handle by a bit of string: 'Sidi Bou Zid 14/2/43'. An Afrika Korps Enigma, captured by the Eighth Army during their

371

attack on Rommel last month. He laid it carefully on the table and unfastened the metal clasps. The lid opened easily.

This one was in perfect condition: a beauty. The letters on the keys were unworn, the black metal casing unscratched, the glass bulbs clear and gleaming. The three rotors – stopped, he saw, at ZDE – glinted silver beneath the naked light. He stroked it tenderly. It must only just have left its makers. 'Chiffreirmaschine Gesellschaft,' read their label. 'Heimsoeth und Rinke, Berlin-Wilmersdorf, Uhlandstrasse 138.'

He pushed a key. It was stiffer than on a normal typewriter. When he had depressed it far enough, the machine emitted a clunk and the right-hand rotor moved on a notch. At the same time, one of the bulbs lit up.

Hallelujah!

The battery was charged. The Enigma was live.

He checked the mechanism. He stooped and typed C. The letter J lit up. He typed L and got a U. A, I, R and E yielded, successively, X, P, Q and Q again.

He lifted the Enigma's inner lid and detached the spindle, set the rotors back at ZDE and locked them into place. He typed the cryptogram JUXPQQ and C-L-A-I-R-E was spelled out letter by letter on the bulbs in little bursts of light.

He fumbled through his pockets for his watch. Two minutes to twelve.

He folded the lid back into place and hoisted the Enigma up on its shelf. He made sure to lock the door behind him.

To the people whom he ran past in the mansion's corridors, who was he? Nothing. Nobody. Just another peculiar cryptanalyst in a flap.

Hester Wallace, as agreed, was in the telephone box at midnight, the receiver in her hand, feeling more foolish than afraid as she pretended to make a call. Beyond the glass, two currents of pale sparks were flowing quietly in the dark, as one shift streamed in from the main gate and the other ebbed towards it. In her pocket was a sheet of Bletchley's wood-flecked, brownish notepaper on which were jotted six entries.

Cordingley had swallowed her story whole – indeed, he had been, if anything, a little *too* eager to help. Unable at first to locate the relevant file, he had called in aid a pimply, jug-eared youth with wispy yellow hair. Could this child, she had wondered, this foetus-face, really be a cryptanalyst? But Donald had whispered yes, he was one of the best: now the professions and the universities had all been picked over, they were turning to boys straight out of school. Unformed. Unquestioning. The new elite.

The file had been procured, a space cleared in a corner, and never had Miss Wallace made a pencil move more quickly. The worst part had been at the end: keeping her nerve and not fleeing when she'd finished, but checking the figures, returning the file to the Foetus, and observing the normal social code with Donald –

'*We really must have a drink one of these evenings.*'
'*Yes really we must.*'

'I'll be in touch, then.'

'Absolutely. So shall I.'

– neither, of course, having the slightest intention of ever doing so.

Come on, Tom Jericho.

Midnight passed. The first of the buses lumbered by – invisible, almost, except for its exhaust fumes, which made a puff of pink cloud in its red rear lights.

And then, just as she was beginning to give up hope, a blur of white. A hand tapped softly on the glass. She dropped the telephone and shone her torch on to the face of a lunatic pressed close to the pane. Dark wild eyes and a convict mask of shadowed beard. 'There's really no need to scare me half to death,' she muttered, but that was in the privacy of the phone booth. As she came out, all she said was: 'I've left your numbers on the telephone.'

She held the door open for him. His hand rested on hers. A brief moment of pressure signalled his thanks – too brief for her to tell whose fingers were the coldest.

'Meet me here at five.'

Exhilaration gave a fresh energy to her tired legs as she pedalled up the hill away from Bletchley.

He needed to see her at five. How else could one interpret that, except as meaning he had found a way? A victory! A victory against the Mermagens and the Cordingleys!

The gradient steepened. She rose to tread the pedals. The bicycle waved from side to side like a metronome. The light danced on the road.

Afterwards, she was to reproach herself severely for this premature jubilation, but the truth was she would probably never have seen them anyway. They had positioned themselves quite carefully, drawn up parallel with the track and hidden by the hawthorn hedge – a professional job – so that when she came round the corner and began to bounce over the potholes towards the cottage she passed them in the shadows without a glance.

She was six feet from the door when the headlights came on – slitted blackout headlights, but dazzling enough to splash her shadow against the whitewashed wall. She heard the engine cough and turned, shielding her eyes, to see the big car coming at her – calm, unhurried, implacable, nodding over the bumpy ground.

5

Jericho told himself to take his time. There's no hurry. You've given yourself five hours. Use them.

He locked himself into the cellar room, leaving the key half turned in the keyhole, so that anyone trying to insert *their* key from the other side would find it blocked. He knew he'd have to open up eventually – otherwise, what was he? Just a rat in a trap. But at least he would now have thirty seconds' warning, and to give himself a cover story, he reopened the Naval Section safe and spread the handful of maps and code books across the narrow table. To these he added the stolen cryptograms and key settings, and his watch, which he placed before him with its lid open. Like preparing for an examination, he thought. *'Candidates must write on one side of the paper only; this margin to be left blank for the use of the examiner.'*

Then he lifted down the Enigma and removed the cover.

He listened. Nothing. A dripping pipe somewhere, that was all. The walls bulged with the pressure of the cold earth; he could smell the soil, taste the spores of damp lime plaster. He breathed on his fingers and flexed them.

He would work backwards, he decided, deciphering the last cryptogram first, on the theory that whatever had caused Claire's disappearance was contained somewhere in those final messages.

He ran his fingers down the columns of notation to find the Vulture settings for 4 March – panic day in the Bletchley Registry.

            III V IV GAH CX AZ DV KT HU LW GP EY MR FQ

The Roman numerals told him which three out of the machine's five rotors were to be used that day, and what order they were to be placed in. GAH gave him the rotor starting positions. The next ten letter pairs represented the cross-pluggings he needed to make on the plugboard at the back of the Enigma. Six letters were left unconnected which, by some mysterious and glorious fold in the laws of statistics, actually increased the number of potential different cross-pluggings from almost 8 million million (25 x 23 x 21 x 19 x 17 x 15 x 13 x 11 x 9 x 7 x 5 x 3) to more than 150 million million.

He did the plugging first. Short lengths of corded, chocolate-coloured flex, tipped at either end by brass plugs sheathed in bakelite that sank with satisfying precision into the lettered sockets: C to X, A to Z . . .

Next he lifted the Enigma's inner lid, unlocked the spindle, and slid off the three rotors that were already loaded. From a separate compartment he withdrew the two spares.

Each rotor was the size and thickness of an ice-hockey puck, but heavier: a code wheel with twenty-six terminals – pin-shaped and spring-loaded on one side, flat and circular on the other – with the letters of the alphabet engraved around the edge. As the rotors turned against one another, so the shape of the electrical circuit they completed varied. The right-hand rotor always moved on a letter each time a key was struck. Once every twenty-six letters, a notch in its alphabet ring caused the middle rotor also to move on a place. And when, eventually, the middle rotor reached its turnover position, the third rotor would move. Two rotors moving together was known at Bletchley as a crab; three was a lobster.

He sorted the rotors into the order of the day – III, V and IV – and slipped them on to the spindle. He twirled III and set it at the letter G, V at A and IV at H, and closed the lid.

The machine was now primed just as its twin had been in Smolensk on the evening of 4 March.

He touched the keys.

He was ready.

The Enigma worked on a simple principle. If, when the machine was set in a particular way, pressing key A completed a circuit that illuminated bulb X, then it followed – because electric current is reciprocal – that, in the same position, pressing key X would illuminate bulb A. Decoding was designed to be as easy as encoding.

Jericho realised quite quickly that something was going wrong. He would type a letter of the cryptogram with his left index finger and with his right hand make a note of the character illuminated on the display panel. T gave him H, R gave him Y, X gave him C . . . This was no German he recognised. Still, he went on in the increasingly desperate hope it would start to come right. Only after forty-seven letters did he give up.

HYCYKWPIOROKDZENAJEWICZJPTAKJHRUTBPYSJMOTYLPCIE

He ran his hands through his hair.

Sometimes an Enigma operator would insert meaningless padding around proper words to disguise the sense of his message, but never this much, surely? There *were* no proper words that he could discern hidden anywhere in this gibberish.

He groaned, leaned back in his chair and stared at the flaking plaster ceiling.

Two possibilities, each equally unpleasant.

One: the message had been super-enciphered, its

plaintext scrambled once, and then again to make its meaning doubly obscure. A time-consuming technique, usually reserved for only the most secret communications.

Two: Hester had made a mistake in transcription – had got, perhaps, just one letter wrong – in which case he could sit here, literally for the rest of his life, and still he would never make the cryptogram disgorge its secrets.

Of the two explanations, the latter was the more likely.

He paced around his cell for a while, trying to get some circulation back into his legs and arms. Then he set the rotors back at GAH and made an attempt to decipher the second message from 4 March. The same result:

                    SZULCJK UKAH _

He didn't even bother with the third and fourth but instead played around with the rotor settings – GEH, GAN, CAH – in the hope she might simply have got one letter wrong, but all the Enigma winked at him was more gobbledygook.

Four in the car. Hester in the back seat next to Wigram. Two men in the front. The doors all locked, the heater on, a stench of cigarette smoke and sweat so strong that Wigram had his paisley scarf pressed delicately to his nose. He kept his face half-turned from her all journey and didn't say a word until they reached the main road. Then they pulled across the white lines to overtake another car and their driver switched on a police bell.

'Oh, for Christ's sake, Leveret, cut it out.'

The noise stopped. The car swerved left, then right. They jolted down a rutted track and Hester's fingers sank deeper into the leather upholstery as she strained to avoid toppling into Wigram. She hadn't spoken, either – it was her single, token gesture of defiance, this silence. She was damned if she was going to show her nerves by babbling like a girl.

After a couple of minutes they stopped somewhere and Wigram sat motionless, a statesman, while his men in the front seats scrambled out. One of them opened his door. Torches flashed in the darkness. Shadows appeared. A welcoming committee.

'Got those lights up yet, inspector?' asked Wigram.

'Yes, sir.' A deep male voice; a Midlands accent. 'A lot of complaints from the air raid people, though.'

'Well, they can frig off for a start. Jerry wants to bomb this place, he's welcome. Got the plans?'

'Yes, sir.'

'Good-oh.' Wigram grabbed the roof and hoisted himself out on the running board. He waited a second or two and when Hester didn't move he ducked back inside and flexed his fingers irritably. 'Come on, come on. D'you expect me to carry you?'

She slid across the seat.

Two other cars – no, *three* other cars with their headlights on, showing the cut-out patterns of men moving, plus a small Army truck and an ambulance. It was the ambulance that shook her. Its doors were open and, as Wigram guided her past it, his hand lightly on her elbow, she caught the smell of disinfectant, saw the dun-coloured oxygen cylinders, the stretchers with their coarse brown blankets, their leather straps, their innocent white sheets. Two men sat on the rear bumper, legs outstretched, smoking. They stared at her without interest.

'Been here before?' said Wigram.

'Where are we?'

'Lovers' lane. Not your scene, I fancy.'

He was holding a flashlight and as he stood aside to usher her through a gate she saw a sign: DANGER: FLOODED CLAY PIT – VERY DEEP WATER. She could hear a guttural engine somewhere ahead, and the cry of sea-birds. She started to shake.

'The hand of the Lord was upon me, and carried me out in the spirit of the Lord, and set me down in the midst of the valley which was full of bones.'

'D'you say something?' asked Wigram.

'I don't believe so.'

Oh, Claire, Claire, Claire . . .

The engine noise was louder now, and seemed to be coming from inside a brick building to her left. A faint white light shone up through the gaps in its roof to reveal a tall, square chimney, its lower part engulfed by ivy. She was vaguely aware that they were at the head of a procession. Behind them came the driver, Leveret, and then the second man from the car wearing a belted gaberdine, and then the police inspector.

'Mind yourself here,' warned Wigram, and he tried

381

to take her arm again but she shook him off. She picked her own way between the clumps of brick and the towering weeds, heard voices, turned a corner, and was confronted by a dazzling line of arc lights illuminating a broad path. Six policemen were working their way along it, in parallel, on their hands and knees among a glitter of broken glass and rubble. Behind them, one soldier tended a shuddering generator; another unreeled a drum of cable; a third was rigging more lights.

Wigram grinned and winked at her, as if to say: See what I can command. He was pulling on a pair of light brown, calfskin gloves. 'Got something to show you.'

In a corner of the building, a police sergeant stood beside a rumpled heap of sacks. Hester had to will her legs to move forwards. *Please, Lord, don't let it be her.*

'Get your notebook out,' said Wigram to the sergeant. He hoisted the tails of his overcoat and squatted on his haunches. 'I am showing the witness, first, one lady's coat, ankle-length by the look of it, colour grey, trimmed with black velvet.' He drew it completely out of the sack and turned it over. 'Grey satin lining. Quite badly stained. Probably blood. Need to check it. Collar label: "Hunters, Burlington Arcade". And the witness responded?' He held it up, without looking round.

Remember, I said, 'That's too beautiful to put on every day,' and you said, 'Silly old Hester, that's the only reason there is to wear it'?

'And the witness *responded?*'

'It's hers.'

' "It's hers." Got that? Good. OK. Next. One lady's

shoe. Left foot. Black. High heel. Heel snapped off. Hers, d'you think?'

'How can I tell? One shoe –'

'Largish. Say, size seven. Eight. What size did she take?'

A pause, then Hester, quietly: 'Seven.'

'We've found the other one outside, sir,' said the inspector. 'Near the water's edge.'

'And a pair of knickers. White. Silk. Badly blood-stained.' He held them out at arm's length between finger and thumb. 'Recognise these, Miss Wallace?' He let them drop and rummaged in the bottom of the sack. 'Final item. One brick.' He shone his flashlight onto it; something glinted. 'Also bloodstained. Blonde hairs attached.'

'Eleven main buildings,' said the inspector. 'Eight of them with kilns, four with chimneys still standing. Rail spur here with sidings, linking into the main line, and a branch going off here, right through the site.'

They were outside now, at the spot where the second shoe had been found, and the map was spread over a rusting water rank. Hester stood away from them, Leveret watching her, his hands hanging loosely by his sides. There were more men moving down by the water's edge, torches stabbing the night.

'Local fishing club use a shed here, near the jetty. Three rowing boats usually stored.'

'Usually?'

'Door's been kicked in, sir. Season's over. That's why nobody discovered it. A boat's missing.'

'Since?'

383

'Well, there was some fishing on Sunday. Deep ledgering for carp. That was the last day of the season. Everything was all right then. So any time from Sunday night onwards.'

'Sunday. And we're now into Wednesday.' Wigram sighed and shook his head.

The inspector spread his hands. 'With respect, sir, I have three men stationed in Bletchley. Bedford lent us six, Buckingham nine. We're two miles from the centre of town. There is a limit. Sir.'

Wigram didn't seem to hear him. 'And how big's the lake?'

'About a quarter of a mile across.'

'Deep?'

'Yes, sir.'

'What – twenty, thirty feet?'

'At the edges. Shelving to sixty. Could be seventy. It's an old working. They built the town with what they dug out here.'

'Did they really?' Wigram flashed his light across the lake. 'Makes sense, I suppose. Making one hole out of another.' Mist was rising, swirling in the breeze like steam above a cauldron. He swung the beam round and pointed it back at the building. 'So what happened here?' he said softly. 'Our man lures her out for a shag on Sunday night. Kills her, probably with that brick. Drags her down here . . .' The beam traced the path from the kilns to the water. 'Strong man – must have been, she was a big girl. Then what? Gets a boat. Stuffs the body in a sack maybe. Weights it with bricks. That's obvious. Rows it out. Dumps it. A muffled splash at midnight, just like in the pictures . . . He probably meant to come back for the clothes as well, but something put him off. Perhaps the next pair of lovebirds had already arrived.' He played the light over the mist again. 'Seventy feet deep. Frigging hell! We'll need to put a submarine down there to find her.'

'May I go now?' said Hester. She had kept herself very quiet and composed so far, but now the tears had started and she was drawing in great gulps of air.

Wigram aimed the beam at her wet face. 'No,' he said sadly. 'I'm rather afraid you can't.'

Jericho was replugging the cipher machine as quickly as his numb fingers would permit him.

Enigma settings for German Army key Vulture, 6 February 1943:

```
I V III DMR EY JL AK NV FZ CT HP MX BQ GS
```

The final four cryptograms were hopeless, a disaster, mere chaos out of chaos. He had wasted too much time on them already. He would begin again, this time with the first signal. E to Y, J to L. And if this didn't work? Don't even think it. A to K, N to V . . . He lifted the lid, unfastened the spindle, slid off the rotors. Above his head, the great house was silent. He was too deeply entombed to hear a footstep. He wondered what they were doing up there. Looking for him? Probably. And if they woke up Logie it wouldn't take them long to find him. He slid the rotors into place – first, fifth, third – and clicked them round to DMR.

Almost at once he began to sense success. First C and X, which were nulls, and then A, N, O, K, H.

An OKH . . .

To OKH. *Oberkommando des Heeres.* The High Command of the Army.

A miracle.

His finger hammered away at the key. The lights flashed.

An OKH/BEFEHL. To the office of the Commander-in-Chief.

Dringend.

Urgent.

Melde Auffindung zahlreicher menschlicher Überreste zwölf Km westlich Smolensk . . .

Discovered yesterday twelve kilometres west Smolensk human remains . . .

Hester was locked in the car with Wigram, Leveret standing guard outside.

Jericho. He was asking her about Jericho. Where was he? What was he doing? When did she last see him?

'He's left the hut. He's not at his digs. He's not at the cottage. I ask you: Where the hell else is there to go in this frigging town?'

She said nothing.

He tried shouting at her, pounding his fist on the seat in front, and then, when that didn't work, he gave her his handkerchief and tried sympathy, but the scent of cologne on the silk and the memory of the blonde hair gilding the brick made her want to be sick and he had to wind his window down and get

Leveret to come round and open her door.

'They've found the boat, sir,' said Leveret. 'Blood in the bottom.'

Just before three o'clock, Jericho had the first message deciphered.

```
TO THE OFFICE OF THE COMMANDER IN CHIEF. URGENT.
DISCOVERED TWELVE KILOMETRES WEST SMOLENSK
EVIDENCE HUMAN REMAINS. BELIEVED EXTENSIVE,
POSSIBLY THOUSANDS. HOW AM I TO PROCEED?
LACHMAN, OBERST, FIELD POLICE.
```

Jericho sat back and contemplated this marvel. Well, yes, Herr Oberst, how are you to proceed? I die to know.

Once again he began the tedious procedure of replugging and re-rotoring the Enigma. The next signal had been sent from Smolensk three days later, on 9 February. A, N, O, K, H, B, E, F, E, H, L . . . The exquisite formality of the German armed forces unfolded before him. And then a null, and then G, E, S, T, E, R, N, U, N, D, H, E, U, T, E.

Gestern und heute. Yesterday and today.

And so on, letter by letter, inescapably, remorselessly – press, *clunk*, light, note – stopping occasionally to massage his fingers and straighten his back, the whole ghastly story made worse by the slowness with which he had to read it, his eyeballs pressed to the crime. Some of the words gave him difficulty. What was *mumifiziert?* Could it be 'mummified'? And *Sagemehl geknebelt?* 'Gagged with sawdust'?

```
PRELIMINARY EXCAVATION UNDERTAKEN IN FOREST
NORTH DNIEPER CASTLE YESTERDAY AND TODAY. SITE
APPROXIMATELY TWO HUNDRED SQUARE METRES. TOPSOIL
COVERING TO DEPTH OF ONE POINT FIVE METRES
PLANTED PINE SAPLINGS. FIVE LAYERS CORPSES.
UPPER MUMMIFIED LOWER LIQUID. TWENTY BODIES
RECOVERED. DEATH CAUSED BY SINGLE SHOT HEAD.
HANDS BOUND WIRE. MOUTHS GAGGED CLOTH AND
SAWDUST. MILITARY UNIFORMS, HIGH BOOTS AND
MEDALS INDICATE VICTIMS POLISH OFFICERS. SEVERE
FROST AND HEAVY SNOWFALL OBLIGE US SUSPEND
OPERATIONS PENDING THAW. I SHALL CONTINUE MY
INVESTIGATIONS. LACHMAN, OBERST, FIELD POLICE.
```

Jericho took a tour around his little cell, flapping his arms and stamping his feet. It seemed to him to be peopled with ghosts, grinning at him with toothless mouths blasted into the backs of their heads. He was walking in the forest himself. The cold sliced his flesh. And when he stopped and listened he could hear the sound of trees being uprooted, of spades and pickaxes ringing on frozen earth.

Polish officers?

Puck?

The third signal, after a gap of eleven days, had been sent on 20th February. *Nach Eintreten Tauwetter Exhumierungen im Wald bei Katyn fortgesetzt . . .*

Enigma

FOLLOWING THAW KATYN FOREST EXCAVATIONS RESUMED
EIGHT HUNDRED YESTERDAY. FIFTY-TWO CORPSES
EXAMINED. QUANTITIES OF PERSONAL LETTERS,
MEDALS, POLISH CURRENCY RECOVERED. ALSO SPENT
PISTOL CARTRIDGE CASES SEVEN POINT SIX FIVE
MILLIMETRE STAMPED QUOTE GECO D UNQUOTE.
INTERROGATION LOCAL POPULATION ESTABLISHES ONE
EXECUTIONS CONDUCTED NKVD DURING SOVIET
OCCUPATION MARCH AND APRIL NINETEEN HUNDRED AND
FORTY. TWO VICTIMS BELIEVED BROUGHT FROM
KOZIELSK DETENTION CAMP BY RAIL TO GNIEZDOVO
STATION TAKEN INTO FOREST AT NIGHT IN GROUPS ONE
HUNDRED SHOTS HEARD. THREE TOTAL NUMBER VICTIMS
ESTIMATED TEN THOUSAND REPEAT TEN THOUSAND.
ASSISTANCE URGENTLY REQUIRED IF FURTHER
EXCAVATION DESIRED.

Jericho sat motionless for fifteen minutes, gazing at the
Enigma, trying to comprehend the scale of the
implications. This was a secret it was dangerous to
know, he thought. This was a secret big enough to
swallow a person whole. Ten thousand Poles – our
gallant Allies, survivors of an army that had charged the
Wehrmacht's Panzers on horseback, waving swords –
ten thousand of them trussed, gagged and shot by our
other, more recent, gallant Allies, the heroic Soviet
Union? No wonder the Registry had been cleared.

An idea occurred to him and he went back to the
first cryptogram. For if one looked at it thus:

HYCYKWPIOROKDZENAJEWICZJPTAKJHRUTBPYSJMOTYLPCIE

it was meaningless, but if one rearranged it thus:

```
HYCYK, W . , PIORO, K . , DZENAJEWICZ, J . ,
PTAK, J . , HRUT, B . , PYS, J . , MOTYL, P . , _
```

then out of the chaos was conjured order. Names.

He had enough now. He could have stopped. But he went on anyway, for he was never a man to leave a mystery partially solved, a mathematical proof only half worked-out. One had to sketch in the route to the answer, even if one had guessed at the destination long before the journey's end.

Enigma settings for German Army key Vulture, 2 March 1943:

```
III IV II LUK JP DY QS HL AE NW CU IK FX BR
```

An Ostubaf Dorfmann. Ostubaf for *Obersturmbann-führer.* A Gestapo rank.

```
TO OBERSTURMBANNFUHRER DORFMANN RHSA
ON ORDERS OFFICE COMMANDER IN CHIEF NAMES OF
POLISH OFFICERS IDENTIFIED TO DATE IN KATYN
FOREST AS FOLLOWS
```

He didn't bother to write them down. He knew what he was looking for and he found it after an hour, buried in a babble of other names. It wasn't sent to the Gestapo on the 2nd, but on the 3rd:

```
PUKOWSKI, T.
```

6

A few minutes after 5 a.m., Tom Jericho surfaced, molelike, from his subterranean hole, and stood in the passage of the mansion, listening. The Enigma had been returned to its shelf, the safe locked, the door to the Black Museum locked as well. The cryptograms and the settings were in his pocket. He had left no trace. He could hear footsteps and male voices coming towards him and he drew back against the wall, but whoever they were they didn't come his way. The wooden staircase creaked as they passed on, out of sight, up to the offices in the bedrooms.

He moved cautiously, keeping close to the wall. If Wigram had gone looking for him in the hut at midnight and failed to find him, what would he have done? He would have gone to Albion Street. And seeing Jericho hadn't turned up there, he might by now have roused a considerable search party. And Jericho didn't want to be found, not yet. There were too many questions he had to ask, and only one man had the answers.

He passed the foot of the staircase and opened the double doors that led to the lobby.

You became her lover, didn't you, Puck? The next after me in the great revolving door of Claire Romilly's men. And somehow – how? – you knew that something terrible was going on in that ghastly forest. Wasn't that why you sought her out? Because she had access to information you couldn't get to? And she

391

must have agreed to help, must have started copying out anything that looked of interest. ('*She'd really been much more attentive of late . . .*') And then there came the nightmare day when you realised – who? your father? your brother? – was buried in that hideous place. And then, the next day, all she could bring you was cryptograms, because the British – the British: your trusty Allies, your loyal protectors, to whom the Poles had entrusted the secret of Enigma – the British had decided that in the higher interest they simply didn't want to know any more.

Puck, Puck, what have you done?

What have you done with her?

There was a sentry in the Gothic entry hall, a couple of cryptanalysts talking quietly on a bench, a WAAF with a stack of box files struggling to find the doorhandle with her elbow. Jericho opened it for her and she smiled her thanks and made a rolling motion with her eyes, as if to say: *What a place to find ourselves at five o'clock on a spring morning*, and Jericho smiled and nodded back, a fellow sufferer: *Yes, indeed, what a place . . .*

The WAAF went one way and he went the other, towards the morning star and the main gate. The sky was black, the telephone box almost invisible in the shadows of the arboretum. It was empty. He walked straight past it and pushed his way into the vegetation. Sir Herbert Leon, the last Victorian master of the Park, had been a dedicated arborist, planting his realm with three hundred different species of tree. Forty years of re-seeding, followed by four years without pruning, had turned the arboretum into a labyrinth of secret chambers, and here Jericho squatted on the dry earth and waited for Hester Wallace.

By five fifteen it was clear to him she wasn't coming, which suggested she had been detained. In which case, they were almost certainly looking for him.

He had to get out of the Park, and he couldn't risk the main gate.

At five twenty, when his eyes were thoroughly used to the dark, he began to move northwards through the arboretum, back towards the house, his bundle of secrets heavy in his pocket. He could still feel the effects of the Benzedrine – a lightness in his muscles, an acuteness in his mind, especially to danger – and he offered a prayer of thanks to Logie for making him take it, because otherwise by now he'd be half-dead.

Puck, Puck, what have you done?

What have you done with her?

He came out cautiously from between two sycamores and stepped on to the lawn at the side of the mansion. Ahead of him was the long, low outline of the old Hut 4, with the mass of the big house behind it. He skirted it and went around the back, past some rubbish bins and into the courtyard. Here were the stables where he'd started work in 1939, and beyond those the cottage where Dilly Knox had first pried into the mysteries of the Enigma. Drawn up in a semicircle on the cobbles he could just make out the gleaming cylinders and exhausts of half a dozen motorcycles. A door opened and in the brief glow he saw a dispatch rider, padded, helmeted and gauntleted, like a medieval knight. Jericho pressed himself against the brickwork and waited while the motorcyclist adjusted his pillion, then kicked the machine into life and revved it. Its red light dwindled and disappeared through the rear gate.

He considered, briefly, trying to get out using the same exit, but reason told him that if the main entrance was probably being watched, then so was this. He stumbled on past the cottage, past the back of the tennis courts, and finally past the bombe hut, throbbing like an engine shed in the darkness.

By now a faint blue stain had begun to seep up from the rim of the sky. Night – his friend and ally, his only cover – was preparing to desert him. Ahead, he could begin to make out the contours of a building site. Pyramids of earth and sand. Squat rectangles of bricks and sweet-smelling timber.

Jericho had never before paid much notice to Bletchley's perimeter fence, which turned out, on inspection, to be a formidable stockade of seven-foot-high iron stakes, tapering at their tips into triple spears, bent outwards to deter incursion. It was as he was running his hands over the galvanised metal that he heard a swish of movement in the undergrowth just beyond it, to his left. He took a few steps backwards and retreated behind a stack of steel girders. A moment later, a sentry ambled past, in no great state of alertness, to judge by his slouched silhouette and the shuffle of his step.

Jericho crouched lower, listening as the sounds faded. The perimeter was perhaps a mile long. Say, fifteen minutes for a sentry to complete a circuit. Say, two sentries patrolling. Possibly three.

If there were three, he had five minutes.

He looked around to see what he could see.

A two-hundred-gallon drum proved too heavy for him to shift, but there were planks, and some thick sections of concrete drainage pipe, both of which he found he was able to drag over to the fence. He started to sweat again. Whatever they were building here, it was going to be vast – vast and bombproof. In the gloom the excavations were fathomless. 'FIVE LAYERS CORPSES. UPPER MUMMIFIED LOWER LIQUID . . .'

He upended the pipes and stood them about five feet apart. He laid a plank on top. Then he hefted a second set of pipes on to the first, picked up another length of timber and staggered over with it balanced on his shoulder. He set it down carefully, making a platform with two steps – about the first practical thing he had made since boyhood. He climbed on to the rickety structure and seized the iron spears. His feet scrabbled for a purchase on the rails. But the fence was designed to keep people out, not in. Fuelled by chemicals and desperation, Jericho was just able to pull himself astride it, twist, and lower himself down the other side. He dropped the last three feet and stayed there, squatting in the long grass, recovering his breath, listening.

His final act was to put his foot through the railings and kick away the planks.

He didn't wait to see if the noise had attracted attention. He set off across the field, walking at first, then trotting and finally running, sliding and skidding over the dewy grass. There was a big military camp to his right, concealed by a line of trees only just now materialising. Behind him, he could sense the dawn on his shoulders, brightening by the minute. He looked back only when he reached the road, and that was his last impression of Bletchley Park: a thin line of low, black buildings – mere dots and dashes along the horizon – and above them in the eastern sky an immense arc of cold blue light.

He had been to Puck's digs once before, on a Sunday afternoon a year ago, for a game of chess. He had a vague memory of an elderly landlady who doted on Puck pouring them tea in a cramped front room, while her invalid husband wheezed and coughed and retched upstairs. He could remember the game quite clearly, it had a curious shape to it – Jericho very strong in the opening, Puck in the middle, and Jericho again at the end. A draw agreed.

Alma Terrace. That was it. Alma Terrace. Number nine.

He was moving quickly – long strides and an occasional, loping run – keeping to the side of the pavement, down the hill and into the sleeping town. Outside the pub lingered a soapy smell of last night's beer. The Methodist chapel a few doors down was dark and bolted, its blistered sign unchanged since the outbreak of war: 'Repent ye: for the Kingdom of Heaven is at hand.' He went under the railway bridge. On the opposite side of the road was Albion Street, and a little further along the Bletchley Working Men's Club ('The Co-Operative Society Presents a Talk by Councillor A. E. Braithwaite: The Soviet Economy, Its Lessons for Us'). After another twenty yards he turned left into Alma Terrace.

It was a street like so many others: a double row of tiny red-brick houses running parallel with the railway. Number nine was a clone of all the rest: two little windows upstairs and one downstairs, all three swathed in blackout curtains as though in mourning, a spade's length of front yard with a dustbin in it, and a wooden gate to the road. The gate was broken, the timber splintered grey and smooth like driftwood, and Jericho had to hoist it open. He tried the door – locked – and hammered on it with his fist.

A loud coughing – as loud and immediate as a woken guard dog. He stepped back a pace and after a couple of seconds one of the upstairs curtains flickered open. He shouted: 'Puck, I need to talk to you.'

A steady clop-clop of hooves. He glanced up the road to see a coal dray turning into the street. It passed by slowly and the driver took a good, long look at him, then flicked the reins and the big horse responded, the tempo of its hooves increasing. Behind him Jericho heard a bolt being worked and drawn back. The door opened a crack. An old woman peered out.

'I'm so sorry,' said Jericho, 'but it's an emergency, I need to speak to Mr Pukowski.'

She hesitated, then let him in. She was less than five feet tall, a wraith, with a pale blue, quilted housecoat clutched across her nightdress. She spoke with her

397

hand held in front of her mouth and he realised she was embarrassed because she didn't have her teeth in.

'He's in his room.'

'Could you show me?'

She shuffled down the passage and he followed. The coughing from upstairs had intensified. It seemed to shake the ceiling, to swing the grimy lampshade.

'Mr Puck?' She tapped on the door. 'Mr Puck?' She said to Jericho: 'He must be still asleep. I heard him come in late.'

'Let me. May I?'

The little room was empty. Jericho was across it in three strides, pulling back the curtains. Grey light lit the kingdom of the exile: a single bed, a washstand, a wardrobe, a wooden chair, a small mirror of thick, pink, crystalled glass with birds carved into it, suspended above the mantelpiece by a metal chain. The bed had been lain on rather than slept in, and a saucer by the bedhead was filled with cigarette stubs.

He turned back to the window. The inevitable vegetable patch and hooped bomb shelter. A wall.

'What's over there?'

'But the door was bolted —'

'On the other side of the wall? What's over there?'

With her hand in front of her mouth she looked aghast. 'The station.'

He tried the window. It was jammed shut.

'Is there a back door?'

She led him through a kitchen that couldn't have altered much since Victorian days. A mangle. A hand pump for raising water to the sink . . .

The back door was unlocked.

'He's all right, isn't he?' She'd stopped worrying about her teeth. Her mouth was trembling, the skin around it furrowed, sunken, brown.

'I'm sure. You go back to your husband.'

He was following Puck's trail now. Footprints – large footprints – led across the vegetable patch. A tea chest stood against the wall. It bowed and splintered as Jericho mounted it, but he was just able to fold himself over the top of the sooty brickwork. For a moment he almost tumbled head first on to the concrete path, but then he managed to brace himself and brought his legs up.

In the distance: the whistle of a train.

He hadn't run like this for fifteen years, not since he was a schoolboy being screamed at on a five-mile steeplechase. But here they were again, as grim as ever, the familiar instruments of torture – the knife in his side, the acid in his lungs, the taste of rust in his mouth.

He tore through the back entrance into Bletchley Station and flailed around the corner on to the platform, through a cloud of leaden-coloured pigeons that flapped and rose heavily and settled again. His feet rang on the ironwork of the footbridge. He took the stairs two at a time and ran across the gantry. A fountain of white smoke spurted up to his left, his right, and filtered through the floorboards, as the locomotive passed slowly underneath.

The hour was early, the waiting crowd was small, and Jericho was halfway down the steps to the northbound platform when he spotted Puck about fifty yards away, standing close to the tracks, holding a small suitcase, his head turning to follow the slow parade of compartments. Jericho stopped and clutched the hand rail, bent forwards, struggling for air. The Benzedrine, he realised, was wearing off. When the train at last jolted to a stop, Puck looked around, walked casually towards the front, opened a door and disappeared.

Using the rail to support himself, Jericho picked his way down the last few steps and almost toppled into an empty compartment.

He must have blacked out, and for several minutes, because he never heard the door slam behind him or the whistle blow. The next thing he was conscious of was a rocking motion. The banquette was warm and dusty to his cheek and through it he could feel the soothing rhythm of the wheels – *dah-dah-dee-dee, dee-dee-dah-dah, dah-dah-dee-dee* . . . He opened his eyes. Smudges of bluish cloud edged in pink slipped slowly across a square of white sky. It was all very beautiful, like a nursery, and he could have fallen asleep again, but for a vague recollection that there was something dark and threatening he was supposed to be afraid of, and then he remembered.

Levering himself up, he ministered to his aching head – shook it, rotated it in a figure of eight, then pushed down the window and thrust it into the cold draught of rushing air. No sign of any town. Just flat, hedged countryside, interspersed with barns and ponds that glinted in the morning light. The track was curving slightly and ahead he could see the locomotive

400

flying its long pennant of smoke above a black wall of carriages. They were heading north on the main west-coast line, which meant – he tried to recall – Northampton next, then Coventry, Birmingham, Manchester (probably), Liverpool . . .

Liverpool?

Liverpool. And the ferry across the Irish Sea.

Jesus.

He was stunned by the unreality of it all, yet at the same time by its simplicity, its obviousness. There was a communication cord above the opposite row of seats ('Penalty for improper use: £20') and his immediate reaction was to pull it. But then what? *Think.* He would be left, unshaven, ticketless, drug-eyed, trying to convince some sceptical guard there was a traitor on board, while Puck – what would Puck do? He would climb down from the train and disappear. Jericho suddenly saw the full absurdity of his own situation. He didn't even have enough money to buy a ticket. All he had was a pocketful of cryptograms.

Get rid of them.

He pulled them from his pocket and tore them into fragments, then hung his head back out of the window and released them into the slipstream. They were whipped away, borne up and over the top of the carriage and out of sight. Craning his head the other way, he tried to guess how far up the train Puck was. The force of the wind stifled him. Three carriages? Four? He pulled back in and closed the window, then crossed the swaying compartment and slid open the door to the corridor.

He peered out, carefully.

The rolling stock was standard, pre-war, dark and filthy. The corridor, lit for the blackout by faint blue bulbs, was the colour of a poison bottle. Four compartments off to one side. A connecting door at the front and rear led into the adjacent carriages.

Jericho lurched towards the head of the train. He glanced into each compartment as he passed. Here were a pair of sailors playing cards, there a young couple asleep in one another's arms, there again a family – mother, father, boy and girl – sharing sandwiches and a flask of tea. The mother had a baby at her breast and turned away, embarrassed, when she saw him looking.

He opened the door leading to the next carriage and stepped into no man's land. The floor shifted and pitched beneath his feet like a catwalk at a funfair. He stumbled and banged his knee. Through a three-inch gap he could see the couplings clanking and, beneath them, the rushing ground. He let himself into the other carriage in time to see the big, unsmiling face of the guard emerging from a compartment. Jericho slipped smartly into the lavatory and locked himself in. For a moment he thought he was sharing it with some tramp or derelict but then he realised that this was *him* – the yellowish face, the dwindled and feverish eyes, the windblown hair, the two days' growth of blue-black beard – this was *his* reflection. The toilet was blocked and stinking. A trail of sodden, soiled paper curled from its bowl and wrapped around his feet like an unravelled bandage.

'Ticket please.' The guard rapped loudly. 'Slide your ticket under the door, please.'

'It's in my compartment.'

'Oh, is it then?' The handle rattled. 'You'd better come and show me.'

'I'm not feeling awfully well.' (Which was true.) 'I've left it out for you.' He pressed his burning forehead to the cool mirror. 'Just give me five minutes.'

The guard grunted. 'I'll be back.' Jericho heard the rush of wheels as the connecting door opened, then the slam of it closing. He waited a few seconds then flipped open the lock.

There was no sign of Puck in this carriage, or in the next, and by the time he'd leaped the gyrating iron plates into the third he could sense the train beginning to slow. He moved on down the corridor.

Two compartments filled with soldiers, six in each, sullen-looking, their rifles stacked at their feet.

Then one empty compartment.

Then Puck.

He was sitting with his back to the engine, leaning forwards – the same old Puck, handsome, intense, his elbows on his knees, engrossed in conversation with someone just out of Jericho's line of sight.

It was Claire, thought Jericho. It had to be Claire. It would be Claire. He was taking her with him.

He turned his back on the compartment and moved discreetly crabwise, pretending to look out of the dirty window. His eyes registered an approaching town – scrubland, goods wagons, warehouses – and then an anonymous platform with a clock frozen at ten to twelve, and faded posters with jolly, buxom girls advertising long-dead holidays in Bournemouth and Clacton-on-Sea.

The train crawled along for a few more yards, then stopped abruptly opposite the station buffet.

'Northampton!' shouted a man's voice. 'Northampton Station!'

And if it was Claire, what would he do?

But it wasn't her. He looked and saw a *man*, a young man – neat, dark, tanned, aquiline: in every essence, *foreign* – saw him only briefly because the man was already up on his feet and releasing Puck's hand from a double clasp. The young man smiled (he had very white teeth) and nodded – some transaction had been completed – and then he was stepping out of the compartment and was moving quickly across the platform, sharp shoulders slicing through the crowd. Puck watched him for a moment, then pulled the door shut and sank back into his seat, out of sight.

Whatever his escape plans, they did not appear to include Claire Romilly.

Jericho jerked his gaze away.

Suddenly he saw what must have happened. Puck cycling over to the cottage on Saturday night to retrieve the cryptograms – and instead finding Jericho. Puck returning later to discover the cryptograms were missing. And Puck assuming, naturally, that Jericho had them and was about to do what any loyal servant of the state would do: run straight to the authorities and turn Claire in.

He glanced back at the compartment. Puck must have lit a cigarette. Films of smoke were settling into wide, steel-blue strata.

But you couldn't allow that, could you, because she was the only link between you and the stolen papers? And you needed time to plan this escape with your foreign friend.

So what have you done with her?

A whistle. A frantic working-up of steam. The platform shuddered and began to slide away. Jericho barely noticed, unconscious of everything except the inescapable sum of his calculations.

What happened next happened very quickly and if there was never to be a single, coherent explanation of events, that was due to a combination of factors: the amnesia induced by violence, the deaths of two of the participants, the bureaucratic fog-machine of the Official Secrets Act.

But it went something like this.

About two miles north of Northampton Station, close to the village of Kingsthorpe, a set of points connected the west-coast main line with the branch line to Rugby. With five minutes' notice, the train was diverted off its scheduled course, westwards down the branch line, and very shortly afterwards a red signal warned the driver of an obstruction on the tracks ahead.

The train was therefore already slowing, although he didn't recognise it, when Jericho slid open the door to Puck's compartment. It moved very easily, at a finger's pressure. The layers of smoke rippled and erupted.

Puck was just extinguishing the cigarette (his ashtray was subsequently found to contain five stubs) and he was pushing down the window – presumably because he had noticed the loss of speed, and maybe the diversion, and was suspicious and wanted to see what was happening. He heard the door behind him and turned, and his face, in that instant, became a skull. His flesh was shrunken, tautened, masklike. He was already a dead man, and he knew it. Only his eyes were still alive, glittering beneath his high forehead. They flickered from Jericho to the corridor to the window and back to Jericho. A frantic effort was going on behind them, you could see, a mad and hopeless attempt to compute odds, angles, trajectories.

Jericho said: 'What have you done with her?'

Puck had the stolen Smith and Wesson in his hand, safety catch off. He brought it up. His eyes went through the same routine: Jericho, corridor, window, then Jericho again and finally the window. He tilted his head back, keeping the gun held out at arm's length, and tried to see up the track.

'Why are we stopping?'

'What have you done with her?'

Puck waved him back with the gun, but Jericho didn't care what happened now. He took a step closer.

Puck began to say something like 'Please don't make me' and then – farce, as the door slid open and the guard came in for Jericho's ticket.

For a long moment they stood there, this curious trio – the guard with his large, bland face, creasing with surprise; the traitor with his wavering pistol; the cryptanalyst between them – and then several things happened more or less at once. The guard said 'Give me that' and made a lunge at Puck. The gun went off. The noise of it was like a physical blow. The guard said 'Ooof?' in a puzzled way, and looked down at his stomach as if he had a bad twinge of indigestion. The wheels of the train locked and screamed and suddenly they were all on the floor together.

It may have been that Jericho was the first to crawl free. Certainly he had a memory of actually helping Puck to his feet, of pulling him out from beneath the guard, who was making a ghastly keening sound and leaking blood everywhere – from his mouth and his nose, from the front of his tunic, even from the bottom of his trouser legs.

Jericho knelt over him and said, rather fatuously, because he'd never seen anyone injured before: 'He needs a doctor.' There was a commotion in the corridor. He turned to find that Puck had the outside door open and the Smith and Wesson pointed at him. He was clasping the wrist of his gun hand and wincing as if he'd sprained it. Jericho closed his eyes for the bullet and Puck said – and this Jericho was sure of, because he spoke the words very deliberately, in his precise English: 'I killed her, Thomas. I am so terribly sorry.'

Then he vanished.

The time by now was just after a quarter past seven – 7.17, according to the official report – and the day was coming up nicely. Jericho stood on the threshold of the carriage and he could hear blackbirds singing in the nearby copse, and a skylark above the field. All along the train, doors were banging open in the sunshine and people were jumping out. The locomotive was leaking steam and beyond it a group of soldiers were scrambling down the slight embankment, led – Jericho was surprised to see – by Wigram. More soldiers were deploying from the train itself, to Jericho's right. Puck was only about twenty yards away. Jericho jumped down to the grey stones of the track and set off after him.

Someone shouted, very loudly, almost directly behind him: 'Get out of the fucking way, you fucking idiot!' – wise advice, which Jericho ignored.

It couldn't end here, he thought, not with so much still to know.

He was all in. His legs were heavy. But Puck wasn't making much progress either. He was hobbling across a meadow, trailing a left ankle which autopsy analysis would later show had a hairline fracture – whether from his fall in the compartment or his leap from the train, no one would ever know, but every step must have been agony for him. A small herd of Jersey cattle watched him, chewing, like spectators at a running track.

The grass smelled sweet, the hedges were in bud, and Jericho was very close to him when Puck turned and fired his pistol. He couldn't have been aiming at Jericho – the shot went wide of anything. It was just a parting gesture. His eyes were dead now. Sightless, blank. There was an answering crackle from the train. Bees buzzed past them in the spring morning.

Five bullets hit Puck and two hit Jericho. Again, the order is obscure. Jericho felt as though he had been struck from behind by a car – not painfully, but terrifically hard. It winded him and pitched him forward. He somehow kept on going, his legs cartwheeling, and saw tufts flying out of Puck's back, one, two, three, and then Puck's head exploded in a red blur, just as a second blow – irresistible this time – spun Jericho from his right shoulder round in a graceful arc. The sky was wet with spray and his final thought was what a pity it was, what a *pity* it was, *what a pity it was* that rain should spoil so fine a morning.

SEVEN

PLAINTEXT

PLAINTEXT: The original,
intelligible text, as it was
before encipherment, revealed
after successful decoding or
cryptanalysis.

A Lexicon of Cryptography
('Most Secret', Bletchley Park, 1943)

THE APPLE TREES wept blossom in the wind. It drifted across the graveyard and piled like snow against the slate and marble tombs.

Hester Wallace leaned her bicycle beside the low brick wall and surveyed the scene. Well, this was life, she thought, and no mistake about it; this was nature going on regardless. From inside the church rolled the booming notes of the organ. 'O God, Our Help in Ages Past . . .' She hummed to herself as she tugged on her gloves, tucked a few stray hairs under the band of her hat, straightened her shoulders and strode on up the flagstone path towards the porch.

The truth was, if it hadn't been for her, there would never have been a memorial service. It was she who persuaded the vicar to open the doors of St Mary's, Bletchley, even though she had to concede that 'the deceased', as the vicar primly put it, was not a believer. It was she who booked the organist and told him what to play (Bach's Prelude and Fugue in E flat major to see them all in, the Sanctus from Fauré's *Requiem* to get them all out). It was she who chose the hymns and the readings and had the service cards printed, she who decorated the nave with spring flowers, she who wrote out the notices and posted them around the Park ('a short service of remembrance will be held on Friday 16

413

April at 10 o'clock . . .'), she who lay awake the night
before, worrying in case nobody bothered to come.

But they came all right.

Lieutenant Kramer came in his American naval
uniform, and old Dr Weitzman came from the Hut 3
Watch, and Miss Monk and the girls from the German
Book Room, and the heads of the Air Index and the
Army Index, and various rather sheepish-looking
young men in black ties, and many others whose names
Hester never knew but whose lives had clearly been
touched by the six-month presence at Bletchley Park of
Claire Alexandra Romilly, born 21.12.22 and died
(according to the police's best estimate) 14.3.43: Rest
in Peace.

Hester sat in the front pew with her Bible marked at
the passage she intended to read (I Corinthians 15.li-lv:
'Behold, I show you a mystery . . .') and every time
someone new came in she turned to see if it was *him*,
only to glance away in disappointment.

'We really ought to begin,' said the vicar, fussing
with his watch. 'I've a christening due at half past.'

'Another minute, vicar, if you'd be so good. Patience
is a Christian virtue.'

The scent of the Easter lilies rose above the nave –
virgin-white lilies with green, fleshy stems, white tulips,
blue anemones . . .

It was a long time since she had seen Tom Jericho.
He might be dead for all she knew. She had only
Wigram's word that he was still alive, and Wigram
wouldn't even tell her which hospital he was in, let
alone allow her to visit. He had, though, agreed to pass

on an invitation to the service, and the following day he announced that the answer was yes, Jericho would love to come. 'But the poor chap's still quite sick, so don't count on it is my advice.' Soon Jericho would be going away, said Wigram, going away for a good long rest. Hester hadn't cared for the way he had said this, as if Jericho had somehow become the property of the state.

By five past ten the organist had run out of music to play and there was an awkward hiatus of shuffling and coughing. One of the German Book Room girls began to giggle until Miss Monk told her loudly to hush.

'Hymn number 477,' said the vicar, with a glare at Hester. '"The Day Thou gavest, Lord, is ended."'

The congregation stood. The organist hit a shaky D. They started to sing. From somewhere near the back she could hear Weitzman's rather beautiful tenor. It was only as they reached the fifth verse ('So be it, Lord; thy throne shall never,/Like earth's proud empires, pass away') that Hester heard the door scrape open behind them. She turned, and so did half the others, and there, beneath the grey stone arch – thin and frail and supported by the arm of Wigram, but alive, thank God: indisputably alive – was Jericho.

Standing at the back of the church, in his overcoat with its bullet holes freshly darned, Jericho wished several things at once. He wished, for a start, that Wigram would take his bloody hands off him, because the man made his flesh crawl. He wished they weren't playing this particular hymn because it always reminded him of the last day of term at school. And he wished it hadn't been necessary to come. But it was. He couldn't have avoided it.

He detached himself politely from Wigram's arm and walked, unaided, to the nearest pew. He nodded to Weitzman and to Kramer. The hymn was ending. His shoulder ached from the journey. 'Thy Kingdom stands and grows for ever,' sang the congregation, 'Till all Thy creatures own Thy sway.' Jericho closed his eyes and inhaled the rich aroma of the lilies.

The first bullet, the one that had hit him like a blow from a car, had struck him in the lower left-hand quadrant of his back, had passed through four layers of muscle, nicked his eleventh rib and had exited through his side. The second, the one that had spun him round, had buried itself deep in his right shoulder, shredding part of the deltoid muscle, and that was the bullet they had to cut out surgically. He lost a lot of blood. There was an infection.

He lay in isolation, under guard, in some kind of military hospital just outside Northampton – isolated, presumably, in case, in his delirium, he babbled about Enigma; guarded in case he tried to get away: a ludicrous notion, as he didn't even know where he was.

His dream – it seemed to him to go on for days, but perhaps that was just a part of the dream: he could never tell – his dream was of lying at the bottom of a sea, on soft white sand, in a warm and rocking current. Occasionally he would float up and it would be light, in a high-ceilinged room, with a glimpse of trees through tall, barred windows. At other times, he would rise to find it dark, with a round and yellow moon, and someone bending overhead.

The first morning he woke up he asked to see a doctor. He wanted to know what had happened.

The doctor came and told him he had been involved in a shooting accident. Apparently, he had wandered too close to an Army firing range ('you bloody silly fool') and he was lucky he hadn't been killed.

No, no, protested Jericho. It wasn't like that at all. He tried to struggle up but the pain in his back made him cry out loud.

They gave him an injection and he went back to the bottom of the sea.

Gradually, as he started to recover, the equilibrium of his pain began to shift. In the beginning, it was nine-tenths physical to one-tenth mental; then eight-tenths to two-tenths; then seven to three, and so on, until the original proportions were reversed and he almost looked forward to the daily agony of the changing of his dressings, as an opportunity to burn away the memory of what had happened.

He had part of the picture, not all of it. But any attempt to ask questions, any demand to see someone in authority – any behaviour, in short, that might be construed as 'difficult' – and out would come the needle with its little cargo of oblivion.

He learned to play along.

He passed the time by reading mystery stories, Agatha Christie mostly, which they brought him from the hospital library – little red-bound volumes, warped with use, with mysterious stains on their pages which he preferred not to study too closely. *Lord Edgeware Dies, Parker Pyne Investigates, The Seven Dials Mystery, Murder at the Vicarage.* He got through two, sometimes three a day. They also had some Sherlock Holmes and one afternoon he lost himself for a blissful couple of hours by trying to solve the Abe Slaney cipher in *The Adventure of the Dancing Men* (a simplified Playfair grid system, he concluded, using inverted and mirror images) but he couldn't check his findings as they wouldn't let him have pencil and paper.

By the end of the first week, he was strong enough to take a few steps down the corridor and visit the lavatory unaided.

In all this time, he had only two visitors: Logie and Wigram.

Logie must have come to see him some time at the beginning of April. It was early evening, but still quite light, with shadows dividing the little room – the bed of tubular metal, painted white and scratched; the trolley with its jug of water and metal basin; the chair. Jericho was dressed in blue-striped pyjamas, very faded; his wrists on the counterpane were frail. After the nurse had gone, Logie perched uneasily on the edge of the bed and told him that everyone sent their best.

'Even Baxter?'

'Even Baxter.'

'Even Skynner?'

'Well, no, maybe not Skynner. But then I haven't seen much of Skynner to be honest. He's got other things on his mind.'

Logie talked for a bit about what everyone was

doing, then started telling him about the convoy battle, which had gone on for most of the week, just as Cave had predicted. Twenty-two merchantmen sunk by the time the convoys reached air-cover and the U-boats could be driven off. 150,000 tons of Allied shipping destroyed and 160,000 tons of cargo lost – including the two weeks' supply of powdered milk that Skynner had made that disastrous joke about, remember? Apparently, when the ship went down, the sea had turned white. '*Die grösste Geleitzugschlacht aller Zeiten,*' German radio had called it, and for once the buggers weren't lying. The greatest convoy battle of all time.

'How many dead?'

'About four hundred. Mostly Americans.'

Jericho grunted. 'Any U-boats sunk?'

'Only one. We think.'

'And Shark?'

'Hanging in there, old love.' He patted Jericho's knee through the bedclothes. 'You see, it *was* worth it in the end, thanks to you.'

It had taken the bombes forty hours to solve the settings, from midnight on Tuesday until late on the Thursday afternoon. But by the weekend the Crib Room had made a partial recovery of the Weather Code Book – or enough of it to give them a toehold – and now they were breaking Shark six days out of seven, although sometimes the breaks came in quite late. But it would do. It would do until they got the first of the Cobra bombes in June.

A plane passed low overhead – a Spitfire, to judge by the crack of its engine.

After a while, Logie said quietly: 'Skynner's had to hand over the plans for the four-wheel bombes to the Americans.'

'Ah.'

'Well, *of course*,' said Logie, folding his arms, 'it's all *dressed up* as cooperation. But nobody's fooled. Leastways, *I'm not*. From now on, we're to teleprinter a copy of all Atlantic U-boat traffic to Washington the moment we receive it, then it's two teams working in friendly consultation. Blah, blah, blah. What bloody have you. But it'll come down to brute force in the end. It always does. And when they've got ten times the bombes we have – which won't take very long, I reckon, six months at the outside – what chance do we stand? We'll just do the interception and they'll do all the breaking.'

'We can hardly complain.'

'No, no. I know we can't. It's just . . . Well, we've seen the best days, you and I.' He sighed and stretched out his legs, contemplating his vast feet. 'Still, there is one bright side, I suppose.'

'What's that?' Jericho looked at him, then saw what he meant, and they both said 'Skynner!' simultaneously, and laughed.

'He is *bloody* upset,' said Logie contentedly. 'Sorry about your girl, by the way.'

'Well . . .' Jericho made a feeble gesture with his hand and winced.

There was a difficult silence, mercifully ended by the nurse coming in and telling Logie his time was up. He got to his feet with relief and shook Jericho's hand.

'Now you get well, old love, d'you hear what I'm saying, and I'll come and see you again soon.'

'Do that, Guy. Thank you.'

But that was the last time he saw him.

Miss Monk approached the pulpit to give the first reading: 'Say Not the Struggle Naught Availeth' by Arthur Hugh Clough, a poem she declaimed with great determination, glaring at the congregation from time to time, as if defying them to contradict her. It was a good choice, thought Jericho. Defiantly optimistic. Claire would have enjoyed it:

> 'And not by eastern windows only,
>   When daylight comes, comes in the light,
> In front the sun climbs slow, how slowly,
>   But westward, look, the land is bright.'

'Let us pray,' said the vicar.

Jericho lowered himself carefully to his knees. He covered his eyes and moved his lips like all the others, but he had no faith in any of it. Faith in mathematics, yes; faith in logic, of course; faith in the trajectory of the stars, yes, perhaps. But faith in a God, Christian or otherwise?

Beside him, Wigram uttered a loud 'Amen'.

Wigram's visits had been frequent and solicitous. He would shake Jericho's hand with the same peculiar and tenuous grip. He would plump his pillows, pour his water, fuss with his sheets. 'They treating you well? You

421

want for nothing?' And Jericho would say yes, thank you, he was being well looked after, and Wigram would always smile and say *super*, how *super* everything was – how *super* he was looking, what a *super* help he had been, even, once, how *super* the view was from the sickroom window, as if Jericho had somehow created it. Oh yes, Wigram was charming. Wigram dispensed charm like soup to the poor.

In the beginning it was Jericho who did most of the talking, answering Wigram's questions. Why hadn't he reported the cryptograms in Claire's room to the authorities? Why had he gone to Beaumanor? What had he taken? How? How had he broken the inter-cepts? What had Puck said to him as he leaped from the train?

Wigram would then go away, and the next day, or the day after, come back and ask him some more. Jericho tried to mix in some questions of his own, but Wigram always brushed them away. Later, he would say. Later. All in good time.

And then one afternoon he came in beaming even more broadly than usual to announce that he had completed his enquiries. A little web of wrinkles appeared at the edges of his blue eyes as he smiled down at Jericho. His lashes were thick and sandy, like a cow's.

'So, my dear chap, if you're not too exhausted, I suppose I should tell you the story.'

Once upon a time, said Wigram, settling himself at the bottom of the bed, there was a man called Adam Pukowski, whose mother was English and whose father was Polish, who lived in London until he was ten, and who, when his parents divorced, went away with his father to live in Cracow. The father was a professor of mathematics, the son showed a similar aptitude, and in due course found his way into the Polish Cipher Bureau at Pyry, south of Warsaw. War came. The father was called up with the rank of major to rejoin the Polish Army. Defeat came. Half the country was occupied by the Germans, the other half by the Soviet Union. The father disappeared. The son escaped to France to become one of the fifteen Polish cryptanalysts employed at the French cipher centre at Gretz-Armainvillers. Defeat came again. The son escaped via Vichy France to neutral Portugal, where he made the acquaintance of one Rogerio Raposo, a junior member of the Portuguese diplomatic service and an extremely dodgy character.

'The man on the train,' murmured Jericho.

'Indeed.' Wigram sounded irritated at being interrupted: this was his moment of glory, after all. 'The man on the train.'

From Portugal, Pukowski made his way to England.

Nineteen-forty passed with no news of Pukowski's father or, indeed, of any of the other ten thousand missing Polish officers. In 1941, after Germany invaded Russia, Stalin unexpectedly became our ally. Representations were duly made about the vanished Poles. Assurances were duly given: there were no such prisoners in Soviet hands; any there might have been had been released long ago.

'Anyway,' said Wigram, 'to cut a long story a whole

lot shorter, it appears that at the end of last year, rumours began to circulate among the Poles in exile in London that these officers had been shot and then buried in a forest near Smolensk. I say, is it hot in here or is it me?' He got up and tried to open the window, failed, and returned to his perch on the bed. He smiled. 'Tell me, was it you who introduced Pukowski to Claire?'

Jericho shook his head.

'Ah, well,' sighed Wigram, 'I don't suppose it matters. A lot of the story is lost to us. Inevitably. We don't know how they met, or when, or why she agreed to help him. Or even what she showed him exactly. But I think we can guess what must have happened. She'd make a copy of these signals from Smolensk, and sneak them out in her knickers or whatever. Hide them under her floorboards. Lover-boy would collect them. This may have gone on for a week or two. Until the day came when Pukowski saw that one of the dead men was his own father. And then the next day Claire had nothing to bring him but the undecoded intercepts, because *someone* –' Wigram shook his head in wonder '– someone very, very senior *indeed*, I have since discovered, had decided they just didn't want to know.'

He suddenly reached over and picked up one of Jericho's discarded mystery stories, flicked through it, smiled, replaced it.

'You know, Tom,' he said thoughtfully, 'there's never been anything like Bletchley Park in the history of the world. There's never been a time when one side knew so much about its enemy. In fact, sometimes, I think, it's possible to know too much. When Coventry was bombed, remember? Our beloved Prime Minister discovered from Enigma what was going to happen about four hours in advance. Know what he did?

Again Jericho shook his head.

'Told his staff that London was about to be attacked and that they should go down to the shelters, but that he was going upstairs to watch. Then he went out on to the Air Ministry roof and spent an hour waiting in the freezing cold for a raid he *knew* was going to happen somewhere else. Doing his bit, d'you see? To protect the Enigma secret. Or, another example: take the U-boat tankers. Thanks to Shark, we know where they're going to be, and when, and if we knocked them out we might save hundreds of Allied lives – in the short term. But we'd jeopardise Enigma, because if we did that, Dönitz would know we must be reading his codes. You see what I'm driving at? So Stalin has killed ten thousand Poles? I mean, *please*, Uncle Joe's a national hero. He's winning the frigging war for us. Third most popular man in the country, after Churchill and the King. What's that Hebrew proverb? "My enemy's enemy is my friend"? Well, Stalin's the biggest enemy Hitler's got, so as far as we're concerned, for present purposes, he's a bloody good friend of ours. Katyn massacre? Katyn frigging *massacre?* Thanks awfully, but, really, do shut up.'

'I don't suppose Puck would have seen it quite like that.'

'No, old chap, I don't suppose he would. Shall I tell you something? I think he rather hated us. After all, if it hadn't been for the Poles, we might not even have broken Enigma in the first place. But the people he really hated were the Russians. And he was prepared to do anything to get revenge. Even if it meant helping the Germans.'

'"My enemy's enemy is my friend,"' murmured Jericho, but Wigram wasn't listening.

'And how could he help the Germans? By warning them Enigma wasn't safe. And how could he do *that*?' Wigram smiled and spread his hands. 'Why, with the assistance of his old friend from 1940, Rogerio Raposo, recently transferred from Lisbon and now employed as a courier at the Portuguese legation in London. How about some tea?

> For the dear ones parted from us
> We would raise our hymns of prayer;
> By the tender love which watcheth
> Round thy children everywhere . . .

Senhor Raposo, said Wigram, sipping his tea after the nurse had gone, Senhor Raposo, presently a resident of His Majesty's Prison, Wandsworth, had confessed to everything.

On 6 March, Pukowski had gone to see Raposo in London, handed him a thin, sealed envelope and told him he could make a great deal of money if he delivered it to the right people.

The following day, Raposo flew on the scheduled British Imperial Airways flight to Lisbon carrying said envelope, which he passed to a contact of his on the staff of the German naval attaché.

Two days after that, the U-boat service changed its Short Weather Code Book, and a general review of cipher security began – Luftwaffe, Afrika Korps . . . Oh, the Germans were interested, of course they were. But they weren't about to abandon what their experts still insisted was the most secure enciphering system ever devised. Not on the basis of one letter. They suspected a trick. They wanted proof. They wanted this mysterious informant in Berlin, in person.

'That's our best guess, anyway.'

On 14 March, two days before the start of the convoy battle, Raposo made his next weekly trip to Lisbon and returned with specific instructions for Pukowski. A U-boat would be waiting to pick him up off the coast of northwest Ireland on the night of the 18th.

'And that was what they were discussing on the train,' said Jericho.

'And that was what they were discussing on the train. Quite right. Our man Puck was collecting his ticket, so to speak. And shall I tell you the really frightening thing?' Wigram took another sip of tea, his little finger delicately crooked, and looked at Jericho over the rim of his cup. 'If it hadn't been for you, he might just have got away with it.'

'But Claire would never have gone along with this,' protested Jericho. 'Passed on a few intercepts – yes. For a lark. For love, even. But she wasn't a *traitor*.'

'Lord, no.' Wigram sounded shocked. 'No, I'm sure Pukowski never even told her for *one minute* what he was planning to do. Consider it from his point of view.

She was the weak link. She could have given him away at any moment. So imagine how he must have felt when he saw *you* walk back through the door from Cambridge on that Friday night.'

Jericho remembered the look of horror on Puck's face, that desperate attempt to force a smile. He had already seen what must have happened: Puck leaving a message at the cottage that he needed to talk to her, Claire hurrying back into the Park at four in the morning – *click click click* on her high heels in the darkness. He said quietly, almost to himself: 'I was her death warrant.'

'I suppose you were. He must've known you'd try and get in touch with her. And then, the next night, when he went round to the cottage to get rid of the evidence, the stolen cryptograms, and found you there . . . Well . . .'

Jericho lay back and stared at the ceiling as Wigram rattled through the rest of the story. How, on the night the convoy battle had started, just before midnight, he'd been called by the police and told that a sack full of women's clothing had been found. How he'd tried to find Jericho, but Jericho had disappeared, so he'd grabbed Hester Wallace instead and taken her down to the lakeside. How it had been obvious at once what had happened, that Claire had been bludgeoned, or maybe bludgeoned and strangled, and her body rowed out into the lake and dumped.

'Mind if I smoke?' He lit up without waiting for a reply, using his saucer as an ashtray. He examined the tip of his cigarette for a moment. 'Where was I exactly?'

Jericho didn't look at him. 'The night of the convoy battle.'

Ah, yes. Well, Hester had refused to talk at first, but there's nothing like shock to loosen the tongue and eventually she'd told him everything, at which point Wigram had realised that Jericho wasn't a traitor; realised, in fact, that if Jericho had broken the cryptograms he was probably closer to discovering the traitor than *he* was.

So he had deployed his men. And watched.

This would have been about five in the morning.

First, Jericho was seen hurrying down Church Green Road into the town. Then he was observed going into the house in Alma Terrace. Then he was identified boarding the train.

Wigram had men on the train.

'After that, the three of you were just flies in a jam jar, frankly.'

All passengers disembarking at Northampton were stopped and questioned, and that took care of Raposo. By then, Wigram had arranged for the train to be diverted into a branch line where he was waiting to search it at leisure.

His men had orders not to shoot unless they were shot at first. But no chances were going to be taken. Not with so much at stake.

And Pukowski had used his pistol. And fire had been returned.

'You got in the way. I'm sorry about that.' Still, as he was sure Jericho would agree, preserving the Enigma secret had been the most important objective. And that had been accomplished. The U-boat that had been sent to pick up Puck had been intercepted and sunk off the coast of Donegal, which was a double bonus, as the Germans probably now thought that the whole business had been a set-up all along, designed to trap one of their submarines. At any rate, they hadn't abandoned Enigma.

'And Claire?' Jericho was still staring at the ceiling. 'Have you found her yet?'

'Give us time, my dear fellow. She lies under at least sixty feet of water, somewhere in the middle of a lake a quarter of a mile across. That may take us a while.'

'And Raposo?'

'The Foreign Secretary spoke to the Portuguese ambassador that morning. Under the circumstances, he agreed to waive diplomatic immunity. By noon we'd taken Raposo's flat apart. Dreary place at the wrong end of Gloucester Road. Poor little sod. He really was only in it for the money. We found two thousand dollars the Germans had given him, stuffed in a shoe box on top of his wardrobe. Two grand! Pathetic.'

'What will happen to him?'

'He'll hang,' said Wigram pleasantly. 'But never mind about him. He's history. The question is, what are we going to do with *you*?'

After Wigram had gone, Jericho lay awake for a long time, trying to decide which parts of his story had been true.

'Behold, I show you a mystery,' said Hester.

430

'We shall not all sleep, but we shall all be changed,

'In a moment, in the twinkling of an eye, at the last trump: for the trumpet shall sound, and the dead shall be raised incorruptible, and we shall be changed.

'For this corruptible must put on incorruption, and this mortal must put on immortality.

'So when this corruptible shall have put on incorruption, and this mortal shall have put on immortality, then shall be brought to pass the saying that is written, Death is swallowed up in victory.

'O death, where is thy sting? O grave, where is thy victory?'

She closed her Bible slowly and regarded the congregation with a dry and level eye. In the end pew she could just make out Jericho, white-faced, staring straight ahead.

'Thanks be to God.'

She found him waiting for her outside the church, the white blossom raining down on him like confetti. The other mourners had gone. He had his face raised to the sun and she guessed from the way he seemed to be drinking in the warmth that he hadn't seen it for a long while. As he heard her approach, he turned and smiled and she hoped her own smile hid her shock. His cheeks were concave, his skin as waxy as one of the candles in church. The collar of his shirt hung loosely from his gaunt neck.

'Hello, Hester.'

'Hello, Tom.' She hesitated, then held out her gloved hand.

'Super service,' said Wigram. 'Absolutely super. Everybody's said so, haven't they, Tom?'

'Everybody. Yes.' Jericho closed his eyes for a second and she understood immediately what he was signalling: that he was sorry Wigram was there, but that he couldn't do anything about it. He released her hand. 'I didn't want to leave,' he said, 'without seeing how you were.'

'Oh, well,' she said, with a jollity she didn't feel, 'bearing up, you know.'

'Back at work?'

'Yes, yes. Still blisting away.'

'And still in the cottage?'

'For now. But I think I'll move out, as soon as I can find myself another billet.'

'Too many ghosts?'

'Something like that.'

She suddenly found herself loathing the banality of the conversation but she couldn't think of anything better to say.

'Leveret's waiting,' said Wigram. 'With the car. To run us to the station.' Through the gate Hester could see the long black bonnet. The driver was leaning against it, watching them, smoking a cigarette.

'You're catching a train, Mr Wigram?' asked Hester.

'*I'm* not,' he said, as if the notion was offensive. 'Tom is. Aren't you, Tom?'

'I'm going back to Cambridge,' explained Jericho. 'For a few months' rest.'

'In fact we really ought to push off,' continued Wigram, looking at his watch. 'You never know – there's always a *chance* it may be on time.'

Jericho said, irritably: 'Will you excuse us for just one minute, Mr Wigram?' Without waiting for a reply, he guided Hester away from Wigram, back towards the church. 'This bloody man won't leave me alone for a second,' he whispered. 'Listen, if you can bear it, will you give me a kiss?'

'What?' She wasn't sure she could have heard him correctly.

'A kiss. Quickly. Please.'

'Very well. It's no great hardship.'

She took off her hat, reached over and brushed his thin cheek with her lips. He held her shoulders and said softly in her ear: 'Did you invite Claire's father to the service?'

'Yes.' He had gone mad, she thought. The shock had affected his mind. 'Of course I did.'

'What happened?'

'He didn't reply.'

'I knew it,' he whispered. She felt his grip tighten.

'Knew what?'

'*She isn't dead* . . .'

'How touching,' said Wigram loudly, coming up behind them, 'and I hate to break things up, but you're going to miss your train, Tom Jericho.'

Jericho released her and took a step back. 'Look after yourself,' he said.

For a moment she couldn't speak. 'And you.'

'I'll write.'

'Yes. Please. Be sure you do.'

Wigram tugged at his arm. Jericho gave her a final smile and a shrug, then allowed himself to be led away.

She watched him walk painfully up the path and through the gate. Leveret opened the car door and as he did so, Jericho turned and waved. She raised her hand in return, saw him manoeuvre himself stiffly into the back seat, then the door slammed shut. She let her hand drop.

She stayed there for several minutes, long after the big car had pulled away, then she replaced her hat and went back into the church.

2

'I almost forgot,' said Wigram, as the car turned down the hill. 'I bought you a paper. For the journey.'

He unlocked his briefcase and took out a copy of *The Times*, opened it to the third page and handed it to Jericho. The story consisted of just five paragraphs, flanked by an illustration of a London bus and an appeal for the Poor Clergy Relief Corporation:

MISSING POLISH OFFICERS

GERMAN ALLEGATIONS

The Polish Minister of National Defence, Lieutenant-General Marjan Kukiel, has issued a statement concerning some 8,000 missing Polish officers who were released from Soviet prison camps in the spring of 1940. In view of German allegations that the bodies of many thousands of Polish officers had been found near Smolensk and that they had been murdered by the Russians, the Polish Government has decided to ask the International Red Cross to investigate the matter . . .

'I particularly like that line,' said Wigram, 'don't you: "released from Soviet prison camps"?'

'That's one way of putting it, I suppose.' Jericho tried to give him back the paper, but Wigram waved it away.

'Keep it. A souvenir.'

'Thanks.' Jericho folded the paper and slipped it into his pocket, then stared firmly out of the window to forestall any further conversation. He'd had enough of Wigram and his lies. As they passed under the blackened railway bridge for the final time he surreptitiously touched his cheek and he suddenly wished he could have brought Hester with him for this last act.

At the station, Wigram insisted on seeing him on to the train, even though Jericho's luggage had been sent on ahead at the beginning of the week and there was nothing for him to carry. And Jericho consented in return to have Wigram's hand for support as they crossed the footbridge and strolled along the length of the Cambridge train in search of an empty seat. Jericho was careful to make sure that he, rather than Wigram, chose the compartment.

'Well, then, my dear Tom,' said Wigram, with

mock sadness, 'I'll bid you goodbye.' That peculiar handshake again, the little finger somehow tucked up into the palm. Final things: did Jericho have his travel warrant? Yes. And he knew that Kite would be meeting him at Cambridge to escort him by taxi to King's? Yes. And he'd remembered that a nurse would be coming in from Addenbrooke's Hospital every morning to change the dressing on his shoulder? Yes, yes, yes.

'Goodbye, Mr Wigram.'

He settled his aching back into a seat facing away from the engine. Wigram closed the door. There were three other passengers in the compartment: a fat man in a dirty fawn raincoat, an elderly woman in a silver fox, and a dreamy-looking girl reading a copy of *Horizon*. They all looked innocent enough, but how could one tell? Wigram tapped on the window and Jericho struggled to his feet to lower it. But the time he had it open, the whistle had blown and the train was beginning to pull away. Wigram trotted alongside.

'We'll be in touch when you're fit again, all right? You know where to get hold of me if anything comes up.'

'I certainly do,' said Jericho, and slid the window up with a bang. But still Wigram kept pace with the compartment – smiling, waving, running. It had become a challenge for him, a terrific joke. He didn't stop until he reached the end of the platform, and that was Jericho's final impression of Bletchley: of Wigram leaning forwards, his hands on his knees, shaking his head and laughing.

*

Thirty-five minutes after boarding the train at Bletchley, Jericho disembarked at Bedford, bought a one-way ticket to London, then waited in the sunshine at the end of the platform, filling in *The Times* crossword. It was hot, the tracks shimmered; there was a strong smell of baking coal dust and warm steel. When he'd finished the final clue he stuffed the newspaper, unread, into a rubbish bin and walked slowly up and down the platform, getting used to the feel of his legs. A crowd of passengers was beginning to build up around him and he scanned each face automatically, even though logic told him it was unlikely he was being followed: if Wigram had feared he might abscond, he surely would have arranged for Leveret to drive him all the way to Cambridge.

The tracks began to whine. The passengers surged forwards. A military train passed slowly southwards, with armed soldiers on the engine footplate. From the carriages peered a line of gaunt, exhausted faces, and a murmur went through the crowd. German prisoners! German prisoners under guard! Jericho briefly met the eyes of one of the captives – owlish, bespectacled, unmilitary: more clerk than warrior – and something passed between them, some flash of recognition across the gulf of war. A second later the white face blurred and disappeared, and soon afterwards the London express pulled in, packed and filthy. 'Worse than the bloody Jerries' train,' complained a man.

Jericho couldn't find a seat, so he stood, leaning against the door to the corridor, until his chalk complexion and the sheen of perspiration on his forehead prompted a young Army officer to give up his place. Jericho sat down gratefully, dozed, and dreamed of the German prisoner with his sad owl's face, and then of Claire on that first journey, just before Christmas, their bodies touching.

By 2.30 he was in London, at St Pancras Station, moving awkwardly through the mass of people towards the entrance to the Underground. The lift was out of action so he had to take the stairs, stopping on every landing to recover his strength. His back was throbbing and something wet was trickling down his spine, but whether it was sweat or blood he couldn't tell.

On the eastbound Circle Line platform, a rat scurried through the rubbish beneath the rails towards the tunnel mouth.

When Jericho failed to emerge from the Bletchley train, Kite was irritated but unconcerned. The next train was due in within a couple of hours, there was a good pub just around the corner from the station, and that was where the college porter chose to do his waiting, in the amiable company of two halves of Guinness and a pork pie.

But when the second train terminated at Cambridge, and still there was no sign of Jericho, Kite went into a sulk that lasted him throughout the half hour it took him to trudge back to King's.

He informed the domestic bursar of Jericho's non-appearance, and the domestic bursar told the Provost, and the Provost dithered over whether or not to call the Foreign Office.

438

'No consideration,' complained Kite to Dorothy Saxmundham in the Porter's Lodge. 'Just no bloody consideration at all.'

With the solution in his pocket, Tom Jericho left Somerset House and made his slow way westwards, along the Embankment, towards the heart of the city. The south bank of the Thames was a garden of ruins. Above the London docks, silver-coloured barrage balloons turned and glinted and nodded in the late afternoon sun.

Just beyond Waterloo Bridge, outside the entrance to the Savoy, he managed at last to find a taxi for hire and directed the driver to Stanhope Gardens in South Kensington. The streets were empty. They reached it quickly.

The house was big enough to be an embassy, wide and stucco-fronted, with a pillared entrance. It must have been impressive once, but now the plasterwork was grey and flaking and in places great chunks of it had been blasted away by shrapnel. The windows of the top two storeys were curtained, blind. The house next door was bombed out, with weeds growing in the base-ment. Jericho climbed the steps and pressed the bell. It seemed to ring a long way off, deep within the bowels of the dead house, and left a heavy silence. He tried again, even though he knew it was useless, then retreated across the road to wait, sitting on the steps of the opposite house.

Fifteen minutes passed, and then, from the direction of Cromwell Place, a tall, bald man appeared, startlingly thin – a skeleton in a suit – and Jericho knew at once it must be him. Black jacket, grey-striped trousers, a grey silk tie: all that was needed to complete the cliché was a bowler hat and a rolled umbrella. Instead, incongruously, he carried, as well as his briefcase, a string bag full of groceries. He approached his vast front door wearily, unlocked it and vanished inside.

Jericho stood, brushed himself down and followed.

The door bell tolled again; again, nothing happened. He tried a second time, and a third, and then, with difficulty, got down on his knees and opened the letter flap.

Edward Romilly was standing at the end of a gloomy passage with his back to the door, perfectly still.

'Mr Romilly?' Jericho had to shout through the flap. 'I need to speak to you. Please.'

The tall man didn't move. 'Who are you?'

'Tom Jericho. We spoke once on the telephone. Bletchley Park.'

Romilly's shoulders sagged. 'For God's sake, will you people just *leave me alone!*'

'I've been to Somerset House, Mr Romilly,' said Jericho, 'to the Registry of Births, Marriages and Deaths. I have her death certificate here.' He pulled it out of his pocket. 'Claire Alexandra Romilly. Your daughter. Died on 14 June 1929. At St Mary's Hospital, Paddington. Of spinal meningitis. At the age of six.' He propelled it through the letter flap and watched it slither across the black and white tiles towards Romilly's feet. 'I'm going to have to stay here, sir, I'm afraid, for as long as it takes.'

He let the flap snap shut. Weary with self-disgust, he turned away and leaned his good shoulder against one of the pillars. He looked across the street to the little communal gardens. From beyond the houses opposite came the pleasant hum of the early-evening traffic on Cromwell Road. He grimaced. The pain had begun to move out from his back now, establishing lines of communication into his legs, his arms, his neck; everywhere.

He wasn't sure how long he knelt there, looking at the budding trees, listening to the cars, until at last behind him Romilly unlocked the door.

He was fifty or thereabouts, with an ascetic, almost monkish face, and as Jericho followed him up the wide staircase, he found himself thinking, as he often did on meeting men of that generation, that this would be roughly the age of his father now, if he had lived. Romilly led Jericho through a doorway into darkness and tugged open a pair of heavy curtains. Light spilled into a drawing room full of furniture draped in white sheets. Only a sofa was uncovered, and a table, pushed up close to a marble fireplace. On the table was some dirty crockery; on the mantelpiece, a large pair of matching silver photograph frames.

'One lives alone,' said Romilly apologetically, fanning away the dust. 'One never entertains.' He hesitated, then walked over to the fireplace and picked up one of the photographs. 'This is Claire,' he said, quietly. 'Taken a week before she died.'

A tall, thin girl with dark ringlets smiled up at Jericho.

441

'And this is my wife. She died two months after Claire.'

The mother had the same colouring and bone-structure as the daughter. Neither looked remotely like the woman Jericho knew as Claire.

'She was driving alone in a motorcar,' went on Romilly, 'when it ran off an empty road and struck a tree. The coroner was kind enough to record it as an accident.' His Adam's apple bobbed as he swallowed. 'Does anyone know you're here?'

'No, sir.'

'Wigram?'

'No.'

'I see.' Romilly took the pictures from him and replaced them on the mantelpiece, realigning them precisely as they had been. He stared from mother to daughter and back again.

'This will sound absurd to you,' he said eventually, without looking at Jericho, 'it sounds absurd to *me*, now – but it seemed to be a way of *bringing her back*. Can you understand that? I mean, the idea that another girl of exactly her age would be going around, using her name, doing what she might have done . . . Living her life . . . I thought it might make sense of what had happened, d'you see? Give her death a purpose, after all these years. Foolish, but . . .' He raised a hand to his eyes. It was a minute before he could speak. 'What exactly do you want from me, Mr Jericho?'

Romilly lifted a dustsheet and found a bottle of whisky

and a pair of tumblers. They sat on the sofa together staring at the empty fire.

'What exactly do you want from me?'

The truth, at last, perhaps? Confirmation? Peace of mind? An ending . . .

And Romilly seemed to want to give it, as if he recognised in Jericho a fellow sufferer.

It had been Wigram's bright idea, he said, to put an agent into Bletchley Park. A woman. Someone who could keep an eye on this peculiar collection of characters, so essential to the defeat of Germany, yet so alien to the tradition of intelligence; who had, indeed, destroyed that tradition, turning what had been an art – a game, if you like, for gentlemen – into a science of mass production.

'Who *were* you all? *What* were you? Could *all* of you be trusted?'

No one at Bletchley was to know she was an agent, that was important, not even the commander. And she had to come from the right kind of background, that was absolutely vital, otherwise she might have been dumped at some wretched out-station somewhere, and Wigram needed her *there*, at the heart of the place.

Romilly poured himself another drink and offered to top up Jericho's, but Jericho covered his glass.

Well, he said, sighing, putting the bottle at his feet, it was harder than one might think to manufacture such a person: to conjure her into life complete with identity card and ration books and all the other paraphernalia of wartime life, to give her the right background ('the right *legend*,' as Wigram had termed

443

it), without at the very least dragging in the Home Office and half a dozen government agencies who knew nothing of the Enigma secret.

But then Wigram had remembered Edward Romilly.

Poor old Edward Romilly. The widower. Barely known outside the Office, abroad these past ten years, with all the right connections, initiated into Enigma – and, more importantly, with the birth certificate of a girl of exactly the right age. All that was required of him, apart from the use of his daughter's name, was a letter of introduction to Bletchley Park. In fact, not even that, since Wigram would write her letter: a signature would suffice. And then Romilly could continue with his solitary existence, content to know he had done his patriotic duty. And given his daughter a kind of life.

Jericho said: 'You never met her, I suppose? The girl who took your daughter's name?'

'Good God, no. In fact, Wigram assured me I'd never hear another word about it. I made that a condition. And I didn't hear anything, for six months. Until you called one Sunday morning and told me my daughter had disappeared.'

'And you got straight on the telephone to Wigram to report what I'd said?'

'Of course. I was horrified.'

'And naturally you demanded to know what was happening. And he told you.'

Romilly drained his scotch and frowned at the empty tumbler. 'The memorial service was today, I think?'

444

Jericho nodded.

'May I ask how it went?'

'"For the trumpet shall sound,"' said Jericho, '"and the dead shall be raised incorruptible, and we shall be changed . . ."' He looked away from the photograph of the little girl above the fireplace. 'Except that Claire – my Claire – isn't dead, is she?'

The room darkened, the light was the colour of the whisky, and now Jericho was doing most of the talking.

Afterwards, he realised he never actually told Romilly how he had worked it all out: that host of tiny inconsistencies that had made a nonsense of the official version, even though he recognised that much of what Wigram had told him must have been the truth.

The oddity of her behaviour, for a start; and the failure of her supposed father to react to her disappearance, or to show up at her memorial service; the puzzle of why her clothes had been so conveniently discovered when her body had not; the suspicious speed with which Wigram had been able to halt the train . . . All these had clicked and turned and rearranged themselves into a pattern of perfect logic.

Once one accepted she was an informer, everything else followed. The material which Claire – he still called her Claire – had passed to Pukowski had been leaked with Wigram's approval, hadn't it?

'Because really – in the beginning, anyway – it was nothing, just chickenfeed, compared with what Puck already knew about naval Enigma. Where was the harm? And Wigram let her go on handing it over

445

because he wanted to see what Puck would do with it. See if anyone else was involved. It was bait, if you like. Am I right?'

Romilly said nothing.

It was only later that Wigram had realised he'd made the most almighty miscalculation – that Katyn, and more especially the decision to stop monitoring it, had tipped Puck over the edge into treason, and that somehow he'd managed to tell the Germans about Enigma.

'I assume it wasn't Wigram's decision to stop the monitoring?'

Romilly gave a barely perceptible shake of his head. 'Higher.'

How high?

He wouldn't say.

Jericho shrugged. 'It doesn't matter. From that point on, Puck must have been under twenty-four-hour watch, to find out who his contact was and to catch them both red-handed

'Now, a man under round-the-clock surveillance is not in a position to murder anyone, least of all an agent of the people doing the watching. Not unless they are spectacularly incompetent. No. When Puck discovered I had the cryptograms he knew Claire would have to disappear, otherwise she'd be questioned. She had to vanish for at least a week, so he could get away. And preferably for longer. So between them they *staged* her murder – stolen boat, bloodstained clothes beside the lake. He guessed that would be enough to make the police call off their hunt. And he was right: they have

446

stopped looking for her. He never suspected she was betraying *him* all the time.'

Jericho took a sip of whisky. 'Do you know, I really think he may have loved her – that's the joke of it. So much so that his last words, literally, were a lie – "*I killed her, Thomas, I'm so very sorry*" – a deliberate lie, a gesture from the edge of the grave, to give her a chance to get away.

'And that, of course, was the cue for Wigram, because from his point of view, that confession neatly tied up everything. Puck was dead. Raposo would soon be dead. Why not leave "Claire" to rest at the bottom of the lake as well? All that he needed to do to round the story off was to pretend that it was *me* who led him to the traitor.

'So to say that she's still alive is not an act of faith, but merely logical. She *is* alive, isn't she?'

A long pause. Somewhere a trapped fly barged against a window pane.

Yes, said Romilly, hopelessly. Yes, he understood that to be the case.

What was it Hardy had written? That a mathematical proof, like a chess problem, to be aesthetically satisfying, must possess three qualities: inevitability, unexpectedness and economy; that it should 'resemble a simple and clear-cut constellation, not a scattered cluster in the Milky Way'.

Well, Claire, thought Jericho, here is my proof.

Here is my clear-cut constellation.

*

Poor Romilly, he didn't want Jericho to leave. He had bought some food, he said, on his way home from the office. They could have supper together. Jericho could stay the night – God knew, he had enough room . . .

But Jericho, looking around at the furniture dressed as ghosts, the dirty plates, the empty whisky bottle, the photographs, was suddenly desperate to get away.

'Thank you, but I'm late.' He managed to push himself to his feet. 'I was due back in Cambridge hours ago.'

Disappointment settled like a shadow across Romilly's long face. 'If you're sure I can't persuade you . . .' His words were slightly slurred. He was drunk. On the landing he bumped against a table and switched on a tasselled lamp, then conducted Jericho, unsteadily, down the stairs to the hall.

'Will you try and find her?'

'I don't know,' said Jericho. 'Perhaps.'

The death certificate was still lying on the letter-stand in the hall. 'Then you'll need this,' said Romilly, picking it up. 'You must show it to Wigram. If you like, you can tell him you've seen me. In case he tries to deny everything. I'm sure he'll have to let you see her then. If you insist.'

'Won't that get you into trouble?'

'Trouble?' Romilly gave a laugh. He gestured behind him, at his mausoleum of a house. 'D'you think I care about *trouble*? Come on, Mr Jericho. Take it.'

Jericho hesitated, and in that moment he had a vision of himself – a few years older, another Romilly, struggling vainly to breathe life into a ghost. 'No,' he said at last. 'You are very kind. But I think I ought to leave it here.'

He left the silent street with relief and walked towards the sound of traffic. On Cromwell Road he hailed a cab.

The spring evening had brought out the crowds. Along the wide pavements of Knightsbridge and in Hyde Park it was almost like a festival: a profusion of uniforms, American and British, Commonwealth and exile – dark blue, khaki, grey – with everywhere the splashes of colour from the summer dresses.

She was probably here, he thought, tonight, somewhere in the city. Or perhaps that would have been considered too risky, and she had been sent abroad by now, to lie low until the whole business had been forgotten. It occurred to him that a lot of what she had told him might actually be true, that she could well be a diplomat's daughter.

On Regent Street, a blonde-haired woman on the arm of an American major came out of the Café Royal.

He made a conscious effort to look away.

ALLIED SUCCESS IN NORTH ATLANTIC read a newspaper placard on the opposite side of the street. NAZI U-BOATS SUNK.

He pulled down the window and felt the warm night air on his face.

And here was something very odd. Staring out at the teeming streets he began to experience a definite sense of – well, he could not call it *happiness*, exactly. *Release*, perhaps, would be a better word.

449

He remembered their last night together. Lying beside her as she wept. What had that been? Remorse, was it? In which case, perhaps she *had* felt something for him.

'She never talked about you,' Hester had said.

'I'm flattered.'

'Given the way she used to talk about the others, you should be . . .'

And then there had been that birthday card: 'Dearest Tom . . . always see you as a friend . . . perhaps in the future . . . Sorry to hear about . . . in haste . . . Much love . . .'

It was a solution, of a sort. As good a solution, at any rate, as he was likely to get.

At King's Cross Station he bought a postcard and a book of stamps and sent a message to Hester asking her to visit him in Cambridge as soon as she could.

On the train he found an empty compartment and stared at his reflection in the glass, an image which gradually became clearer as the dusk gathered and the flat countryside disappeared, until he fell asleep.

The main gate to the college was closed. Only the little doorway cut into it was unlocked and it must have been ten o'clock when Kite, dozing beside the coke stove, was woken by the sound of it opening and closing. He lifted the corner of the blackout curtain in time to see Jericho walking into the great court.

Kite quietly let himself out of the Porter's Lodge to get a better view.

It was unexpectedly bright – there were a lot of stars

– and he thought for a moment that Jericho must have heard him, for the young man was standing at the edge of the lawn and seemed to be listening. But then he realised that Jericho was actually looking up at the sky. The way Kite told it afterwards, Jericho must have stood that way for at least five minutes, turning first towards the chapel, then the meadow, and then the hall, before moving off purposefully towards his staircase, passing out of sight.

Acknowledgements

I OWE A debt of gratitude to all those former employees of Bletchley Park who spoke to me about their wartime experiences. In particular, I would like to thank Sir Harry Hinsley (Naval Section, Hut 4), Margaret Macintyre and Jane Parkinson (Hut 6 Decoding Room), the late Sir Stuart Milner-Barry (former head of Hut 6), Joan Murray (Hut 8) and Alan Stripp (Japanese ciphers).

Roger Bristow, Tony Sale and their colleagues at the Bletchley Park Trust answered my questions with great patience and allowed me to wander about the site at will.

None of these kind people bears any responsibility for the contents of this book, which is a work of the imagination, not of reference.

For those readers who would like the facts on which this novel is based, I strongly recommend *Top Secret Ultra* by Peter Calvocoressi (London, 1980), *Codebreakers* edited by F. H. Hinsley and Alan Stripp (Oxford, 1993), *Seizing the Enigma* by David Kahn (Boston, USA, 1991), *The Enigma Symposium* by Hugh Skillen (Middlesex, two volumes, 1992 and 1994), *The Hut 6 Story* by Gordon Welchman (New York, 1982) and *GCHQ* by Nigel West (London, 1986).

Details of the action in the North Atlantic are drawn from the original, decoded signals of the U-boats, held at the Public Record Office in London, and also from *Convoy* by Martin Middlebrook (London, 1976) and *The Critical Convoy Battles of March 1943* by Jürgen Rohwer (English translation, London, 1977).

Finally, I would like to record my special thanks to Sue Freestone and David Rosenthal, neither of whom ever lost faith in *Enigma,* even on those occasions when it was a mystery to its author.

Robert Harris
June 1995

ARCHANGEL

IN MEMORY OF

Dennis Harris
1923–1996

and for

Matilda

Prologue

Rapava's story

'Death solves all problems – no man, no problem.'
J. V. Stalin, 1918

LATE ONE NIGHT a long time ago – before you were even born, boy – a bodyguard stood on the verandah at the back of a big house in Moscow, smoking a cigarette. It was a cold night, without stars or moon, and he smoked for the warmth of it as much as anything else, his big, farm lad's hands cupped around the burning cardboard tube of a Georgian *papirosa*.

This bodyguard's name was Papu Rapava. He was twenty-five years old, a Mingrelian, from the north-eastern shoreland of the Black Sea. And as for the house – well, *fortress* would have been a better word. It was a tsarist mansion, half a block long, in the diplomatic sector, not far from the river. Somewhere in the frosty darkness at the bottom of the walled garden was a cherry orchard, and beyond it a wide street – Sadovaya-Kudrinskaya – and beyond that the grounds of the Moscow Zoo.

There was no traffic. Very faintly in the distance, when it was quiet, like now, and the wind was in the right direction, you could hear the howling of caged wolves.

By this time the girl had stopped screaming, which was a mercy, for it had got on Rapava's nerves. She couldn't have been more than fifteen, not much older than his own kid sister, and when he had picked her up and delivered her, she had looked at him – looked at him – well, to be honest, boy, he preferred not to talk of it, even now, nearly fifty years later.

Anyway, the girl had finally shut up and he was enjoying his cigarette when the telephone rang. This must have been about two a.m. He would never forget it. Two o'clock in the

3

morning on the second of March, 1953. In the cold stillness of the night the bell sounded as loud as a fire alarm.

Now, normally – you have to understand this – there were four guards on duty during an evening shift: two in the house and two in the street. But when there was a girl, the Boss liked his security kept to a minimum, at least indoors, so on this particular night Rapava was alone. He threw down his cigarette, sprinted through the guard room, past the kitchen and into the hall. The phone was old-fashioned, pre-war, fastened to the wall – Holy Mother, it was making a racket! – and he grabbed the receiver mid-ring.

A man said: 'Lavrenty?'

'He's not here, comrade.'

'Get him. It's Malenkov.' The normally ponderous voice was hoarse with panic.

'Comrade –'

'Get him. Tell him something's happened. Something's happened at Blizhny.'

'KNOW what I mean by Blizhny, boy?' asked the old man.

There were two of them in the tiny bedroom, on the twenty-third floor of the Ukraina Hotel, slumped in a pair of cheap foam armchairs, so close their knees were almost touching. A bedside lamp threw their dim shadows on to the curtained window – one profile bony, picked bare by time, the other still fleshy, middle-aged.

'Yes,' said the middle-aged man, whose name was Fluke Kelso. 'Yes, I know what Blizhny means.' (*Of course I bloody know*, he felt like saying, *I did teach Soviet history at Oxford for ten bloody years –*)

Blizhny is the Russian word for 'near'. 'Near', in the Kremlin of the forties and fifties, was shorthand for the 'Near

Dacha'. And the Near Dacha was at Kuntsevo, just outside Moscow – double-perimeter fence, three hundred NKVD special troops and eight camouflaged 30-millimetre anti-aircraft guns, all hidden in the birch forest to protect the dacha's solitary, elderly resident.

Kelso waited for the old man to carry on, but Rapava was suddenly preoccupied, trying to light a cigarette from a book of matches. He couldn't manage it. His fingers couldn't grasp the flimsy sticks. He had no fingernails.

'So what did you do?' Kelso leaned across and lit Rapava's cigarette for him, hoping to mask the question with the gesture, trying to keep the excitement out of his voice. On the little table between them, hidden among the empty bottles and the dirty glasses and the ashtray and the crumpled packs of Marlboro, was a miniature cassette recorder which Kelso had put there when he thought Rapava wasn't looking. The old man sucked hard on the cigarette and then contemplated the tip with gratitude. He tossed the matches on to the floor.

'You know about Blizhny?' he said at last, settling back in his chair. 'Then you know what I did.'

Thirty seconds after answering the telephone, young Papu Rapava was knocking on Beria's door.

POLITBURO member Lavrenty Pavlovich Beria, draped in a loose red silk kimono through which his belly sloped like a great white sack of sand, called Rapava a cunt in Mingrelian, and gave him a shove in the chest that sent him stumbling backwards into the corridor. Then he pushed past him and padded off towards the stairs, his sweaty white feet leaving prints of moisture on the parquet flooring.

Through the open door, Rapava could see into the bedroom – the big wooden bed, a heavy brass lampstand in the form of a dragon, the crimson sheets, the white limbs of the girl, sprawled like a sacrifice. Her eyes were wide open, dark and vacant. She made no effort to cover herself. On the bedside table was a jug of water and an array of medicine bottles. A scattering of large white pills had fallen across the pale yellow Aubusson carpet.

He couldn't remember anything else, or exactly how long he had stood there before Beria came panting back up the stairs, all fired up by his conversation with Malenkov, throwing the girl's clothes at her, shouting at her to *get out, get out,* ordering Rapava to bring round the car.

Rapava asked who else he wanted. (He had in mind Nadaraya, the head of the bodyguard, who normally went everywhere with the Boss. And maybe Sarsikov, who at that moment was deep in a vodka stupor, snoring in the guard house at the side of the building.) At this, Beria, who had his back to Rapava and was beginning to shrug off his dressing gown, stopped for a moment, and glanced over his fleshy shoulder – thinking, thinking – you could see his little eyes flickering behind their rimless pince-nez.

'No,' he said at last. 'Just you.'

The car was American – a Packard, twelve cylinders, dark green bodywork, running-board a half-metre wide – a beauty. Rapava backed it out of the garage and reversed it down Vspolnyi Street until he was directly outside the front entrance. He left the engine running to try to get the heater going, jumped out and took up the standard NKVD position beside the rear passenger door: left hand on hip, coat and jacket pulled slightly open, shoulder holster exposed, right hand on the butt of his Makarov pistol, checking the street up and down. Beso Dumbadze, another of the Mingrelian boys, came running round the corner to see what was going on, just as the Boss stepped out of the house and on to the pavement.

'WHAT was he wearing?'

'What the hell do I know what he was wearing, boy?' said the old man, irritably. 'What the hell does it matter what he was wearing?'

ACTUALLY, now he stopped to think of it, the Boss was wearing grey – grey coat, grey suit, grey pullover, no tie – and what with this, and his pince-nez, and his sloping shoulders, and his big, domed head, he looked like nothing so much as an owl – an old, malevolent grey owl. Rapava opened the door and Beria got in the back, and Dumbadze – who was about ten yards away – made a little *what the fuck do I do?* gesture with his hands, to which Rapava gave a shrug – what the fuck did *he* know? He ran round the car to the driver's seat, slid behind the wheel, jammed the gear stick in to first, and they were off.

He had driven the fifteen miles out to Kuntsevo a dozen times before, always at night and always as part of the General Secretary's convoy – and *that* was some performance, boy, I can tell you. Fifteen cars with curtained rear windows, half the Politburo – Beria, Malenkov, Molotov, Bulganin, Khrushchev – plus bodyguards: out of the Kremlin, through the Borovitskiy Gate, down the ramp, accelerating to 75 miles an hour, the militia holding back the traffic at every intersection, two thousand plainclothes NKVD men lining the government route. And you never knew which car the GenSec was in until, at the last minute, just as they turned off the highway into the woods, one of the big ZiLs would pull out and accelerate to the front of the cortège, and the rest of them would all slow down to let the Rightful Heir of Lenin go in first.

But there was nothing like that tonight. The wide road was empty and once they were across the river Rapava was able to let the big Yankee car have its head, the speedo flickering up to nearly 90, while Beria sat in the back as still as a rock. After twelve minutes, the city was behind them. After fifteen, at the end of the highway from Poklonnaya Gora, they slowed for the hidden turning. The tall white strips of the silver birches strobed in the headlights.

How quiet the forest was, how dark, how limitless – like a gently rustling sea. Rapava felt that it might stretch all the way to the Ukraine. A half-mile of track took them to the first perimeter fence where a red-and-white pole lay waist-high across the road. Two NKVD specials in capes and caps carrying sub-machine guns strolled out of the sentry box, saw Beria's stone face, saluted smartly and raised the barrier. The road curved for another hundred yards, past the hunched shadows of big shrubs, and then the Packard's powerful lights picked out the second fence, a fifteen foot high wall with gun-slits. Iron gates were swung open from the inside by unseen hands.

And then the dacha.

Rapava had been expecting something unusual – he wasn't sure what – cars, men, uniforms, the bustle of a crisis. But the two-storey house was in darkness, save for one yellow lantern above the entrance. In this light, a figure waited – the unmistakable plump and dark-haired form of the Deputy Chairman of the Council of Ministers, Georgiy Maksimilanovich Malenkov. And here was an odd thing, boy: he had taken off his shiny new shoes and had them wedged under one fat arm.

Beria was out of the car almost before it had stopped and in a flash he had Malenkov by the elbow and was listening to him, nodding, talking quietly, looking this way and that. Rapava heard him say, 'Moved him? Have you moved him?' And then Beria snapped his fingers in Rapava's direction, and Rapava realised he was being summoned to follow them inside.

Always before on his visits to the dacha he had either waited in the car for the Boss to emerge, or had gone to the guardhouse for a drink and a smoke with the other drivers. You have to understand that *inside* was forbidden territory. Nobody except the GenSec's staff and invited guests ever went *inside*. Now, moving into the hall, Rapava suddenly felt almost suffocated by panic – physically choked, as if someone had their hands around his windpipe.

Malenkov was walking ahead in his stockinged feet and even the Boss was on tiptoe, so Rapava played follow-my-leader and tried not to make a sound. Nobody else was about. The house seemed empty. The three of them crept down a passage, past an upright piano, and into a dining room with chairs for eight. The light was on. The curtains were drawn. There were some papers on the table, and a rack of Dunhill pipes. A wind-up gramophone was in one corner. Above the fireplace was a blown up black and white photograph in a cheap wooden frame: the GenSec as a younger man, sitting in a garden somewhere on a sunny day with Comrade Lenin. At the far end of the room was a door. Malenkov turned to them and put a pudgy finger to his lips, then opened it very slowly.

THE old man closed his eyes and held out his empty glass for a refill. He sighed.

'You know, boy, people criticise Stalin, but you've got to say this for him: he lived like a worker. Not like Beria – *he* thought he was a prince. But Comrade Stalin's room was a plain man's room. You've got to say that for Stalin. He was always one of us.'

CAUGHT in the draught of the opening door, a red candle flickered in the corner beneath a small icon of Lenin. The only other source of light was a shaded reading lamp on a desk. In the centre of the room was a large sofa that had been made up as a bed. A coarse brown army blanket trailed off it on to a tiger-skin rug. On the rug, on his back, breathing heavily and apparently asleep, was a short, fat, elderly, ruddy-faced man in a dirty white vest and long woollen underpants. He had soiled himself. The room was hot and stank of human waste.

Malenkov put his podgy hand to his mouth and stayed close to the door. Beria went quickly over to the rug, unbuttoned his overcoat and fell to his knees. He put his hands on Stalin's forehead and pulled back both eyelids with his thumbs, revealing sightless, bloodshot yolks.

'Josef Vissarionovich,' he said softly, 'it's Lavrenty. Dear comrade, if you can hear me, move your eyes. Comrade?' Then to Malenkov, but all the while looking at Stalin: 'And you say he could have been like this for *twenty hours?*'

Behind his palm, Malenkov made a gagging sound. There were tears on his smooth cheeks.

'Dear comrade, move your eyes . . . Your eyes, dear comrade . . . Comrade? Ah, fuck it.' Beria pulled his hands away and stood up, wiping his fingers on his coat. 'It's a stroke right enough. He's meat. Where are Starostin and the boys? And Butusova?'

Malenkov was blubbing by now and Beria had to stand between him and the body – literally had to block his view to get his attention. He grasped Malenkov by the shoulders and began talking very quietly and very fast to him, as one would to a child – told him to forget Stalin, that Stalin was history, Stalin was meat, that the important thing was what they did next, that they had to stand together. Now: where were the boys? Were they still in the guard room?

Malenkov nodded and wiped his nose on his sleeve.

'All right,' said Beria. 'This is what you do.'

Malenkov was to put on his shoes and go tell the guards that Comrade Stalin was sleeping, that he was drunk and why the fuck had he and Comrade Beria been dragged out of their beds for nothing? He was to tell them not to touch the telephone, and not to call any doctors. ('You listening, Georgiy?') Especially no doctors, because the GenSec thought all doctors were Jewish poisoners – remember? Now, what was the time? Three? All right. At eight – no, better, seven-thirty – Malenkov was to start calling the leadership. He was to say that he and Beria wanted a full Politburo meeting here, at Blizhny, at nine. He was to say they were worried about Josef Vissarionovich's health and that a collective decision on treatment was necessary.

Beria rubbed his hands. 'That should start them shitting themselves. Now let's get him up on the couch. You,' he said to Rapava. 'Get hold of his legs.'

THE old man had been sinking deeper into his chair as he talked, his feet sprawled, his eyes shut, his voice a monotone. Suddenly he let out a long breath and hauled himself upright again. He looked around the hotel bedroom in a panic. 'Need to have a piss, boy. Gotta piss.'

'In there.'

He rose with a drunk's careful dignity. Through the flimsy wall, Kelso heard the sound of his urine drilling into the back of the toilet bowl. Fair enough, he thought. There was a lot to unload. He had been lubricating Rapava's memory for the best part of four hours by now: Baltika beer first, in the Ukraina's lobby bar, then Zubrovka in a café across the street, and finally single-malt Scotch in the cramped intimacy of his room. It was like playing a fish: playing a fish through a river of booze. He noticed the book of matches lying on the floor where Rapava had thrown it and he reached down and picked it up. On the back flap was the name of a bar or a nightclub – ROBOTNIK – and an address near the Dinamo Stadium. The lavatory flushed and Kelso quickly slipped the matches into his pocket, then Rapava reappeared, leaning against the door jamb, buttoning his flies.

'What's the time, boy?'

'Nearly one.'

'Gotta go. They'll think I'm your fucking boyfriend.' Rapava made an obscene gesture with his hand.

Kelso pretended to laugh. Sure, he'd call down for a taxi in a minute. Sure. But let's just finish this bottle first – he reached over for the Scotch and surreptitiously checked that the tape was still running – finish the bottle, comrade, *and finish the story.*

The old man scowled and looked at the floor. The story was finished already. There was nothing more to say. They got Stalin up on to the couch – so, what of it? Malenkov went off to talk to the guards. Rapava drove Beria home. Everyone knows the rest. A day or two later, Stalin was dead. And not long after that, Beria was dead. Malenkov – well, Malenkov hung around for years after his disgrace (Rapava saw him once, in the seventies, shuffling through the Arbat) but now even Malenkov was dead. Nadaraya, Sarsikov, Dumbadze, Starostin, Butusova – dead, dead. The Party was dead. The whole fucking country was dead, come to that.

'But there's more to your story, surely,' said Kelso. 'Please sit down Papu Gerasimovich, and let us finish the bottle.'

He spoke politely and hesitantly, for he sensed that the anaesthetic of alcohol and vanity might be wearing off, and that Rapava, on coming round, might suddenly realise he was talking far too much. He felt another spasm of irritation. Christ, they were always so bloody *difficult*, these old NKVD men – difficult and maybe even still *dangerous*. Kelso was a historian, in his middle forties, thirty years younger than Papu Rapava. But he was out of condition – to be truthful, he had never really been *in* condition – and he wouldn't have fancied his chances if the old man turned rough. Rapava, after all, was a survivor of the Arctic Circle camps. He wouldn't have forgotten how to hurt someone – hurt someone very quickly, guessed Kelso, and probably very badly.

He filled Rapava's glass, topped up his own, and forced himself to keep on talking.

'I mean, here you are, twenty-five years old, in the General Secretary's bedroom. You couldn't get any closer to the centre than that – that was the inner sanctum, that was *sacred*. So what was Beria up to, taking you in there?'

'You deaf, boy? I said. He needed me to move the body.'

'But why you? Why not one of Stalin's regular guards? It was they who'd found him, after all, and alerted Malenkov in the first place. Or why didn't Beria take one of his more senior boys out to Blizhny? Why did he specifically take *you?*'

Rapava was swaying, staring now at the glass of Scotch,

and afterwards Kelso decided that the whole night really turned upon this one thing: that Rapava needed another drink, and he needed it at that precise instant, and he needed these two things in combination more than he needed to leave. He came back and sat down heavily, drained the glass in one, then held it out to be filled again.

'Papu Rapava,' continued Kelso, pouring another three fingers of scotch. 'Nephew of Avksenty Rapava, Beria's oldest crony in the Georgian NKVD. Younger than the others on the staff. A new boy in the city. Maybe a little more naïve than the rest? Am I right? Precisely the sort of eager young fellow the Boss might have looked at and thought: *yes, I could use him, I could use Rapava's boy, he would keep a secret.*'

The silence lengthened and deepened until it was almost tangible, as if someone had come into the room and joined them. Rapava's head began to rock from side to side, then he leaned forward and clasped the back of his scrawny neck with his hands, staring at the worn carpet. His grey hair was cropped close to his skull. An old, puckered scar ran from his crown almost to his temple. It looked as if it had been stitched up by a blind man using string. And those fingers: blackened yellow tips and not a nail on one of them.

'Turn off your machine, boy,' he said, quietly. He nodded towards the table. 'Turn it off. Now take out the tape – that's it – and leave it where I can see it.'

COMRADE Stalin was only a short man – five foot four – but he was heavy. Holy Mother, he was heavy! It was as if he wasn't made of fat and bone, but of some denser stuff. They dragged him across the wooden floor, his head lolling and banging on the polished blocks, and then they had to lever him up, legs first. Rapava noticed – couldn't help noticing, as

14

they were almost in his face – that the second and third toes of the GenSec's left foot were webbed – the Devil's mark – and when the others weren't looking, he crossed himself.

'Now, young comrade,' said Beria, when Malenkov had gone, 'do you like standing on the ground, or would you prefer to be under it?'

At first, Rapava couldn't believe he had heard properly. That was when he knew his life would never be the same again, and that he'd be lucky to survive this night. He whispered, 'I like standing on it, Boss.'

'Good lad.' Beria made a pincer of his thumb and forefinger. 'We need to find a key. About so big. Looks like the sort of key you might use to wind a clock. He keeps it on a brass ring with a piece of string attached. Check his clothes.'

The familiar grey tunic was hanging off the back of a chair. Grey pants were neatly folded over it. Beside them was a pair of high black cavalry boots, their heels built up an inch or so. Rapava's limbs moved jerkily. What kind of dream was this? The Father and Teacher of the Soviet People, the Inspirer and Organiser of the Victory of Communism, the Leader of All Progressive Humanity, with half his iron brain destroyed, lying filthy on the sofa, while the two of them went through his room like a pair of thieves? Nevertheless, he did as he was ordered and started on the tunic while Beria attacked the desk with an old Chekist's skill – pulling out drawers, upending them, scavenging through their contents, sweeping back the detritus and replacing them on their runners.

There was nothing in the tunic and nothing in the trousers, either, apart from a soiled handkerchief, brittle with dried phlegm. By now, Rapava's eyes had grown used to the gloom, and he was better able to see his surroundings. On one wall was a large Chinese print of a tiger. On another – and this was the strangest thing of all – Stalin had stuck up photographs of children. Toddlers, mostly. Not proper prints, but pictures roughly torn out of magazines and newspapers. There must have been a couple of dozen of them.

'Anything?'

'No, Boss.'

'Try the couch.'

They had put Stalin on his back, with his hands folded on his paunch, and you'd have thought the old fellow was merely asleep. His breathing was heavy. He was almost snoring. Close up, he didn't look much like his pictures. His face was mottled red and fleshy, pitted with shallow cratered scars. His moustache and eyebrows were whitish grey. You could see his scalp through his thin hair. Rapava leaned over him – ah! the smell: it was as if he were already rotting – and slid his hand down into the gap between the cushions and the sofa's back. He worked his fingers all the way down, leaning left towards the GenSec's feet then moving right again, up towards the head until, at last, the tip of his forefinger touched something hard and he had to stretch to retrieve it, his arm pressing gently against Stalin's chest.

And then – an awful thing: the most horrible, terrible thing. As he withdrew the key and called in a whisper to the Boss, the GenSec gave a grunt and his eyes jerked open – an animal's yellow eyes, full of rage and fear. Even Beria faltered when he saw them. No other part of the body moved, but a kind of straining growl came from the throat. Hesitantly, Beria came closer and peered down at him, then passed his hand in front of Stalin's eyes. That seemed to give him an idea. He took the key from Rapava and let it dangle at the end of its cord a few inches above Stalin's face. The yellow eyes locked on to it at once, and followed it, never left it, through all the points of the compass. Beria, smiling now, let it circle slowly for at least half a minute, then abruptly snatched it away and caught it in his palm. He closed his fingers around it and offered his clenched fist to Stalin.

Such a sound, boy! More animal than human! It pursued Rapava out of that room and along the passage and down all the years, from that night to this.

THE bottle of Scotch was drained and Kelso was on his knees now before the mini-bar like a priest before his altar. He wondered how his hosts at the historical symposium would feel when they got the bar bill, but that was less important right now than the task of keeping the old man fuelled and talking. He pulled out handfuls of miniatures – vodka, more Scotch, gin, brandy, something German made of cherries – and cradled them across the room to the table. As he sat down and released them a couple of bottles rolled on to the floor but Rapava paid them no heed. He wasn't an old man in the Ukraina any more; he was back in fifty-three – a frightened twenty-five-year-old at the wheel of a dark green Packard, the highway to Moscow shining white in the headlights before him, Lavrenty Beria rocklike in the rear.

THE big car flew along the Kutuzovskiy Prospekt and through the silent sweep of the western suburbs. At three-thirty it crossed the Moskva at the Borodinskiy Bridge and headed at speed towards the Kremlin, entering through the south-western gate on the opposite side to Red Square.

Once they had been waved inside, Beria leaned forward

and gave Rapava directions – left past the Armoury, then sharp right through a narrow entrance into an inner courtyard. There were no windows, just half a dozen small doors. The icy cobbles in the darkness glowed crimson like wet blood. Looking up, Rapava saw they were beneath a giant red neon star.

Beria was quickly through one of the doors and Rapava had to scramble to follow him. A little flagstoned passage took them to a cage-lift that was older than the Revolution. A rattle of iron and the drone of an engine accompanied their slow ascent through two silent, unlit floors. They jolted to a stop and Beria wrenched back the gate. Then he was off again, down the corridor, walking fast, swinging the key on the end of its length of string.

Don't ask me where we went, boy, because I can't tell you. There was a long, carpeted corridor lined with fancy busts on marble pedestals, then an iron spiral staircase which had to be climbed down, and then a huge ballroom, as vast as an ocean liner, with giant mirrors ten yards high, and fancy gilt chairs set around the walls. Finally, not long after the ballroom, came a wide corridor with lime-green, shiny plaster, a floor that smelt of wood-polish and a big, heavy door that Beria unlocked with a key he kept in a bunch on a chain.

Rapava followed him in. The door, on an old imperial pneumatic hinge, closed slowly behind them.

It wasn't much of an office. Eight yards by six. It might have done for some factory director at the arse-end of Vologda or Magnitogorsk – a desk with a couple of telephones, a bit of carpet on the floor, a table and a few chairs, a heavily-curtained window. On the wall was one of those big, pink, roll-up maps of the USSR – this was back in the days when there *was* a USSR – and next to the map was another, smaller door, to which Beria immediately headed. Again, he had a key. The door opened into a kind of walk-in cupboard in which there was a blackened samovar, a bottle of Armenian brandy and some stuff for making herbal teas. There was also a wall-safe, with a sturdy brass front on which was a manufacturer's label – not in Russian Cyrillic but in some western language. The safe wasn't very big – a foot across, if that. Square. Well fashioned. Straight handle, also brass.

Beria noticed Rapava staring at it and told him roughly to clear off back outside.

NEARLY an hour passed.

Standing in the corridor, Rapava tried to keep himself alert, practising drawing his pistol, imagining every little creak of the great building was a footstep, every moan of wind a voice. He tried to picture the GenSec striding down this wide, polished corridor in his cavalry boots, and then he tried to reconcile that image with the ruined figure lying imprisoned in his own rancid flesh out at Blizhny.

And you know something, boy? I cried. I might have cried a bit for myself as well – I can't deny it, I was scared – I was shitless – but really I cried for Comrade Stalin. I cried more over Stalin than I did when my own father died. And that goes for most of the boys I knew.

A distant bell chimed four.

At around half-past, Beria at last emerged. He was carrying a small leather satchel stuffed with something – papers, certainly, but there might have been other objects: Rapava couldn't tell. The contents, presumably, had come from the safe, and the satchel might have come from there,

too. Or it might have come from the office. Or it might –
Rapava couldn't swear to this, but it was possible – it might
have been in Beria's hand right from the moment he got out
of the car. At any rate, he had what he wanted, and he was
smiling.

Smiling?

Like I say, boy. Yes – smiling. Not a smile of pleasure, mark
you. More a kind of –

Rueful?

– That's it, a rueful kind of smile. A would-you-fucking-
believe-it? kind of a smile. Like he'd just been beaten at cards.

They went back the way they had come, only this time in
the bust-lined passage they ran into a guard. He practically
dropped to his knees when he saw the Boss. But Beria just
dead-eyed the man and kept on walking – the coolest piece
of thievery you ever saw. In the car he said, 'Vspolnyi Street.'

By now it was nearly five, still dark, but the trams had
started running and there were people on the streets –
babushkas, mostly, who had cleaned the government offices
under the Tsar and under Lenin, and who, after tomorrow,
would be cleaning them under somebody else. Outside the
Lenin Library a vast poster of Stalin, in red, white and black,
gazed down upon a line of workers queuing outside the
metro station. Beria had the satchel open on his lap. His head
was bent. The interior light was on. He was reading
something, tapping his fingers with anxiety.

'Is there a shovel in the back?' he asked, suddenly.

Rapava said there was. For snowdrifts.

'And a toolbox?'

'Yes, Boss.' A big one: car jack, wheel wrench, wheel nuts,
spare starting handle, spark plugs . . .

Beria grunted and returned his attention to his reading.

*

BACK at the house, the surface of the ground was diamond-hard, set with glittering points of ice, much too hard for the shovel, and Rapava had to hunt around the outbuildings at the bottom of the garden for a pick-axe. He took off his coat and wielded the axe like he used to when he worked his father's patch of Georgian dirt, bringing it down in a great smooth arc over his head, letting the weight and the velocity of the tool do the job, the edge of the blade burying itself in the frozen earth almost to the shaft. He wrestled it back and forth and pulled it free, adjusted his stance, then brought it down again.

He worked in the little cherry orchard by the light of a hurricane lamp suspended from a nearby branch, and he worked at a frantic pace, conscious that in the darkness behind him, invisible on the far side of the light, Beria was sitting on a stone bench watching him. Soon he was sweating so heavily that despite the March cold he had to stop and take off his jacket and roll up his sleeves. A large patch of his shirt was stuck to his back and he had an involuntary memory of other men doing this while he nursed his rifle and watched – other men on a much hotter day, hacking away at the ground in a forest, then lying obediently on their faces in the freshly dug earth. He remembered the smell of moist soil and the hot drowsy silence of the wood and he wondered how cold it would be if Beria made him lie down now.

A voice came out of the darkness. 'Don't make it so wide. It's not a grave. You're making work for yourself.'

After a while, he began alternating between the axe and the shovel, hacking off chunks of earth and jumping into the hole to clear the debris. At first the ground came up to his knees, and then it lapped his waist, and finally it was at his chest – at which point Beria's moon face appeared above him and told him to stop, that he had done well, it was enough. The Boss was actually smiling and held out his hand to pull Rapava from the hole, and Rapava at that moment, as he grasped that soft palm, was filled with such love – such a surge of gratitude and devotion: he would never feel anything like it again.

It was as comrades, in Rapava's memory, that they each took hold of one end of the long metal toolbox and lowered it into the ground. They kicked the earth in after it, stamped it tight, and then Rapava hammered the mound flat with the back of the shovel and scattered dead leaves over the site. By the time they turned to walk across the lawn to the house, the faintest gleams of grey were beginning to infiltrate the eastern sky.

BETWEEN them, Kelso and Rapava had drained the miniatures and had moved on to a kind of home-made pepper vodka, which the old man had produced from a battered tin flask. God alone knew what he had made it from. It could have been shampoo. He sniffed it, sneezed, then winked and poured a brimming, oily glass for Kelso. It was the colour of a pigeon's breast and Kelso felt his stomach lurch.

'And Stalin died,' he said, trying to avoid taking a sip. His words slurred into one another. His jaw was numb.

'And Stalin died.' Rapava shook his head in sorrow. He suddenly leaned forward and clinked glasses. 'To Comrade Stalin!'

'To Comrade Stalin!'

They drank.

AND Stalin died. And everyone went mad with grief. Everyone, that is, except Comrade Beria, who delivered his eulogy to the thousands of hysterical mourners in Red Square like he was reading a railway announcement, and had a good laugh about it afterwards with the boys.

Word of this got around.

Now Beria was a clever man, much cleverer even than you are, boy – he'd have eaten you for breakfast. But clever people all make one mistake. They all think everyone else is stupid. And everyone isn't stupid. They just take a bit more time, that's all.

The Boss thought he was going to be in power for twenty years. He lasted three months.

It was late one morning in June and Rapava was on duty with the usual team – Nadaraya, Sarsikov, Dumbadze – when word came through that there was a special meeting of the Presidium in Malenkov's office in the Kremlin. And because it was at Malenkov's place, the Boss thought nothing of it. Who was fat Malenkov? Fat Malenkov was nothing. He was just a dumb brown bear. The Boss had Malenkov on the end of a rope.

So when he got in to the car to go to the meeting, he wasn't even wearing a tie, just an open-necked shirt and a worn-out old suit. Why should he wear a tie? It was a hot day and Stalin was dead and Moscow was full of girls and he was going to be in power for twenty years.

The cherry orchard at the bottom of the garden had not long finished flowering.

They arrived at Malenkov's building and the Boss went upstairs to see him, while the rest of them sat around in the ante-room by the entrance. And one by one the big guys arrived, all the comrades Beria used to laugh about behind their backs – old 'Stone Arse' Molotov and that fat peasant Khrushchev and the ninny Voroshilov, and finally Marshal Zhukov, the puffed-up peacock, with his boards of tin and ribbon. They all went upstairs and Nadaraya rubbed his hands and said to Rapava: 'Now then, Papu Gerasimovich, why don't you go to the canteen and get us some coffee?'

The day passed and from time to time Nadaraya would wander upstairs to see what was happening, and always he came back with the same message: meeting still in progress. And again: so what? It wasn't unusual for the Presidium to sit for hours. But by eight o'clock, the chief of the bodyguard was starting to look worried and, at ten, with the summer darkness gathering, he told them all to follow him upstairs.

They crashed straight past Malenkov's protesting secretaries and into the big room. It was empty. Sarsikov tried the phones and they were dead. One of the chairs had been tipped back and on the floor around it were some folded scraps of paper, on each of which, in red ink, in Beria's writing, was the single word 'Alarm!'

THEY could have made a fight of it, perhaps, but what would have been the point? The whole thing was an ambush, a Red Army operation. Zhukov had even brought up tanks – stationed twenty T34s at the back of the Boss's house (Rapava heard this later). There were armoured cars inside the Kremlin. It was hopeless. They wouldn't have lasted five minutes.

The boys were split up there and then. Rapava was taken to a military prison in the northern suburbs where they proceeded to beat ten kinds of shit out of him, accused him of procuring little girls, showed him witness statements and photographs of the victims and finally a list of thirty names that Sarsikov (great big swaggering Sarsikov – some tough guy *he* turned out to be) had written down for them on the second day.

Rapava said nothing. The whole thing made him sick.

And then, one night, about ten days after the coup – for a coup was how Rapava would always think of it – he was patched up and given a wash and a clean prison uniform and taken up in handcuffs to the director's office to meet some big shot from the Ministry of State Security. He was a tough-looking, miserable bastard, aged between forty and fifty – said he was a Deputy Minister – and he wanted to talk about Comrade Stalin's private papers.

Rapava was handcuffed to the chair. The guards were sent out of the room. The Deputy Minister sat behind the director's desk. There was a picture of Stalin on the wall behind him.

It seems, said the Deputy Minister – after looking at Rapava for a while – that Comrade Stalin, in recent years, to assist him in his mighty tasks, had got into the habit of making notes. Sometimes these notes were confided to ordinary sheets of writing paper and sometimes to an exercise book with a black oilskin cover. The existence of these notes was known only to certain members of the Presidium, and to Comrade Poskrebyshev, Comrade Stalin's long-standing secretary, whom the traitor Beria recently had falsely imprisoned on fraudulent charges. All witnesses agree that Comrade Stalin kept these papers in a personal safe in his private office, to which he alone had the key.

The Deputy Minister leaned forwards. His dark eyes searched Rapava's face.

Following Comrade Stalin's tragic death, attempts were made to locate this key. It could not be found. It was therefore agreed by the Presidium to have this safe broken into, in the presence of them all, to see if Comrade Stalin had left behind material that might be of historical value, or which might assist the Central Committee in its stupendous responsibility of appointing Comrade Stalin's successor.

The safe was duly broken open, under the supervision of the Presidium, and found to be empty, apart from a few minor items, such as Comrade Stalin's party card.

'And now,' said the Deputy Minister, getting slowly to his feet, 'we come to the crux of the matter.'

He walked around and sat on the edge of the desk directly in front of Rapava. Oh, he was a big bastard, boy, a fleshy tank.

We know, he said, from Comrade Malenkov that in the early hours of the second of March, you went to the Kuntsevo dacha in the company of the traitor, Beria, and that you were both left alone with Comrade Stalin for several minutes. Was anything removed from the room?

No, comrade.

Nothing at all?

No, comrade.

And where did you go when you left Kuntsevo?

I drove Comrade Beria back to his house, comrade.

Directly back to his house?

Yes, comrade.

You are lying.

No, comrade.

You are lying. We have a witness who saw you both inside the Kremlin shortly before dawn. A sentry who met you in a corridor.

Yes, comrade. I remember now. Comrade Beria said he needed to collect something from his office –

Something from Comrade Stalin's office!

No, comrade.

You are lying! You are a traitor! You and the English spy Beria broke into Stalin's office and stole his papers! Where are those papers?

No, comrade –

Traitor! Thief! Spy!

Each word accompanied by a punch in the face.

And so on.

I'LL tell you something, boy. Nobody knows the full truth of what happened to the Boss, even now – even after Gorbachev and Yeltsin have sold off our whole fucking birthright to the capitalists and let the CIA go picnicking in our files. The papers on the Boss are still closed. They smuggled him out of the Kremlin on the floor of a car, rolled up in a carpet, and some say Zhukov shot him that very night. Others say they shot him the following week. Most say they kept him alive for five months – *five months!* – sweated him in a bunker underneath the Moscow Military District – and shot him after a secret trial.

Either way, they shot him. He was dead by Christmas Day.

And this is what they did to me.

Rapava held up his mutilated fingers and wiggled them. Then he clumsily unbuttoned his shirt, pulled it from the waistband of his pants, and twisted his scrawny torso to show his back. His vertebrae were criss-crossed with shiny roughened panes of scar-tissue – translucent windows on to the flesh beneath. His stomach and chest were whorls of blue-black tattoos.

Kelso didn't speak. Rapava sat back leaving his shirt unbuttoned. His scars and his tattoos were the medals of his lifetime. He was proud to wear them.

NOT a word, boy. You listening? They did not get. One. Single. Word.

Throughout it all, he didn't know if the Boss was still alive, or if the Boss was talking. But it didn't matter: Papu Gerasimovich Rapava, at least, would hold his silence.

Why? Was it loyalty? A bit, perhaps – the memory of that reprieving hand. But he wasn't such a young fool that he didn't also realise that silence was his only hope. How long do you think they'd have let him live if he'd led them to that place? It was his own death warrant he'd buried under that tree. So, softly, softly: not a word.

He lay shivering on the floor of his unheated cell as the winter came and dreamed of cherry trees, the leaves dying and falling now, the branches dark against the sky, the howling of the wolves.

And then, around Christmas, like bored children, they suddenly seemed to lose interest in the whole business. The beating went on for a while – by now it was a matter of honour on both sides, you must understand – but the questions stopped, and finally, after one prolonged and imaginative session, the beating stopped as well. The Deputy Minister never came again and Rapava guessed that Beria must be dead. He also guessed that someone had decided that Stalin's papers, if they did exist, were better left unread.

Rapava expected to get his seven grams of lead at any moment. It never occurred to him that he wouldn't, not after Beria had been liquidated. So of his journey, in a snowstorm, to the Red Army building on Kommissariat Street, and of the makeshift courtroom, with its high, barred windows and its troika of judges, he remembered nothing. He blanked his mind with snow. He watched it through the window, advancing in waves up the Moskva and along the embankment, smothering the afternoon lights on the opposite side of the river – high white columns of snow on a death march from the east. Voices droned around him. Later, when it was dark and he was being taken outside, he assumed to be shot, he asked if he could stop for a minute on the steps and bury his hands in the drifts. A guard asked why, and Rapava said: 'To feel snow between my fingers one last time, comrade.'

They laughed a lot at that. But when they found out he was serious they laughed a whole lot more. 'If there's one thing you'll never go hungry for, Georgian,' they told him, as they pushed him into the back of the van, 'it's snow.' That was how he learned he had been sentenced to fifteen years' hard labour in the Kolyma territory.

KHRUSHCHEV amnestied a whole bunch of Gulag prisoners in fifty-six, but nobody amnestied Papu Rapava. Papu Rapava was forgotten. Papu Rapava alternately rotted and froze in the forests of Siberia for the next decade and a half – rotted in the short summer, when each man worked in his own private fever-cloud of mosquitoes, and froze in the long winter when the ice made rock of the swamps.

They say that people who survive the camps all look alike because, once a man's skeleton has been exposed, it doesn't matter how well-padded his flesh subsequently becomes, or how carefully he dresses – the bones will always poke through. Kelso had interviewed enough Gulag survivors in his time to recognise the camp skeleton in Rapava's face even now, as he talked, in the sockets of his eyes and in the crack of his jaw. He could see it in the hinges of his wrists and ankles, and the flat blade of his sternum.

He wasn't amnestied, Rapava was saying, because he killed

a man, a Chechen, who tried to sodomise him – gutted him with a shank he'd made from a piece of saw.

And what happened to your head? said Kelso.

Rapava fingered the scar. He couldn't remember. Sometimes, when it was especially cold, the scar ached and gave him dreams.

What kind of dreams?

Rapava showed the dark glint of his mouth. He wouldn't say.

Fifteen years . . .

They returned him to Moscow in the summer of sixty-nine, on the day the Yankees put a man on the moon. Rapava left the ex-prisoners' hostel and wandered round the hot and crowded streets and couldn't make sense of anything. Where was Stalin? That was what amazed him. Where were the statues and the pictures? Where was the respect? The boys all looked like girls and the girls all looked like whores. Clearly, the country was already halfway in the shit. But still – you have to say – at least in those days there were jobs for everyone, even for old *zeki* like him. They sent him to the engine sheds at the Leningrad Station, to work as a labourer. He was only forty-one and as strong as a bear. Everything he had in the world was in a cardboard suitcase.

Did he ever marry?

Rapava shrugged. Sure, he married. That was the way you got an apartment. He married and got himself fixed up with a place.

And what happened? Where was she?

She died. It was a decent block in those days, boy, before the drugs and the crime.

Where was his place?

Fucking criminals . . .

And children?

A son. He died as well. In Afghanistan. And a daughter.

His daughter was dead?

No. She was a whore.

And Stalin's papers?

Drunk as he was, there was no way Kelso could make *that* question casual and the old man shot him a crafty look; a peasant's look.

Rapava said softly, 'Go on, boy. Yes? And Stalin's papers? What about Stalin's papers?'

Kelso hesitated.

'Only that if they still existed – if there was a chance – a possibility –'

'You'd want to see them?'

'Of course.'

Rapava laughed.

'And why should I help you, boy? Fifteen years in Kolyma, and for what? To help you spin more lies? For love?'

'No. Not for love. For history.'

'For history? Do me a favour, boy!'

'All right – for money, then.'

'What?'

'For money. A share in the profits. A lot of money.'

The peasant Rapava stroked the side of his nose.

'How much money?'

'A lot. If this is true. If we could find them. Believe me: a lot of money.'

THE momentary silence was broken by the sound of voices in the corridor, voices talking in English, and Kelso guessed who this would be: his fellow historians – Adelman, Duberstein and the rest – coming back late from dinner, wondering where he'd got to. It suddenly seemed overwhelmingly important to him that no one else – least of all his colleagues – should know anything at all about Papu Rapava.

Someone tapped softly on the door and he held up a warning hand to the old man. Very quietly he reached over and turned off the bedside lamp.

They sat together and listened to the whispers, magnified by the darkness but still muffled and indistinct. There was another knock, and then a splutter of laughter, hushed by the others. Maybe they had seen the light go out. Perhaps they thought he was with a woman – such was his reputation.

After a few more seconds, the voices faded and the corridor was silent again. Kelso turned on the light. He smiled and patted his heart. The old man's face was a mask, but then he smiled and began to sing – he had a quavering, unexpectedly melodious voice –

> *Kolyma, Kolyma,*
> *What a wonderful place!*
> *Twelve months of winter*
> *Summer all the rest . . .*

AFTER his release, he was this and no more: Papu Rapava, railway worker, who had done a spell in the camps, and if anyone wanted to take it further – well? yes? come on, then, comrade! – he was always ready with his fists or an iron spike.

Two men watched him from the start. Antipin, who was a foreman in the Lenin No. 1 shed, and a cripple in the downstairs flat called Senka. And they were as pretty a pair of canaries as you could ever hope to meet. You could practically hear them singing to the KGB before you were

out of the room. The others came and went – the men on
foot, the men in parked cars, the men asking 'routine
questions, comrade' – but Antipin and Senka were the
faithful watchers, though they never got a thing, neither of
them. Rapava had buried his past in a hole far deeper than
the one he'd dug for Beria.

Senka died five years ago. He never knew what became of
Antipin. The Lenin No. 1 shed was now the property of a
private collective, importing French wine.

Stalin's papers, boy? Who gives a shit? He wasn't afraid of
anything any more.

A lot of money, you say? Well, well –

He leaned over and spat into the ashtray, then seemed to
fall asleep. After a while, he muttered, My lad died. Did I tell
you that?

Yes.

He died in a night ambush on the road to Mazar-i-Sharif.
One of the last to be sent. Killed by stone-age devils with blackened faces and Yankee missiles. Could anyone imagine Stalin
letting the country be humiliated by such savages? Think of it!
He'd have crushed them into dust and scattered the powder in
Siberia! After the lad was gone, Rapava took to walking. Great
long hikes that could last a day and a night. He criss-crossed the
city, from Perovo to the lakes, from Bittsevskiy Park to the
Television Tower. And on one of these walks – it must have
been six or seven years ago, around the time of the coup – he
found himself walking into one of his own dreams. Couldn't
figure it out at first. Then he realised he was on Vspolnyi Street.
He got out of there fast. His lad was a radio man in a tank unit.
Liked fiddling with radios. No fighter.

And the house? said Kelso. Was the house still standing?

He was nineteen.

And the house? What had happened to the house?

Rapava's head drooped.

The *house,* comrade –

There was a red sickle moon, and a single red star. And the place was guarded by devils with blackened faces –

KELSO could get no more sense out of him after that. The old man's eyelids fluttered and closed. His mouth slackened. Yellow saliva leaked across his cheek.

Kelso watched him for a minute or two, feeling the pressure build in his stomach, then rose suddenly from his chair and moved as quickly as he could to the lavatory, where he was violently and copiously sick. He rested his hot forehead against the cold enamel bowl and licked his lips. His tongue felt huge to him, and bitter, like a swollen piece of black fruit. There was something stuck in his throat. He tried to clear it by coughing but that didn't work so he tried swallowing and was promptly sick again. When he pulled his head back, the bathroom fixtures seemed to have detached themselves from their moorings and to be revolving around him in a slow tribal dance. A line of silver mucus extended in a shimmering arc from his nose to the toilet seat.

Endure, he told himself. This, too, will pass.

He clutched again at the cool white bowl, a drowning man, as the horizon tilted and the room darkened, slid –

A RUSTLE in the blackness of his dreams. A pair of yellow eyes.

'Who are you,' said Stalin, 'to steal my private papers?'

He sprang from his couch like a wolf.

KELSO jerked awake and cracked his head on the protruding lip of the bath. He groaned and rolled on to his back, dabbing at his skull for signs of blood. He was sure he felt some tacky liquid, but when he brought his fingers up close to his eyes and squinted at them they were clean.

As always, even now, even as he lay sprawled on the floor of a Moscow bathroom, there was a part of him that remained mercilessly sober, like the wounded captain on the bridge of a stricken ship, calling calmly through the smoke of battle for damage assessments. This was the part of him which concluded that, bad as he felt, he had – amazingly – sometimes felt worse. And this was the part of him that also heard, beyond the dusty thump of his pulse, the creak of a footstep and the click of a door being quietly closed.

Kelso set his jaw and rose, by force of will, through all the stages of human evolution – from the slime of the floor, to his hands and knees, to a kind of shuffling, simian crouch – and propelled himself into the empty bedroom. Grey light seeped through thin orange curtains and lit the detritus of the night. The sour reek of spilled booze and stale smoke made his stomach coil. Still – and there was heroism as well as desperation in the effort – he headed for the door.

'Papu Gerasimovich! Wait!'

The corridor was dim and deserted. From the end of it, around the corner, came the ping of an arriving elevator. Wincing, Kelso loped towards it, arriving just in time to see the doors close. He tried to prise them open with his fingers, shouting into the crevice for Rapava to come back. He punched the call button with the heel of his hand a few times, but nothing happened so he took the stairs. He got as far as the twenty-first floor before he acknowledged he was beaten. He stopped on the landing and summoned the express elevator, and stood there waiting for it, leaning against the wall, breathless, nauseous, with a knife behind his eyes. The car was a long time coming and when, at last, it did arrive, it promptly took him back up the two floors he had just run down. The doors slid open mockingly on to the empty passage.

By the time Kelso reached ground level, his ears popping from the speed of his descent, Rapava was gone. In the marble vault of the Ukraina's reception there was nobody about except for a babushka, hoovering ash from the red carpet, and a platinum-blonde hooker with a fake sable curled over her shoulders, arguing with a security man. As he made for the entrance he was aware that all three had stopped what they were doing and were staring at him. He put his hand to his forehead. He was dripping with sweat.

It was cold outside and barely light. A sharp October morning. A damp chill rising off the river. Yet already the rush-hour traffic was beginning to build along the Kutuzovskiy Prospekt, backing up from the Kalininskiy Bridge. He walked on for a while until he came to the main road, and there he stood for a minute or two, shivering in his shirtsleeves. There was no sign of Rapava. Along the sidewalk to his right, an old grey dog, big and half-starved, went slouching past the heavy buildings, heading east, towards the waking city.

Part One

Moscow

'To choose one's victims, to prepare one's plans minutely,
to slake an implacable vengeance, and then to go to bed . . .
there is nothing sweeter in the world.'

J. V. Stalin
in conversation with Kamenev and Dzerzhinsky

Chapter One

OLGA KOMAROVA OF the Russian Archive Service, Rosarkhiv, wielding a collapsible pink umbrella, prodded and shooed her distinguished charges across the Ukraina's lobby towards the revolving door. It was an old door, of heavy wood and glass, too narrow to cope with more than one body at a time, so the scholars formed a line in the dim light, like parachutists over a target zone, and as they passed her, Olga touched each one lightly on the shoulder with her umbrella, counting them off one by one as they were propelled into the freezing Moscow air.

Franklin Adelman of Yale went first, as befitted his age and status, then Moldenhauer of the Bundesarchiv in Koblenz, with his absurd double-doctorate – Doctor Doctor Karl-bloody-Moldenhauer – then the neo-Marxists, Enrico Banfi of Milan and Eric Chambers of the LSE, then the great cold warrior, Phil Duberstein of NYU, then Ivo Godelier of the Ecole Normale Superieure, followed by glum Dave Richards of St Antony's, Oxford – another Sovietologist whose world was rubble – then Velma Byrd of the US National Archive, then Alastair Findlay of Edinburgh's Department of War Studies, who still thought the sun shone out of Comrade Stalin's arse, then Arthur Saunders of Stanford, and finally – the man whose lateness had kept them waiting in the lobby for an extra five minutes – Dr C. R. A. Kelso, commonly known as Fluke.

The door banged hard against his heels. Outside the weather had worsened. It was trying to snow. Tiny flakes, as hard as grit, came whipping across the wide grey concourse

and spattered his face and hair. At the bottom of the flight of
steps, shuddering in a cloud of its own white fumes, was a
dilapidated bus, waiting to take them to the symposium.
Kelso stopped to light a cigarette.

'Jesus, Fluke,' called Adelman, cheerfully, 'you look just
awful.'

Kelso raised a fragile hand in acknowledgement. He could
see a huddle of taxi drivers in quilted jackets stamping their
feet against the cold. Workmen were struggling to lift a roll
of tin off the back of a lorry. One Korean businessman in a
fur hat was photographing a group of twenty others,
similarly dressed. But of Papu Rapava: no sign.

'Doctor Kelso, please, we are waiting again.' The umbrella
wagged at him in reproof. He transferred the cigarette to the
corner of his mouth, hitched his bag up on to his shoulder
and moved towards the bus.

'A battered Byron' was how one Sunday newspaper had
described him when he had resigned his Oxford lectureship
and moved to New York, and the description wasn't a bad
one – curly black hair too long and thick for neatness, a
moist, expressive mouth, pale cheeks and the glow of a
certain reputation – if Byron hadn't died on Missolonghi but
had spent the next ten years drinking whisky, smoking,
staying indoors and resolutely avoiding all exercise, he, too,
might have come to look a little like Fluke Kelso.

He was wearing what he always wore: a faded dark blue
shirt of heavy cotton with the top button undone, a loosely
knotted and vaguely stained dark tie, a black corduroy suit
with a black leather belt over which his stomach bulged
slightly, red cotton handkerchief in his breast pocket, scuffed
boots of brown suede, an old blue raincoat. This was Kelso's
uniform, unvaried for twenty years.

'Boy,' Rapava had called him, and the word was both absurd for a middle-aged man and yet oddly accurate. *Boy.*

The heater was going full blast. Nobody was saying much. He sat on his own near the back of the bus and rubbed at the wet glass as they jolted up the slip-road to join the traffic on the bridge. Across the aisle, Saunders made an ostentatious display of batting Kelso's smoke away. Beneath them, in the filthy waters of the Moskva, a dredger with a crane mounted on its aft deck beat sluggishly upstream.

He nearly hadn't come to Russia. That was the joke of it. He knew well enough what it would be like: the bad food, the stale gossip, the sheer bloody tedium of academic life – of more and more being said about less and less – that was one reason why he had chucked in Oxford and gone to live in New York. But somehow the books he was supposed to write had not quite materialised. And besides, he never could resist the lure of Moscow. Even now, sitting on a stale bus in the Wednesday rush-hour, he could feel the charge of history beyond the muddy glass: in the dark and renamed streets, the vast apartment blocks, the toppled statues. It was stronger here than anywhere he knew; stronger even than in Berlin. That was what always drew him back to Moscow – the way history hung in the air between the blackened buildings like sulphur after a lightning-strike.

'*You think you know it all about Comrade Stalin, don't you boy? Well, let me tell you: you don't know fuck.*'

Kelso had already delivered his short paper, on Stalin and the archives, at the end of the previous day: delivered it in his trademark style – without notes, with one hand in his pocket, extempore, provocative. His Russian hosts had looked gratifyingly shifty. A couple of people had even walked out. So, all in all, a triumph.

Afterwards, finding himself predictably alone, he had decided to walk back to the Ukraina. It was a long walk, and it was getting dark, but he needed the air. And at some point – he couldn't remember where: maybe it was in one of the back streets behind the Institute, or maybe it was later, along the Noviy Arbat – but at some point he had realised he was being followed. It was nothing tangible, just a fleeting impression of something seen too often – the flash of a coat, perhaps, or the shape of a head – but Kelso had been in Moscow often enough in the bad old days to know that you were seldom wrong about these things. You always knew if a film was out of synch, however fractionally; you always knew if someone fancied you, however improbably; and you always knew when someone was on your tail.

He had just stepped into his hotel room and was contemplating some primary research in the mini-bar when the front desk had called up to say there was a man in the lobby who wanted to see him. Who? He wouldn't give his name, sir. But he was most insistent and he wouldn't leave. So Kelso had gone down, reluctantly, and found Papu Rapava sitting on one of the Ukraina's imitation leather sofas, staring straight ahead, in his papery blue suit, his wrists and ankles sticking out as thin as broomsticks.

'*You think you know it all about Comrade Stalin, don't you, boy . . .?*'Those had been his opening words.

And that was the moment that Kelso had realised where he had first seen the old man: at the symposium, in the front row of the public seats, listening intently to the simultaneous translation over his headphones, muttering in violent disagreement at any hostile mention of J. V. Stalin.

Who are you? thought Kelso, staring out of the grimy window. Fantasist? Con man? The answer to a prayer?

*

42

THE symposium was only scheduled to last one more day – for which relief, in Kelso's view, much thanks. It was being held in the Institute of Marxism–Leninism, an orthodox temple of grey concrete, consecrated in the Brezhnev years, with Marx, Engels and Lenin in gigantic bas-relief above the pillared entrance. The ground floor had been leased to a private bank, since gone bust, which added to the air of dereliction.

On the opposite side of the street, watched by a couple of bored-looking militia men, a small demonstration was in progress – maybe a hundred people, mostly elderly, but with a few youths in black berets and leather jackets. It was the usual mixture of fanatics and grudge-holders – Marxists, nationalists, anti-semites. Crimson flags bearing the hammer and sickle hung beside black flags embroidered with the tsarist eagle. One old lady carried a picture of Stalin; another sold cassettes of SS marching songs. An elderly man with an umbrella held over him was addressing the crowd through a bullhorn, his voice a distorted, metallic rant. Stewards were handing out a free newspaper called *Aurora*.

'Take no notice,' instructed Olga Komarova, standing up beside the driver. She tapped the side of her head. 'These are crazy people. Red fascists.'

'What's he saying?' demanded Duberstein, who was considered a world authority on Soviet communism even though he had never quite got round to learning Russian.

'He's talking about how the Hoover Institution tried to buy the Party archive for five million bucks,' said Adelman. 'He says we're trying to steal their history.'

Duberstein sniggered. 'Who'd want to steal *their* goddamned history?' He tapped on the window with his signet ring. 'Say, isn't that a TV crew?'

The sight of a camera caused a predictable, wistful stir among the academics.

'I believe so . . . '

'How very flattering . . .'

'What's the name,' said Adelman, 'of the fellow who runs *Aurora*? Is it still the same one?' He twisted round in his seat and called up the aisle. 'Fluke – you should know. What's his name? Old KGB –'

'Mamantov,' said Kelso. The driver braked hard and he had to swallow to stop himself being sick. 'Vladimir Mamantov.'

'Crazy people,' repeated Olga, bracing herself as they came to a stop. 'I apologise on behalf of Rosarkhiv. They are not representative. Follow me, please. Ignore them.'

They filed off the bus and a television cameraman filmed them as they trudged across the asphalt forecourt, past a couple of drooping, silvery fir trees, pursued by jeers.

Fluke Kelso moved delicately at the rear of the column, nursing his hangover, holding his head at a careful angle, as if he was balancing a pitcher of water. A pimply youth in wire spectacles thrust a copy of *Aurora* at him and Kelso got a quick glimpse of the front page – a cartoon caricature of Zionist conspirators and a weird cabalistic symbol that was something between a swastika and a red cross – before he rammed it back in the young man's chest. The demonstrators jeered.

A thermometer on the wall outside the entrance read minus one. The old nameplate had been taken down and a new one had been screwed in its place, but it didn't quite fit so you could tell that the building had been renamed. It now proclaimed itself 'The Russian Centre for the Preservation and Study of Documents Relating to Modern History'.

Archangel

Once again, Kelso lingered behind after the others had gone in, squinting at the hate-filled faces across the street. There were a lot of old men of a similar age, pinched and raw-cheeked in the cold, but Rapava wasn't among them. He turned away and moved inside, into the shadowy lobby, where he gave his coat and bag to the cloakroom attendant, before passing beneath the familiar statue of Lenin towards the lecture hall.

Another day began.

There were ninety-one delegates at the symposium and almost all of them seemed to be crowded into the small ante-room where coffee was being served. He collected his cup and lit another cigarette.

'Who's up first?' said a voice behind him. It was Adelman.

'Askenov, I think. On the microfilm project.'

Adelman groaned. He was a Bostonian, in his seventies, at that twilight stage in his career when most of life seemed to be spent in airplanes or foreign hotels: symposia, conferences, honorary degrees – Duberstein maintained that Adelman had given up pursuing history in favour of collecting air miles. But Kelso didn't begrudge him his honours. He was good. And brave. It had taken courage to write his kind of books, thirty years ago, on the Famine and the Terror, when every other useful idiot in academia was screeching for détente.

'Listen, Frank,' he said, 'I'm sorry about dinner.'

'Forget it. You got a better offer?'

'Kind of.'

The refreshment room was at the back of the Institute and looked out on to an inner courtyard, in the centre of which, dumped on their sides amid the weeds, were a pair of statues, of Marx and Engels – a couple of Victorian gentlemen taking

45

time off from the long march of history for a morning doze.

'They don't mind taking down those two,' said Adelman. 'That's easy. They're foreigners. And one of them's a Jew. It's when they take down Lenin – that's when you'll know the place has really changed.'

Kelso took another sip of coffee. 'A man came to see me last night.'

'A man? I'm disappointed.'

'Could I ask your advice, Frank?'

Adelman shrugged. 'Go ahead.'

'In private?'

ADELMAN stroked his chin. 'You got his name, this guy?'

'Of course I got his name.'

'His real name?'

'How do I know if it's his real name?'

'His address, then? You got his address?'

'No, Frank, I didn't get his address. But he did leave these.'

Adelman took off his glasses and peered closely at the book of matches. 'It's a set-up,' he said at last, handing them back. 'I wouldn't touch it. Whoever heard of a bar called "Robotnik", anyhow? "Worker"? Sounds phoney to me.'

'But if it was a set-up,' said Kelso, weighing the match-book in his palm, 'why would he run away?'

'Obviously, because he doesn't want it to *look* like a set-up. He wants you to have to work at it – track him down, persuade him to help you. That's the psychology of a clever fraud – the victims wind up doing so much chasing around, they start *wanting* to believe it's true. Remember the Hitler diaries. Either that or he's a lunatic.'

'He was very convincing.'

'Lunatics often are. Or it's a practical joke. Someone wants to make you look a fool. Have you thought of that? You're not exactly the most popular kid in the school.'

Kelso glanced up the corridor towards the lecture hall. It wasn't a bad theory. There were plenty in there who didn't like him. He had appeared on too many television programmes, knocked out too many newspaper columns, reviewed too many of their useless books. Saunders was loitering at the corner, pretending to talk to Moldenhauer, both men obviously straining to overhear what he was saying to Adelman. (Saunders had complained bitterly after Kelso's paper about his 'subjectivity': 'Why was he even invited, that's what one wants to know. One had been given to understand this was a symposium for *serious* scholars . . .')

'They don't have the wit,' he said. He gave them a wave and was pleased to see them duck out of sight. 'Or the imagination.'

'You sure have a genius for making enemies.'

'Ah well. You know what they say: more enemies, more honour.'

Adelman smiled and opened his mouth to say something, but then seemed to think better of it. 'How's Margaret, dare one ask?'

'Who? Oh, you mean *poor* Margaret? She's fine, thank you. Fine and feisty. According to the lawyers.'

'And the boys?'

'Entering the springtime of their adolescence.'

'And the book? That's been a while. How much of this new book have you actually written?'

'I'm writing it.'

'Two hundred pages? A hundred?'

'What is this, Frank?'

'How many pages?'

47

'I don't know.' Kelso licked his dry lips. Almost unbelievably, he realised he could do with a drink. 'A hundred maybe.' He had a vision of a blank grey screen, a cursor flashing weakly, like a pulse on a life-support machine begging to be switched off. He hadn't written a word. 'Listen, Frank, there *could* be something in this, couldn't there? Stalin was a hoarder, don't forget. Didn't Khrushchev find some letter in a secret compartment in the old man's desk after he died?' He rubbed his aching head. 'That letter from Lenin, complaining about Stalin's treatment of his wife? And then there was that list of the Politburo, with crosses against everyone he was planning to purge. And his library – remember his library? He made notes in almost every book.'

'So what are you saying?'

'I'm just saying it's possible, that's all. That Stalin wasn't Hitler. That he wrote things down.'

'*Quod volimus credimus libenter,*' intoned Adelman. 'Which means –'

'I know what it means –'

' – which *means,* my dear Fluke, we always believe what we want to believe.' Adelman patted Kelso's arm. 'You don't want to hear this, do you? I'm sorry. I'll lie if you prefer it. I'll tell you he's the one guy in a million with a story like this who turns out not to be full of shit. I'll tell you he's going to lead you to Stalin's unpublished memoirs, that you'll rewrite history, millions of dollars will be yours, women will lie at your feet, Duberstein and Saunders will form a choir to sing your praises in the middle of Harvard Yard . . .'

'All right, Frank.' Kelso leaned the back of his head against the wall. 'You've made your point. I don't know. It's just – Maybe you had to be there with him –' He pressed on, reluctant to admit defeat. 'It's just it rings a bell with me somewhere. Does it ring a bell with you?'

'Oh sure. It rings a bell, okay. An alarm bell.' Adelman pulled out an old pocket watch. 'We ought to be getting back. D'you mind? Olga will be frantic.' He put his arm round Kelso's shoulders and led him down the corridor. 'In any case, there's nothing you can do. We're flying back to New York tomorrow. Let's talk when we get back. See if there's anything for you in the faculty. You were a great teacher.'

'I was a lousy teacher.'

'You were a great teacher, until you were lured from the path of scholarship and rectitude by the cheap sirens of journalism and publicity. Hello, Olga.'

'So here you are! The session is almost starting. Oh, Doctor Kelso – now this is not so good – no smoking, thank you.' She leaned over and removed the cigarette from his lips. She had a shiny face with plucked eyebrows and a very fine moustache, bleached white. She dropped the stub into the dregs of his coffee and took away his cup.

'Olga, Olga, why so bright?' groaned Kelso, putting his hand to his brow. The lecture hall exuded a tungsten glare.

'Television,' said Olga, with pride. 'They are making a programme of us.'

'Local?' Adelman was straightening his bow tie. 'Network?'

'Satellite, professor. *International.*'

'Say, now, where are our seats?' whispered Adelman, shielding his eyes from the lights.

'Doctor Kelso? Any chance of a word, sir?' An American accent. Kelso turned to find a large young man he vaguely recognised.

'I'm sorry?'

'R. J. O'Brian,' said the young man, holding out his hand. 'Moscow correspondent, Satellite News System. We're making a special report on the controversy –'

'I don't think so,' said Kelso. 'But Professor Adelman, here – I'm sure he'd be delighted –'

At the prospect of a television interview, Adelman seemed physically to swell in size, like an inflating doll. 'Well, as long as it's not in any *official* capacity . . .'

O'Brian ignored him. 'You sure I can't tempt you?' he said to Kelso. 'Nothing you want to say to the world? I read your book on the fall of communism. When was that? Three years ago?'

'Four,' said Kelso.

'Actually, I believe it was five,' said Adelman.

Actually, thought Kelso, it was nearer six: dear God, where were all the years going? 'No,' he said, 'thanks all the same, but I'm keeping off television these days.' He looked at Adelman. 'It's a cheap siren, apparently.'

'Later, please,' hissed Olga. 'Interviews are later. The director is talking. Please.' Kelso felt her umbrella in his back again as she steered him into the hall. 'Please. *Please –*'

By the time the Russian delegates were added in, plus a few diplomatic observers, the press, and maybe fifty members of the public, the hall was impressively full. Kelso sank heavily into his place in the second row. Up on the platform, Professor Valentin Askenov of the Russian State Archives had launched into a long explanation of the microfilming of the Party records. O'Brian's cameraman walked backwards down the central aisle, filming the audience. The sharp amplification of Askenov's sonorous voice seemed to pierce some painful chamber of Kelso's inner ear. Already, a kind of metallic, neon torpor had descended over the hall. The day stretched ahead. He covered his face with his hands.

Twenty-five million sheets . . . recited Askenov, *twenty-five thousand reels of microfilm . . . seven million dollars . . .*

Kelso slid his hands down his cheeks until his fingers converged and covered his mouth. *Frauds!* he wanted to shout. *Liars!* Why were they all just sitting here? They knew as well as he did that nine-tenths of the best material was still locked up, and to see most of the rest required a bribe. He'd heard that the going rate for a captured Nazi file was $1,000 and a bottle of Scotch.

He whispered to Adelman, 'I'm getting out of here.'

'You can't.'

'Why not?'

'It's discourteous. Just sit there, for pete's sake, and pretend to be interested like everyone else.' Adelman said all this out of the side of his mouth, without taking his eyes off the platform. Kelso stuck it for another half minute.

'Tell them I'm ill.'

'I shall not.'

'Let me by, Frank. I'm going to be sick.'

'Jesus . . .'

Adelman swung his legs to one side and pressed himself back in his seat. Hunched in a vain effort to make himself less conspicuous, Kelso stumbled over the feet of his colleagues, kicking in the process the elegant black shin of Ms Velma Byrd.

'Aw, fuck, Kelso,' said Velma.

Professor Askenov looked up from his notes and paused in mid-drone. Kelso was conscious of an amplified, humming silence, and of a kind of collective movement in the audience, as if some great beast had turned in its field to watch his progress. This seemed to last a long time, for at least as long as it took him to walk to the back of the hall. Not until he had passed beneath the marble gaze of Lenin and into the deserted corridor did the droning begin again.

KELSO sat behind the bolted door of a lavatory cubicle on the ground floor of the former Institute of Marxism–Leninism and opened his canvas bag. Here were the tools of his trade: a yellow legal pad, pencils, an eraser, a small Swiss army knife, a welcome pack from the organisers of the symposium, a dictionary, a street map of Moscow, his cassette recorder, and a Filofax that was a palimpsest of ancient numbers, lost contacts, old girlfriends, former lives.

There *was* something about the old man's story that was familiar to him, but he couldn't remember what it was. He picked up the cassette recorder, pressed REWIND, let it spool back for a while, then pressed PLAY. He held it to his ear and listened to the tinny ghost of Rapava's voice.

'. . . *Comrade Stalin's room was a plain man's room. You've got to say that for Stalin. He was always one of us . . .* '

REWIND. PLAY.

'. . . *and here was an odd thing, boy – he had taken off his shiny new shoes and had them wedged under one fat arm . . .* '

REWIND. PLAY.

'. . . *Know what I mean by Blizhny, boy? . . .* '

'. . . *by Blizhny, boy? . . .* '

'. . . *by Blizhny . . .* '

Chapter Two

THE MOSCOW AIR tasted of Asia – of dust and soot and eastern spices, cheap petrol, black tobacco, sweat. Kelso came out of the Institute and turned up the collar of his raincoat. He walked across the rutted concourse, skirting the frozen puddles, resisting the temptation to wave at the sullen crowd – that would have been 'a western provocation'.

The street sloped southwards, down towards the centre of the city. Every other building was encased in scaffolding. Beside him, debris hurtled down a metal chute and exploded into a fountain of dust. He passed a shady casino, anonymous except for a sign showing a pair of rolling dice. A fur boutique. A shop selling nothing but Italian shoes. A single pair of handmade loafers would have cost any one of the demonstrators a whole month's wages and he felt a stab of sympathy. He remembered a line of Evelyn Waugh's he had used before about Russia: 'The foundations of Empire are often occasions of woe; their dismemberment, always.'

At the bottom of the hill he turned right, into the wind. The snow had stopped but the cold blast was hard and unyielding. He could see tiny figures bent into it, across the road, beneath the red rock-face of the Kremlin wall, while the golden domes of the churches rose above the parapet like the globes of some vast meteorological machine.

His destination lay straight ahead. Like the Institute of Marxism–Leninism, the Lenin Library had been renamed. It was now the Central Library of the Russian Federation, but everyone still called it the Lenin. He stepped through the familiar triple doors, gave his bag and coat to the babushka behind the cloakroom counter, then showed his old reader's ticket to an armed guard in a glass booth.

He signed his name in the register and added the time. It was eleven minutes past ten.

They had yet to get around to computerising the Lenin, which meant forty million titles were still on index cards. At the top of a wide flight of stone steps, beneath the vaulted ceiling, was a sea of wooden cabinets, and Kelso moved among them as he had done years ago, sliding open one drawer after another, riffling through the familiar titles. Radzinsky he would need, and the second volume of Volkogonov, and Khrushchev and Alliluyeva. The cards for these last two were marked with the Cyrillic symbol '¢' which meant they had been held in the secret index until 1991. How many titles was he allowed? Five, wasn't it? Finally, he decided on Chuyev's series of interviews with the ancient Molotov. Then he took his request slips to the issuing desk and watched as they were fitted into a metal canister and fired down the pneumatic tube into the Lenin's lower depths.

'What's the wait today?'

The assistant shrugged. Who was she to say?

'An hour?'

She shrugged again.

He thought: nothing changes.

He wandered back across the landing into Reading Room No. 3, and trod softly down the path of worn green carpet that led to his old seat. And nothing had changed here, either – not the rich brownness of the wood-panelled, galleried hall, nor the dry smell of it, nor its sacrilegious hush. At one end was a statue of Lenin reading a book, at the other an astrological clock. Maybe two hundred people were bent over their desks. Through the window to his left he could see the dome and spire of St Nicholas's. He might never have left; the past eighteen years might have been a dream.

He sat down and laid out his things and in that instant he was a student of twenty-six again, living in a single room in Corpus V of Moscow University, paying 260 roubles a month for a desk, a bed, a chair and a cupboard, taking meals in the basement canteen that was overrun by cockroaches, spending his days in the Lenin and his nights with a girlfriend – with Nadya, or Katya, or Margarita, or Irina. *Irina*. Now there was a woman. He ran his hand over the scratched surface of the desk and wondered what had become of Irina. Perhaps he should have stuck with her – serious, beautiful Irina, with her *samizdat* magazines and her basement meetings, making love to the accompaniment of a rattling Gestetner duplicator and afterwards vowing that they would be different, that they would change the world.

Irina. He wondered what she would make of the new Russia. The last he had heard she was a dental assistant in South Wales.

He glanced around the reading room and closed his eyes, trying to keep hold of the past for a minute longer, a fattening and hungover middle-aged historian in a black corduroy suit.

HIS books arrived at the issuing stack just after eleven, or at any rate four of them did: they had fetched up volume one of Volkogonov rather than volume two and he had to send it back. Still, he had enough. He carried the books back to his desk and gradually he became absorbed in his task, reading, noting and cross-referencing the various eyewitness accounts of Stalin's death. He found, as usual, an aesthetic pleasure in the sheer detective work of research. Secondhand sources and

speculation he discarded. He was only interested in those
people who had actually been in the same room as the
GenSec and had left behind a description he could match
against Rapava's.

By his reckoning there were seven: the Politburo members,
Khrushchev and Molotov; Stalin's daughter, Svetlana
Alliluyeva; two of Stalin's bodyguards, Rybin and Lozgachev;
and two of his medical staff: the physician, Myasnikov, and
the recuscitator, a woman named Chesnokova. The other
eyewitnesses had either killed themselves (like the
bodyguard, Khrustalev, who drank himself to death after
watching the autopsy), or had died soon afterwards, or had
disappeared.

The accounts all differed in detail but were in essence the
same. Stalin had suffered a catastrophic haemorrhage in the
left cerebral hemisphere some time when he was alone in his
room between 4 a.m. and 10 p.m. on Sunday March 1 1953.
Academician Vinogradov, who examined the brain after
death, found serious hardening of the cerebral arteries which
suggested Stalin had probably been half-crazy for a long
while, maybe even years. Nobody could tell what time the
stroke had hit. His door had stayed closed all day and his staff
had been too scared to enter his room. The bodyguard
Lozgachev told the writer Radzinsky that he had been the
first to pluck up the courage:

I opened the door . . . and there was the Boss lying on
the floor holding up his right hand like this. I was
petrified. My hands and legs wouldn't obey me. He had
probably not yet lost consciousness but he couldn't
speak. He had good hearing, he'd obviously heard me
coming, and probably raised his hand slightly to call me

in to help him. I hurried up to him and said 'Comrade Stalin, what's wrong?' He'd – you know – wet himself while he was lying there, and was trying to straighten something with his left hand. I said, 'Shall I call the doctor, maybe?' He made some incoherent noise – like 'Dz – dz . . . ,' all he could do was keep on 'dz'-ing.

It was immediately after this that the guards had called in Malenkov. Malenkov had called in Beria. And Beria's order, tantamount to murder by negligence, had been that Stalin was drunk and should be left to sleep it off.

Kelso made a careful note of the passage. Nothing here contradicted Rapava. That didn't prove Rapava was telling the truth, of course – he could have got hold of Lozgachev's testimony for himself, and tailored his story to fit. But it didn't suggest he was lying, either, and certainly the details tallied – the time frame, the order not to call for medical help, the way Stalin had wet himself, the way he would regain consciousness but be unable to speak. This happened at least twice over the three days it took Stalin to die. Once, according to Khrushchev, when the doctors at last brought in by the Politburo were spoon-feeding him soup and weak tea, he had raised his hand and pointed at one of the pictures of children on the wall. The second return to consciousness occurred just before the end and was noted by everyone, especially his daughter, Svetlana:

At what seemed like the very last moment he suddenly opened his eyes and cast a glance over everyone in the room. It was a terrible glance, insane or perhaps angry and full of fear of death and the unfamiliar faces of the doctors bent over him. The glance swept over everyone in a second. Then something incomprehensible and terrible happened that to this day I can't forget and don't understand. He suddenly lifted his left hand as though he were pointing to something up above and bringing down a curse on us all. The gesture was incomprehensible and full of menace, and no one could say to whom or what it might be directed. The next moment, after a final effort, the spirit wrenched itself free of the flesh.

That had been written in 1967. After his heart had stopped, the doctors had ordered the resuscitator, Chesnokova – a strong young woman – to pound at Stalin's chest and blow into his mouth, until Khrushchev had heard the old man's ribs snap and had told her to pack it in. '... *no one could say to whom or what it might be directed ...*' Kelso underlined the words lightly with his pencil. If Rapava was telling the truth, it was fairly obvious whom Stalin must have been cursing: the man who had stolen the key to his private safe – Lavrenty Beria. Why he should have pointed at a picture of a child was less clear.

Kelso tapped the pencil against his teeth. It was all very circumstantial. He could imagine Adelman's reaction if he tried to offer it as any sort of supporting evidence. The thought of Adelman made him look at his watch. If he set off now he could be back at the symposium comfortably in time for lunch and there was a good chance they wouldn't even have missed him. He gathered up the books and took them back to the issuing desk, where the second volume of Volkogonov had just arrived.

'Well,' said the librarian, her thin lips crimped with irritation, 'do you want it or not?'

Kelso hesitated, almost said no, then decided he might as well finish what he'd started. He handed over the other books and carried the Volkogonov back into the reading room.

It lay before him on his desk like a dull brown brick. *Triyumf i Tragediya: politicheskii portret I. V. Stalina,* Novosti publishers, Moscow 1989. He had read it when it first came out and hadn't felt the need to look at it since. He regarded it now without enthusiasm, then flicked the cover open with his finger. Volkogonov was a three-star Red Army general with powerful contacts inside the Kremlin, granted special access to the archives under Gorbachev and Yeltsin which he had used to produce a trio of tombstone lives – Stalin, Trotsky, Lenin – each one more revisionist than the last. Kelso picked it up and leafed through it to the index, looked up the relevant entries for Stalin's death – and a moment later there it was, the memory that had been niggling at the back of his mind ever since Papu Rapava disappeared into the Moscow dawn:

A. A. Yepishev, who was at one time deputy Minister of State Security, told me that Stalin kept a black oilskin exercise book in which he would make occasional notes, and that for some time Stalin kept letters from Zinoviev, Kamenev, Bukharin and even Trotsky. All efforts to discover either the notebook or these letters have failed, and Yepishev did not reveal his source.

Yepishev did not reveal his source but he did, according to Volkogonov, have a theory. He believed that Stalin's private papers had been removed from his Kremlin safe by Lavrenty Beria, while the General Secretary lay paralysed by his stroke.

Beria made a dash for the Kremlin where it is reasonable to assume he cleaned out the safe, removing the Boss's personal papers and with them, one assumes, the black notebook . . . Having destroyed Stalin's notebook, if indeed it was there, Beria would have cleared the path to his own ascendancy. Perhaps the truth will never be known, but Yepishev was convinced that Beria cleaned out the safe before the others could get to it.

*

Now calm yourself, and don't get excited, because this proves nothing, you understand? Nothing whatever.

But it does make it a thousand times more likely.

Back outside the entrance to the reading room, Kelso yanked open the narrow wooden drawer and searched through it quickly until he found the index cards to Yepishev, A. A. (1908–85). The old man had written a score of books, of uniform dullness and hackery: *History Teaches: The Lessons of the Twentieth Anniversary of Victory in the Great Patriotic War* (1965), *Ideological Warfare and Military Problems* (1974), *We Are True to the Ideas of the Party* (1981) . . .

Kelso's hangover had gone, to be replaced by that familiar phase of post-alcoholic euphoria – always, in the past, his most productive time of day – a feeling that alone was enough to make getting drunk worthwhile. He ran down the flight of steps and along the wide and gloomy corridor that led to the Lenin's military section. This was a small and self-contained area, neon-lit, with a subterranean feel to it. A young man in a grey pullover was leaning against the counter, reading a 1970s *MAD* comic.

'What do you have on an army man named Yepishev?' asked Kelso. 'A. A. Yepishev?'

'Who wants to know?'

Kelso handed over his reader's card and the young man examined it with interest.

'Hey, are you the Kelso who wrote that book a few years back on the end of the Party?'

Kelso hesitated – this could go either way – but finally he admitted he was. The young man put down the comic and shook his hand. 'Andrei Efanov. Great book. You really stuffed the bastards. I'll see what we have.'

THERE were two reference books with entries for Yepishev: the *Military Encyclopaedia of the USSR* and the *Directory of Heroes of the Soviet Union*, and both told pretty much the same story, if you knew how to read between the lines, which was that Aleksey Alekseevich Yepishev had been an armour-plated, ocean-going Stalinist of the old school: Komsomol and Party instructor in the twenties and thirties; Red Army Military Academy, 1938; Commissar of the Komintern Factory in Kharkov, 1942; Military Council of the Thirty-Eighth Army of the 1st Ukrainian Front, 1943; Deputy People's Commissar for Medium Machine Building, also 1943 –

'What's a "medium machine",' asked Efanov, who was peering at the books over Kelso's shoulder. Efanov turned out to have done his military service in Lithuania – two years of hell – and to have been refused admittance to Moscow University in the communist time on the grounds he was a Jew. Now he was taking a huge delight in poking over the dust and ashes of Yepishev's career.

'Cover-name for the Soviet atomic bomb programme,' said Kelso. 'Beria's pet project.' *Beria.* He made a note.

– Secretary of the Central Committee of the Ukrainian Communist Party, 1946 –

'That was when they purged the Ukraine of collaborators, after the war,' said Efanov. 'A bloody time.'

– First Secretary of the Odessa Regional Party Committee, 1950; Deputy Minister of State Security, 1951 –

Deputy Minister . . .

Each entry was illustrated with the same official photograph of Yepishev. Kelso looked again at the the square jaw, the thick brow, the grim face set above the boxer's neck.

'Oh, he was a big bastard, boy. A fleshy tank . . . '

'Gotcha,' whispered Kelso to himself.

After Stalin's death, Yepishev's career had taken a dive. First he had been sent back to Odessa, then he had been packed off abroad. Ambassador to Romania, 1955-61. Ambassador to Yugoslavia, 1961-62. And then, at last, the long-awaited summons back to Moscow, as Head of the Central Political Department of the Soviet Armed Forces – its ideological commissar – a position he held for the next twenty-three years. And who had served as his deputy? None other than Dmitri Volkogonov, three-star general and future biographer of Josef Stalin.

To extract these small plums of information it was necessary to dig through a great pudding of cliché and jargon, praising Yepishev for his 'important role in shaping the necessary political attitudes and enforcing Marxist–Leninist orthodoxy in the Armed Forces, in strengthening military discipline and fostering ideological readiness'. He had died aged seventy-seven. Volkogonov, Kelso knew, had died ten years later.

The list of Yepishev's honours and medals took up the rest of his entry: Hero of the Soviet Union, winner of the Lenin Prize, holder of four Orders of Lenin, the October Revolution Order, four Orders of the Red Banner, two

Orders of the Great Patriotic War (1ˢᵗ class), the Order of the Red Banner, three Orders of the Red Star, the Order of Service to the Motherland . . .

'It's a wonder he could stand up.'

'And I'll bet you he never shot anyone,' sneered Efanov, 'except on his own side. So what's so interesting about Yepishev, if you don't mind me asking?'

'What's this?' said Kelso suddenly. He pointed to a line at the foot of the column: 'V. P. Mamantov.'

'He's the author of the entry.'

'Yepishev's entry was written by Mamantov? *Vladimir* Mamantov? The KGB man?'

'That's him. So what? The entries are usually written by friends. Why? D'you know him?'

'I don't *know* him. I've *met* him.' He frowned at the name. 'His people were demonstrating – this morning –'

'Oh, them? They're always demonstrating. When did you meet Mamantov?'

Kelso reached for his notebook and began skimming back through the pages. 'About five years ago, I suppose. When I was researching my book on the Party.'

Vladimir Mamantov. My God, he hadn't thought about Vladimir Mamantov in half a decade, and suddenly here he was, crossing his path twice in a morning. The years fluttered through his fingers – *ninety-five, ninety-four* . . . Some details of the meeting were starting to come back to him now: a morning in late spring, a dead dog revealed in the thawing snow outside an apartment block in the suburbs, a gorgon of a wife. Mamantov had just finished serving fourteen months in Lefortovo for his part in the attempted coup against Gorbachev, and Kelso had been the first to interview him when he came out of jail. It had taken an age to fix the appointment and then it had proved, as so often in these cases, not worth the effort. Mamantov had refused point-blank to talk about himself, or the coup, and had simply spouted Party slogans straight out of the pages of *Pravda*.

He found Mamantov's home telephone number from 1991, next to an office address for a lowly Party functionary, Gennady Zyuganov.

'You're going to try to see him?' asked Efanov, anxiously. 'You know he hates all Westerners? Almost as much as he hates the Jews.'

'You're right,' said Kelso, staring at the seven digits. Mamantov had been a formidable man even in defeat, his Soviet suit hanging loose off his wide shoulders, the grey pallor of prison still dull on his cheeks, murder in his eyes. Kelso's book had not been flattering about Vladimir Mamantov, to put it mildly. And it had been translated into Russian – Mamantov must have seen it.

'You're right,' he repeated. 'It would be stupid even to try.'

FLUKE Kelso walked out of the Lenin Library a little after two that afternoon, pausing briefly at a stall in the lobby to buy a couple of bread rolls and a bottle of warm and salty mineral water.

He remembered passing a row of public telephones opposite the Kremlin, close to the Intourist office, and he ate his lunch as he walked – first down into the gloom of the metro station to buy some plastic tokens for the phone, and then back along Mokhavaya Street towards the high red wall and the golden domes.

He was not alone, it seemed to him. His younger self was ambling alongside him now – floppy-haired, chain-smoking, forever in a hurry, forever optimistic, a writer on the rise.

('Dr Kelso brings to the study of contemporary Soviet history the skills of a first-rate scholar and the energy of a good reporter' – *The New York Times*.) This younger Kelso wouldn't have hesitated to call up Vladimir Mamantov, that was for sure – by God, he would have battered his bloody door down by now if necessary.

Think about it: if Yepishev had told Volkogonov about Stalin's notebook, might he not also have told Mamantov? Might he not have left behind papers? Might he not have a family?

It had to be worth a try.

He wiped his mouth and fingers on the little paper napkin and as he picked up the receiver and inserted the tokens he felt a familiar tightening of his stomach muscles, a butteriness around his heart. Was this sensible? No. But who cared about that? Adelman – he was sensible. And Saunders – he was *very* sensible.

Go for it.

He dialled the number.

The first call was an anti-climax. The Mamantovs had moved and the man who now lived at their old address was reluctant to give out their new number. Only after he had held a whispered consultation with someone at his end did he pass it on. Kelso hung up and dialled again. This time the phone rang for a long time before it was answered. The tokens dropped and an old woman with a trembling voice said, 'Who is this?'

He gave his name. 'Could I speak with Comrade Mamantov?' He was careful to say 'comrade': 'mister' would never do.

'Yes? Who is this?'

Kelso was patient. 'As I said, my name is Kelso. I'm using a public telephone. It's urgent.'

65

'Yes, but who is this?'

He was about to repeat his name for a third time when he heard what sounded like a scuffle at the other end of the line and a harsh male voice cut in. 'All right. This is Mamantov. Who are you?'

'It's Kelso.' There was a silence. 'Doctor Kelso? You may remember me?'

'I remember you. What do you want?'

'To see you.'

'Why should I see you after that shit you wrote?'

'I wanted to ask you some questions.'

'About?'

'A black oilskin notebook that used to belong to Josef Stalin.'

'Shut up,' said Mamantov.

'What?' Kelso frowned at the receiver.

'I said shut up. I'm thinking it over. Where are you?'

'Near the Intourist building, on Mokhavaya Street.'

There was another silence.

Mamantov said, 'You're close.'

And then he said, 'You'd better come.'

He gave his address. The line went dead.

THE line went dead and Major Feliks Suvorin of the Russian intelligence service, the SVR, sitting in his office in the south-eastern suburb of Yasenevo, carefully slipped off his headphones and wiped his neat pink ears with a clean white handkerchief. On the notepad in front of him he had written: *A black oilskin notebook that used to belong to Josef Stalin . . .*

Chapter Three

'Confronting the Past'
An International Symposium on the
Archives of the Russian Federation

Tuesday 27 October,
final afternoon session

DR KELSO: *Ladies and gentlemen, whenever I think of Josef Stalin, I find myself thinking of one image in particular. I think of Stalin, as an old man, standing beside his gramophone.*

He would finish working late, usually at nine or ten, and then he would go to the Kremlin movie theatre to watch a film. Often, it was one of the Tarzan series – for some reason Stalin loved the idea of a young man growing up and living among wild animals – then he and his cronies in the Politburo would drive out to his dacha at Kuntsevo for dinner, and, after dinner, he would go over to his gramophone and put on a record. His particular favourite, according to Milovan Djilas, was a song in which howling dogs replaced the sound of human voices. And then Stalin would make the Politburo dance.

Some of them were quite good dancers. Mikoyan, for example: he was a lovely dancer. And Bulganin wasn't bad; he could follow a beat. Khrushchev, though, was a lousy dancer – 'like a cow on ice' – and so was Malenkov and so was Kaganovich, for that matter.

Anyway, one evening – drawn, we might speculate, by the peculiar noise of grown men dancing to the baying of hounds – Stalin's daughter, Svetlana, put her head round the door, and

67

Stalin made her start dancing, too. Well, after a time, she grew tired, and her feet were hardly moving, and this made Stalin angry. He shouted at her, 'Dance!' And she said, 'But I've already danced, papa, I'm tired.' At which Stalin – and here I quote Khrushchev's description – 'grabbed her like this, by the hair, a whole fistful, I mean by her forelock, as it were, and pulled, you understand, very hard . . . pulled, jerked and jerked.'

Now keep that image in your mind for a moment, and let us consider the fate of Stalin's family. His first wife died. His oldest son, Yakov, tried to shoot himself when he was twenty-one, but only succeeded in inflicting severe wounds. (When Stalin saw him, according to Svetlana, he laughed. 'Ha!' he said. 'Missed! Couldn't even shoot straight!') Yakov was captured by the Germans during the war and, after Stalin refused a prisoner exchange, he tried suicide again – successfully this time, by hurling himself at the electrified fence of his prison camp.

Stalin had one other child, a son, Vasily, an alcoholic, who died aged forty-one.

Stalin's second wife, Nadezhda, refused to bear her husband any more children – according to Svetlana, she had a couple of abortions – and late one night, aged thirty-one, she shot herself through the heart. (Or perhaps it would be more accurate to say that someone *shot her: no suicide note has ever been found.)*

Nadezhda was one of four children. Her older brother, Pavel, was murdered by Stalin during the purges; the death certificate recorded a heart attack. Her younger brother, Fyodor, was driven insane when a friend of Stalin's, an Armenian bank robber named Kamo, handed him a gouged-out human heart. Her sister, Anna, was arrested on Stalin's orders and sentenced to ten years in solitary confinement. By the time she came out she was no longer capable of recognising her own children. So that was one set of Stalin's relatives.

And what of the other set? Well, there was Aleksandr Svanidze, the brother of Stalin's first wife – he was arrested in thirty-seven and shot in forty-one. And there was Svanidze's wife, Maria, who was also arrested; she was shot in forty-two. Their surviving child, Ivan – Stalin's nephew – was sent into exile, to a ghastly state orphanage for the children of 'enemies of the state', and when he emerged, nearly twenty years later, he was profoundly psychologically damaged. And finally there was Stalin's sister-in-law, Maria – she was also arrested in thirty-seven and died mysteriously in prison.

Now let us go back to that image of Svetlana. Her mother is dead. Her half-brother is dead. Her other brother is an alcoholic. Two uncles are dead and one is insane. Two aunts are dead and one is in prison. She is being dragged around by her hair, by her father, in front of a roomful of the most powerful men in Russia, all of whom are being forced to dance, maybe to the sound of howling dogs.

Colleagues, whenever I sit in an archive or, more rarely these days, attend a symposium like this one, I always try to remember that scene, because it reminds me to be wary of imposing a rational structure on the past. There is nothing in the archives here to show us that the Deputy Chairman of the Council of Ministers, or the Commissar for Foreign Affairs, when they made their decisions, were shattered by exhaustion, and very probably terrified – that they had been up until three a.m. dancing for their lives, and knew they might well be dancing again that evening.

Not that I am saying that Stalin was crazy. On the contrary. One could argue that the man who worked the gramophone was the sanest person in the room. When Svetlana asked him why her Aunt Anna was being held in solitary confinement, he answered, 'Because she talks too much.' With Stalin, there was usually a logic to his actions. He didn't need a sixteenth-century English philosopher to tell him that 'knowledge is power'. That realisation is the absolute essence of Stalinism. Among other things, it explains why Stalin murdered so many of his own family and close colleagues – he wanted to destroy anyone who had any first-hand knowledge of him.

And this policy, we must concede, was remarkably successful. Here we are, gathered in Moscow, forty-five years after Stalin's death, to discuss the newly-opened archives of the Soviet era. Above our heads, in fire-proofed strong-rooms, maintained at a constant temperature of eighteen degrees celsius and sixty per cent humidity, are one and a half million files – the entire archive of the Central Committee of the Communist Party of the Soviet Union.

Yet how much does this archive really tell us about Stalin? What can we see today that we couldn't see when the communists were in power? Stalin's letters to Molotov – we can see those – and they are not without interest. But clearly they have been heavily censored. And not just that: they end in thirty-six, at precisely the point when the real killing started.

We can also see the death lists that Stalin signed. And we have his appointments book. So we know that on the eighth of December, nineteen thirty-eight, Stalin signed thirty death lists containing five thousand names, many of them of his so-called friends. And we also know, thanks to his appointments book, that on that very same evening he went to the Kremlin movie theatre and watched, not Tarzan this time, but a comedy called Happy Guys.

But between these two events, between the killing and the laughter, there lies – what? who? We do not know. And why? Because Stalin made it his business to murder almost everyone who might have been in a position to tell us what he was like . . .

Chapter Four

MAMANTOV'S NEW PLACE turned out to be just across the river, in the big apartment complex on Serafimovich Street known as the House on the Embankment. This was the building to which Comrade Stalin, with typical generosity, had insisted that leading Party members go to live with their families. There were ten floors with twenty-five different entrances at ground level, at each of which the GenSec had thoughtfully posted an NKVD guard – purely for your security, comrades.

By the time the purges were finished, six hundred of the building's tenants had been liquidated. Now the flats were privately owned and the good ones, with a view across the Moskva to the Kremlin, sold for upwards of half a million dollars. Kelso wondered how Mamantov could afford it.

He came down the steps from the bridge and crossed the road. Parked outside the entrance to Mamantov's staircase was a boxy white Lada, its windows open, two men in the front seat, chewing gum. One had a livid scar running almost from the corner of his eye to the edge of his mouth. They watched Kelso with undisguised interest as he walked past them towards the entrance.

Inside the apartment block, next to the elevator, someone had written, neatly, in English, in capitals and lower case, 'Fuck Off'. A tribute to the Russian education system, thought Kelso. He whistled nervously, a made-up tune. The lift rose smoothly and he got out at the ninth floor to be met by the distant thump of western rock music.

Mamantov's apartment had an outer door of steel plate. A

red aerosol swastika had been sprayed on to the metal. The paint was old and faded but no attempt had been made to clean it off. Set in the wall above it was a small remote TV camera.

There was already plenty about this set-up that Kelso didn't like – the heavy security, the guys in the car downstairs – and for a moment he could almost smell the terror from sixty years ago, as if the sweat had seeped into the brickwork: the clattering footsteps, the heavy knocking, the hurried goodbyes, the sobs, silence. His hand paused over the buzzer. What a place to choose to live.

He pressed the button.

After a long wait, the door was opened by an elderly woman. Madame Mamantov was as he remembered her – tall and broad, not fat, but heavily built. She was draped in a shapeless, flowery smock and looked as though she had just finished crying. Her red eyes rested on him briefly, distractedly, but before he could even open his mouth she had wandered off and suddenly there was Vladimir Mamantov, looming down the dark passage, dressed as if he still had an office to go to – white shirt, blue tie, black suit with a small red star pinned in his lapel.

He didn't say anything, but he offered his hand. He had a crushing handshake, perfected, it was said, by squeezing balls of vulcanized rubber during KGB meetings. (A lot of things were said about Mamantov: for example – and Kelso had put it in his book – that at the famous meeting in the Lubyanka on the night of 20 August 1991, when the plotters of the coup had realised the game was up, Mamantov had offered to fly down to Gorbachev's dacha at Foros on the Black Sea and shoot the Soviet President personally; Mamantov had dismissed the story as 'a provocation'.)

A young man in a black shirt with a shoulder holster appeared in the gloom behind Mamantov, and Mamantov said, without looking round, 'It's all right, Viktor. I'm dealing with the situation.' Mamantov had a bureaucrat's face – steel-coloured hair, steel-framed glasses and pouched cheeks, like a suspicious hound's. You could pass it in the street a hundred times and never notice it. But his eyes were bright: a fanatic's eyes, thought Kelso; he could imagine Eichmann or some other Nazi desk-murderer having eyes like these. The old woman had started making a curious howling noise from the other end of the flat, and Mamantov told Viktor to go and sort her out.

'So you're part of the gathering of thieves,' he said to Kelso.

'What?'

'The symposium. *Pravda* published a list of the foreign historians they invited to speak. Your name was on it.'

'Historians are hardly thieves, Comrade Mamantov. Even foreign historians.'

'No? Nothing is more important to a nation than its history. It is the earth upon which any society stands. Ours has been stolen from us – gouged and blackened by the libels of our enemies until the people have become lost.'

Kelso smiled. Mamantov hadn't changed at all. 'You can't seriously believe that.'

'You're not Russian. Imagine if your country offered to sell its national archive to a foreign power for a miserable few million dollars.'

'You're not selling your archive. The plan is to microfilm the records and make them available to scholars.'

'To scholars *in California*,' said Mamantov, as if this settled the argument. 'But this is tedious. I have an urgent appointment.' He looked at his watch. 'I can only give you five minutes, so get to the point. What's all this about Stalin's notebook?'

'It comes into some research I'm doing.'

'Research? Research into what?'

Kelso hesitated. 'The events surrounding Stalin's death.'

'Go on.'

'If I could just ask you a couple of questions, then perhaps I could explain the relevance –'

'No,' said Mamantov. 'Let us do this the other way round. You tell me about this notebook and then I might answer your questions.'

'You *might* answer my questions?'

Mamantov consulted his watch again. 'Four minutes.'

'All right,' said Kelso, quickly. 'You remember the official biography of Stalin, by Dmitri Volkogonov?'

'The traitor Volkogonov? You're wasting my time. That book is a piece of shit.'

'You've read it?'

'Of course not. There's enough filth in this world without my volunteering to go jump in it.'

'Volkogonov claimed that Stalin kept certain papers – private papers, including a black oilskin exercise book – in his safe at the Kremlin, and that these papers were stolen by Beria. His source for this story was a man you're familiar with, I think. Aleksey Alekseevich Yepishev.'

There was a slight movement – a flicker, no more – in Mamantov's hard grey eyes. He's heard of it, thought Kelso, he knows about the notebook –

'And?'

'And I wondered if you'd come across this story while you were writing your entry on Yepishev for the biographical guide. He was a friend of yours, I assume?'

'What's it to you?' Mamantov glanced at Kelso's bag. 'Have you found the notebook?'

'No.'

'But you know someone who may know where it is?'

'Someone came to see me,' began Kelso, then stopped. The apartment was very quiet now. The old woman had finished wailing, but the bodyguard hadn't reappeared. On the hall table was a copy of *Aurora*.

Nobody in Moscow knew where he was, he realised. He had dropped off the map.

'I'm wasting your time,' he said. 'Perhaps I might come back when I've –'

'That's unnecessary,' said Mamantov, softening his tone. His sharp eyes were checking Kelso up and down – flickering across his face, his hands, gauging the potential strength of his arms and chest, darting up to his face again. His conversational technique was pure Leninism, thought Kelso: *'Push out a bayonet. If it strikes fat, push deeper. If it strikes iron, pull back for another day.'*

'I'll tell you what, Doctor Kelso,' said Mamantov. 'I'll show you something. It will interest you. And then I'll tell you something. And then you'll tell me something.' He waved his fingers back and forth between them. 'We'll trade. Is it a deal?'

AFTERWARDS, Kelso tried to make a list of it all, but there was too much of it for him to remember: the immense oil painting, by Gerasimov, of Stalin on the ramparts of the Kremlin, and the neon-lit glass cabinet with its miniatures of Stalin – its Stalin dishes and its Stalin boxes, its Stalin stamps and Stalin medals – and the case of books by Stalin, and the books about Stalin, and the photographs of Stalin – signed and unsigned – and the scrap of Stalin's handwriting – blue pencil, lined paper, quarto-sized and framed – that hung above the bust of Stalin by Vuchetich ('. . . don't spare individuals, no matter what position they occupy, spare only the cause, the interests of the cause . . .').

He moved among the collection while Mamantov watched him closely.

The handwriting sample, said Kelso – that . . . that was a note for a speech, was it not? Correct, said Mamantov: October 1920, address to the Worker–Peasant Inspection. And the Gerasimov? Wasn't it similar to the artist's 1938 study of Stalin and Voroshilov on the Kremlin Wall? Mamantov nodded again, apparently pleased to share these moments with a fellow connoisseur: yes, the GenSec had ordered Gerasimov to paint a second version, leaving out Voroshilov – it was Stalin's way of reminding Voroshilov that life (how to put it?) could always be *rearranged* to imitate art. A collector in Maryland and another in Dusseldorf had each offered Mamantov $100,000 for the picture but he would never permit it to leave Russian soil. Never. One day, he hoped to exhibit it in Moscow, along with the rest of his collection – 'when the political situation is more favourable'.

'And you think one day the situation will be favourable?'

'Oh yes. Objectively, history will record that Stalin was right. That is how it is with Stalin. From the subjective perspective, he may seem cruel, even wicked. But the glory of the man is to be found in the objective perspective. There he is a towering figure. It is my unshakeable belief that when the proper perspective is restored, statues will be raised again to Stalin.'

'Goering said the same of Hitler during the Nuremberg trial. I don't see any statues –'

'Hitler lost.'

'But surely Stalin lost? In the end? From the "objective perspective"?'

'Stalin inherited a nation with wooden ploughs and bequeathed us an empire armed with atomic weapons. How can you say he lost? The men who came after him – they lost. Not Stalin. Stalin foresaw what would happen, of course. Khrushchev, Molotov, Beria, Malenkov – they thought they were hard, but he saw through them. "After I've gone, the capitalists will drown you like blind kittens." His analysis was correct, as always.'

'So you think that if Stalin had lived –'

'We would still be a superpower? Absolutely. But men of Stalin's genius are only given to a country perhaps once in a century. And even Stalin could not devise a strategy to defeat death. Tell me, did you see the survey of opinion to mark the forty-fifth anniversary of his passing?'

'I did.'

'And what did you think of the results?'

'I thought they were –' Kelso tried to find a neutral word ' – remarkable.'

(Remarkable? Christ. They were horrifying. One third of Russians said they thought Stalin was a great war leader. One in six thought he was the greatest ruler the country had ever had. Stalin was seven times more popular than Boris Yeltsin, while poor old Gorbachev hadn't even scored enough votes to register. This was in March. Kelso had been so appalled he had tried to sell an op-ed piece to the *New York Times* but they weren't interested.)

'Remarkable,' agreed Mamantov. 'I should even say astounding, considering his vilification by so-called "historians".'

There was an awkward silence.

'Such a collection,' said Kelso, 'it must have taken years to assemble.' And cost a fortune, he almost added.

'I have a few business interests,' said Mamantov, dismissively. 'And a considerable amount of spare time, since my retirement.' He put out his hand to touch the bust, but then hesitated and drew it back. 'The difficulty, of course, for any collector, is that he left so little behind in the way of personal possessions. He had no interest in private property, not like these corrupt swine we have in the Kremlin nowadays. A few sticks of government-issue furniture was all he had. That and the clothes he stood up in. And his private notebook, of course.' He gave Kelso a crafty look. 'Now that would be something. Something – what is the American phrase? – *to die for?*'

'So you have heard of it?'

Mamantov smiled – an unheard-of occurrence – a narrow, thin, rapid smile, like a sudden crack in ice. 'You're interested in Yepishev?'

'Anything you can tell me.'

Mamantov crossed the room to the bookshelf and pulled down a large, leather-bound album. On a higher shelf Kelso could see the two volumes of Volkogonov – of course Mamantov had read them.

'I first met Aleksey Alekseevich,' he said, 'in fifty-seven, when he was ambassador in Bucharest. I was on my way back from Hungary, after we'd sorted things out there. Nine months work, without a break. I needed a rest, I can tell you. We went shooting together in the Azuga region.'

He carefully peeled back a layer of tissue paper and offered the heavy album to Kelso. It was open at a small photograph, taken by an amateur camera, and Kelso had to stare at it closely to make out what was happening. In the background, a forest. In the foreground, two men in leather hunting caps with fleece-lined jackets, smiling, holding rifles, dead birds piled at their booted feet. Yepishev was on the left, Mamantov next to him – still hard-faced but leaner then, a cold war caricature of a KGB man.

'And somewhere there's another.' Mamantov leaned over Kelso's shoulder and turned a couple of pages. Close up, he smelled elderly, of mothballs and carbolic, and he had shaved badly, as old men do, leaving grey stubble in the shadow of his nose and in the cleft of his broad chin. 'There.'

This was a much bigger, professional picture, showing maybe two hundred men, arranged in four ranks, as if at a graduation. Some were in uniform, some in civilian suits. A caption underneath said 'Sverdlovsk, 1980'.

'This was an ideological collegium, organised by the Central Committee Secretariat. On the final day, Comrade Suslov himself addressed us. This is me.' He pointed to a grim face in the third row, then moved his finger to the front, to a relaxed, uniformed figure sitting cross-legged on the ground. 'And this – would you believe? – is Volkogonov. And here again is Aleksey Alekseevich.'

It was like looking at a picture of Imperial officers in the tsarist time, thought Kelso – such confidence, such order, such masculine arrogance! Yet within ten years, their world had been atomised: Yepishev was dead, Volkogonov had renounced the Party, Mamantov was in jail.

Yepishev had died in 1985, said Mamantov. He had passed on just as Gorbachev came to power. And that was a good time for a decent communist to die, in Mamantov's opinion: Aleksey Alekseevich had been *spared*. Here was a man whose whole life had been devoted to Marxism–Leninism, who had helped plan the fraternal assistance to Czechoslovakia and Afghanistan. What a mercy he hadn't lived to see the whole lot thrown away. Writing Yepishev's entry for the *Book of Heroes* had been a privilege, and if nobody ever read it nowadays – well, that was what he meant. The country had been robbed of its history.

'And did Yepishev tell you the same story about Stalin's papers as he told Volkogonov?'

'He did. He talked more freely towards the end. He was often ill. I visited him in the leadership clinic. Brezhnev and he were treated together by the parapsychic healer, Davitashvili.'

'I don't suppose he left any papers.'

'Papers? Men like Yepishev didn't keep papers.'

'Any relatives?'

'None that I knew of. We never discussed *families.*' Mamantov pronounced the word as if it was absurd. 'Did you know that one of the things Aleksey had to do was interrogate Beria? Night after night. Can you imagine what that must have been like? But Beria never cracked, not once in nearly half a year, until right at the very end, after his trial, when they were strapping him to the board to shoot him. He hadn't believed they'd dare to kill him.'

'How do you mean, he cracked?'

'He was squealing like a pig – that's what Yepishev said. Shouting something about Stalin and something about an archangel. Can you imagine that? Beria, of all people, getting religious! But then they put a scarf in his mouth and shot him. I don't know any more.' Mamantov closed the albums tenderly and placed them back on the shelf. 'So,' he said, turning to face Kelso with a look of menacing innocence, 'someone came to see you. When was this?'

Kelso was on his guard at once. 'I'd prefer not to say.'

'And he told you about Stalin's papers? He *was* a man, I assume? An eyewitness, from that time?'

Kelso hesitated.

'Named?'

Kelso smiled and shook his head. Mamantov seemed to think he was back in the Lubyanka.

'His profession, then?'

'I can't tell you that, either.'

'Does he know where these papers are?'

'Perhaps.'

'He offered to show you?'

'No.'

'But you *asked* him to show you?'

'No.'

'You're a very disappointing historian, Dr Kelso. I thought you were famous for your diligence –'

'If you must know, he disappeared before I had the chance.'

He regretted the words the instant they were out of his mouth.

'What do you mean, he "disappeared"?'

'We were drinking,' muttered Kelso. 'I left him alone for a minute. When I came back he'd run away.'

It sounded implausible, even to his own ears.

'Run away?' Mamantov's eyes were as grey as winter. 'I don't believe you.'

'Vladimir Pavlovich,' said Kelso, meeting his gaze and holding it, 'I can assure you this is the truth.'

'You're lying. Why? *Why?*' Mamantov rubbed his chin. 'I think it must be because you have the notebook.'

'If I had the notebook, ask yourself: Would I be here?

Wouldn't I be on the first flight back to New York? Isn't that what thieves are supposed to do?'

Mamantov continued to stare at him for a few more seconds, then looked away. 'Clearly we need to find this man.'

We . . .

'I don't think he wants to be found.'

'He will contact you again.'

'I doubt it.' Kelso badly wanted to get out of here now. He felt compromised, somehow; complicit. 'Besides, I'm flying back to America tomorrow. Which, now I come to think of it, really means I ought –'

He made a move towards the door but Mamantov barred it. 'Are you excited, Dr Kelso? Do you feel the force of Comrade Stalin, even from the grave?'

Kelso laughed unhappily. 'I don't think I quite share your . . . obsession.'

'Go fuck your mother! I've read your work. Does that surprise you? I'll pass no comment on its quality. But I'll tell you this: you're as obsessed as I am.'

'Perhaps. But in a different way.'

'Power,' said Mamantov, savouring the word in his mouth like wine, 'the absolute mastery and understanding of *power.* No man ever matched him for it. Do this, do that. Think this, think that. Now I say you live, and now I say you die, and all you say is, "Thank you for your kindness, Comrade Stalin." *That's* the obsession.'

'Yes, but then there's the difference, if you'll permit me, which is you want him back.'

'And you just like to watch, is that it? I like fucking and you like pornography?' Mamantov jerked his thumb at the room. 'You should have seen yourself just now. "Isn't this a note for a speech?" "Isn't that a copy of an earlier painting?" Eyes wide, tongue out – the western liberal, getting his safe thrill. Of course, *he* understood that, too. And now you tell me you're going to give up trying to find his private notebook and just run away back to America?'

'May I get by?'

Kelso stepped to his left but Mamantov moved smartly to block him.

'This could be one of the greatest historical discoveries of the age. And you want to run away? It *must* be found. We must find it *together*. And then you must present it to the world. I want no credit – I promise you: I prefer the shadows – the honour will be yours alone.'

'So, what's all this then, Comrade Mamantov?' said Kelso, with forced cheerfulness. 'Am I a prisoner?'

Between him and the outside world there were, he calculated, one fit and obviously crazy ex-KGB man, one armed bodyguard, and two doors, one of them armour-plated. And for a moment, he thought that Mamantov might indeed be intending to keep him: that he had everything else connected with Stalin, so why not a Stalin historian, pickled in formaldehyde and laid out in a glass case, like V. I. Lenin? But then Madame Mamantov shouted from the passage – 'What's going on in there?' – and the spell was broken.

'Nothing,' called Mamantov. 'Stop listening. Go back to your room. Viktor!'

'But who is everyone?' wailed the woman. 'That's what I want to know. And why is it always so dark?' She started to cry. They heard the shuffle of her feet and the sound of a door closing.

'I'm sorry,' said Kelso.

'Keep your pity,' said Mamantov. He stood aside. 'Go on,

then. Get out of here. Go.' But when Kelso was halfway down the passage he shouted after him: 'We'll talk again about this matter. One way or another.'

THERE were three men now in the car downstairs, although Kelso was too preoccupied to pay them much attention. He paused in the gloomy portal of the House on the Embankment, to hoist his canvas bag more firmly on to his shoulder, then set off in the direction of the Bolshoy Kamenniy bridge.

'That's him, major,' said the man with the scar, and Feliks Suvorin leaned forward in his seat to get a better look. Suvorin was young to be a full major in the SVR – he was only in his thirties – a dapper figure, with blond hair and cornflower blue eyes. And he wore a western aftershave, that was the other thing that was very noticeable at this moment: the little car was fragrant with the smell of Eau Sauvage.

'He had that bag with him when he went in?'

'Yes, major.'

Suvorin glanced up at the Mamantovs' ninth-floor apartment. What was needed here was better coverage. The SVR had managed to get a bug into the flat at the start of the operation, but it had lasted just three hours before Mamantov's people had found it and ripped it out.

Kelso had begun climbing the flight of stairs that led up to the bridge.

'Off you go, Bunin,' said Suvorin, tapping the man in front of him lightly on the shoulder. 'Nothing too obvious, mind you. Just try to keep him in view. We don't want a diplomatic protest.'

Grumbling under his breath, Bunin levered himself out of the car.

Kelso was moving rapidly now, had almost reached road-level, and the Russian had to jog across to the bottom of the steps to make up part of the distance.

Well, well, thought Suvorin, he's certainly in a hurry to get somewhere. Or is it just that he wants to get away from here?

He watched the blurred pink faces of the two men above the stone parapet as they headed north across the river into the grey afternoon and then were lost from view.

Chapter Five

KELSO PAID HIS two-rouble fare at the Borovitskaya metro station, collected his plastic token, and descended gratefully into the Moscow earth. At the entrance to the northbound platform something made him glance back up the moving staircase to see if Mamantov was following, but there was no sign of him among the tiers of exhausted faces.

It was a stupid thought – he tried to smile at himself for his paranoia – and he turned away, towards the welcoming dimness and the warm gusts of oil and electricity. Almost at once, a yellow headlight danced around a bend in the track and the rush of the train sucked him forwards. Kelso let the crowd jostle him into a carriage. There was an odd comfort in this dowdy, silent multitude. He hung on to the metal handrail and pitched and swayed with the rest as they plunged back into the tunnel.

They hadn't gone far when the train suddenly slowed and stopped – a bomb scare, it turned out, at the next station: the militia had to check it out – and so they sat there in the semi-darkness, nobody speaking, just the occasional cough, the tension rising by imperceptible degrees.

Kelso stared at his reflection in the dark glass. He was jumpy, he had to admit it. He couldn't help feeling he had just put himself into some kind of danger, that telling Mamantov about the notebook had been a reckless mistake. What had the Russian called it? Something *to die for?*

It was a relief to his nerves when the lights eventually flickered back on and the train jolted forwards. The soothing rhythm of normality resumed.

By the time Kelso emerged above ground it was after four. Low in the western sky, barely clearing the tops of the dark trees that fringed the Zoopark, was a lemony crack in the clouds. A winter sunset was little more than an hour away. He would have to hurry. He folded the map into a small square and twisted it so that the metro station was to his right. Across the road was the entrance to the zoo – red rocks, a waterfall, a fairy tower – and, a little further along, a beer garden, closed for the season, its plastic tables stacked, its striped umbrellas down and flapping. He could hear the roar of the traffic on the Garden Ring road, about two hundred yards straight ahead. Across that, sharp left, then right, and there it ought to be. He stuffed the map into his pocket, picked up his bag and climbed the cobbled slope that led to the big intersection.

Ten lanes of traffic formed an immense, slow-moving river of light and steel. He crossed it in a dog-leg and suddenly he was into diplomatic Moscow: wide streets, grand houses, old birch trees weeping dead leaves on to sleek black cars. There wasn't much life. He passed a silvery-headed man walking a poodle and a woman in green rubber boots that poked incongruously from beneath her Muslim robe. Behind the thick gauze of the curtained windows, he could see the occasional yellow constellation of a chandelier. He stopped at the corner of Vspolnyi Street and peered along it. A militia car drove towards him very slowly and passed away to his right. The road was deserted.

He located the house at once, but he wanted to get his bearings and to check if anyone was about, so he made himself walk past it, right to the end of the street before returning along the opposite side. *'There was a red sickle moon, and a single red star. And the place was guarded by devils with blackened faces . . .* 'Suddenly he saw what the old man must have meant. A red sickle moon and a single red star – that would be a flag: a Muslim flag. And black faces? The place must have been an embassy – it was too big for anything else – an embassy of a Muslim country, perhaps in North Africa. He was certain he was right. It was a big building, that was for sure, forbidding and ugly, built of sandy-coloured stone which made it look like a bunker. It ran for at least forty yards along the western side of the road. He counted thirteen sets of windows. Above the massive entrance was an iron balcony with double doors leading on to it. There was no nameplate and no flag. If it had been an embassy it was abandoned now; it was lifeless.

He crossed the street and went up close to it, patting the coarse stone with his palm. He stood on tiptoe and tried to see through the windows. But they were set too high and besides were blanked off by the ubiquitous grey netting. He gave up and followed the façade around the corner. The house went on down this street, too. Thirteen windows again, no door, thirty or forty yards of heavy masonry – immense, impregnable. Where this elevation of the house eventually ended there was a wall made of the same stone, about eight feet high, with a locked, iron-studded wooden door set into it. The wall ran on – down this street, along the side of the ring-road, and finally back up the narrow alley which formed the fourth side of the property. Walking round it, Kelso could see why Beria had chosen it, and why his rivals had decided the only place to capture him was inside the Kremlin. Holed up in this fortress he could have withstood a siege.

In the neighbouring houses, the lights were becoming sharper as the afternoon faded into dusk. But Beria's place remained a square of darkness. It seemed to be gathering the shadows into itself. He heard a car door slam and he walked back up to the corner of Vspolnyi Street. While he had been at the back of the property, a small van had arrived at the front.

He hesitated, then began to move towards it.

The van was a Russian model – white, unmarked, unoccupied. Its engine had just been switched off and it was making a slight ticking noise as it cooled. As he came level with it, he glanced towards the door of the house and saw that it was slightly open. Again he hesitated, looking up and down the quiet street. He went over and put his head into the gap and shouted a greeting.

His words echoed in the empty hall. The light inside was weak and bluish, but even without taking another step he could see that the floor was of black and white tiles. To his left was the start of a wide staircase. The house smelled strongly of sour dust and old carpets, and there was an immense stillness to it, as though it had been shut up for months. He pushed the door wide open and took a step inside.

He called out again.

He had two options now. He could stay by the door, or he could go further inside. He went further inside and immediately, like a laboratory rat in a maze, he found his options multiplied. He could stay where he was, or he could take the door to his left, or the stairs, or the passage that led off into the darkness beyond the stairs, or one of the three doors to his right. For a moment, the weight of choice paralysed him. But the stairs were straight ahead and seemed the obvious course – and perhaps, subconsciously, he also wanted to get the advantage of height, to get above whoever might be on the ground floor, or at least to get on equal terms with them if they were already above.

The stairs were stone. He was wearing brown suede boots with leather soles he'd bought in Oxford years ago and no matter how quietly he tried to walk his steps seemed to ring like gunshots. But that was good. He wasn't a thief, and to emphasise the point he called out again. *Pree-vyet! Kto tam?* Hello? Is anybody there? The stairs curled round to his right and he had a good, high view now, looking down into the dark blue well of the hall, pierced by the softer shaft of blue that shone from the open door. He reached the top of the stairs and came out into a wide corridor that stretched to right and left, vanishing at either end into Rembrandt gloom. Ahead of him was a door. He tried to take his bearings. That must lead to the room above the front entrance, the one with the iron balcony. What was it? A ballroom? The master bedroom? The corridor floor was parquet and he remembered Rapava's description of Beria's damp footprints on the polished wood as he hurried off to take the call from Malenkov.

Kelso opened the heavy door and the stale air hit him like a wall. He had to clamp a hand to his mouth and nose to keep from gagging. The smell that pervaded the whole house seemed to have its source in here. It was a big room, bare, lit from the opposite wall by three tall, net-curtained windows, high oblongs of translucent grey. He moved towards them. The floor seemed to be strewn with pools of tiny black husks. His idea was that if he pulled back the curtain, he could throw light on the room, and see what he was treading on. But as his hand touched the rough nylon net, the material seemed to split and ripple downwards and a shower of black granules went pattering across his hand and brushed the back of his neck. He twitched the curtain again and the shower became a cascade, a waterfall of dead, winged insects. Millions of them must have hatched and died in here over the summer, trapped in the airless room. They had a papery, acid smell. They were in his hair. He could feel them rustling under his feet. He stepped backwards, furiously brushing at himself and shaking his head.

Down in the lobby, a man shouted. *Kto idyot?* Is somebody up there?

Kelso knew he should have shouted back. What greater proof could he have offered of his blameless intentions – of his innocence – than to have stepped at once out on to the landing, identified himself and apologised? He was very sorry. The door was open. This was an interesting old house. He was a historian. Curiosity had got the better of him. And obviously, there was nothing here to steal. Really, he was truly sorry –

That was Kelso's alternative history. He didn't take it. He didn't *choose* not to take it. He merely did nothing, which was a form of choice. He stood there, in Lavrenty Beria's old bedroom, frozen, half bent, as if the creaking of his bones might give him away, and listened. With each second that passed, his chances of talking his way out of the building dwindled. The man began to climb the staircase. He came up seven steps – Kelso counted them – then stopped and stayed very still for perhaps a minute.

Then he walked down again and crossed the lobby and the front door closed.

Kelso moved now. He went to the window. Without touching the curtain he found it was possible, by pressing his cheek to the wall, to peer around the edge of the dusty nylon mesh, down into the street. From this oblique angle, he could see a man in a black uniform, standing on the pavement next to the van, holding a flashlight. The man stepped off the kerb and into the gutter and squinted up at the house. He was squat and simian. His arms seemed too long for his thick trunk. Suddenly, he was looking directly at Kelso – a brutal, stupid face – and Kelso drew back. When he next dared to risk a look, the man was bending to open the door on the driver's side. He threw in the flashlight and climbed in after it. The engine started. The van drove off.

Kelso gave him thirty seconds then hurried downstairs. He was locked in. He couldn't believe it. The absurdity of his predicament almost made him smile. He was locked inside Beria's house! The front door was huge, with a big iron ball for a handle and a lock the size of a telephone directory. He tried it hopelessly, then looked around. What if there was an intruder alarm? In the gloom, he couldn't see anything attached to the walls, but maybe it was an old-fashioned system – that would be more likely, wouldn't it? – something triggered by pressure-pads rather than beams? The idea froze him.

What set him moving again was the gathering darkness and the realisation that if he didn't find an escape route now he might be trapped by his blindness all night. There was a light switch by the door but he didn't dare try it – the guard was obviously suspicious: he might drive by for a second look. In any case, something about the silence of the place, its utter deadness, made him sure all forms of life-support had been disconnected, that the house had been left to rot. He tried to recall Rapava's description of the lay-out when he came in to answer Malenkov's call. Something about coming in off a verandah, through a duty room, past a kitchen and into the hall.

He headed into the blackness of the passage beyond the stairs, feeling his way along the left-hand wall. The plaster was cool and smooth. The first door he encountered was locked. The second wasn't – he felt a draught of cold air, but sensed a drop, into a cellar, presumably – and closed it quickly. The third opened on to the dull blue gleam of metal surfaces and a faint smell of old food. The fourth was at the end, facing him, and revealed the room where he guessed that Beria's guards must once have sat.

Unlike the rest of the house, which seemed to have been stripped bare, there was furniture here – a plain wooden table and a chair, and an old sideboard – and some signs of life. A copy of *Pravda* – he could just make out the familiar masthead – a kitchen knife, an ashtray. He touched the table and felt crumbs. Pale light leaked through a pair of small windows. Between them was a door. It was locked. There was no key. He looked again at the windows. Too narrow for him to squeeze through. He took a breath. Some habits, surely, are international? He ran his hand along the sill to the right of the door and it was there and it turned easily in the lock.

When the door was opened he removed the key, and – a nice touch this, he remembered thinking – replaced it on the sill.

HE emerged on to a narrow verandah, about two yards wide, with weathered floorboards and a broken handrail. He could hear traffic at the bottom of the garden and the laborious whine of a big jet, dropping towards Sheremetevo Airport. The breeze was cold, scented by the smoke of a bonfire. There was a last pale flush of daylight in the sky.

He guessed the garden must have been abandoned at the same time as the house. Nobody could have worked in it for months. To his left was an ornate greenhouse with an iron chimney, partially overgrown by Russian vines. To his right, a ragged thicket of dark green shrubs. Ahead were trees. He stepped down off the verandah on to the carpet of leaves that covered the lawn. The wind stirred and lofted some of them, sent a detachment cartwheeling towards the house. He kicked through the drifts towards the orchard – a cherry orchard he could see now as he came closer: big old trees, maybe twenty feet high, at least a hundred of them, a Chekhovian scene. Suddenly he stopped. The ground beneath the trees was flat and level except in one place. At the base of one tree, close to a stone bench, was a patch of blackness, darker than the surrounding shadows. He frowned. Was he sure he wasn't imagining it?

He went over, knelt and slowly sank his hands into the leaves. On the surface they were dry but the lower levels were damp and mulchy. He brushed them back, releasing a rich smell of moist soil – the black and fragrant earth of Mother Russia.

'Don't make it so wide. It's not a grave. You're making work for yourself . . . '

He cleared away the leaves from an area about a yard square, and although he couldn't see much, he could see enough, and he could feel it. The grass had been removed and a hole had been dug. And then it had been filled in again and an attempt had been made to jam the turfs back into their original positions. But some parts had crumbled and others overlapped the lip of the hole and the result was a mess, like a broken, muddy jigsaw. It had been done in a hurry, thought Kelso, and it had been done recently, possibly even today. He stood and brushed the wet leaves from his coat.

'*Do you feel the force of Comrade Stalin, even from the grave . . .?*'

Beyond the high wall he could hear the traffic on the wide highway. Normality seemed close enough to touch. He used the side of his foot to scrape a covering of leaves back across the scarred surface, grabbed his bag and stumbled through the orchard towards the end of the garden, towards the sounds of life. He had to get out now. He didn't mind admitting it. He was rattled. The cherry trees stretched almost to the wall which rose up blank and sheer before him, like the perimeter of a Victorian gaol. There was no way he could scale it.

A narrow cinder path followed the line of the wall. He headed left. The path turned the corner and took him back in the direction of the house. About halfway along, he could see a darkened oblong – the garden door he had noticed from the street – but even this was overgrown and he had to pull back the trailing branches of a bush to get at it. It was locked, maybe even rusted shut. The big iron ring of the handle wouldn't turn. He flicked his cigarette lighter and held it close to get a better view. The door was solid but the frame looked weak. He stood back and aimed a kick at it, but nothing happened. He tried again. Hopeless.

He stepped back on to the path. He was now about thirty yards from the house. Its low roof was clearly silhouetted. He could see an aerial and the bulk of a tall chimney with a satellite dish attached to it. It was too big to be an ordinary domestic receiver.

It was while he was staring distractedly at the dish that his eye was caught by a glimmer of light in an upstairs window. It vanished so quickly he thought he might have imagined it and he told himself to keep his nerve, just find a tool, get out

of here. But then it flashed again, like the beam of a
lighthouse – pale, then bright, then pale again – as someone
holding a powerful torch swivelled anti-clockwise towards
the window then back towards the blackness of the room.

The suspicious security guard was back.

'God.' Kelso's lips were so tightly drawn he could barely
shape his breath into the syllable. 'God, God, God.'

He ran up the path towards the greenhouse. A rickety
door slid back just far enough for him to slip through. The
vines made it darker inside than out. Trestle tables, an old
trug, empty trays for seedlings, terracotta pots – nothing,
nothing. He blundered down a narrow aisle, a frond of
something brushed his face and then he collided with an
object immense and metal. An old bulbous, cast-iron stove.
And next to it, a heap of discarded implements – shovel,
scuttle, riddling iron, poker. *Poker.*

He squeezed back on to the path, holding his prize, and
jammed the poker into the gap between the garden door and
the frame, just above the lock. He heaved and heard a crack.
The poker came loose. He jammed it back and pulled again.
Another crack. He worked it downwards. The frame was
splintering.

He took a few paces back and ran at the door, rammed it
with his shoulder, and some force that seemed to him beyond
the physical – some fusion of will and fear and imagination
– carried him through the door and out of the garden and
into the quiet emptiness of the street.

Chapter Six

AT SIX O'CLOCK that evening, Major Feliks Suvorin, accompanied by his assistant, Lieutenant Vissari Netto, presented an account of the day's developments to their immediate boss, the chief of the RT Directorate, Colonel Yuri Arsenyev.

The atmosphere was informal, as usual. Arsenyev sprawled sleepily behind his desk, on which had been placed a map of Moscow and a cassette player. Suvorin reclined on the sofa next to the window, smoking his pipe. Netto worked the tape machine.

'The first voice you'll hear, colonel,' Netto was saying to Arsenyev, 'is that of Madame Mamantov.'

He pressed PLAY.

'*Who is this?*'

'*Christopher Kelso. Could I speak with Comrade Mamantov?*'

'*Yes? Who is this?*'

'*As I said, my name is Kelso. I'm using a public telephone. It's urgent.*'

'*Yes, but who is this?*'

Netto pressed PAUSE.

'Poor Ludmilla Fedorova,' said Arsenyev, sadly. 'Did you know her, Feliks? I knew her when she was at the Lubyanka. Oh, she was a piece of work! A body like a pagoda, a mind like a razor and a tongue to match.'

'Not any more,' said Suvorin. 'Not the mind, anyway.'

Netto said, 'The next voice will be even more familiar, colonel.'

PLAY.

'All right, this is Mamantov. Who are you?'

'It's Kelso. Doctor Kelso? You may remember me?'

'I remember you. What do you want?'

'To see you.'

'Why should I see you after that shit you wrote?'

'I wanted to ask you some questions.'

'About?'

'A black oilskin notebook that used to belong to Josef Stalin.'

'Shut up.'

'What?'

'I said shut up. I'm thinking it over. Where are you?'

'Near the Intourist building, on Mohavaja Street.'

'You're close. You'd better come.'

STOP.

'Play it again,' said Arsenyev. 'Not Ludmilla. The latter part.'

Through the armoured glass at Arsenyev's back Suvorin could see the ripple of the office lights reflected in Yasenevo's ornamental lake, and the massive floodlit head of Lenin, and beyond these, almost invisible now, the dark line of the forest, its edge serrated against the evening sky. A pair of headlights winked through the trees and disappeared. A security patrol, thought Suvorin, suppressing a yawn. He was happy to let Netto do the talking. Give the lad a chance.

'A black oilskin notebook that used to belong to Josef Stalin . . .'

'Fuck me,' said Arsenyev, softly, and his flabby face tautened.

'The call was initiated this afternoon, at fourteen-fourteen, by this man,' continued Netto, handing out two flimsy buff-coloured folders. 'Christopher Richard Andrew Kelso, commonly known as "Fluke".'

'Now this is nice,' said Suvorin, who hadn't seen the photograph before. It was still glistening from the darkroom, and reeked of sodium thiosulphate. 'Where are we?'

'Third floor, inner courtyard, opposite the entrance to Mamantov's staircase.'

'So now we can afford an apartment in the House on the Embankment?' grumbled Arsenyev.

'It's empty. Doesn't cost us a rouble.'

'How long did he stay?'

'Arrived at fourteen-thirty-two, colonel. Left at fifteen-seven. One of our operatives, Lieutenant Bunin, was then detailed to follow him. Kelso caught the metro at Borovitskaya, here, changed once, got out at Krasnopresnenskaya, and walked to a house here –' Netto again put his finger on the map ' – in Vspolnyi Street. A deserted property. He made an illegal entry and spent approximately forty-five minutes inside. He was last reported here, heading south on foot along the Garden Ring. That was ten minutes ago.'

'What does that mean exactly? "Fluke"?'

'"A lucky stroke", colonel,' said Netto, smartly. '"An unexpected success."'

'Sergo? Where's that damned coffee?' Arsenyev, immensely fat, had a habit of falling asleep if he didn't have caffeine every hour.

'It's coming, Yuri Semonovich,' said a voice from the intercom.

'Kelso's parents were both in their forties, sir, when he was born.'

Arsenyev turned a tiny and astonished eye towards Vissari Netto. 'Why do we care about his parents?'

'Well –' The young man wilted, stalled, appealed to Suvorin.

'Kelso was a fluke,' said Suvorin. 'The joke. It's a joke.'

'And that is funny?'

They were spared by the arrival of the coffee, borne in by Arsenyev's male assistant. The blue mug said 'I LOVE NEW YORK' and Arsenyev raised it towards them, as if drinking their health. 'So tell me,' he said, blinking through the steam over the rim, 'about Mister Fluke.'

'Born Wimbledon, England, nineteen fifty-four,' said Netto, reading from the file (he had done well, thought Suvorin, to get all this together in the space of an afternoon – the lad was keen, you couldn't fault him on ambition). 'Father, a typical petit-bourgeois, a clerk in legal chambers; three sisters, all older; standard education; nineteen seventy-three, scholarship to study history at the college of St John, Cambridge; starred first class honours degree, nineteen seventy-six –'

Suvorin had already skimmed through all of this – the personal file dredged up from the Registry, a few newspaper cuttings, the entry in *Who's Who* – and now he tried to reconcile the biography with this snatched picture of a figure in a raincoat leaving an apartment. The graininess of the picture had a pleasing, fifties feel: the man, glancing across the street, a cigarette in his mouth, had the appearance of a slightly seedy French actor playing a dodgy cop. *Fluke*. Does a name stick because it suits a man or does the man, unconsciously, evolve into his name? Fluke, the spoiled and lazy teenager, doted on by all these family women, who astonishes his teachers by winning a scholarship to Cambridge – the first in the history of his minor grammar school. Fluke, the carousing student who, after three years of no apparent effort, walks away with the best history degree of his year. Fluke, who just happens to turn up on the doorstep of one of the most dangerous men in Moscow – although, naturally, as a foreigner he would have felt invulnerable. Yes, one would have to be wary of this *Fluke* –

' – scholarship to Harvard, nineteen seventy-eight; admitted to Moscow University, under the "Students for Peace" scheme, nineteen eighty; dissident contacts – see annex "A" – led to recategorisation from "bourgeois-liberal" to "conservative and reactionary"; doctoral thesis published eighty-four, *Power in the Land: The Peasantry of the Volga Region, 1917–22*; lecturer in modern history, Oxford University, eighty-three to ninety-four; now resident in New York City; author of the *Oxford History of Eastern Europe, 1945–87; Vortex: The Collapse of the Soviet Empire*, published ninety-three; numerous articles –'

'All right, Netto,' said Arsenyev, holding up a hand. 'It's getting late. Did we ever make a pass at him?' This question was addressed to Suvorin.

'Twice,' said Suvorin. 'Once at the University, obviously, in nineteen eighty. Again in Moscow in ninety-one, when we tried to sell him on democracy and the New Russia.'

'And?'

'And? Looking at the reports? I should say he laughed in our faces.'

'He's a western asset, do we think?'

'Unlikely. He wrote an article in the *New Yorker* – it's in the file – describing how the Agency and SIS both tried to sign him. Rather a funny piece, in fact.'

Arsenyev frowned. He disapproved of publicity, on either side. 'Wife? Kids?'

Netto jumped in again: 'Married three times.' He glanced at Suvorin, and Suvorin made a little 'go ahead' gesture with his hand: he was happy to take a back seat. 'First, as a student, Katherine Jane Owen, marriage dissolved, seventy-nine. Second, Irina Mikhailovna Pugacheva, married eighty-one – '

'He married a Russian?'

'Ukrainian. Almost certainly a marriage of convenience. She was expelled from the University for anti-state activity. This is the beginning of Kelso's dissident contact. She was granted a visa in eighty-four.'

'So we blocked her entry into Britain for three years?'

'No, colonel, the British did. By the time they let her in, Kelso was living with one of his students, an American, a Rhodes Scholar. Marriage to Pugacheva dissolved in eighty-five. She is now married to an orthodontist in Glamorgan. There is a file but I'm afraid I haven't –'

'Forget it,' said Arsenyev. 'We'll drown in paper. And the third marriage?' He winked at Suvorin. 'A real romeo!'

'Margaret Madeline Lodge, an American student –'

'This is the Rhodes Scholar?'

'No, this is a different Rhodes Scholar. He married this one in eighty-six. The marriage was dissolved last year.'

'Kids?'

'Two sons. Resident with their mother in New York City.'

'One cannot help but admire this fellow,' said Arsenyev, who, despite his bulk, had a mistress of his own in Technical Support. He contemplated the photograph, the corners of his mouth turned down in admiration. 'What's he doing in Moscow?'

'Rosarkhiv are holding a conference,' said Netto, 'for foreign scholars.'

'Feliks?'

Major Suvorin had his right ankle swung up on to his left knee, his elbows resting casually on the sofa back, his sports jacket unbuttoned – easy, confident, Americanized: his style. He took a pull on his pipe before he spoke.

'The words used on the telephone are ambiguous, obviously. The implication could be that Mamantov has this notebook, and the historian wishes to see it. Or the historian himself has the notebook, or has heard of it, and wishes to check some detail with Mamantov. Whichever is the case, Mamantov is clearly aware of our surveillance, which is why he cuts the conversation short. When is Kelso due to leave the Federation, Vissari, do we know yet?'

'Tomorrow lunchtime,' said Netto. 'Delta flight to JFK, leaves Sheremetevo-2 at thirteen-thirty. Seat booked and confirmed.'

'I recommend we arrange for Kelso to be stopped and searched,' said Suvorin. 'Strip-searched, it had better be – delay the flight if necessary – on suspicion of exporting material of historical or cultural interest. If he's taken anything from this house in Vspolnyi Street, we can get it off him. In the meantime, we maintain our coverage of Mamantov.'

A buzzer sounded on Arsenyev's desk; Sergo's voice.

'There's a call for Vissari Petrovich.'

'All right, Netto,' said Arsenyev. 'Take it in the outer office.' When the door was closed, he scowled at Suvorin, 'Efficient little bastard, isn't he?'

'He's harmless enough, Yuri. He's just keen.

Arsenyev grunted, took two long squirts from his inhaler, unhitched his belt a notch, let his flesh sag towards his desk. The colonel's fat was a kind of camouflage: a blubbery, dimpled netting thrown over an acute mind, so that while other, sleeker men had fallen, Arsenyev had safely waddled on – through the cold war (KGB chief resident in Canberra and Ottawa), through glasnost and the failed coup and the break-up of the service, on and on, beneath the armoured soft protective shell of his flesh, until now, at last, he was into the final stretch: retirement in one year, dacha, mistress, pension, and the rest of the world could go fuck its collective mother. Suvorin rather liked him.

'All right, Feliks. What do you think?'

'The purpose of the Mamantov operation,' said Suvorin, carefully, 'is to discover how five hundred million roubles were siphoned out of KGB funds, where Mamantov hid them, and how this money is being used to fund the anti-democratic opposition. We already know he bankrolls that red fascist mucksheet –'

'*Aurora* –'

' – *Aurora* – if it now turns out he's spending it on guns as well, I'm interested. If he's buying Stalin memorabilia, or selling it, for that matter – well, it's sick, but –'

'This isn't just *memorabilia*, Feliks. This – this is famous – there was a file on this notebook – it was one of "the legends of Lubyanka".'

Suvorin's first reaction was to laugh. The old man couldn't be serious, surely? Stalin's *notebook?* But then he saw the expression on Arsenyev's face and hastily turned his laughter into a cough. 'I'm sorry, Yuri Semonovich – forgive me – if you take it seriously, then, of course, I take it seriously.'

'Run the tape again, Feliks, would you be so good? I never could work these damned machines.'

He slid it across the desk with a hairy, pudgy forefinger. Suvorin came over from the sofa and they listened to it together, Arsenyev breathing heavily, tugging at the thick flesh of his fat neck, which was what he always did when he scented trouble.

'*... a black oilskin notebook that used to belong to Josef Stalin...*'

They were still bent over the tape when Netto crept back in, his complexion three shades paler than usual, to announce he had bad news.

FELIKS Stepanovich Suvorin, with Netto at his heels, walked back, grim-faced, to his office. It was a long trek from the leadership suites in the west of the building to the operational block in the east, and in the course of it at least a dozen people must have nodded and smiled at him, for in the Finnish-designed, wood and white-tile corridors of Yasenevo, the major was the golden boy, the coming man. He spoke English with an American accent, subscribed to the leading American magazines and had a collection of modern American jazz, which he listened to with his wife, the daughter of one of the President's most liberal economic advisers. Even Suvorin's clothes were American – the button-down shirt, the striped tie, the brown sports jacket – each one a legacy of his years as the KGB resident in Washington.

Look at Feliks Stepanovich!, you could see them thinking, as they struggled into their winter coats and hurried past to catch the buses home. Put in as number two to that fat old timer, Arsenyev, primed to take over an entire directorate at the age of thirty-eight. And not just any directorate, either, but RT – one of the most secret of them all! – licensed to conduct foreign intelligence operations on Russian soil. Look at him, the coming man, hurrying back to his office to work, while we go off home for the night...

'Good evening to you, Feliks Stepanovich!'
'So long, Feliks! Cheer up!'
'Working late again, I see, comrade major!'

Suvorin half-smiled, nodded, gestured vaguely with his pipe, preoccupied.

The details, as Netto had relayed them, were sparse but eloquent. Fluke Kelso had left the Mamantovs' apartment at fifteen-seven. Suvorin had also left the scene a few minutes later. At fifteen-twenty-two, Ludmilla Fedorova Mamantova, in the company of the bodyguard, Viktor Bubka, was also observed to leave the apartment for her customary afternoon stroll to the Bolotnaya Park (given her confused condition, she had always to be accompanied). Since there was only one man on duty, they were not followed.

They did not return.

Shortly after seventeen hundred, a neighbour in the apartment beneath the Mamantovs' reported hearing prolonged, hysterical screams. The porter had been summoned, the apartment – with difficulty – opened and Madame Mamantov had been discovered alone, in her undergarments, locked inside a cupboard, through the door of which she had nevertheless managed to kick a hole using her bare feet. She had been taken to the Diplomatic Policlinic in a state of extreme distress. Both her ankles were broken.

'This must be an emergency escape plan,' said Suvorin, as they reached his office. 'He's clearly had this up his sleeve for quite a while, even down to establishing a routine for his wife. The question is: what's the emergency?'

He pressed the light switch. Neon panels stuttered into life. The leadership's side of the building had the view of the lake and the trees while Suvorin's office looked north, towards the Moscow ring road and the squat and crowded tower blocks of a housing estate. Suvorin threw himself into his chair, grabbed his tobacco pouch and swung his feet up on to the window sill. He saw Netto, reflected, coming in and closing the door. Arsenyev had given him a blasting, which wasn't really fair. If anyone was to blame, it was Suvorin, for sending Bunin after Kelso.

'How many men do we have at Mamantov's apartment right now?'

'Two, major.'

'Split them. One to the Policlinic to keep an eye on the wife, one to stay in place. Bunin's to stick with Kelso. What's his hotel?'

'The Ukraina.'

'Right. If he's heading south down the Garden Ring he's probably on his way back. Call Gromov at the Sixteenth and tell him we want a full communications intercept on Kelso. He'll tell you he hasn't the resources. Refer him to Arsenyev. Have the authorisation papers on my desk within fifteen minutes.'

'Yes, major.'

'Leave the Tenth to me.'

'The Tenth, major?' The Tenth was the archives branch.

'According to the colonel, there should be a file on this Stalin notebook.' Legend of the Lubyanka, indeed! 'I'll need to dream up some excuse to see it. Check on this place in Vspolnyi Street: what is it exactly? God, we need more men!' Suvorin banged his desk in frustration. 'Where's Kolosov?'

'He left for Switzerland yesterday.'

'Anybody else around? Barsukov?'

'Barsukov's in Ivanovo with his Germans.'

Suvorin groaned. This operation was running on paraffin and thin air, that was the trouble with it. It didn't have a name, a budget. Technically, it wasn't even legal.

Netto was writing rapidly. 'What do you want to do with Kelso?'

'Just continue to keep an eye on him.'

'Not pick him up?'

'For what exactly? And where do we take him? We have no cells. We have no legal basis to make arrests. How long's Mamantov been loose?'

'Three hours, major. I'm sorry, I –' Netto looked close to tears.

'Forget it, Vissi. It's not your fault.' He smiled at the young man's reflection. 'Mamantov was pulling stunts like that while we were in the womb. We'll find him,' he added, with a confidence he did not feel, 'sooner or later. Now off you go. I've got to call my wife.'

After Netto had gone, Suvorin removed the photograph of Kelso from its folder and pinned it to the noticeboard beside his desk. Here he was, with so much else to do, on issues which really mattered – economic intelligence, bio-technology, fibre optics – reduced to worrying about whether and why Vladimir Mamantov was after Stalin's notebook. It was absurd. It was worse than absurd. It was shaming. What kind of a country was this? Slowly, he tamped the tobacco in his pipe and lit it. And then he stood there for a full minute, his hands clasped behind his back, his pipe between his teeth, regarding the historian with an expression of pure loathing.

Chapter Seven

FLUKE KELSO LAY on his back, on his bed, in his room on the twenty-third floor of the Ukraina Hotel, smoking a cigarette and staring at the ceiling, the fingers of his left hand curled around the comforting and familiar shape of a quarter-bottle of Scotch.

He hadn't bothered to take off his coat, nor had he turned on the bedside lamp. Not that he needed to. The brilliant white floodlights that lit the Stalinist–Gothic skyscraper shone into his room and provided a feverish illumination. Through the closed window he could hear the sound of the early evening traffic on the wet road far below.

A melancholy hour this, he always thought, for a stranger in a foreign city – nightfall, the brittle lights, the temperature dropping, the office workers hurrying home, the business-men trying to look cheerful in the hotel bars.

He took another swig of Scotch, then reached over for the ashtray and balanced it on his chest, tapping the end of his cigarette into it. The bowl hadn't been cleaned properly. Still stuck to its dusty bottom, like a small green egg, nested a gobbet of Papu Rapava's phlegm.

It had taken Kelso only a few minutes – the length of one short visit to the Ukraina's business centre and the time it took to flick through an old Moscow telephone directory – to establish that the house on Vspolnyi Street had indeed once been an African embassy. It was listed under the Republic of Tunisia.

And it had taken him only slightly longer to extract the rest of the information he needed – sitting on the edge of his hard and narrow bed, talking earnestly on the telephone to the press attaché at the new Tunisian Embassy, pretending an intense interest in the booming Moscow property market and the precise design of the Tunisian flag.

According to the press attaché, the Tunisians had been offered the mansion on Vspolnyi Street by the Soviet government in 1956, on a short-term lease, renewable every seven years. In January, the ambassador had been notified that the lease would not be extended when it came up for renegotiation, and in August they had moved out. And in truth, sir, they had not been too sorry to go, no indeed, not after that unfortunate business in 1993 when workmen had dug up twelve human skeletons, victims of the Stalinist repression, buried beneath the pavement outside. No explanation for the eviction had been offered, but, as everyone knew, great swathes of state property were now being privatised in central Moscow and sold on to foreign investors; fortunes were being made.

And the flag? The flag of the Tunisian Republic, honourable sir, was a red crescent and a red star in a white orb, all on a red ground.

'... *there was a red sickle moon and a single red star* ... '

The blue shaving of cigarette smoke curled and broke against the dusty plaster.

Oh, he thought, how prettily it all hung together – Rapava's story and Yepishev's story and the convenient emptiness of the Beria mansion and the freshly turned earth and the bar named 'Robotnik'.

He finished the Scotch and stubbed out his cigarette and lay there for a while, turning the book of matches over and over, anti-clockwise in his fingers.

*

STILL unsure of what he should do, Kelso went down to the front desk and changed the last of his travellers' cheques into roubles. He would need to have cash, whatever happened. He would need ready money. His credit card was not entirely reliable these days – witness that unfortunate incident at the hotel shop, when he had tried to use it to buy his Scotch.

He thought he saw someone he recognised – from the symposium, presumably – and he raised his hand but they had already turned away.

On the counter of the reception was a sign – *Any guest requiring to make an international telephone call must please to leave a cash deposit* – and seeing it gave him a second stab of homesickness. So much happening, nobody to tell. On impulse he handed over $50 and made his way back through the crowded lobby towards the elevators.

Three marriages. He contemplated this extraordinary feat as the elevator shot him skywards. Three divorces in ascending order of bitterness.

Kate – well, Kate, that hardly counted, they were students, it was doomed from the start. She had even sent him Christmas cards until he moved to New York. And Irina – she at least had got her passport, which was always, he suspected, the main point of the exercise. But Margaret – poor Margaret – she was pregnant when he married her, which was why he married her, and no sooner had one boy arrived than the next was coming, and suddenly they were stuck in four cramped rooms off the Woodstock Road: the history teacher and the history student who between them had no history. It had lasted twelve years – 'as long as the Third Reich,' Fluke, drunk, had told an inquiring gossip columnist on the day that Margaret's petition for divorce had been published. He had never been forgiven.

Still, she was the mother of his children. Maggie. Margaret. He would call poor Margaret.

The line sounded strange from the moment the operator got on to the international circuit, and his first reaction was, *Russian phones!* He shook it hard as the New York number began to ring.

'Hello.' The familiar voice, sounding unfamiliarly bright.

'It's me.'

'Oh.' Flat, suddenly; dead. Not even hostile.

'Sorry to ruin your day.' It was meant to be a joke, but it came out badly, bitter and self-pitying. He tried again. 'I'm calling from Moscow.'

'Why?'

'Why am I calling or why am I calling from Moscow?'

'Are you drinking?'

He glanced at the empty bottle. He had forgotten her capacity to smell breath at four thousand miles. 'How are the boys? Can I talk to them?'

'It's eleven o'clock on a Tuesday morning. Where do you think they are?'

'School?'

'Well done, *dad.*' She laughed, despite herself.

'Listen,' he said, 'I'm sorry.'

'For what in particular?'

'For last month's money.'

'*Three* months' money.'

'It was some cock-up at the bank.'

'Get a job, Fluke.'

'Like you, you mean?'

'Fuck you.'

'All right. Withdrawn.' He tried again. 'I spoke to Adelman this morning. He might have something for me.'

'Because things can't go on like this, you know?'

'I know. Listen. I may be on to something here –'

'What's Adelman offering?'

'Adelman? Oh, teaching. But that's not what I mean. I'm on to something here. In Moscow. It could be nothing. It could be huge.'

'What is it?'

There was definitely something odd about the line. Kelso could hear his own voice playing back in his ear, too late to be an echo. *It could be huge,* he heard himself say.

'I don't want to talk about it on the phone.'

'You don't want to talk about it on the phone –'

'I don't want to talk about it on the phone.'

' – no, sure you don't. You know why? Because it's just more of the same old shit –'

'Hold on, Maggie. Are you hearing me twice?'

' – and here's Adelman offering you a proper job, but of course you don't want that, because that means facing up –'

'Are you hearing me twice?'

' – to your responsibilities –'

Quietly, Kelso replaced the receiver. He looked at it for a moment, and chewed his lip, then lay back on the bed and lit another cigarette.

STALIN, as you know, was dismissive of women.

Indeed, he believed the very notion of an intelligent woman was an oxymoron: he called them 'herrings with ideas'. Of Lenin's wife, Nadezhda Krupskaya, he once observed to Molotov: 'She may use the same lavatory as Lenin, but that doesn't mean she knows anything about Leninism.' After Lenin's death, Krupskaya believed her status as the great man's widow would protect her from Stalin's purges, but Stalin quickly disabused her. 'If you don't shut your mouth,' he told her, 'we'll get the Party a new Lenin's widow.'

However, this is not the whole story. And here we come to one of those strange reversals of the accepted wisdom which occasionally make our profession so rewarding. For while the common view of Stalin has always been that he was largely indifferent to sex – the classic case of the politician who channels all his carnal appetites into the pursuit of power – the truth appears to have been the opposite. Stalin was a womaniser.

The recognition of this facet of his character is recent. It was Molotov, in 1988, who coyly told Chuyev (Sto sorok besed s Molotovym, Moscow) that Stalin had 'always been attractive to women'. In 1990, Khrushchev, with the posthumous publication of his last set of interviews (The Glasnost Tapes, Boston) lifted the curtain a little further. And now the archives have added still more valuable detail.

Who were these women, whose favours Stalin enjoyed both before and after the suicide of his second wife? Some we know of. There was the wife of A. I. Yegorov, First Deputy People's Commissar of Defence, who was notorious in Party circles for her numerous affairs. And then there was the wife of another military man – Gusev – a lady who was allegedly in bed with Stalin on the night Nadezhda shot herself. There was Rosa Kaganovich, whom Stalin, as a widower, seems for a time to have thought of marrying. Most interesting of all, perhaps, there was Zhenya Alliluyeva, the wife of Stalin's brother-in-law, Pavel. Her relationship with Stalin is described in a diary which was kept by his sister-in-law, Maria. It was seized on Maria's arrest and only recently declassified (F45 O1 D1).

These, of course, are only the women we know something about. Others are mere shadows in history, like the young maidservant, Valechka Istomina, who joined Stalin's personal staff in 1935 ('whether or not she was Stalin's wife is nobody else's business,' Molotov told Chuyev), or the 'beautiful young woman with dark skin' Khrushchev once saw at Stalin's dacha. 'I was told later she was a tutor for Stalin's children,' he said, 'but she was not there for long. Later she vanished. She was there on Beria's recommendation. Beria knew how to pick tutors . . .'

'Later she vanished . . .'

Once again, the familiar pattern asserts itself: it was never very wise to know too much about Comrade Stalin's private life. One of the men he cuckolded, Yegorov, was shot; another, Pavel Alliluyev, was poisoned. And Zhenya herself, his mistress and his sister-in-law by marriage – 'the rose of the Novgorod fields' – was arrested on Stalin's orders and spent so long in solitary confinement that when eventually she was released, after his death, she could no longer talk – her vocal cords had atrophied . . .

HE must have fallen asleep because the next he knew the telephone was ringing.

The room was still in semi-darkness. He switched on the lamp and looked at his watch. Nearly eight.

He swung his legs off the bed and took a couple of stiff paces across the room to the little desk next to the window.

He hesitated, then picked up the receiver.

But it was only Adelman, wanting to know if he was coming down to dinner.

'Dinner?'

'My dear fellow, it's the great symposium farewell supper, not to be missed. Olga's going to come out of a cake.'

'Christ. Do I have a choice?'

'Nope. The story, by the way, is that you had a hangover of such epic proportions this morning you had to go back to your room and sleep it off.'

'Oh, that's lovely, Frank. Thank you.'

Adelman paused. 'So what happened? You find your man?'

'Of course not.'

'It's all balls?'

'Absolutely. Nothing in it.'

'Only – you know – you were gone all day –'

'I looked up an old friend.'

'Oh, I *get* you,' said Adelman, with heavy emphasis. 'Same old Fluke. Say, are you looking at this view?'

A glittering nightscape spread out at Kelso's feet, neon banners hoisted across the city like the standards of an invading army. Philips, Marlboro, Sony, Mercedes-Benz . . . There was a time when Moscow after sunset was as gloomy as any capital in Africa. Not any more.

There wasn't a Russian word in sight.

'Never thought I'd live to see this, did you?' Adelman's voice crackled down the receiver. 'This is victory we're looking at, my friend. You realise that? Total victory.'

'Is it really, Frank? It just looks like a lot of lights to me.'

'Oh no. It's more than that, believe me. They ain't coming back from this.'

'You'll be telling me next it's "the end of history".'

'Maybe it is. But not the end of historians, thank God.' Adelman laughed. 'Okay, I'll see you in the lobby. Say twenty minutes?' He hung up.

The searchlight on the opposite side of the Moskva, next to the White House, shone fiercely into the room. Kelso reached across and opened the wooden frame of the inner window and then of the outer, admitting a particulate breath of yellow mist and the white noise of the distant traffic. A few snowflakes fluttered across the sill and melted.

The end of history, my arse, he thought. This was

History's town. This was History's bloody *country*.

He stuck his head into the cold, leaning out to see as much of the city as he could across the river, before it was lost in the murk of the horizon.

If one Russian in six believed that Stalin was their greatest ruler, that meant he had about twenty million supporters. (The sainted Lenin, of course, had many more.) And even if you halved that figure, just to get down to the hard core, that still left ten million. Ten million Stalinists in the Russian Federation, after forty years of denigration?

Mamantov was right. It was an astounding figure. Christ, if one in six Germans had said they thought Hitler was the greatest leader they'd ever had, the *New York Times* wouldn't just have wanted an op-ed piece. They'd have put it on the front page.

He closed the window and began gathering together what he would need for the evening: his last two packets of duty free cigarettes, his passport and visa (in case he was picked up), his lighter, his bulging wallet, the book of matches with Robotnik's address.

It was no use pretending he was happy about this, especially after that business at the embassy, and if it hadn't been for Mamantov, he might have been tempted to leave matters as they stood – to play it safe, the Adelman way, and to come back to find Rapava in a week or two, perhaps after wangling a commission in New York from some sympathetic publisher (assuming such a mythical creature still existed).

But if Mamantov was on the trail, he couldn't afford to wait. That was his conclusion. Mamantov had resources at his disposal Kelso couldn't hope to beat. Mamantov was a collector, a fanatic.

And it was the thought of what Mamantov might do with

this notebook, if he found it first, that was also beginning to nag at him. Because the more Kelso turned matters over in his mind, the more obvious it became that whatever Stalin had written was important. It couldn't be some mere compendium of senile jottings, not if Beria wanted it enough to steal it and then, having stolen it, was willing to risk hiding it, rather than destroying it.

'He was squealing like a pig . . . shouting something about Stalin and something about an archangel . . . Then they put a scarf in his mouth and shot him . . .'

Kelso took a last look around the bedroom and turned out the light.

It wasn't until he got down to the restaurant that he realised how hungry he was. He hadn't had a proper meal for a day and a half. He ate cabbage soup, then pickled fish, then mutton in a cream cheese sauce, with the Georgian red wine, Mukuzani, and sulphurous Narzan mineral water. The wine was dark and heavy and after a couple of glasses on top of the whisky he could feel himself becoming dangerously relaxed. There were more than a hundred diners at four big tables and the noise of the conversation and the clink and chime of glass and cutlery were soporific. Ukrainian folk music was being played over loudspeakers. He started to dilute his wine.

Someone – a Japanese historian, whose name he didn't know – leaned across and asked if this was Stalin's favourite drink and Kelso said no, that Stalin preferred the sweeter Georgian wines, Kindzmarauli and Hvanchkara. Stalin liked sweet wines and syrupy brandies, sugared herbal teas and strong tobacco –

'And Tarzan movies . . .' said someone.

'And the sound of dogs singing . . .'

Kelso joined in the laughter. What else could he do? He clinked glasses with the Japanese across the table, bowed and sat back, sipping his watery wine.

'Who's paying for all this?' someone asked.

'The sponsor who paid for the symposium, I guess.'

'Who's that?'

'American?'

'Swiss, I heard . . .'

The conversation resumed around him. After about an hour, when he thought no one was looking, he folded his napkin and pushed back his chair.

Adelman looked up and said, 'Not again? You can't run out on them again?'

'A call of nature,' said Kelso, and then, as he passed behind Adelman, he bent down and whispered, 'What's the plan for tomorrow?'

'The bus leaves for the airport after breakfast,' said Adelman. 'Check-in at Sheremetevo at eleven-fifteen.' He grabbed Kelso's arm. 'I thought you said this was all balls?'

'I did. I just want to find out what kind of balls.'

Adelman shook his head. 'This just isn't history, Fluke –'

Kelso gestured across the room. 'And this is?' Suddenly there was the sound of a knife being rapped against a glass, and Askenov pushed himself heavily to his feet. Hands banged the table in approval.

'Colleagues,' began Askenov.

'I'd sooner take my chances, Frank. I'll see you.'

He detached himself gently from Adelman's grip and headed towards the exit.

The cloakroom was by the toilets, next door to the dining room. He handed over his token, put down a tip and collected his coat, and he was just shrugging it on when he saw, at the end of the passage leading to the hotel lobby, a man. The man wasn't looking in his direction. He was pacing backwards and forwards across the corridor, talking into a mobile phone. If Kelso had seen him full-face he probably wouldn't have recognised him, and then everything would have turned out differently. But in profile the scar on the side of his face was unmistakable. He was one of the men who had been parked outside Mamantov's apartment.

Through the closed door behind him, Kelso could hear laughter and applause. He backed towards it, until he could feel the doorhandle – all this time keeping his eyes on the man – then he turned and quickly re-entered the restaurant.

Askenov was still on his feet and talking. He stopped when he saw Kelso. 'Doctor Kelso,' he said, 'seems to have a deep aversion to the sound of my voice.'

Saunders called out, 'He has an aversion to the sound of everyone's voice, except his own.'

There was more laughter. Kelso strode on.

Through the swing doors the kitchen was in pandemonium. He had an overpowering impression of heat and steam and of noise and the hot stink of cabbage and boiled fish. Waiters were lining up with trays of cups and coffee pots, being screamed at by a red-faced man in a stained tuxedo. Nobody paid Kelso any attention. He walked quickly across the huge room to the far end, where a woman in a green apron was unloading trays of dirty crockery off a trolley.

'The way out?' he said.

'*Tam*,' she said, gesturing with her chin. '*Tam*.' Over there.

The door had been wedged open to let in some cold air. He went down a dark flight of concrete steps and then he was outside, in the slushy snow, moving through a yard of overflowing trash bins and burst plastic sacks. A rat went scrabbling for safety in the shadows. It took him a minute or so to find his way out, and then he was in the big, enclosed courtyard at the rear of the hotel. Dark walls studded with lit windows rose on three sides of him. The low clouds above his head seemed to boil a yellowish-grey where they were struck by the beam of the searchlight.

He got out down a side-street on to Kutuzovskiy Prospekt and trudged through the wet snow beside the busy highway trying to find a taxi. A dirty, unmarked Volga swerved across two lanes of traffic and the driver tried to persuade him to get in, but Kelso waved him away and kept on walking until he came to the taxi rank at the front of the hotel. He couldn't be bothered to haggle. He climbed into the back of the first yellow cab in the queue and asked to be driven off, quickly.

Chapter Eight

THERE WAS A big football match in progress at the Dinamo stadium – an international, Russia playing someone-or-other, two-all, extra time. The taxi driver was listening to the commentary on the radio and as they came closer to the stadium, the cheers on the cheap plastic loudspeaker were subsumed into the roar of eighty thousand Muscovite throats less than two hundred yards away. The flurries of snow swelled and lifted like sails in the floodlights above the stands.

They had to go up Leningradskiy Prospekt, make a U-turn and come back down the other side to reach the stadium of the Young Pioneers. The taxi, an old Zhiguli that stank of sweat, turned off right, through a pair of iron gates, and bounced down a rutted track and into the sports ground. A few cars were drawn up in the snow in front of the grandstand, and there was a queue of people, mostly girls, outside an iron door with a peep-hole set into it. A sign above the entrance said 'Robotnik'.

Kelso paid the taxi driver a hundred roubles – a ludicrous amount, the price of not haggling before the journey started – and watched with some dismay as the red lights bucked across the rough surface, turned and disappeared. An immense noise, like a breaking wave, came from the phosphorescent sky above the trees and rolled across the white sweep of the pitch. 'Three–two,' said a man with an Australian accent. 'It's over.' He pulled out a tiny black earpiece and stuffed it into his pocket. Kelso said to the nearest person, a girl, 'What time does it open?' and she

122

turned to look at him. She was startlingly beautiful: wide dark eyes and wide cheekbones. She must have been about twenty. Snow flecked her black hair.

'Ten,' she said, and slipped her arm through his, pressing her breast against his elbow. 'Can I have a cigarette?'

He gave one to her and took one himself and their heads brushed as they bent to share the flame. He inhaled her perfume with the smoke. They straightened. 'One minute,' he said, smiling, and moved away, and she smiled back, waving the cigarette at him. He walked along the edge of the pitch, smoking, looking at the girls. Were they *all* hookers? They didn't seem like hookers. What were they, then? Most of the men were foreigners. The Russians looked rich. The cars were big and German, apart from one Bentley and one Rolls. He could see men in the back of them. In the Bentley, a red tip the size of a burning coal glowed and faded as someone smoked an immense cigar.

At five past ten, the door opened – a yellow light, the silhouettes of the girls, the steamy glow of their perfumed breath – a festive sight, thought Kelso, in the snow. And from the cars now came the serious money. You could tell the seriousness not just by the weight of the coats and the jewellery, but by the way their owners carried themselves, straight to the head of the queue, and by the amount of protection they left hanging around at the door. Clearly, the only guns allowed on the premises belonged to the management, which Kelso found reassuring. He went through a metal detector, then his pockets were checked for explosives by a goon with a wand. The admission fee was three hundred roubles – fifty dollars, the average weekly wage, payable in either currency – and in return for this he got an ultra-violet stamp on his wrist and a voucher for one free drink.

A spiral staircase led down to darkness, smoke and laser beams, a wall of techno-music pitched to make the stomach shake. Some of the girls were dancing listlessly together, the men were standing, drinking, watching. The idea of Papu Rapava showing his scowling face in here was a joke, and Kelso would have turned round there and then, but he felt in need of another drink, and fifty dollars was fifty dollars. He gave his voucher to the barman and took a bottle of beer. Almost as an afterthought, he beckoned the bartender towards him.

'Rapava,' he said. The barman frowned and cupped his ear, and Kelso bent closer. 'Rapava,' he shouted.

The barman nodded slowly, and said in English, 'I know.'

'You know?'

He nodded again. He was a young man, with a wispy blond beard and a gold earring. He began to turn away, to serve another customer so Kelso pulled out his wallet and put a one-hundred thousand rouble note on the bar. That got his attention. 'I want to find Rapava,' he shouted.

The money was carefully folded and tucked into the barman's breast pocket. 'Later,' said the young man. 'Okay? I tell you.'

'When?'

But the young man smirked and moved further up the bar.

'Bribing bartenders?' said an American voice at Kelso's elbow. 'That's smart. Never thought of that. Get served first? Impress the ladies? Hello, Dr Kelso. Remember me?'

In the half-light, the handsome face was patched with colour and it took Kelso a couple of seconds to work out who he was. 'Mr O'Brian.' A television reporter. Wonderful. This was all he needed.

They shook hands. The young man's palm was moist and

fleshy. He was wearing his off-duty uniform – pressed blue jeans, white T-shirt, leather jacket – and Kelso registered broad shoulders, pectorals, thick hair glistening with some aromatic gel.

O'Brian gestured across the dance floor with his bottle. 'The new Russia,' he shouted. 'Whatever you want, you buy, and someone's always selling. Where're you staying?'

'The Ukraina.'

O'Brian made a face. 'Save your bribe for later's my advice. You'll need it. They're strict on the door at the old Ukraina. And those beds. Boy.' O'Brian shook his head and drained his bottle, and Kelso smiled and drank as well.

'Any other advice?' he yelled.

'Plenty, since you ask.' O'Brian beckoned him in close. 'The good ones'll ask for six hundred. Offer two. Settle on three. And we're talking all-night rates, remember, so keep some money back. As an incentive, let's say. And be careful of the real, *real* babes, 'cause they may be spoken for. If the other fellow's Russian, just walk away. It's safer, and there's plenty more – we're not talking life partners here. Oh, and they don't do triples. As a rule. These are respectable girls.'

'I'm sure.'

O'Brian looked at him. 'You don't get it, do you, professor? This ain't a whorehouse. Anna here –' he curled his arm around the waist of a blonde girl standing next to him and used his beer bottle as a microphone ' – Anna, tell the professor here what you do for a living.'

Anna spoke solemnly into the bottle. 'I lease property to Scandinavian businesses.'

O'Brian nuzzled her cheek and licked her ear and released her. 'Galina over there – the skinny one in the blue dress? – she works at the Moscow stock exchange. Who else? Damnit, they all look alike, after you've been here a time. Nataliya, the one you spoke to outside – oh, yes, I was watchin' you, professor, you sly old dog – Anna, darlin', what does Nataliya do?'

'Comstar, R.J.,' said Anna. 'Nataliya works for Comstar, remember?'

'Sure, sure. And what was the name of that cute kid at Moscow U? The psychologist, you know the one –'

'Alissa.'

'Alissa, right. Alissa – she in tonight?'

'She got shot, R.J.'

'Boy! Did she? *Really?*'

'Why were you watching me outside?' asked Kelso.

'That's commerce, I guess. You wanna make money, you gotta take risks. Three hundred a night. Let's say three nights a week. Nine hundred dollars. Give three hundred for protection. Still leaves six hundred clear. Twenty thousand dollars a year – that's not hard. What's that – seven times the average annual wage? And no tax? Gotta pay a price for that. Gotta take a risk. Like working on an oil rig. Let me get you a beer, professor. Why shouldn't I watch you? I'm a reporter, goddamnit. Everyone comes here watches everyone else. There's half a billion dollars worth of custom here tonight. And that's just the Russians.'

'Mafia?'

'No, just business. Same as any place else.'

The dance floor was packed now, the noise louder, the smoke denser. A new kind of lightshow had been switched on – lights that made everything that was white stand out dazzlingly bright. Teeth and eyes and nails and banknotes flashed in the gloom like knives. Kelso felt disorientated and vaguely drunk. But not, he thought, as drunk as O'Brian was pretending to be. There was something about the reporter that gave him the creeps. How old was he? Thirty? A young man in a hurry, if ever he'd seen one.

He said to Anna, 'What time does this finish?'

She held up five fingers. 'You want to dance, Mister Professor?'

'Later,' said Kelso. 'Maybe.'

'It's the Weimar Republic,' said O'Brian, coming back with two bottles of beer and a can of Diet Coke for Anna. 'Isn't that what you wrote? Look at it. Christ. All we need is Marlene Dietrich in a tuxedo and we might as well be in Berlin. I liked your book, professor, by the way. Did I say that already?'

'You did. Thanks. Cheers.'

'Cheers.' O'Brian raised his bottle and took a swig, then he leaned over and shouted in Kelso's ear. 'Weimar Republic, that's how I see it. Like you see it. Six things the same, okay? One: you have a big country, proud country, lost its empire, really lost a war, but can't figure out *how* – figures it must've been stabbed in the back, so there's a lot of resentment, right? Two: democracy in a country with no tradition of democracy – Russia doesn't know democracy from a fuckin' hole in the ground, frankly – people don't like it, sick of all the arguing, they want a strong line, *any* line. Three: border trouble – lots of your own ethnic nationals suddenly stuck in other countries, saying they're getting picked on. Four: anti-semitism – you can buy SS marchin' songs on the street corners, for Christ's sake. That leaves two.'

'All right.' It was disconcerting, hearing your own views so crudely parroted; like an Oxford tutorial –

'Economic crash, and that's coming, don't you think?'

'And?'

127

'Isn't it obvious? *Hitler*. They haven't found their Hitler yet. But when they do, it's watch out, world, I reckon.' O'Brian put his left forefinger under his nose and raised his right arm in a Nazi salute. Across the bar, a group of Russian businessmen whooped and cheered.

AFTER that, the evening accelerated. Kelso danced with Anna, O'Brian danced with Nataliya, they had more drinks – the American stuck to beer while Kelso tried the cocktails: B-52s, Kamikazes – they swapped girls, danced some more and then it was after midnight. Nataliya was in a tight red dress that was slippery, like plastic, and her flesh beneath it, despite the heat, felt cold and hard. She had taken something. Her eyes were wide and poorly focused. She asked if he wanted to go somewhere – she liked him a lot, she whispered, she'd do it for five hundred – but he just gave her fifty, for the pleasure of the dance, and went back to the bar.

Depression stalked him. He wasn't sure why. He could smell desperation, that was it: desperation stank as strongly as the perfume and the sweat. Desperation to buy. Desperation to sell. Desperation to pretend you were having a good time. A young man in a suit, so drunk he could barely walk, was being led away by his tie by a hard-faced girl with long blonde hair. Kelso decided he would have a smoke at the bar and then go – no, on second thoughts, forget the cigarette – he stuffed it back into the pack – he would go.

'Rapava,' yelled the barman.

'What?' Kelso cupped his hand to his ear.

'That's her. She's here.'

'What?'

Kelso looked to where the barman was pointing and saw her at once. *Her.* He let his gaze travel past her and then come back. She was older than the others: close-cropped black hair, black eyeshadow like bruises, black lipstick, a dead white face at once broad and thin, with cheekbones as sharp as a skull. Asiatic-looking. Mingrelian.

Papu Rapava: released from the camps in 1969. Married, say 1970, 1971. A son just old enough to fight in Afghanistan. And a daughter?

'My daughter's a whore . . . '

'Night night, professor –' O'Brian swept past with a wink over his shoulder, Nataliya on one arm, Anna on the other. The rest of his words were lost in the noise. Nataliya turned, giggled, blew Kelso a kiss. Kelso smiled vaguely, waved, put down his drink and moved along the bar.

A black cocktail dress – fabric shiny, knee-length, sleeve-less – bare white throat and arms (not even a wrist watch), black stockings, black shoes. And something not quite right about her, some disturbance in the atmosphere around her, so that even at the crowded bar she was in a space, alone. No one was talking to her. She was drinking a bottle of mineral water without a glass and looking at nothing, her dark eyes were blank, and when he said hello she turned to face him, without interest. He asked if she wanted a drink.

No.

A dance, then?

She looked him over, thought about it, shrugged.

Okay.

She drained the bottle, set it on the bar, and pushed past him on to the dance floor, turned, waited for him. He followed her.

She didn't make much of a pretence and he rather liked her for that. The dance was merely a polite prelude to business, like a broker and a client spending ten seconds inquiring after each other's health. For about a minute she moved idly, at the edge of the pack, then she leaned over and said, 'Four hundred?'

No trace of perfume, just a vague scent of soap.

Kelso said, 'Two hundred.'

'Okay.'

She walked straight off the floor without looking back and he was so surprised by her failure to haggle that for a moment he was left alone. Then he went after her, up the spiral staircase. Her hips were full in the tight black dress, her waist thick, and it occurred to him that she didn't have long to go at this end of the game, that it was a mistake to invite immediate comparison with women eight, ten, maybe even twelve years her junior.

They collected their coats in silence. Hers was cheap, thin, too short for the season.

They went out into the cold. She took his arm. That was when he kissed her. He was slightly drunk and the situation was so surreal that he actually thought for a moment that he might combine business and pleasure. And he was curious, he had to admit it. She responded immediately, and with more passion than he'd expected. Her lips parted. His tongue touched her teeth. She tasted unexpectedly of something sweet and he remembered thinking that maybe her lipstick was flavoured with liquorice: was that possible?

She pulled away from him.

'What's your name?' he said.

'What name do you like?'

He had to smile at that. His luck: to find the first post-modern whore in Moscow. When she saw him smiling, she frowned.

'What's your wife's name?'

'I don't have a wife.'

'Girlfriend?'

'No girlfriend, either.'

She shivered and thrust her hands deep into her pockets. It had stopped snowing, and now that the metal door had closed behind them the night was silent.

She said, 'What's your hotel?'

'The Ukraina.'

She rolled her eyes.

'Listen,' he began, but he had no name to ease the conversation. 'Listen, I don't want to sleep with you. Or rather,' he corrected himself, 'I do, but that isn't what I had in mind.'

Was that clear?

'Ah,' she said, and looked knowing – looked like a whore for the first time, in fact. 'Whatever you want, it's still two hundred.'

'Do you have a car?'

'Yes.' She paused. 'Why?'

'The truth is,' he said, wincing at the lie, 'I'm a friend of your father's. I want you to take me to see him –'

That shocked her. She reeled back, laughing, panicky. 'You don't know my *father*.'

'Rapava. His name's Papu Rapava.'

She stared at him, slack mouthed, then slapped his face – hard, the heel of her hand connecting with the edge of his cheekbone – and started walking away, fast, stumbling a little: it couldn't have been easy in high heels on freezing snow. He let her go. He wiped his mouth with his fingers. They came away black with something. Not blood he realised: lipstick. Oh, but she packed a punch, though: he was hurting. Behind him, the door had opened. He was aware of people watching, and a murmur of disapproval. He could guess what they were thinking: rich westerner gets honest Russian girl outside, tries to renegotiate the terms, or suggests something so disgusting she can only turn and run – *bastard*. He set off after her.

She had veered on to the virgin snow of the pitch and had stopped, somewhere near the halfway line, staring into the dark sky. He trod along the path of her small footprints, came up behind her and waited, a couple of yards away.

After a while, he said, 'I don't know who you are. And I don't want to know who you are. And I won't tell your father how I found him. I won't tell anyone. I give you my word. I just want you to take me to where he lives. Take me to where he lives and I'll give you two hundred dollars.'

She didn't turn. He couldn't see her face.

'Four hundred,' she said.

Chapter Nine

FELIKS SUVORIN, IN a dark blue Crombie overcoat from Saks of Fifth Avenue, had arrived at the Lubyanka in the snow a little after eight that evening, sweeping up the slushy hill in the back of an official Volga.

His path had been eased by a call from Yuri Arsenyev to his old buddy, Nikolai Oborin – hunting crony, vodka partner and nowadays chief of the Tenth Directorate, or the Special Federal Archive Resource Bureau, or whatever the Squirrels had decided to call themselves that particular week.

'Now listen, Niki, I've got a young fellow in the office with me, name of Suvorin, and we've come up with a ploy . . . That's him . . . Now, listen, Niki, I can't say more than this: there's a foreign diplomat – western, highly placed – he's got a racket going, smuggling . . . No, not icons, this time, wait for it – documents – and we thought we'd lay a trap . . . That's it, that's it, you're way ahead of me, comrade – something big, something irresistible . . . Yes, that's an idea, but what about this: what about that notebook the old NKVDers used to go on about, what was it? . . . That's it, "Stalin's testament" . . . Well, this is why I'm calling now. We've got a problem. He's meeting the target tomorrow . . . *Tonight?* He can do tonight, Niki, I'm certain – I'm looking at him now, he's nodding – he can do tonight . . .'

Suvorin hadn't even had to repeat the tale, let alone elaborate upon it. Once inside the Lubyanka's marble hall, his papers checked, he'd followed his instructions and called a man named Blok, who was expecting him. He stood around the empty lobby, watched by the silent, uncurious

133

guards and contemplated the big white bust of Andropov, and presently there were footsteps. Blok – an ageless creature, stooped and dusty, with a bunch of keys on his belt – led him into the depths of the building, then out into a dark, wet courtyard and across it and into what looked like a small fortress. Up the stairs to the second floor: a small room, a desk, a chair, a wood-block floor, barred windows –

'How much do you want to see?'

'Everything.'

'That's your decision,' said Blok, and left.

Suvorin had always preferred to look ahead rather than to live in the past: something else he admired about the Americans. What was the alternative for a modern Russian? Paralysis! The end of history struck him as an excellent idea. History couldn't end soon enough, as far as Feliks Suvorin was concerned.

But even he could not escape the ghosts in this place. After a minute he got to his feet and prowled around. Craning his head at the high window he found he could see up to the narrow strip of night sky, and then down to the tiny windows, level with the earth, that marked the old Lubyanka cells. He thought of Isaak Babel, down there somewhere, tortured into betraying his friends, then frantically retracting, and of Bukharin, and his final letter to Stalin (*'I feel, toward you, toward the Party, toward the cause as a whole nothing but great and boundless love: I embrace you in my thoughts, farewell forever . . .'*) and of Zinoviev, disbelieving, being dragged away by his guard to be shot (*'Please comrade, please, for God's sake call Josef Vissarionovich . . .'*)

He pulled out his mobile phone, tapped in the familiar number and spoke to his wife.

'Hi, you'll never guess where I am . . . Who's to say?' He

felt better immediately for hearing her voice. 'I'm sorry about tonight. Hey, kiss the babies for me, will you . . .? And one for you, too, Serafima Suvorina . . .'

The secret police was beyond the reach of time and history. It was protean. *That* was its secret. The Cheka had become the GPU, and then the OGPU, and then the NKVD, and then the NKGB, and then the MGB, and then the MVD, and finally the KGB: the highest stage of evolution. And then, lo and behold!, the mighty KGB itself had been obliged by the failed coup to mutate into two entirely new sets of initials: the SVR – the spies – stationed out at Yasenevo, and the FSB – internal security – still here, in the Lubyanka, amid the bones.

And the view in the Kremlin's highest reaches was that the FSB, at least, was really nothing more than the latest in the long tradition of rearranged letters – that, in the immortal words of Boris Nikolaevich himself, delivered to Arsenyev in the course of a steam bath at the Presidential dacha, 'those motherfuckers in the Lubyanka are still the same old motherfuckers they always were'. Which was why, when the President decreed that Vladimir Mamantov had to be investigated, the task could not be entrusted to the FSB, but had to be farmed out to the SVR – and never mind if they hadn't the resources.

Suvorin had four men to cover the city. He called Vissari Netto for an update. The situation hadn't changed: the primary target – No. 1 – had still not returned to his apartment, the target's wife – No. 2 – was still under sedation, the historian – No. 3 – was still at his hotel and now having dinner.

'Lucky for some,' muttered Suvorin. There was a clatter in the corridor. 'Keep me informed,' he added firmly, and pressed END. He thought it sounded like the right kind of thing to say.

He had been expecting one file, maybe two. Instead, Blok threw open the door and wheeled in a steel trolley stacked with folders – twenty or thirty of them – some so old that when he lost control of the heavy contraption and collided with the wall, they sent up protesting clouds of dust.

'That's your decision,' he repeated.

'Is this the lot?'

'This goes up to sixty-one. You want the rest?'

'Of course.'

HE couldn't read them all. It would have taken him a month. He confined himself to untying the ribbon from each bundle, riffling through the torn and brittle pages to see if they contained anything of interest, then tying them up again. It was filthy work. His hands turned black. The spores invaded the membrane of his nose and made his head ache.

Highly confidential
28 June 1953
To Central Committee, Comrade Malenkov
I hereby enclose the deposition of the cross-examination of prisoner A. N. Poskrebyshev, former assistant to J. V. Stalin, concerning his work as an anti-Soviet spy.
The investigation is continuing.
USSR Deputy Minister of State Security,
A. A. Yepishev

This had been the start of it – a couple of pages, in the middle of Poskrebyshev's interrogation, underscored in red ink almost half a century ago, by an agitated hand:

Interrogator: Describe the demeanour of the General
Secretary in the four years, 1949-53.
Poskrebyshev: The General Secretary became increasingly
withdrawn and secretive. After 1951, he never left the
Moscow district. His health deteriorated sharply, I
should say from his 70th birthday. On several occasions I
witnessed cerebral disturbances leading to blackouts,
from which he quickly recovered. I told him: "Let me call
the doctors, Comrade Stalin. You need a doctor." The
General Secretary refused, stating that the 4th Main
Administration of the Ministry of Health was under the
control of Beria, and that while he would trust Beria to
shoot a man, he would not trust him to cure one. Instead
I prepared for the General Secretary herbal infusions.
Interrogator: Describe the effect of these health
problems upon the General Secretary's conduct of his
duties.
Poskrebyshev: Before the blackouts commenced, the
General Secretary would sustain a workload of
approximately two hundred documents each day.
Afterwards, this number declined sharply and he ceased
to see many of his colleagues. He made numerous
writings of his own, to which I was not permitted
access.
Interrogator: Describe the form of these private
writings.
Poskreybshev: These private writings took various forms.
In his final year, for example, he acquired a notebook.
Interrogator: Describe this notebook.
Poskrebyshev: This notebook was of an ordinary sort,

which might be bought in any stationers, with a black oilskin cover.

Interrogator: Which other persons knew of the existence of this notebook?

Poskrebyshev: The chief of his bodyguard, General Vlasik, knew of it. Beria also knew of it and asked me on several occasions to obtain a copy of it. This was not possible, even for me, as the General Secretary confined it to an office safe to which he alone possessed the key.

Interrogator: Speculate as to the contents of this notebook.

Poskrebyshev: I cannot speculate. I do not know.

Highly Confidential
30 June 1953
To USSR Deputy Minister of State Security, A. A. Yepishev
You are instructed to investigate the whereabouts of the personal writings of J. V. Stalin referred to by A. N. Poskrebyshev as a matter of supreme urgency and using all appropriate measures.
Central Committee,
Malenkov

Cross-examination of prisoner Lieutenant-General N. S. Vlasik
1 July 1953 [Extract]
Interrogator: Describe the black notebook belonging to J. V. Stalin.
Vlasik: I do not remember such a notebook.
Interrogator: Describe the black notebook belonging to J. V. Stalin.

Vlasik: I remember now. I first became aware of this in December 1952. One day I saw this notebook on Comrade Stalin's desk. I asked Poskrebyshev what it contained, but Poskrebyshev could not tell me. Comrade Stalin saw me looking at it and asked me what I was doing. I replied that I was doing nothing, that my eye had merely fallen upon this notebook, but that I had not touched it. Comrade Stalin said: "You as well, Vlasik, after more than thirty years?" I was arrested the following morning and brought to the Lubyanka.

Interrogator: Describe the circumstances of your arrest.

Vlasik: I was arrested by Beria, and subjected to numberless cruelties at his hands. Beria questioned me repeatedly about the notebook of Comrade Stalin. I was unable to tell him details. I know nothing further of this matter.

Statement of Lieutenant A. P. Titov, Kremlin Guard
6 July 1953 [Extract]
I was on duty in the leadership area of the Kremlin from 22:00 on 1 March 1953 until 06:00 the following day. At approximately 04:40, I encountered in the Passage of Heroes Comrade L. P. Beria and a second comrade whose identity is not known to me. Comrade Beria was carrying a small case or bag.

Interrogation of Lieutenant P. G. Rapava, NKVD
7 July 1953 [Extract]
Interrogator: Describe what happened following your departure from J. V. Stalin's dacha with the traitor Beria.

Rapava: I drove Comrade Beria to his home.

Interrogator: Describe what happened following your departure from J. V. Stalin's dacha with the traitor Beria.

Rapava: I remember now. I drove Comrade Beria to the Kremlin to enable him to collect material from his office.

Interrogator: Describe what happened following your departure from J. V. Stalin's dacha with the traitor Beria.

Rapava: I have nothing to add to my previous statement.

Interrogator: Describe what happened following your departure from J. V. Stalin's dacha with the traitor Beria.

Rapava: I have nothing to add to my previous statement.

Interrogation of L. P. Beria
8 July 1953 [Extract]
Interrogator: When did you first become aware of the personal notebook belonging to J. V. Stalin?

Beria: I refuse to answer any questions until I have been allowed to express myself before a full meeting of the Central Committee.

Interrogator: Both Vlasik and Poskrebyshev have confirmed your interest in this notebook.

Beria: The Central Committee is the proper forum in which all these matters should be addressed.

Interrogator: You do not deny your interest in this notebook.

Beria: The Central Committee is the proper forum.

Highly Confidential
30 November 1953
To USSR Deputy Minister of State Security, A. A. Yepishev
You are instructed to bring the investigation into the anti-Party criminal and traitor Beria to a rapid conclusion, and to move this matter to trial.
Central Committee,
Malenkov
Khrushchev

Interrogation of L. P. Beria
2 December 1953 [Extract]
Interrogator: We know that you took possession of the notebook of J. V. Stalin, yet you continue to deny this matter. What was your interest in this notebook?
Beria: End it.
Interrogator: What was your interest in this notebook?
Beria: [The accused indicated by gesture his refusal to co-operate]

Highly confidential
23 December 1953
To Central Committee, Comrades Malenkov, Khrushchev
I beg to report that the sentence of death by shooting imposed on L. P. Beria was carried out today at 01:50.
T. R. Falin,
Procurator General

27 December 1953
Judgement of the People's Special Court in the case of

Lieutenant P. G. Rapava: 15 years' penal servitude.

SUVORIN couldn't bear the filth of his hands any longer. He wandered the empty corridor until he found a toilet with a sink where he could wash himself down. He was still in there, trying to get the last of the dust out from under his fingernails, when his mobile phone rang. In the silence of the Lubyanka it made him jump.

'Suvorin.'

'It's Netto. We've lost him. No. 3.'

'Who? What're you talking about?'

'No. 3. The historian. He went in to eat with the others. He never came out. It looks as though he left through the kitchens.'

Suvorin groaned, turned, leaned against the wall. This whole business was spinning out of control.

'How long ago?'

'About an hour. In defence of Bunin, he has been on duty for eighteen hours.' A pause. 'Major?'

Suvorin had the phone wedged between his chin and shoulder. He was drying his hands, thinking. He didn't blame Bunin, actually. To mount a decent surveillance took at least four watchers; six for safety.

'I'm still here. Stand him down.'

'Do you want me to tell the chief?'

'I think not, don't you? Not twice in one day. He might begin to think we're incompetent.' He licked his lips, tasting dust. 'Why don't you go home yourself, Vissari? We'll meet in my office, eight tomorrow.'

'Have you discovered anything?'

'Only that when people go on about "the good old days" they're talking shit.'

He rinsed his mouth, spat, went back to work.

BERIA was shot, Poskrebyshev released, Vlasik got a sentence of ten years, Rapava was sent to Kolyma, Yepishev was taken off the case, the investigation meandered on.

Beria's house was searched from attic to cellar and yielded no further evidence, apart from some pieces of human remains (female) that had been partially dissolved by acid and bricked up. He had his own private network of cells in the basement. The property was sealed. In 1956, the Ministry for Foreign Affairs asked the KGB if it had any suitable premises which might be offered as an embassy to the new Republic of Tunisia, and, after a final brief investigation, Vspolnyi Street was handed over.

Vlasik was interrogated twice more about the notebook, but added nothing new. Poskrebyshev was watched, bugged, encouraged to write his memoirs and, when he had finished, the manuscript was seized 'for permanent retention'. An extract, a single page, had been clipped to the file:

What went through the mind of this incomparable genius in that final year, as he confronted the obvious fact of his own mortality, I do not know. Josef Vissarionovich may have confided his most private thoughts to a notebook, which rarely left his side during his final months of unstinting toil for his people and the cause of progressive humanity. Containing, as it may do, the distillation of his wisdom as the leading theoretician of Marxism–Leninism, it must be hoped that this remarkable document will one day be discovered and published for the benefit . . .

Suvorin yawned, closed the bundle and put it to one side, grabbed another. This turned out to be the weekly reports of a Gulag stool-pigeon named Abidov, assigned to keep an eye on the prisoner Rapava during his time at the Butugychag uranium mine. There was nothing of interest in the smudged carbons, which ended abruptly with a laconic note from the camp KGB officer, recording Abidov's death from a stab wound, and Rapava's transfer to a forestry labour detail.

More files, more stoolies, more of nothing. Papers authorising Rapava's release at the conclusion of his sentence, reviewed by a special commission of the Second Chief Directorate – passed, stamped, authorised. Appropriate work selected for the returning prisoner at the Leningrad Station engine sheds; KGB informer-in-place: Antipin, foreman. Appropriate housing selected for the returning prisoner at the newly built Victory of the Revolution complex; KGB informer-in-place: Senka, building supervisor. More reports. Nothing. Case reviewed and classified as 'diversion of resources', 1975. Nothing on file until 1983, when Rapava was briefly re-examined at the request of the deputy chief of the Fifth Directorate (Ideology and Dissidents).

Well, well . . .

Suvorin pulled out his pipe and sucked at it, scratched his forehead with the stem, then went searching back through the files. How old was this fellow? Rapava, Rapava, Rapava – here it was, Papu Gerasimovich Rapava, born 9.9.27.

Old, then – in his seventies. But not *that* old. Not so old that even in a country where the average male life expectancy was fifty-eight and falling – worse than it had been in Stalin's time – not so old that he need necessarily be *dead*.

He flipped back to the 1983 report, and scanned it. It told him nothing he didn't know already. Oh, he was a tight one, this Rapava – not a word in thirty years. Only when he reached the bottom, and saw the recommendation to take no further action, and the name of the officer accepting this recommendation did he jolt up in his chair.

He swore and fumbled for his mobile, tapped out the number of the SVR's night duty officer and asked to be patched through to the home of Vissari Netto.

Chapter Ten

THEY SETTLED ON three hundred, and for that he insisted on two things: first, that she drove him there herself and, secondly, that she waited an hour. An address on its own would be useless at this time of night, and if Rapava's neighbourhood was as rough as the old man had implied it was (*'it was a decent block in those days, boy, before the drugs and the crime...'*) then no foreigner in his right mind would go stumbling around there alone.

Her car was a battered, ancient Lada, sand-coloured, parked in the dark street that led to the stadium, and they walked to it in silence. She opened her door first and then reached across to let him in. There was a pile of books on the passenger seat – legal textbooks, he noticed – and she moved them quickly into the back.

He said, 'Are you a lawyer? Are you studying the law?'

'Three hundred dollars,' she said, and held out her hand. 'US.'

'Later.'

'Now.'

'Half now,' he said, cunningly, 'half later.'

'I can get another fuck, mister. Can you get another ride?'

It was her longest speech of the night.

'Okay, okay.' He pulled out his wallet. 'You'll make a good lawyer.' Jesus. Three hundred to her, after more than a hundred at the club – it just about cleaned him out. He had thought he might try offering the old man some cash, this evening, as a downpayment for the notebook, but that wouldn't be possible now.

She re-counted the notes, folded them carefully and put them away in her coat pocket. The little car rattled down to the Leningradskiy Prospekt. She made a right into the quiet traffic, then did a U-turn, and now they were heading out of the city, back past the deserted Dinamo stadium, north-west, towards the airport.

She drove fast. He guessed she wanted to be rid of him. Who was she? The Lada's interior offered him no clues. It was fastidiously clean, almost empty. He gave her profile a surreptitious look. Her face was tilted downwards slightly. She was scowling at the road. The black lips, the white cheeks, the small and delicately pointed ears below the lick of short black hair – she had a vampirish look: disturbing, he thought again. Disturbed. He still had the taste of her in his mouth and he couldn't help wondering what the sex would have been like – she was so utterly out of reach now, yet fifteen minutes earlier she would have done whatever he asked.

She glanced up at the mirror and caught him looking at her. 'Cut that out.'

He continued to stare anyway – more frankly now: he was making a point, he had paid for the ride – but then he felt cheap and turned away.

The streets beyond the glass had become much darker. He didn't know where they were. They had passed the Park of Friendship, he knew that, and passed a power station, a railway junction. Thick pipes carrying communal hot water ran beside the road, across the road, along the other side, steam leaking from their joints. Occasionally, in the patches of blackness, he could see the flames of bonfires and people moving around them. After another ten minutes, they turned off left into a street as wide and rough as a field, with scruffy birch trees on either side. They hit a pothole and the chassis cracked, scraped rock. She spun the wheel and they hit another. Orange lights beyond the trees dimly lit the gantries and stairwells of a giant housing complex.

She had slowed the car now almost to walking pace. She stopped beside a broken-down wooden bus shelter.

'That's his place,' she said. 'Block number nine.'

It was about a hundred yards away, across a snowy strip of waste ground.

'You'll wait here?'

'Entrance D. Fifth floor. Apartment twelve.'

'But you'll wait?'

'If you want.'

'We did agree.'

Kelso looked at his watch. It was twenty-five past one. Then he looked again at the apartment block, trying to think what he would say to Rapava, wondering what reception he would get.

'So this is where you grew up?'

She didn't answer. She switched off the engine and turned up her collar, put her hands in her pockets, stared ahead. He sighed and got out of the car, walked around it. The powdery snow creaked as it compacted under his feet. He shivered and began to pick his way over the rough ground.

He was about halfway across when he heard the grating of an ignition and an engine firing up. He swung round to see the Lada moving off slowly, lights doused. She hadn't even bothered to wait until he was out of sight. *Bitch*. He began running towards her. He shouted – not loudly, and not in anger really: it was more a groan at his own stupidity. The little car was shuddering, stalling, and for a moment he thought he might catch up with it, but then it coughed, lurched, the lights came on and it accelerated away from him. He stood and watched it helplessly as it vanished into the labyrinth of concrete.

He was alone. Not a soul in view.

He turned and began quickly retracing his steps, crunching across the snow towards the building. He felt vulnerable in the open and panic sharpened his senses. Somewhere to his left, he could hear the bark of a dog and a baby's cry, and ahead of him there was music – it was faint, there was scarcely more than a thread of it, but it was coming from Block Nine and it was getting louder with each step. His eyes were making out details now – the ribbed concrete, the shadowed doorways, the stacked balconies crammed with junk: bed frames, bike frames, old tyres, dead plants; three windows were lit, the rest in darkness.

At Entrance D something crunched beneath his foot and he bent to pick it up, then dropped it, fast. A hypodermic syringe.

The stairwell was a sump of piss and vomit, stained newsprint, limp condoms, dead leaves. He covered his nose with the back of his hand. There was an elevator, and it might have been working – a Moscow miracle that would have been – but he didn't propose to try. He climbed the stairs, and by the time he reached the third floor he could hear the music much more clearly. Someone was playing the old Soviet national anthem – the *old* old anthem, that was – the one they used to sing before Khrushchev had it censored. 'Party of Lenin!' shouted the chorus. 'Party of Stalin!' Kelso took the last two flights more quickly, with a sudden rush of hope. She hadn't entirely tricked him, then, for who else but Papu Rapava would be playing the greatest hits of Josef Stalin at half-past one in the morning?

He came out on to the fifth floor and followed the noise along the dingy passage to number twelve. The block was largely derelict. Most of the doors were boarded over, but not Rapava's. Oh no, boy. Rapava's door wasn't boarded over. Rapava's door was open and outside it, for reasons Kelso couldn't begin to fathom, there were feathers on the floor.

The music stopped.

COME on then, boy. What're you waiting for? What's up? Don't tell me you haven't the balls –

For several seconds, Kelso stood on the threshold, listening.

Suddenly there was a drumroll.

The anthem began again.

Cautiously, he pushed at the door. It was partially open, but it wouldn't go back any further. There was something behind it, blocking it.

He squeezed around the edge. The lights were on.

Dear God –

Thought you'd be impressed, boy! Thought you'd be surprised! If you're going to get fucked over, you might as well get fucked over by professionals, eh?

At Kelso's feet were more feathers, leaking from a cushion that had been disemboweled. These feathers could not be said to be on the floor, however, because there was no floor. The boards were all prised up and stacked around the edges of the room. Strewn across the rib-cage of the joists were the remains of Rapava's few possessions – books with splayed and shattered spines, punched-through pictures, the skeletons of chairs, an exploded television, a table with its legs in the air, bits of crockery, shards of glass, shredded fabric. The interior walls had been skinned to expose the cavities. The exterior walls were

bruised and dented, apparently by a sledgehammer. Much of
the ceiling was hanging down. Plaster dust frosted the room.

Balanced in the centre of this chaos, amid a black and
jagged pool of broken records, was a bulky 1970s Telefunken
record player, set to automatic replay.

Party of Lenin!

Party of Stalin!

Kelso stepped carefully from rib to rib and lifted the
needle.

In the silence: the dripping of a broken tap.

The extent of the destruction was so overwhelming, so
utterly beyond anything he had ever seen, that once he was
satisfied the apartment was empty, it barely occurred to him
that he ought to be scared. Not at first. He peered around
him, baffled.

*So where am I, boy? That's the question. What have they done
with poor old Papu? Come on then, come and get me. Chop,
chop, comrade – we haven't got all night!*

Kelso, wobbling, tightrope-walked along a joist, into the
kitchen alcove: slashed packets, upended ice-box, wrenched-
down cupboards . . .

He edged backwards and round the corner into a little
passage, scrabbling at the broken wall to stop himself from
slipping.

Two doors here, boy – right and left. You take your pick.

He swayed, indecisive, then reached out a hand.

The first – a bedroom.

*Now you're getting warm, boy. By the way: did you want to
fuck my daughter?*

Slashed mattress. Slashed pillow. Overturned bed. Empty
drawers. Small and tatty nylon carpet, rolled and stacked.
Clumps of plaster everywhere. Floor up. Ceiling down.

Kelso back in the passage, breathing hard, balanced on a rib, summoning the nerve.

The second door –

Very warm now, boy!

– the second door: the bathroom. Cistern lid off, propped against the toilet. Sink dragged away from the wall. A white plastic tub brimming with pinkish water that made Kelso think of diluted Georgian wine. He dipped his finger in and pulled it out sharply, shocked at the coldness, his fingertip sheathed in red.

Floating on the surface: a ring of hair still attached to a small flap of skin.

Let's go, boy.

Rib to rib, plaster dust in his hair, on his hands, all over his coat, his shoes –

He stumbled in his panic, lost his footing on the beam, and his left shoe punched a hole into the ceiling of the flat beneath. A piece of debris detached itself. He heard it fall into the darkness of the empty apartment. It took him half a minute and both hands to pull his foot free, and then he was out of there.

He squashed himself around the door and into the corridor and moved quickly back along the passage, past the abandoned apartments, towards the stairs. He heard a thump.

He stopped and listened.

Thump.

Oh, you're hot, now, boy, you're very, very hot . . .

It was the elevator. It was someone inside the elevator.

Thump.

*

Archangel

THE Lubyanka, the still of night, the long black car with the
engine running, two agents in overcoats charging down the
steps – *was there no escaping the past?* thought Suvorin,
bitterly, as they accelerated away. He was surprised there were
no tourists on hand to record this traditional scene of life in
Mother Russia. *Why not put it in the album, darling, between
St Basil's Cathedral and a troika in the snow?*

They thumped into a dip at the bottom of the hill near the
Metropol Hotel, and his head connected with the cushioned
roof. In the front seat, next to the driver, Netto was unfolding
a large-scale map of the Moscow streets of a detail that no
tourist would ever see because it was still officially secret.
Suvorin snapped on the interior light and leaned forward for
a better look. The apartment blocks of the Victory of the
Revolution complex were scattered like postage stamps
across the Tagansko–Krasno metro line, in the north-west
outer suburb.

'How long do you reckon? Twenty minutes?'

'Fifteen,' said the driver, showing off. He gunned the
engine, shot the lights, swung right, and Suvorin was pitched
the other way, against the door. He had a brief impression of
the Lenin Library flashing past.

'Relax,' he said, 'for pity's sake. We don't want to get a
ticket.'

They sped on. Once they were clear of the centre, Netto
unlocked the glove compartment and handed Suvorin a well-
oiled Makarov and a clip of ammunition. Suvorin took it
reluctantly, felt the unfamiliar weight in his hand, checked
the mechanism and sighted briefly at a passing birch tree. He
hadn't joined the service because he enjoyed this kind of
thing. He had joined because his father was a diplomat who
had taught him early on that the best thing to do if you lived

153

in the Soviet Union was to get a posting abroad. Guns? Suvorin hadn't set foot on the Yasenevo range inside a year. He gave the weapon back to Netto who shrugged and stuffed it in his own pocket.

A blue dot grew noisily in the road behind them, swelled and flashed past like an angry fly – a patrol car of the Moscow militia. It dwindled into the distance.

'Asshole,' said their driver.

A few minutes later they turned off the main road and headed into the wilderness of concrete and wasteland that was the Victory of the Revolution. Fifteen years in Kolyma, thought Suvorin, then welcome home to this. And the joke was, it must have seemed like paradise.

Netto said, 'According to the map, Block Nine should be just round this corner.'

'Slow down,' ordered Suvorin, suddenly, putting his hand on the driver's shoulder. 'Can you hear something?'

He wound down his window. Another siren, off to the left. It faded for a moment, muffled by a building, then became very loud, and colours burst ahead – a blue and yellow light-show, rather pretty, moving fast. For a couple of seconds the patrol car seemed to be coming straight at them but then it swung off the road and bounced over the rough ground, and a moment later they were level with it and could see the entrance to the block themselves, lit up like a fairyland – three cars, an ambulance, people moving, shadowed tracks in the snow.

They cruised round the building a couple of times, a trio of ghouls, unnoticed, as the stretcher men brought out the body and then Kelso was driven away.

Chapter Eleven

SIMONOV TELLS THE *following story.*

At meetings of the Council of People's Commissars, it was Comrade Stalin's habit to rise from his place at the head of the long table and to pace behind the backs of the participants. Nobody dared to look round at him: they could establish where he was only by the soft squeak of his leather boots or by the passing fragrance of his Dunhill pipe. On this particular occasion, the conversation concerned the large number of recent plane crashes. The head of the air force, Rychagov, was drunk. 'There will continue to be a high level of accidents,' he blurted out, 'as long as we're compelled by you to go up in flying coffins.' There was a long silence, at the end of which Stalin murmured, 'You really shouldn't have said that.' A few days later, Rychagov was shot.

One could quote any number of such stories. His favourite technique, according to Khrushchev, was suddenly to look at a man and say: 'Why is your face so shifty today? Why can't you look Comrade Stalin directly in the eyes?' That was the moment when one's life hung in the balance.

Stalin's use of terror seems to have been partly instinctive (he was naturally physically violent: he sometimes struck his subordinates in the face) and partly calculated. 'The people,' he told Maria Svanidze, 'need a tsar.' And the tsar upon whom he modelled himself was Ivan the Terrible. We have written confirmation of that here in this archive, in Stalin's personal library, which contains a copy of A. M. Tolstoy's 1942 play, Ivan Grozny *(F558 O3 D350). Not only has Stalin corrected the speeches of Ivan to make them sound more clipped and laconic –*

to sound more like himself, in fact – but he has also scrawled repeatedly over the title page 'Teacher'.

Indeed, he had only one criticism of his role model: that he was too weak. As he told the director, Sergei Eisenstein: 'Ivan the Terrible would execute someone and then spend a long time repenting and praying. God got in his way in this matter. He ought to have been still more decisive!' (Moskovskie novosti, no. 32, 1988).

Stalin was nothing if not decisive.

Professor I. A. Kuganov estimates that some sixty-six million people were killed in the USSR between 1917 and 1953 – shot, tortured, starved mostly, frozen or worked to death. Others say the true figure is a mere forty-five million. Who knows?

Neither estimate, by the way, includes the thirty million now known to have been killed in the Second World War.

To put this loss in context: the Russian Federation today has a population of roughly 150 million. Assuming the ravages inflicted by communism had never occurred, and assuming normal demographic trends, the actual population should be about 300 million.

And yet – and this is surely one of the most astounding phenomena of the age – Stalin continues to enjoy a wide measure of popular support in this half-empty land. His statues have been taken down, true. The street names have been changed. But there have been no Nuremberg Trials, as there were in Germany. There has been no process here equivalent to de-Nazification. There has been no Truth Commission, of the sort established in South Africa.

And the opening of the archives? 'Confronting the past'? Come, ladies and gentlemen, let us say frankly what we all know to be the case. That the Russian government today is scared, and that it is actually harder to gain access to the archives now than it was six or seven years ago. You all know the facts as well as I do. Beria's files: closed. The Politburo's files: closed. Stalin's files – the real files, I mean, not the window dressing on offer here: closed.

I can see my remarks are not being well received by one or two colleagues –

All right, I shall draw them to a conclusion, with this observation: that there can now be no doubt that it is Stalin rather than Hitler who is the most alarming figure of the twentieth century.

I say this –

I say this not merely because Stalin killed more people than Hitler – although clearly he did – and not even because Stalin was more of a psychopath than Hitler – although clearly he was. I say it because Stalin, unlike Hitler, has not yet been exorcised. And also because Stalin was not a one-off like Hitler, an eruption from nowhere. Stalin stands in a historical tradition of rule by terror which existed before him, which he refined, and which could exist again. His, not Hitler's, is the spectre that should worry us.

Because, you know, you think about it. You hail a taxi in Munich – you don't find the driver displaying Hitler's portrait in his cab, do you? Hitler's birthplace isn't a shrine. Hitler's grave isn't piled with fresh flowers every day. You can't buy tapes of Hitler's speeches on the streets of Berlin. Hitler isn't routinely praised as 'a great patriot' by leading German politicians. Hitler's old party didn't receive more than forty per cent of the votes in the last German election –

But all these things are true of Stalin in Russia today, which is what makes the words of Yevtushenko, in 'The Heirs of Stalin', more relevant now than ever:

'So I ask our government
  To double
    To treble
      The guard
        Over this tomb.'

FLUKE Kelso was escorted into the headquarters of the central division of the Moscow City Militia shortly before three a.m. And there he was left, washed up with the rest of the night's detritus – half a dozen hookers, a Chechen pimp, two white-faced Belgian bankers, a troupe of transsexual dancers from Turkestan and the usual midnight chorus of outraged lunatics, tramps and bloodied addicts. High-corniced ceilings and half-blown chandeliers gave proceedings a Revolutionary epic look.

He sat alone on a hard wooden bench, his head leaning back on the peeling plaster, staring ahead, unseeing. So that – *that* was what it looked like? Oh, you could spend half a lifetime *writing* about it all, about the millions – about Marshal Tukhachevsky, say, beaten to a pulp by the NKVD: there was his confession in the archives, still sprinkled with his dried blood: you even held it in your hands – and you thought for a moment you had a sense of what it must have been like, but then you confronted the reality and you realised you hadn't understood it at all, you hadn't even *begun* to know what it was like.

After a while two militia men wandered up and stood at the metal drinking fountain next to him, discussing the case of the Uzbeki bandit, Tsexer, apparently machine-gunned earlier that evening in the cloakroom of the Babylon.

'Is anyone dealing with my case?' interrupted Kelso. 'It is a murder.'

'Ah, a murder!' One of the men rolled his eyes in mock surprise. The other laughed. They dropped their paper cones in the trash can and moved off.

'Wait!' shouted Kelso.

Across the corridor, an elderly woman with a bandaged hand started screaming.

He sank back on to the bench.

Presently, a third officer, powerfully built, with a Gorky moustache, came wearily downstairs and introduced himself as Investigator Belenky, a homicide detective. He was holding a piece of grubby paper.

'You're the witness in the business involving the old man, Rapazin?'

'Rapava,' corrected Kelso.

'Right. That's it.' Belenky squinted at the top and bottom of the paper. Perhaps it was the walrus moustache or maybe it was his watery eyes but he seemed immensely sad. He sighed. 'Okay. We'd better have a statement.'

Belenky led him up a grand staircase to the second floor, to a room with flaking green walls and an uneven, shiny woodblock floor. He gestured to Kelso to sit, and put a pad of lined forms in front of him.

'The old man had Stalin's papers,' began Kelso, lighting a cigarette. He exhaled quickly. 'You ought to know that. Almost certainly he had them hidden in his apartment. That's why –'

But Belenky wasn't listening. 'Everything you can remember.' He slapped a blue biro down on the table.

'But you hear what I'm saying? Stalin's papers –'

'Right, right.' The Russian still wasn't listening. 'We'll sort out the details later. Need a statement first.'

'All of it?'

159

'Of course. Who you are. How you met the old man. What you were doing at the apartment. The whole story. Write it down. I'll be back.'

After he had gone, Kelso stared at the blank paper for a couple of minutes. Mechanically, he wrote his full name, his date of birth and his address in neat Cyrillic script. His mind was a fog. '*I arrived,*' he wrote, and paused. The plastic pen felt as heavy between his fingers as a crowbar. '*I arrived in Moscow on –*' He couldn't even remember the date. He who was normally so good at dates! (25 October 1917, the battle-cruiser *Aurora* shells the Winter Palace and begins the Revolution; 17 January 1927, Leon Trotsky is expelled from the Politburo; 23 August 1939: the Molotov–Ribbentrop pact is signed . . .) He bent his head to the desk. '*– I arrived in Moscow on the morning of Monday October 26 from New York at the invitation of the Russian Archive Service to deliver a short lecture on Josef Stalin . . .*'

He finished his statement in less than an hour. He did as he was told and left nothing out – the symposium, Rapava's visit, the Stalin notebook, the Lenin Library, Yepishev and the meeting with Mamantov, the house on Vspolnyi Street, the freshly dug earth, Robotnik and Rapava's daughter . . . He filled seven pages with his tiny scrawl, and took the final section even quicker, hurrying over the scene in the apartment, the discovery of the body, his desperate search for a working telephone in the next-door block, eventually rousing a young woman with a baby on her hip. It felt good to be writing again, to be imposing some kind of rational order on the chaos of the past.

Belenky put his head round the door just as Kelso added the final sentence.

'You can forget that now.'

'I've done.'

'No?' Belenky stared at the small pile of sheets and then at Kelso. There was a commotion in the corridor behind him. He frowned, then yelled over his shoulder, 'Tell him to wait.' He came into the room and closed the door.

Something had happened to Belenky, that much was obvious. His tunic was unbuttoned, his tie loose. Dark patches of sweat stained his khaki shirt. Without taking his eyes off Kelso's face, he held out his massive hand and Kelso gave him the statement. He sat down with a grunt on the opposite side of the table and took a plastic case from his breast pocket. From the case he withdrew a surprisingly deli-cate pair of gold-framed, half-moon glasses, shook them open, perched them on the end of his nose, and began to read.

His heavy chin jutted forwards. Occasionally, his eyes would flicker up from the page to Kelso, study him for a moment, then return to the text. He winced. His moustache sagged lower over his tightening lips. He chewed the knuckle of his right thumb.

When he laid the final page aside he gave a sigh.

'And this is true?'

'All of it.'

'Well, fuck your mother.' Belenky took off his glasses and rubbed his eyes with the side of his hand. 'Now what am I supposed to do?'

'Mamantov,' said Kelso. 'He must have been involved. I was careful not to give him any details but –'

The door opened and a small, thin man, a Laurel to Belenky's Hardy, said, in a frightened voice, 'Sima! Quick! They're here!'

Belenky gave Kelso a significant look, gathered the statement together and pushed back his chair. 'You'll have to

161

go down to the cells for a bit. Don't be alarmed.'

At the mention of cells Kelso felt a spasm of panic. 'I'd like to speak to someone from the embassy.'

Belenky stood and slid his tie back up into a tight knot, fastened the buttons of his tunic, tugged the jacket down in a hopeless attempt to straighten it.

'Can I speak to someone from the embassy?' repeated Kelso. 'I'd like to know my rights.'

Belenky squared his shoulders and moved towards the door. 'Too late,' he said.

IN the cells beneath the headquarters of the Central Division of the Moscow City Militia, Kelso was roughly frisked and parted from his passport, wallet, watch, fountain pen, belt, tie and shoelaces. He watched them shovelled into a cardboard envelope, signed a form, was handed a receipt. Then, with his boots in one hand, his chit in the other and his coat over his arm, he followed the guard down a whitewashed passage lined on either side with steel doors. The guard was suffering from a plague of boils – his neck above his greasy brown collar looked like a plate of red dumplings – and at the sound of his footsteps, the inmates of some of the cells began a frantic shouting and banging. He took no notice.

The eighth cubicle on the left. Three yards by four. No window. A metal cot. No blanket. An enamel pail in the corner with a square of stained wood for a lid.

Kelso went slowly into the cell on his stockinged feet, threw his coat and boots down on the cot. Behind him, the door swung shut with a submarine clang.

Acceptance. That, he had learned in Russia many years ago, was the secret of survival. At the frontier, when your papers were being checked for the fifteenth time. At the road block, when you were pulled over for no reason and kept waiting for an hour and a half. At the ministry, when you went to get your visa stamped and no one had bothered to show up. Accept it. Wait. Let the system exhaust itself. Protest will only raise your blood pressure.

The spyhole in the centre of the door clicked open, stayed open for a moment, clicked shut. He listened to the guard's footsteps retreat.

He sat on the bed and closed his eyes and saw, at once, unbidden, like the after-image of a bright light imprinted on his retina, the white and naked body revolving in the down draught of the elevator shaft – shoulders, heels and trussed hands rebounding gently off the walls.

He sprang at the door and hammered on it with his empty boots and yelled for a while, until he'd got something out of himself. Then he turned and rested his back against the metal, confronting the narrow limits of his cell. Slowly he allowed himself to slide down until he was resting on his haunches, his arms clasped around his knees.

TIME. Now here is a peculiar commodity, boy. The measurement of time. Best accomplished, obviously, with a watch. But, lacking a watch, a man may use instead the ebb and flow of light and dark. Lacking, however, a window through which to see such movement, the reliance must be devolved upon some inner mechanism of the mind. But if the mind has received a shock, the mechanism is disturbed, and time becomes as the ground is to a drunkard, variable.

Thus Kelso, at some point indeterminate, transferred his body from the doorway to the cot and drew his coat across himself. His teeth were chattering.

His thoughts were random, disconnected. He thought of Mamantov, going back over their meeting again and again, trying to remember if he had said anything that could have led him to Rapava. And he thought about Rapava's daughter and the way he had broken his word in his statement. She had abandoned him. Now he had revealed her as a whore. So the world turns. Somewhere, presumably, the militia would have her address on file. Her name as well. The news about her father would be broken to her, and she would be – what? Dry-eyed, he was fairly sure. Yet vengeful.

In his dreams he moved to kiss her again but she evaded his embrace. She danced jerkily across the snow outside the apartment block while O'Brian paraded up and down pretending to be Hitler. Madame Mamantov raged against her madness. And behind a door somewhere, Papu Rapava went on knocking to be let out. In here, boy! Thump. Thump. *Thump.*

HE woke to find a cool blue eye regarding him through the spyhole. The metal eyelid drooped and closed, the lock rattled.

Behind the pustulous guard there stood a second man – blond-headed, well-dressed – and Kelso's first thought was a happy one: *The embassy, they've come to get me out.* But then blond-head said, in Russian, 'Dr Kelso, put your boots on, please,' and the guard shook the contents of the envelope out on to the cot.

Kelso bent to thread his laces. The stranger, he noticed, was wearing a smart pair of western brogues. He straightened and strapped on his watch and saw that it was only six-twenty. A mere two hours in the cells, but enough to last him a lifetime. He felt more human with his boots on. A man can face the world with something on his feet. They passed down the corridor, triggering the same desperate hammering and shouting.

He assumed he would be taken back upstairs for more questioning, but instead they came out into a rear courtyard where a car was waiting with two men in the front seats. Blond-head opened the rear passenger door for Kelso – 'Please,' he said, with cold politeness – then went round and got in the other side. The interior of the car was hot and fetid, as if at the end of a long journey, sweetened only by blond-head's delicate aftershave. They pulled away, out of militia headquarters and into the quiet street. Nobody spoke.

It was beginning to get light – light enough, at least, for Kelso to recognise roughly where they were heading. He had already marked this trio down as secret police, which meant the FSB, which meant the Lubyanka. But to his surprise he realised they were travelling east, not west. They came down the Noviy Arbat, past the deserted shops, and the Ukraina came into view. So they were taking him back to the hotel, he thought. But he was wrong again. Instead of crossing the bridge they turned right and followed the course of the Moskva. Dawn was coming on quickly now, like a chemical reaction, darkness dissolving across the river, first to grey and then to a dirty alkali blue. Streaks of smoke and steam from the factory chimneys on the opposite bank – a tannery, a brewery – turned a corrosive pink.

They drove on in silence for a few more minutes and then suddenly swung off the embankment and parked in a derelict patch of reclaimed land that jutted out into the water. A couple of big sea-birds flapped and rose, and span away, crying. Blond-head was out first and then, after a brief hesitation, Kelso followed him. It crossed his mind that they had brought him to the perfect spot for an accident: a simple push, a flurry of news reports, a long investigation for a London colour supplement, suspicions raised and then forgotten. But he put a brave face on it. What else could he do?

Blond-head was reading the statement Kelso had given to the militia. It flapped in the breeze that was coming off the river. Something about him was familiar.

'Your plane,' he said, without turning round, 'leaves Sheremetevo-2 at one-thirty. You will be on board it.'

'Who are you?'

'You'll be taken back to your hotel now, and then you'll catch the bus to the airport with your colleagues.'

'Why are you doing this?'

'You may try to re-enter the Russian Federation in the near future. In fact, I'm sure you will: you're a persistent fellow, anyone can see that. But I must tell you that your application for a visa will be rejected.'

'This is a bloody *outrage*.' It was stupid, of course, to lose his temper, but he was too tired and shaken-up to help himself. 'A complete bloody *disgrace*. Anyone would think that I was the killer.'

'But you *did* kill him.' The Russian turned round. 'You *are* the killer.'

'This is a joke, is it? I didn't have to come forward. I didn't have to call the militia. I could have run away.'

And don't think I didn't consider it —

'It's here in your own words.' Blond-head slapped the statement. 'You went to Mamantov yesterday afternoon and told him a "witness from the old time" had approached you with information about Stalin's papers. That was a death sentence.'

Kelso faltered. 'I never gave a name. I've been over that conversation in my mind a hundred times –'

'Mamantov didn't need a name. He already *had* the name.'

'You can't be certain –'

'Papu Rapava,' said the Russian, with exaggerated patience, 'was re-investigated by the KGB in nineteen eighty-three. The investigation was at the request of the deputy chief of the Fifth Directorate – Vladimir Pavlovich Mamantov. Do you see?'

Kelso closed his eyes.

'Mamantov knew precisely who you were talking about. There is no other "witness from the old time". Everyone else is dead. So: fifteen minutes after you left Mamantov's apartment, Mamantov also left. He even knew where the old man lived, from his file. He had seven, possibly eight hours to question Rapava. With the assistance of his friends. Believe me, a professional like Mamantov can do a lot of damage to a person in eight hours. Would you like me to give you some of the medical details? No? Then go back to New York, Dr Kelso, and play your games of history in somebody else's country, because this isn't England or America, the past isn't safely dead here. In Russia, the past carries razors and a pair of handcuffs. Ask Papu Rapava.'

A gust of wind swept the surface of the river, raised waves, set a nearby buoy clanking against its rusting chains.

'I can testify,' said Kelso after a while. 'To arrest Mamantov, you'll need my evidence.'

For the first time, the Russian smiled. 'How well do you know Mamantov?'

'Hardly at all.'

'You know him hardly at all. That is your good fortune. Some of us have come to know him well. And I can assure you that Comrade V. P. Mamantov will have no fewer than six witnesses – none of them below the rank of full colonel – who will swear that he spent the whole of last evening with them, discussing charity work, one hundred miles from Papu Rapava's apartment. So much for the value of your testimony.'

He tore Kelso's statement in half, then halved it again, and again – kept on until it couldn't be reduced further. He crumpled the pieces between his hands, cupped them and threw the fragments out across the water. The wind caught them. The seagulls swooped in the hope of food then wheeled away, shrieking with disappointment.

'Nothing is as it was,' he said. 'You ought to know that. The investigation begins again from scratch this morning. This statement was never taken. You were never detained by the militia. The officer who questioned you has been promoted and is being transferred, even as we speak, by military transport plane to Magadan.'

'Magadan?' Magadan was on the eastern rim of Siberia, four thousand miles away.

'Oh, we'll bring him back,' said the Russian, airily, 'when this is sorted out. What we don't want is the Moscow press corps trampling over everything. That really would be embarrassing. Now, I tell you all this, knowing there's nothing we can do to prevent you publishing your version of events abroad. But there will be no official corroboration from here, you understand? Rather the contrary. We reserve the right to make public *our* record of your day's activity, in which your motives will be made to look quite different. For example: you were arrested for indecent exposure to a couple of children in the Zoopark, the daughters of one of my men. Or you were picked up drunk on the Smolenskaya embankment, urinating into the river, and had to be locked up for violent and abusive behavior.'

'Nobody will believe it,' said Kelso, trying to summon a last vestige of outrage. But, of course, they would. He could make a list now of everyone who would believe it. He said, bitterly, 'So that's it then? Mamantov goes free? Or perhaps you'll try to find Stalin's papers yourselves, so you can bury them somewhere, like you people bury everything else that's "embarrassing"?'

'Oh, but you *irritate* me,' said the Russian, and now it was his turn to lose his temper. 'People like you. How much more is it you want of us? You've won, but is that enough? No, you have to rub our faces in it – Stalin, Lenin, Beria: I'm sick of hearing their damn names – make us turn out all our filthy closets, wallow in guilt, so you can feel superior –'

Kelso snorted, 'You sound like Mamantov.'

'I *despise* Mamantov,' said the Russian. 'Do you understand me? For the same reason I despise you. We want to put an end to Comrade Mamantov and his kind – what d'you suppose this is all about? But now you've come along – blundered into something much bigger – something you can't even begin to understand –'

He stopped – goaded, Kelso could tell, into saying more than he intended – and then Kelso realised where he must have seen him before.

'You were there, weren't you?' he said. 'When I went to see him. You were one of the men outside his apartment –'

But he was talking to himself. The Russian was striding back to the car.

'Take him to the Ukraina,' he said to the driver, 'then come back here and pick me up. I need some air.'

'Who *are* you?'

'Just go. And be grateful.'

Kelso hesitated but suddenly he was too tired to argue. He climbed, weary and defeated, into the back seat as the engine started. The Russian slammed the door on him, emphatically. He felt numb and shut his eyes again and there was Rapava's corpse swinging in the darkness. Thump. *Thump.* He opened his eyes and saw that it was the blond-headed man, knocking on the window. Kelso wound it down.

'A final thought.' He was making an effort to be polite again. He even smiled. 'We're working on the assumption, obviously, that Mamantov now has this notebook. But have you considered the alternative? Remember, Papu Rapava withstood six months of interrogation back in fifty-three, and then fifteen years in Kolyma. Suppose Mamantov and his friends didn't manage to break him in one evening. It's a possibility: it would explain the . . . ferocity of their behaviour: frustration. In that case, if you were Mamantov, who would you want to question next?' He banged on the roof. 'Sleep well in New York.'

SUVORIN watched the big car as it bounced over the rough ground and out of sight. He turned away, towards the river, and walked along the quayside, smoking his pipe, until he came to a big metal post set into the concrete, to which ships had moored in the communist time, before economics had accomplished what Hitler's bombers had never managed, and laid waste the docks. His performance had exhausted him. He wiped the surface with his handkerchief, sat down, and pulled out his photocopy of Kelso's statement. To have written so much – perhaps two thousand words – so quickly and with such clarity, after such an experience . . . Well, it proved his hunch: he was a clever one, this fellow, Fluke.

Troublesome. Persistent. *Clever.*

He went through the pages again with a gold propelling pencil and made a list of matters for Netto to check. They needed to visit the house on Vspolnyi Street – Beria's place, well, well. They ought to find this daughter of Rapava's. They should compile a list of every forensic document examiner in the Moscow region to whom Mamantov might take the notebook for authentication. And every handwriting expert. And they should find a couple of tame historians and ask them to make the best guess possible as to what this notebook might contain. *And and and . . .* He felt as though he was trying to stuff gas back into a cylinder with his hands.

He was still writing when Netto and the driver returned. He rose stiffly. To his dismay he found that the mooring-post had left a rust-coloured mark on the back of his beautiful coat, and he spent much of the journey to Yasenevo picking at it obsessively, trying to make it clean.

Chapter Twelve

KELSO'S HOTEL ROOM was in darkness, the curtains closed. He pulled aside the cheap nylon drapes. There was an odd smell of something – talcum powder? Aftershave? Someone had been in here. Blond-head, was it? Eau Sauvage? He lifted the telephone receiver. The line hummed. He felt breathless. His skin was crawling. He could have done with a whisky but the mini-bar was still empty after his night with Rapava; there was nothing in it apart from soda and orange juice. And he could have done with a bath but there wasn't a plug.

He guessed now who the blond-headed man was. He knew the species – smooth and sharply-dressed, westernised, *deracinated* – too sharp for the secret police. He had been meeting men like that at embassy receptions for more than twenty years, dodging their discreet invitations for lunch and drinks, listening to their carefully indiscreet jokes about life in Moscow. They used to be called the First Chief Directorate of the KGB. Now they called themselves the SVR. The name had changed but the job had not. Blond-head was a spy. And he was investigating Mamantov. They had set the spies on Mamantov, which was not much of a vote of confidence in the FSB.

At the thought of Mamantov, he stepped quickly over to the door and turned the heavy lock and set the chain. Through the spy-hole he took a fish-eyed squint down the empty corridor.

'*But you* did *kill him . . . You* are *the killer.*'

He was shaking now with delayed shock. He felt filthy,

somehow, defiled. The memory of the night was like grit against his skin.

He went into the little green-tiled bathroom, took off his clothes and turned on the shower, set the water as hot as he could bear, and soaped himself from head to foot. The suds turned grey with the Moscow grime. He stood under the steaming jet and let it scourge him for another ten minutes, thrashing his shoulders and his chest, then he stepped out of the tub, slopping water over the uneven lino. He lit a cigarette and smoked as he shaved, transferring it from one side of his mouth to the other, working his razor around it, standing in a puddle. Then he dried himself off, got into bed and pulled the cover up to his chin. But he didn't sleep.

A little after nine o'clock the telephone began to ring. The bell was shrill. It rang for a long while, stopped, then started again. This time, though, whoever it was hung up quickly.

A few minutes later, someone knocked softly on his bedroom door.

Kelso felt vulnerable now, naked. He waited ten minutes, threw off the sheet, dressed, packed – that didn't take long – then sat in one of the foam rubber chairs facing the door. The cover of the other chair was rucked, he noticed, the seat still slightly depressed from the imprint of poor Papu Rapava.

AT ten-fifteen, carrying his suitcase in one hand and with his raincoat over his arm, Kelso unlocked and unchained his door, checked the corridor and descended via the express elevator into the hubub of the ground floor.

He handed in his key at the reception desk and was in the act of turning away, towards the main entrance, when a man shouted 'Professor!'

It was O'Brian, hurrying over from the news-stand. He

was still wearing his clothes from the night before – jeans a little less pressed, T-shirt no longer as white – and he had a couple of newspapers tucked under his arm. He hadn't shaved. He seemed even bigger in the daylight. 'Morning, professor. So. What's new?'

Kelso made a groaning noise in the back of his throat but managed to hoist up a smile. 'Leaving, I'm afraid.' He displayed his suitcase, bag and coat.

'Now I'm sorry to hear that. Let me help you with those.'

'I'm fine.' He began to move around O'Brian. 'Really.'

'Aw, come on.' The reporter's arm flashed out, grabbing the handle, squeezing Kelso's fingers out of the way. In a second he had the suitcase. He quickly transferred it to his other hand, out of Kelso's reach. 'Where to, sir? Outside?'

'What the fuck are you playing at?' Kelso strode after him. People sitting in reception turned to watch. 'Give me back my case –'

'That was some night, though, wasn't it? That place? Those girls?' O'Brian shook his head and grinned as they walked. 'And then you go and find that body and all – must've been one hell of a shock. Look out, professor, here we go.'

He plunged through the revolving door and Kelso, after a hesitation, followed him. He came out the other side to find O'Brian looking serious.

'All right,' said O'Brian, 'don't let's embarrass one another. I know what's going on.'

'I will take my case now, thank you.'

'I decided to hang around outside Robotnik last night. Forgo the pleasures of the flesh.'

'My *case* –'

'Let's say I had a hunch. Saw you leave with the girl. Saw

you kiss her. Saw her *hit* you – what was that all about, by the way? Saw you get in her car. Saw you go into the apartment block. Saw you run out ten minutes later like all the hounds of hell were after you. And then I saw the cops arrive. Oh, professor, you are a character, you are a man of surprises.'

'And you're a creep.' Kelso began pulling on his raincoat, making an effort to seem unconcerned. 'What were you doing at Robotnik anyway? Don't tell me: it was a coincidence.'

'I go to Robotnik, sure,' said O'Brian. 'That's how I like my relationships: on a business footing. Why get a girl for free when you can pay for one, that's my philosophy.'

'God.' Kelso held out his hand. 'Just give me my case.'

'Okay, okay.' O'Brian glanced over his shoulder. The bus was in its usual place, waiting to ferry the historians to the airport. Moldenhauer was taking a picture of Saunders with the hotel in the background, Olga was watching them, fondly. 'If you want to know the truth, it was Adelman.'

Kelso drew his head back slowly. '*Adelman?*'

'Yeah, at the symposium yesterday, during the morning break, I asked Adelman where you were and he told me you were after some Stalin papers.'

'*Adelman* said that?'

'Oh, come on, don't tell me you trusted Adelman?' O'Brian grinned. 'One sniff of a scoop and you guys make the paparazzi look like choirboys. Adelman proposed a deal. Fifty-fifty. He said I should try to find the papers, see if there was anything in it, and if there was then he'd authenticate them. He told me everything you'd told him.'

'Including Robotnik?'

'Including Robotnik.'

'Bastard.'

Now Olga was taking a picture of Moldenhauer and Saunders. They stood shyly, side by side, and it struck Kelso for the first time that they were gay. Why hadn't he realised it before? This trip was nothing but surprises –

'Come on, professor. Don't get all shocked on me. And don't get shocked about Adelman, either. This is a story. This is a *hell* of a story. And it just keeps on getting better. Not only d'you find this poor bastard hanging in the elevator shaft with his pecker in his mouth, you also tell the militia that the guy who did it is none other than Vladimir Mamantov. And not only that – the whole investigation's now been canned on the orders of the Kremlin. Or so I hear. What's so funny?'

'Nothing.' Kelso couldn't help smiling, thinking of the blond-headed spy. ('*What we don't want is the Moscow press corps trampling over everything. . .*') 'Well, I'll say this for you, Mr O'Brian: you have good contacts.'

O'Brian made a dismissive gesture. 'There's not a secret in this town that can't be bought for a bottle of Scotch and fifty bucks. And man, I tell you, they're in a *rage* down there, you know? They're leaking like a *nuclear reactor*. They don't like being told what to do.'

The driver of the bus sounded his horn. Saunders was on board now. Moldenhauer had taken out his handkerchief to wave goodbye. Kelso could see the faces of the other historians through the glass, like pale fish in an aquarium.

He said, 'You really had better give me my case now. I've got to go.'

'You can't just run out, professor.' But there was a defeated tone to his appeal and this time he let Kelso take the handle. 'Come on, Fluke, just one little interview? One brief comment?' He followed at Kelso's heels, an importunate

176

beggar. 'I need an interview, to stand this thing up.'

'It would be irresponsible.'

'Irresponsible? Balls! You won't talk because you want to keep it all for yourself! Well, you're crazy. The cover-up isn't working. This story's going to blow – if not today, tomorrow.'

'And you want it today, naturally, ahead of everyone else?'

'That's my job. Oh, come on, professor. Stop being so goddamn snooty. We're not so very different –'

Kelso was at the door of the bus. It opened with a pneumatic sigh. From the interior came a ragged, ironic cheer.

'Goodbye, Mr O'Brian.'

Still O'Brian wouldn't give up. He climbed up on to the first step. 'Take a look at what's happening here.' He jammed his roll of newspapers into Kelso's coat pocket. 'Take a look. That's Russia. Nothing here keeps until *tomorrow*. This place might not be here *tomorrow*. You're – oh, shit –'

He had to jump to avoid the closing door. He gave a last, despairing thump on the bodywork from outside.

'Dr Kelso,' said Olga, stonily.

'Olga,' said Kelso.

He pushed his way down the aisle. When he came level with Adelman he stopped, and Adelman, who must have watched his whole encounter with O'Brian, glanced away. Beyond the muddy glass the reporter was trudging towards the hotel, his hands in his pockets. Moldenhauer's white handkerchief fluttered in farewell.

The bus lurched. Kelso turned, half-walking, half-tumbling, towards his usual place, alone and at the back.

*

FOR five minutes he did nothing except stare out of the window. He knew he ought to write this down, prepare another record while it was still clear in his mind. But he couldn't, not yet. For now, all roads of thought seemed to lead back to the same image of the figure in the elevator-shaft.

Like a side of beef in a butcher's shop –

He patted his pockets to find his cigarettes and pulled out O'Brian's newspapers. He threw them on the seat beside him and tried to ignore them. But after a couple of minutes he found himself reading the headlines upside down, then reluctantly he picked them up.

They were nothing special, just a couple of English-language freesheets, given away in every hotel lobby.

The *Moscow Times*. Domestic news: the President was ill again, or drunk again, or both. A serial cannibal in the Kemerovo region was believed to have killed and eaten eighty people. Interfax reported that 60,000 children were sleeping on the streets each night in Moscow. Gorbachev was recording another television commercial for Pizza Hut. A bomb had been planted at the Nagornaya metro station by a group opposed to plans to remove Lenin's mummified body from public display in Red Square.

Foreign news: The IMF was threatening to withold $700 million in aid unless Moscow cut its budget deficit.

Business news: interest rates had tripled, stock market prices halved.

Religious news: A nineteen-year-old nun with ten thousand followers was predicting the end of the world on Hallowe'en. A statue of the Virgin Mother was trundling around the Black Earth region, weeping real blood. There was a holy man from Tarko-Sele who spoke in tongues.

There were fakirs and Pentecostalists, faith healers, shamans, workers of miracles, anchorites and marabouts and followers of the *skoptsy*, who believed themselves the Lords Incarnate . . . It was like Rasputin's time. The whole country was a tumult of bloody auguries and false prophets.

He picked up the other paper, *The eXile*, this one written for young westerners like O'Brian working in Moscow. No religion here, but a lot of crime:

> In the village of Kamenka, in the Smolenskaya Oblast, where the local collective farm is bankrupt and state employees haven't been paid all year, the big summer activity for kids is hanging around the Moscow–Minsk highway and sniffing gasoline, bought in half-litre jugs for a rouble. In August, two of the biggest gasoline addicts, Pavel Mikheenkov, 11, and Anton Malyarenko, 13, graduated from their favourite pastime – torturing cats – to tying a five year-old boy named Sasha Petrochenkov to a tree and burning him alive. Malyarenk was deported to his native Tashkent, but Mikheenkov has had to stay in Kamenka, unpunished: sending him to reform school would cost 15,000 roubles and the town doesn't have the money. The victim's mother, Svetlana Petrochenkova, has been told she can have her son's killer sent away if she digs up the money herself, but failing that must live with him in the village. According to police, Mikheenkov had been drinking vodka regularly with his parents since the age of four.

He turned the page quickly and found a guide to Moscow night life. Gay bars – Dyke, The Three Monkeys, Queer

Nation; strip clubs – Navada, Rasputin, The Intim Peep Show; nightclubs – the Buchenwald (where the staff wore Nazi uniforms), Bulgakov, Utopiya. He looked up Robotnik: *'No place could better exemplify the excesses of the New Russia than Robotnik: bitchin interior, ear-splitting techno, Babe-O-Litas and their flathead keepers, Die Hard security, black-eyed patrons sucking down Evians. Get laid and see someone get shot.'*

That sounded about right, he thought.

THE departure terminal at Sheremetevo-2 was crammed with people trying to get out of Russia. Queues formed like cells under a microscope – grew from nothing, wormed back on themselves, broke, re-formed, and merged into other queues: queues for customs, for tickets, for security, for passport controls. You finished one and joined the next. The hall was dark and cavernous, sour with the reek of aviation spirit and the thin acid of anxiety. Adelman, Duberstein, Byrd, Saunders and Kelso, plus a couple of Americans who had been staying at the Mir – Pete Maddox of Princeton and Vobster of Chicago – stood in a group at the end of the nearest line while Olga went off to see if she could speed things up.

After a couple of minutes, they still hadn't moved. Kelso ignored Adelman who sat on his suitcase reading a biography of Chekhov with extravagant intensity. Saunders sighed and flapped his arms with frustration. Maddox wandered away and came back to report that customs seemed to be opening every bag.

'Shit, and I bought an icon,' complained Duberstein. 'I knew I shouldn't've bought an icon. I'll never get it through.'

'Where'd you get it?'

'That big bookstore on the Noviy Arbat.'

'Give it to Olga. She'll get it out. How much d'you pay?'

'Five hundred bucks.'

'Five *hundred?*'

Kelso remembered he hadn't any money. There was a news-stand at the end of the terminal. He needed more cigarettes. If he asked for a seat in smoking he could keep clear of the others.

'Phil,' he said to Duberstein, 'you couldn't lend me ten dollars, could you?'

Duberstein started laughing. 'What're you going to do, Fluke? Buy Stalin's notebook?'

Saunders sniggered. Velma Byrd raised her hand to her mouth and looked away.

'You told them as well?' Kelso stared at Adelman in disbelief.

'And why not?' Adelman licked a finger and turned over a page without looking up. 'Is it a secret?'

'Tell you what,' said Duberstein, pulling out his wallet. 'Here's twenty. Buy one for me as well.'

They all laughed at that, and openly this time, watching Kelso to see what he would do. He took the money.

'All right, Phil,' he said, quietly. 'I'll tell you what. Let's make a deal. If Stalin's notebook turns up by the end of the year, I'll just keep this and then we're quits. But if it doesn't, I'll pay you back a thousand dollars.'

Maddox gave a low whistle.

'Fifty to one,' said Duberstein, swallowing. 'You're offering me fifty to one?'

'We've got a deal?'

'Well, you bet.' Duberstein laughed again, but nervously this time. He glanced around at the others. 'You hear that everyone?'

They'd heard. They were staring at Kelso. And for him, at that moment, it was worth a thousand dollars – worth it just for the way they looked: open-mouthed, stricken, panicked. Even Adelman had temporarily forgotten his book.

'Easiest twenty dollars I ever made,' said Kelso. He stuffed the bill into his pocket and picked up his suitcase. 'Save my place for me, will you?'

He moved off across the crowded terminal, quickly, quitting while he was still ahead, easing his way through the people and the piles of luggage. He felt a childish pleasure. A few fleeting victories here and there – what more could a man hope for in this life?

Over the loudspeaker, a woman with a harsh voice made a deafening announcement about the departure of an Aeroflot flight to Delhi.

At the news-stand he made a quick check to see if they had the paperback of his book. They did not. Naturally. He turned his attention to a rack of magazines. Last week's *Time* and *Newsweek*, and the current *Der Spiegel*. So. He would take *Der Spiegel*. It would do him good. It would certainly last him an eleven-hour plane ride. He fished in his pocket for Duberstein's $20 and turned towards the till. Through the plate glass window he could see the wet sweep of concrete, a jammed line of cars and taxis and buses, grey buildings, abandoned trolleys, a girl with cropped dark hair, a white face watching him. He looked away casually. Frowned. Checked himself.

He stuffed the magazine back into the rack and returned to the window. It was her, all right, standing alone, in jeans and a fleece-lined leather jacket. His breath misted on the cold glass. *Wait*, he mouthed at her. She stared at him blankly. He pointed at her feet. *Stay there.*

To get to her he had to walk away from her, following the line of the glass wall, trying to find an exit. The first set of doors was chained shut. The second opened. He came out into the cold and wet. She was standing about fifty yards away. He looked back at the crowded terminal – he couldn't see the others – and then at her, and now she was moving away from him, heading across a pedestrian crossing, heedless of the cars. He hesitated: what to do? A bus momentarily wiped her from view and that made his mind up for him. He hoisted his luggage and set off after her, breaking into a trot. She drew him on, always maintaining the same distance, until they were into the big outdoor car park, and then he lost her.

Grey light, snow and frozen slush. The stink of fuel much sharper here. Row upon row of boxy cars, some muffled white, others thinly wrapped in a film of mud and grit. He walked on. The air shook. A big old Tupolev jet swept directly over his head, so low he could see the lines of rust where the plates of the fuselage were welded together. Instinctively, he ducked, just as a sandy-coloured Lada emerged slowly from the end of the line and stopped, its engine running.

SHE didn't make it easy for him, even then. She didn't drive over to where he was; he had to walk to her. She didn't open the door; he had to do it. She didn't speak; it was left to him to break the silence. She didn't even tell him her name – not then, at least, although he discovered it later. She was called Zinaida. Zinaida Rapava.

She knew what had happened, that was obvious by the strain on her face, and he felt guiltily relieved at that, because at least he wouldn't have to break the news. He had always been a coward when it came to breaking bad news – that was one reason he'd been married three times. He sat in the front passenger seat, his suitcase wedged across his knees. The heater was running. The windscreen wiper flicked intermittently across the dirty glass. He knew he would have to say something soon. Delta to New York was the one event of the symposium he had no intention of missing.

'Tell me what I can do to help.'

'Who killed him?'

'A man named Vladimir Mamantov. Ex-KGB. He knew of your father from the old time.'

'The old time,' she said, bitterly.

Silence – long enough for the wiper to scrape back and forth, back and forth.

'How did you know where to find me?'

'Always, all my life: the *old time*.'

Another Tupolev rumbled low overhead.

'Listen,' he said, 'I've got to go in a minute. I've got to catch a plane to New York. When I get there, I'm going to write everything down – are you listening? I'll send you a copy. Tell me where to send it. You need anything, I'll help.'

It was hard to move with his case on his lap. He unbuttoned his coat and reached awkwardly into his inside pocket for his pen. She wasn't listening to him. She was staring straight ahead, talking almost to herself.

'It'd been years since I saw him. Why would I want to? I hadn't been near that dump in eight years till you asked me to take you.' She turned to him for the first time. She had washed off her makeup. She looked younger, more pretty. Her leather jacket was old, brown, zipped tight to the neck. 'After I left you, I went home. Then I went back to his place again. I had to find out – you know – what was going on.

Never saw so many cops in my life. You'd been taken away by then. I didn't say who I was. Not to the cops. I had to think things through. I –' She stopped. She seemed baffled, lost.

'What's your name?' he said. 'Where can I reach you?'

'Then, this morning, I went to the Ukraina. I rang you. Went up to your room. When they said you'd checked out I came here and waited.'

'Can't you just tell me your name?' He looked at his watch, hopelessly. 'Only I've got to catch this plane, you see.'

'I don't ask favours,' she said fiercely. 'I never ask favours.'

'Listen, don't worry. I want to help. I feel responsible.'

'Then help me. He said you'd help me'

'*He?*'

'The thing is, mister, he's left me something.' Her leather jacket creaked as she unzipped it. She felt around inside and brought out a scrap of paper. 'Something worth a lot? In a toolbox? He says that you can tell me what it is.'

Chapter Thirteen

THEY DROVE OUT of the airport perimeter onto the St Petersburg highway and turned south towards the city. A big truck overtook them, its wheels as high as their roof, rocking them in its wake, soaking them in a filthy spray.

Kelso had promised himself he wouldn't look back, but of course he did – looked back and saw the terminal building, like a great grey ocean liner, sink out of sight behind a line of birch trees until only a few watery lights were visible, and then they disappeared.

He winced and nearly asked the girl to take him back. He gave her a sideways glance. In her scuffed flying jacket she looked intrepid: an aviatrix at the controls of her battered plane.

He said, 'Who's Sergo?'

'My brother.' She glanced in the rear-view mirror. 'He's dead.'

He turned the note over and read it again. Rough paper. Pencil scrawl. Written quickly. Stuffed under the door of her apartment, or so she said: she had found it when she got back after dropping Kelso outside her father's block.

My little one, Greetings!
I have been a bad one, you're right. All you said was right. So don't think I don't know it! But here is a chance to do some good. You wouldn't let me tell you yesterday, so listen now. Remember that place I used to have, when Mama was alive? It's still there! And there's a toolbox with a present for you that's worth a lot.

186

Are you listening, Zinaida?
Nothing will happen to me, but if it does – take the box and hide it safe. But it could be dangerous, so mind yourself. You'll see what I mean.
Destroy this note.
I kiss my little one,
Papa.
– There's a Britisher called Kelso, get him through the Ukraina, he knows the story. Remember your papa!
I kiss you again, Zinaida.
Remember Sergo!!

'So he came to see you – when was it? The day before yesterday?'

She nodded, without looking round at him, concentrating on the road. 'It was the first time I'd seen him in nearly ten years.'

'You didn't get on, then?'

'Oh, you're a smart one.' Her laugh was brief, sarcastic: a short expulsion of breath. 'No, we didn't get on.'

He ignored her aggression. She was entitled to it. 'What was he like, the last time you saw him?'

'Like?'

'His mood.'

'A bastard. Same as always.' She frowned at the oncoming traffic. 'He must have been waiting for me all night, outside my place. I got back about six. I'd been at the club, you know, been working. The moment he saw me he started shouting. Saw my clothes. Called me a whore.' She shook her head at the memory.

'Then what happened?'

'He followed me in. Into my place. I said to him, I said:

187

"You hit me, I'll take your fucking eye out, I'm not your little girl any more." That calmed him down.'

'What did he want?'

'To talk, he said. It was a shock after all that time. I didn't think he knew where I lived. I didn't even know he was still alive. Thought I'd got away from him for good. Oh, but he'd known, he said – known where I was for a long time. Said he used to come and watch me sometimes. He said, "You don't get away from the past that easily." Why did he come to see me?' She looked at Kelso for the first time since they'd left the airport. 'Can you tell me that?'

'What did he want to talk about?'

'I don't know. I wouldn't listen. I didn't want him in my place, looking at my things. I didn't want to hear his stories. He started going on about his time in the camps. I gave him some cigarettes to get rid of him and told him to go. I was tired and I'd got to go to work.'

'Work?'

'I work at GUM in the daytime. I learn law at college in the evenings. Some nights, I screw. Why? Is it a problem?'

'You lead a full life.'

'I have to.'

He tried to picture her behind the counter at GUM. 'What do you sell?'

'What?'

'At the store. What do you sell?'

'Nothing.' She checked the mirror again. 'I work the switchboard.'

Closer to the city, the road was clogged. They slowed to a crawl. There had been an accident up ahead. A rickety Skoda had run into the back of a big old Zhiguli. Broken glass and bits of metal were scattered across two lanes. The militia were on the scene. It looked as though one of the drivers had punched the other: he had splashes of blood on the front of his shirt. As they passed the policemen, Kelso turned his head away. The road cleared. They picked up speed.

He tried to fit all this together: Papu Rapava's last two days on earth. Tuesday 27 October: he goes to see his daughter for the first time in a decade, because, he says, he wants to talk. She throws him out, buys him off with a pack of cigarettes and a book of matches labelled 'Robotnik'. In the afternoon, he turns up, of all places, at the Institute of Marxism–Leninism and listens to Fluke Kelso deliver a paper on Josef Stalin. Then he follows Kelso back to the Ukraina and sits up all night drinking. And talking. He certainly talked. *Perhaps he told me what he would have told his daughter if she'd only listened.*

And then it's dawn and he leaves the Ukraina. This is now Wednesday 28 October. And what does he do after he's slipped away into the morning? Does he go to the deserted house on Vspolnyi Street and dig up the secret of his life? He must have done. And then he hides it, and he leaves a note for his daughter, telling her where to find it (*'remember that place I used to have when Mama was alive?'*) and then, late in the afternoon, his killers come for him. And either he had told them everything, or he hadn't, and if he hadn't, then it must have been partly out of love, surely? To make certain that the only thing he had in the world that might be worth anything should go not to them but to his daughter.

God, thought Kelso, what an ending. What a way to leave a life – and how in keeping with the rest of it.

'He must have cared for you,' said Kelso. He wondered if she knew how the old man had died. If she didn't, he couldn't bring himself to tell her. 'He must have cared for you, to have come to find you.'

'I don't think so. He used to hit me. And my mother. And my brother.' She glared at the oncoming traffic. 'He used to hit me when I was little. What does a child know?' She shook her head. 'I don't think so.'

Kelso tried to imagine the four of them in the one-bedroom apartment. Where would her parents have slept? On a mattress in the sitting-room? And Rapava, after a decade and a half in Kolyma – violent, unstable, confined. It didn't bear contemplating.

'When did your mother die?'

'Do you ever stop asking questions, mister?'

They came off the highway and down a slip road. Half of it had never been completed. One lane curved like a water-chute, ending abruptly in a row of dripping metal rods and a ten-yard drop to waste ground.

'When I was eighteen, if that makes any difference.'

The ugliness around them was heroic. In Russia it could afford to be – could afford to take its time, stretch out a bit. Minor roads ran as wide as motorways, with flooded potholes the size of ponds. Each concrete stack of apartments, each belching industrial plant had an entire wilderness to itself to pollute. Kelso remembered the night before – the endless run from Block Nine to Block Eight to raise the alarm: it had gone on and on, like a journey in a nightmare.

Rapava's place in the daylight looked even more derelict than it had seemed in the darkness. Scorch marks shot up the wall from a set of windows on the second floor where an apartment had been torched. There was a crowd outside and Zinaida slowed so they could take a look.

O'Brian was right. The word was out. That much was obvious. A solitary militia man blocked the doorway, holding at bay a dozen cameramen and reporters, who were themselves being watched by a straggling semi-circle of apathetic neighbours. Some kids kicked a ball on the waste ground. Others hung around the media's fancy western cars.

'What was he to them?' Zinaida said suddenly. 'What was he to any of you? You're all vultures.'

She gave a grimace of disgust, and for the third time Kelso noticed her adjusting the rear-view mirror.

'Is someone behind us?' He turned round sharply.

'Maybe. A car from the airport. But not any more.'

'What sort of a car?' He tried to keep his voice calm.

'A BMW. Seven series.'

'You know about cars?'

'More questions?' She shot him another look. 'Cars were my father's interest. Cars and Comrade Stalin. He was a driver, wasn't he, for some big shot in the old days? You'll see.'

She put her foot down.

She knows nothing, thought Kelso. She has no idea of the risks. He began making promises to himself of what he would do: you take a quick look now to see if this toolbox is here (it wouldn't be) then ask her to take you back to the airport and see if you can talk your way on to the next flight out –

Two minutes from Rapava's apartment they turned off the main street and on to a muddy track that led through a scrappy copse of birch to a field that had been divided into small-holdings. A pig snuffled in the earth in an enclosure made of old car doors tied together with wire. There were a few scrawny chickens, some frost-blasted vegetables. Children had made a snowman out of yesterday's fall. It had melted in the light rain and looked grotesque in the dirt, like a lump of white fat.

Facing this rural scene was a row of lock-up garages. On the long flat roof sat the remains of half a dozen small cars – rusted red skeletons picked bare of windows, engines, tyres, upholstery. Zinaida switched off the engine and they climbed out into the mud. An old man leaned on his shovel and watched them. Zinaida stared him down, her hands on her hips. Eventually, he spat on the ground and returned to his digging.

She had a key. Kelso looked back along the deserted track. His hands felt numb. He stuffed them into his coat pockets. She was the calm one. She was wearing a pair of knee-length leather boots and to avoid getting them dirty she stepped carefully across the lumpy ground. He looked around again. He didn't like it: the encroaching trees, the derelict cars, this bewildering woman with her kaleidoscope of roles – GUM telephonist, would-be lawyer, part-time hooker and now griefless daughter.

He said, 'Where did you get the key?'

'It was with the note.'

'I don't understand why you didn't come here on your own straight away. Why do you need me?'

'Because I don't know what I'm looking for, do I? Are you coming or not?' She was fitting the key into a big padlock on the nearest lock-up. 'What are we looking for, anyway?'

'A notebook.'

'What?' She stopped fiddling with the key and stared at him.

'A black oilskin notebook that used to belong to Josef Stalin.' He repeated the familiar phrase. It was becoming his mantra. (It wouldn't be here, he told himself again. It was the Holy Grail. The quest was all that mattered. It wasn't supposed to be found.)

'Stalin's notebook? And what's that worth?'

'Worth?' He tried to make it sound as if the question had never occurred to him. 'Worth?' he repeated. 'It's hard to put an exact figure on it. There are some rich collectors. It depends what's in it.' He spread his hands. 'Half a million, maybe.'

'Roubles?'

'Dollars.'

'Dollars? Shit. *Shit.*' She resumed her efforts to undo the padlock, clumsy now with her eagerness.

And suddenly, watching her, he caught her mood and then of course he knew why he had come. Because it was everything, really, wasn't it? It was much more than mere money. It was vindication. Vindication for twenty years of freezing his arse off in basement archives, and dragging himself to lectures in the winter dark – first to listen, then to give them – twenty years of teaching and faculty politics and trying to write books that mostly didn't sell and all the while hoping that one day he would produce something worthwhile – something true and big and definitive – a piece of history that would explain *why things had happened as they did.*

'Here,' he said, almost pushing her out of the way, 'let me try.'

He jiggled the key in the lock. At last it turned and the arm sprang open. He pulled the chain through the heavy eye-bolts.

COLD, oily darkness. No window. No electricity. An ancient paraffin lamp hanging on a nail by the door.

He took down the lamp and shook it – it was full – and she said she knew how to light it. She knelt on the earth floor

193

and struck a match, applied it to the wick. A blue flame, then yellow. She held it up while he dragged the door shut behind them.

The garage was a bone-yard of old spare parts, stacked around the walls. At the far end in the shadows was a row of car seats arranged to form a bed, with a sleeping bag and a blanket, neatly folded. Suspended from a beam in the roof was a block and tackle, a chain, a hook. Beneath the hook were floorboards forming a rectangle a yard and a half wide by two yards long.

She said, 'He's had this place for as long as I've been alive. He used to sleep here, when things were bad.'

'How bad did they get?'

'Bad.'

He took the lamp and walked around, shining it into the corners. There was nothing like a toolbox that he could see. On a work bench was a tin tray with a metal brush, some rods, a cylinder, a small coil of copper wire: what was all that? Fluke Kelso's ignorance of mechanics was deep and carefully maintained.

'Did he have a car of his own?'

'I don't know. He fixed them up for people. People gave him things.'

He stopped next to the makeshift bed. Something glinted above it. He called to her, 'Look at this,' and raised the light to the wall. Stalin's sombre face gazed down at them from an old poster. There were a dozen more pictures of the General Secretary, torn from magazines. Stalin looking thoughtful behind a desk. Stalin in a fur hat. Stalin shaking hands with a general. Stalin, dead, lying in state.

'And who's this? This is you?'

It was a photograph of Zinaida, aged about twelve, in

school uniform. She stepped closer to it, surprised.

'Who'd have thought it?' She laughed uneasily. 'Me up there with Stalin.'

She stared at it a while longer.

'Let's find this thing,' she said, turning away. 'I want to get out of here.'

Kelso was prodding one of the floorboards with his foot. It rested loosely on a wooden frame set into the earth. This was it, he thought. This had to be the place.

They worked together, watched by Stalin, stacking the short planks against the wall, uncovering a mechanic's pit. It was deep. In the weak light it looked like a grave. He held the lamp over it. The floor was sand, stamped smooth and hard, stained black with oil. The sides were shored up with old timber, into which Rapava had let alcoves for tools. He gave her the lamp and wiped his palms on his coat. Why was he so damned nervous? He sat on the edge for a moment, legs dangling, before cautiously lowering himself. He knelt on the floor of the pit, his bones cracking, and felt around in the damp gloom. His hands touched sacking.

He called up to her, 'Shine the light here.'

The rough cloth pulled away easily. Next came something solid, wrapped in newspaper. He passed it up to Zinaida. She set down the lamp and unwrapped a gun. She was surprisingly deft with it, he noticed, sliding out the clip of ammunition, checking it – eight rounds loaded – sliding it back again, pushing the safety catch down then up.

'You know how it works?'

'Of course. It's his. A Makarov. When we were little, he taught us how to strip it, clean it, fire it. He always kept it by him. He said he'd kill if he had to.'

'That's a nice memory.' He thought he heard a sound

195

outside. 'Did you hear that?'

But she shook her head, preoccupied with the gun.

He sank back down to his knees.

And here, jammed into the aperture, was the square end of a metal box, flaking with rust and dried mud. If you didn't know what you were looking for, you would never have bothered with it. Rapava had hidden well. He put his hands on either side of it and tugged.

Well, *something* was heavy. Either the box or what was in it. The handles had rusted flat. It was hard to get a grip. He dragged it into the centre of the pit and hoisted it up to the edge. His cheek was close to it. He could taste the smell of rusted steel, like blood in his mouth. Zinaida bent to help. And this was peculiar: for an instant he thought that the box was exuding an unearthly, blue-grey light. There was a rush of cold air. But then he saw that the garage door was open and that framed in it was the silhouette of a man, watching them.

AFTERWARDS, Kelso was to recognise this as the decisive moment: as the point at which he lost control of events. If he didn't see it at the time it was because his main concern was simply to stop her blowing a hole in R. J. O'Brian's chest.

The reporter stood against the garage wall, his hands above his head. Kelso could tell he didn't quite believe she would shoot. But a gun was a gun. They could go off accidentally. And this one was old.

'Professor, do me a favour, would you, and tell her to put that thing down?'

But Zinaida jabbed it again towards his chest and O'Brian, groaning, raised his hands still further.

Okay, okay, he said. He was sorry. He had followed them

from the airport. It hadn't been hard, for Christ's sake. He was only doing his job. *Sorry.*

His eyes flickered to the toolbox. 'Is that it?'

Kelso's immediate reaction on seeing the American had been relief: thank God it was only O'Brian who had followed them from Sheremetevo and not Mamantov. But Zinaida had grabbed the gun and had backed him against the wall.

She said, 'Shut up.'

'Look, professor, I've seen these suckers go off. And I have to tell you: they really make a mess.'

Kelso said to her, in Russian, 'Put it away, Zinaida.' It was the first time he had used her name. 'Put it away and let's sort this out.'

'I don't trust him.'

'Neither do I. But what can we do? Put it away.'

'Zinaida? Who is she? Don't I know her from someplace?'

'She goes to the Robotnik.' Kelso spoke through his teeth. 'Will you let me handle this?'

'Does she, by God?' O'Brian passed his tongue across his thick lips. In the yellow lamplight his broad and well-fed face looked like a Hallowe'en pumpkin. 'That's right. Of course she does. She's the babe you were with last night. I thought I knew her.'

'Shut up,' she said again.

O'Brian grinned. 'Listen, Zinaida, we don't have to be in competition. We can share, can't we? Split this three ways? I just want a story. Tell her, Fluke. Tell her I can keep her name out of it. She knows me. She'll understand. She's a business-minded kind of a girl, aren't you, darlin'?'

'What's he saying?'

He told her.

'*Nyet,*' she said. And then, in English, to O'Brian, 'No way.'

'You two,' said O'Brian. 'You make me laugh. The historian and the whore. Okay, tell her this. Tell her she can either deal with me or we can stand around like this for an hour or two and you'll have half the Moscow press pack on your back. And the militia. And maybe the guys who killed the old man. Tell her that.'

But Kelso didn't need to translate. She understood.

She stood there for another quarter of a minute, frowning, then clicked on the safety catch and slowly lowered the gun. O'Brian let out a breath.

'What's she doing in all this anyway?'

'She's Papu Rapava's daughter.'

'Ah.' O'Brian nodded. Now he got the picture.

THE toolbox lay on the earth floor. O'Brian wouldn't let them open it, not right away. He wanted to capture the great moment, he said – 'for posterity and the evening news'. He went off to get his camera.

Once he'd gone, Kelso shook a cigarette out of his half-empty pack and offered it to Zinaida. She took it and leaned towards him, looking at him steadily as he lit it for her, the flame reflected in her dark eyes. He thought: less than twelve hours ago you were going to go to bed with me for $200 – who the hell are you?

She said, 'What's on your mind?'

'Nothing. Are you all right?'

'I don't trust him,' she repeated. She threw back her head and blew smoke at the roof. 'What's he doing?'

'I'll tell him to hurry up.'

Outside, O'Brian was sitting in the front seat of a four-wheel drive Toyota Land Crusier, snapping a new battery on to the back of a tiny video camera. At the sight of the Toyota,

Kelso felt a fresh sweat of anxiety.

'You don't drive a BMW?'

'A BMW? I'm not a businessman. Why should I?'

The field was deserted. The old man who had been digging had gone.

'Zinaida thought we were followed from the airport by a BMW. Seven series.'

'Seven series? That's a mafia car.' O'Brian got out of the Toyota and put the camera to his eye. 'I wouldn't pay any attention to Zinaida. She's crazy.' The pig emerged from its sty and trotted over for a look at them, hopeful of some food. 'Here, piggy piggy.' He began filming it. 'Remember what the man said? "A dog looks up to you, a cat looks down on you, but a pig looks you straight in the eye"?' He swung round and pointed the camera at Kelso's face. 'Smile, professor. I'm going to make you famous.'

Kelso put his hand over the lens. 'Listen, Mr O'Brian –'

'R. J.'

'And what does that stand for?'

'Everybody calls me R. J.'

'All right, *R. J.* I'm going to do this. I'll let you film me. If you insist. But on three conditions.'

'Which are?'

'One, you stop calling me bloody *professor*. Two, you keep her name out of it. And three, none of this is shown – not a second, you hear? – until this notebook, or whatever it is, has been forensically verified.'

'Agreed.' O'Brian slipped the camera into his pocket. 'Actually, it may surprise you to hear this, but I've got a reputation of my own to consider. And from what I hear, *doctor*, it's one hell of a sight better than yours.'

He pointed a remote key at the Toyota. It bleeped and

locked. Kelso took a last look around and followed him into the garage.

O'BRIAN made Kelso put the toolbox back in its hiding place and drag it out again. He made him do this twice, filming him once from the front and then from the side. Zinaida watched them closely but was careful to keep out of shot. She smoked incessantly, one arm clasped defensively across her stomach. When O'Brian had what he needed, Kelso carried the box over to the workbench and brought the lamp up close to it. There wasn't a lock. There were two spring-loaded catches at either end of the lid. They had been cleaned up recently, and oiled. One was broken. The other opened.

Here we go, boy.

'What I want you to do,' said O'Brian, 'is describe what you see. Talk us through it.'

Kelso contemplated the box.

'D'you have any gloves?'

'Gloves?'

'If what's inside is genuine, Stalin's fingerprints should be on it. And Beria's. I don't want to contaminate the evidence.'

'Stalin's *fingerprints?*'

'Of course. Don't you know about Stalin's fingers? The Bolshevik poet, Demyan Bedny, once complained that he didn't like lending his books to Stalin because they always came back with such greasy finger marks on them. Osip Mandelstam – a much greater poet – got to hear about this, and put the image into a poem about Stalin: "His fingers are fat as grubs".'

'What did Stalin think of that?'

'Mandelstam died in a labour camp.'

'Right. I guess I should have figured that out.' O'Brian dug around in his pockets. 'Okay: gloves. There you go.'

Kelso pulled them on. They were dark blue leather, slightly too big, but they would do. He flexed his fingers – a surgeon before a transplant, a pianist before a concert. The thought made him smile. He glanced at Zinaida. Her face was clenched. O'Brian's expression was hidden by the camera.

'Okay. I'm running. In your own time.'

'Right. I'm opening the lid, which is . . . *stiff*, as you'd . . . *expect*.' Kelso winced with the effort. The top wrenched up a crack, just wide enough for him to jam his fingers into the gap, and then it took all his strength to break the two edges apart. It came open suddenly, like a broken jaw, with a scream of oxidised metal. 'There's only one object inside . . . a bag of some kind . . . leather, by the look of it . . . badly moulded.'

The satchel had grown a shroud of fungus – of different fungi – pale blues and greens and greys, vegetative filaments and white patches mottled black. It stank of decay. He lifted it clear of the box and turned it round in the light. He rubbed at the surface with his thumb. Very faintly, the ghost of an image began to appear. 'It's embossed here with the hammer and sickle . . . That suggests it's an official document pouch of some kind . . . Oil here on the buckle . . . Some of the rust has been cleaned off . . . ' He imagined Rapava's nail-less fingers, fumbling to discover what had cost him so much of his life.

The strap unthreaded through the pitted metal, leaving a floury residue. The satchel opened. The hyphae had spread inside, feeding off the dank skin, and as he lifted out the contents he knew, whatever else it was, that this was genuine, that no forger would have done all this, would have allowed so much damage to be inflicted on his work: it went against nature. What had once been a packet of papers had fused together, swollen, and was covered in the same destructive cancer of spores as the leather. The pages of the notebook had also warped, but less badly, protected as they were by a smooth outer layer of black oilskin.

The cover opened, the binding split.

On the first page: nothing.

On the second: a photograph, neatly cut out of a magazine, glued down in the centre of the page. A group of young women, in their late teens, dressed as athletes – shorts, singlets, sashes – marching in step, eyes right, carrying a picture of Stalin. Parading in Red Square by the look of it. Caption: *Komsomol Unit No. 2 from Archangel oblast display their paces! Front row, l. to r. I. Primakova, A. Safanova, D. Merkulova, K. Til, M. Arsenyeva* . . . Against the youthful face of A. Safanova there was a tiny red cross.

He picked up the notebook and blew, to separate the second page from the third. His hands were sweating inside the gloves. He felt absurdly clumsy, as if he were trying to thread a needle while wearing gauntlets.

On the third page: writing, in faint pencil.

O'Brian touched his shoulder, prompting him to say something.

'It's not Stalin's writing, I'm sure of that . . . It reads more like someone writing *about* Stalin . . .' He held it closer to the lamp. '"He stands apart from the others, high on the roof of Lenin's tomb. His hand is raised in greeting. He smiles. We pass beneath him. His glance falls across us like the rays of the sun. He looks directly into my eyes. I am pierced by his power. All around us, the crowd breaks into stormy applause." The next part is smudged. And then it's written, "Great Stalin lived! Great Stalin lives! Great Stalin will live for ever! . . .'"

Chapter Fourteen

> *... Great Stalin lived!*
> *Great Stalin lives!*
> *Great Stalin will live for ever!*

12.5.51 Our picture is in Ogonyok! Maria runs in at the end of the first class to show me. I am displeased with my appearance and M. chides me for my vanity. (She always says I think too much of being pretty: it is not fitting for a candidate-member of the Party. Fine for her to say, who always looks like a tank!) All morning comrades hurry up to us to offer their congratulations. The usual trouble of this time is forgotten for once. We are so happy . . .

5.6.51 The day is hot and sunny. The Dvina is gold. I return home from the Institute. Papa is there, much earlier than usual, looking grave. Mama is strong, as ever. With them is a stranger, a comrade from the organs of the Central Committee in Moscow! I am not afraid of him. I know I have done nothing wrong. And the stranger is smiling. A little man – I like him. Despite the heat he is carrying a hat and wears a leather coat. This stranger is named, I think, Mekhlis. He explains that after a thorough investigation, I have been selected for special tasks relating to the high Party leadership. He cannot say more for reasons of security. If I accept, I must travel to Moscow and stay for one year, perhaps for two. Then I may return to Archangel and resume my studies. He offers to come back the next morning for my answer, but I give it now, with all my heart: Yes! But because I am nineteen, he needs the permission of my parents. Oh, please papa! Please,

please! Papa is deeply moved by the scene. He goes with Comrade Mekhlis into the garden, and when he returns his face is solemn. If it is my wish, and if it is the will of the Party, he will not prevent me. Mama is so proud.

To Moscow, then, for the second time in my life!

I know His hand is behind this.

I am so happy, I could die . . .

10.6.51 Mama brings me to the station. Papa stays behind. I kiss her dear cheeks. Farewell to her, farewell to childhood. The carriages are crowded. The train moves off. Others run along the platform, but mama stays still and is quickly lost. We cross the river. I am alone. Poor Anna! And this is the worst of days to travel. But I have my clothes, some food, a book or two, and this journal, in which I shall record my thoughts – this will be my friend. We plunge south through the forest, the tundra. A great red sunset blazes like a fire through the trees. Isakogorka. Obozerskiy. And now I have written down everything that has happened until this time and I can no longer see to write.

11.6.51 Monday morning. The town of Vozhega appears with the dawn. Passengers alight to stretch their legs, but I stay where I am. From the corridor comes a smell of smoke. A man watches me write from the opposite seat, pretending to be asleep. He is curious about me. If only he knew! And still there are eleven hours to Moscow. How can one man rule such a nation? How could such a nation exist without such a man to rule it?

Konosha. Kharovsk. Names on a map become real to me.

Vologda. Danilov. Yaroslavl.

A fear has come upon me. I am so far from home. Last time there were twenty of us, silly laughing girls. O, papa!

Alexandrov.

And now we reach the outskirts of Moscow. A tremor of excitement runs through the train. The blocks and factories stretch as far and wide as the tundra. A hot haze of metal and smoke. The June sun is much warmer than at home. I am excited again.

4.30! Yaroslavskaya station! And now what?

LATER. *The train halts, the man opposite, who had been watching me all journey, leans forward. 'Anna Mikhailovna Safanova?' For a moment I am too amazed to speak. Yes? 'Welcome to Moscow. Come with me, please.' He wears a leather coat, like Comrade Mekhlis. He carries my case along the platform to the station entrance on Komsomolskaya Square. A car is waiting, with a driver. We drive for a long while. An hour at least. I don't know where. Right across the city it seems to me, and out again. Along a highway that leads to a birch forest. There is a high fence and soldiers who check our papers. We drive some more. Another fence. And then a house, in a large garden.*

(And Mama, yes, it is a modest house! Two storeys only. Your good Bolshevik heart would rejoice at its simplicity!)

I am taken around the side of the house to the back. A servants' wing, connected to the main quarters by a long passageway. Here in the kitchen a woman is waiting. She is grey-haired, almost old. And kindly. She calls me 'child'. Her name is Valechka Istomina. A simple meal has been prepared – cold meat and bread, pickled herring, kvas. She watches me. (Everyone here watches everyone else: it is strange to look up and find a pair of eyes regarding you.) From time to time, guards come by to take a look at me. They don't talk much but when they do they sound like Georgians. One asks, 'Well, now, Valechka, and what was the Boss's humour this morning?' but Valechka hushes him and nods to me.

I am not such a young fool as to ask any questions. Not yet.

Valechka says: 'Tomorrow we shall talk. Now rest.'

I have a room to myself. The girl who had it before has gone away. Two plain black blouses and skirts have been left behind for me.

I have a view of a corner of the lawn, a tiny summer house, the woods. The birds sing in the early summer evening. It seems so peaceful. Yet every couple of minutes a guard goes past the window.

I lie on my little bed in the heat and try to sleep. I think of Archangel in the winter: the coloured lanterns strung out across the frozen river, skating on the Dvina, the sound of ice cracking at night, hunting for mushrooms in the forest. I wish I was at home. But these are foolish thoughts.

I must sleep.

Why did that man watch me on the train for all that time?

LATER: In the darkness, the sound of cars.

He is home.

12.6.51 This is a day! I can hardly set it down. My hand shakes so. (It did not at the time but now it does!) At seven I go to the kitchen. Valechka is already up, sorting through a great mess of broken crockery, glass, spilled food, which lies in a heap in the centre of a big tablecloth. She explains how the table is cleared every night: two guards each take two corners of the cloth and carry everything out! So our first task every morning is to rescue all that isn't broken, and wash it. As we work, Valechka explains the routine of the house. He rises quite late and sometimes likes to work in the garden. Then he goes to the Kremlin and his quarters are cleaned. He never returns before nine or ten in the evening, and then there is a dinner. At two or three He goes to bed. This happens seven days a week. The rules: when one approaches Him, do so openly, He hates it when people creep up on Him. If a door has to be knocked on, knock upon it loudly. Don't stand around. Don't speak unless you are spoken to. And if you do have to speak, always look Him in the eyes.

She prepares a simple breakfast of coffee, bread and meat, and takes it out. Later, she asks me to collect the tray. Before I go, she makes me tie up my hair and turn around while she examines me. I will do, she says. She says He is working at a table at the edge of the lawn on the south side of the house. Or was. He moves restlessly, from place to place. It is His way. The guards will know where to look.

What can I write of this moment? I am calm. You would have been proud of me. I remember what to do. I walk around the edge of the lawn and approach Him in plain view. He's sitting on a bench, alone, bent over some papers. The tray is on a table beside Him. He glances up at my approach, then returns to His work. But as I walk away across the grass – then, I swear, I feel His eyes upon my back, all the way, until I'm out of sight. Valechka laughs at my white face.

I don't see Him again after that.

Just now (it is after ten): the sound of cars.

14.6.51 Last night. Late. I'm in the kitchen with Valechka when Lozgachev (a guard) comes rushing in, all steamed up, to say the Boss is out of Ararat. Valechka fetches a bottle, but instead of giving it to Lozgachev, she gives it to me: 'Let Anna take it in.' She wants to help me – dear Valechka! So Lozgachev takes me down the passage to the main part of the house. I can hear male voices. Laughter. He knocks hard on the door and stands aside. I go in. The room is hot, stuffy. Seven or eight men around a table – familiar faces, all of them. One – Comrade Khrushchev,

I think – is on his feet, proposing a toast. His face is flushed, sweating. He stops. There is food all over the place, as if they have been throwing it. All look at me. Comrade Stalin is at the head of the table. I set the brandy next to him. His voice is soft and kindly. He says, 'And what is your name, young comrade?' 'Anna Safanova, Comrade Stalin.' I remember to look into his eyes. They are very deep. The man next to him says, 'She's from Archangel, Boss.' And Comrade Khrushchev says, 'Trust Lavrenty to know where she's from!' More laughter. 'Ignore these rough fellows,' says Comrade Stalin. 'Thank you, Anna Safanova.' As I close the door, their talk resumes. Valechka is waiting for me at the end of the passage. She puts her arm around me and we go back in to the kitchen. I am shaking, it must be with joy.

16.6.51 Comrade Stalin has said that from now on I am to bring him breakfast.

21.6.51 He is in the garden as usual this morning. How I wish the people could see him here! He likes to listen to the birdsong, to prune the flowers. But his hands shake. As I am setting down the tray, I hear him curse. He has cut himself. I pick up the napkin and take it over to him. At first, he looks at me suspiciously. Then he holds out his hand. I wrap it in the white linen. Bright spots of blood soak through. 'You are not afraid of Comrade Stalin, Anna Safanova?' 'Why should I be afraid of you, Comrade Stalin?' 'The doctors are afraid of Comrade Stalin. When they come to change a dressing on Comrade Stalin, their hands shake so much, he has to do it himself. Ah, but if their hands didn't shake – well then, what would that mean? Thank you, Anna Safanova.'

O, mama and papa, he is so lonely! Your hearts would go out to him. He is only flesh and blood, after all, like us. And close-up he is old. Much older than he appears in his pictures. His moustache is grey, the underside stained yellow by his pipe smoke. His teeth are almost all gone. His chest rattles when he breathes. I fear for him. For all of us.

30.6.51 Three a.m. A knock at my door. Valechka is outside, in her nightdress, with a pocket torch. He has been in the garden, pruning by moonlight, and he has cut himself again! He is calling for me! I dress quickly and follow her along the passage. The night is warm. We pass through the dining room and in to his private quarters. He has three rooms and he moves between them, one night in this one, one night in another. Nobody is ever sure where. He sleeps beneath a blanket on a couch. Valechka leaves us. He is sitting on the couch, his hand outstretched. It is only a graze. It takes me half a minute to bind it with my handkerchief. 'The fearless Anna Safanova . . .'

I sense he wants me to stay. He asks me about my home and parents, my Party work, my plans for the future. I tell him of my interest in the law. He snorts: he doesn't think much of lawyers! He wants to know of life in Archangel in the winter. Have I seen the lights of the Northern Aurora? (Of course!) When do the first snows come? At the end of September, I tell him, and by the end of October, the city is snowbound and only the trains can get through. He is hungry for details. How the Dvina freezes and wooden tracks are laid across it and there is light for only four hours a day. How the temperature drops to 35 below and people go into the forests for ice-fishing . . .

He listens most intently. 'Comrade Stalin believes the soul of Russia lies in the ice and solitude of the far north. When Comrade Stalin was in exile – this was before the Revolution, in Kureika, within the Arctic Circle – it was his happiest time. It was here Comrade Stalin learned how to hunt and fish. That swine Trotsky maintained that Comrade Stalin used only traps. A filthy lie! Comrade Stalin set traps, yes, but he also set lines in the ice holes, and such was his success in the detection of fish that the local people credited him with supernatural powers. In one day, Comrade Stalin travelled forty-five versts on skis and killed twelve brace of partridge with twenty-four shots. Could Trotsky claim as much?'

I wish I could remember all he said. Perhaps this should be my destiny: to record his words for History?

By the time I leave him to return to my bed, it is light.

8.7.51 The same performance as last time. Valechka at my door at 3 a.m.: he has cut himself, he wants me. But when I get there, I can see no wound. He laughs at my face – his joke! – and tells me to bind his hand in any case. He strokes my cheek, then pinches it. 'You see, fearless Anna Safanova, how you make a prisoner of me?!'

He is in a different room from the last time. On the walls are pictures of children, torn from magazines. Children playing in a cherry orchard. A boy on skis. A girl drinking goat's milk from a horn. Many pictures. He notices me staring at them and this prompts him to talk frankly of his own children. One son dead. One a drunkard. His daughter married twice, the first time to a Jew: he never even allowed him in to the house! What has Comrade Stalin done to deserve this? Other men produce normal children. Was it bad blood or bad upbringing? Was there something wrong with the mothers? (He thinks so, to judge from their families, who have been a constant plague to him.) Or was it impossible for the children of Comrade Stalin ever to develop normally, given his high position in the State and Party? Here is the age-old conflict, older even than the struggle between the classes.

He asks if I have heard of Comrade Trofim Lysenko's 1948 speech to the Lenin All-Union Academy of Agricultural Sciences? I say that I have. My answer pleases him.

'But Comrade Stalin wrote this speech! It was Comrade Stalin's insight, after a lifetime of study and struggle, that acquired characteristics are inheritable. Though naturally these discoveries must be put into the mouths of others, just as it is for others to turn the principle into a practical science.'

'Remember Comrade Stalin's historic words to Gorky: "It is the task of the proletarian state to produce engineers of human souls."'

'Are you a good Bolshevik, Anna Safanova?'

I swear to him that I am.

'Will you prove it? Will you dance for Comrade Stalin?'

There is a gramophone in the corner of the room. He goes to it. I —

Chapter Fifteen

'AND THAT'S HOW it ends?' said O'Brian. His voice was heavy with disappointment. 'Just like that?'

'See for yourself.' Kelso turned the book round and showed it to the other two. 'The next twenty pages have been removed. And here – look – you can see the way it's been done. The torn edges attached to the spine are all different lengths.'

'What's so significant about that?'

'It means they weren't torn out all at once, but one by one. Methodically.' Kelso resumed his examination. 'There are some pages left at the back, about fifty, but they've not been written on. They've been drawn on – doodled on, I should say – in red pencil. The same image again and again, d'you see?'

'What are they?' O'Brian moved in closer with the camera running. 'They look like wolves.'

'They are wolves. The heads of wolves. Stalin often drew wolves in the margins of official documents when he was thinking.'

'Jesus. So it's genuine, you think?'

'Until it's been forensically tested, I'm not prepared to say. I'm sorry. Not officially.'

'Unofficially, then – not for attribution until later – what d'you think?'

'Oh, it's genuine,' said Kelso, without hesitation. 'I'd stake my life on it.'

O'Brian switched the camera off.

*

THEY had left the lock-up by this time and were sitting in the Moscow bureau of the Satellite News System which occupied the top floor of a ten-storey office block just south of the Olympic Stadium. A glass partition separated O'Brian's room from the main production office, where a secretary sat listlessly before a computer screen. Next to her, a mute television, tuned to SNS, was showing clips of the previous night's baseball games. Through a skylight Kelso could see a big satellite dish, raised like an offertory plate to the bulging Moscow clouds.

O'Brian said, 'And how long is it going to take us to get this stuff tested?'

'A couple of weeks, perhaps,' said Kelso. 'A month.'

'No way,' said O'Brian. 'No way can we wait that long.'

'Well, think about it. First of all this material technically belongs to the Russian government. Or Stalin's heirs. Or someone. Anyway, it isn't ours – Zinaida's, I mean.'

Zinaida was standing at the window, staring out through a gap she had made with her fingers in the slatted blinds. At the mention of her name she glanced briefly in Kelso's direction. She had barely said a word in the last hour – not when they were still in the garage, not even on their cautious drive across Moscow, following O'Brian.

'So it isn't safe to keep it here,' continued Kelso. 'We've got to get it out of the country. That's the first priority. God knows who's after it now. Just being in the same *room* is bloody dangerous as far as I'm concerned. The tests themselves – well, we can have those done anywhere. I know some people in Oxford who can check the ink and paper. There are document examiners in Germany, Switzerland –'

O'Brian didn't seem to be listening. He had his feet up on his desk, his long body lolling back in his chair, his hands clasped behind his head. 'You know what we've really got to do?' he mused. 'We've got to find the girl.'

Kelso stared at him for a moment. 'Find the girl? What are you talking about? There isn't going to be a girl. The girl's going to be dead.'

'You can't be sure of that. She'd only be – what? – sixty-something?'

'She'd be sixty-six. But that's hardly the point. It's not *old age* she'll have died of. Who d'you think she was getting mixed up with here? Prince Charming? She won't have lived happily ever after.'

'Maybe not, but we still need to find out what happened to her. What happened to her folks. Human interest. *That's* the story.'

The wall behind O'Brian's head was plastered with photographs: O'Brian with Yasser Arafat, O'Brian with Gerry Adams, O'Brian in a flak jacket next to a mass grave in the Balkans somewhere and another of him, in protective gear, stepping through a minefield with the Princess of Wales. O'Brian in a tuxedo, collecting an award – for the sheer genius of simply being O'Brian, perhaps? Citations for O'Brian. Reviews of O'Brian. A herogram from the Chief Executive of SNS, praising O'Brian for his 'relentless dedication to triumphing over our competitors'. For the first time, and far too late, Kelso began to get a measure of the man's ambition.

'Nothing,' said Kelso very deliberately, so there was no room for misunderstanding, '*nothing* is to be made public until this material is out of the country and has been forensically verified. Do you hear me? That's what we agreed.'

O'Brian clicked his fingers. 'Yeah, yeah, yeah. All right.

But in the meantime we should find out what happened to the girl. We've got to do that anyway. If we go on air with the notebook before we find out what happened to Anna, someone else'll come along and get the best part of the story.' He lifted his feet off the desk and spun around in his chair to a set of bookshelves beside his desk. 'Now where the hell is Archangel, anyway?'

IT happened with a kind of inexorable logic so that later, when Kelso had the time to review his actions, he still could never identify a precise moment when he could have stopped it, when he could have diverted events on to a different course –

"'Archangel,'" said O'Brian, reading aloud from a guidebook. "'Northern Russian port city. Population: four hundred thousand. Situated on the River Dvina, thirty miles upstream from the White Sea. Principal industries: timber, shipbuilding and fishing. From the end of October until the beginning of April, Archangel is snowbound." Shit. What's the date?'

'October the twenty-ninth.'

O'Brian picked up the telephone and jabbed out a number. From his position on the sofa Kelso watched through the thick glass wall as the secretary reached silently for the receiver.

'Sweetheart,' said O'Brian, 'do me a favour will you? Get on to the System's weather centre in Florida and get the latest weather prediction for Archangel.' He spelt it out for her. 'That's it. Quick as you can.'

Kelso closed his eyes.

The point was – he knew it in his heart – that O'Brian was right. The story *was* the girl. And the story couldn't be

216

pursued in Moscow. If the trail could be picked up anywhere, it could only be in the north, on her home territory, where it was possible there might still be some family or friends who would remember her: remember the Komsomol girl of nineteen and the dramatic summons to Moscow in the summer of 1951 –

'"Archangel,"' resumed O'Brian, '"was founded by Peter the Great and named after Archangel Michael, the Warrior-Angel. See the Book of Revelation, chapter twelve, verses seven to eight: 'And there was war in heaven: Michael and his angels fought against the dragon; and the dragon fought and his angels,/And prevailed not.' In the nineteen-thirties – "'

'Do we really have to listen to this?'

But O'Brian held up his finger.

'" – in the nineteen-thirties, Stalin exiled two million Ukrainian kulaks into the Archangel oblast, a region of forest and tundra larger than the whole of France. After the war, this vast area was used for testing nuclear weapons. Archangel's outport is Severodvinsk, centre of Russia's nuclear submarine construction programme. Until the fall of communism, Archangel was a closed city, forbidden to all outside visitors.

'"Traveller's tip,"' concluded O'Brian. '"When arriving at the Archangel Railway Station, always be sure to check the digital radiation meter – if it shows 15 microRads per hour or below, it's safe."' He closed the book with a cheerful snap. 'Sounds like a fun place. What d'you think? You up for this?'

I am trapped, thought Kelso. *I am a victim of historical inevitability. Comrade Stalin would have approved.*

'You know I've no money – ?'

'I'll lend you money.'

'No winter clothes –'

'We've got clothes.'

'No *visa* –'

'A detail.'

'A *detail?*'

'Come on, Fluke. You're the Stalin expert. I need you.'

'Well that's touching. And if I say no, presumably you'll go anyway?'

O'Brian grinned. The telephone rang. He picked it up, listened, made a few notes. When he put it down, he was frowning and Kelso entertained a brief hope of reprieve. But no.

The weather in Archangel at 11:00 GMT that day (3 p.m. local time) was being reported as partly cloudy, minus four degrees, with light winds and snow flurries. However, a deep depression was rolling westwards from Siberia and that was promising snow heavy enough to close the city within a day or two.

In other words, said O'Brian, they would have to hurry.

HE fetched an atlas and opened it on his desk.

The fastest way into Archangel, obviously, was by air, but the Aeroflot flight didn't leave until the following morning and the airline would require Kelso to show his visa which would expire at midnight. So that was out. The train took more than twenty hours, and even O'Brian could see the risks in that – trapped on board a slow-moving sleeper for the best part of a day.

Which left the road – specifically, the M8 – which ran nearly 700 miles, more or less direct, according to the map, swerving slightly to take in the city of Yaroslavl, then following the river plateaux of the Vaga and the Dvina, across the taiga and the tundra and the great virgin forests of northern

218

Russia, directly into Archangel itself, where the road ended.

Kelso said, 'It's not a freeway, you know. There are no motels.'

'It's nothing, man. It'll be a breeze, I promise. What've we got now – let's see – couple of hours of daylight left? That should get us well clear of Moscow. You drive, don't you?'

'Yes.'

'There you go. We'll take turns. These journeys, I tell you, they always look worse on paper. Once we're in the groove, we'll eat those miles. You'll see.' He was making a calculation on a pad. 'I figure we could hit Archangel about nine or ten tomorrow morning.'

'So we drive through the night?'

'Sure. Or we can stop if you'd sooner. The thing is to quit talking and start moving. Quicker we hit the road, quicker we get there. We need to pack that book in something –'

He came round from behind his desk and headed towards the notebook that was lying on the coffee table, next to the congealed mass of papers. But before he could reach it, Zinaida grabbed it.

'This,' she said in English, 'mine.'

'What?'

'Mine.'

Kelso said, 'That's right. Her father left it for her.'

'I only want to borrow it.'

'*Nyet!*'

O'Brian appealed to Kelso. 'Is she crazy? Supposing we find Anna Safanova?'

'Supposing we do? What do you have in mind exactly? Stalin's grey-haired old lover in a rocking chair, reading aloud for the viewers?'

'Oh, funny guy. Listen: people are a whole lot more likely

to talk to us if we're carrying proof. I say that book should come with us. Why's it hers, anyhow? It's no more hers than mine. Or anybody else's.'

'Because that was the deal, remember?'

'Deal? Seems to me it's you two've got the only *deal* going round here.' He slipped back into his wheedling mode. 'Come on, Fluke, it's not safe for her in Moscow. Where's she gonna keep it? What if Mamantov comes after her?'

Kelso had to concede this point. 'Then why doesn't she come with us?' He turned to Zinaida, 'Come with us to Archangel –'

'With him?' she said in Russian. 'No way. He'll kill us all.'

Kelso was beginning to lose patience. 'Then let's postpone Archangel,' he said irritably to O'Brian, 'until we can get the material copied.'

'But you heard the forecast. In a day or two we won't be able to move up there. Besides, this is a story. Stories don't keep.' He raised his hands in disgust. 'Shit, I can't stand around here bitching all afternoon. Need to get some equipment together. Need supplies. Need to get going. Talk some sense into her, man, for God's sake.'

'I told you,' said Zinaida, after O'Brian had stamped out of the office, banging the glass door behind him. 'I told you we couldn't trust him.'

Kelso sank back into the sofa. He rubbed his face with both hands. This was starting to get dangerous, he thought. Not physically – in a curious way that was still unreal to him – but professionally. It was professional danger he scented now. Because Adelman was right: these big frauds did usually follow a pattern. And part of it involved being rushed to judgement. Here he was – a trained scholar, supposedly – and what had he done? He'd read through the notebook once. *Once.* He hadn't even done the most basic check to see whether the dates in the journal tallied with Stalin's known movements in the summer of 1951. He could just imagine the reaction of his former colleagues, probably leaving Russian airspace right now. If they could see how he was handling this –

The thought bothered him more than he cared to admit.

And then there was the other bundle of papers, lying on the table, mouldering and congealed. Those he hadn't even begun to look at.

He pulled on O'Brian's gloves and leaned forwards. He ran his forefinger experimentally through the grey spores on the top sheet. There was writing underneath. He rubbed again and the letters NKVD appeared.

'Zinaida,' he said.

She was sitting behind O'Brian's desk, turning the pages of the notebook, *her* notebook. At the sound of her name she looked up.

KELSO borrowed her tweezers to peel away the outer layer of paper. It came off like dead skin, flaking here and there, but cleanly enough for him to make out some of the words on the page underneath. It was a typed document, a surveillance report of some kind by the look of it, dated 24 May 1951, signed by Major I. T. Mekhlis of the NKVD.

'*. . . summary of finding to the 23rd instant . . . Anna Mikhailovna Safanova, born Archangel 27.2.32 . . . Maxim Gorky Academy . . . reputation (see attached). Health: good . . . diptheria, aged 8 yrs. 3 mths . . . Rubella, 10yrs. 1 mth . . . No family history of genetic disorder. Party work: outstanding . . . Pioneers . . . Komsomol . . .*'

Kelso peeled back more layers. Sometimes they came away

singly, sometimes fused in twos or threes. It was painstaking work. Through the glass partition he caught occasional glimpses of O'Brian, lugging suitcases across the outer office to the elevator doors, but he was too absorbed to pay much attention. What he was reading was as full a record of a nineteen-year-old girl's life as it was possible for a secret police force to compile. There was something almost pornographic about it. Here was an account of every childhood ailment, details of her blood group (O), the state of her teeth (excellent), her height and weight and hair-colour (light auburn), her physical aptitude ('in gymnastics she displays a particularly high aptitude ...'), mental abilities ('overall, in the 90th percentile ... '), ideological correctness ('the firmest grasp of Marxist theory ... '), interviews with her doctor, coach, teachers, Komsomol group leader, schoolfriends.

The worst that could be said about her was that she had, perhaps 'a slightly dreamy temperament' (Comrade Oborin) and 'a certain tendency to subjectivity and bourgeois sentimentalism rather than objectivity in all her personal relations' (Elena Satsanova). Against a further criticism from the same Comrade Satsanova, that she was 'naïve,' a marginal comment had been appended, in red pencil: 'Good!' and, later, 'Who is this old bitch?' There were numerous other underlinings, exclamation marks, queries and marginalia: 'Ha ha ha', 'And so?', 'Acceptable!'

Kelso had spent enough time in the archives to recognise this hand and style. The jagged scrawl was Stalin's. There was no question of it.

After half an hour he put the papers back in their original order and took off his gloves. His hands felt claw-like, raw and sweaty. He was suddenly overcome with self-disgust.

Zinaida was watching him.

'What do you think happened to her?'

'Nothing good.'

'He brought her down from the north to screw her?'

'That's one way of putting it.'

'Poor kid.'

'Poor kid,' he agreed.

'So why did he keep her book?'

'Obsession? Infatuation?' He shrugged. 'Who's to say. He was a sick man by then. He only had twenty months to live. Maybe she described what happened to her, then thought better of it, and tore out the pages. Or, more likely, he got hold of her book and ripped them out himself. He didn't like people knowing too much about him.'

'Well, I can tell you one thing: he didn't screw her that night.'

Kelso laughed. 'And how do you know that?'

'Easy. Look.' She opened the notebook. 'Here on the twelfth of May, she's got "the usual trouble of this time", right? On the tenth of June, on the train, it's "the worst of days to travel". Well, you can work it out for yourself, can't you? There's exactly twenty-eight days between the two. And twenty-eight days after the tenth of June is July the eighth. Which is the last entry.'

Kelso stood slowly and went over to the desk. He peered over her shoulder at the childish writing.

'What are you talking about?'

'She was a regular girl. A regular little Komsomol girl.'

Kelso absorbed this information, put the gloves back on, took the book from her, flicked between the two pages. Well, now, this was crazy, wasn't it? This was *sick*. He could barely bring himself to acknowledge the suspicion that was forming in the back of his mind. But why else would Stalin have been so interested in whether or not she had had *rubella*, of all things? Or whether her family had any history of congenital disorders?

'Tell me,' he said, quietly, 'when would she have been fertile?'

'Fourteen days later. On the twenty-second.'

AND suddenly she couldn't get out of there fast enough.

She pushed her chair back from the desk and stared at the notebook with revulsion.

'Take the damned thing,' she said. 'Take it. Keep it.'

She didn't want to touch it again. She didn't even want to *see* it.

It was *cursed*.

In a couple of seconds she had her bag over her shoulder and was flinging open the door and Kelso had to scramble to catch up with her as she strode across the office towards the elevators. O'Brian came out of an editing suite to see what was going on. He was in a heavy waterproof jacket with two pairs of binoculars slung around his thick neck. He started to follow them but Kelso waved him back.

'I'll handle this.'

She was standing in the corridor, her back to him.

'Listen Zinaida,' he said. The lift door opened and he stepped in after her. 'Listen. It's not safe for you out there –'

Almost immediately the car stopped and a man got in – heavy-set, middle-aged, black leather coat and a black leather cap. He stood between them, glanced at Zinaida, then at Kelso, sensing the edge to their silence. He looked straight ahead and stuck out his chin, smiling slightly. Kelso could tell what he was thinking: *a lovers' tiff – well, that was life, they'd get over it.*

When they reached the ground floor he stood back politely to let them out first and Zinaida clattered quickly across the marble in her knee-length boots. A security guard pressed a switch to unlock the doors.

'You,' she said, zipping up her jacket, 'should worry about yourself.'

It was just after four. People were beginning to leave from work. In the offices across the road Kelso could see the green glow of computer screens. A woman had shrunk herself into a doorway and was talking into a mobile phone. A motorcyclist went past, slowly.

'Zinaida, listen.' He grabbed her arm, stopping her from walking away. She wouldn't look at him. He pulled her close to the wall. 'Your father died badly, do you understand what I'm saying? The people who did it – Mamantov and his people – they're after this notebook. They know there's something important about it – don't ask me how. If they realise your father had a daughter – and they're bound to because Mamantov used to have access to his file – well, think about it. They're going to come after you.'

'And they killed him for *that?*'

'They killed him because he wouldn't tell them where it was. And he wouldn't tell them where it was because he wanted you to have it.'

'But it wasn't worth *dying* for. The stupid old fool.' She glared at him. Her eyes were wet for the first time that day. 'Stupid *stubborn* old fool.'

'Is there someone you can stay with? Family?'

'My family are dead.'

'A friend maybe?'

'Friend? I've got this, remember?' She lifted the flap of her bag, showing him her father's pistol.

Kelso said, as calmly as he could, 'At least give me your address, Zinaida. Your phone number –'

She looked at him suspiciously. 'Why?'

'Because I feel responsible.' He glanced around. This was madness, talking in the street. He felt in his pocket for a pen, couldn't find any paper, tore the side off a pack of cigarettes. 'Come on, write it for me. Quickly.'

He thought she wouldn't do it. She turned to go. But then, abruptly, she swung back and scribbled something down. She had a place near Izmaylovo Park, he saw, where the big flea market was.

She didn't say goodbye. She set off up the street, dodging the pedestrians, walking fast. He watched her, waiting to see if she might look back. But of course she didn't. He knew she wouldn't. She wasn't the looking-back kind.

Part Two

Archangel

'If you are afraid of wolves, keep out of the woods.'

J. V. Stalin, 1936

Chapter Sixteen

BEFORE THEY COULD get out of Moscow they had to take on fuel – because, as O'Brian said, you never knew what kind of rusty, watered-down *horse's piss* they might try to sell you once you got out of town. So they stopped at the new Nefto Agip on Prospekt Mira and O'Brian filled the Land Cruiser's tank and four big jerrycans with forty gallons of high-octane, lead-free gasoline. Then he checked the tyres and the oil, and by the time they were back on the road the evening rush was in full and sluggish spate.

It took them the best part of an hour to reach the outer ring, but there, at last, the traffic thinned, the monotonous apartment blocks and factory chimneys fell away, and suddenly they were out and free – into the flat open countryside, with its grey-green fields and giant pylons and a vast sky: a Kansas sky. It was more than ten years since Kelso had ventured north on the M8. Village churches, used as grain stores since the Revolution, were being restored, encased in webworks of wooden scaffolding. Near Dvoriki, a golden dome gathered the weak afternoon light and shone from the horizon like an autumn bonfire.

O'Brian was in his element. 'On the road,' he would say occasionally, 'and out of town – it's great, isn't it? Just great.' He drove at a steady sixty-five miles an hour, talking constantly, one hand on the wheel, the other beating time to a tape of thumping rock music.

'Just great . . . '

The satchel was on the back seat, wrapped in plastic. Heaped around it was an extravagant array of equipment and provisions: a couple of sleeping bags, thermal underwear ('Got any thermals, Fluke? Gotta have those thermals!'), two waterproof and fur-lined jackets, rubber boots and army boots, ordinary binoculars, binoculars with night-imaging, a shovel, a compass, water bottles, water purification tablets, two six-packs of Budweiser, a box of Hershey chocolate bars, two vacuum flasks filled with coffee, pot noodles, a torch, a short-wave transistor radio, spare batteries, a travelling kettle that could be plugged into the car's cigarette lighter – Kelso lost count after that.

In the rear section of the Toyota were the jerrycans and four rigid cases stamped SNS, whose contents O'Brian described with professional relish: a miniaturised, digital camcorder; an Inmarsat satellite telephone; a laptop-sized DVC-PRO video editing machine; and something he called a Toko Video Store and Forward Unit. Total value of these four items: $120,000.

'Ever hear of travelling light?' asked Kelso.

'Light?' O'Brian grinned. 'You can't get any lighter. Give me four suitcases and I can do what it used to take six guys and a truckful of equipment to do. If there's any excess baggage around here, my friend, it's you.'

'It wasn't my idea to come.'

But O'Brian wasn't listening. Thanks to these four cases, he said, his beat was the *world*. African famines. The genocide in Rwanda. The bomb in the village in Northern Ireland that he'd actually filmed go off (he'd won an award for that one). The mass graves in Bosnia. The cruise missiles in Baghdad, trundling down the streets at roof-top level – left, then right, then right again, and which way, please, for the presidential palace? And then of course there was Chechnya. Now, the trouble with Chechnya –

(You are a bird of ill-omen, thought Kelso. You circle the world and wherever you land there is famine and death and destruction: in an earlier and less credulous age, the local citizens would have gathered at the first sight of you and driven you off with stones –)

– the trouble with Chechnya, O'Brian was saying, was that the sucker had ended just as he arrived, so he had pitched up in Moscow for a while. Now *that* was a scary town: 'Give me Sarajevo any day.'

'How long are you planning to stay in Moscow?'

'Not long. Till the presidential elections. Should be fun, I reckon.'

Fun?

'And then where are you going?'

'Who knows? Why d'you ask?'

'I just want to make sure I'm nowhere around, that's all.'

O'Brian laughed and put his foot down. The speedometer flickered up towards seventy.

THEY maintained this pace as the afternoon turned to dusk, O'Brian still prattling on. (Jesus, did the man *never* shut up?) At Rostov the road ran beside a great lake. Boats, moored and tarpaulined for the winter, lined a jetty, close to a row of shuttered, timbered buildings. Far out on the water Kelso could see a lone sailboat with a light at its stern. He watched it swing about in the wind and tack for the shore and he felt again the familiar depression of nightfall starting to creep over him.

He could sense Stalin's papers behind him now almost as a physical presence, as if the GenSec were in the car with them. He worried about Zinaida. He would have liked a drink, or a cigarette, come to that, but O'Brian had declared the Toyota a smoke-free zone.

'You're jumpy,' said O'Brian, interrupting himself. 'I can tell.'

'Do you blame me?'

'Why? Because of Mamantov?' The reporter flicked his hand. 'He doesn't scare me.'

'You didn't see what he did to the old man.'

'Yeah, well he wouldn't do that to us. Not to a Brit and a Yank. He's not completely nuts.'

'Maybe not. But he might do it to Zinaida.'

'I wouldn't worry about Zinaida. Besides, she hasn't got the stuff any more. We have.'

'You're a nice man, you know that? And what if they don't believe her?'

'I'm just saying you should quit bothering about Mamantov, that's all. I've interviewed him a couple of times and I can tell you, he's a busted flash. The man lives in the past. Like you.'

'And you? You don't live in the past, I suppose?'

'Me? No way. Can't afford to, in my job.'

'Now let's just analyse that,' said Kelso, pleasantly. In his mind he was opening a drawer, selecting the sharpest knife he could find. 'So all these places you've been boasting about for the past two hours – Africa, Bosnia, the Middle East, Northern Ireland – the past isn't important there, is that what you're saying? You think they're all living in the present? They all just woke up one morning, saw you were there with your four little suitcases, and decided to have a war? It wasn't happening till you arrived? "Gee, hey, look everyone, I'm R. J. O'Brian and I just discovered the fucking *Balkans* – "'

'Okay,' muttered O'Brian, 'there's no need to be offensive about it.'

'Oh but there is.' Kelso was warming up. 'This is the great

myth, you see, of our age. The great western myth. The arrogance of our time, personified – if you'll excuse me for saying so – in *you*. That just because a place has a McDonalds and MTV and takes American Express it's exactly the same as everywhere else – it doesn't have a past any more, it's Year Zero. But it's not true.'

'You think you're better than me, don't you?'

'No.'

'Smarter then?'

'Not even that. Look. You say Moscow is a scary town. It is. Why? I'll tell you. Because there's no tradition of private property in Russia. First of all there were workers and peasants who had nothing and the nobility owned the country. Then there were workers and peasants with nothing and the Party owned the country. Now there are still workers and peasants with nothing and the country's owned, as it's always been owned, by whoever has the biggest fists. Unless you understand that, you can't begin to understand Russia. You can't make sense of the present unless a part of you lives in the past.' Kelso sat back in his seat. 'End of lecture.'

And for half an hour, as O'Brian pondered this, there was blessed peace.

THEY reached the big town of Yaroslavl just after nine and crossed the Volga. Kelso poured them each a cup of coffee. It slopped across his lap as they hit a rough patch of road. O'Brian drank as he drove. They ate chocolate. The headlights that had blazed towards them around the city gradually dwindled to the occasional flash.

Kelso said, 'Do you want me to take over?'

O'Brian shook his head. 'I'm fine. Let's change at midnight. You should get some sleep.'

They listened on the radio to the news at ten o'clock. The communists and the nationalists in the lower senate, the Duma, were using their majority to block the President's latest measures: another political crisis threatened. The Moscow stock exchange was continuing its plunge. A secret report from the Interior Ministry to the President, warning of a danger of armed rebellion, had been leaked and printed in *Aurora*.

Of Rapava, Mamantov or Stalin's papers there was no mention.

'Shouldn't you be in Moscow, covering all this?'

O'Brian snorted. 'What? "New Political Crisis in Russia"? Give me a break. R. J. O'Brian won't be on the hour every hour with *that*.'

'But he will with this?'

'"Stalin's Secret Lover, Mystery Girl Revealed"? What do you think?'

O'Brian switched off the radio.

Kelso reached over to the back seat and dragged one of the sleeping bags into the front. He opened it out and wrapped it around him like a blanket, then pressed a button and his seat slowly reclined.

He closed his eyes but he couldn't sleep. Images of Stalin gradually invaded his mind. Stalin as an old man. Stalin as glimpsed by Milovan Djilas after the war, leaning forward in his limousine while he was being driven back to Blizhny, turning on a little light in the panel in front of him to see the time on a pocket watch hanging there – 'and I observed directly in front of me his already hunched back and the bony grey nape of his neck with its wrinkled skin above the stiff marshal's collar . . .' (Djilas thought Stalin was senile that night: cramming his mouth with food, losing the thread of his stories, making jokes about the Jews.)

And Stalin, less than six months before he died, delivering his last, rambling speech to the Central Committee, describing how Lenin faced the crises of 1918 and repeating the same word over and over – 'he thundered away in an incredibly difficult situation, he thundered on, fearing nothing, he just thundered away . . .' – while the delegates sat stunned, transfixed.

And Stalin, alone in his bedroom, at night, tearing pictures of children out of magazines and plastering them around his walls. And then Stalin making Anna Safanova dance for him –

It was curious, but whenever Kelso tried to picture Anna Safanova dancing, the face he always gave her was that of Zinaida Rapava.

Chapter Seventeen

ZINAIDA RAPAVA WAS sitting in her parked car in Moscow in the darkness with her bag on her lap and her hands in that bag, feeling the outline of her father's Makarov pistol.

She had discovered that she could still strip and load it without looking at it – like riding a bicycle, it seemed: one of those childish accomplishments you never forgot. Release the spring at the bottom of the grip, pull out the magazine, squeeze in the bullets (six, seven, *eight* of them, smooth and cold to the touch), push the magazine back up, click, slide, then press the safety catch down to fire. *There.*

Papa would have been proud of her. But then she always had been better at this game than Sergo. Guns made Sergo nervous. Which was a joke, seeing as he was the one who had to do military service.

Thinking of Sergo made her cry again, but she wouldn't let herself give in to it for long. She pulled her hands out of her bag and wiped each eye irritably – so then so – on either sleeve of her jacket, then went back to her task.

Push. Click. Slide. Press . . .

SHE was scared. So scared, in fact, that when she had walked away from the westerner that afternoon she had wanted to look back at him standing outside the office block – had wanted to *go* back to him – but if she'd done that he would have known she was afraid, and fear, she had been taught, was something you must never show. Another of her father's lessons.

So she had hurried on to her car and had driven around

236

for a while without thinking until presently she had found herself heading in the direction of Red Square. She had parked in Bolshaya Lubyanka and had walked uphill to the little white Church of the Icon of the Virgin of Vladimir, where a service was in progress.

The place was packed. The churches were always packed now, not like in the old days. The music washed over her. She lit a candle. She wasn't sure why she did this because she had no faith; it was the sort of thing her mother used to do. *'And what has your god ever done for us?'* – her father's sneering voice. She thought of him, and of the girl who wrote the journal, Anna Safanova. Silly bitch, she thought. Poor silly bitch. And she lit a candle for her, too, and much good might it do her, wherever she was.

She wished her memories were better but they weren't and there was nothing to be done. She could remember him drunk, mostly, his eyes like worm holes, his fists flying. Or tired from work at the engine sheds, as rank as an old dog, too weary to rise from his chair to go to bed, sitting on a sheet of *Pravda* to keep the oil off the cover. Or paranoid, up half the night, staring out of the window, prowling the corridors – who was that looking at him? who was that talking about him? – spreading yet more sheets from *Pravda* down on the floor and obsessively cleaning his Makarov. (*'I'll kill them if I have to . . .'*)

But sometimes, when he wasn't drunk or exhausted or mad – in the mellow hour, between mere inebriation and oblivion – he'd talk about life in Kolyma: how you survived, traded favours and scraps of tobacco for food, wangled the easier jobs, learned to smell a stoolie – and then he'd take her on his lap and sing to her, some of the Kolyma songs, in his fine Mingrelian tenor.

That was a better memory.

At fifty he had seemed so *old* to her. He always had been an old man. His youth had gone when Stalin died. Maybe that was why he went on about him so much? He even had a picture of Stalin on the wall – remember that? – Stalin with his glossy moustaches, like great black slugs? Well, she could never take her friends back *there*, could she? Never let them see the pig state in which they lived. Two rooms, and her in the only bedroom, sharing first with Sergo and then, when he was too big and too embarrassed to look at her, with mama. And mama a wraith even before the cancer got her, then turning to gossamer and finally melting to nothing.

She'd died in eighty-nine when Zinaida was eighteen. And six months later they were back at the Troekurovo cemetery putting Sergo in the earth beside her. Zinaida closed her eyes and remembered papa, drunk, at the funeral, in the rain, and a couple of Sergo's army comrades, and a nervous young lieutenant, just a kid himself, who had been Sergo's commanding officer, talking about how Sergo had died for the motherland whilst rendering fraternal assistance to the progressive forces of the People's Republic of –

– oh, fuck it, what did it matter? The lieutenant had cleared off as soon as he decently could, after about ten minutes, and Zinaida had moved her things out of the ghost-filled apartment that night. He had tried to stop her, hitting her, sweating vodka through his open pores, stinking even more like an old dog from his soaking in the rain, and she had never seen him again. Never seen him again until last Tuesday morning when he had turned up on her doorstep and called her a whore. And she had thrown him out like a beggar, sent him away with a couple of packs of cigarettes, and now he was dead and she really would never see him again.

She bent her head, lips moving, and anyone watching might have thought she was praying, but actually she was reading his note and talking to herself.

'I have been a bad one, you're right. All you said was right. So don't think I don't know it —'

Oh, papa, you were, you know that? You really were.

'But here is a chance to do some good —'

Good? Is that what you call it? Good? That's a joke. They killed you for it and now they're going to kill me.

'Remember that place I used to have, when mama was alive?'

Yes, yes, I remember.

'And remember what I used to tell you? Are you listening to me, girl? Rule number one? What's rule number one?'

She folded away the note and glanced around. This was stupid.

'Speak up, girl!'

She bowed her head meekly.

Never show them you're afraid, papa.

'Again!'

'Never show them you're afraid.'

'And rule number two? What's rule number two?'

You've only got one friend in this world.

'And that friend is?'

Yourself.

'And what else?'

This.

'Show me.'

This, papa. This.

In the concealed darkness of the bag her fingers began to work her rosary, clumsily at first but with increasing dexterity —

Push. Click. Slide. Press —

*

239

SHE had left the church when the service ended and hurried down into Red Square, knowing what she had to do, much calmer now.

The westerner was right. She didn't dare risk her apartment. There wasn't a friend she knew well enough to ask if she could stay. And in a hotel she would have to register, and if Mamantov had friends in the FSB –

That only left one option.

It was nearly six and the shadows were beginning to collect and deepen around the base of Lenin's tomb. But across the cobbles the lights of the GUM department store blazed brighter by the minute – a line of yellow beacons, it seemed to her, in the gloom of the late October afternoon.

She made her purchases quickly, starting with a knee-length black cocktail dress of raw silk. She also bought herself sheer black tights, short black gloves, a black purse, a pair of black high-heeled shoes and make-up.

She paid for it all in cash, in dollars. She never went out with less than $1,000 in cash. She refused to use a credit card: they left too many traces. And she didn't trust the banks, either: thieving alchemists, the lot of them, who would take your precious dollars and conjure them into roubles, turn gold into base metal.

At the cosmetic counter one of the salesgirls recognised her – Hi, Zina! – and she had to turn and flee.

She went back into the boutique and took off her jeans and shirt and tugged herself into her new dress. It was hard to fasten the zip – she had to twist her left arm half way up her back and push her right hand down between her shoulder blades until her fingers touched, but it fastened eventually, pinching her flesh, and she stepped back a pace to look at herself – her hand on her hip, her chin tilted, her profile turned to the mirror.

Good.

Well: *good enough.*

The make-up took another ten minutes. She stuffed her old warm clothes into the GUM carrier bag, slipped on her leather jacket, and headed back into Red Square, tottering on her high heels over the big stones.

She was careful not to look at the Lenin mausoleum, nor at the Kremlin wall behind it, where her father used to take her when she was a girl to file past Stalin's tomb. Instead she walked quickly through the gate in the northern edge of the square, turned right and headed towards the Metropol. She wanted to have a drink at the hotel bar but the security men wouldn't let her through.

'No way, darling. Sorry.'

She could hear them laughing as she walked away.

'Starting early tonight?' one of them called after her.

It was dark by the time she reached her car.

WHICH was where she now sat.

Strange, she thought, looking back, the deaths of mama and Sergo – these two little deaths. *Strange.* They were like two small pebbles at the start of an avalanche. Because not long after they went, everything went – all the old, familiar world slid after them into the wet ground.

Not that Zinaida took much notice of the politics of it all. The first couple of years after leaving papa were a haze in her memory. She lived in a squat out in the Krasnogorsk district. Got pregnant twice. Had two abortions. (And not many days had gone by since when she hadn't wondered what they might have been like, those two – they'd be nearly nine and seven now – and whether they could have been any more clamorous than the spaces they'd left behind.)

Still: if she didn't notice the politics, she did notice the money that was now beginning to appear around the rich hotels – the Metropol, the Kempinski and the rest. And the money noticed her, like it noticed all the Moscow girls. Zinaida wasn't one of the most beautiful, maybe, but she was *good enough*: sufficiently Mingrelian to have an almost Oriental sharpness to her face, sufficiently Russian to have a padding of voluptuousness despite her skinny frame.

And as no girl in Moscow could earn in a month what a western businessman might spend in a night on a bottle of wine, you didn't have to be a genius at economics – you didn't have to be one of the hard-faced management consultants drinking at the bar – to see there was a market in the making here. Which was why one night in December 1992, at the age of twenty-one, in the hotel suite of a German engineer from Ludwigshafen am Rhein, Zinaida Rapava became a whore, tottering down the corridor after ninety sweaty minutes with $125 hidden in her bra, which was more money than she had ever even *seen.*

And shall I tell you something else, papa, now that we're talking at last? It was fine. *I* was fine. Because what was I doing, really, that ten million other girls don't do every night, only they don't have the sense to get paid for it? *That* was decadent. *This* was business – *kapitalism* – and it was fine, and it was like you said, I only had one friend: myself.

After a time, the trade moved out of the hotels and into the clubs, and that was easier. The clubs paid protection to the mafia, collecting a percentage from the girls, and in return the mafia kept the pimps out of it, so it all looked nice and respectable and everyone could pretend it was pleasure, not business.

Tonight, almost six years after that first encounter, hidden in her apartment – which was bought and paid for, by the way – Zinaida Rapava had nearly $30,000 in cash. And she had plans. She was studying law. She was going to be a lawyer. She was going to give up Robotnik, and Moscow with it, and move to St Petersburg and become a proper legal whore – a lawyer.

She was going to do all this until, on Tuesday morning, Papu Rapava had turned up out of nowhere, wanting to talk, calling her filthy names, bringing with him from the street the familiar, stinking dog's breath stench of *the past*.

SHE listened to the ten o'clock news, then switched on the ignition and drove slowly out of Bolshaya Lubyanka, heading north-west across Moscow to the Stadium of the Young Pioneers, where she parked in her usual spot, just off the darkened track.

The night was cold. The wind whipped the thin dress tight around her legs. She held on to her bag as she stumbled towards the lights. She would be safer inside.

Outside Robotnik there was a good crowd for a Thursday night, a nice line of rich western sheep all waiting to be fleeced. Normally her eyes would have flashed as sharp across them as a pair of shears, but not tonight, and she had to force herself forwards.

She went round to the back entrance, as normal, and the barman, Aleksey, let her in. She checked her jacket into the cloakroom and hesitated over her bag but then gave that to the old woman attendant as well: the floor of the Robotnik was not the wisest place in Moscow to be caught carrying a gun.

She could always pretend to be someone else when she

came to the club, and apart from the money that was the other good thing about it. (*'What's your name?'* they would say, trying to make some human contact. *'What name do you like?'* she would always reply.) She could leave her history at the door of the Robotnik, and hide behind this other Zinaida: sexy, self-possessed, hard. But not tonight. Tonight, as she stood in the ladies' toilet, freshening her make-up, the trick didn't seem to be working, and the face that stared back at her was indisputably her own: raw-eyed, frightened Zinaida Rapava.

SHE sat in one of the shadowy booths for an hour or more, watching. What she needed was someone who would take her for the whole night. Someone decent and respectable, with an apartment of his own. But how could you ever judge what men were really like? It was the young ones with the swaggering walks and the loud mouths who ended up bursting into tears and showing you pictures of their girlfriends. It was the bespectacled bankers and lawyers who liked to knock you around.

Just after half-past eleven, when the place was at its busiest, she made her move.

She circled the dance floor, smoking, holding a bottle of mineral water. Holy Mother, she thought, there were girls in here tonight who barely looked fifteen. She was practically old enough to have given them birth.

She was coming to the end of this life.

A man with dark curly hair poking through the straining buttons of his shirt came over to her but he reminded her of O'Brian and she side-stepped him through a cloud of aftershave, in favour of a big south-east Asian in an Armani suit.

He drained his drink – vodka, neat, no ice, she noticed: noticed it too late – and he got her on the dance floor. He quickly grabbed her backside, a cheek in either hand, and began digging his fingers into her, almost lifting her out of her new shoes. She told him to cut it out but he didn't seem to understand. She tried to press her arms against him, push him back, but he only increased his grip and something gave in her then, or rather joined – a kind of merging of the two Zinaidas –

'Are you a good Bolshevik, Anna Safanova? Will you prove it? Will you dance for Comrade Stalin?'

– and suddenly she raked the fingers of her right hand down his smooth cheek, so deep she was sure she could feel the glossy flesh clogging beneath her nails.

He released her then all right – roared and doubled over, shaking his head, spraying beads of blood around him in a series of perfect arcs, like a wet dog shaking off water. Someone screamed and people rippled away to give him space.

This was what they had come to see!

Zinaida ran – across the bar, up the spiral staircase, past the metal detectors and out into the cold. Her legs splayed like a cow's and gave way on the ice. She was sure he was coming after her. She dragged herself back up on to her feet and somehow made it to her car.

THE Victory of the Revolution apartment complex. Block Nine. In darkness. The cops had gone. The little crowd had gone. And soon the place itself would be gone – it had been jerrybuilt even by Soviet standards; it was going to be pulled down in a month or two.

She parked across the street, in the spot where she had

brought the westerner the night before, and stared at it across the roughened, freezing snow.

Block Nine.

Home.

She was so tired.

She grasped the top of the steering wheel with both hands and laid her forehead on her bare arms. She was done with crying by then. She had a very strong sense of her father's presence, and that stupid song he used to sing.

> *Kolyma, Kolyma,*
> *What a wonderful place!*
> *Twelve months of winter*
> *Summer all the rest . . .*

And wasn't there another verse? Something about twenty-four hours of work each day and sleeping all the rest? And so on and on? She knocked her head against her arms in time to the imagined beat, then rested her cheek against the wheel, and that was the moment that she remembered that she had left her bag with her gun in it back at the club.

She remembered it because a car, a big car, had drawn alongside her, very close, preventing her from pulling out, and a man's face was staring at her – a white blur distorted through two panes of dirty wet glass.

Chapter Eighteen

SILENCE WOKE HIM.

'What time is it?'

'Midnight.' O'Brian yawned noisily. 'Your shift.'

They were parked beside the deserted highway with the engine off. Kelso could see nothing, apart from a few faint stars up ahead. After the noise of the journey the stillness was almost physical, a pressure in the ears.

He pulled himself upright. 'Where are we?'

'About a hundred, maybe a hundred and twenty miles north of Vologda.' O'Brian snapped on the interior light, making Kelso flinch. 'Should be about here, I figure.'

He leaned over with the map, his big fingernail pressed to a spot that looked entirely blank, a white space split by the red line of the highway, with a few symbols for marshland dotted on either side of it. Further north the map turned green for the forest.

'I need a piss,' said O'Brian. 'You coming?'

It was much colder than in Moscow, the sky even bigger. A great fleet of vast clouds, pale-edged by the moonlight, moved slowly southwards, occasionally unveiling patches of stars. O'Brian had a torch. They scrambled down a short bank and stood urinating, companionably, side by side, for half a minute, steam rising from the ground before them, then O'Brian zipped up his flies and shone his torch around. The powerful beam stretched for a couple of hundred yards into the darkness, then dissipated; it lit nothing. A freezing mist hung low to the ground.

'Can you hear anything?' said O'Brian. His breath

flickered in the cold.

'No.'

'Neither can I.'

He switched off the torch and they stood there for a while.

'Oh, daddy,' whispered O'Brian, in a little boy's voice, 'I'm so *scared.*'

He turned the light back on and they climbed the bank to the Toyota. Kelso poured them both more coffee while O'Brian lifted up the rear door and dragged out a couple of the jerrycans. He found a funnel and began filling the tank.

Kelso, nursing his coffee, moved away from the gasoline fumes and lit a cigarette. In the darkness, in the cold, under the immense Eurasian sky, he felt disconnected from reality, frightened yet strangely exhilarated, his senses sharpened. He heard a rumble far away and a yellow dot appeared far back on the straight highway. He watched it grow slowly, saw the gleam divide and become two big headlights, and for a moment he thought they were coming directly at him, and then a big truck, a sixteen-wheeler, rushed past, the driver merrily sounding his horn. The noise of the engine was still faintly audible in the distance long after the red tail lights had vanished in the dark.

'Hey, Fluke! Give us a hand here, will you?'

Kelso took a last draw on his cigarette and flicked it away, spinning orange sparks across the road.

O'Brian wanted help lifting down one of his precious pieces of equipment, a white polycarbonate case, about two feet long and eighteen inches wide, with a small pair of black wheels mounted on one end. Once they'd pulled it out of the Toyota, O'Brian trundled it round to the front passenger door.

'Now what?' said Kelso.

'Don't tell me you've never seen one of these before?'

O'Brian opened the lid of the box and removed what looked like four white plastic trays, of the kind that fold out of aircraft seats. He slotted these together, creating a flat square about a yard across, which he then attached to the side of the case. Into the centre of the square he screwed a long, telescopic prong. He ran a cable from the side of the box to the Toyota's cigarette lighter, came back, flicked a switch and a variety of small lights blinked on.

'Impressed?' He produced a compass from his jacket pocket and shone his torch on it. 'Now where the hell is the Indian Ocean?'

'What?'

O'Brian glanced back along the M8. 'Right the way down there, by the look of it. Directly down there. A satellite in stationary orbit twenty thousand miles above the Indian Ocean. Think of that. Oh, but the world's a small place, is it not, Fluke? I swear I can almost hold it in my hand.' He grinned and knelt by the box, moving it around by degrees until the antenna was pointing directly south. At once the machine began to emit a whine. 'There you go. She's locked on to the bird.' He pressed a switch and the whining stopped. 'Now, we plug in the handset – so. We dial zero-four for the ground station at Eik in Norway – so. And now we dial the number. Easy as that.'

He stood and held out the handset and Kelso cautiously put his ear to it. He could hear a number ringing in America, and then a man said, 'Newsroom.'

KELSO lit another cigarette and walked away from the Toyota. O'Brian was in the front seat with the light on and even with the windows closed his voice carried in the cold silence.

'Yeah, yeah, we're on the road . . . About halfway I guess
. . . Yeah, he's with me . . . No, he's fine.' The door opened
and O'Brian shouted, 'You're fine, aren't you, professor?'
Kelso raised his hand.

'Yeah,' resumed O'Brian, 'he's fine.' The door slammed
and he must have lowered his voice because Kelso couldn't
catch much after that. 'Be there about nine . . . sure . . . good
stuff . . . looking good . . .'

Whatever it was, Kelso didn't like the sound of it. He
walked back to the car and flung open the door.

'Whoops. Gotta go, Joe. Bye.' O'Brian hung up quickly
and winked.

'What are you telling them exactly?'

'Nothing.' The reporter looked like a guilty boy.

'What d'you mean, nothing?'

'Come on, I had to give them the bones, Fluke. Give them
the gist –'

'The *gist?*' Kelso was shouting now. 'This was supposed to
be confidential –'

'Well, they're not going to tell anyone, are they? Come on,
I can't just take off without giving them an idea of what I'm
doing.'

'Christ.' Kelso slumped against the side of the Toyota and
appealed to the sky. 'What am I *doing?*'

'Want to make a call, Fluke?' O'Brian waved the handset
at him. 'Call a wife? On us?'

'No. There's no one I want to call right now. Thank you.'

'Zinaida?' said O'Brian craftily. 'Why don't you call
Zinaida?' He climbed out of the seat and pressed the telephone into Kelso's hand. 'Go ahead. I can tell you're worried.
It's *sweet*. Zero-four, then the number. Only don't take all
night about it. A fellow could freeze his balls off out here.'

He wandered away, flapping his arms against the cold, and Kelso, after a second's hesitation, hunted through his pockets for the scrap of paper with her address on it.

As he waited for the number to connect he tried to visualise her apartment, but he couldn't do it, he didn't know enough about her. He stared southwards down the M8 at the shadowy mass of departing clouds, fleeing as if from some calamity, and he imagined the route his call was taking – from the middle of nowhere to a satellite above the Indian Ocean, down to Scandinavia, across the earth to Moscow. O'Brian was right: you could stand in a great wilderness and the world still felt small enough to hold in your hand.

He let the number ring for a long time, alternately willing her to answer it so that he'd know she was safe, and hoping that she wouldn't, because her apartment was the least safe place of all.

She didn't answer and after a couple of minutes he hung up.

AND then it was Kelso's turn to drive while O'Brian slept, and even then the reporter couldn't be quiet. The sleeping bag was drawn tight up to his chin. His seat was tilted back almost to the horizontal. 'Yeah,' he'd mutter, and then, almost immediately, and with greater emphasis, *'yeah.'* He grunted. He curled up and flopped around like a landed fish. He snorted. He scratched his groin.

Kelso gripped the steering wheel hard. 'Can you shut up, O'Brian?' he said into the windscreen. 'I mean, just for once, could you possibly, as a favour to humanity, and more particularly to me, put a sock in your great fat mouth?'

There was nothing to see except the shifting patch of road in the headlights. Occasionally a car appeared in the opposite carriageway, lights full beam, blinding him. After about an hour he overtook the big truck that had passed them earlier. The driver hooted cheerfully again, and Kelso hooted back.

'Yeah,' said O'Brian, turning over at the sound of the horn, 'oh *yeah* –'

The drumming of the tyres was hypnotic and Kelso's thoughts were random, disconnected. He wondered what O'Brian would have been like in a *real* war, one in which he actually had to fight rather than just take pictures. Then he wondered what *he* would have been like. Most of the men he knew asked themselves that question, as if never having fought somehow made them incomplete – left a hole in their lives where a war should have been.

Was it possible that this *absence* of war – marvellous though it was and so forth: that went without saying – was it possible that it had actually *trivialised* people? Because everything was so bloody trivial now, wasn't it? This was The Trivial Age. Politics was trivial. What people worried about was trivial – mortgages and pensions and the dangers of passive smoking. Jesus! – he shot a look at O'Brian – is this what we've been reduced to, worrying about passive smoking, when our parents and our grandparents had to worry about being shot or bombed?

And then he began to feel guilty, because what was he implying here? That he wanted a war? Or a cold war, come to that? But it was true, he thought: he *did* miss the cold war. He was glad it was over, of course, in a way – glad the right side had won and all that – but at least while it was on people like him had known where they stood, could point to something and say: well, we may not know what we do believe in, but we don't believe in *that*.

The fact was, almost nothing had gone right for him since

the cold war ended. Here was a good joke. He and Mamantov: twin career victims of the end of the USSR! Both bemoaning the trivia of the modern world, both preoccupied with the past, and both in search of the mystery of Comrade Stalin –

He frowned, remembering something Mamantov had said.

'I'll tell you this, you're as obsessed as I am.'

He had laughed it off at the time. But now that he thought of it again, the line struck him as unexpectedly shrewd – unsettling, even, in the quality of its insight – and he found himself returning to it again and again as the temperature dropped and the road uncoiled endlessly from the freezing darkness.

HE drove for more than four hours, until his legs were numb and at one point he actually fell asleep, jerking awake to find the Toyota veering across the centre of the highway, the white lines flashing up at them like spears in the headlights.

A few minutes later they passed a kind of truckers' lay-by. He braked hard, stopped, and reversed back into it. Beside him, O'Brian struggled blearily into consciousness.

'Why're we stopping?'

'The tank's empty. And I've got to rest.' Kelso turned off the ignition and massaged the back of his neck. 'Why don't we stop here for a bit?'

'No. We need to keep moving. Fix us some coffee, will you? I'll fill her up.'

They went through the same ritual as before, O'Brian stumbling out into the cold and hoisting a pair of jerrycans from the back of the Toyota, while Kelso wandered away for a cigarette. The wind had a sharper edge to it this far north.

He could hear it slicing through trees he couldn't see. Running water splashed somewhere, softly.

When he got back into the car, O'Brian was in the driver's seat with the interior light on, running an electric shaver over his big chin, studying the map. It was an unnatural time to be awake, thought Kelso. It meant nothing good. He associated it with emergency, bereavement, conspiracy, flight; the sad skulk away at the end of a one-night affair.

Neither man spoke. O'Brian put away his shaver and stuffed the map into the pocket beside him.

The reclined seat was warm and so was the sleeping bag and within five minutes, despite his anxieties, Kelso was asleep – a dreamless, falling sleep – and when he awoke a few hours later it was as if they had crossed a barrier and entered another world.

Chapter Nineteen

A LITTLE TIME before this, when Kelso was still at the wheel, Major Feliks Suvorin had bent to kiss his wife, Serafima.

She offered him merely her cheek at first but then seemed to think the better of it. A warm, soft arm snaked up from beneath the duvet, a hand cupped the back of his head and drew him down. He kissed her mouth. She was wearing Chanel. Her father had brought it back from the last G8 meeting.

She whispered, 'You won't be back tonight.'

'I will.'

'You won't.'

'I'll try not to wake you.'

'Wake me.'

'Sleep.'

He put his finger to her lips and turned off the bedside lamp. The light from the passage showed him the way out of the bedroom. He could hear the sound of the boys' breathing. An ormolu clock announced it was one-thirty-five. He had been home two hours. *Hell.* He sat down on a gilt chair beside the door and put his shoes on, then collected his coat from its carved wooden hanger. The decor was copied from some glossy western magazine and it all cost far more than he earned as a major in the SVR; in fact, on his salary, they could barely afford the magazine. His father-in-law had paid.

On his way out, Suvorin glimpsed himself in the hall mirror, framed against a Jackson Pollock print. The lines and shadows of his exhausted face seemed to merge with those of the picture. He was getting too old for this kind of game, he thought: the golden boy no longer.

THE news that the Delta flight had taken off without Fluke Kelso had reached Yasenevo shortly after two in the afternoon. Colonel Arsenyev had expressed in various colourful colloquialisms – and had no doubt minuted elsewhere, for the record, more discreetly – his amazement that Suvorin had not arranged for the historian to be escorted on to the aircraft. Suvorin had choked back his response, which would have been to inquire, acidly, how he was supposed to locate Mamantov, control the militia, find the notebook *and* nursemaid an independent-minded western academic through Sheremetevo-2, all with the assistance of four men.

Besides, by then this was of less pressing importance than the discovery that the Interfax news agency was putting out a story on Papu Rapava's death, quoting unnamed 'militia sources' to the effect that the old man had been murdered while trying to sell some secret papers of Josef Stalin to a western author. Three outraged communist deputies had already attempted to raise the matter in the Duma. The Office of the President of the Federation had been on the line to Arsenyev, demanding to know (a direct quote from Boris Nikolaevich, apparently) *what the fuck was going on?* Ditto the FSB. Half a dozen reporters were camped outside Rapava's apartment block, more were besieging militia HQ, while the militia's official position was to hold up their hands and whistle.

For the first time, Suvorin had begun to see the merit of the old ways, when news was what Tass was pleased to announce and everything else was a state secret.

He had made one last attempt to play devil's advocate.

Weren't they in danger of getting this out of proportion? Weren't they playing Mamantov's game? What could Stalin's notebook possibly contain that would have any modern relevance?

Arsenyev had smiled: always a dangerous sign.

'When were you born, Feliks?' he had asked, pleasantly. 'Fifty-eight? Fifty-nine?'

'Sixty.'

'Sixty. You see, I was born in thirty-seven. My grandfather . . . he was shot. Two uncles went to the camps . . . never came back. My father died in some crazy business at the start of the war, trying to stop a German tank outside Poltava with a bit of rag and a bottle, and all because Comrade Stalin said that any soldier who surrendered would be considered a traitor. So I don't underestimate Comrade Stalin.'

'I'm sorry –'

But Arsenyev had waved him away. His voice was rising, his face red. 'If that bastard kept a notebook in his safe, he kept it for a reason, I can tell you that. And if Beria stole it, he had a reason. And if Mamantov is willing to risk torturing an old man to death, then he has a damned good reason for wanting to get his hands on it, too. So find it, Feliks Stepanovich, please, if you would be so good. *Find it.*'

And Suvorin had done his best. Every forensic document examiner in Moscow had been contacted. Kelso's description had been circulated, discreetly, to all the capital's militia posts, as well as to the traffic cops, the GAI. Technically, the SVR was now 'liaising' with the militia's murder inquiry, which meant at least he now had some resources to draw on: he had worked out a common line with the militia which they could spin to the media. He had spoken to a friend of his father-in-law's – the owner of the biggest chain of newspapers in the Federation – to plead for a little restraint. He had sent Netto to poke around Vspolnyi Street. He had arranged for a watch to be put on the apartment of Rapava's daughter, Zinaida, who had disappeared, and when she still hadn't turned up by nightfall he had sent Bunin to hang around the club she worked in, Robotnik.

Shortly after eleven o'clock, Suvorin had gone home.

And at one twenty-five he got the call that told him she had been found.

'WHERE was she?'

'Sitting in her car,' said Bunin. 'Outside her father's place. We followed her from the club. Waited to see if she was meeting anyone, but nobody else showed, so we picked her up. She's been in a fight, I reckon.'

'Why?'

'Well, you'll see when you go up. Take a look at her hand.'

They were standing, talking quietly, in the downstairs lobby of her apartment block, in the Zayauze district, a drab hinterland of eastern Moscow. She had a place close to the park – privatised, to judge by the neatness of its common parts; respectable. Suvorin wondered what the neighbours would think if they knew the girl on the third floor was a tart.

'Anything else?'

'The apartment's clean, and so's her car,' said Bunin. 'There's a bag of clothes in the back – jeans, T-shirt, pair of boots, knickers. But she's got a lot of money stashed up there. She doesn't know I found it yet.'

'How much?'

'Twenty, maybe thirty thousand dollars. Bound up tight in polythene and hidden in the lavatory cistern.'

'Where is it now?'

'I've got it.'

'Let's have it.'

Bunin hesitated, then handed it over: a thick bundle, all hundreds. He looked at it hungrily. It would take him four or five years to make that much and Suvorin guessed he had probably been on the point of helping himself to a percentage. Maybe he already had. He stuffed it into his pocket. 'What's she like?'

'A hard bitch, major. You won't get a lot out of her.' He tapped the side of his head. 'She's cracked, I reckon.'

'Thank you, lieutenant, for that valuable psychological insight. You can wait down here.'

Suvorin climbed the stairs. On the landing of the second floor, a middle-aged woman with her hair in curlers stuck her head round her door.

'What's going on?'

'Nothing, madam. Routine inquiries. You're perfectly safe.'

He carried on climbing. He had to make something of this, he thought. He must. It was the only lead he had. Outside the girl's apartment he squared his shoulders, knocked politely on the open door and went inside. A militia man got to his feet.

'Thank you,' said Suvorin. 'Why don't you go down and keep the lieutenant company?'

He waited until the door had closed before he took a proper look at her. She had a grey woollen cardigan on over her dress and she was sitting in the only chair, her legs crossed, smoking. In a dish on the little table next to her were the stubbed remains of five cigarettes. The apartment consisted of only this one room but it was neat and nicely done, with plenty of evidence of money spent: a western-made television with a satellite decoder, a video, a CD-player, a rack of dresses, all black. A little kitchen was off in one corner. A door led to the bathroom. There was a couch that presumably folded into a bed. Bunin was right about her hand, he noticed. The fingers that held the cigarette had blood crusted under the nails. She saw him looking.

'I fell,' she said, and uncrossed her legs, displaying a scraped knee, torn tights. 'All right?'

'I'll sit down.' She didn't reply, so he sat down anyway, on the edge of the couch, moving a couple of toys out of the way, a soldier and a ballerina. 'You have children?' he asked.

No answer.

'I have children. Two boys.' He searched the room for some other point of contact, some way of opening, but there was no evidence of any personality anywhere: no photographs, no books apart from legal manuals, no ornaments or knick-knacks. There was a row of CDs, all western and all by artists he'd never heard of. It reminded him of one Yasenevo's safe houses – a place to spend a night in and then move on.

She said, 'Are you a cop? You don't look like a cop.'

'No.'

'What are you, then?'

'I'm sorry about your father, Zinaida.'

'Thanks.'

'Tell me about your father.'

'What's to tell?'

'Did you get on with him?'

She looked away.

'Only I'm wondering, you see, why you didn't come forward when his body was discovered. You went to his apartment last night, didn't you, when the militia were there? And then you just drove away.'

'I was upset.'

'Naturally.' Suvorin smiled at her. 'Where's Fluke Kelso?'

'Who?'

Not bad, he thought: she didn't even flicker. But then she didn't know he had Kelso's statement.

'The man you drove to your father's apartment last night.'

'Kelso? Was that his name?'

'Oh you're a sharp one, Zinaida, aren't you? Sharp as a knife. So where have you been all day?'

'Driving around. Thinking.'

'Thinking about Stalin's notebook?'

'I don't know what you –'

'You've been with Kelso, haven't you?'

'No.'

'Where's Kelso? Where's the notebook?'

'Don't know what you're talking about. What d'you mean, anyway – you're not a cop? You got some papers that tell me who you are?'

'You spent the day with Kelso –'

'You've no right to be in my place without the proper papers. It says so in there.' She pointed to her legal books.

'Studying the law, Zinaida?' She was beginning to irritate him. 'You'll make a good lawyer.'

She seemed to find that funny: perhaps she had heard it before? He pulled out the bundle of dollars and that stopped her laughing. He thought she was going to faint.

'So what's the Federation statute on prostitution, Zinaida Rapava?' Her eyes on the money were like a mother's on her baby. 'You're the lawyer: you tell me. How many men in this little pile? A hundred? A hundred and fifty?' He flicked through the notes. 'Must be a hundred and fifty, surely – you're not getting any younger. But the others are, aren't they? They're getting younger every day. You know, I think you might never make this much back.'

'Bastard –'

He weighed the dollars from hand to hand. 'Think about it. A hundred and fifty men in return for telling me where I can find one? A hundred and fifty for one. That's not such a bad deal.'

'Bastard,' she said again, but with less conviction this time.

He leaned forward, soft-voiced, coaxing. 'Come on Zinaida: where's Fluke Kelso? It's important.'

And for a moment he thought she was going to tell him. But then her face hardened. '*You*,' she said. 'I don't care who *you* are. There's more honesty in whoring.'

'Now that may be true,' conceded Suvorin. Suddenly, he threw her the money. It bounced off her lap and on to the floor between her legs. She didn't even bend to pick it up, just looked at him. And he felt a great sadness then: sad for himself, that it should have come to this, sitting on a tart's bed in the Zayauze district, trying to bribe her with her own money. And sad for her, because Bunin was right, she *was* cracked, and now he would have to break her.

Chapter Twenty

IT NEVER SEEMED to get properly light, even two hours after dawn. It was as if the day had given up on itself before it even started. The sky stayed grey and the long concrete ribbon of road that ran straight ahead of them dwindled into a damp murk. On either side of the highway lay a wrinkled dead land of rust-coloured swamps and sickly, yellowish plains – the sub-Arctic tundra – that turned in the middle distance to dense, dark green forests of pine and fir.

It started to snow.

There was a lot of military traffic on the road. They passed a long column of armoured cars with watery headlights and soon afterwards began to see evidence of human settlement – shacks, barns, bits of agricultural machinery – even a collective farm with a broken hammer and sickle over the gate, and an old slogan: PRODUCTION IS VITAL FOR THE VICTORY OF SOCIALISM.

After a couple of miles the road crossed a railway line and a row of big chimneys appeared up ahead in the murk, gushing black soot into the snowy sky.

'That must be it,' said Kelso, looking up from the map. 'The M8 ends here, in the southern outskirts.'

'Shit,' said O'Brian.

'What?'

The reporter gestured with his chin. 'Road block.'

A hundred yards ahead a couple of GAI cops with lighted sticks and guns were waving down every vehicle to check the occupants' papers. O'Brian looked quickly in his mirror, but he couldn't reverse – there was too much traffic slowing

ROBERT HARRIS

behind them. And concrete sleepers laid across the centre of the road made it impossible to perform a U-turn and join the southbound carriageway. They were being forced into a single-lane queue.

'What did you call it?' said Kelso. 'My visa? A *detail?*'

O'Brian tapped his fingers on the top of the steering wheel.

'Is this check permanent, do you think, or just for us?'

Kelso could see a glass booth with a GAI man in it, reading a newspaper.

'I'd say permanent.'

'Well, that's something.' O'Brian began rummaging in the glove compartment. 'Pull your hood up,' he said, 'and get that sleeping bag up over your face. Pretend to be asleep. I'll tell 'em you're my cameraman.' He hauled out a crumpled set of papers. 'You're Vukov, okay? Foma Vukov.'

'Foma Vukov? What kind of a name is that?'

'You want to go straight back to Moscow? Well, do you? I'd say you've got two seconds to make up your mind.'

'And how old is this Foma Vukov?'

'Twentysomething.' O'Brian reached behind him and grabbed the leather satchel. 'You got a better idea? Stick this under your seat.'

Kelso hesitated, then wedged the satchel behind his legs. He lay back, drew up the sleeping bag and closed his eyes. Travelling without a visa was one crime. Travelling without a visa and using someone else's papers – that, he suspected, was quite another.

The car edged forwards, braked. He heard the engine switch off and then the hum of the driver's window being lowered. A blast of cold air. A gruff male voice said in Russian, 'Get out of the car please.'

The Toyota rocked as O'Brian clambered out.

With his heel, Kelso gently pushed at the satchel, jamming it further out of sight.

There was a second rush of cold as the rear door was lifted.

The sound of boxes being swung out, of catches snapping. Footsteps. A quiet conversation.

The door next to Kelso opened. He could hear the pattering of snowflakes, a man breathing. And then the door was closed – closed softly, with consideration, so as not to wake a sleeping passenger, and Kelso knew that he was safe.

He heard O'Brian load up the back and come round to the driver's seat. The engine started.

'It is surely most amazing,' said O'Brian, 'the effect of a hundred bucks on a cop who ain't been paid for six months.' He pulled the sleeping bag away from Kelso. 'This is your wake-up call, professor. Welcome to Archangel.'

THEY thumped across an iron bridge above the Northern Dvina. The river was wide, stained yellow by the tundra. Swollen currents rolled and flexed like muscles beneath its dirty skin. A couple of big black cargo barges, chained together, steamed north towards the White Sea. On the opposite bank, through the filter of snow and the spars of the bridge, they could see factory chimneys, cranes, apartment blocks, a big television tower with a winking red light.

As the vista broadened, even O'Brian's spirits seemed to fall. He called it a dump. He declared it a hole. He said it was the worst goddamn place he had ever seen.

A goods train clanked along the railroad track beside them. At the end of the bridge they turned left, towards what seemed to be the main part of the city. Everything had decayed. The façades of the buildings were pitted and peeling. Parts of the road had subsided. An ancient tram, in a brown and mustard livery, went rattling by, making a sound like a chain being dragged over cobbles. Pedestrians tilted drunkenly into the snow.

O'Brian drove slowly, shaking his head, and Kelso wondered what more he had been expecting. A press centre? A media hotel? They came out into the wide open space of a bus station. On the far side of it, on the waterfront, four giant Red Army men, cast in bronze, stood back to back, facing the four points of the compass, their rifles raised in triumph. At their feet, a pack of wild dogs scavenged among the trash. Nearby was a long, low building of white concrete and plate glass with a big sign: 'Harbour Master of Archangel'. If the city had a centre, this was probably it.

'Let's pull up over there,' suggested Kelso.

They cruised around the edge of the square and parked with their front bumper up close to the bent railings, looking directly out across the water. A husky watched them with detached interest, then brought its hind paw up to its neck and vigorously scratched its fleas. In the distance, through the snow, it was just possible to make out the flat shape of a tanker.

'You do realise,' said Kelso quietly, staring straight ahead across the water, 'that we are at the edge of the world? That at this point we are one hundred miles south of the Arctic Circle and there is nothing between us and the North Pole but sea and ice? You are aware of that?'

He started to laugh.

'What's funny?'

'Nothing.' He glanced at O'Brian and tried to stop himself, but it was no good, there was something about the reporter's utter dejection that set him off again. His vision was blurred by tears. 'I'm sorry,' he gasped. 'Sorry –'

'Oh, go ahead, enjoy yourself,' said O'Brian, bitterly. 'This is my idea of a perfect fucking Friday. Drive eight hundred miles to some dump that looks like Pittsburgh after a nuclear strike to try to find Stalin's fucking *girlfriend* –'

He snorted and started to laugh as well.

'You know what we haven't done?' O'Brian managed to say after a while.

Kelso took a breath and swallowed. 'What?'

'We haven't been to the railway station and checked the radiation meter . . . We're probably . . . being . . . fucking . . . *irradiated!*'

They roared. They cried. The Toyota rocked with it. The snow fell and the husky watched them, its head cocked in surprise.

O'BRIAN locked the car and they hurried through the snow, across the treacherous expanse of subsiding concrete, into the port authority building.

Kelso carried the satchel.

They were both still slightly shaky and the advertised ferry sailings – to Murmansk and the Groaning Islands – briefly set them off again.

The Groaning Islands?

'Oh come on, man. Stop it. We've got to do some work here.'

The building was bigger than it looked from the outside. On the ground floor there were shops – little kiosks selling clothes and toiletries – plus a café and a ticket booth. Downstairs, beneath banks of fluorescent lights, most of which had blown, was a gloomy underground market – stalls offering seeds, books, pirated cassettes, shoes, shampoo, sausages and some immense, sturdy Russian brassières in black and beige: miracles of cantilevered engineering.

O'Brian bought a couple of maps, one of the city and the other of the region, then they both went back upstairs to the ticket office where Kelso, in return for offering a dollar bill to a suspicious man in a greasy uniform, was permitted a brief look at the Archangel telephone directory. The book was small, red-bound, with hard covers and it took him less than thirty seconds to establish that no Safanov or Safanova was listed.

'Now what?' said O'Brian.

'Food,' said Kelso.

The café was an old-style *stolovaya*, a self-service workers' canteen, its floor wet and filthy with melted snow. There was a warm fug of strong tobacco. At the next door table a couple of German seamen were playing cards. Kelso had a big bowl of *shchi* – cabbage soup with a dollop of sour cream bobbing in its centre – black bread, a couple of hard-boiled eggs, and the effect of all this on his empty stomach was immediate. He began to feel almost euphoric. This was going to be all right, he thought. They were safe up here. Nobody could find them. And if they played it properly, they could be in and out in a day.

He tipped half a miniature of cognac into his instant coffee, looked at it, thought, *Sod it, why not?* and added the rest. He lit a cigarette and glanced around. The people up here appeared shabbier than they did in Moscow. They stared at foreign strangers. But when you attempted to meet their eyes they looked away.

O'Brian pushed his plate to one side. 'I've been thinking about this college, whatever it was – this "Maxim Gorky Academy". They'll have old records, right? And there was this girl she knew – what was her name, the ugly kid?'

'Maria.'

'Maria. Right. Let's find her class yearbook and find Maria.'

Class yearbook? thought Kelso. Who did O'Brian think she was? The Maxim Gorky prom queen, 1950? But he was too full of goodwill to pick a fight. 'Or,' he said, diplomatically, '*or* we could try the local Party. She was in Komsomol, remember. They might still have the old files.'

'Okay. You're the expert. How d'we find 'em?'

'Easy. Give me the town plan.'

O'Brian pulled the map from his inside pocket and scraped his chair round until he was sitting next to Kelso. They spread out the city plan.

The bulk of Archangel was crammed into a wide headland, about four miles across, with ribbons of development running out along either bank of the Dvina.

Kelso put his finger on the map. 'There,' he said. 'That's where they are. Or were. On the ploshchad Lenina, in the biggest building on the square. That's where the bastards always were.'

'And you think they'll help?'

'No. Not willingly. But if you can provide a little financial lubrication . . . It's worth a try, anyway.'

On the map it looked like a five-minute walk.

'You're really getting into this, aren't you?' said O'Brian. He gave Kelso's arm an affectionate pat. 'We make a good team, you know that? We'll show 'em.' He folded away the map and put a five roubles note under his plate as a tip.

Kelso finished his coffee. The cognac gave him a warm glow. O'Brian really wasn't such a bad fellow, he thought. Sooner him than Adelman and the rest of those waxworks, no doubt safely stowed in New York by now.

History wasn't made without taking risks, that much he knew. So maybe sometimes you had to take risks to write it, too?

O'Brian was right.

He would show them.

Chapter Twenty-one

THEY WENT BACK out into the snow, past the Toyota and past the shuttered front of a decaying hospital: the Northern Basin Seamen's Policlinic. The wind was driving the snow inshore across the water, whining through the steel rigging of the boats on the wooden jetty, bending the stumpy trees that had been planted along the promenade to protect the buildings. The two men had to struggle to keep their feet.

A couple of the boats had sunk, and so had the wooden hut at the end of the jetty. Benches had been heaved by vandals over the railings into the river. There was graffiti on the walls: a Star of David, dripping blood, with a swastika daubed across it; SS flashes; KKK.

One thing was sure: there wouldn't be any Italian shoe boutiques up here.

They turned inland.

Every Russian town still had its statue of Lenin. Archangel's portrayed the Leader, fifteen yards high, rising out of a block of granite, his face determined, his overcoat flapping, a roll of papers in his outstretched hand. He looked as if he were trying to hail a taxi. The square that still carried his name was huge, and smooth with snow, and deserted; in one corner, a couple of tethered goats nibbled at a bush. Fronting it were a big museum, the city's central post office, and a huge office block with the hammer and sickle still attached to the balcony.

Kelso led the way towards it and they had almost made it when a sandy-coloured jeep with a searchlight mounted on its hood came round the corner: Interior Ministry troops, the

271

MVD. That sobered him up. He could be stopped at any minute, he realised, and forced to show his visa. The pale faces of the soldiers stared at them. He bowed his head and trotted up the steps, O'Brian close behind him, as the jeep completed its cautious circuit of the square and passed out of sight.

THE communists had not been forced entirely from the building; they had merely moved round to the back. Here they maintained a small reception area presided over by a big, middle-aged woman with a froth of dyed yellow hair. Beside her, along the window sill, was a row of straggling spider plants in old tin cans; opposite her, a big colour poster of Gennady Zyuganov, the Party's pudding-faced candidate in the last presidential election.

She studied O'Brian's business card intently, turning it over, holding it to the light, as if she suspected forgery. Then she picked up the telephone and spoke quietly into the receiver.

Outside, through the double glass, the snow was beginning to pile in the courtyard. A clock ticked. Beside the door Kelso noticed a bundle of the latest issue of *Aurora*, tied up with string, awaiting distribution. The headline was a quote from the Interior Ministry's report to the president: 'VIOLENCE IS INEVITABLE'.

After a couple of minutes, a man appeared. He must have been about sixty – an odd-looking figure. His head was too small for his heavy torso, his features too small for his face. His name was Tsarev, he said, holding out a hand stained black with ink. *Professor* Tsarev. Deputy First Secretary of the Regional Committee.

Kelso asked if they could have a word.

Yes. Perhaps. That would be possible.

Now? In private?

Tsarev hesitated, then shrugged. 'Very well.'

He led them down a dark corridor and into his office, a little time warp from the Soviet days, with its pictures of Brezhnev and Andropov. Kelso reckoned he must have visited a score of offices like this over the years. Wood block flooring, thick water pipes, a heavy radiator, a desk calendar, a big green Bakelite telephone, like something out of a 1950s science fiction movie, the smell of polish and stale air – every detail was familiar, right down to the model Sputnik and the clock in the shape of Zimbabwe left behind by some visiting Marxist delegation. On the shelf behind Tsarev's head were six copies of Mamantov's memoirs, *I Still Believe.*

'I see you have Vladimir Mamantov's book.' It was a stupid thing to say but Kelso couldn't help himself.

Tsarev turned round, as if noticing them for the first time. 'Yes. Comrade Mamantov came to Archangel and campaigned for us, during the presidential elections. Why? Do you know him?'

'Yes. I know him.'

There was a silence. Kelso was aware of O'Brian looking at him, and of Tsarev waiting for him to speak. Hesitantly, he began his rehearsed speech. First of all, he said, he and Mr O'Brian would like to thank Professor Tsarev for seeing them at such short notice. They were in Archangel for one day only, making a film about the residual strength of the Communist Party. They were visiting various towns in Russia. He was sorry they had not been in contact earlier to make a proper appointment, but they were working quickly –

'And Comrade Mamantov sent you?' interrupted Tsarev.

'Comrade Mamantov sent you *here?*'

'I can truthfully say we would not be here without Vladimir Mamantov.'

Tsarev began nodding. Well, this was a most excellent subject. This was a subject *wilfully ignored* in the west. How many people in the west knew, for example, that in the Duma elections, the communists had taken thirty per cent of the votes, and then, in 1996, in the presidential elections, forty per cent? Yes, they would be in power again soon. Sharing power to begin with, perhaps, but afterwards – who could say?

He became more animated.

Take the situation here in Archangel. They had millionaires, of course. Wonderful! Unfortunately, they also had organised crime, unemployment, AIDS, prostitution, drug addiction. Were his visitors aware that life expectancy and child-mortality in Russia had now reached African levels? Such progress! Such freedoms! Tsarev had been a professor of Marxist theory in Archangel for twenty years – the post was now abolished, naturally – so he had taught Marxism in a Marxist state, but it was only now, as they were literally tearing down Marx's statues, that he had come to appreciate the genius of the man's insight: that money robs the whole world, both the human world and nature, of their own proper value –

'Ask him about the girl,' whispered O'Brian. 'We haven't got time for all this bullshit. Ask him about Anna.'

Tsarev had halted in mid-speech and was looking from one man to the other.

'Professor Tsarev,' said Kelso, 'to illustrate our film we need to look at particular human stories –'

That was good. Yes. He understood. The human element.

There were many such stories in Archangel.

'Yes, I'm sure. But we have in mind one in particular. A girl. Now a woman in her sixties. She would be about the same age as you. Her unmarried name was Safanova. Anna Mikhailovna Safanova. She was in the Komsomol.'

Tsarev stroked the end of his squat nose. The name, he said, after a moment's thought, was not familiar. This would have been some time ago, presumably?

'Almost fifty years.'

Fifty years? It was not possible! Please! He would find them other persons –

'But you must have records?'

– he would show them females who fought the fascists in the Great Patriotic War, Heroes of Socialist Labour, Holders of the Order of the Red Banner. Magnificent people –

'Ask him how much he wants,' said O'Brian, not even bothering to whisper now. He was pulling out his wallet. 'To look in his files. What's his price?'

'Your colleague,' said Tsarev, 'is not happy?'

'My colleague was wondering,' said Kelso, delicately, 'if it would be possible for you to undertake some research work for us. For which we would be happy to pay you – to pay the Party, that is – a fee . . .'

IT would not be easy, said Tsarev.

Kelso said he was sure it would not be.

The membership of the Communist Party in the last years of the Soviet Union comprised seven per cent of the adult population. Apply those figures to Archangel and what did you get? Maybe 20,000 members in the city alone, and perhaps the same number again in the oblast. And to those figures you had to add the membership of Komsomol and of all the other Party outfits. And then, if you included all the people who had been members over the past eighty years – the people who had died or dropped out, been shot, imprisoned, exiled, purged – you had to be looking at a really large number. A huge number. Still –

Two hundred dollars was the sum they agreed on. Tsarev insisted on providing a receipt. He locked the money into a battered cash box which he then locked in a drawer, and Kelso realised, with a curious sense of admiration, that Tsarev probably did intend to give the money to Party funds. He wouldn't keep it for himself: he was a true believer.

The Russian conducted them back along the passage and into reception. The woman with the dyed blonde hair was watering her tinned plants. *Aurora* still proclaimed that violence was inevitable. Zyuganov's fat smile remained in place. Tsarev collected a key from a metal cupboard and they followed him down two flights of stairs into the basement. A big, blast-proof iron door, studded with bolts, thickly painted a battleship grey, swung open to show a cellar, lined with wooden shelving, piled with files.

Tsarev put on a pair of heavy-framed spectacles and began pulling down dusty folders of documents while Kelso looked around with wonder. This was not a storeroom, he thought. This was a catacomb, a necropolis. Busts of Lenin, and of Marx and Engels, crowded the shelves like perfect clones. There were boxes of photographs of forgotten Party appa-ratchiks and stacked canvases of socialist realism, depicting bosomy peasant girls and worker-heroes with granite mus-cles. There were sacks of decorations, diplomas, membership cards, leaflets, pamphlets, books. And then there were the flags – little red flags for children to wave, and swirling crim-son banners for the likes of Anna Safanova to parade with.

It was as if a great world religion had been suddenly obliged to strip its temples and hide everything underground – to preserve its texts and icons out of sight, in the hope of better times, the Second Coming –

The Komsomol lists for 1950 and 1951 were missing.

'What?'

Kelso wheeled round to find Tsarev frowning over a pair of folders, one in either hand.

It was most curious, Tsarev was saying. This would need to be investigated further. They could see for themselves – he held out the files for their inspection – the lists were here for 1949 and here, also, for 1952. But in neither of those years was there an Anna Safanova listed.

'She was too young in forty-nine,' said Kelso, 'she wouldn't have qualified.' And by 1952 God alone knew what might have happened to her. 'When were they removed?'

'April, fifty-two,' said Tsarev, frowning. 'There's a note. "To be transferred to the archives of the Central Committee, Moscow."'

'Is there a signature?'

Tsarev showed it him: '"A. N. Poskrebyshev."'

O'Brian said, 'Who's Poskrebyshev?'

Kelso knew. And so, he could see, did Tsarev.

'General Poskrebyshev,' said Kelso, 'was Stalin's private secretary.'

'So,' said Tsarev, a little too quickly, 'a mystery.' He began putting the files back up on the shelf. Even after fifty years and all that had happened the signature of Stalin's secretary was still enough to unsettle a man of the right age. His hands shook. One of the folders slipped through his fingers and flopped to the floor. Pages spilled. 'Leave it, please. I'll attend to it.' But Kelso was already on his knees, gathering the loose sheets.

'There is one other thing you could do for us,' he said.

'I don't think so –'

'We believe that Anna Safanova's parents were probably both Party members.'

It was impossible, said Tsarev. He couldn't let them look. Those records were confidential.

'But you could look for us –'

No. He didn't think so.

He held out his inky hand for the missing pages and suddenly O'Brian was beside him, bending, and pressing into his outstretched palm another two hundred dollars.

'It really would help us very much,' said Kelso, desperately waving O'Brian away and nodding to emphasise each word, '*help us very much with our film*, if you could look them up.'

But Tsarev ignored him. He was staring at the two one-hundred dollar bills, and the face of Benjamin Franklin, shrewd and appraising, gazed back up at him.

'There isn't anything, is there,' he said slowly, 'that you people don't think you can buy with money?'

'No insult was intended,' said Kelso. He gave O'Brian a murderous look.

'Yeah,' muttered O'Brian, 'no offence.'

'You buy our industries. You buy our missiles. You try to buy our archives –'

His fingers contracted around the notes, screwing them tight, then he let the money fall.

'Keep your money. To hell with you and your money.'

He turned and bent his head, busied himself with putting all the records in the proper order. There was silence save for the rustling of dried paper.

Well done, mouthed Kelso at O'Brian. *Congratulations –*

A minute passed.

And then, unexpectedly, Tsarev spoke. 'What did you say their names were?' he said, without looking round. 'The parents?'

'Mikhail,' said Kelso quickly, 'and –' And, hell, what was the mother called? He tried to remember the NKVD report. Vera? Varushka? No, Vavara, that was it. 'Mikhail and Vavara Safanova.'

Tsarev hesitated. He turned to look at them, an expression on his narrow face that mingled dignity with contempt. 'Wait here,' he said. 'Don't touch anything.'

He disappeared to another part of the storeroom. They could hear him moving around.

O'Brian said, 'What's going on?'

'I think,' said Kelso, 'I *think* it's called making a point. He's gone to see if there are any records on Anna's parents. And no bloody thanks to you. Didn't I tell you: *leave the talking to me?*'

'Well, it worked didn't it?' O'Brian stooped and picked up the crumpled dollars, smoothed them out and replaced them in his wallet. 'Jesus, what a boneyard.' He picked up a nearby head of Lenin. 'Alas, poor Yorick . . .' He stopped. He couldn't remember the rest of the quotation. 'Here you go, professor. Have a souvenir.' He tossed the bust to Kelso, who caught it and quickly set it down.

'Don't,' he said. His good mood had gone. He was sick of O'Brian, but it wasn't only that. There was something else – something about the atmosphere down here. He couldn't define it exactly.

O'Brian sneered. 'What's up with you?'

'I don't know. "God is not mocked."'

'And neither is Comrade Lenin? Is that it? Poor old Fluke. You know what? I think you're beginning to lose it.'

Kelso would have told him to go to hell, but Tsarev was on his way back, carrying another file and now he was looking triumphant.

Here was a subject who would be suitable for their filming. Here was a woman who had never been bought – he glared at O'Brian – a person who was a lesson to them all. Vavara Safanova had joined the Communist Party in 1935 and had stayed with it, through good times and bad. She had a list of citations bestowed by the Archangel Central Committee that took up half a page. Oh yes: here was the indomitable spirit of socialism that could never be conquered!

Kelso smiled at him. 'When did she die?'

Ah! That was the thing. She hadn't died.

'Vavara Safanova?' repeated Kelso. He couldn't believe it. He exchanged a look with O'Brian. 'Anna Safanova's *mother?* Still *alive?*'

Still alive last month, said Tsarev. Still alive at eighty-five! It was written here. They could take a look. More than sixty years a faithful member – she had just paid her Party dues.

Chapter Twenty-two

IT WAS MORNING in Moscow.

Suvorin was in the back of the car with Zinaida Rapava. Militia liaison was sitting up front with the driver. The doors were locked. The Volga was wedged in the stream of sluggish traffic on the road heading south towards Lytkarino.

The militia man was complaining. They should have come in a different car – to force their way through this lot needed revolving lights and sound effects.

And who do you think you are? thought Suvorin. The President?

Zinaida's eyes looked bruised and puffy from lack of sleep. She wore a raincoat over her dress and her knees were turned towards the door, putting as much seat leather as she could between herself and Suvorin. He wondered if she knew where they were going. He doubted it. She seemed to have gone off somewhere into the heart of herself and barely to be aware of what was happening.

Where was Kelso? What was in the notebook? The same two questions, over and over, first at her place, then upstairs in the front office that the SVR maintained in downtown Moscow – the place where visiting western journalists were entertained by the Service's smiling, Americanized public relations officer. (See, gentlemen, how democratic we are! Now what can we do to help?) No coffee for her and no cigarettes, either, once she had smoked the last of her own. Write a statement, Zinaida, then we tear it up and we write it again, and again, as the clock drags on till nine, which is when Suvorin can play his ace.

281

She was as stubborn as her father.

In the old days, in the Lubyanka, they had operated a system called The Conveyer Belt: the suspect was passed between three investigators working eight-hour shifts in rotation. And after thirty-six hours without sleep most people would sign anything, incriminate anyone. But Suvorin didn't have back-up and he didn't have thirty-six hours. He yawned. His eyes seemed full of grit. He guessed he was as tired as she was.

His mobile telephone rang.

'Go ahead.'

It was Netto.

'Good morning, Vissari. What do you have?'

A couple of things, said Netto. One: the house in Vspolnyi Street. He had established that it belonged to a medium-sized property company called Moskprop, who were trying to let it for $15,000 a month. No takers so far.

'At that price? I'm not surprised.'

Two: it looked as though something *had* been dug up in the garden in the past couple of days. There was loose soil in one spot to a depth of five feet, and forensics reported traces of ferrous oxide in the earth. Something had been rusting away down there for years.

'Anything else?'

'No. Nothing on Mamantov. He's evaporated. And the colonel's agitated. He's been asking for you.'

'Did you tell him where I was?'

'No, lieutenant.'

'Good man.' Suvorin rang off. Zinaida was watching him.

'You know what I think?' said Suvorin, 'I think your old papa went and dug up that toolbox just before he died. And then I think he gave it to you. And then I reckon you gave it to Kelso.'

It was only a theory, but he thought he saw something flicker in her eyes before she turned away.

'You see,' he said, 'we *will* get there in the end. And we'll get there without you, if necessary. It's just going to take us more time, that's all.'

He settled back in his seat.

Wherever Kelso was, he thought, the notebook would be. And wherever the notebook was, Vladimir Mamantov would be as well – if not now, then very soon. So the answer to one question – where was Kelso? – would provide the solution to all three problems.

He glanced at Zinaida. Her eyes were closed.

And *she* knew it, he was sure of it.

It was so infuriatingly simple.

He wondered if Kelso had any idea how physically close Mamantov might be to him at that moment, and how much danger he was in. But of course he wouldn't, would he? He was a westerner. He would think he was immune.

The journey dragged on.

'THAT'S it,' said the militia man, pointing a thick forefinger. 'Up there, on the right.'

It looked a grim place in the rain, a warehouse of dull red brick, with small windows set behind the usual cobweb of iron bars. There was no nameplate beside the dingy entrance.

'Let's drive round the back,' suggested Suvorin. 'See if you can park.'

They swung right and right again, through open wooden gates, into an asphalt courtyard glistening in the wet. There was an old green ambulance with its windows painted out parked in one corner, next to a large black van. Big drums of corrugated metal were piled with white plastic sacks, tied with tape and stamped SURGICAL WASTE in red letters. Some had toppled off and split open, or been torn open by dogs, more like. Sodden, bloodied linen soaked up the rain.

The girl was sitting erect now, staring about her, beginning to guess where she was. The militia man levered his big frame out of the front seat and came round to open her door. She didn't move. It was Suvorin who had to take her gently by her arm and coax her out of the car.

'They've had to convert this place. And there's another warehouse out in Elektrostal, apparently. But there you are. That's the crime-wave for you. Even the dead are obliged to sleep rough. Come on, Zinaida. It's a formality. It has to be done. Besides, I'm told it often helps. We must always look our terrors in the eye.'

She shook her arm free of him and gathered her coat around herself and he realised that actually he was more nervous than she was. He had never seen a corpse before. Imagine it: a major of the former First Chief Directorate of the KGB and he had never seen a dead man. This whole case was proving an education.

They picked their way through the refuse, past a goods lift, and into the back of the warehouse – the militia man in the lead, then Zinaida, then Suvorin. It had been a cold store originally, for fish trucked north from the Black Sea, and there was still a slight tang of brine to the air, despite the smell of chemicals.

The policeman knew the drill. He put his head into a glassed-in office and shared a brief joke with whoever was inside, then another man appeared, shrugging on a white coat. He held back a high curtain of thick black rubber strips and they passed into a long corridor, wide enough to take a fork-lift truck, with heavy refrigerated doors off to either side.

In America – Suvorin had seen this on a video of a cops-and-robbers programme Serafima liked to watch – the bereaved could view their loved ones on a monitor, comfortably screened from the physical reality of death. In Russia, no such delicacy attended the extinct. But, there again, in fairness to the authorities, it had to be said that they had done their best with limited resources. The viewing room – if approached from the street entrance – was out of sight of the refrigerators. Also, a couple of bowls of plastic flowers had been placed on a covered table, on either side of a brass cross. The trolley was in front of these, the outline of the body clear beneath the white sheet. *Small,* thought Suvorin. He had expected a larger man.

He made sure he stood next to Zinaida. The militia man was beside his friend, the morgue technician. Suvorin nodded and the technician folded back the top part of the sheet.

Papu Rapava's mottled face, his thin grey hair combed back and neatly parted, stared through blackened eyelids at the peeling roof.

The militia man intoned the formal words in a bored voice, 'Witness, is this Papu Gerasimovich Rapava?'

Zinaida, her hand to her mouth, nodded.

'Speak please.'

'It is.' They could hardly hear her. And then, more loudly: 'Yes. It is.'

She glanced sideways at Suvorin, defiantly.

The technician began to replace the sheet.

'Wait,' said Suvorin.

He reached out for the edge of the sheet that was closest to him and pulled, hard. The thin nylon whisked away, billowed clear of the body and settled on the floor.

A silence, and then her scream split the room.

'And is *this* Papu Gerasimovich Rapava? Take a look, Zinaida.' He didn't look himself – he had only a vague impression, thankfully – his eyes were fixed on her. 'Take a look at what they did to him. This is what they'll do to you. And to your friend Kelso, if they catch him.'

The technician was shouting something. Zinaida, yelling, reeled away, towards the corner of the room, and Suvorin went after her – this was his moment, his only moment: he had to strike. 'Now, tell me where he is. I'm sorry, but you've got to tell me. Tell me where he is. I'm sorry. Now.'

She turned and her arm flailed out at him, but the militia man had her by her coat and was pulling her backwards. 'Eh, eh,' he said, 'enough of that,' and he spun her round and on to her knees.

Suvorin got on to his knees as well and shuffled after her. He cupped her face between his hands. 'I'm so sorry,' he said. Her face seemed to be dissolving beneath his fingers, her eyes were liquid, blackness was trickling down her cheeks, her mouth a black smear. 'It's all right. I'm sorry.'

She went still. He thought she might have fainted but her eyes were still open.

She wouldn't break. He knew it at that moment. She was her father's daughter.

After maybe half a minute, he released her and sat back on his heels, head bowed, breathing hard. Behind him, he heard the noise of the trolley being wheeled away.

'You're a madman,' said the technician, incredulously. 'You're fucking mad, you are.'

Suvorin raised his arm in weary acknowledgement. The door slammed shut. He rested his palms on the cold stone floor. He hated this case, he realised, not simply because it was so damned impossible and freighted with risk, but because it made him realise just how much he hated his own country: hated all those old-timers turning out on Sunday mornings with their pictures of Marx and Lenin, and the hard-faced fanatics like Mamantov who just wouldn't give up, who just didn't get it, couldn't see that the world had changed.

The dead weight of the past lay across him like a toppled statue.

It took an effort, pressing hard on the smooth stone, to push himself up on to his feet.

'Come on,' he said. He offered her his hand.

'Archangel.'

'What?' He looked down at her. She was watching him from the floor. There was a frightening calmness about her. He moved closer to her. 'What was that?'

She said it again.

'Archangel.'

HE held on to the tails of his overcoat and carefully lowered himself back to the floor and sat close to her. They both had their backs propped up against the wall, like a couple of survivors after an accident.

She was staring straight ahead and was talking in an odd monotone. He had his notebook open and his pen was working fast, tearing across the page, filling one sheet then flicking it over to start another. Because she might stop, he thought, stop talking as suddenly as she'd started –

He had gone to Archangel, she said. Driving. Gone up north, him and the reporter from the television.

Fine, Zinaida, take your time. And when was this?

Yesterday afternoon.

When exactly?

Four, maybe. Five. She couldn't remember. Did it matter?

What reporter?

O'Brian. An American. He was on the television. She didn't trust him.

And the notebook?

Gone. Gone with them. It was hers but she didn't want it. She wouldn't touch it. Not after she had worked out what it was about. It was cursed. The thing was cursed. It killed everyone who touched it.

She paused, staring at the spot where her father's body had been. She covered her eyes.

Suvorin waited, then said, Why Archangel?

Because that was where the girl had lived.

Girl? Suvorin stopped writing. What was she talking about? What *girl?*

'LISTEN,' he said, a few minutes later, when he had put his notebook away, 'you're going to be all right. I'm going to see to that, personally, do you understand me? The Russian government *guarantees* it.'

(What was he talking about? The Russian government couldn't guarantee a damned thing. The Russian government couldn't guarantee its president wouldn't drop his pants at a diplomatic reception and try to set light to one of his farts –)

'Now what I'm going to do is this. Here's my office number: it's a direct line. I'm going to get one of my men to take you back to your apartment, okay? And you can get some sleep. And I'll make sure there's a guard outside on the landing and one in the street. So no one's going to be able to get at you and harm you in any way. Right?'

He rushed on, making more promises he couldn't keep. I

should go into politics, he thought. I'm a natural.

'We're going to make sure Kelso is safe. And we're going to find the people – the man – who did this terrible thing to your father, and we're going to lock him up. Are you listening, Zinaida?'

He was on his feet again, surreptitiously looking at his watch.

'I've got to set things moving now. I've got to go. All right? I'm going to call Lieutenant Bunin – you remember Bunin, from last night? – and I'll get him to take you home.'

Halfway out the door he looked back at her.

'My name is Suvorin, by the way. Feliks Suvorin.'

THE militia man and the morgue assistant were waiting in the corridor. 'Leave her alone,' he said. 'She'll be fine.' They were looking at him strangely. Was it contempt, he wondered, or a wary respect? He wasn't sure which he deserved and he didn't have time to decide. He turned his back on them and called Arsenyev's number at Yasenevo.

'Sergo? I need to speak to the colonel . . . Yes, it's urgent. And I need you to fix some transport for me . . . Yes – are you ready? – I need you to fix me a *plane*.'

Chapter Twenty-three

ACCORDING TO HER Party record, Vavara Safanova had lived at the same address for more than sixty years, a place in the old part of Archangel, about ten minutes' drive from the waterfront, in a neighbourhood built of wood. Wooden houses were reached by wooden steps from wooden pavements – ancient timber, weathered grey, that must have been floated down the Dvina from the forests upstream long before the Revolution. It looked picturesque in the winter weather, if you could close your eyes to the concrete apartment blocks towering in the background. There were stacks of cordwood beside some of the houses and here and there a curl of smoke rose to lick the falling snow.

The roads were broad and empty, guarded on either side by sentinels of silver birch, and the surface in the snow was deceptively smooth. But the roads weren't made. The Toyota plunged into potholes as deep as a man's shin, jarring and bouncing down the wide track, until Kelso suggested they pull over and continue the search on foot.

He stood shivering on the duckboards as O'Brian rummaged around in the back. Across the street were a dozen railroad freight cars. Suddenly a homemade door in the side of one of them opened and a young woman climbed out, followed by two small children so thickly bundled against the cold they were almost spherical. She set off across the snowy field, the children dawdling behind her and staring at Kelso with solemn curiosity, until she turned and shouted sharply for them to follow her.

O'Brian locked the car. He was carrying one of the

aluminium cases. Kelso still had the satchel.

'Did you see that?' said Kelso. 'There are people actually living over there in those freight cars. Did you see that?'

O'Brian grunted and pulled up his hood.

They trudged down the side of the road, past a row of patched and tumbledown houses, each tilted at its own mad angle to the ground. Every summer the land must thaw, thought Kelso, and shift, and the houses with it. And then fresh boards would have to be nailed over the new cracks, so that some of the walls had skins of repairs that must date back to the Tsars. He had a sense of time frozen. It wasn't hard to imagine Anna Safanova, fifty years ago, walking where they walked, with a pair of ice skates slung around her shoulders.

It took them another ten minutes to find the old woman's street – an alley, really, no more, running off the main road, behind a clump of birch trees, and leading to the back of the house. In the yard were some animal coops: chickens, a pig, a couple of goats. And looming over it all, ghostly in the snow, a slab-sided fourteen-storey tower block, with a few yellow lights visible on the lower floors.

O'Brian unlocked his case, took out his video camera and started filming. Kelso watched him, unhappily.

'Shouldn't we check she's in first? Shouldn't you get her permission?'

'You ask her. Go ahead.'

Kelso glanced at the sky. The flakes seemed to be getting bigger – thick and soft as a baby's hand. He could feel a knot of tension in his stomach the size of his fist. He picked his way across the yard, past the hot stink of the goats, and started to climb the half-dozen loose wooden steps that led to the back porch. On the third step he paused. The door was partially open and in the narrow gap he could see an old woman, bent forwards, two hands resting on a stick, watching him.

He said, 'Vavara Safanova?'

She didn't say anything for a moment. Then she muttered, 'Who wants her?'

He took this as an invitation to climb the remaining steps. He wasn't a tall man but when he reached the rickety porch he soared above her. She had osteoporosis, he could see now. The tops of her shoulders were on a level with her ears and it gave her a watchful look.

He tugged down his hood and for the second time that morning he launched into his carefully prepared lie – they were in town to make a film about the communists; they were looking for people with interesting memories; they had been given her name and address by the local Party – and all the time he was appraising her, trying to reconcile this hunched figure with the matriarch who featured briefly in the girl's journal.

'Mama is strong, as ever . . . Mama brings me to the station . . . I kiss her dear cheeks . . .'

She had opened the door a crack wider to get a better look at him, and he could see more of her. Apart from her shawl the clothes she wore were masculine – old clothes: her dead husband's clothes, perhaps – with a man's thick socks and boots. Her face was still handsome. She might have been stunning once – the evidence was there, in the sharpness of her jaw and cheekbones, in the keenness of her one good blue-green eye; the other was milky with a cataract. It didn't take much effort to imagine her as a young communist in the 1930s, pioneer builder of a new civilisation, a socialist heroine to warm the hearts of Shaw or Wells. He bet she would have worshipped Stalin.

*'And Mama, yes, it is a modest house! Two storeys only. Your
good Bolshevik heart would rejoice at its simplicity . . . '*

' – so if it would be possible,' he concluded, 'for us to take
up some of your time, we would be very grateful.'

He transferred the satchel uneasily, from hand to hand. He
was conscious of the snow settling in a cold clump on his
back, of water trickling from his scalp, and of O'Brian at the
foot of the steps, filming them.

Oh God, throw us out, he thought suddenly. Tell us to go
to hell, and take our lies with us: I would if I were you. You
must know why we're here.

But all she did was turn and shuffle back into the room,
leaving the door wide open behind her.

KELSO went in first, and then O'Brian, who had to duck to
get through the low entrance. It was dark. The solitary
window was thickly glazed with snow.

If they wanted tea, she said, setting herself down heavily in
a hard-backed wooden chair, then they would have to make
it themselves.

'Tea?' said Kelso softly to O'Brian. 'She's offering to let us
make her tea. I think yes, don't you?'

'Sure. I'll do it.'

She issued a stream of irritated instructions. Her voice,
emanating from her buckled frame, was unexpectedly deep
and masculine.

'Well, get the water from the pail, then – no, not *that* jug:
that one, the *black* one – use the ladle, that's it – no, no *no* –'
she banged her stick on the floor ' – not that much, *that*
much. Now put it on the stove. And you can put some wood
on the fire, too, while you're about it.' Another two bangs of
the stick. '*Wood? Fire?*'

O'Brian appealed helplessly to Kelso for a translation.

'She wants you to put some wood on the fire.'

'Tea in that jar. No, no. Yes. *That* jar. Yes. *There.*'

Kelso couldn't get a handle on any of this – on the town, on her, on this place, on the speed with which everything seemed to be happening. It was like a dream. He thought he ought to start taking some notes, so he pulled out his yellow pad and began making a discreet inventory of the room. On the floor: a large square of grey linoleum. On the linoleum: one table, one chair and a bed covered with a woollen blanket. On the table: a pair of spectacles, a collection of pill-bottles and a copy of the northern edition of *Pravda*, open at the third page. On the walls: nothing, except in one corner, where a flickering red candle on a small sideboard punctuated the gloom, lighting a wood-framed photograph of V. I. Lenin. Hanging next to it were two medals for Socialist Labour and a certificate commemorating her fiftieth anniversary in the Party in 1984; by the time of her sixtieth, presumably, they couldn't run to such extravagance. The bones of communism and of Vavara Safanova had crumbled together.

The two men sat awkwardly on the bed. They drank their tea. It had a peculiar, herbal flavour, not unpleasant – cloudberries in it somewhere: a taste of the forest. She seemed to find nothing surprising in the fact of two foreigners arriving in her yard with a Japanese video camera, claiming to be making a film about the history of the Archangel Communist Party. It was as if she had been expecting them. Kelso guessed she would find no surprise in anything any more. She had the resigned indifference of extreme old age. Buildings and empires rose and fell. It snowed. It stopped snowing. People came and went. One day death would come for her, and she would not find that surprising, either, and she would not care – not so long as He trod in the proper places: 'No, not *there. There . . .*'

WELL, yes, she remembered the past, she said, settling back. Nobody in Archangel remembered the past better than she did. She remembered *everything*.

She could remember the Reds in 1917 coming out on to the street, and her uncle wheeling her up in the air, and kissing her and telling her the Tsar had gone and Paradise was on the way. She could remember her uncle and her father running away into the forest to hide when the British came to stop the Revolution in 1918 – a great grey battleship moored in the Dvina and runty little English soldiers swarming ashore. She *played* to the sound of gunfire. And then she remembered early one morning walking down to the harbour and the ship had gone. And that afternoon her uncle came back – but not her father: her father had been taken by the Whites and he never came back.

She remembered all these things.

And the kulaks?

Yes, she remembered the kulaks. She was seventeen. They arrived at the railway station, thousands of them, in their strange national dress. Ukrainians: you never saw so many people – covered in sores and carrying their bundles – they were locked in the churches and the townspeople were forbidden to approach them. Not that they wished to. The kulaks carried contamination, they all knew that.

Their sores were contagious?

No. The *kulaks* were contagious. Their *souls* were contagious. They carried the spores of counter-revolution. Bloodsuckers, spiders and vampires: that was what Lenin called them.

And so what happened to the kulaks?

It was like the English battleship. You went to bed at night and they were there, and you got up in the morning and they were gone. The churches were all closed after that. But now the churches were open again – she had seen it with her own eyes. The kulaks had come back. They were *everywhere*. It was a *tragedy*.

And the Great Patriotic War, she remembered that – the Allied ships moored out beyond the mouth of the river, and the docks working all day and all night, under the heroic direction of the Party, and the fascist planes dropping fire-bombs over the old wooden town and burning it, burning so much of it down. Those were the hardest times – her husband away fighting at the front, herself working as an auxiliary nurse at the Seamen's Policlinic, no food in the town and not much fuel, the black-out, the bombs and a daughter to bring up on her own . . .

ALL of this, of course, took much longer to extract than the printed record would suggest. There was a lot of banging of her stick and doubling-back and repitition and meandering, and Kelso was acutely aware of O'Brian fidgeting beside him and of the snow piling up and muffling the sounds outside. But he let her talk. Indeed, he kicked O'Brian twice on the ankle to warn him to be patient. He wanted to let her come to things in her own time.

Fluke Kelso was an expert at this. This was how the whole business had started, after all.

He sipped his cold tea.

So you had a daughter, Comrade Safanova? That's interesting. Tell us about your daughter.

Vavara prodded the linoleum with her stick. Her mouth turned down.

That was of no consequence to the history of the Archangel Regional Party.

'But it was of consequence to you?'

Well, naturally it was of consequence to *her*. She was the child's *mother*. But what was a child when set against the forces of history? It was a matter of *subjectivity* and *objectivity*. Of *who* and *whom*. And of various other slogans of the Party she could no longer fully remember, but which she knew to be true and which had been a comfort to her at the time.

She sat back, hunched in her chair.

Kelso reached for the satchel.

'Actually, I know something of what happened to your daughter,' he began. 'We have found a book, a journal, that Anna kept. That was her name, wasn't it? Anna? I wonder – can I show it you?'

Her eyes followed the movement of his hands, warily, as he began to unfasten the straps.

HER fingers were spotted with age, like the book itself, but they didn't tremble as she opened the cover. When she saw the picture of Anna, she touched it hesitantly, then her knuckle went to her mouth. She sucked on it. Slowly she brought the page up level with her face and held it close.

'I ought to be getting this on camera,' whispered O'Brian.

'Don't you dare even move,' hissed Kelso.

He couldn't see her expression, but he could hear her laboured breathing and again he had the odd sensation that she had been waiting for them – for years, maybe.

Eventually, she said, 'Where did you get this?'

'It was dug up. In a garden in Moscow. It was with some papers belonging to Stalin.'

When she lowered the book, her eyes were dry. She closed it and held it out to him.

'No. Read it,' he said. 'Please. It's hers.'

But she shook her head. She didn't want to.

'But that *is* her writing?'

'Yes, it's hers. Take it away.'

She waved the book at him and wouldn't rest until it was safely put back in the satchel. Then she sat back, leaning to her right, one hand covering her good eye, stabbing at the floor with her stick.

ANNA, she said, after a time.

Well. Anna.

Where to begin?

Truth to tell, she had been pregnant with Anna when she married. But people didn't care about such things in those times – the Party had done away with *priests*, thank God.

She was eighteen. Mikhail Safanov was five years older – a metallurgist in the shipyards and a member of the Party's factory committee.

A good-looking man. Their daughter took after him. Oh yes, Anna was a pretty thing. *That* was her tragedy.

'Tragedy?'

Clever, too. And growing up a good young communist. She was following her parents into the Party. She had served her time as a Pioneer. She was in the Komsomol: she looked like something out of a poster in her uniform. So much so that she had been picked for the Archangel Komsomol delegation to pass through Red Square – oh, a great honour, this – picked to pass beneath the eyes of the *Vozhd* himself, on May Day 1951.

Anna's picture had been in *Ogonyok* afterwards and

questions had been asked. That had been the start of it. Nothing had been the same after that.

Some comrades had come up from the Central Committee in Moscow the following week and had started asking around about her. And about the Safanovs.

And once word of this got out, some of their neighbours had started to avoid them. After all, though the arch-fiend Trotsky was dead at last, his spies and saboteurs might not be. Perhaps the Safanovs were wreckers or deviationists?

But of course nothing could have been further from the truth.

Mikhail had come home early from the shipyard one afternoon in the company of a comrade from Moscow – Comrade Mekhlis: she would never forget his name – and it was this comrade who had given them the good news. The Safanovs had been thoroughly checked and found to be loyal communists. Their daughter was a particular credit to them. So much so that she had been selected for special Party work in Moscow, attending to the needs of the senior leadership. Domestic service, but still: the work required intelligence and discretion, and afterwards the girl could resume her studies with good words on her file.

Anna – well, once Anna got to hear of it – there was no stopping her. And Vavara was in favour of it, too. Only Mikhail had been opposed. Something had happened to Mikhail. It pained her to say it. Something during the war. He had never spoken of it, except once, when Anna was talking, full of wonder, about the genius of Comrade Stalin. Mikhail said he had seen a lot of comrades die at the front: could she tell him, then, if Comrade Stalin was such a genius, why so many millions had had to die?

Vavara had made him rise from this very table – she struck

it with her hand – and go outside into the yard for his foolishness. No. He was not the man he had been before the war. He wouldn't even go to the railway station to see his daughter off.

She fell silent.

Kelso said quietly, 'And you never saw her again?'

Oh yes, said Vavara, surprised at the question. They saw her again.

She made a curving motion with her hands, outwards from her belly.

They saw her again when she came home to have the baby.

SILENCE.

O'Brian coughed and bent forwards, head down, his hands clasped tight in front of him, his elbows on his knees. 'Did she just say what I thought she said?'

Kelso ignored him. With great effort, he managed to keep his voice neutral.

'And when was this?'

Vavara thought for a while, tapping her stick against her boot.

The spring of 1952, she said eventually. That was it. She got through on the train in March 1952, when it was starting to thaw a bit. They had had no warning, she had just turned up, with no explanation. Not that she needed to explain anything. You only had to look at her. She was seven months gone by then.

'And the father . . . ? Did she say . . . ?'

No.

A vigorous shake of the head.

But you guessed, didn't you? thought Kelso.

No, she didn't say anything about the father, or about

what had happened in Moscow, and after a while they gave up asking. She just sat in the corner and waited for her term to come. She was very silent, this new girl, not like their old Anna. She wouldn't see her friends, or step outside. The truth was, she was scared.

'Scared? What was she scared of?'

Of giving birth, of course. And why not? Men! she said – and some of her old fire returned – what did men know of life? Naturally she was scared. Anyone with eyes in their head and a mind to think would be *scared*. And that baby didn't give her an easy time, either, the little devil. It sucked the goodness out of her. Oh, a proper little devil – what a kick it had! They would sit here in the evening and watch her belly heave.

Mekhlis came by sometimes to keep an eye on her. Most weeks there was a car at the bottom of the street with a couple of his men it.

No, they didn't ask who the father was.

She started to bleed at the beginning of April. They took her to the clinic. And that was the last time they saw her. She had a haemorrhage in the delivery room. The doctor told them everything about it afterwards. There was nothing to be done. She died on the operating table two days later. She was twenty.

'And the baby?'

The baby lived. A boy.

THE arrangements were all made by Comrade Mekhlis.

It was the least he could do, he told them. He felt responsible.

It was Mekhlis who provided the doctor – an academician, no less, the country's leading expert, flown up specially from

301

Moscow – and Mekhlis who arranged the adoption. The Safanovs would have reared the child themselves, willingly – they asked to do so: they begged – but Mekhlis had a paper, signed by Anna, in which she said that if anything happened to her, she wanted the baby to be adopted. She named some relatives of the father, a couple named Chizhikov.

'Chizhikov?' said Kelso. 'You're sure of that name?'

Certain.

They never even saw the baby. They weren't allowed inside the hospital.

Now she was willing to accept all this, because Vavara Safanova believed in the discipline of the Party. She still did. She would believe in it until the day she died. The Party was her god, and sometimes, like a god, the Party moved in a mysterious way.

But Mikhail Safanov no longer accepted the doctrine of infallibility. He was set on finding these Chizhikovs, whatever Mekhlis said, and he still had enough friends in the regional Party to help him do it. And that was how he discovered that the Chizhikovs were not fancy Moscow folk at all – which was what he had expected – but were northerners, like them, and had gone to live in a village in the forest outside Archangel. The whisper in the town was that Chizhikov was not their real name. That they were NKVD.

By this time it was winter and there was nothing Mikhail could do. And then one morning in early spring, while he was still looking out each day for the first signs of a thaw, they woke to solemn music on the radio and the news that Comrade Stalin was dead.

She had wept, and he had, too. Did that surprise him? Oh, they had howled and clutched at one another! They had cried in a way they never had before, not even for Anna. The whole of Archangel was in grief. She could still remember the day of the funeral. The long silence, broken by a thirty-gun salute. The echo of the gunfire had rolled across the Dvina like a distant storm in the forest.

Two months later, in May, when the ice had gone, Mikhail had filled a backpack and had set off to find his grandson.

She had known nothing good could come of it.

One day passed, then two, then three. He was a fit man, strong and healthy – he was only forty-five.

On the fifth day some fishermen had found his body, about thirty *versts* upstream, rushing along in the yellow meltwater that was pouring out of the forest, not far from Novodvinsk.

KELSO unfolded O'Brian's map and laid it out on the table. She put on her spectacles and hunted up and down the blue line of the Dvina, her good eye held very close.

There, she said, after a while, and pointed. That was the place where her husband's body had been found. A wild spot! There were wolves here in the forest, and lynx and bear. In some places the trees were too dense for a man to move. In others, there were swamps that could eat you in a minute. And here and there the grey weathered bones of the old kulak settlements. Almost all of the kulaks had perished, of course. There was not much of a living to be scratched in such a place.

Mikhail knew the forest as well as any man. He had been roaming the taiga since he was a child.

It had been a heart attack, according to the militia. That was what they said. Maybe he had been trying to fill his water bottle? He had fallen into the cold yellow water and the shock had stopped his heart.

She had buried him in the Kuznecheskoye Cemetery, next to Anna.

'And what,' said Kelso, conscious again of O'Brian just behind them, filming them now with his wretched miniature camera, 'what was the name of the village where your husband said the Chizhikovs lived?'

Ah! This was crazy! How could she be expected to remember that? It was so long ago – nearly fifty years . . .

She brought her face down close to the map again.

Here somewhere – she placed a wavering finger on a spot just north of the river – somewhere around here: a place too small to be worth recording. Too small to have a name, even.

She had never tried to find it herself?

Oh no.

She looked at Kelso in horror.

Nothing good could come of it. Not then. And not now.

Chapter Twenty-four

THE BIG CAR braked hard and swerved off the south Moscow highway into the Zhukovsky military airbase shortly before noon, Feliks Suvorin hanging grimly to the strap in the rear. Beyond the checkpoint, a jeep waited. It pulled away as the barrier rose, its tail lights flashing, and they followed it around the side of the terminal building, through a wire fence and on to the concrete apron.

A small grey aircraft, as requested – six-seater, prop-driven – was being fuelled by a tanker. Beyond the plane was a line of dark green army helicopters with drooping rotors; parked next to it, a big ZiL limousine.

Well, well, thought Suvorin. Some things still work round here.

He stuffed his notes into his briefcase and darted through the wind and rain towards the limousine where Arsenyev's driver was already opening the rear door.

'And?' said Arsenyev from the warmth of the interior.

'And,' said Suvorin, sliding along the seat to join him, 'it's not what we thought it was. And thank you for fixing the plane.'

'Wait in the other car,' said Arsenyev to his chauffeur.

'Yes, colonel.'

'What's not as who thought it was?' said Arsenyev, when the door was shut. 'Good morning, by the way.'

'Good morning, Yuri Semonovich. The notebook. Everybody's always believed it was Stalin's. Actually it turns out to have been a journal kept by a girl servant of Stalin's, Anna Mikhailovna Safanova. He had her brought down

305

from Archangel to work for him in the summer of '51, about eighteen months before he died.'

Arsenyev blinked at him.

'And that's it? That's what Beria stole?'

'That's it. That and some papers about her, apparently.'

Arsenyev stared at Suvorin for a second or two, then started laughing. He shook his head with relief. 'Go fuck your mother! The old bastard was screwing his maid? Is that what he was up to?'

'Apparently.'

'That is priceless. That is brilliant!' Arsenyev punched the seat in front of him. 'Oh, let me be there! Let me be there to see Mamantov's face when he finds out his great Stalin testament is nothing more than a maid's account of getting screwed by the mighty *Vozhd!*' He glanced at Suvorin, his fat cheeks flushed with mirth, diamonds glistening in his eyes. 'What's the matter, Feliks? Don't tell me you can't see the funny side?' He stopped laughing. 'What's the matter? You are sure this is true, aren't you?'

'Pretty well sure, colonel, yes. This is all according to the woman we picked up last night, Zinaida Rapava. She read the notebook yesterday afternoon – her father left it hidden for her. I can't think that she would invent such a story. It defies imagination.'

'Right, right. So cheer up, eh? And where's this notebook now?'

'Well, that's the first complication.' Suvorin spoke hesitantly. It seemed such a shame to spoil the old fellow's mood. 'That's why I needed to talk to you. It seems she showed it to the historian, Kelso. According to her, he's taken it with him.'

'With him?'

'To Archangel. He's trying to find the woman who wrote it, this Anna Safanova.'

Arsenyev tugged nervously at his thick neck. 'When did he leave?'

'Yesterday afternoon. Four or five. She can't remember exactly.'

'How?'

'Driving.'

'Driving? That's all right. You'll catch him easily. By the time you land, you'll only be a few hours behind him. He's a rat in a trap up there.'

'Unfortunately, it's not just him. He's got a journalist with him. O'Brian. You know him? That correspondent with the satellite television station.'

'Ah.' Arsenyev stuck out his lower lip and pulled at his neck some more. After a while he said, 'But even so, the chances of this woman still being alive are small. And if she is – well, so, so, it's no disaster. Let them write their books and make their fucking news reports. I can't see Stalin entrusting his *maid* with a message for future generations. Can you?'

'Well, this is my worry –'

'His *maid?* Come on, Feliks! He was a Georgian, after all, and an old one at that. Women were good for only three things, as far as Comrade Stalin was concerned. Cooking, cleaning and having kids. He –' Arsenyev stopped. 'No –'

'It's insane,' said Suvorin, holding up his hand. 'I know that. I've been telling myself all the way over that it's crazy. But then, he *was* crazy. And he was a Georgian. Think about it. Why would he go to so much trouble to check out one girl? He had her medical records, apparently. And he wanted her checked for congenital abnormalities. Also, why would he keep her diary in his safe? And then there's more, you see –'

'More?' Arsenyev was no longer punching the front seat. He was clutching it for support.

'According to Zinaida, there are references in the girl's journal to Trofim Lysenko. You know: "the inheritability of acquired characteristics" and all that rubbish. And apparently he also goes on about how useless his own children are, and how "the soul of Russia is in the north".'

'Stop it, Feliks. This is too much.'

'And then there's Mamantov. I've never understood why Mamantov should have taken such an insane risk – to murder Rapava, and in such a way. Why? This is what I tried to say to you yesterday: what could Stalin possibly have written that could have any effect upon Russia nearly fifty years later? But if Mamantov knew – had heard some rumour years ago, maybe, from some of the old timers at the Lubyanka – that Stalin might deliberately have left behind an heir –'

'An *heir?*'

' – well, that would explain everything, wouldn't it? He'd take the risk for that. Let's face it, Yuri, Mamantov's just about sick enough to – oh, I don't know –' he tried to think of something utterly absurd ' – to run Stalin's son for the Presidency, or something. He does have half a billion roubles, after all . . .'

'Wait a minute,' said Arsenyev. 'Let me think about this.' He looked across the airfield to the line of helicopters. Suvorin could see a muscle like a fish hook twitching deep in his fleshy jaw. 'And we still have no idea where Mamantov is?'

'He could be anywhere.'

'Archangel?'

'It's a possibility. It must be. If Zinaida Rapava had the brains to find Kelso at the airport, why not Mamantov? He could have been tailing them for twenty-four hours. They're not professionals; he is. I'm worried, Yuri. They'd never know a thing until he made his hit.'

Arsenyev groaned.

'You got a phone?'

'Sure.' Suvorin dug in his pocket and produced it.

'Secure?'

'Supposedly.'

'Call my office for me, will you?'

Suvorin began punching in the number. Arsenyev said, 'Where's the Rapava girl?'

'I got Bunin to take her back home. I've fixed up a guard, for her own protection. She's not in a good state.'

'You saw this, I suppose?' Arsenyev pulled a copy of the latest *Aurora* out of the seat pocket. Suvorin saw the headline: 'VIOLENCE IS INEVITABLE'.

'I heard it on the news.'

'Well, you can imagine how pleasantly *that's* gone down –'

'Here,' said Suvorin, giving him the phone. 'It's ringing.'

'Sergo?' said Arsenyev. 'It's me. Listen. Can you patch me through to the President's office . . . ? That's it. Use the second number.' He put his hand over the mouthpiece. 'You'd better go. No. Wait. Tell me what you need.'

Suvorin spread his hands. He barely knew where to begin. 'I could do with the militia or someone up in Archangel to check out every Safanov or Safanova and have the job finished by the time I arrive. That would be a start. I'll need a couple of men to meet me at the airfield. Transport I'll need. And some place to stay.'

'It's done. Go carefully, Feliks. I hope –' But Suvorin never did discover what the colonel hoped, because Arsenyev suddenly held up a warning finger. 'Yes . . . Yes, I'm ready.' He took a breath and forced a smile; if he could have stood up and saluted, he would have done so. 'And good day to you, Boris Nikolaevich –'

Suvorin climbed quietly out of the car.

The tanker had been unhooked from the little aircraft and the hose was being wound up. There were rainbows of oil in the puddles beneath the wings. Close up, the dented, rust-streaked Tupolev looked even older than he expected. Forty, at least. Older than he was, in fact. Holy Mother, what a bucket!

A couple of ground crew watched him without curiosity. 'Where's the pilot?'

One of the men gestured with his head to the plane. Suvorin pulled himself up the steps and into the fuselage. It was cold inside and smelled like an old bus that hadn't been driven for years. The door to the cockpit was open. He could see the pilot idly pressing switches on and off. He ducked his head and went forward and tapped him on the shoulder. The airman had a pouchy face, with the sandy, dull-eyed, bloodshot look of a heavy drinker. Great, thought Suvorin. They shook hands.

'What's the weather like in Archangel?'

The pilot laughed. Suvorin could smell the booze: it was not only on his breath – he was sweating it. 'I'll risk it if you will.'

'Shouldn't you have a navigator or someone?'

'There's nobody about.'

'Great. Terrific.'

Suvorin went aft and took his seat. One engine coughed and started with a spurt of black smoke, and then the other.

Arsenyev's limousine had already gone, he noticed. The Tupolev turned and taxied across the deserted apron, out towards the runway. They turned again, the sawing whine of the propellers falling then rising, rising, rising. The wind whipped the rain like dirty laundry, in horizontal sheets across the concrete. He could see the narrow trunks of silver birches on the airfield perimeter, grown close together like a white palisade. He closed his eyes – it was stupid to be scared of flying, but there it was: he always had been – and they were off, scuttling and swaying down the runway, the pressure pushing him back in his seat, and then there was a lurch and they were airborne.

He opened his eyes. The plane rose beyond the edge of the airfield and banked across the city. Objects seemed to rush into his field of vision, only to dwindle and tilt away – yellow headlights reflecting on the wet streets, flat grey roofs and the dark green patches of trees. So many trees! It always surprised him. He thought of all the people he knew down there – Serafima at home in the apartment they couldn't quite afford and the boys at school and Arsenyev trembling after his call to the President and Zinaida Rapava and her silence when he left her in the morgue –

They hit the sudden underside of the low cloud and he was permitted one, two, three last glimpses through the shreds of thickening gauze before Moscow was blanked from view.

Chapter Twenty-five

R. J. O'BRIAN stood on the street corner at the end of the alleyway leading to Vavara Safanova's yard, his metal case on the ground between his legs, his head bent over the map.

'How long d'you figure it'll take us to get there? A couple of hours?'

Kelso looked back at the tiny wooden house. The old woman was still standing at her open door, leaning on her stick, watching them. He raised his hand to wave goodbye and the door slowly closed.

'Get where?'

'The Chizhikov place,' said O'Brian. 'How long d'you figure?'

'In this?' Kelso raised his eyes to the heavy sky. 'You want to try to find it now?'

'There's only one road. See for yourself. She said it was a village, right? If it's a village, it'll be on the road.' He brushed a dusting of snowflakes off the map and gave it to Kelso. 'I'd say two hours.'

'That's not a road,' said Kelso. 'That's a dotted line. That's a track.' It wandered eastwards through the forest, parallel with the Dvina for perhaps fifty miles, then struck north and ended nowhere – just stopped in the middle of the taiga after about two hundred miles. 'Take a look around you, man. They haven't even made most of the roads in the city. What d'you think they'll be like out there?'

He thrust the map back at O'Brian and began walking in the direction of the Toyota. O'Brian came after him. 'We got four-wheel drive, Fluke. We got snow chains.'

'And what if we break down?'

'We got food. We got fuel for a fire and a whole damn forest to burn. We can always drink the snow. We've got the satellite phone.' He clapped Kelso on the shoulder. 'Tell you what, how about this: you get scared, you can call your mommy. How's that?'

'My mommy's dead.'

'Zinaida then. You can call Zinaida.'

'Tell me, *did* you screw her, O'Brian? As a matter of interest?'

'What's that got to do with anything?'

'I just want to know why she doesn't trust you. Whether she's right. Is it sex or is it something personal?'

'Oh-ho. Is that what all this is about?' O'Brian smirked. 'Come on, Fluke. You know the rules. A gentleman never talks.'

Kelso huddled further into his jacket and increased his pace.

'It's not a question of being scared.'

'Oh really?'

They were within sight of the car now. Kelso stopped and turned to face him. 'All right, I admit it. I am scared. And you know what scares me most? The fact you're *not* scared. That *really* scares me.'

'Bullshit. A bit of snow –'

'Forget the snow. I'm not bothered about the snow.' Kelso glanced around at the tumbling houses. The scene was entirely brown and white and grey. And silent, like an old movie. 'You just don't get it, do you?' he said. 'You don't understand. You've no history, that's your problem. It's like this name "Chizhikov". What's that to you?'

'Nothing. It's just a name.'

'But it's not, you see. "Chizhikov" was one of Stalin's aliases before the Revolution. Stalin was issued with a passport in the name of P. A. Chizhikov in 1911.'

(*'Are you excited, Dr Kelso? Do you feel the force of Comrade Stalin, even from the grave?'* And he did. He did feel it. He felt as if a hand had reached out from the snow and touched his shoulder.)

O'Brian was quiet for a few seconds, but then he gave a dismissive sweep of his metal case. 'Well, you can stand here and *commune* with history if you want. I'm going to go and *find* it.' He set off across the street, turning as he walked. 'You coming or not? The train to Moscow leaves at ten past eight tonight. Or you can come with me. Make your choice.'

Kelso hesitated. He looked up again at the tumbling sky. It wasn't like any snowfall he had ever known in England or the States. It was as if something was disintegrating up there – flaking to pieces and crashing around them.

Choice? he thought. For a man with no visa and no money, no job, no book? For a man who had come this far? And what *choice* would that be, exactly?

Slowly, reluctantly, he began to walk towards the car.

THEY headed back out of the city, along a minor road, and northwards, so at least there was no GAI checkpoint to negotiate.

By now it must have been about one o'clock.

The road ran alongside an overgrown railroad track lined with ancient freight cars, and to start with it wasn't too bad. It could almost have been romantic, in the right company.

They overtook a gaily painted cart being pulled by a pony, its head down into the wind, and soon there were more wooden houses, also bright with paint – blue, green, red –

leaning in a picturesque way out in the marshland at the end of wooden jettys. In the snow it wasn't possible to tell where the solid ground ended and water began. Boats, cars, sheds, chicken coops and tethered goats were jumbled together. Even the big wood pulp mill across the wide Dvina, on the southern headland, had a kind of epic beauty, its cranes and smoking chimneys silhouetted against the concrete sky.

But then, abruptly, the houses disappeared and so did their view of the river. At the same time the hard surface gave way beneath their wheels and they began jolting along a rutted track. Birch and pine trees closed around them. In less than fifteen minutes they might have been a thousand miles from Archangel rather than a mere ten. The road wound on through the muffled forest. Sometimes the trees grew high and fine. But occasionally the woodland would thin and they would find themselves in a wilderness of blackened, blighted stumps, like a battlefield after heavy shelling. Or – and this was oddly more disconcerting – they would suddenly come across a small plantation of tall radio antennae.

Listening posts, O'Brian said, eavesdropping on Northern NATO.

He started to sing. *Walking in a Winter Wonderland.*

Kelso stood it for a couple of verses. 'Do you have to?'

O'Brian stopped.

'Gloomy sonofabitch,' he muttered under his breath.

The snow was still falling steadily. Occasional gunshots cracked and echoed in the distance – hunters in the woods – sending panicky birds flapping and crying across the track.

They went through several small villages, each smaller and more dilapidated than the last – a barracks in one with graffiti on its walls, and a satellite dish: a little chunk of Archangel dropped in the middle of nowhere. There was no one to be seen except a couple of gawping children and an old woman dressed entirely in black who stood at the roadside and tried to wave them down. When O'Brian didn't slow she shook her fist and cursed them.

'Hag.' O'Brian looked back at her in the mirror. 'What's eating her? Where are all the men, anyway? Drunk?' He meant it as a joke.

'Probably.'

'No? What? *All* of them?'

'Most of them, I should think. Home-made vodka. What else is there to do?'

'Jesus, what a country.'

After a while O'Brian began to sing again, but under his breath now and less confidently than before.

'We're walking in a winter wonderland . . .'

ONE hour passed, then another.

A couple of times the river came back briefly into view, and that, as O'Brian said, was a sight and a half – the swampy land, the wide and sluggish mass of water and, far beyond it, the flat, dark mass of trees picking up again, only to dissolve into the waves of snow. It was a primordial landscape. Kelso could imagine a dinosaur moving slowly across it.

From the map it was hard to tell exactly where they were. No habitations were recorded, no landmarks. He suggested they stop at the next village and try to regain their bearings.

'Whatever you want.'

But the next village was a long time coming, it never came, and Kelso noticed that the snow on the track was virgin: there hadn't been any traffic this far out for hours. They hit a drift for the first time – a pothole disguised by snow – and the Toyota slewed, its rear tyres flailing, until they bit on

something solid. The car lurched. O'Brian spun the wheel
and brought them back on course. He laughed – 'Whoa, that
was fun!' – but Kelso could tell that even he was starting to
feel unsettled now. The reporter slowed the engine, switched
on the headlights and shifted forwards in his seat, peering
into the swirling flakes.

'Fuel's low. I'd say we've got about fifteen minutes.'

'Then what?'

'Either we head back to Archangel, or we go on and try to
find some place to stay the night.'

'Oh, what? You mean a Holiday Inn?'

'Fluke, Fluke –'

'Listen, if we try to stay the night here, we'll end up staying
the winter.'

'Oh, come on, man, they have to send a snow plough,
don't they? Surely? At some point?'

'*At some point?*' repeated Kelso. He shook his head. And
there would have been another row if, just then, they hadn't
rounded a curve and seen, above the snow-topped trees, a
smudge of smoke.

O'BRIAN stood in the doorway of the Toyota, leaning on the
roof, staring ahead through his binoculars. It looked as if
there might be a settlement of some sort, he said, about half
a mile off the road, along a rough track.

He slipped back behind the wheel. 'Let's take a look.'

The passage through the trees was like a tunnel, barely
wide enough for a single vehicle, and O'Brian drove down it
slowly. The branches clawed at them, slapping the
windscreen, raking the sides of the car. The track worsened.
They rocked sharply – hard left, hard right – and suddenly
the Toyota plunged forwards and Kelso was thrown at the

windscreen; only the seat belt saved him. The engine revved helplessly for a second, then stalled.

O'Brian turned the ignition, put the car into reverse and cautiously pressed the accelerator. The back wheels whined in the loose snow. He tried it again, harder. A howl like an animal trapped.

'Get out, could you, Fluke? Take a look.' He couldn't quite keep the edge of panic out of his voice.

Kelso had to push hard even to open the door. He jumped out and immediately sank up to his knees. The drift was axle-deep.

He banged on the back door and gestured to O'Brian to switch off the engine.

In the silence he could hear the snowflakes pattering in the trees. His knees were wet and cold. He trod awkwardly, bow-legged, through the deep drift round to the driver's door and had to dig away the snow with his gloved hands before he could drag it open. The Toyota was tilted forwards at an angle of at least twenty degrees. O'Brian struggled out.

'What'd we hit?' he demanded. He waded round to the front of the car. 'Jesus, it's like someone's dug a tank-trap. Will you look at this?'

It was indeed as if a trench had been laid across the track. A few paces further on the snow became more solid again.

'Maybe they were laying a cable or something,' said Kelso. But a cable for what? He cupped his hands above his eyes and stared through the snow towards the huddle of wooden huts about three hundred yards ahead. They didn't look as though they were connected to electricity, or to anything else. He noticed that the smoke had disappeared.

'Someone's put that fire out.'

'We're gonna need a tow.' O'Brian gave the side of the

Toyota a gloomy kick. 'Heap of junk.'

He held on to the car for support and edged round to the back, opened it up and pulled out a couple of pairs of boots, one of green rubber, the other of leather, high-sided, army-issue. He threw the rubber boots to Kelso. 'Get these on,' he said. 'Let's go parley with the natives.'

Five minutes later, their hoods up, the car locked, and each with a pair of binoculars hung round his neck, they set off down the track.

The settlement had been abandoned for at least a couple of years. The handful of wooden shacks had been ransacked. Rubbish poked through the snow – rusting sheets of corrugated tin roofing, shattered window frames, rotting planks, a torn fishing net, bottles, tin cans, a holed rowing boat, bits of machinery, ripped sacking and, bizarrely, a row of cinema seats. A timber-framed greenhouse fitted with polythene instead of glass had blown over on to its side.

Kelso ducked his head into one of the derelict buildings. It was roofless, freezing. It stank of animal excreta.

As he came out O'Brian caught his eye and shrugged.

Kelso stared towards the edge of the clearing. 'What's that over there?'

Both men raised their binoculars and trained them on what appeared to be a row of wooden crosses, half-hidden by the trees – Russian crosses, with three pairs of arms: short at the top, longer in the centre, and slanted downwards, left to right, at the bottom.

'Oh, that's marvellous,' said Kelso, trying to laugh. 'A cemetery. That's bloody perfect.'

'Let's take a look,' said O'Brian.

He set off eagerly with long, determined strides. Kelso, more reluctant, followed as best he could. Twenty years of cigarettes and Scotch seemed to have convened a protest meeting in his heart and lungs. He was sweating with the effort of moving through the snow. He had a pain in his side.

It was a cemetery right enough, sheltered by the trees, and as they came closer he could see six – or was it eight? – graves, arranged in twos, with a little wooden fence around each pair. The crosses were home-made but well done, with white enamel name-plates and small photographs covered in glass, in the traditional Russian manner. *A. I. Sumbatov,* read the first one, *22.1.20 – 9.8.81.* The picture showed a man, in middle age, in uniform. Next to him was *P. J. Sumbatova, 6.12.26 – 14.11.92.* She, too, was in uniform: a heavy-faced woman with a severe central parting. Next to them were the Yezhovs. And next to the Yezhovs, the Golubs. They were married couples, all about the same age. They were all in uniform. T. Y. Golub had been the first to die, in 1961. It was impossible to see his face. It had been scratched out.

'This must be the place,' said O'Brian, quietly. 'No question. This is it. Who are they all, Fluke? Army?'

'No.' Kelso shook his head slowly. 'The uniform is NKVD, I think. And here, look. Look at this.'

It was the final pair of graves, the ones furthest from the clearing, set slightly apart from the others. They had been the last survivors. *B. D. Chizhikov* – a major, by the look of his insignia – *19.2.19 – 9.3.96.* And next to him *M. G. Chizhikova, 16.4.24 – 16.3.96.* She had outlasted her husband by exactly one week. Her face was also obliterated.

They stood like mourners for a while: silent, their heads bowed.

'And then there were none,' murmured O'Brian.

'Or one.'

'I don't think so. No way. This place has been empty quite

a while. Shit,' he said suddenly, and took a kick at the snow, 'would you believe it, after all that? We *missed* him?'

The trees were thick here. It was impossible to see beyond a few dozen yards.

O'Brian said, 'I'd better get a shot of this while it's light. You wait here. I'll go back to the car.'

'Oh, great,' said Kelso. 'Thank you.'

'Scared, Fluke?'

'What do you think?'

'Whoo,' said O'Brian. He raised his arms and fluttered his fingers above his head.

'If you try playing any jokes, O'Brian, I'm warning you, I'll kill you.'

'Ho ho ho,' said O'Brian, moving away towards the track. 'Ho ho ho.' He disappeared beyond the trees. Kelso heard his stupid laugh for a few more seconds and then there was silence – just the rustle of the snow and the sound of his own breathing.

My God, what a set-up *this* was, just look at these dates: they were a story in themselves. He walked back to the first grave, pulled off his gloves, took out his notebook. Then he went down on one knee and began to copy the details from the crosses. An entire troop of bodyguards had been dispatched into the forest more than forty years earlier to protect one solitary baby boy, and all of them had stuck it out, had stayed at their posts, out of loyalty or habit or fear, until eventually they had dropped down dead, one after another. They were like those Japanese soldiers who stayed hidden in the jungle, unaware that the war was over.

He began to wonder how close Mikhail Safanov might have managed to get in the spring of 1953, and then he consciously abandoned this line of thought. It didn't bear contemplating – not yet; not *here*.

It was hard to hold the pencil between his cold fingers, and difficult to write as the snowflakes settled across the page. Still, he worked his way along to the final crosses.

'*B. D. Chizhikov*,' he wrote. '*Tough-looking, brutal face. Dark-skinned. A Georgian?? Died aged 77 . . .*'

He wondered what Comrades Golub and Chizhikova might have looked like, and who had blacked out their faces, and why. There was something infinitely sinister about their featureless silhouettes. He found himself writing, '*Could they have been purged?*'

Oh, where the hell was O'Brian?

His back was aching. His knees were wet. He stood and another thought occurred to him. He brushed the page clear of snow again and licked the end of his pencil.

'*The graves are all well kept*,' he wrote, '*plots appear to be weeded. If this place is abandoned, like the buildings, shouldn't they have grown over?*'

'O'Brian?' he called. 'R. J.?'

The snow deadened his shout.

He put away the notebook and began walking quickly away from the cemetery, pulling on his gloves. The wind stirred in the abandoned buildings ahead of him, catching the snow and lifting it here and there like the corner of a curtain. He picked his way across the ground, following O'Brian's large footprints until he came to the start of the track. The prints led off clearly in the direction of the Toyota. He raised the binoculars to his eyes and twisted the focus. The stricken car filled his vision, so still and distant it seemed unreal. There was no sign of anyone around it.

Odd.

He turned round very slowly, a complete 360 degrees,

scanning through the binoculars. Forest. Tumbled walls and wreckage. Forest. Graves. Forest. Track. Toyota. Forest again.

He lowered the binoculars, frowning, then began walking towards the car, still following O'Brian's trail. It took him a couple of minutes. Nobody else had been this way in the snow, that much was obvious: there were two pairs of tracks heading up to the clearing and one pair heading back. He approached the car and, by lengthening his stride and planting his feet in the prints of the bigger man, he was able to retrace O'Brian's movements exactly: so and so . . . and . . . *so* . . .

Kelso stopped, arms outstretched, wobbling. The American had definitely come this way, round to the back of the Toyota, had taken out the metal camera case – it was missing, he could see – and then it looked as though something had distracted him, because instead of heading back up the track to the settlement his footprints turned sharply and led directly away from the vehicle, at a right angle, straight into the forest.

He called O'Brian's name, softly. And then, in a spasm of panic, he cupped his hands and bellowed it as loud as he could.

Again, that same curious deadening effect, as if the trees were swallowing his words.

Cautiously, he stepped into the undergrowth.

Oh, but he had always hated forests, hadn't he? Hated even the woodland around Oxford, with its poetic shafts of dusty bloody sunlight, and its mossy vegetation, and the way things suddenly flew up at you or rustled away! And branches slapping back into your face . . . *Sorry, sorry* . . . Oh yes, give him a wide open space any day. Give him a hill. Give him a cliff-top. Give him the sparkling sea!

'R. J.?' What a damned silly name to have to yell, but he yelled it louder anyway: 'R. J.!'

There were no footprints visible here. The ground was rough. He could smell the decay of a swamp somewhere, as rank as dog's breath, and it was dark, too. He would have to watch himself, he thought, keep his back firmly to the road, because if he went too far, he would lose his bearings, and maybe end up walking further and further away from the car, until there would be nothing left to do but lie down in the darkness and freeze.

There was a sudden heavy crash off to his left, and then a succession of smaller bursts, like echoes. It sounded at first like someone running but then he realised it was only snow dislodging from the tops of some branches and plunging to the earth.

He cupped his hands.

'R. J . . . !'

And then he heard a human sound. A moan, was that it? A sob?

He tried to place where it was coming from. And then he heard it again. Nearer, and behind him now, it seemed to be. He pushed through a gap between a couple of close-growing trees into a tiny clearing, and there was O'Brian's camera case lying open on the ground and there, beyond it, was O'Brian himself, upside down and swinging gently, his fingertips barely brushing the surface of the snow, suspended by his left leg from a length of oily rope.

Chapter Twenty-six

THE ROPE WAS attached to the top of a tall birch sapling, bent almost double by O'Brian's weight. The reporter was groaning. He was barely conscious.

Kelso knelt by his head. At the sight of him, O'Brian began struggling feebly. He didn't seem able to form a sentence.

'It's all right,' said Kelso. He tried to sound calm. 'Don't worry. I'll get you down.'

Get him down. Kelso took off his gloves. Get him down. Right. Using what? He had a knife for sharpening pencils, but it was in the car. He patted his pockets and found his lighter. He flicked it on, showed the flame to O'Brian.

'We'll get you down. Look. You'll be all right.'

He stood and reached up, grabbing O'Brian by his booted ankle. A noose of thin rope had dug deep into the leather. It took all Kelso's weight to drag him down far enough for him to apply the flame to the taut rope just above his sole. O'Brian's shoulders rested in the snow.

'Asornim,' he was saying. 'Asornim.'

The rope was wet. It seemed to take an age for the lighter to have any effect. Kelso had to stop and shake it. The flame was beginning to turn blue and die before the first strands started to smoulder. But then under the strain they parted fast. The last of them snapped and the sapling whipped back and Kelso tried to support the legs with his free hand but he couldn't manage it and O'Brian's body crashed heavily into the snow.

The reporter struggled to sit up, managed to prop himself

on his elbows, then slumped back again. He was still mumbling something. Kelso knelt beside him.

'You're okay. You'll be fine. We'll get you out of here.'

'Asornim.'

I sore nim?

I saw him.

'Saw who? Who did you see?'

'Oh, Jesus. Oh, fuck.'

'Can you bend your leg? Is it broken?' Kelso shuffled on his knees through the snow and began digging with his fingernails at the knot of the noose, embedded in the side of O'Brian's boot.

'Fluke –' O'Brian held up his arm, desperately flexing his fingers. 'Give me a lift here, will you?'

Kelso took his hand and pulled until O'Brian was sitting upright. Then he put his arm round the reporter's broad chest and together they managed to get him up on to his feet. O'Brian stood, leaning heavily against Kelso, putting his weight on his right leg.

'Can you walk?'

'Not sure. Think so.' He hobbled a few steps. 'Just give me a minute.'

He stayed where he was, with his back to Kelso, staring into the trees. When he seemed to be breathing more normally, Kelso said, 'Saw *who?*'

SAW *him,* said O'Brian, turning round. His eyes were wild and fearful now, searching the forest behind Kelso's head. Saw *the man.* Saw him staring out of the fucking trees next to the car. *Jesus.* Just about jumped out of my fucking *skin.*

'What do you mean? What man?'

Took one step towards him – hands up, let's be friends,

white-man-he-come-in-peace – and presto! he was *gone*. I mean, he *vanished*. Never saw him properly again after that. Heard him, though, and kind of glimpsed him once – moving fast through the forest up ahead, away to the right – sort of a sawn-off figure, like a quarterback, built low to the ground. And *quick*. So quick you wouldn't believe it. Man, he seemed to move like an *ape*. Next thing I know, the world's turned upside down.

'He led me on, Fluke, you know that, don't you? Led me right into his fucking *trap*. He's probably out there now, *watching us*.'

He was getting his strength back, his recovery speeded by fear.

He hobbled a few steps. When he tried to put his left leg down properly he winced. But he could move it, that was something. It definitely wasn't broken.

'We gotta go. We gotta get out of here.' He bent awkwardly and closed the catches on the camera case.

Kelso needed no persuading. But they would have to go carefully, he said. They had to *think*. They had blundered into two of his traps already – one on the track and one here – and who could guess how many more there might be. In this snow it was so damned hard to see.

'Maybe,' said Kelso, 'if we try to follow my footprints –'

But his tracks were already beginning to be lost beneath the ceaseless soft downpour.

'Who is he, Fluke?' whispered O'Brian, as they went back into the trees. 'I mean, *what* is he? What is he so goddamned scared of?'

He's his father's son, thought Kelso, that's who he is. He's a forty-five-year-old paranoid psychopath, if such a thing is possible.

'Oh man,' said O'Brian, 'what was *that?*'

Kelso stopped.

It wasn't another avalanche of snow from the treetops, that was for sure. It went on too long. A heavy, sustained rustling, somewhere in front of them.

'It's him,' said O'Brian. 'He's moving again. He's trying to head us off.' The noise stopped abruptly and they stood, listening. 'Now what's he doing?'

'Watching us, at a guess.'

Again, Kelso strained his eyes into the gloom, but it was hopeless. Dense undergrowth, great patches of shadow, occasionally broken by torrents of snow – he couldn't get a fix on anything, it was so unlike any place he had ever seen. He was really sweating now, despite the cold. His skin was prickling.

That was when the howling started – a deafening, inhuman wail. It took Kelso a couple of seconds to realise it was the car alarm.

Then came two loud gunshots in rapid succession, a pause, and then a third.

Then silence.

AFTERWARDS, Kelso was never sure how long they stood there. He remembered only the immobilising sense of terror: the paralysis of thought and action that came from the realisation there was nothing they could do. He – whoever *he* was – knew where they were. He had shot up their car. He had booby-trapped the forest. He could come for them whenever he wanted. Or he could leave them where they were. There was no prospect of rescue from the outside world. He was their absolute master. Unseen. All-seeing. Omnipotent. *Mad.*

After a minute or two they risked a whispered conference. The telephone, said O'Brian, what if he had damaged the Inmarsat telephone? It was their only hope and it was in the back of the Toyota.

Maybe he wouldn't know what a satellite telephone looked like, said Kelso. Maybe if they stayed where they were until dark and then went to retrieve it —

Suddenly O'Brian grabbed him hard by the elbow.

A face was looking at them through the trees.

Kelso didn't see it at first, it was so perfectly still — so unnaturally, perfectly immobile, it took a moment for his mind to register it, to separate the pieces from the shapes of the forest, to assemble them and declare the composite human:

Dark impassive eyes that didn't blink. Black, arched brows. Coarse black hair hanging loose across a leathery forehead. A beard.

There was also a hood made of some kind of brown animal fur.

The apparition coughed. It grunted.

'Com-rades,' it said. The word was slurred, the voice harsh, like a tape being played at too slow a speed.

Kelso could feel the hair stirring on his scalp.

'Aw, Jesus,' said O'Brian, 'Jesusjesusjesus —'

There was another cough and a great gathering of phlegm. A gobbet of yellow spit was ejected into the undergrowth. 'Com-rades, I am a rude fell-ow. I cannot deny it. And I have been out of the way of hu-man com-pany. But there it is. Well then? D'yer want me to shoot yer? Yes?'

He stepped out in front of them — quickly, sharply: he barely disturbed a twig. He was wearing an old army greatcoat — patched, hacked off above the knees and belted with a length of rope – and cavalry boots into which his baggy trousers were stuffed. His hands were bare and huge. In one he carried an old rifle. In the other was the satchel with Anna Safanova's notebook and the papers.

Kelso felt O'Brian's grip tighten on his arm.

'This is the book of which it is spok-en? Yes? And the papers prove it!' The figure leaned towards them, rocking his head this way and that, studying them intently. 'You are the ones, then? You are truly the ones?'

He came closer, peering at them with his dark eyes, and Kelso could smell the stench of his body, sour with stale sweat.

'Or are you, perhaps, *spiders?*'

He took a pace back and swiftly raised the rifle, aiming it from his waist, his finger on the trigger.

'We are the ones,' said Kelso, quickly.

The man cocked an eyebrow in surprise. 'Imperialists?'

'I am an English comrade. The comrade here is American.'

'Well, well! England and America! And Engels was a Jew!' He laughed, showing black teeth, then spat. 'And yet you have not asked me for proof. Why so?'

'We trust you.'

'"We trust you."' He laughed again. 'Imperialists! Always sweet words. Sweet words and then they kill you for a kopek. For a kopek! If you *were* the ones, you would *demand* proof.'

'We demand proof.'

'I have *proof*,' he said defiantly. He glanced from one man to the other, then lowered the rifle, turned and began moving quickly back towards the trees.

'Now what?' whispered O'Brian.

'God knows.'

'Can we get that rifle off him? Two of us, one of him?'

Kelso stared at him in astonishment. 'Don't even *think* it.'

'Boy, but he's quick, though, isn't he? And completely fucking crazy.' O'Brian gave a nervous giggle. 'Look at him. Now what's he doing?'

But he was doing nothing, merely standing impassively at the edge of the trees, waiting.

THERE didn't seem to be much else for them to do except follow him, which wasn't easy, given his speed across the ground, the roughness of the forest floor, the handicap of O'Brian's injured leg. Kelso carried the camera case. Once or twice they seemed to lose him, but never for long. He must have kept stopping to let them catch up.

After a few minutes they came back out on to the track, but further up, roughly midway between the abandoned Toyota and the empty settlement.

He didn't pause. He led them straight across the snowy track and into the trees on the other side.

This was not good, thought Kelso, as they passed out of the grey light and back into the shadows. Surreptitiously, without slackening pace, he put his hand into his pocket and tore a page out of his yellow notebook, screwed it into a ball and dropped it behind him. He did this every fifty yards or so – hare and hounds: an old school game – only now he was hare *and* hound.

O'Brian, panting at his back, whispered, 'Nice work.'

They emerged into a small clearing, with a wooden cabin in the centre. He had built this well – and recently, by the look of it – cannibalising the old encampment for his materials. Why he had done this, Kelso never discovered. Perhaps the other place was too full of ghosts. Or, maybe he wanted a spot even more secluded, and more easily defensible. In the silence, Kelso thought he could hear running water and he guessed they must be near the river.

The cabin was made of the familiar grey timber, with one small window and a door to suit his height, set a yard above the ground and approached by four wooden steps. At the base of these he picked up a branch and prodded deep into the snow. There was a spurt of white powder as something jumped and snapped. He withdrew the branch. Clamped around the end was a large animal trap, the rusty metal teeth stuck deep into the wood.

He laid this carefully to one side, climbed the steps to his door, unfastened the padlock and went inside. After a brief exchange of looks with O'Brian, Kelso followed, ducking his head to pass through the low entrance, emerging into the one small room. It was dark and cold and he could smell the insanity – he inhaled the lonely madness, as sharp and sour as the lingering stink of unwashed flesh. He put his hand to his mouth. Behind him he heard O'Brian suck in his breath.

Their host had lit a kerosene lamp. The whitened skulls of a bear and a wolf shone from the shadows. He put the notebook on the table, next to a half-eaten plate of some dark and bony fish, put a pot of water on the hob and bent to rekindle the old iron stove, keeping his rifle close to hand.

Kelso could imagine him an hour ago: hearing the distant sound of their car on the track, abandoning his meal, grabbing his gun and heading for the forest, his fire doused, his trap set –

There wasn't a bed, merely a thin mattress, leaking stuffing, rolled and tied with string. Beside it was an ancient Soviet-made transistor radio, the size of a packing case, and next to that a wind-up gramophone with a tarnished brass horn.

The Russian unfastened the satchel and took out the notebook. He opened it at the picture of the girl gymnasts in Red Square and held it up for them: there, you see? They nodded. He set it down on the table. Then he pulled on a length of greasy leather hanging round his neck and kept on pulling until he hauled from somewhere deep in the fetid folds of his clothes a small piece of clear plastic. He offered it to Kelso. It was warm from the heat of his body: the same picture, but folded very small, so that only Anna Safanova's face was visible.

'You are the ones,' he said. 'I am the one you seek. And now: the proof.'

He kissed the home-made locket and lowered it back into his clothes. Then, from the belt of his greatcoat, he drew out a short, wide-bladed knife with a leather hilt. He turned it, showing them the sharpness of the edge. He grinned at them. He kicked back the bit of carpet at his feet, dropped to his knees and prised up a crude trapdoor.

He reached down and pulled out a large and shabby suitcase.

HE unpacked his reliquary like a priest, reverently placing each object on the crude wooden table as if it were an altar.

The holy texts came out first: the thirteen volumes of Stalin's collected works and thoughts, the *Sochineniya*, published in Moscow after the war. He showed the title page of each book to Kelso and then to O'Brian. All of them were signed in the same way – 'To the future, J. V. Stalin' – and all, clearly, had been read and re-read endlessly. On some of the volumes, the spines were badly cracked or hanging off. The pages were swollen by markers and bent corners.

Then came the uniform, each part carefully wrapped in

yellowing tissue paper. A pressed grey tunic with red epaulets. A pair of black trousers, also pressed. A greatcoat. A pair of black leather boots, gleaming like polished anthracite. A marshal's cap. A gold star in a crimson leather case embossed with the hammer and sickle, which Kelso recognised as the Order of Hero of the Soviet Union.

And then came the mementoes. A photograph (in a wooden frame, glazed) of Stalin standing behind a desk: signed, like the books, 'To the future, J. V. Stalin'. A Dunhill pipe. An envelope containing a lock of coarse grey hair. And finally a stack of gramophone records, old 78s, as thick as dinner plates, each still in its original paper sleeve: 'Mother, the Fields are Dusty', 'I'm Waiting For You', 'Nightingale of the Taiga,' 'J. V. Stalin: Speech to the First All-Union Congress of Collective Farm Shock Workers, February 19 1933', 'J. V. Stalin: Report to the Eighteenth Congress of the Communist Party of the Soviet Union, March 10 1939' . . .

Kelso couldn't move. He couldn't speak. It was O'Brian who took the first step. He glanced at the Russian, touched himself on his chest, gestured at the table, and received in return a nod of approval. Tentatively, he reached out to pick up the photograph. Kelso could see what he was thinking: the likeness was indeed striking. Not exact, of course – no man ever looks exactly like his father – but there was *something* there, no doubt about it, even with the younger man's beard and straggling hair. Something in the cast of the eyes and the bone structure, perhaps, or in the play of the expression: a kind of ponderous agility, a genetic shadow that was beyond the skills of any actor.

The Russian grinned again at O'Brian. He picked up his knife and pointed at the photograph, then mimed hacking at his beard. Yes?

For a moment, Kelso wasn't sure what he meant, but O'Brian did. O'Brian knew at once.

Yes. He nodded vigorously. Oh, yes. Yes, please.

The Russian promptly scythed away a great swathe of coarse black facial hair and held it out, with childish pleasure, for their inspection. He repeated the stroke, again and again, and there was something shocking about the way he did this, in the casual manipulation of the razor-edged knife – this side, that, and then the throat – in the careless self-mutilation of it. *There is nothing*, thought Kelso, with a flash of certainty, *there is no act of violence this man is not capable of.* The Russian reached behind his head and grabbed his hair into a thick ponytail and sliced it off as close to the roots as he could. Then he crossed the cabin in a couple of strides, opened the door of the iron stove, and flung the mass of hair on to the burning wood where it flared for an instant before shriveling to dust and smoke.

'Bloody hell,' whispered Kelso. He watched, disbelieving, as O'Brian began opening the camera case. 'Oh no. Not that. You can't be serious.'

'I can.'

'But he's mad.'

'So are half the people we put on television.' O'Brian pushed a new cassette into the side of the camera and smiled as it clicked home. 'Showtime.'

Behind him, the Russian had his head bent over the bowl of hot water steaming on the stove. He had stripped to a dirty yellow vest and had lathered his face with something. The rasp of the knife-blade on his bristle made Kelso's own flesh ache.

'Look at him,' said Kelso. 'He probably doesn't even know what television *is*.'

'Fine by me.'

'God.' Kelso closed his eyes.

The Russian turned towards them, wiping himself on his shirt. His face was blotchy, beaded with pinheads of blood, but he had left himself a heavy moustache, as black and oily as a crow's wings, and the transformation was stunning. Here stood the Stalin of the 1920s: Stalin in his prime, an animal force. What was it Lenin had predicted? *'This Georgian will serve us a peppery stew.'*

He tucked his hair under the marshal's cap. He slipped on the tunic. A little loose around the front, perhaps, but otherwise a perfect fit. He buttoned it and strutted up and down the room a couple of times, his right hand circling modestly in an imperial wave.

He picked up a volume of the *Collected Works*, opened it at random, glanced at the page and handed it to Kelso.

Then he smiled, held up a finger, coughed into his hand, cleared his throat and began to speak. And he was good. Kelso could tell that straight away. He was not merely word perfect. He was better than that. He must have studied the recordings, hour after hour, year after year since childhood. He had the familiar, flat, remorseless delivery; the brutal, incantatory beat. He had the expression of heavy sarcasm, the dark humour, the strength, the *hate*.

'This Trotsky–Bukharin bunch of spies, murderers and wreckers,' he began slowly, 'who kow-towed to the foreign world, who were possessed by a slavish instinct to grovel before every foreign bigwig, and who were ready to enter his employ as a spy –' his voice began to rise ' – this handful of people who did not understand that the *humblest* Soviet citizen, being free from the fetters of capital, stands head and shoulders above any high-placed foreign *bigwig* whose neck wears the yoke of capitalist slavery –' and now he was shouting ' – who needs this *miserable* band of venal *slaves*, of what value can they be to the people, and whom can they demoralise?'

He glared around, defying any of them – Kelso with the open book, O'Brian with the camera to his eye, the table, the stove, the skulls – any one of them to dare to answer him back.

He straightened, thrusting out his chin.

'In 1937 Tukhachevsky, Yakir, Uborevich and other fiends were sentenced to be shot. After that, the elections to the Supreme Soviet of the U.S.S.R. were held. In these elections, 98.6 per cent of the total vote was cast for the Soviet power!

'At the beginning of 1938 Rosengoltz, Rykov, Bukharin and other fiends were sentenced to be shot. After that, the elections to the Supreme Soviets of the Union Republics were held. In these elections 99.4 per cent of the total vote was cast for the Soviet power! Where are the symptoms of demoralisation, we would like to know?'

He placed his fist on his heart.

'Such was the *inglorious* end of the opponents of the line of our Party, who finished up as *enemies of the people!*'

'*Stormy applause,*' read Kelso. '*All the delegates rise and cheer the speaker. Shouts of "Hurrah for Comrade Stalin!" "Long live Comrade Stalin!" "Hurrah for the Central Committee of our Party!"*'

The Russian swayed before the rhythm of the dead crowd. He could hear the roars, the stamping feet, the cheers. He nodded modestly. He smiled. He applauded in return. The imaginary tumult rang around the narrow cabin and rolled out across the snowy clearing to split the silent trees.

Chapter Twenty-seven

FELIKS SUVORIN'S AIRCRAFT dropped through the base of low cloud and banked to starboard, following the line of the White Sea coast.

A stain of rust appeared in the snowy wilderness and spread, and he began to make out details. Drooping cranes, empty submarine pens, derelict construction sheds . . . Severodvinsk, it must be – Brezhnev's big nuclear junkyard, just along the coast from Archangel, where they built the subs in the 1970s that were supposed to bring the imperialists to their knees.

He stared down at it as he fastened his seatbelt. Some mafia middlemen had been sniffing around up here, about a year ago, trying to buy a warhead for the Iraqis. He remembered the case. Chechens in the taiga! Unbelievable! And yet they would manage it one day, he thought. There was too much spare hardware, too little supervision, too much money chasing it. The law of supply and demand would mate with the law of averages and they would get something, sometime.

The wingflaps shuddered. There was a whine of cables. They descended further, yawing and pitching through the snowstorm. Severodvinsk slid away. He could see grey discs of freezing water, flat blank swampland, white-capped trees and more trees, running away for ever. What could live down there? Nothing, surely? No one. They were at the edge of the earth.

The old plane trundled on for another ten minutes, barely fifty yards above the forest ceiling, and then ahead Suvorin saw a pattern of lights in the snow.

It was a military airfield, secluded in the trees, with a snow plough parked at the edge of the apron. The runway had just been cleared but already a thin white skin was beginning to form again. They came in low to take a look then lifted once more, the engine straining, and turned to make a final approach. As they did so, Suvorin had a tilting glimpse of Archangel – of distant, shadowy tower blocks and filthy chimneys – and then in they came, bouncing off the runway, once, twice, before settling, turning, the propellers conjuring miniature blizzards from the snow.

When the pilot switched off the engine there was a quality of silence that Suvorin had never experienced before. Always in Moscow there was something to hear, even in the so-called still of night – a bit of traffic, maybe, a neighbour's quarrel. But not here. Here the quiet was absolute, and he loathed it. He found himself talking just to fill it.

'Good work,' he called up to the pilot. 'We made it.'

'You're welcome. By the way, there's a message for you from Moscow. You're to call the colonel before you go. Make any sense?'

'Before I go?'

'That's it.'

Before I go where?

There wasn't enough room to stand upright. Suvorin had to crouch. Drawn up beside a big hangar he could see a line of bi-planes painted in arctic camouflage.

The door at the back of the plane swung open. The temperature dropped about five degrees. Snowflakes billowed up the fuselage. Suvorin grabbed his attaché case and jumped down to the concrete. A technician in a fur hat pointed him towards the hangar. Its heavy sliding door was pulled a quarter open. Waiting in the shadows, next to a couple of jeeps, sheltering from the snow, was a reception committee: three men in MVD uniforms with AK-74 assault rifles, a guy from the militia and, most bizarrely, an elderly lady in thick male clothing, hunched like a vulture, leaning on a stick.

SOMETHING had happened, Suvorin could tell that right away, and whatever it was, it was not good. He knew it when he offered his hand to the senior Interior Ministry soldier – a surly-lipped, bull-necked young man named Major Kretov – and received in reply a salute of just sufficient idleness to imply an insult. And as for Kretov's two men, they never even bothered to acknowledge his arrival. They were too busy unloading a small armoury from the back of one of the jeeps – extra magazines for their AK-74s, pistols, flares and a big old RP46 machine gun with cannisters of belt-fed ammunition and a metal bipod.

'So, what are we expecting here, major?' Suvorin said, in an effort to be friendly. 'A small war?'

'We can discuss it on the way.'

'I'd prefer to discuss it now.'

Kretov hesitated. Clearly he would have liked to tell Suvorin to go to hell, but they had the same rank, and besides he hadn't quite got the measure yet of this civilian-soldier in his expensive western clothes. 'Well, quickly then.' He clicked his fingers irritably in the direction of the gangly young militia man. 'Tell him what's happened.'

'And you are?' said Suvorin.

The militia man came to attention. 'Lieutenant Korf, major.'

'So, Korf?'

The lieutenant delivered his report quickly, nervously.

Shortly after midday, the Archangel militia had been notified by Moscow central headquarters that two foreigners were believed to be in the vicinity of the city, possibly seeking to make contact with a person or persons named Safanov or Safanova. He had undertaken the inquiry himself. Only one such citizen had been located: the witness Vavara Safanova – he indicated the old woman – who had been picked up within ninety minutes of receipt of the telex from Moscow. She had confirmed that two foreigners had been to see her and had left her barely an hour earlier.

Suvorin smiled in a kindly way at Vavara Safanova. 'And what were you able to tell them, Comrade Safanova?'

She looked at the ground.

'She told them her daughter was dead,' cut in Kretov, impatiently. 'Died in childbirth, forty-five years ago, having a kid. A boy. Now: can we go? I've got all this out of her already.'

A boy, thought Suvorin. It had to be. A girl wouldn't have mattered. But a boy. An heir –

'And the boy lives?'

'Reared in the forest, she says. Like a wolf.'

Suvorin turned reluctantly from the silent old woman to the major. 'And Kelso and O'Brian have gone into the forest to find this "wolf", presumably?'

'They're about three hours ahead of us.' Kretov had a large-scale map spread over the hood of the nearest jeep. 'This is the road,' he said. 'There's no way out except back the way they went, and the snow will hold them up. Don't worry. We'll have them by nightfall.'

'And how do we reach them? Can we use a helicopter?'

Kretov winked at one of his men. 'I fear the major from

Moscow has not adequately studied our terrain. The taiga is not well supplied with *helicopter pads*.'

Suvorin tried to stay calm. 'Then we reach them how?'

'By snow plough,' said Kretov, as if it was obvious. 'Four of us can just fit in the cab. Or three, if you prefer not to wet your fancy footwear.'

Again, and with difficulty, Suvorin controlled his temper. 'So what's the plan? We clear a way for them to drive back into town behind us, is that it?'

'If that proves necessary.'

'If that proves necessary,' repeated Suvorin, slowly. Now he was beginning to understand. He gazed into the major's cold grey eyes, then looked at the two MVD men who had finished unloading the jeep. 'So what are you people running nowadays? Death squads, is that it? It's a little bit of South America you've got going up here?'

Kretov began folding up the map. 'We must move out immediately.'

'I need to speak to Moscow.'

'We've already spoken to Moscow.'

'*I* need to speak to Moscow, major, and if you attempt to leave without me, I can assure you that you will spend the next few years *building* helicopter pads.'

'I don't think so.'

'If it comes to a trial of strength between the SVR and the MVD, be aware of this: the SVR will win every time.' Suvorin turned and bowed to Vavara Safanova. 'Thank you for your assistance.' And then, to Korf, who was watching all this, goggle-eyed: 'Take her home, please. You did well.'

'I told them,' said the old woman suddenly. 'I told them nothing good could come of it.'

'That may be true,' said Suvorin. 'All right, lieutenant, off you go. Now,' he said to Kretov, 'where's that fucking telephone?'

O'BRIAN had insisted on shooting another twenty minutes of footage. By sign language he had persuaded the Russian to pack up his relics and then to unpack them again, holding each object up to the camera and explaining what it was. ('His book.' 'His picture.' 'His hair.' Each was dutifully kissed and arranged on the altar.) Then O'Brian showed him how he wanted him to sit at the table smoking his pipe and to read from Anna Safanova's journal. (*Remember Comrade Stalin's historic words to Gorky: "It is the task of the proletarian state to produce the engineers of human souls . . ."*)

'Great,' said O'Brian, moving around him with the camera. 'Fantastic. Isn't this fantastic, Fluke?'

'No,' said Kelso, 'it's a bloody circus.'

'Ask him a couple of questions, Fluke.'

'I shall not.'

'Go on. Just a couple. Ask him what he thinks of the new Russia.'

'No.'

'Two questions and we're out of here. I promise.'

Kelso hesitated. The Russian stared at him, stroking his moustache with the stem of his pipe. His teeth were yellowish and stumpy. The underside of his moustache was wet with saliva.

'My colleague would like to know,' Kelso said, 'if you have heard of the great changes that have taken place in Russia and what you think of them.'

For a moment, he was silent. Then he turned from Kelso and stared directly into the lens.

'One feature of the history of the old Russia,' he began,

'was the continual beatings she suffered. All beat her for her backwardness. She was beaten because to do so was profitable and could be done with impunity. Such is the law of the exploiters – to beat the backward and the weak. It is the jungle law of capitalism. You are backward, you are weak – therefore you are wrong; hence, you can be beaten and enslaved.'

He sat back, sucking on his pipe, his eyes half closed. O'Brian was standing directly behind Kelso, holding the camera, and Kelso felt the pressure of his hand on his shoulder, urging him to ask another question.

'I don't understand,' Kelso said. 'What are you saying? That the new Russia is beaten and enslaved? But surely most people would say the opposite: that however hard life might be, at least they now have freedom?'

A slow smile, directly into the camera. The Russian removed his pipe from his mouth and leaned forwards, jabbing it at Kelso's chest.

'That is very good. But, unfortunately, freedom alone is not enough, by far. If there is a shortage of bread, a shortage of butter and fats, a shortage of textiles, and if housing conditions are bad, freedom will not carry you very far. It is very difficult, comrades, to live on freedom alone.'

O'Brian whispered, 'What's he saying? Does it make sense?'

'It makes a kind of sense. But it's odd.'

O'Brian persuaded Kelso to ask a couple more questions, each of which drew similar, stilted replies, and then, when Kelso refused to translate any more, he insisted on taking the Russian outside for a final shot.

Kelso watched them for a minute through the narrow, dirty window: O'Brian making a mark in the snow and then walking towards the cabin, returning, pointing to the line, trying to make the Russian understand what he wanted him to do. It was almost as if he had been expecting them, Kelso thought. *'You are the ones,'* he had said. *'You are truly the ones . . .'*

'This is the book of which it is spoken . . .'

He had been educated, obviously – indoctrinated, perhaps, a better word. He could read. He seemed to have been brought up with a sense of destiny: a messianic certainty that one day strangers would appear in the forest, bearing a book, and that they, whoever they were – even if they were a couple of imperialists – *they would be the ones . . .*

The Russian was apparently in a great good humour, bringing his index finger up close to his eye and wiggling it at the camera, grinning, stooping and making a snowball, tossing it playfully at O'Brian's back.

Homo Sovieticus, thought Kelso. Soviet man.

He tried to remember something, a passage in Volkogonov's biography, quoting Sverdlov, who had been exiled with Stalin to Siberia in 1914. Stalin wouldn't associate with the other Bolsheviks, that was what had struck Sverdlov. Here he was: unknown, almost forty, had never done a day's work in his life, had no skills, no profession, yet he would simply go off on his own to hunt or fish, and 'gave the impression that he was waiting for something to happen'.

Hunting. Fishing. *Waiting.*

Kelso turned from the window and quickly slipped the notebook back into the satchel, stuffed the satchel into his jacket. He checked the window again, then stepped over to the table and began leafing through Stalin's *Collected Works*.

It took him a couple of minutes to find what he was looking for: a pair of dog-eared pages in different volumes, both passages heavily underlined with black pencil. And it was as he thought: the Russian's first answer was a direct quotation from a Stalin speech – to the All-Union Conference of Managers of Socialist Industry, February 4 1931, to be exact – while the second was lifted from an address to three thousand Stakhanovites, November 17 1935.

The son was speaking the words of the Father.

He heard the sound of Stalin's boots on the wooden steps and hastily replaced the books.

SUVORIN followed one of the MVD men out of the hangar and across the runway towards a single-storey block next to the control tower. The wind tore through his coat. Snow leaked through the tops of his shoes. By the time they reached the office he was freezing. A young corporal looked up as they came in, without interest. Suvorin was beginning to feel thoroughly sick of this tin pot, backwoods town, this *Archangel.* He slammed the door.

'Salute, man, damn you, when an officer comes into the room!'

The corporal leapt up so quickly he knocked over his chair.

'Get me a line to Moscow. Now. Then wait outside. Both of you wait outside.'

Suvorin didn't start to dial until they had gone. He picked up the chair and righted it and sat down heavily. The corporal had been reading a German pornographic magazine. A stockinged foot poked out glossily from beneath a pile of flight logs. He could hear the number ringing faintly. There was heavy static on the line.

'Sergo? It's Suvorin. Give me the chief.'

A moment later, Arsenyev came through. 'Feliks, listen.' His tone was strained. 'I've been trying to reach you. You've heard the news?'

'I've heard the news.'

'Unbelievable! You've talked to the others? You must move quickly.'

'Yes, I've talked to them, and I mean to say, what is this, colonel?' Suvorin had to put his finger into his other ear and shout into the receiver. 'What's going on? I've landed in the middle of nowhere and I'm looking out of the window here at three cut-throats loading a snow plough with enough firepower to take out a battalion of NATO –'

'Feliks,' said Arsenyev, 'it's out of our hands.'

'So what is this? Now we are supposed to take our orders from the MVD?'

'They're not MVD,' said Arsenyev quietly. 'They're Special Forces in MVD uniforms.'

'Spetsnaz?' Suvorin put his hand to his head. Spetsnaz. Commandos. Alpha Brigade. *Killers.* 'Who decided to turn them loose?'

As if he didn't know.

Arsenyev said, 'Guess.'

'And was His Excellency drunk as usual? Or was this a rare interlude of sobriety?'

'Have a care, major!' Arsenyev's voice was sharp.

The snow plough's heavy diesel cracked into life. The revving engine shook the double glass, briefly obliterating Arsenyev's voice. Big yellow headlights turned and flashed through the snow then began moving ponderously across the runway towards Suvorin.

'So what are my orders exactly?'

'To proceed as you think fit, using all force necessary.'

'All force necessary to achieve what?'

'Whatever you think fit.'

'Which is what?'

'That's for you to decide. I'm relying on you, major. I'm allowing you complete operational freedom –'

Oh but he was a wily one, wasn't he? The wiliest. A real survivor. Suvorin lost his temper.

'So how many are we supposed to kill then, colonel? One man is it? Two? *Three?*'

Arsenyev was shocked. He was profoundly disturbed. If the tape of the call was ever played back – which it would be, the following day – his expression would be obvious for all to hear. 'Nobody said anything about killing, major! Has anyone there said such a thing? Have I?'

'No, you haven't,' said Suvorin, finding within himself a depth of sarcasm and bitterness he didn't know he possessed, 'so obviously whatever happens is my responsibility alone. I haven't been guided by my superior officers in any way. And neither, I am sure, has the exemplary Major Kretov!'

Arsenyev started to say something but his voice was drowned out by the roar of the engine being revved again. The snow plough was nearly up against the window now. Its blade rose and fell like a guillotine. Suvorin could see Kretov in the driver's seat, passing his finger across his throat. The horn sounded. Suvorin waved at him irritably and turned his back.

'Say again, colonel.'

But the line was dead and all attempts to reconnect it failed. And that was the sound that Suvorin afterwards could never quite get out of his ears, as he sat squashed in the jumpseat of the snow plough, bouncing into the forest: the cold, implacable buzz of a number unobtainable.

Chapter Twenty-eight

THE SNOW HAD eased and it was much colder – it must have been minus three or four. Kelso pulled up his hood and set off as fast as he could towards the edge of the clearing. Ahead of him through the trees his paper trail of yellow markers blossomed every fifty yards in the snowy undergrowth like winter flowers.

Getting out of the cabin had not been easy. When he had told the Russian they needed to go back to their car – 'only to collect some more equipment, comrade,' he had added, quickly – he had received a look of such glinting suspicion he had almost quailed. But somehow he held the other man's gaze and eventually, after a final, searching glance, he was given a brief nod of permission. And even then O'Brian had lingered – 'you know, we could do with one more shot from over here . . .' – until Kelso had grabbed him hard by the elbow and steered him towards the door. The Russian watched them go, puffing on his pipe.

Kelso could hear O'Brian, breathing hard, stumbling after him, but he didn't stop to let him catch up until they were out of sight of the hut.

O'Brian said, 'You got the notebook?'

Kelso patted the front of his jacket. 'In here.'

'Oh, nice work,' said O'Brian. He performed a little victory shuffle in the snow. 'Jesus, this is a story, isn't it? This is a hell of a story.'

'A hell of a story,' repeated Kelso, but all he wanted was to get away. He resumed his walk, but more urgently now, his legs aching with the effort of pushing through the snow.

They came out on to the track and there was the Toyota, a hundred yards away, wrapped in a wet, white layer more than an inch deep, thicker towards the rear where the wind was blowing from, and as they came closer they could see that the surface was beginning to crystalise to ice. It was still tilting forwards, its back tyres almost clear of the snow, and it took them a while to locate all the damage. The Russian had fired three bullets into the car. One had blown off the lock on the back door. Another had opened up the driver's side. A third had gone through the hood into the engine, presumably to silence the alarm.

'That crazy sonofabitch,' said O'Brian, staring at the ugly holes. 'This is a forty-thousand-dollar vehicle –'

He squeezed behind the steering wheel, put the key in the ignition and turned it. Nothing. Not even a click.

'No wonder he didn't mind if we came back to the car,' said Kelso, quietly. 'He knew we weren't going anywhere.'

O'Brian had started looking worried again. He struggled out of the front seat and sank deep into the drift. He waded round to the back, lifted the rear door and blew out a long sigh of relief, his breath condensing in the cold air.

'Well, it doesn't look as though he's damaged the Inmarsat, thank Christ. That's something.' He glanced around, frowning.

Kelso said, 'Now what?'

O'Brian muttered, 'Trees.'

'*Trees?*'

'Yeah. The satellite's not straight above our heads, remember? She's over the equator. This far north, that means you need to keep the dish at a real low angle to send a signal. Trees, if they're close up – they, ah, well, they kind of *get in the way*.' He turned to Kelso, and Kelso could have murdered him then: killed him just for the nervous, sheepish grin on his big, handsome, stupid face. 'We're gonna need a space, Fluke. Sorry.'

A space?

Yeah. A space. They would have to return to the clearing.

O'BRIAN insisted they took the rest of the equipment back with them. That, after all, was what Kelso had told the Russian they were going to do, and they didn't want to make him suspicious, did they? Besides, no way was O'Brian going to leave over a hundred-grand's-worth of electronic gear sitting in a shot-up Toyota in the middle of nowhere. He wasn't going to let it out of his *sight*.

And so they struggled back along the track, O'Brian in the lead carrying the Inmarsat and the heavier of the big cases, with the Toyota's battery, wrapped in a black plastic sheet, jammed under his arm. Kelso had the camera case and the lap-top editing machine and he did his best to keep up, but it was heavy going. His arms ached. The snow sucked at him. Soon, O'Brian had turned into the forest and was out of sight, while Kelso had to keep stopping to transfer the damned bloody swine of an edit case from one hand to the other. He sweated and cursed. On his way back through the trees he stumbled over a hidden root and dropped to his knees.

By the time he reached the clearing, O'Brian already had the satellite dish connected to the battery and was trying to twist it into the right direction. The trajectory of the antenna pointed directly at the snowy tops of some big firs, about fifty yards away, and he was hunched over it, his jaw working with anxiety, holding the compass in one hand, pressing switches with the other. The snow had almost stopped and there was a faint blueness to the freezing air. Behind him, framed against the shadows of the trees, was the grey wooden cabin – utterly still, deserted apparently, apart from the thread of smoke rising from its narrow iron chimney.

Kelso let the cases drop and leaned forwards, his hands on his knees, trying to recover his breath.

'Anything?' he said.

'Nope.'

Kelso groaned.

A bloody circus –

'If that thing doesn't work,' he said, 'we're here for the duration, you realise that? We'll be stuck here till next April with nothing to do except listen to extracts from Stalin's *Complete Works*.'

It was such an appalling prospect, he actually found himself laughing, and for the second time that day, O'Brian joined in.

'Oh man,' he said, 'the things we do for glory.'

But he didn't laugh for long, and the machine stayed silent.

AND it was in this silence, about thirty seconds later, that Kelso thought he heard again the faint sound of rushing water.

He held up his hand.

'What?' said O'Brian.

'The river.' He closed his eyes and raised his face to the sky, straining to hear. 'The river, I *think* –'

It was hard to separate it from the noise of the wind in the trees. But it was more sustained than wind, and deeper, and it seemed to be coming from somewhere on the other side of the cabin.

'Let's go for it,' said O'Brian. He snatched the pair of crocodile clips off the battery terminals and began rapidly rolling up the cable. 'Makes sense, if you think of it. Must be how he gets about. A boat.'

Kelso hoisted the two cases and O'Brian called out, 'Watch yourself, Fluke.'

'What?'

'Traps. Remember? He's got this whole wood wired.'

Kelso stood, looking at the ground, uncertain, remembering the spurt of snow, the snap of the metal jaws. But it was hopeless to worry about that, he thought, just as there was no way they could avoid passing directly by the door of the cabin. He waited for O'Brian to finish packing up the Inmarsat, and then they started walking together, treading warily. And Kelso could sense the Russian everywhere now: at the window of his squalid hut, in the crawlspace underneath it, behind the stack of cordwood piled against the back wall, in the dank and mossy water barrel and in the darkness of the nearby trees. He could imagine the rifle trained on his back and he was acutely aware of the softness of his own skin, of its babyish vulnerability.

They reached the edge of the clearing and followed the perimeter of the forest. Dense undergrowth. Fallen, rotted logs. Strange white fungoid growths like melted faces. And occasionally, in the distance, crashes, as the wind shifted and brought down falls of frozen snow. It was impossible to see much further than a hand's reach. They couldn't find a path. There was nothing to do but plunge between the trees.

O'Brian went first and had the worst of it, lugging the two heavy cases and the big battery, having to twist his bulky body sideways to edge through the narrow gaps, sometimes left, sometimes right, ducking abruptly, no free hand to protect his face from the low branches. Kelso tried to follow in his footsteps and after half a dozen paces he was conscious of the forest swinging shut behind them like a solid door.

They stumbled on for a few minutes in the semi-darkness. Kelso wanted to stop and transfer the edit machine to his other hand but he didn't dare lose sight of O'Brian's back and soon he had forgotten about everything except the pain in his right shoulder and the acid in his lungs. Trickles of sweat and melted snow were running into his eyes, blurring his vision, and he was trying to bring his arm up to wipe his forehead on his wet sleeve when O'Brian gave a shout and lurched forwards, and suddenly – it was like passing through a wall – the trees parted and they were in the light again, standing on the ridge of a steep bank that fell away at their feet to a tumbling plain of yellowish-grey water a clear quarter-mile across.

IT was an awesome sight – God's work, truly – like finding a cathedral in the middle of a jungle – and for a while neither man spoke. Then O'Brian set down his cases and the battery and took out his compass. He showed it to Kelso. They were on the northern bank of the Dvina facing almost exactly due south.

Ten yards below them, and a hundred yards to their left, dragged clear of the water and covered in a dark green tarpaulin, was a small boat. It looked as though it had been taken out for the winter, and that would make sense, thought Kelso, because already ice was beginning to extend out into the river – a shelf maybe ten or fifteen yards across that seemed to be widening even as he watched.

On the opposite bank there was a similar strip of whiteness, and then the dark line of the trees began again.

Kelso raised his binoculars and inspected the far shore for signs of habitation but there was none. It looked utterly forbidding and gloomy. A wilderness.

He lowered the binoculars. 'Who're you going to call?'

'America. Get them to call the bureau in Moscow.' O'Brian already had the case of the Inmarsat open and was slotting together the plastic dish. He had taken off his gloves. In the extreme cold his hands looked raw. 'When's it gonna be dark?'

Kelso looked at his watch. 'It's nearly five now,' he said. 'An hour perhaps.'

'Okay, let's face it, even if the battery holds on this thing and I get through to the States and they fix us a rescue party – we're stuck here for the night. Unless we take some pretty dramatic action.'

'Meaning?'

'We take his boat.'

'You'd steal his boat?'

'I'd borrow it, sure.' He sat on his haunches, unwrapping the battery, refusing to meet Kelso's eyes. 'Oh, come on, man, don't look at me like that. Where's the harm? He's not going to need it till the spring anyhow – not if the temperature keeps on dropping like this – that river'll be iced over in a day or two. Besides, he shot up our car, didn't he? We'll use his boat – that's fair.'

'And you can work a boat, can you?'

'I can work a boat, I can work a camera, I can make pictures fly through the air – I'm fucking superman. Yeah, I can sail. Let's do it.'

'And what about him? He'll just stand there, will he, while we do it? He'll wave us off?' Kelso glanced back the way they had come. 'You realise he's probably watching us right now?'

'Okay. So you go keep him talking while I get everything ready.'

'Oh, thank you,' said Kelso. 'Thank you very much indeed.'

'Well, at least I've had a fucking idea. What's yours?'

A fair point, Kelso had to concede.

He hesitated, then focused his binoculars on the boat.

So this was how the Russian survived – how he made his occasional forays into the outside world. This was how he acquired the fuel for his lamp, the tobacco for his pipe, the ammunition for his guns, the battery for his transistor radio. What did he use for money? Did he barter what he caught or trapped. Or had the encampment been set up in the 1950s with a treasury of some sort – NKVD gold – which they had been eking out ever since?

The boat was concealed in a small depression, protected from the river by a low screen of trees: to anyone drifting by, she would be invisible. She was resting on her keel, propped up to port and starboard by logs – a sturdy-looking vessel, not big, room for four people, at a pinch. A bulge at her stern suggested an outboard motor, and if that was the case, and if O'Brian could make it work, they might reach Archangel in a couple of hours – less, probably, with the current flowing so fast through its narrowing channel.

He thought of the crosses in the cemetery, the dates, the obliterated faces.

It did not look as though many people had ever left this place.

It was worth a try.

'All right,' he said, reluctantly, 'let's do it.'

'That's my boy.'

When he stepped back into the trees, he left O'Brian

aiming the antenna across the river, and he had not gone far when he heard behind him the blissful, rising note of the Inmarsat locking on to the satellite.

THE snow plough was coming on fast now, thirty, forty miles an hour, rushing down the track, throwing up a great white bow wave of freezing surf that went smashing into the trees on either side. Kretov was driving. His men were jammed together next to him, nursing their guns. Suvorin was hanging on to the metal moorings of the jump seat at the back of the cab, the barrel of the RP46 poking into his thigh, feeling sick from the vibration and the diesel fumes. He marvelled at the complexities that had overwhelmed his life in so short a time, and pondered nervously the wisdom of the old Russian proverb: 'We are born in a clear field and die in a dark forest.'

He had plenty of time for his thoughts because none of the other three had addressed a word to him since they left the airfield. They passed chewing gum to one another and TU-144 cigarettes and talked quietly so he couldn't hear what they were saying above the racket of the engine. An intimate trio, he thought: clearly a partnership with some history. Where had they been last? Grozny, maybe, taking Moscow's peace to the Chechen rebels? (*'The terrorist gunmen all died at the scene . . .'*) In which case this would be a holiday for them. A picnic in the woods. And who was giving them their orders? *Guess . . .*

Arsenyev's joke.

It was hot in the cab. The single windscreen wiper batted away the pawprints of snow with a soporific beat.

He tried to shift his leg away from the machine gun.

Serafima had been on at him for months to get out of the

service and make some money – her father knew a man on the board of a big privatised energy consortium and, well, let's just say, my dear Feliks, that – how should we put this? – a number of *favours* are owed. So what would that be worth, papa, exactly? Ten times his official salary and a tenth of the work? To hell with Yasenevo. Perhaps it was time.

A heavy male voice started grunting from the radio. Suvorin leaned forwards. He couldn't make out exactly what was being said. It sounded like co-ordinates. Kretov was holding the microphone in one hand, steering with the other, craning his neck to study the map on the knee of the man sitting next to him, watching the road. 'Sure, sure. No problem.' He hung up.

Suvorin said, 'What was that?'

'Ah,' said Kretov, in mock-surprise, 'you're still here? You got it, Aleksey?' This was to the man with the map, and then, to Suvorin, 'That was the listening post at Onega. They just intercepted a satellite transmission.'

'Fifteen miles, major. It's right on the river.'

'You see?' said Kretov, grinning at Suvorin in the mirror. 'What did I tell you? Home by nightfall.'

Chapter Twenty-nine

KELSO CAME OUT of the trees and walked towards the wooden cabin. The surface of the snow had frozen to a thin crust and the wind had picked up slightly, sending little twisters of powder dancing across the clearing. Rising from the iron chimney the thin brown coil of smoke jerked and snagged in the breeze.

'When one approaches Him, do so openly.' That was the advice of the maidservant, Valechka. *'He hates it when people creep up on Him. If a door has to be knocked upon, knock upon it loudly . . .'*

Kelso tried his best to make his rubber boots thump on the wooden steps, and he hammered on the door with his gloved fist. There was no reply.

Now what?

He knocked again, waited, then raised the latch and pushed open the door, and immediately, the now-familiar smell – cold, close, *animal,* with an underlay of stale pipe tobacco – rose to overwhelm him.

The cabin was empty. The rifle was gone. It looked as though the Russian had been working at his table: papers were laid out, and a couple of stubby pencils.

Kelso stood just inside the doorway, eyeing the papers, trying to decide what to do. He checked over his shoulder. There was no sign of movement in the clearing. The Russian was probably down at the river's edge, spying on O'Brian. This was their only tactical advantage, he thought: the fact that there were two of them and only one of him and he couldn't watch them both at once. Hesitantly, he stepped

359

over to the table.

He only meant to look for a minute, and probably that was all he did – just long enough to run his fingers through it all:

A pair of passports – red, stiff-backed, six inches by four, lion-crested, marked 'PASS' and 'NORGE', issued in Bergen, 1968 – a young couple, identical-looking: long hair, blond, hippyish, the girl quite pretty in a washed-out kind of way; he didn't register their names; entered the USSR via Leningrad, June 1969 –

Identity papers – old-style, Soviet Union, three different men: the first, a youngish, jug-eared fellow in spectacles, a student by the look of him; the second, old, in his sixties, weathered, self-reliant, a sailor perhaps; the third, bug-eyed, unkempt, a gypsy or a drifter; the names a blur –

And, finally, a stack of sheets, which, as he fanned them out, he saw were six sets of documents, of five or six pages each, pinned together and written in pencil or ink, in various hands – this one neat, that one hesitant, another a wild and desperate scrawl – but always, at the top of the first sheet, in neat Cyrillic capitals, the same word: '*Confession*'.

Kelso could feel the freezing draught from the open door shifting the hairs on the back of his scalp.

He replaced the pages carefully and backed away from them, his hands raised slightly as if to ward them off, and at the doorway he turned and stumbled out on to the steps. He sat down on the weathered planking and when he raised the binoculars and scanned the rim of the clearing he found that he was shaking.

He stayed there for a couple of minutes, recovering his nerve. It occurred to him that what he ought to do – the calm, rational, sensible thing: the not-leaping-to-any-hysterical-conclusions kind of thing, that a serious scholar would do – was to return and briefly make a note of the names for checking later.

So when he had satisfied himself for the twentieth time that not a soul was moving in the trees, he stood and ducked back through the low door, and the first thing he saw on re-entry was the rifle propped against the wall, and the second was the Russian, sitting at the table, perfectly still, watching him.

'He possessed in a high degree the gift for silence,' according to his secretary, *'and in this respect he was unique in a country where everybody talks far too much . . .'*

He was still in full uniform, still in his greatcoat and cap. The gold star of the Order of Hero of the Soviet Union was pinned to his lapel and shone in the dull light of the kerosene lamp.

How had he done that?

Kelso started gabbling into the silence. 'Comrade – you – I'm startled – I – came to find you – I wanted –' He fumbled with the zipper on the front of his jacket and held out the satchel. 'I wanted to return to you the papers of your mother, Anna Mikhailovna Safanova –'

Time stretched. Half a minute passed, a minute, and then the Russian said, softly, 'Good, comrade,' and made a note on the sheet of paper beside him. He indicated the table and Kelso took a pace towards it and laid the satchel down, like an offering placed to appease some unreliable and vengeful god.

Another endless silence followed.

'Capitalism,' said the Russian eventually, putting down his stub of pencil and reaching for his pipe, 'is thievery. And imperialism is the highest form of capitalism. Thus it follows that the imperialist is the greatest thief of all mankind. Steal a man's papers, he will. Oh, easily! Pick the last kopek from yer pocket! Or steal a man's boat, eh, comrade?'

He winked at Kelso and continued staring at him as he struck a match, sucking the fire into the bowl of his pipe, producing great spurts of smoke and flame.

'Close the door would you, comrade?'

It was beginning to get dark.

If we have to stay here the night, thought Kelso, we shall never leave.

Where the hell was O'Brian?

'Now,' the Russian continued, 'and this is the decisive question, comrade: how do we protect ourselves from these capitalists, these imperialists, these thieves? And we say the answer to this decisive question must be equally decisive.' He extinguished the match with one shake and leaned forwards. 'We protect ourselves from these capitalists, these imperialists, and these stinking, crawling thieves of all mankind only by the most ferocious vigilance. Take, for example, the Norway couple, with their serpenty smiles – crawling on their maggoty bellies through the undergrowth to ask for "directions, comrade," if you please! On a "walking holiday" if you please!'

He waved their open passports in Kelso's face and Kelso had a second glimpse of the two young people, the man in a psychedelic headband –

'Are we such *fools*,' he demanded, 'such backward *primitives*, not to recognise the capitalist–imperialist thief–spy when it worms its way among us? No, comrade, we are not such backward primitives! To such people we administer a hard lesson in socialist realities – I have their confessions here before me, they denied it at first but they admitted it all in the end – and we need say no more of them. They are as Lenin predicted they would be: dust on the dunghill of history. Nor need we say anything of him!' He waved a set of identity papers – the older man. 'And nor of him! Nor him!' The faces of the victims flashed briefly. '*That*,' said the Russian, 'is our decisive answer to the decisive question posed by all capitalists, imperialists and stinking thieves!'

He sat back with his arms folded, smiling grimly.

The rifle was almost within Kelso's reach but he didn't move. It might not be loaded. And even if it was loaded he wouldn't know how to fire it. And even if he fired it he knew he could never injure the Russian: he was a supernatural force. One minute he was ahead of you, one minute behind; now he was in the trees and now he was here, sitting at his table, poring over his collection of confessions, making the occasional note.

'Worse by far however,' said the Russian after a while, 'is the canker of the right-deviationism.' He relit his pipe, sucking noisily on the stem. 'And here Golub was the first.'

'Golub was the first,' repeated Kelso, numbly.

He was remembering the row of crosses: T. Y. Golub, his face blacked out, died November-the-something, 1961.

The essence of Stalin's success was really very simple, he thought, built around an insight that could be reduced to a mere three words: *people fear death*.

'Golub was the first to succumb to the classic conciliationist tendencies of the right-deviationism. Of course, I was merely a child at the time, but his whining still clamours in my ears: "Oh, comrades, they are saying in the villages that Comrade Stalin's body has been removed from his rightful place next to Lenin! Oh, comrades, what are we going to do? It is hopeless, comrades! They will come and

363

they will kill us all! It's time for us to give up!"

'Have you ever seen fishermen when a storm is brewing on a great river? I have seen them many a time. In the face of a storm one group of fishermen will muster all their forces, encourage their fellows and boldly put out to meet the storm: "Cheer up, lads, hold tight to the tiller, cut the waves, we'll pull her through!" But there is another type of fishermen – those who, on sensing a storm, lose heart, begin to snivel and demoralise their own ranks: "What a misfortune, a storm is brewing; lie down, boys, in the bottom of the boat, shut your eyes; let's hope she'll make the shore somehow."'

The Russian spat on the floor.

'Chizhikov took him out into the dark part of the forest that very night and in the morning there was a cross and that was the end of Golub and that put an end to the bleatings of the right-deviationists – even that old hag his widow put a sock in her mouth after that. And for a few years more, the steady work went on, under our four-fold slogans: the slogan of *the fight against defeatism and complacency*, the slogan of *the struggle for self-sufficiency*, the slogan of *constructive self-criticism is the foundation of our Party*, and the slogan of *out of the fire comes steel*. And then the sabotage began.'

'Ah,' said Kelso. 'The sabotage. Of course.'

'It began with the poisoning of the sturgeon. This was soon after the trial of the foreign spies. Late in the summer this was. We came out one morning and there they were – white bellies floating in the river. And time without number we discovered that food had been taken from the traps and yet no animals were caught. The mushrooms were shrivelled, useless things – scarcely a *pood* to be had all year – and that had never happened before, either. Even the berries on the two-*verst* track were gone before we could pick them. I

discussed the crisis confidentially with Comrade Chizhikov
– I was older now, you understand, and able to take a hand
– and his analysis was identical to mine: that this was a classic
outbreak of Trotskyite wreckerism. And when Yezhov was
discovered with a flashlight – out walking, after curfew: the
swine – the case was made. And this,' he held up a thick pile
of barely legible scrawl and slapped it against the table, 'this
is his confession – you can see it, here, in his own hand – how
he received his signals by torch-transmission from some
spiderish associates he had made contact with while out
fishing.'

'And Yezhov – ?'

'His widow hanged herself. They had a child.' He looked
away. 'I don't know what became of it. They're all dead now,
of course. Even Chizhikov.'

More silence. Kelso felt like Scheherazade: as long as he
could keep talking, there was a chance. Death lay in the
silences.

'Comrade Chizhikov,' he said. 'He must have been a –' he
nearly said *'a monster'* ' – a formidable man?'

'A shock-worker,' said the Russian, 'a Stakhanovite, a
soldier and a hunter, a red expert and a theoretician of the
highest calibre.' His eyes were almost closed. His voice fell to
a whisper. 'Oh, and he *beat* me, comrade. He beat me and he
beat me, until I was *weeping* blood! On instructions that were
given to him, as to the manner of my upbringing, by the
highest organs: "You are to give him a good shaking every
now and again!" All that I am, he made me.'

'When did Comrade Chizhikov die?'

'Two winters ago. He was clumsy and half-blind by then.
He stepped into one of his own traps. The wound turned
black. His leg turned black and stank like maggoty meat.

There was delirium. He raged. In the end, he begged us to leave him outside overnight, in the snow. A dog's death.'

'And his wife – she died soon afterwards?'

'Within the week.'

'She must have been like a mother to you?'

'She was. But she was old. She couldn't work. It was a hard thing to have to do – but it was for the best.'

'He never ever loved a human being,' said his schoolfriend, Iremashvili. *'He was incapable of feeling pity for man or beast, and I never knew him cry . . .'*

A hard thing –

For the best –

He opened one yellow eye.

'You are shifty, comrade. I can tell.'

Kelso's throat was dry. He looked at his watch. 'I was wondering what had become of my colleague –'

It was now more than half an hour since he had left O'Brian by the river.

'The Yankee? Take my tip there, comrade. Don't trust him. You'll see.'

He winked again, put his finger to his lips and stood. And then he moved across the cabin with an extraordinary speed and agility – it was grace, really: one, two, three steps, yet the soles of his boots barely seemed to connect with the boards – and he flung open the door and there was O'Brian.

And later Kelso was to wonder what might have happened next. Would it all have been treated as some terrific joke? (*'Your ears must be flapping like boards in this cold, comrade!'*) Or would O'Brian have been the next interloper in the miniature Stalinist state required to sign a confession?

But it was impossible to say what might have happened, because what did happen was that the Russian suddenly pulled O'Brian roughly into the cabin. Then he stood alone at the open door, his head tilted to one side, nostrils dilated, sniffing the air, listening.

SUVORIN never even saw the smoke. It was Major Kretov who spotted it.

He braked and pointed to it, put the snow plough into first gear, and they crawled forwards for a couple of hundred yards until they drew level with the entrance to the track. Halfway along it, the sharp white outline of the Toyota's roof showed up clear against the shadows of the trees.

Kretov stopped, reversed a short distance, and left the engine idling as he scanned the way ahead. Then he swung the wheel hard and the big vehicle lurched forwards again, off the road and down the track, clearing a path to within a few paces of the empty car. He turned the engine off and for a few moments Suvorin heard again that unnatural silence.

He said, 'Major, what *are* your orders, exactly?'

Kretov was opening the door. 'My orders are plain Russian good sense. "To stuff the cork back in to the bottle at the narrowest point."' He jumped down easily into the snow and reached back for his AK-74. He stuffed an extra magazine into his jacket. He checked his pistol.

'And this is the narrowest point?'

'Stay here and keep your backside warm, why don't you? This won't take us long.'

'I won't be a party to anything illegal,' said Suvorin. The words sounded absurdly prim and official, even to his ears, and Kretov took no notice. He was already beginning to move off with his men. 'The westerners, at least,' Suvorin called after them, 'are not to be harmed!'

He sat there for a few more seconds, watching the backs of

the soldiers as they fanned out across the track. Then, cursing, he shoved the front seat forwards and squeezed himself into the open door. The cab was unexpectedly high off the ground. He leapt and felt himself jerked backwards, heard a tearing sound. The lining of his coat had snagged on a bit of metal. He swore again and detached himself.

It was hard to keep up with the other three. They were fit and he was not. They had army boots and he had leather-soled brogues. It was difficult to maintain his footing in the snow and he wouldn't have caught them at all if they hadn't stopped to inspect something on the ground beside the track.

Kretov smoothed out the screwed-up yellow paper and turned it this way and that. It was blank. He balled it up again and dropped it. He inserted a small, flesh-coloured miniature receiver, like a hearing-aid, into his right ear. From his pocket he took out a black ski-mask and pulled it over his head. The others did the same. Kretov made a chopping motion with his gloved hand towards the forest and they set off again: Kretov first with his assault rifle held before him, turning as he walked, ducking this way and that, ready to rake the trees with bullets; then one soldier, then another, both keeping up the same wary surveillance, their faces like skulls in the masks; and finally Suvorin in his civilian clothes – stumbling, slipping, in every way absurd.

CALMLY the Russian closed the door and collected his rifle. He pulled out a wooden box from beneath the table and filled his pockets with bullets. In the same unhurried manner, he rolled back the carpet, lifted the trapdoor and leapt, cat-like, into the space.

'We stand for peace and champion the cause of peace,' he said. 'But we are not afraid of threats and are prepared to answer the instigators of war blow for blow. Those who try to attack us will receive a crushing repulse to teach them not to poke their pig snouts into our Soviet garden. Replace the carpet, comrade.'

He disappeared, closing the trapdoor after him.

O'Brian gaped at the floorboards and then at Kelso.

'What the fuck – ?'

'And where the hell have *you* been?' Kelso grabbed the satchel and quickly stuffed it back into his jacket. 'Never mind him,' he said, rolling back the carpet. 'Let's just get out of here.'

But before either of them could move a skull appeared at the cabin windows – two round eyes and a slit for a mouth. A boot kicked wood. The door splintered.

THEY were made to stand against the wall – shoved against the rough planked wall – and Kelso felt cold metal jabbed into the nape of his neck. O'Brian was a bit too slow on the uptake so he had his forehead banged against the planking, just to mend his manners and teach him a little Russian.

Their wrists were trussed tightly behind their backs with thin plastic.

A man said roughly, 'Where's the other?' He raised the butt of his rifle.

'Under the floorboards!' shouted O'Brian. 'Tell 'em, Fluke, he's under the fucking floorboards!'

'He's under the floorboards,' said a well-educated voice in Russian that Kelso thought he recognised.

Heavy boots clumped on the wooden floor. Turning his head, Kelso saw one of the masked men walk to the end of the cabin, point his gun at the ground and casually begin firing. He flinched at the deafening noise in the confined space and when he looked again the man was walking backwards, spraying bullets into the floor in neat rows, his weapon leaping in his hands like a pneumatic drill. Wood chips sprouted, ricocheted, and Kelso felt something strike the side of his head, just below his ear. Blood started trickling down his neck. He turned the other way and pressed his cheek to the wall. The noise stopped, there was a rattle of a fresh magazine being fitted, then it started again, then stopped. Something crashed to the floor. There was a stink of cordite. Acrid smoke made him clench his eyes and when he opened them again he could see the blond-headed spy from Moscow. The spy shook his head in disgust.

The man who had been firing kicked aside the shredded carpet and lifted the trapdoor. He shone a flashlight down through the rising dust, then clambered into the hole and disappeared. They could hear him moving around beneath their feet. After thirty seconds he reappeared at the door of the cabin, pulling off his mask.

'There's a tunnel. He's got out.'

He produced a pistol and gave it to the blond man.

'Watch them.'

Then he gestured to the other two and they clattered out into the snow.

Chapter Thirty

SUVORIN FELT WET. He glanced down and saw that he was standing in a puddle of melted snow. His trousers were sodden. So was the bottom of his overcoat. A piece of frayed silk lining trailed on the floor. And his shoes – his shoes were leaking and scuffed – they were *ruined.*

One of the two bound men – the reporter: O'Brian, wasn't that his name? – started to turn and say something.

'Shut up!' said Suvorin, furiously. He clicked off the safety catch and waved the gun. 'Shut up and face the wall!'

He sat down at the table and wiped his damp sleeve across his face.

Absolutely *ruined . . .*

He noticed Stalin glowering at him. He picked up the framed photograph with his free hand and tilted it to the light. It was signed. And what was all this other stuff? Passports, identity papers, a pipe, old gramophone records, an envelope with a piece of hair in it . . . It looked as though someone had been trying to perform a conjuring trick. He sprinkled the hair into his palm and rubbed it between his thumb and forefinger. The fibres were dry, grey, coarse, like a clump of bristles. He let them fall and wiped his hands on his coat. Then he laid the pistol on the table and massaged his eyes.

'Sit down,' he said, wearily, 'why don't you?'

Outside in the forest there was a long jabbering burst of gunfire.

'You know, he said sadly to Kelso, 'you really should have caught that plane.'

*

371

'WHAT happens next?' said the Englishman. It was obviously difficult for them to sit properly. They were on their knees, next to the wall. The stove had gone out. It was getting very cold. Suvorin had slid one of the records out of its paper sleeve and put it on the turntable of the ancient gramophone.

'It's a surprise,' he said.

'I am an accredited member of the foreign press corps –' began O'Brian.

The crack-crack of a high velocity rifle was answered by a heavier bang.

'The American ambassador –' said O'Brian.

Suvorin wound the handle of the gramophone very fast – anything to block out the noise from outside – and placed the needle on the record. Through a hailstorm of crackles, a tinny orchestra struck up a wavering tune.

More gunfire. Someone was screaming, far away, through the trees. Two shots followed in rapid succession. The screaming stopped and O'Brian started whining, 'They're going to shoot us. They'll shoot us, too!' He struggled against the plastic wire and tried to rise, but Suvorin put his wet shoe on O'Brian's chest and gently pushed him down again.

'Let us,' he said, in English, 'at least try to act like civilised men.'

This was not what I dreamed for myself, either, he wanted to say. It formed no part of my life's dreams, I do assure you, to arrive in some stinking madman's hovel and hunt him down like an animal. Honestly, I believe you would find me an amusing fellow, if only circumstances were different.

He made an effort to follow the beat of the music, conducting with his forefinger, but he couldn't find any rhythm, there seemed to be no sense to it.

'You'd better have brought an army,' said the Englishman,

'because if it's just three against one out there, they don't stand a chance.'

'Nonsense,' said Suvorin, patriotically. 'They're our special forces. They'll get him. And yes, if necessary, they *will* send an army.'

'Why?'

'Because I work for frightened men, Dr Kelso, some of whom are just about old enough to have been touched by Comrade Stalin.' He frowned at the gramophone. What a racket. It sounded like howling dogs. 'Do you know what Lenin called the Tsarovich, when the Bolsheviks were deciding the fate of the Imperial Family? He called the boy "the living banner". And there's only one way, Lenin said, to deal with a living banner.'

Kelso shook his head. 'You don't understand this man. Believe me – you should see him – he is criminally insane. He's probably killed half a dozen people over the past thirty years. He's nobody's banner. He's crazy.'

'Everyone said Zhirinovsky was crazy, remember? His foreign policy towards the Baltic States was to bury nuclear waste along the Lithuanian border and blow it into Vilnius every night using giant fans. He still got twenty-three per cent of the vote in the ninety-three election.'

Suvorin couldn't stand this unearthly, bestial music a moment more. He lifted the needle.

They heard a solitary shot.

Suvorin held his breath for an answering salvo.

'Perhaps,' he said doubtfully, after waiting a long while, 'I should think about calling up that army –'

'THERE are traps,' said Kelso.

'What?'

Suvorin was at the doorway, peering tentatively into the twilight. He looked back into the cabin. He had looped some rope around their wrists and attached it to the cold stove.

'He's put down traps. Be careful where you tread.'

'Thank you.' Suvorin planted his foot on the top step. 'I'll be back.'

His plan – and that was a good word, he thought, that had a certain ring to it: his *plan* – was to get back to the snow plough and use the radio to summon reinforcements. So he headed towards the entrance to the clearing, the only fixed point he had. There were good footprints to follow here, although it was getting dark, and he must have been midway along the rough path when he felt the explosion and a second later he heard it, a great rush of snow marking the passage of the shock wave as it travelled through the forest. Cascades of crystal pattered down from the higher branches and bounced off into space, leaving tiny clouds of particles hanging in the air like puffs of breath.

He spun around, the gun held out in a double grip, pointing uselessly in the direction of the blast.

He panicked then and began to run – a comic figure, a jerking marionette – trying to bring his knees up as high as they would go to avoid the sucking, clinging snow. His breath was coming in sobs.

He was so intent on keeping going he almost tripped over the first body.

It was one of the soldiers. He had been caught in a trap – a huge trap: a bear trap, maybe – so big and powerfully sprung, the jaws of it had actually clamped into the bone above his knee. There was a lot of blood smeared around in the flattened snow, blood from the shattered leg and blood from a big head wound that gaped through the back of the knitted ski-mask like a second mouth.

The corpse of the other soldier was a few paces further on. Unlike the first man, he was lying on his back, his arms outstretched, his legs arranged in a perfect figure 4. There was a puddle of blood on his chest.

Suvorin put down his gun, took off his gloves and checked the pulses of both men – although he knew it was useless – pulling aside the layers of clothing to feel their warm, dead wrists.

How had he ambushed them *both?*

He looked around.

Like this, probably: he had laid the trap on the path, buried in the snow, and had lured them over it; the man in the lead had missed it, somehow, the man in the rear had been caught – that was the screaming – and the lead man had turned to help only to find their quarry behind them – that was what was cunning: they wouldn't have expected that. And so he had been shot full in the front, and then the second man had been taken out at leisure, executioner-style, with a bullet at point-blank range in the back of the head.

And then he had taken their AK-74s.

What kind of creature *was* this?

Suvorin knelt by the head of the first soldier and pulled off his ski-mask. He took out his ear-piece and pressed it to his own ear. He thought he could hear something. A rushing sound. He found the little microphone attached to the inside cuff of the dead man's left hand.

'Kretov?' he whispered. 'Kretov?' But the only voice he could hear was his own.

Then the gunfire started up again.

*

THE fire was like a red dawn through the trees, and when Suvorin stepped out on to the track he could feel the heat of the burning snow plough, even at a range of a hundred yards. The fuel tank must have exploded and the inferno had melted the winter all around it. The vehicle stood blazing in the centre of its own scorched spring.

The gunfire was continuing sporadically, but that wasn't Kretov returning fire. That was boxes of ammunition, exploding in the cab. Kretov himself was sitting down, doubled over in the centre of the track, beside the RP46, as dead as his comrades. He looked as though he had been shot while trying to set up the machine gun. He had got as far as mounting it on to the bipod but he hadn't had time to open the cannister of ammunition.

Suvorin went up to him and touched his arm and Kretov toppled over, his grey eyes open, a look of astonishment on his broad, pink face. Suvorin couldn't see a wound, not at first, anyway. Perhaps the heroic major of the Spetsnaz had simply died of fright?

Another loud bang from the direction of the fire made him look up, to find himself being watched by Comrade Stalin, in his generalissimo's uniform and cap.

The GenSec was some way up the track, standing before the fire, his left hand on his hip, his right holding a rifle almost casually across his shoulder. His shadow was long in proportion to his squat torso. It danced and flickered on the churned snow.

Suvorin thought he would choke on his own heart. They looked at one another. Then Stalin started marching towards him. And *marching* – that was the word for the way he walked: quickly, but without hurrying, swinging his arms up across his barrel chest, left-right, left-right: look lively there, comrade, here I come!

Suvorin fumbled in his pocket for his pistol and realised he had left it in the trees, beside the first two corpses.

Left-right, left-right – the living banner, kicking up the snow –

Suvorin didn't dare look at him an instant longer. He knew that if he did he would never move.

'Why is your face so shifty, comrade?' called the advancing figure. 'Why can't you look Comrade Stalin directly in the eyes?'

Suvorin swung the barrel of the RP46, his memory toiling back twenty years, to his compulsory army training, shivering on some godforsaken range on the outskirts of Vitebsk. '*Cock gun by pulling operating handle to the rear. Pull rear sight base to the rear and lift cover. Lay belt, open side up, on the feed plate so that the leading round contacts the cartridge stop and close cover. Pull trigger and gun will fire . . .*'

He closed his eyes and squeezed the trigger and the machine gun jumped in his hands, sending a couple of dozen bullets sawing into a birch tree at a range of twenty yards.

When he dared to check the track again Comrade Stalin had disappeared.

IF Suvorin's memory served him right, the ammunition belt of the RP46 carried 250 rounds, which the gun would dispatch at a rate of, say, 600 rounds per minute. So, given he'd already used a few, he probably had something less than thirty seconds of firepower with which to cover 360 degrees of track and forest, with night coming on and the temperature plunging to a level that would kill him in a couple of hours.

He had to get out of the open, that was for sure. He couldn't keep on like this, scrambling round and round like a tethered goat in a tiger shoot, trying to see through the gloom of the trees.

He seemed to remember some abandoned wooden huts at the far end of the track. They might provide a bit of cover. He needed to get his back against a wall somewhere, needed time to *think*.

A wolf howled in the forest.

He disconnected the machine gun from the bipod and hoisted the long barrel up on to his shoulder, the ammunition belt heavy on his arm, his knees almost buckling under the weight, his feet sinking deeper into the snow.

The full-throated howling came again. It was not a wolf at all, he thought. It was a man – a man's exultant shout: a blood cry.

He started wading up the track, away from the burning snow plough, and he sensed that there was someone walking parallel with him through the trees, keeping an easy pace, laughing at his ponderous attempt at flight. He was being played with, that was all. He would be allowed to get within a few paces of his destination, then he would be shot.

He came out of the neck of the track and into the abandoned settlement and headed for the nearest wooden building. The windows were out, the door had gone, half the roof was missing, it stank. He put down the gun and crawled into the corner, then turned and dragged the weapon after him. He wedged himself against the wall and pointed the barrel at the door, his finger on the trigger.

KELSO heard the big explosion, gunfire, a long pause, and then the short and heavy clatter of a much bigger weapon opening up. He and O'Brian were on their feet by now, frantically trying to find some way of cutting the rope that bound them to the stove chimney. Each sound from the forest drove them to more desperate efforts. The thin plastic was digging into his wrists, his fingers were slippery with blood.

There was blood on the Russian, too, when he appeared in the doorway. Kelso saw it as he came towards them, unsheathing his knife – smeared across his face, on his forehead and on either cheek, like a hunter who had dipped himself in his kill.

'Comrades,' he reported, 'we are dizzy with success. Three are dead. Only one still lives. Are there more?'

'More coming.'

'How many more?'

'Fifty,' said Kelso. 'A hundred.' He tugged against the rope. 'Comrade, we must get clear of this place, or they will kill us all. Even you cannot stop so many. They are going to send an army.'

ACCORDING to Suvorin's watch, about fifteen minutes had elapsed.

The temperature was plunging as the light faded. His body began to vibrate with the cold – a steady, violent shaking he couldn't stop.

'Come on,' he whispered. 'Come on and finish the job.'

But nobody came.

Comrade Stalin's capacity for springing surprises was truly endless.

THE next thing Suvorin heard was a distant click, followed by a whirr.

Click-whirr. Click-whirr.

379

Now what was he doing?

Suvorin found it hard to move at first. The frost had locked his joints and starched his wet clothes to board. Still, he was on his feet in time to hear the mysterious click-whirr turn suddenly into a cough and then a roar as an engine started.

No, no, not an engine exactly: a motor – an outboard motor –

He was baffled for a moment, but then he realised.

'Fifteen miles, major. It's right on the river . . . '

WELL, the RP46 didn't get any lighter, nor the snow any easier, and now he had the oncoming darkness to contend with, but he tried. He made a valiant effort.

'Bastard, bastard, bastard,' he chanted as he ran, following the pulse of the revving outboard as it led him through the fifty yards or so of trees that screened the deserted fishing settlement from the river.

He crashed through the last barrier of undergrowth and came out on to the crest of a bank that sloped down steeply to the water's edge. He stumbled along the ridge, heading upstream. Some pieces of electronic equipment lay spread out in the snow. Grey ice extended for a little distance and the black water rushed beyond his reach – an immensity of it: he couldn't see the trees on the opposite shore. And already the little boat was heading towards the centre, and turning now, carving a great white sickle of spray in the darkness. He could just make out three crouched figures. One seemed to be trying to struggle to his feet, but another pulled him down.

Suvorin dropped to his knees and unshouldered the machine gun, fumbling to close the cover on the ammunition belt, which promptly jammed. By the time he had it free and ready to fire the boat had rounded the curve of the river – and then he couldn't see it any more, he could only hear it.

He put down the gun and bent his head.

Beside him, like a space probe landed on some hostile planet, the antenna of a satellite dish pointed low across the Dvina to the dissolving horizon. One set of cables connected the dish to a car battery. Another was linked to a small grey box labelled 'Transportable Video & Audio Transmission Terminal'. Even as he watched, a row of ten red zeros in a digital display winked at him briefly, faded and died.

He had an overwhelming sense of emptiness, squatting there, as if some malevolent force had erupted from this place and escaped for ever, a comet trailing darkness.

For perhaps half a minute he listened to the sound of the outboard motor and then that too was gone and he was left alone in the utter silence.

Chapter Thirty-one

THE FIGURE SUVORIN had seen trying to rise in the boat was O'Brian – *my gear!,* he shouted, *the tapes!* – and the figure who had pulled him down was Kelso – *forget the bloody gear, forget the tapes.* For a moment the boat rocked dangerously, and the Russian cursed them both, and then O'Brian moaned and sat down quickly and put his head in his hands.

Kelso couldn't make out anyone on the shore as they roared away from it. All he could see was the sky pulsing red above the tips of the darkening firs where something big was burning fiercely, and then very quickly a bend in the river obliterated even that and he was conscious only of speed – of the racket of the outboard motor and the rushing current hurtling them downstream through the forest.

He was thinking with great clarity now, everything else in his life irrelevant, everything narrowed to this one single point: survival. And it seemed to him that all that counted was to put as much distance as possible between themselves and this spot. He didn't know how many men were left alive behind them, but the best he reckoned they could hope for was that a search party wouldn't set out till the morning. The worst scenario was that the blond-headed man had radioed for help and Archangel would already be sealed.

There was no food or water in the boat, just a couple of oars, a boathook, the Russian's suitcase, his rifle, and a small tank that smelled as though it was leaking cheap fuel. In the darkness he had to hold his watch up very close to his eyes. It was just after half-past six. He leaned over and said to O'Brian, 'What time did you say the Moscow train left Archangel?'

O'Brian lifted his head long enough from his despair to mutter, 'Ten past eight.'

Kelso twisted round and shouted above the engine and the wind, 'Comrade, could we get to Archangel?' There was no reply. He tapped his watch. 'Could we get to the centre of Archangel in an hour?'

The Russian didn't seem to have heard. His hand was on the tiller and he was staring straight ahead. With his collar turned up and his cap pulled down, it was impossible to make out his expression. Kelso tried shouting again and then gave up. It was a new kind of horror, he thought, to realise that they probably owed their lives to him – that he was now their ally – and that their futures were at the mercy of his unfathomable mind.

THEY were heading roughly north-west and the cold was being hammered into them from all sides – a Siberian wind at their backs, the freezing water beneath their feet, the rushing air on their faces. O'Brian remained monosyllabic, inconsolable. There was a light in the prow, and Kelso found himself concentrating on that – on the shifting yellow path and the roiling water, black and viscous as it began to solidify.

After half an hour the snow resumed, the flakes huge and luminous in the dark, like falling ash. Occasionally something knocked against the hull and Kelso spotted lumps of ice drifting in the current. It was as if winter was clutching at them, determined not to let them go, and Kelso wondered if fear was the reason for the Russian's silence. Killers could be frightened, like anyone else, perhaps more than anyone else. Stalin lived half his life in a state of terror – scared of aeroplanes, scared of visiting the front, never eating food unless it had been tasted for poison, changing his guards, his routes, his beds – when you had murdered so many, you knew how easily death could come. And it could come for them here very easily, he thought. They would run into an ice barrier, the water would freeze behind them, they would be trapped; the ice-crust would be too thin to risk crawling across, and here they would die, covered for decency under a shroud of snow.

He wondered what people would make of it. Margaret – what would she say when she learned her ex-husband's body had been found in a forest nearly a thousand miles from Moscow. And his boys? He cared what they would think: he wouldn't miss much, but he would miss his sons. Perhaps he should try to scrawl them a heroic final note, like Captain Scott in Antarctica: 'These rough notes and our dead bodies must tell the tale –'

He thought that perhaps he didn't fear dying as much as he had expected he would, which surprised him as he had little physical courage and no religious faith. But a man would have to be a rare fool – wouldn't he? – to spend a lifetime studying history without acquiring at least some sense of perspective on his own mortality. Perhaps that was why he'd done it – devoted so many years to writing about the dead. He'd never thought of it that way.

He tried to imagine his obituaries: *'never quite fulfilled his early promise . . . never published the major work of scholarship of which he was once judged capable . . . the bizarre circumstances of his premature death may never be fully explained . . .'* The memorialising articles would all be the same and he would know every one of their grudging, time-serving authors.

The Russian opened the throttle wider and Kelso could hear him, muttering to himself.

*

ANOTHER half hour passed.

Kelso had his eyes closed and it was O'Brian who saw the lights first. He nudged Kelso and pointed, and after a second or two, Kelso saw them as well – high gantry lights on the chimneys and cranes of the big wood pulp factory on the headland outside the city. Presently more lights began to appear in the darkness on either bank and the night sky ahead became fractionally paler. Perhaps they would make it after all?

His face was frozen. It was hard to speak.

He said, 'Got the Archangel map?'

O'Brian turned stiffly. He looked like a white marble statue coming to life and as he moved small slabs of frozen snow cracked and slid off his jacket into the bottom of the boat. He dragged the city plan out of his inside pocket and Kelso shifted forwards off the thin plank that served as a seat, fell on to his hands and knees, and crawled awkwardly to the prow. He held the map to the light. The Dvina bulged as it came into the city, and a pair of islands split it into three channels. They needed to keep to the northern one.

It was a quarter to eight.

He moved back to the stern and managed to shout, 'Comrade!' He made a chopping motion with his hand to starboard. The Russian gave no sign of having understood but a minute later, as the dark mass of the island emerged out of the snow, he steered to the north of it and soon afterwards Kelso made out a rusty buoy and beyond that a line of lights in the sky.

He cupped his hand to O'Brian's ear. 'The bridge,' he said. O'Brian pulled down his hood and squinted at him. 'The bridge,' repeated Kelso. 'The one we came over this morning.'

He pointed and very quickly they were passing beneath it
– a double-bridge, half-rail, half-road: heavy ironwork
dangling stalactites of ice, a strong smell of sewage and
chemicals, the drumming of vehicles overhead – and when
he looked back he could see the headlights of traffic moving
slowly through the snow.

The familiar shape of the Harbour Master's building
appeared ahead of them on the starboard side, with a jetty
stretching out and boats moored to it. They hit an invisible
sheet of thick ice and Kelso and O'Brian were bounced
forwards. The engine cut out. The Russian restarted it and
reversed, then found a channel which must have been cut by
a bigger boat earlier in the evening. There was still ice but it
was thinner and it splintered as their prow sliced into it.
Kelso looked back at the Russian. He was standing now,
peering intently at the dark corridor, his hand on the tiller,
taking them in. They came alongside the jetty and he put the
outboard into reverse again, slowing them, stopping. He cut
the motor and leapt nimbly on to the wooden planking,
holding a length of rope.

O'BRIAN was out of the boat first, with Kelso after him. They
stamped and brushed the snow off themselves and tried to
stretch some life back into their frozen limbs. O'Brian started
to say something about finding a hotel, maybe, calling the
office, but Kelso cut him off.

'No hotel. Are you listening to me? No office. And no
bloody story. We're getting out of here.'

They had thirteen minutes to catch the train.

'And him?'

O'Brian nodded to the Russian who was standing quietly,
holding his suitcase, watching them. He looked oddly

forlorn – vulnerable, even, now that he was out of his home territory. He was obviously expecting to come with them.

'Christ almighty,' muttered Kelso. He had the map open. He didn't know what to do. 'Let's just go.' He set off along the jetty towards the shore. O'Brian hurried after him.

'You still got the notebook?'

Kelso patted the front of his jacket.

'D'you think he's got a gun?' said O'Brian. He glanced back. 'Shit. He's following us.'

The Russian was trotting about a dozen paces behind them, wary and fearful, like a stray dog. It looked as though he had left his rifle behind in the boat. So what would he be armed with, wondered Kelso? His knife? He pushed his stiff legs forwards as hard as he could.

'But we can't just leave him –'

'Oh yes we bloody can,' said Kelso. He realised O'Brian didn't know about the Norwegian couple, or any of the others. 'I'll explain later. Just believe me – we don't want him anywhere near us.'

They almost ran off the jetty and came into the big bus park in front of the Harbour Master's building – a bleak expanse of snow, a few sorrowful orange sodium lights catching the whirling flakes, nobody else about. Kelso struck north, slithering on the ice, holding on to the map. The station was at least a mile away and they were never going to make it in time, not on foot. He looked around. A ubiquitous, boxy, sand-coloured Lada, spattered with mud and grit, was emerging slowly from the street to their right, and Kelso ran towards it, flapping his arms.

In the Russian provinces, every car is a potential taxi, most drivers willing to hire themselves out on the spur of the moment, and this one was no exception. He swerved towards them, throwing up a fountain of dirty snow, and even as he pulled up he was winding down his window. He looked respectable enough, muffled against the cold – a schoolteacher, maybe, a clerk. Weak eyes blinked at them through thick-framed spectacles. 'Going to the concert hall?'

'Do us a favour, citizen, and take us to the railway station,' said Kelso. 'Ten dollars US if we catch the Moscow train.' He opened the passenger door without waiting for an answer and tipped forward the seat, shoving O'Brian into the back, and suddenly he saw that this was their chance, because the Russian, caught by surprise, had fallen behind slightly, and was making heavy progress through the snow with his case.

'Comrade!' he shouted.

Kelso didn't hesitate. He rammed back the seat and got in, slamming the door.

'Don't you want –' began the driver, looking in his mirror.

'No,' said Kelso. 'Go.'

The Lada skidded away and he turned to look back. The Russian had set down his case and was staring after them, seemingly bewildered, a lost figure in the widening vista of the alien city. He dwindled and disappeared into the night and snow.

'Can't help but feel sorry for the poor bastard,' said O'Brian, but Kelso's only emotion was relief.

'"Gratitude,"' he said, quoting Stalin, '"is a dog's disease."'

THE Archangel railway station was at the northern edge of a big square, directly opposite a huddle of apartment blocks and wind-blasted birch trees. O'Brian threw a $10 bill in the direction of the driver and they sprinted into the gloomy terminal. Seven wood-fronted ticket kiosks with net curtains, five of them closed, a long queue outside the two that were open, a baby crying. Students, backpackers, soldiers, people of all ages and races, families with their home-made luggage – huge cardboard boxes trussed with string – children running everywhere, sliding on the dirty, melted snow.

O'Brian pushed his way to the front of the nearest line, spraying dollars, playing the westerner: 'Sorry, lady. Excuse me. There you go. Sorry. Gotta catch this train –'

Kelso had an impression of a fortune changing hands – three hundred, four hundred dollars, murmurs from the people standing round – and then, a minute later, O'Brian was striding back through the crowd, waving a pair of tickets, and they ran up the stairs to the platform.

If they were going to be stopped then this would be the place. At least a dozen militia men were standing around, all of them young, all with their caps pushed back like Imperial Army privates off to war in 1914. They stared at Kelso and O'Brian as they hurried through the terminal, but it was no more than the frank stare that all foreigners received up here. They made no move to detain them.

No alert had been issued. *Whoever is running this show,* thought Kelso, as they came back out into the open air, *must be convinced we're already dead –*

Doors were being closed all the way along the great train; it must have been a quarter of a mile long. Low yellow lighting, snow falling, lovers embracing, army officers hurrying up and down with their cheap briefcases – he felt they had stepped back seventy years into some revolutionary tableau. Even the giant locomotive still had the hammer and sickle welded to its side. They found their carriage, three cars back from the engine, and Kelso held the door open while O'Brian darted across the platform to one of the babushkas selling food for the journey. She had a wart on her cheek the size of a walnut. He was still stuffing his pockets as the whistle blew.

The train pulled away so slowly it was hard at first to tell it was moving. People walked alongside it down the platform, heads bent into the snow, waving handkerchiefs. Others were holding hands through the open windows. Kelso had a sudden image of Anna Safanova here, almost fifty years ago – '*I kiss mama's dear cheeks, farewell to her, farewell to childhood*' – and the full sadness and the pity of it came home to him for the first time. The people ambling along the platform began to jog and then to run. He stretched out his hand and pulled O'Brian aboard. The train lurched forwards. The station disappeared.

Chapter Thirty-two

THEY SWAYED ALONG the narrow, blue-carpeted corridor until they found their compartment – one of eight, about halfway down the carriage. O'Brian pulled back the sliding wooden door and they lurched inside.

It was not too bad. A thousand roubles per head in 'soft' class bought two dusty, crimson banquettes facing one another, a white nylon sheet, a rolled mattress and a pillow neatly folded on each; a lot of laminated, imitation-wood panelling; green-shaded reading lamps; a little fold-up table; privacy.

Through the window they could see the spars of the iron bridge clicking past but once they were across the river there was nothing visible in the snowstorm except their own reflections staring back at them – haggard, soaking, unshaven. O'Brian drew the yellow curtains, unfastened the table and laid out their food – a grubby loaf, some kind of dried fish, a sausage, tea-bags – while Kelso went in search of hot water.

A blackened samovar stood at the far end of the corridor, opposite the cubicle of the carriage's female attendant, their *provodnik*: a hefty, unsmiling woman, like a camp guard in her grey-blue uniform. She had rigged up a little mirror so she could keep an eye on everyone without stirring from her stool. He could see her watching him as he stopped to study the timetable that was fixed to the wall. They had a journey of more than twenty hours ahead of them, and thirteen stops, not counting Moscow, which they would reach just after four in the afternoon.

Twenty hours.

What were their chances of lasting that long? He tried to calculate. By mid-morning at the latest, Moscow would know that the operation in the forest had been bungled. Then they would be bound to stop the only train out of Archangel and search it. Perhaps he and O'Brian would be wiser to get off at one of these earlier stops – Sokol, maybe, which they would reach at 7 a.m., or, better still, Vologda (Vologda was a big town) – get off the train at Vologda, get to a hotel, call the American Embassy –

He heard a sliding door open behind him and a businessman in a smartly cut blue suit came out of his compartment and went in to the lavatory. His neatness made Kelso aware of his own bizarre appearance – heavy waterproof jacket, rubber boots – and he hurried on down the corridor. It would be best to stay out of sight as much as possible. He begged a couple of plastic cups off the grim-faced guard, filled them with scalding water, and made his way unsteadily back to their sleeping-berth.

THEY sat opposite one another, chewing steadily on the dry, stale food.

Kelso said he thought they should get off the train early.

'Why?'

'Because I don't think we should risk being picked up. Not before people know where we are.'

O'Brian bit off a piece of bread and considered this.

'So you really think – back there in the forest – they'd've shot us?'

'Yes I do.'

O'Brian had apparently forgotten his earlier panic. He began to argue but Kelso cut him off impatiently. 'Think about it for a minute. Think how easy it could have been. All the Russians would have had to say is that some maniac took us hostage in the woods and they sent in the special forces to rescue us. They could have made it look as though he'd murdered us.'

'But nobody would've believed that –'

'Of course they would. He was a psychopath.'

'What?'

'A psychopath. This is why I didn't want to bring him with us. Half the people in that cemetery, he put there. And there were others.'

'Others?' O'Brian had stopped eating.

'At least five. A young Norwegian couple, and three other poor bastards, Russians who just happened to take a wrong turning. I found their papers while you were down at the river. They'd all been made to confess to spying, and then they were shot. I tell you, he's a sick piece of work. I only hope to God I never have to see him again. So should you.'

O'Brian seemed to be having difficulty swallowing. There were bits of fish stuck between his teeth. He said quietly, 'What d'you think's going to happen to him?'

'They'll get him in the end, I imagine. They'll close down Archangel until they find him. And I don't blame them, to be honest. Can you imagine what Mamantov and his people would do if they got hold of a man who looks like Stalin, talks like Stalin and comes with a written guarantee that he's Stalin's son? Wouldn't they have had some fun with that?'

O'Brian had slumped back in his seat, his eyes shut, his face stricken, and Kelso, watching him, felt a sudden twinge of unease. In the rush of events he had entirely forgotten Mamantov. His gaze shifted from O'Brian to the wire luggage rack where the satchel was still carefully wrapped inside his jacket.

He tried to think, but he couldn't. His mind was shutting down on him. It was three days since he'd had a proper sleep – the first night he'd sat up with Rapava, the second he'd ended in the cells beneath Moscow militia HQ, the third had been spent on the road travelling north to Archangel. He ached with exhaustion. It was all he could do to kick off his boots and begin making up his meagre bed.

'I'm all in,' he said. 'Let's work something out in the morning.'

O'Brian didn't answer.

As a flimsy precaution, Kelso locked the door.

It must have been another twenty minutes before O'Brian finally moved. Kelso had his face to the wall by then and was drifting in the hinterland between sleep and wakefulness. He heard him unlace his boots, sigh and stretch out on the banquette. His reading lamp clicked off and the compartment was in darkness save for the blue neon night light that fizzed above the door.

The immense train rocked slowly southwards through the snow and Kelso slept, but not well. Hours passed and the sounds of the journey mingled with his uneasy dreams – the urgent whisperings from the compartments on either side; the *slop slop slop* of some babushka's slippers as she shuffled past in the corridor; the distant, tinny sound of a woman's voice over a loudspeaker as they stopped at the remote stations throughout the night – Nyandoma, Konosha, Yertsevo, Vozhega, Kharovsk – and people clumping on and off the train; the harsh white arc lights of the platforms shining through the thin curtains; O'Brian restless at some point, moving around.

He didn't hear the door open. All he knew was that

something rustled in the compartment for a fraction of a second, and then a hard pad of flesh clamped down over his mouth. His eyes jerked open as the point of a knife began to be inserted into his throat, at that point where the flesh of the under-jaw meets the ridged tube of the windpipe. He struggled to sit up but the hand pressed him down. His arms were somehow pinned beneath the twisted sheet. He couldn't see anyone but a voice whispered close to his ear – so close he could feel the hot wetness of the man's breath – 'A comrade who deserts a comrade is a cowardly dog, and all such dogs should die a dog's death, *comrade* –'

The knife slid deeper.

KELSO was awake in an instant – a cry rising in his throat, his eyes wide, the thin sheet balled and clenched between his sweating hands. The gently swaying compartment was empty above him, the blue-edged darkness faintly tinged by grey. For a moment he didn't move. He could hear O'Brian breathing heavily and when eventually he turned he could see him – head lolling, mouth open, one arm flung down almost to the floor, the other crooked across his forehead.

It took another couple of minutes for his panic to subside. He reached over his shoulder and lifted a corner of the curtain to check his watch. He thought it must be still the middle of the night, but to his surprise it was just after seven. He had slept for the best part of nine hours.

He raised himself up on to his elbow and pushed the curtain a fraction higher and saw at once the head of Stalin floating towards him, disconnected in the pale dawn beside the railway track. It drew level with the window and passed away very quickly.

He stayed at the window but saw nobody else, just the

scrubby land beyond the rails and the faint gleam of the electricity lines strung between the pylons seeming to swoop and rise, swoop and rise as the train trundled on. It wasn't snowing here, but there was a cold, bleached emptiness to the emerging sky.

Someone must have been holding up a picture, he realised. Holding up a picture of Stalin.

He let the curtain drop and swung his legs to the floor. Quietly, so as not to wake O'Brian, he tugged on his rubber boots and cautiously opened the door to the empty corridor. He peered both ways. Nobody about. He closed the latch behind him and began walking towards the rear of the train.

He passed through an empty carriage identical to the one he had just left, all the while glancing at the passing landscape, and then 'soft' class gave way to 'hard'. The accommodation here was much more crowded – two tiers of berths in open compartments down one side of the corridor, a single row arranged lengthwise on the other. Sixty people to a car. Luggage crammed everywhere. Some passengers sitting up, yawning, raw-eyed. Others still snoring, impervious to the waking carriage. People queuing for the stinking toilet. A mother changing a baby's filthy nappy (he caught the sour reek of milky faeces as he pushed past). The smokers huddled at the open windows at the far end of the carriage. The scent of their untipped tobacco. The sweet coldness of the rushing air.

He went through four 'hard' carriages and was on the threshold of the fifth, and had decided this would be the last – had concluded he was worrying about nothing: he must have dreamt it, the countryside was empty – when he saw another picture. Or, rather, he realised it was a pair of pictures coming towards him, one of Stalin, the other of

Lenin, being held aloft by an elderly couple, the man wearing medals, standing on a slight embankment. The train was slowing for a station and he could see them clearly as he passed – creased and leathery faces, almost brown, exhausted. And a couple of seconds later he saw them turn, suddenly years younger, smiling and waving at someone they had just seen in the carriage Kelso was about to enter.

Time seemed to decelerate, dreamily, along with the train. A line of railway workers in quilted jackets, leaning on their pick-axes and shovels, raised their gloved fists in salute. The carriage darkened as it drew alongside a platform. He could hear music, faintly, above the metallic scrape of the brakes – the old Soviet national anthem again –

Party of Lenin!
Party of Stalin!

– and a small band in pale blue uniforms slid past the window.

The train stopped with a sigh of pneumatics and he saw a sign: VOLOGDA. People were cheering on the platform. People were running. He opened the door to the carriage and there facing him was the Russian, still in his father's uniform, asleep, sitting no more than a dozen paces away, his suitcase wedged in the rack above his head, a clear space all around him, passengers standing back, respectful, watching.

The Russian was beginning to wake. His head stirred. He batted something away from his face with his hand and his eyes flickered open. He saw that he was being observed and carefully, warily, he straightened his back. Someone in the carriage started to clap and the applause was taken up by the others, spreading outside to the platform where people had crammed up against the window to watch. The Russian stared around him, the fear in his eyes giving way to bewilderment. A man nodded encouragingly at him, smiling, clapping, and he slowly nodded back, as if gradually beginning to understand some strange foreign ritual, and then he started to applaud softly in return, which only increased the volume of adulation. He nodded modestly and Kelso imagined he must have spent thirty years dreaming of this moment. *Really, comrades,* his expression seemed to say, *I am only one of you – a plain man, rough in my ways – but if venerating me in some way gives you pleasure –*

He wasn't aware of Kelso watching him – the historian was just another face in the crowd – and after a few seconds Kelso turned and began fighting his way back through the jostling throng.

His mind was in a turmoil.

The Russian must have got on board the train in Archangel, a minute or so after them – that was conceivable, if he had copied what they'd done and flagged down a car. That he could understand.

But this?

He knocked into a woman who was pushing her way roughly along the corridor, struggling with a pair of carrier bags, a red flag and an old camera.

He said to her, 'What's happening?'

'Haven't you heard? Stalin's son is with us! It's a miracle!' She couldn't stop smiling. Some of her teeth were metal.

'But how do you know?'

'It's been on the television,' she said, as if this settled matters. 'All night! And when I woke, his picture was still there and they were saying he'd been seen on the Moscow train!'

Someone pushed into her from behind and she was pitched into him. His face was very close to hers. He tried to disentangle himself but she clutched on to him, staring hard into his eyes.

'But you,' she said, 'you know all this! You were on the television, saying it was true!' She threw her heavy arms around him. Her bags jabbed into his back. 'Thank you. Thank you. It's a miracle!'

He could see a bright, white light moving along the platform behind her head and he scrambled past her. A television light. Television cameras. Big grey microphones. Technicians walking backwards, stumbling over one another. And in the middle of this mêlée, striding ahead towards his destiny, talking confidently, surrounded by a phalanx of black-jacketed bodyguards, was Vladimir Mamantov.

IT took Kelso several minutes to claw and squeeze his way back through the crowds. When he opened the door to their compartment O'Brian had his back to him and was staring through the window. At the sound of Kelso entering, he wheeled round quickly, his hands up, his palms outwards – pre-emptive, guilty, apologetic.

'Now, I didn't know this was going to happen, Fluke, I swear to you –'

'What have you done?'

'Nothing –'

'What have you *done*?'

O'Brian flinched and muttered, 'I filed the story.'

'You *what*?'

'I filed the story,' he said, sounding more defiant now. 'Yesterday, from the river bank, while you were talking to him in the hut. I cut the pictures to three minutes forty, laid a commentary, converted them to digital and sent them over the satellite. I nearly told you last night, but I didn't want to upset you –'

'*Upset me?*'

'Come on, Fluke, for all I knew the story might not have gone through. Battery could've failed or something. Gear could've been shot up –'

Kelso was struggling to keep pace with all that was happening – the Russian on the train, the excitement, Mamantov. They still hadn't left Vologda, he noticed.

'These pictures – what time would they have been seen here?'

'Maybe nine o'clock last night.'

'And they would have run – what? Often? "On the hour, every hour"?'

'I guess so.'

'For *eleven hours?* And on other channels, too? Would they have sold them to the Russian networks?'

'They'd've *given* them to the Russians, as long as they were credited. It's good advertising, you know? CNN probably took them. Sky. BBC World –'

He couldn't help looking pleased.

'And you also used the interview with me, about the notebook?'

The hands came back up, defensively.

'Now, I don't know anything about that. I mean, okay, they *had* it, sure. I cut that and sent it back from Moscow before we left.'

'You irresponsible bastard,' said Kelso, slowly. 'You do know Mamantov's on the train?'

'Yeah. I saw him just now.' He glanced nervously at the window. 'Wonder what he's doing here?'

And there was something in the way he said this – a slight

400

falseness of tone: a pretence at being offhand – that made Kelso freeze. After a long pause he said, quietly, 'Did Mamantov put you up to this?'

O'Brian hesitated and Kelso was conscious of swaying slightly, like a boxer about to go down for the final time, or a drunk.

'Christ almighty, you've set me up –'

'No,' said O'Brian, 'that's not true. Okay, I admit Mamantov called me up once – I told you we'd met a few times. But all of this – finding the notebook, coming up here – no: that was all us, I swear. You and me. I knew nothing about what we'd find.'

Kelso closed his eyes. It was a nightmare.

'When did he call?'

'At the very beginning. It was just a tip. He didn't mention Stalin or anything else.'

'The very beginning?'

'The night before I showed up at the symposium. He said: "Go to the Institute of Marxism-Leninism with your camera, Mr O'Brian" – you know the way he talks – "find Dr Kelso, ask him if there is an announcement he wants to make." That was all he said. He put the phone down on me. Anyway, his tips are always good, so I went. Jesus –' he laughed ' – why else d'you think I was there? To film a bunch of historians talking about the archives? Do me a favour!'

'You irresponsible, duplicitous bloody *bastard* –'

Kelso took a step across the compartment and O'Brian backed away. But Kelso ignored him. He'd had a better idea. He dragged down his jacket from the luggage rack.

O'Brian said, 'What're you doing?'

'What I would have done at the beginning, if I'd known the truth. I'm going to destroy that bloody notebook.'

He pulled the satchel out of the inside pocket.

'But then you'll ruin the whole thing,' protested O'Brian. 'No notebook – no proof – no story. We'll look like complete assholes.'

'Good.'

'I'm not sure I can let you do that –'

'Just try and bloody stop me –'

It was the shock of the blow as much as the force of it that felled him. The compartment turned upside down and he was lying on his back.

'Don't make me hit you again,' begged O'Brian, looming over him. 'Please, Fluke. I like you too much for that.'

He held out his hand, but Kelso rolled away. He couldn't get his breath. His face was in the dust. Beneath his hands he could feel the heavy vibrations of the locomotive. He brought his fingers up to his mouth and touched his lip. It was bleeding slightly. He could taste salt. The big engine revved again, as if the driver was bored of waiting, but still the train didn't move.

Chapter Thirty-three

In Moscow, Colonel Yuri Arsenyev, clumsily juggling technologies, had a telephone receiver wedged between his shoulder and his ear, and a television remote control in his plump hands. He pointed it at the big television screen in the corner of his office and tried hopelessly to raise the volume, boosting first the brightness and then the contrast before he was at last able to hear what Mamantov was saying.

'. . . *flew up here from Moscow the moment I heard the news. I am therefore boarding this train to offer my protection, and that of the Aurora movement, to this historic figure, and we defy the great fascist usurper in the Kremlin to try to prevent us from reaching together the once and future seat of Soviet power . . .*'

The past twelve hours had already delivered a succession of unpleasant shocks to the chief of the RT Directorate, but this was the greatest. First, at eight o'clock the previous evening, there had been the anxious call reporting that Spetsnaz HQ had lost all communication with Suvorin and his unit in the forest. Then, an hour later, the first television pictures of the lunatic raving in his hut had begun to be broadcast (*'Such is the law of capitalism – to beat the backward and the weak. It is the jungle law of capitalism . . .'*) Reports that the man had been seen on the Moscow sleeper had reached Yasenevo just before dawn and a scratch force of militia units and MVD had been assembled at Vologda to stop the train. And now this!

Well, to take a man off under cover of darkness in some piddling little halt like Konosha or Yertsevo – that was one thing. But to storm a train in daylight, in full view of the

ROBERT HARRIS

media, in a city as big as Vologda, with V. P. Mamantov and his Aurora thugs on hand to put up a fight – that was something else entirely.

Arsenyev had called the Kremlin.

He was therefore hearing Mamantov's ponderous tones twice – once via the television in his own office and then again, a fraction later, coming down the telephone, filtered through the sound of an ailing man's laboured breathing. In the background at the other end of the line someone was shouting, there were general sounds of panic and commotion. He heard the clink of a glass and a liquid being poured.

Oh, please, he thought. *Not vodka, surely. Please. Not even him. Not this early in the morning –*

On the screen, Mamantov had turned and was boarding the train. He waved at the cameras. The band was playing. People were applauding.

Holy mother –

Arsenyev could feel the lurching of his heart, the clenching of his bronchial tubes. Getting air into his lungs was like sucking mud through a straw.

He took a couple of squirts on his inhaler.

'No,' grunted the familiar voice in Arsenyev's ear, and the line went dead.

'No,' wheezed Arsenyev, quickly, pointing at Vissari Netto.

'No,' said Netto, who was sitting on the sofa, also holding a telephone, patched through on a secure military circuit to the MVD commander in Vologda. 'I repeat: no move to be made. Stand your men down. Let the train go.'

'The right decision,' said Arsenyev, replacing the receiver. 'There could have been shooting. It wouldn't have looked good.'

Looking good was all that mattered now.

For a while Arsenyev said nothing as he contemplated, with increasing unease, this final fork in his life's road. One route, it seemed to him, took him to retirement, pension and a dacha; the other to almost certain dismissal, an official inquiry into illegal assassination attempts and, quite possibly, jail.

'Abandon the whole operation,' he said.

Netto's pen began to move across his pad. Deep in their fleshy sockets, like a pair of berries in dough, Arsenyev's little eyes blinked in alarm.

'No, no, no, man! Don't write any of this down! Just do it. Pull the surveillance off Mamantov's apartment. Remove the protection from the girl. Abort the whole thing.'

'And Archangel, colonel? We've still got a plane waiting up there for Major Suvorin.'

Arsenyev tugged at his thick neck for a few seconds. In his perennially fertile mind, the form of an unattributable briefing for the foreign media was already beginning to take shape: *'reports of shooting in the Archangel forest . . . regrettable incident . . . rogue officer took matters into his own hands . . . disobeyed strict orders . . . tragic outcome . . . profound apologies . . .'*

Poor Feliks, he thought.

'Order it back to Moscow.'

IT was as if the train had been held in check too long, so that when the brakes were finally released it lunged forwards and then stopped abruptly, and O'Brian, like the clapper of a bell, was slammed into the front and back of the compartment. The satchel flew out of his hands.

Very slowly, creaking and protesting, and with the same

infinitesimal speed as when they left Archangel, the locomotive began to haul them out of Vologda.

Kelso was still on the floor.

'*No notebook – no proof – no story –*'

He dived for the satchel and scooped it in one hand, got the fingertips of his other up on to the door handle, and was attempting to rise when he felt O'Brian grab his legs and try to drag him back. The handle tipped, the door slid open and he flopped out on to the carpeted corridor, kicking backwards frantically with his heels at O'Brian's head. He felt a satisfying contact of hard rubber on flesh and bone. There was a howl of pain. The boot came off and he left it behind like a lizard losing the tip of its tail. He limped away down the corridor on his stockinged foot.

The narrow passage was clogged with anxious 'soft' class passengers – '*Did you hear?*' '*Is it true?*' – and it was impossible to make quick progress. O'Brian was coming after him. He could hear his shouts. At the end of the carriage the window of the door was open and he briefly considered hurling the satchel out on to the tracks. But the train hadn't cleared Vologda, was travelling much too slowly – the notebook was bound to land intact, he thought: was certain to be found –

'Fluke!'

He ran into the next carriage and realised too late that he was heading back towards 'hard' again, which was a mistake because 'hard' was where Mamantov and his thugs had boarded – and here, indeed was one of Mamantov's men, hastening down the corridor towards him, pushing people out of his way.

Kelso grabbed the door handle nearest him. It was locked. But the second handle turned and he almost fell into the empty compartment, locking the door after him. Inside it was shaded, the curtains closed, the berths unmade, a stale smell of cold, male sweat – whoever had occupied it must have got off at Vologda. He tried to open the window but it was stuck. The Aurora man was battering at the door, shouting at him to open up. The handle rattled furiously. Kelso unfastened the satchel and tipped out the contents and had his lighter in his hand as the lock gave way.

THE blinds of Zinaida Rapava's apartment were drawn. The lights were off. The television screen flickered in the corner of her tiny flat like a cold blue hearth.

There had been a plainclothes guard outside on the landing all night – Bunin to start with, and then a different man – and a militia car parked ostentatiously opposite the entrance to the apartment block. It was Bunin who had told her to keep the blinds closed and not to go out. She didn't like Bunin and she could tell he didn't like her. When she asked him how long she would have to stay like this, he had shrugged. Was she a prisoner, then? He had shrugged again.

She had lain in a foetal curl on her bed for the best part of twenty hours, listening to her neighbours coming home from work, then some of them going out for the evening. Later, she heard them preparing for bed. And she had discovered, lying in the darkness, that as long as something occupied her eye, she could prevent herself seeing her father: she could block out the image of the broken figure on the trolley. So she had watched television all night. And at one point, hopping between a game show and a black-and-white American movie, she had lighted on the pictures from the forest.

'... *freedom alone is not enough, by far ... It is very difficult, comrades, to live on freedom alone ...*'

She had watched, hypnotised, as the night went on, how the story had spread like a stain across the networks, until she could recite it by heart. There was her father's lock-up, and the notebook, and Kelso turning the pages (*'it's genuine – I'd stake my life on it'*). There was the old woman pointing at a map. There was the strange man walking across the forest clearing and staring into the camera as he spoke. He ranted part of a hate-filled speech and that had nagged at her memory for a while in the early hours, until she remembered that her father had sometimes played a record of it when she was a child.

(*'You should listen to this, girl – you might learn something.'*)

He was frightening, this man, comic and sinister – like Zhirinovsky, or Hitler – and when it was reported that he had been seen on the Moscow train, heading south, she felt almost as if he were coming for *her*. She could imagine him stamping down the halls of the big hotels, his boots hammering on the marble, his coat flying behind him, smashing the windows of the expensive boutiques, hurling the foreigners out on to the pavements, looking for her. She could see him in Robotnik, overturning the bar, calling the girls whores and shouting at them to cover themselves. He would paint out the western signs, shatter the neon, empty the streets, shut down the airport –

She knew they should have burned that notebook.

It was later, when she was in the bathroom, naked from the waist up, splashing cold water into her red eyes, that she heard from the television the name of Mamantov. And her first thought was, naïvely, that he had been arrested. After all, that was what Suvorin had promised her, wasn't it?

'We're going to find the man who did this terrible thing to your father, and we're going to lock him up.'

She grabbed a towel and darted back to the screen, hastily drying her face, and scrutinised him, and, oh yes, she knew it was him right enough, she could believe it of *him* – he looked a pitiless, cold bastard, with his wire-framed glasses and his thin, hard lips, and his Soviet-style hat and coat. He looked capable of anything.

He was saying something about 'the fascist usurper in the Kremlin' and it took her a minute to realise that actually he wasn't being arrested. On the contrary: he was being treated with respect. He was moving towards the train. He was boarding it. Nobody was stopping him. She could even see a couple of militia men, watching him. He turned on the step to the carriage and raised his hand. Lights flickered. He flashed his hangman's smile and disappeared inside.

Zinaida stared at the screen.

She searched through the pockets of her jacket until she found the telephone number Suvorin had given her.

It rang, unanswered.

She replaced the receiver calmly enough, wrapped the towel around her torso and unlocked her door.

Nobody was on the landing.

She went back into the flat and lifted the blind.

No sign of any militia car. Just the normal Saturday morning traffic beginning to build for the Izmaylovo market.

Afterwards, several witnesses came forward who claimed to have heard the sound of her cry, even above the noises of the busy street.

KELSO was overpowered with humiliating ease. He was pushed back on to the banquette, the satchel and the papers were taken from him, the door was wedged shut, and the young man in the black leather jacket took the seat opposite him, stretching one leg across the narrow aisle to prevent his prisoner from moving.

He unzipped the jacket just far enough to show Kelso a shoulder holster, and Kelso recognised him then: Mamantov's personal bodyguard from the Moscow apartment. He was a big, baby-faced lad, with a drooping left eyelid and a blubbery lower lip, and there was something about the way he let his boot rest against Kelso's thigh, cramming him against the window, that suggested hurting people might be his pleasure in life: that he needed violence as a swimmer requires water.

Kelso remembered Papu Rapava's slowly twisting body and began to sweat.

'It's Viktor, isn't it?'

No reply.

'How long am I supposed to stay here, Viktor?'

Again, no answer, and after a couple more half-hearted attempts to demand his release, Kelso gave up. He could hear the sound of boots in the corridor and he had the impression that the whole of the train was being secured.

After that, not much happened for several hours.

At 10.20 they stopped as scheduled at Danilov and more of Mamantov's people poured aboard.

Kelso asked if he could at least go to the lavatory.

No answer.

Later, outside the city of Yaroslavl, they passed a derelict factory with a rusting Order of Lenin pinned to its windowless side. On its roof, a line of youths was silhouetted, their arms raised high in a fascist salute.

Viktor looked at Kelso and smiled, and Kelso looked away.

Archangel

In Moscow, Zinaida Rapava's apartment was empty.

The Klims who lived in the flat beneath afterwards swore they had heard her go out soon after eleven. But old man Amosov, who was fixing his car in the street directly across from the block, insisted it was some time after that: more like noon, he thought. She went straight by him without uttering a word, which wasn't unusual for her – she had her head down, he said, and was wearing dark glasses, a leather jacket, jeans and boots – and she was heading in the direction of the Semyonovskaya metro station.

She didn't have her car: that was still parked outside her father's apartment.

The next authenticated sighting came an hour later, at one o'clock, when she turned up at the back of Robotnik. A cleaner, Vera Yanukova, recognised her and let her in and she went directly to the cloakroom where she retrieved a leather shoulder bag (she showed her ticket; there was no mistake). The cleaner opened up the front entrance for her to leave, but she preferred to go out the way she had come, thus avoiding the metal detectors which were switched on automatically whenever the door was unlocked.

According to the cleaner, she was nervous when she arrived, but once she had the bag she seemed in good spirits, calm and self-possessed.

Chapter Thirty-four

DID KELSO FALL asleep? He afterwards wondered if he might have done, for he had no real recollection of that long afternoon until he heard footsteps in the corridor and the sound of someone knocking softly on the door. And by then they were into the northern fringes of Moscow and the flat October light was already falling on the endless iron and concrete of the city.

Viktor idly swung his foot off the banquette and stood, hitching up his trousers. He removed his knife from the mechanism of the lock and slid back the door a fraction, then pulled it all the way, coming stiffly to attention, and suddenly Vladimir Mamantov was across the threshold and into the compartment, bringing with him that same odd odour of camphor and carbolic that Kelso remembered from his apartment. The same clump of dark bristles still nestled in the cleft of his chin.

He was all false smiles and apologies: so sorry if Kelso had been inconvenienced in any way, such a pity they had not been able to meet much earlier in the journey, but he had had other, more pressing matters to attend to. He was sure that Kelso understood.

His overcoat was unbuttoned. His face was sheened with sweat. He tossed his hat on to the banquette opposite Kelso and sat down next to it, grabbing the satchel, removing the documents, gesturing to Viktor to take the seat next to Kelso, calling to the second bodyguard he had left in the corridor to close the door and not to let anyone in.

This was not the Mamantov Kelso had met seven years ago

412

on his release from prison. This was not even the Mamantov from earlier in the week. This was Mamantov in his prime again. Mamantov rejuvenated. Mamantov *redux*.

Kelso watched him as his thick fingers checked through the notebook and the NKVD reports.

'Good,' he said, briskly, 'excellent. Everything is here, I think. Tell me: were you really were planning to destroy all this?'

'Yes.'

'All of it?'

'Yes.'

He looked at Kelso in wonderment and shook his head.

'And yet you are the one who is always bleating about the need to open every historical document for inspection!'

'Even so, I'd still have destroyed it. In the interests of stopping you.'

Kelso felt the increasing pressure of Viktor's elbow in his ribs, and he knew that the young man was longing for an opportunity to hurt him.

'Ah! So history is only to be permitted where it suits the subjective interests of those who hold the records?' Mamantov smiled again. 'Has the myth of so-called western "objectivity" ever been more completely exposed? I can see I shall have to take these documents back into my possession for safe-keeping.'

'Take them back?' said Kelso. He couldn't keep the incredulity out of his voice. 'You mean you had them before?'

Mamantov inclined his head graciously.

Indeed.

MAMANTOV had replaced the papers in the satchel and had fastened the straps. But he couldn't quite bring himself to leave. Not yet. After all, he had waited so long for this moment. He wanted Kelso know. It was fifteen years since Yepishev had first told him about this 'black oilskin notebook' and he had never lost faith that one day he would find it. And then, like a miracle, in the very darkest hours of the cause, who should turn up on the membership lists of Aurora but the very same Papu Rapava whose name had cropped up so often in the KGB's files? Mamantov had summoned him. And at long last – hesitantly, reluctantly at first, but eventually out of loyalty to his new chief – Rapava had told him the story of the night of Stalin's stroke.

Mamantov had been the first to hear it.

That had been a year ago.

It had taken him a whole nine months to get into the garden of Beria's mansion on Vspolnyi Street. And do you know what he had had to do? No? He had had to set up a property company – Moskprop – and *buy* the goddamn place off its owners, the former KGB, although that hadn't been too hard because Mamantov had plenty of friends at the Lubyanka who, in return for a percentage, were happy to sell state assets for a fraction of their true value. Some might call it corruption, or even robbery. He preferred the western term: privatisation.

The Tunisians had been kicked out, finally, under the terms of their lease, in August, and Rapava had led him to the exact spot in the garden. The toolbox had been retrieved. Mamantov had read the notebook, had flown to Archangel, had followed exactly the same trail as Kelso and O'Brian into the heart of the forest. And he had seen the potential at once. But he also had the sense – the genius, he would almost call it, but he would leave that judgement to others – the *wit*, let's say, to recognise what Kelso had just so aptly proved: that history, in the end, is a matter of subjectivity not objectivity.

'Suppose I had returned to Moscow with our mutual friend, convened a press conference and announced he was Stalin's son. What would have happened? I'll tell you. Nothing. I would have been ignored. Derided. Accused of forgery. And why?' He jabbed his finger at Kelso. 'Because the media is in the grip of cosmopolitan forces that loathe Vladimir Mamantov and all he stands for. Oh, but if Dr Kelso, the darling of the cosmopolitans – ah, yes, if *Kelso* says to the world, "Behold, I give you Stalin's son," then that is a different matter.'

So the son had been prevailed upon to wait a few weeks longer, until some other strangers would appear bearing the notebook.

(And that explained a lot, thought Kelso: the odd sense he had experienced in Archangel that people had been somehow waiting for them – the communist official, Vavara Safanova, the man himself. *'You are the ones, you are truly the ones; and I am the one you seek . . .'*)

'And why me?' he asked.

'Because I remembered you. Remembered you wheedling your way in to see me when I was fresh from Lefortovo after the coup – your fucking arrogance, your certainty that you and your kind had won and I was finished. The shit you wrote about me . . . What was it Stalin said? "To choose one's victims, to prepare one's plans minutely, to slake an implacable vengeance, and then to go to bed . . . there is nothing sweeter in the world." Sweet. That's it. Nothing sweeter in the world.'

ZINAIDA Rapava arrived at Moscow's Yaroslavl Station a few minutes after four o'clock. (What exactly she had been doing in the three hours since leaving Robotnik the authorities were never able to determine, although there were unconfirmed reports of a woman matching her description being seen at the Troekurovo cemetery, where her mother and brother were buried.)

At any rate, at five past four, she approached an employee of the Russian railway network. Afterwards he couldn't say why she stuck in his mind when so many others were milling around that day: perhaps it was the dark glasses she was wearing, despite the perpetual sunken gloom beneath the hooded arches of the railway terminus.

Like the rest, she wanted to know which platform the Archangel train would be arriving at.

The crowds were already beginning to build, and Aurora stewards were doing their best to keep them in order. A gangway had been roped off. A platform had been erected for the cameras. Flags were being distributed – the Tsarist eagle, the hammer and sickle, the Aurora emblem. Zinaida took a little red flag, and maybe it was that, or maybe it was the leather jacket that made her look like a typical Aurora activist, but whatever it was she secured a prime position, at the edge of the rope, and nobody bothered her.

She can be glimpsed, occasionally, on some of the videotape of the crowd, taken before the train arrived – cool, solitary, waiting.

THE train was trundling past the suburban stations. Curious Saturday afternoon shoppers looked to see what all the fuss was about. A man held up a child to wave but Mamantov was too busy talking to notice.

He was describing the way he had lured Kelso to Russia – and that, he said, was the touch he was proudest of: that was a ruse worthy of Josef Vissarionovich himself.

He had arranged for a front company he owned in Switzerland – respectable, a family firm: it had been exploiting the workers for centuries – to contact Rosarkhiv and offer to sponsor a symposium on the opening up of the Soviet archives!

Mamantov slapped his own knee with mirth.

At first, Rosarkhiv hadn't wanted to invite Kelso – imagine that! they thought he was no longer of 'sufficient standing in the academic community' – but Mamantov, through the sponsors, had insisted, and two months later, sure enough, there he was, back in town, in his free hotel room, all expenses paid, like a pig in shit, come to wallow in *our* past, feeling superior to *us*, telling *us* to feel guilty, when all the time the only reason he was there was to bring the past back to life!

And Papu Rapava, asked Kelso, what had he thought of this plan?

For the first time, Mamantov's face darkened.

Rapava had claimed to like the plan. That was what he'd said. To spit in the capitalists' soup and then to watch them drink it? Oh yes please, comrade colonel: that had appealed to Rapava very much! He was supposed to tell Kelso his story overnight, then take him directly to Beria's old mansion, where they would retrieve the toolbox together. Mamantov had tipped off O'Brian who promised to turn up with his cameras at the Institute of Marxism–Leninism the next morning. The symposium was to provide the perfect launch pad. What a story! There would have been a feeding frenzy. Mamantov had the whole thing worked out.

But then: nothing. Kelso had called the following afternoon and that was when Mamantov had learned that

Rapava had failed in his mission: that he had told his story right enough, but then had run away.

'Why?' Mamantov frowned. 'You mentioned money to him, presumably?'

Kelso nodded. 'I offered him a share in the profits.'

A look of contempt spread across Mamantov's face. 'That *you* should seek to enrich yourself – that I'd expected: that was another reason I selected you. But that *he* should?' He shook his head in disgust. 'Human beings,' he murmured. 'They always let you down.'

'He might have felt the same about you,' said Kelso. 'Given what you did to him.'

Mamantov glanced at Viktor and something passed between the older man and the younger in that instant – a look of almost sexual intimacy – and Kelso knew at once that the pair of them had worked on Papu Rapava together. There must have been others but these two were at the centre of it: the craftsman and his apprentice.

He felt himself beginning to sweat again.

'But he never told you where he'd hidden it,' he said.

Mamantov frowned, as if trying to remember something. 'No,' he said, softly. 'No. He came of strong stock. I'll grant him that. Not that it matters. We followed you and the girl the next morning, saw you collect the material. In the end, Rapava's death changed nothing. I have it all now.'

Silence.

The train had slowed almost to walking pace. Beyond the flat roofs, Kelso could see the mast of the Television Tower.

'Time presses,' said Mamantov suddenly, 'and the world is waiting.'

He picked up the satchel and his hat. 'I've given some thought to you,' he said to Kelso, as he stood and began buttoning his coat. 'But really I can't see that you can harm us. You can withdraw your authentication of the papers, of course, but that won't make much difference now, except to make you look a fool – they're genuine: that will be established by independent experts in a day or two. You can also make certain wild allegations about the death of Papu Rapava, but no proof exists.' He bent to examine himself in the small mirror above Kelso's head, straightening the brim of his hat in readiness for the cameras. 'No. I think the best thing I can do is simply leave you to watch what happens next.'

'Nothing's going to happen next,' said Kelso. 'Don't forget I've talked to this creature of yours – the moment he opens his mouth, people will laugh.'

'You want to bet on it?' Mamantov offered his hand. 'No? You're wise. Lenin said: "The most important thing in any endeavour is to get involved in the fight, and in that way learn what to do next." And that's what we're going to do now. For the first time in nearly ten years we're going to be able to start a fight. And such a fight. Viktor.'

Reluctantly, and with a final, wistful glance at Kelso, the young man got to his feet.

The corridor was crowded with figures in black leather jackets.

'It was love,' said Kelso, when Mamantov was halfway out of the door.

'What?' Mamantov turned to stare at him.

'Rapava. That was the reason he didn't take me to the papers. You said he did it for the money, but I don't think he wanted the money for himself. He wanted it for his daughter. To make it up to her. It was love.'

'Love?' repeated Mamantov incredulously. He tested the

word in his mouth as if it was unfamiliar to him – the name
of some sinister new weapon, perhaps, or a freshly discovered
world capitalist–zionist conspiracy. 'Love?' No. It was no use.
He shook his head and shrugged.

The door slid shut and Kelso collapsed back in his seat. A
minute or two later he heard a noise like a high wind roaring
through a forest and he pressed his face to the window. Up
ahead, across an expanse of track, he could see a shifting mass
of colour that gradually became more defined as they drew
alongside the platform – faces, placards, waving flags, a
podium, a red carpet, cameras, people waiting behind ropes,
Zinaida –

SHE spotted him at the same instant and for a few long
seconds their eyes locked. She saw him start to rise,
mouthing something, gesturing at her, but then he was borne
away and out of sight. The procession of dull green carriages,
spattered with mud from the long journey, clanked slowly
past then juddered to a halt, and the crowd, which had been
festively noisy for the past half hour, was suddenly quiet.

Youths in leather jackets leapt from the train immediately
in front of her. She saw the shadow of a marshal's cap move
behind one of the windows.

The gun was out of her bag by now and hidden inside her
jacket and she could feel the cold comfort of its shape against
her palm. There was a ball of something very tight within her
chest but it wasn't fear. It was a tension longing to be released.

In her mind she could see him very clearly, each mark
upon his body a mark of his love for her.

'Who is your only friend, girl?'

There was a movement in the doorway of the carriage.
The two men were coming out together.

'Yourself, papa.'

They stood together on the top step, waving, close enough for her to touch. People were cheering. The crowd surged at her back. She couldn't miss.

'And who else?'

She pulled out the gun very quickly and aimed.

'You, papa. You –'